From

The Women's Press Ltd
34 Great Sutton Street, London EC1V 0DX

Hualing Nieh *Photo: John Zielinski*

Hualing Nieh was born in Hupeh, China, in 1925. From 1949 to 1960 she was Literary Editor of *Free China* fortnightly in Taiwan. After teaching Creative Writing and Modern Literature at Taiwan University and Donghai University, she went to the University of Iowa as Visiting Artist in 1964. In 1967 she launched, with Paul Engle, the International Writing Program at the University of Iowa and she now divides her time between directing the Program and writing.

She has written several novels, books of short stories and essays and has translated works by Henry James, William Faulkner, Stephen Crane and F. Scott Fitzgerald amongst others into Chinese. Her own works have been published in Taiwan, Hong Kong, the United States, Brazil, Poland, Romania, Israel, Italy, Hungary, Yugoslavia and China.

HUALING NIEH

Mulberry and Peach
Two Women of China

The Women's Press

First published in Great Britain by
The Women's Press Limited 1986
A member of the Namara Group
34 Great Sutton Street, London EC1V 0DX

First published in China 1976
This translation first published simultaneously by New World Press,
Peking, and Sino Publishing Company, New York, 1981

British Library Cataloguing in Publication Data
Engle, Hua-ling Nieh
  Mulberry and Peach: two women of China.
  I. Title
  895.1'35[F]   PL2856.N/

  ISBN 0-7043-5005-X
  ISBN 0-7043-4009-7 Pbk

Phototypeset by AKM Associates (UK) Ltd
Ajmal House, Hayes Road, Southall, London
Reproduced, printed and bound in Great Britain by
Hazell Watson & Viney Limited,
Member of the BPCC Group,
Aylesbury, Bucks

Contents

PROLOGUE

The Man from the USA Immigration Service

'I'm not Mulberry. Mulberry is dead!'

'Well, what is your name, then?' asks the man from the Immigration Service.

'Call me anything you like. Ah-chu, Ah-ch'ou, Mei-chuan, Ch'un-hsiang, Ch'iu-hsia, Tung-mei, Hsiu-ying, Ts'ui-fang, Niu-niu, Pao-pao, Pei-pei, Lien-ying, Kuei-fen, Chü-hua. Just call me Peach, OK?' She is dressed only in skin-coloured bikini panties and a peach blouse.

The Immigration agent is standing in her doorway. He is dressed in a dark suit with a black and grey striped tie. He wears sunglasses, although it's an overcast day. The dark lenses disguise the only distinguishing part of his face: eyebrows, eyes, the bridge of his nose. Only the anonymous parts are visible: bald head, sharp chin, high forehead, beak nose, and pencil-thin moustache.

He takes a form out of his briefcase. The form is covered with a cramped script in fountain pen. In the corner is the number: (Alien) number 89–785–462. In the other corner is a woman's photograph. The name Mulberry is written under the photo. One item on the form is checked in red: Application for Permanent Residency.

He points at the woman's photograph. 'This is you in the picture, right? There's a mole under her left eye and her right earlobe has a small notch. You . . .' he says, pointing at Peach, 'have you a mole under your eye and there's a notch in your right earlobe.'

Peach laughs. 'Mr Dark, you have a real good imagination. What you see isn't real. What I see is real. You know what I see when I look at you? A tiger with nine human heads.'

'Please don't make jokes,' the agent says. 'May I come in and talk with you?'

'Only on one condition. You can't call me Mulberry.'

The agent comes in, looks around. 'There's no furniture in here.'

'The furniture belonged to Mulberry. I don't want anything that belonged to a dead person, so I called the Salvation Army to haul it away. Besides, furniture gets in my way. I like it like this.'

Peach moves aside heaps of clothing, boxes, bottles, newspapers, paints, and pieces of paper and sits down on the floor. She pats the floor beside her, 'Sit down here.'

Things are piled all over the room. There isn't any place for him to sit. He stands in the middle of the room, looking around at the walls on which are scrawled crooked columns of words in English and in Chinese.

> A flower but not a flower
> I am the flower
> Mist yet not mist
> I am Everything
>
> When women grow beards
> and men bear children
> the world will be at peace
>
> Who is afraid of Mao Tse-tung?
> Who is afraid of Chiang Kai-shek?
> Who is afraid of Virginia Woolf?
>
> Mulberry murdered her father, murdered
> her mother murdered her husband
> murdered her daughter.
>
> A woman from Lone Tree
> Car accident on a one-way street
> Cause unknown
> Name unknown

There are also drawings on the wall: A naked figure, beheaded, his two nipples, eyes; his protruding navel, a mouth. In one hand he holds a huge axe and hacks at the sky. With his other hand, he gropes for his head on the ground. To one side is a black mountain with a gaping hole. The head lies beside the hole.

A tall man sits stiffly in an armchair. Leopard's face: golden forehead, golden nose, golden cheekbones, black face, black eyes, white eyebrows. Forehead painted with red, white and black stripes. He bares his chest. His chest is an idol's shrine enclosed by bars. A

4

thousand-handed Buddha sits in the shrine. The hands stretch out through the bars. The Buddha is locked inside.

The agent stands in the room, still wearing his sunglasses, pen and notebook in his hands. 'May I copy down the things on the wall?'

'Go ahead. I couldn't care less. If you want to investigate Mulberry, I can give you a lot of information. I know everything about her. Wherever she went, I was always there. What are you after her for, anyway?'

'It's classified. I can't tell you. Can I ask you some questions?'

'If you want to know about me, I won't tell you anything. If you want to know about Mulberry, I'll tell you everything I know.'

'I appreciate your cooperation.' The agent looks over Mulberry's form. 'What is Mulberry's nationality?'

'Chinese.'

'Where was she born?'

'Nanking.'

'Date of birth?'

'October 26, 1929.'

'And you,' he says pointing at Peach, 'where were you born?' The dark glasses flash at her. 'Where were you born, what date?'

Peach laughs. 'Mr Dark, don't try to be so smart! You think I'm going to tell you that I was born in Nanking on 26 October 1929 so you can prove I'm Mulberry? Well, you're wrong, Mr Dark. I was born in a valley when heaven split from the earth. The goddess Nüwa plucked a branch of wild flowers and threw it to the earth. Where the flowers fell, people sprang up. That's how I was born. You people were born from your mothers' wombs. I'm a stranger wherever I go, but I'm happy. There are lots of interesting things to see and do. I'm not some spirit or ghost. I don't believe that nonsense. I only believe in what I can smell, hear, see . . . I . . .'

'Excuse me, Mulberry may I . . .'

'Mulberry is dead. Mr Dark, I won't let you call me by a dead woman's name.'

'You two are the same person all right.' His moustache twitches slightly. He pushes his sunglasses back up on his nose.

'You're wrong. Mulberry is Mulberry and Peach is Peach. They're not the same at all. Their thoughts, manners, interests, and even the way they look are completely different. Mulberry, for instance, was afraid of blood, animals, flashing lights. I'm not afraid of those things. Mulberry shut herself up at home, sighing and carrying on. I go everywhere, looking for thrills. Snow, rain, thunder, birds, animals, I

5

love them all. Sometimes Mulberry wanted to die, sometimes she wanted to live. In the end she gave up. I'd never do that. Mulberry was full of illusions; I don't have any. People and things I can't see don't exist as far as I'm concerned. Even if the sky fell and the world turned upside down, I still wouldn't give up.'

'You smoke?' The agent takes out a cigarette.

'Good idea! Mulberry didn't smoke. Let's have a cigarette to celebrate her death.' She lights her cigarette, stretches out on the floor, staring up at the ceiling while she smokes. The window is open; a gust of air blows in. The newspapers on the floor rustle in the breeze. 'Ooh, what a lovely breeze!' She rolls on the floor in the breeze.

The agent looks away and goes to close the window.

'Mr Dark, please don't close the window. Wind should blow, water should flow. You can't stop it.' Peach unbuttons her blouse, exposing her breasts. 'What a nice breeze! Soft as a deer's skin!' The cigarette in her fingers falls to the floor.

'Mulberry, please behave yourself.' He puts the cigarette out with his foot.

'Mulberry is dead. I am Peach.'

'Please button your blouse.'

'Even if I button it, I'm still naked inside.'

'Don't make jokes. I represent the Immigration Service of the Department of Justice and I am here to investigate Mulberry.' He shivers in the breeze. 'OK, Peach, you win. I need your cooperation. Please tell me everything you know about Mulberry.'

'OK, listen.' Peach sprawls on the floor and pillows her head with her arms. She crosses her legs and swings her calf up and down as she talks. She is speaking in Chinese.

The agent can't understand. He paces back and forth. The papers rustle under his feet. He motions for her to stop, but she goes on speaking in Chinese. Gusts of wind are blowing in.

He finally interrupts her. 'Excuse me, may I use your bathroom?' The glasses slide down his nose, revealing his thick eyebrows. His eyes are still hidden.

'Of course.'

When he comes back, Peach is standing by the window, her blouse half-open, her breasts full. She looks out the window and smiles faintly. Her belly is slightly swollen.

The agent from the Immigration Service picks up his briefcase and walks out, without saying goodbye.

PART I

ONE

Peach's First Letter to the Man from the USA Immigration Service

(January 1970)

CHARACTERS

PEACH, one half of the split personality of the woman Mulberry-Peach. She is running away from the US Immigration Service agent while writing him about her wanders across America.

THE MAN FROM THE IMMIGRATION SERVICE.

Dear Sir:

I'm wandering around these places shown on the map. If you want to chase me, come on. Anyway, I'm not Mulberry. Sometimes I hitchhike. Sometimes I take a bus. As soon as I get somewhere, I leave. I don't have any particular destination. I'm always on the road. You can meet a lot of interesting people on the road. There is so much to see. One by one, the horizons sink behind me and new ones rise ahead of me.

Right now I'm on Highway 70 heading east. We're going 100 miles an hour. The car is black, painted with large red letters: March Against Death.

I got this ride in St. Louis. I was standing by the road and a car came toward me. I waved. The car stopped. Inside were all kinds of people: white, black, yellow. I couldn't tell the men from the women, they all had such long hair.

Conversation with the driver:

9

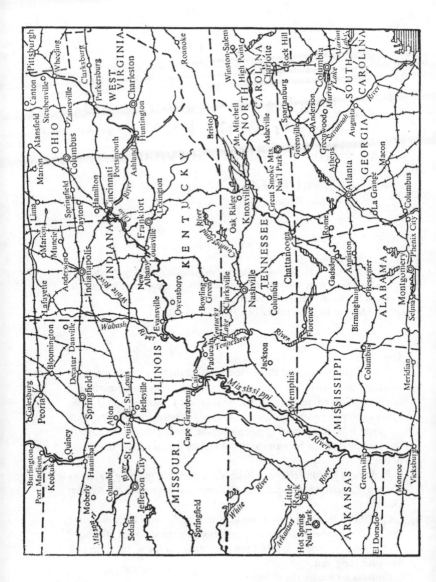

'Hey, you want a ride? Where are you going?'

'I'll go wherever you're going.'

'We're going to Washington to join the March Against Death.'

'I'll come along to watch the excitement!'

'Where are you coming from?'

'The moon.'

'Don't be funny. So you're the moon princess, huh? Why did you come back to earth?'

'I came back to start over. First, I want to have a baby so that human beings won't become extinct.'

'Has the earth changed any since you've been gone?'

'It's weirder, but it's more interesting.'

'OK, Moon Princess, get in!'

Inside the car is a mess strewn with newspapers, paper, coke cans, boxes, cigarettes butts. Overcoats, blankets, and sleeping bags are piled on the seats. Eight people are squeezed together on top of these things. Counting me, that makes nine. I don't know where they are from. They are talking about student demonstrations all over the world: Japan, England, France, Czechoslovakia, Poland, Yugoslavia, and the US. They are talking about the dead. They tell me about the March Against Death, a demonstration against the war in Vietnam They tell me that such protests are becoming increasingly desperate and increasingly useless. But they want to show the world that people don't want to die anymore. Tonight in Washington 45,000 people carrying candles and wearing name tags with the names of soldiers killed in Vietnam, will walk single file from Arlington National Cemetery to the foot of Capitol Hill where there will be twelve coffins. The protest will last forty hours. Each person will place his name tag with the dead soldier's name in a coffin.

I tell them I also want to wear a tag. The name of the dead person is Mulberry.

They yawn one by one. It's boring to talk about death. The sun is shining right in our faces. Powdery snow drifts in the sunlight. If they keep on talking like this, I'm going to get out.

Someone in the front seat holds up a poster:

NOTICE
Office of Civil Defense
Washington, D.C.

Instructions: What to do in case of Nuclear Attack
When the First Warning is Sounded
1. Stay away from all windows.
2. Keep hands free of glasses, bottles, cigarettes, etc.
3. Stand away from bars, tables, musical instruments, equipment, and other furniture.
4. Loosen necktie, unbutton coat and any other restrictive clothing.
5. Remove glasses, empty pockets of all sharp objects: pens, pencils, etc.
6. When you see the flash of nuclear explosion, bend over and place your head firmly between your legs.
7. Then kiss yourself goodbye.

You said you wanted me to tell you about Mulberry. Today I'm sending you her diary. I'll be sending you more material about her, piece by piece. Let me tell you, I know every detail of her life. I know her thoughts, feelings, illusions, dreams, and memories. I even know things she didn't know or remember. We can work together on this. But you'll have to remember one thing: I am not Mulberry. She is afraid of you. But I'm not. As long as you don't call me by a dead woman's name, I can give you a lot of information about her.

I am also enclosing her photo album which she bought from a Japanese prisoner after the war, when she was returning from Chungking to her home in Nanking.

Peach
13 January 1970

12

TWO

Mulberry's Notebook
Chü-t'ang Gorge on the
Yangtze River

(27 July 1945–10 August 1945)

CHARACTERS

MULBERRY, (16 years old), during the Anti-Japanese War, Mulberry is running away from home with her lesbian friend, Lao-shih. Sometime after her parents' marriage, Mulberry's father became impotent as the result of a wound received in a battle between rival Chinese warlords. Later, the mother, who before her marriage had been a prostitute, began an affair with the family butler, and began to abuse her husband and children. As the story opens, Mulberry is running away to Chungking, the wartime capital of China.

LAO-SHIH, (18), a dominating, mannish girl about Mulberry's age. Her father was suffocated in the huge tunnel in which people hid from the continuous Japanese bombing of Chungking in the summer of 1941.

THE OLD MAN, (in his 60s), he represents the traditional type of Chinese. He has been in flight from the Japanese since they occupied Peiping, his home, in 1937.

REFUGEE STUDENT, (in his 20s), he represents the generation growing up during World War II. He is patriotic, aware of his rootless condition. He is rebellious against the old system represented by his father, who had seven wives and forty-six children, and lived in a huge gloomy house in Nanking. His father works for the Japanese. The angry young man reveals the inevitability of the coming revolution.

PEACH-FLOWER WOMAN, (in her 20s), she represents the natural life force, vital, exuberant, sensuous and enduring. It is this spontaneous life force that has enabled the Chinese to survive thousands of years of wars, revolutions

13

and natural disasters. She became the wife of a boy seven years her junior when she herself was a child. She raised the baby husband, and worked hard on the farm. When the husband grew up, he left her and studied in Chungking. The rumour is that he lives with another woman in Chungking. Peach-flower Woman is going there with her baby to look for her husband.

There is no sun. There is no moon. There is no sky. The sky and the water are one, both murky. The river dragon stirs up the water. His hundred hairy legs and clumsy tail swish back and forth, churning the water.

From the window at the inn in Tai-hsi, I can see the mountains across the river, so tall I can't see the top, like a black sword piercing the sky. The sky dies without losing one drop of blood. The gorge suddenly darkens.

A torch flares up along the river. A paddlewheel steamboat, blasted in half by the Japanese, lies stranded in the dark water like a dead cow. Along the river several lamps light up. Near the shore are several old wooden boats. Our boat, crippled while rounding the sandbanks at New Landslide Rapids, is tied up there for repairs.

The village of Tai-hsi is like a delicate chain lying along the cliffs. There is no quay along the river. When you disembark you have to climb up steep narrow steps carved out of the cliff. When I crawled up those steps, I didn't dare look up at the peak, or I might have fallen back into the water, a snack for the dragon.

A torch bobs up the steps. After a while I can see that there is a man on horseback coming up the steps, carrying a torch. The torch flashes under my window and I glimpse a chestnut-coloured horse.

Lao-shih and I ran away together from En-shih to Pa-tung. I am sixteen and she is eighteen. We thought we could get a ship out of Pa-tung right away and be in Chungking in a flash. When we get to Chungking, the war capital, we'll be all right, or at least that's what Lao-shih says. She patted her chest when she said that to show how certain she was. She wears a tight bra and tries to flatten her breasts, but they are as large as two hunks of steamed bread. She said, 'Chungking, it's huge city. The centre of the Resistance! What are you scared about? The hostel for refugee students will take care of our food, housing, school and a job. You can do whatever you want.' We are both from the remote mountains of En-shih and are students at the Provincial High School. Whatever I don't know, she does.

When we got to Pa-tung, we found out that all the steamships have been requisitioned to transport ammunition and troops. Germany has surrendered to the Allies and the Japanese are desperately fighting for their lives. A terrible battle has broken out again in northern Hupeh and western Hunan. There weren't any passenger ships leaving Pa-tung, only a freighter going to Wu-shan, so we took that. When we arrived in Wu-shan, we happened upon an old wooden boat which carried cotton to Feng-chieh, so we took that.

Towering mountains above us, the deep gorge below. Sailing past the Gorges in that old boat was really exciting, but it cracked up on the rocks of New Landslide Rapids and is now at Tai-hsi for repairs.

Lao-shih just went out to find out when the boat will be repaired and when we can sail. A unit of new recruits is camped out in the courtyard of the inn. Tomorrow they'll be sent to the front. I sit by the window and undress, leaving on only a bra and a pair of skimpy panties. The river fog rolls in and caresses me, like damp, cool feathers tickling my body. The river is black and I haven't lit the lamp. I can't see anything in front of me. The few lamps along the river go out one by one. Before me the night is an endless stretch of black cloth, a backdrop for the game I play with my griffin:

> Griffin, griffin, green as oil
> Two horns two wings
> One wing broken
> A beast, yet a bird
> Come creep over the black cloth

And the griffin comes alive in my hand, leaping in the darkness. The wings outstretched, flapping, flapping.

'Hey.'

I turn. Two eyes and a row of white teeth flash at me from the door. I scream.

'No, don't scream. Don't scream. I was just drafted and tomorrow I'm being sent to the front. Let me hide in your room just for tonight.'

I can't stop screaming. My voice is raw. When I finally stop, he is gone, but two eyes and that row of teeth still wink at me in the dark. A whip cracks in the courtyard.

'Sergeant, please, I won't do it again. I won't run away again . . .'

The shadows of the soldiers in the courtyard appear on the paper

15

window. The man hangs upside down, head twitching. Beside him, a man snaps a whip and a crowd of heads looks up.

'Lao-shih,' I pause and stare at the jade griffin in my hand. One of its wings is cracked. 'I don't want to go to Chungking. I want to go home.'

'Chicken. You getting scared?'

'No, it's not that.'

'You can't turn back. You have to go, even if you have to climb the Mountain of Knives. That's all there is to it, you know what I mean. Anyway, you can't go back now. Everyone in En-shih knows you've run away by now. Your mother won't forgive you either. You know when she was drunk, she would beat you for no reason, until you bled. She will kill you if you go back.'

'No. She wouldn't do anything to me. As soon as I ran away, I stopped hating her. And I still have Father. He's always been good to me.'

'Little Berry, don't get mad, but what kind of a man is he, anyway? Can he manage his family? He can't even manage his own wife. He lets her get away with everything while he sits in his study, the old cuckold, meditating. You call that a man? However you look at it, he's not a man.' She starts laughing. 'You said so yourself. Your father wounded his "vital part" during the campaign against the warlords . . .' She is laughing so hard she can't go on.

'Lao-shih, that's not funny.'

'So why can't a daughter talk about her father?'

'Well, I always felt . . .' I rub the jade griffin.

'You always felt guilty, right?'

'Mm . . . but not about his vital part!' I start laughing. 'I mean this griffin I'm holding. I stole it when I left. Father's probably really upset about it.'

'With all these wars and fighting, jewels aren't worth anything anyway. Besides, it's only a piece of broken jade.'

'This isn't an ordinary piece of jade, Lao-shih. This jade griffin was passed down from my ancestors. Originally jade griffins were placed in front of graves in ancient times to scare away devils. My great-grandfather was an only son, really sickly as a child, and he wore this piece of jade around his neck and lived to be eighty-eight. When he died he ordered that it be given to my grandfather and not used as a burial treasure. My grandfather was also an only son. He wore it his whole life and lived to be seventy-five. Then he gave it to my father who was also an only son. He wore the griffin as a pendant on his watch

16

chain. I'll always remember him wearing a white silk jacket and pants, a gold German watch in one pocket and the jade griffin in the other pocket, and the gold chain in between, swishing against the silk. When he wasn't doing anything, he'd take it from his pocket and caress it and caress it and it would come alive. You know what I thought about when he did that?'

Lao-shih doesn't say anything.

'I would think about what my great-grandfather looked like when he died. Isn't that strange? I never even saw him. I would imagine him wearing a black satin gown, black satin cap, with a ruby red pendant dangling from the tip of the cap, black satin shoes. He would have a squarish head, big ears, long chin, and thick eyebrows, his eyes closed, lying in the ruby red coffin with the jade griffin clasped in his hands.'

'Now your younger brother is the only son. Your father will pass it along to him, and you won't get it.'

'Don't I know it. I wasn't even allowed to touch it. I used to get so upset, I would cry for hours. That was before the war when we still lived in Nanking. Mama took the jade griffin from my father's pocket. She said she should be the one to take care of the family heirloom and that father would only break it sooner or later by playing with it. She had it made into a brooch. I really liked to play with cute things like that when I was a kid, you know? I always wanted to wear the brooch. One day I saw it on Mother's dresser. I reached for it and she slapped me and by accident I knocked it to the floor. One of the wings was chipped and she shut me in the attic.

'It was pitchblack in the attic. I knelt on the floor crying. Then I heard a trinket peddler's rattle outside. I stopped crying and got up. I crawled out the window and stood on the roof, looking to see where the rattle was coming from. The peddler passed by right outside our house. I took a broken pot from the windowsill and threw it at him, then went back to the attic. He cursed up and down the street. I knelt on the floor giggling hysterically. Then the door opened.

'Mother stood in the doorway, the dark narrow staircase looming behind her like a huge shadow. She stood motionless, her collar open, revealing a rough red imprint on her neck. She was wearing the jade griffin.

'In my head I recited a poem that my father had taught me. It was like a magic spell to me:

> Child, come back
> Child, come back

17

Child, why don't you come back?
Why do you come back as a bird?
The bird's sad cries fill the mountains.

It's about a stepmother who is mean to her stepson. Her own son turns into a bird. I thought that Mother was my stepmother and that my little brother was her son. I thought if I said this poem, my little brother would turn into a bird. I decided that one day I would smash the griffin.'

'But now you want to give it back.'

'Mmm.'

'Little Berry, I think it's great you stole it. Your family loses twice: they lost their daughter and their jade. This time your mother might stop and think. Maybe she will change her ways.'

'Has the boat been repaired?'

'Not yet.'

'Damn. How long are we going to have to wait here?'

Tai-hsi has only one street, a stone-paved road that runs up the cliff. It's lined with tea houses, little restaurants, and shops for groceries, torches, lanterns, tow-lines. Lao-shih and I are eating noodles at one of the restaurants. The owner's wife clicks her tongue when she hears that our boat was crippled at New Landslide Rapids and will be heading for Feng-chieh once it's repaired.

'Just wait. New Landslide Rapids is nothing. Further on there's Yellow Dragon Rapids, Ghost Gate Pass, Hundred Cage Pass, Dragon Spine Rapids, Tiger Whisker Rapids, Black Rock Breakers and Whirlpool Heap. Some are shallow bars, some are flooded. A shallow bar is dangerous when the water is low, a flooded bar is dangerous when the water is high. If you make it past the shallow bar, you won't make it past the flooded one. If you get past the flooded one, you'll get stuck on the shallow one . . .'

Lao-shih drags me out of the restaurant.

'Little Berry, I know if you hear any more of that kind of talk, you won't want to go on to Chungking.'

'I really don't want to get back on that boat. I want to go home!'

Lao-shih sighs. 'Little Berry, if that's how you feel, why did you ever decide to come in the first place?'

'I didn't know it was going to be like this.'

'All right. Go on back. I'll go to Chungking all by myself.' She turns away and takes off, climbing up the stone-paved path.

18

I have to follow. We get to the end of the path and stop. Before us is a suspension bridge. Beyond it are mountains piled on mountains, below, the valley. There's a stream in the valley and the waters are roaring. Even from this high on the cliff, we can hear the sound of water breaking on the rocks. Six or seven naked boys are playing in the stream below, hopping around on the rocks, skipping stones in the water, swimming, fishing. One of them sits on a rock, playing a folk song about the wanderer, Su Wu, on his flute. There is a heavy fog. The mountains on the other shore are wrapped in mist and all that is visible is a black peak stabbing the sky.

'What do you say? Shall we cross the bridge?' Someone comes up behind us.

It's the young man who boarded with us at Wu-shan. We nicknamed him Refugee Student. He's just escaped from the area occupied by the Japanese. When he gets to Chungking, he wants to join the army and fight the Japanese. He is barechested, showing off his sun-tanned muscular chest. This is the first time we've ever spoken. But I dreamed about him. I dreamed I had a baby and he was the father. When I woke up my nipples itched. A baby sucking at my nipples would probably make them itch like that, itch so much that I'd want someone to bite them. I had another dream about him. It was by the river. A torch was lit, lighting the way for a bridal sedan to be carried up the narrow steps. The sedan stopped under my window. I ran out and lifted up the curtain and he was sitting inside. I told that dream to Lao-shih. She burst out laughing and then suddenly stopped. She said that if you dream of someone riding in a sedan chair, that person will die. A sedan chair symbolises a coffin. I said, damn it, we shouldn't go on the ship with him through the dangerous Chü-t'ang Gorge if he is going to die!

'I was in the tea house drinking tea and I saw you two looking at the bridge,' he says.

'So you've got your eye on us,' says Lao-shih, shoving her hands in the pockets of her black pants and tossing her short hair defiantly. 'Just what do you want, anyway?'

'Hey, I was just trying to be nice. I came over intending to help you two young ladies across this rickety worn-out bridge. Look at it, a few iron chains holding up some rotting planks. I just crossed it myself a while ago. It's really dangerous. When you get to the middle, the planks creak and split apart. The waters roar below you and you're lost if you fall in.'

'That's if you're stupid enough to try it.'

19

'Miss Shih, may I ask what it is about me that offends you?' Refugee Student laughs.

'I'm sorry . . . and my name is Lao-shih.'

'OK, Lao-shih? Let's be friends.'

'How about me?' I say.

'Oh, you!' He smiles at me. 'But I still don't know your name. Lao-shih calls you Little Berry, kind of a weird name if you ask me . . .'

'I don't want you to call me that, either. She's the only person in the whole world who can call me that. Just call me Mulberry.'

'OK, Lao-shih and Mulberry. You've got to cross this bridge at least once. I just crossed it. It's a different experience for everyone. I wanted to see what it felt like to be dangling on a primitive bridge above dangerous water.'

'Well, what's it like?'

'You're suspended there, unable to touch the sky above you or the earth below you, pitch-black mountains all around you and crashing water underneath. You're completely cut off from the world, as if you've been dangling there since creation. And you ask yourself: Where am I? Who am I? You really want to know. And you'd be willing to die to find out.' He takes a stick and draws two mountain peaks in the dust and joins them with two long thin lines.

A burst of flames shoots up towards us from the valley.

'Bravo.' The boys in the valley clap their hands.

'Hey . . .' yells Refugee Student, 'if someone gets killed you'll pay.'

Lao-shih tugs at his arm telling him that the innkeeper told her never to provoke that bunch of kids. There are eleven of them altogether, thirteen or fourteen years old at the most. They live in the forest on the other side of the bridge. No one knows where they come from, only that they are all war orphans and they live by begging along the Yangtze River. They travel awhile, then rest awhile before going on again. They want to go to Chungking to join the Resistance and save the country from the Japanese. They'll kill without batting an eye. They killed a man in Pa-tung. The ferry across the river wasn't running and there was no bridge, so the boys ferried people across. Someone on the boat offended them. They drugged him with some narcotic incense. They dragged him into the forest, cut open his stomach and hid opium inside it. Then they put him in a coffin and pretending they were a funeral procession, they smuggled opium to Wu-shan.

The boys are still laughing and cursing and yelling down the river. The one with the flute climbs up the mountain. His naked body is covered only with a piece of printed cloth frayed into strips. A whistle

20

on a red string dangles on his chest. He leaps onto the bridge, but instead of walking across it, he grabs the iron chains and swings across from chain to chain with the flute clenched in his teeth. He swings to the middle of the bridge, one hand gripping the chain. With his other hand he takes the flute from between his teeth and trills a long signal to the kids in the valley below.

He shouts, 'Hey, you sons of bitches. How about a party tonight?'

'We'll be there in a minute. Let's catch some fish and have a feast.'

He grips the chain and swings on. The frayed cloth flutters as he moves.

The boys scramble up the mountain. One by one they leap onto the bridge and swing across to the other side. They're naked as well, except for the rags around their waists. It's almost dark. The fog is rolling in. They swing on and on, disappearing into the fog.

'Hey, you guys, swing across.' Their voices call to us through the fog.

'OK, here I come,' Refugee Student jumps onto the bridge and swings across.

'Come on!' says Lao-shih tossing her head and walking out onto the bridge. 'We can't let them think we're chicken.'

I go with her onto the bridge. The roar of the water gets louder. The bridge sways violently. I grip the railing and wait for it to stop swinging.

Dangling from the chain, Refugee Student turns and yells: 'Don't stop. Come on. There's no way to stop it. The faster it sways, the faster you have to walk. Try to walk in time to the swaying.' I grip the railing and move forward. I sway the bridge and the bridge sways me. I walk faster. The mountain, the water, the naked boys, Refugee Student, all fuse together in my vision. I want to stop but I can't and I start to run to the other side while the bridge sways and swings.

Finally our boat is repaired. Lao-shih and I climb aboard singing 'On the Sunghua River', a song about the lost homeland. Twelve oarsmen pull at the oars; the captain at the rudder. There are six passengers on board: an old man, a woman in a peach-flowered dress with her baby, Lao-shih, me, and that crazy refugee student.

We get through Tiger Whisker Rapids.

Rocks jut up from Whirlpool Heap. Black Rock Breakers is a sinking whirlpool. We get through it.

21

Our old wooden boat is heading upstream in the gorge. to one side is White Salt Mountain. To the other, Red Promontory Peak. From both sides the mountains thrust upward towards the sky as if they were trying to meet, leaving only a narrow ribbon of blue sky above us. The noon sun dazzles an instant overhead, then disappears. The white light glistens on the cliffs. It's as if you could take a penknife and scrape off the salt. The river mist is white as salt. I stick out my tongue to lick it, but don't taste or touch anything. The water plunges down from heaven, the boat struggles up the water slope, climbing a hill of water. A mountain looms before us, blocking the way, but after a turn to the left and a turn to the right, the river suddenly widens.

The captain says that every June when the flood tides come you can't go upstream in this part of the river. Fortunately for us, the June tides haven't come yet. Clouds move south, water floods the ponds; clouds move north, good sun for wheat. Now the clouds are moving to the north. Rocks stick out from the river like bones.

We reach the City of the White Emperor. From here it's only three miles to our destination, Feng-chieh.

The twelve oarsmen tug at the oars. Their gasps are almost chants, ai-ho, ai-ho. Black sweat streams down their bodies, soaking their skin, plastering their white trousers to their thighs. Their calves bulge like drumsticks.

The captain yells from the bow. 'Everyone, please be careful. Please stay inside the cabin. We're almost to Yellow Dragon Rapids. Don't stand up. Don't move around.'

Some men are struggling to tow our boat through the rapids, filing along the cliff and through the water near shore, the tow-line thrown over their shoulders padded with cloth, hands gripping the rope at their chest, their bodies bending lower and lower, grunting a singsong, hai-yo hai-yo as they pull. Their chant rises and falls with the ai-ho ai-ho of our crew. The whole mountain gorge echoes as if it were trying to help them pull the boat up the rapids. It's useless. Suddenly white foam sprays the rocks and a white wave crashes down on the boat. The tow-line pullers and the oarsmen stop singing. Everyone stares at the water. The men use all their strength to pull the tow-line, curving their bodies, bending their legs, heads looking up at the sky. Pulling and pulling, the men are pinned to the cliff, the boat is pinned to the rocks, twisting in the eddies. The rope lashed to the mast groans.

The captain starts beating a drum.

It's useless. The men are stooped over, legs bent, looking up at the sky. The boat whirls around on the rocks. One big wave passes by, another one rushes forward. The boat is stuck there, twisting and turning. The drum beats faster; it's as if the beating of the drum is turning the boat.

The tow-line snaps. The men on the cliff curse the water.

Our boat lurches along the crest of a wave, bobbing up and down, then lunges downstream like a wild horse set loose.

There's a crash. The boat stops.

The drum stops. The cursing stops.

We're stranded on the rocks.

First Day Aground.

Two rows of rocks rise out of the water, like a set of bared teeth, black and white. Our boat is aground in the gash between the two rows of teeth. Whirlpools surround the rocks. From the boat we toss a chopstick into the whirlpool and in a second the chopstick is swallowed up. Beyond the whirlpools, the river rushes by. One after another, boats glide by heading downstream, turn at the foot of the cliffs and disappear.

The tow-line pullers haul other boats up the rapids. They struggle through it. The tow-line pullers sit by a small shrine on the cliff and smoke their pipes.

'Fuck it! Why couldn't we get through the rocks? All the other boats made it.' Refugee Student stands at the bow waving at the men on the cliff. 'Hey . . .'

A wave billows between the boat and the cliff.

'Help.'

No response.

The oarsmen squatting in the bow stare at him.

'Hey. All you passengers in the hold, come out.' He yells to the cabin. 'We can't stay stranded here waiting to die! Come on out here and let's decide what to do.'

Peach-flower Woman comes out of the cabin holding her child. Lao-shih and I call her Peach-flower Woman because when she boarded the boat that day, she was wearing a flowered blouse, open at the collar, some buttons undone, as if she were about to take off her clothes at any moment.

The old man follows her out.

As Lao-shih and I scurry out of the cabin, Refugee Student claps his hands. 'Great. Everybody's here. We must shout together at the shore. The water is too loud.'

The old man coughs and spits out a thick wad of phlegm into the river. 'Please excuse me. I can only help by mouthing the words. I can't shout.'

'Something wrong with your lungs?' asks Refugee Student.

The old man's moustache twitches. 'Nonsense. I've been coughing and spitting like this for over twenty years. No one's ever dared suggest that I have TB.' He forces up another wad of phlegm and spits it into the river.

'If we're going to yell, let's yell,' I start shouting at the tow-line pullers on the bank. 'Hey!'

Lao-shih jumps up and yells along with me. 'Hey!'

There's no response. Lao-shih picks up a broken bowl from the deck and hurls it at the bank, shouting: 'You sons of bitches. Are you deaf?'

The bowl smashes on the rocks.

Peach-flower Woman sits on the deck, nursing her child. The baby sucks on one breast, patting the other with its hand in rhythm with its sucking, as if keeping time for itself, pressing the milk out. Drops of milk dribble onto the baby's plump arm. Peach-flower Woman lets her milk dribble out. With a laugh she says, 'Us country folk really know how to yell. That's what I'm best at. Hey – yo –'

The tow-line pullers on the bank turn around and stare at our boat.

'Go on singing. Sing. Don't stop now!' The old man waves to Peach-flower Woman. 'You sound like you're singing when you shout! If you don't sing, they'll ignore us.'

'Hey – yo –'

'Hey . . . Yo . . .' The mountains echo.

'Send – bamboo – raft –' shouts Refugee Student. Peach-flower Woman, the old man, Lao-shih and I all join in. 'Send – bamboo – raft –'

'Send . . . Bamboo . . . Raft.' The mountains mock our cry.

The tow-line pullers wave at us and shake their heads.

'Na – yi – na – ya –'

'Na . . . Yi . . . Na . . . Ya . . .'

We point to the bamboo on the mountains. 'Cut – bamboo –'

'Cut . . . Bamboo . . .'

They wave again and shake their heads.

'Na – yi – na – ya –'

'Na . . . Yi . . . Na . . . Ya . . .'

'Cut – bamboo –'

'Cut . . . Bamboo . . .'

They wave again and shake their heads.

24

'Na – yi – na – ya –'

'Na . . . Yi . . . Na . . . Ya . . .'

'Cut – bamboo – make – raft –'

'Cut . . . Bamboo . . . Make . . . Raft . . .'

The men on the cliff stop paying attention to us. The oarsmen squat on the deck, eating.

The captain finally speaks. 'What good will a raft do? There are rocks all around here. A raft can't cross.'

'How come our boat landed here?'

'We're lucky,' says the captain.

'If you're in a great disaster and you don't die, you're sure to have a good fortune later!' says the old man. 'Let's sing to the bank again!'

'Ho – hey – yo –'

'Ho . . . Hey . . . Yo . . .'

'Tell – the – authorities –'

'Tell . . . The . . . Authorities . . .'

Two of the tow-line pullers start climbing the mountain path.

'Good,' says the old man, 'those two will go tell somebody. Go on singing.'

'You sure know how to give orders! But you don't make a sound,' says Refugee Student.

'Forget it,' Lao-shih says, 'here we are fighting for our lives. Let's not fight among ourselves.'

'Hey – you – there – hey –'

'Hey . . . You . . . There . . . Hey . . .'

'Send – life – boats –'

'Send . . . Life . . . Boats . . .'

The two men on the path stop and turn to look at us.

'Good,' says the old man, 'they'll do it.'

'Na – na – hey – yo –'

'Na . . . Na . . . Hey . . . Yo . . .'

'Send – life – boats –'

'Send . . . Life . . . Boats . . .'

The two men on the path turn again and proceed up the mountain. Two others stand up.

'I've been steering boats in these gorges my whole life. I've only seen capsized boats, never life-boats.' The captain puffs away on his pipe.

A boat approaches us, riding the crest of a wave.

'Na – na – hey – yo –'

'Na . . . Na . . . Hey . . . Yo . . .'

'Help! – help! –'

25

'Help! . . . Help! . . .'

The boat ploughs over another large wave, wavers on the crest and glides down.

'There's an air raid alert at Feng-chieh,' someone shouts to us from the boat as it passes, turns a curve, and disappears.

A paddlewheel steamboat comes downstream.

'Hey, I have an idea!' says Refugee Student as he runs into the cabin.

He comes back out carrying the peach-flower blouse. He stands in the doorway of the cabin, the collar of the blouse tucked under his chin; he stretches out a sleeve and playfully tickles the arm hole as the blouse billows in the breeze.

'You imp,' laughs Peach-flower Woman. 'You're tickling me. You make me itch all over.'

Refugee Student waves the blouse in the air. 'I'm going to use this blouse as a flag. Come on, everyone, sing! The steamboat will see it in the distance and hear our song. Come on. Sing: "Rise up, you who will not be slaves." '

'No, no, not that Communist song. I don't know these new songs,' says the old man.

'Well, let's sing an old one, then. "Flower Drum Song",' I say.

'OK!' Lao-shih races over to pick up the drumsticks and pounds several times on the big drum.

We sing in unison.

> A gong in my left hand, a drum in my right
> Sing to the drumbeat, chant to the gong.
> I don't know other songs to sing
> Only the flower drum song.
> Sing now! Sing. Yi – hu – ya – ya – hey –

Refugee Student waves the blouse. The old man taps chopsticks on a metal basin. I beat two chopsticks together. Lao-shih beats the drum. Peach-flower Woman holds her child as she sings and sways back and forth.

The steamboat glides by.

We stop singing and begin shouting. 'We're stranded. Help! Save us! We're stranded! Help!'

The people on the boat lean against the railing and stare at us. Two or three people wave. The boat disappears.

The water gurgles on the rocks.

'It doesn't do any good to sing!' The captain is still puffing on his

26

pipe. 'Even a paddlewheel wouldn't dare cross here. There's only one thing left to do. The oarsmen will divide into two shifts, and day and night take turns watching the level of the water. We have to be ready to push off at any moment. As soon as the water rises over the rocks and the boat floats up, the man at the rudder will hold it steady and the boat will float down with the current. If the water rises and there's no one at the rudder, the boat may be thrown against those big rocks and that'll be the end of us.'

Lumber planks, baskets, basins, and trunks drift down towards us with the current.

'There must be another ship capsized upstream on the rocks.' The captain looks at the black rock teeth jutting out of the water. 'If it rains, we'll make it. When it rains, the water will rise and when the water rises, we'll be saved.'

Someone has lit a bonfire onshore.

The sky is getting dark.

The Second Day Aground.

The sun glistens on the rock teeth. The water churns, boiling around the rocks.

'It's so dry, even the bamboo awning creaks,' an oarsman says.

Our cabin is beneath the awning. It has a low, curved roof and two rows of hard wooden bunks, really planks, on each side. The oarsmen occupy the half at the bow. That half is always empty; they are on deck day and night. The passengers occupy the half in the stern. Our days and nights are spent on these wooden planks. The old man and Refugee Student are on one side. Lao-shih, Peach-flower Woman and I are on the other side. 'The Boys' Dormitory' and 'The Girls' Dormitory'' are separated by a narrow aisle. The old man has been complaining that we are brushing up against each other in the cabin and goes around complaining that 'men and women shouldn't mix.' So he has ordered that men can't go bare-chested and women can't wear clothing open at the neck or low in the back. His own coarse cotton jacket is always snugly buttoned. Refugee Student doesn't pay any attention to him and goes around naked from the waist up. Peach-flower Woman doesn't pay any attention either. She always has her lapels flung open, revealing the top of her smooth chest. The old man puffs hard on his water pipe, although there's no tobacco in it, and makes it gurgle. 'Young people nowadays!'

The old man sits in the cabin doorway all day long, holding his water pipe, looking up towards the small shrine on the shore and occasionally puffing a few empty mouthfuls on his pipe. Refugee Student paces up and down the aisle which is only large enough for one person to pass.

Lao-shih, Peach-flower Woman and I sit in the 'Girls' Dormitory' and stare at the water around us.

'Hey, you've been going back and forth a long time. Have you got to a hundred yet?' asks Lao-shih.

'Ninety-seven, ninety-eight, ninety-nine, one hundred. OK, Lao-shih, it's your turn.'

Lao-shih paces back and forth in the aisle.

Silence.

'. . . Ninety-five, ninety-six, ninety-seven, ninety-eight, ninety-nine, one hundred. OK, I'm done. Little Berry, your turn.'

I walk up and down the aisle.

Silence.

'Ninety-three, ninety-four, ninety-five, ninety-six, ninety-seven, ninety-eight, ninety-nine, one hundred. OK, Peach-flower Lady, your turn.'

She paces up and down with the baby in her arms.

Silence.

The old man begins murmuring, 'Rise, rise, rise, rise.'

'Is the water rising? Really?' Lao-shih and I leap down from the bunks and run to the doorway, jostling each other as we look.

'Who said it's rising?' The old man taps the bowl of his pipe.

'Didn't you just say it's rising?'

'What are you all excited about? Would I be here if the water was rising? I said rise, rise because it's not rising. This morning that little shrine was right next to the water, about to be flooded. But look, it's still safe and dry by the edge of the water. July is the month that waters rise in the Chü-t'ang Gorge. It's now mid-July and the waters haven't risen. So here we are stuck in this Hundred Cage Pass.'

'Hey, I've already counted to a hundred and five,' laughs Peach-flower Woman.

'You're done then. It's my turn again.' Refugee Student jumps down from his plank and starts pacing in the aisle again. 'Hundred Cage Pass! The name itself is enough to depress you! Hey, Captain,' he yells, 'how far is this Hundred Cage Pass from the City of the White Emperor?'

'What is Hundred Cage Pass?'

'What's this place called, then?'

'This place is near Yellow Dragon Rapids. It doesn't have a name. Call it whatever you like!'

'Call it Teeth Pass, then,' he mutters to himself. He calls out again. 'Captain, how far is this place from the City of the White Emperor?'

'Only a couple of miles. Beyond that are Iron Lock Pass, Dragon Spine Rapids, and Fish Belly Beach.'

'Captain, can we see the City of the White Emperor from here?' the old man asks.

'No, Red Promontory Peak is in the way.'

'If only we could see the City of the White Emperor, it would be all right.'

Refugee Student laughs. 'Sir, what good would it do to see it? We'd still be stranded here between these two rows of teeth.'

'If we could see it, we could see signs of human life.'

'We've seen people since we ran aground. The tow-line pullers, the people on the boats, the people on the paddlewheel, but none of them could save us.'

'I've been sitting here all day. I haven't even seen the shadow of a ghost on the bank.'

Lao-shih shouts from the door. 'There's another boat coming.'

The five of us rush to the bow.

The people on that boat wave at us and shout something, but the sound of the water breaking on the rocks is too loud and we can't understand what they're saying.

'A lot of . . .?'

'On the way?'

'It must be that a lot of rescue boats are on the way.'

'Yeah, a lot of rescue boats are coming!'

The boat glides away.

'A lot of rescue boats are coming?' says the captain. 'A lot of Japanese bombers are coming.'

We scurry back into the cabin.

In the distance we hear faint thunder.

'That's not aircraft, that's thunder.'

'Right, it's thunder. It's going to rain.'

'When it rains the water will rise.'

The thunder approaches. Then we hear the anti-aircraft guns and machine guns. Bullets pock the water spitting spray in all directions. The Japanese bombers are overhead. Lao-shih hides under her quilt on the bunk and calls out to me. 'Little Berry, Little Berry, hurry up and get under the covers.'

29

Suddenly Refugee Student shoves me to the floor and sprawls on top of me.

A minute ago, we were standing in the aisle. Now our bodies are pressing against each other. He is bare-chested and I can smell the odour of his armpits. Lao-shih's armpits smell the same way, that smell of flesh mixed with sweat, but smelling it on his body makes my heart pound. I can even feel the hair under his arms. No wonder Mother likes hairy men; I heard her say that once when I was walking by her door. The thick black hair (it must be black) under his arms tickles me. I'm not even scared of the Japanese bombers anymore.

The bombers pass into the distance.

We get up off the floor. Lao-shih sits on the bunk and glares at us.

'The boat that just passed us has capsized at the bend in the river,' shouts the captain from the bow.

'What about the people?' asks Refugee Student.

'They're all dead! Some drowned, some were killed by the Japanese machine gun fire.'

'I wish everybody in the world were dead,' says Lao-shih, still glaring at Refugee Student.

I go back to the 'Girls' Dormitory'. Lao-shih strains to scratch her back.

'I'll scratch it for you!' I stick my hand up under her blouse and scratch her back.

'That's good, just a little bit higher, near the armpit.' I scratch the part between her armpit and her back. She giggles. 'It tickles! Not so hard. It tickles.' She has only a wisp of hair under her arm.

Refugee Student is pacing up and down in the aisle. He raises his head. 'Bombers overhead, the Gorge below. So many boats capsized. So many people dead. Nobody cares if the boats capsize, or if people die. They are playing a game with human lives!'

'May I ask a question?' says the old man. 'Who's playing a game with human lives?'

Refugee Student, taken aback, says, 'Who? The government. Who else?'

'These gorges have been dangerous for thousands of years. What can the government do about it?'

'We're in the twentieth century now! Sir, have you heard of the invention of the helicopter? Just one helicopter could rescue the whole lot of us. A place like the Gorges should have a Gorges Rescue Station. As soon as we get to Chungking, we should all sign a petition of protest

30

and put it in the newspapers. We have a right to protest. We're victims of the Gorges!'

The Peach-flower Woman laughs on her bunk. 'Sign our names to a petition? I can't even write my own name.'

'I'll write it for you!' Lao-shih eyes me. I take my hand out of her blouse.

The old man sits on his bunk, rocking back and forth. 'It's a great virtue for a woman to be without talent. A woman is . . .' he is seized with a coughing fit and gasps for breath.

Lao-shih mutters. 'Serves him right.'

Refugee Student looks at the old man and shakes his head. He turns to Peach-flower Woman. 'I'll write your name down on a piece of paper. If you copy it every day, by the time we get to Chungking, you'll have learned how to write it.'

'Forget it! Forget it! Too much trouble.' Peach-flower Woman waves her hand. 'I'll just make a fingerprint and when we get to Chungking, my man can write my name for me!'

'When we get to Chungking, I'm going to turn somersaults in the mud!' says Lao-shih.

'When we get there, I'm going to walk around the city for three days and three nights,' I say.

'When we get to Chungking, I'm going to go running in the mountains for three days and three nights!' says Refugee Student.

'When we get to Chungking, I'm going to play mahjong for three days and three nights!' says the old man.

'Hey, look at that big fish!' Peach-flower Woman points at a big fish which has just leapt out of the river onto the deck.

'A good omen! A white fish leaps into the boat!' The old man shouts, 'We'll get out of here OK.'

The five of us turn to look at the shrine on the bank.

The water still hasn't risen; the shrine is still dry.

'There's a shrine but nobody offers incense. It would be better if we tore it down,' says Refugee Student.

'You ought to be struck down by lightning for saying such a thing!' The old man's moustache twitches. 'And the fish, where's the fish?'

'The oarsmen just put it in a bucket. We can kill it tomorrow and have fresh fish to eat.'

'It must not be eaten. It must not be eaten. That fish must not be eaten.' The old man walks to the bow of the boat, scoops up the fish with hands, kneels at the side of the boat and spreads his hands open like a mussel shell.

31

The fish slides into the river with a splash, flicks its tail and disappears.

The old man is still kneeling by the side, his two hands spread open like a mussel shell; palms uplifted as if in prayer.

'Dinner time!' yells the captain. 'I'm sorry, but from now on, we're going to have to ration the rice. Each person gets one bowl of rice per meal!'

The two rows of teeth in the river open wider. Even the rocks are hungry!

'One bowl of rice will hardly fill the gaps between my teeth,' says Refugee Student, throwing down his chopsticks. 'I escaped from the Japanese-occupied area, didn't get killed by the Japanese, didn't get hit by bullets or shrapnel, and now I have to starve to death, stranded on this pile of rocks? This is the biggest farce in the world.'

'You can say that again,' I say to myself.

Lao-shih sits down beside me on the bunk. 'Little Berry, I should have let you go back home.'

'Even if I could go back now, I wouldn't do it. I want to go on to Chungking.'

'Why?'

'After going through all this, what is there to be afraid of? Now, I know what I did wrong. This disaster is my own doing. I've been thinking of all the bad things I did to people.'

'I have, too,' says Lao-shih. 'Once my father beat me. When he turned to leave, I clenched my teeth and said, I can't wait until you die.'

'I cursed my father, mother, and brother that way, too. I can't wait until you die,' I say.

'This is the biggest farce in the world,' says Refugee Student as he paces up and down the aisle. 'The first thing I'm going to do when we get to Chungking is call a press conference and expose the serious problems of the Gorges. All of you, please leave your addresses so I can contact you.'

'Leave it for whom?' asks the Peach-flower Woman. She is sitting on the bunk, one breast uncovered. The baby plays with her breast for a while, then grabs it to suck awhile.

We stare at each other. For the first time I ask myself: Will I make it alive to Chungking? If I live, I swear, I'll change my ways.

'Maybe we're all going to die,' says Lao-shih softly.

'Hah,' coughs the old man, turning his head aside, as if one cough could erase what Lao-shih has said. 'Children talk nonsense. All right. Let's do exchange addresses. When we get to Chungking, I invite you all to a banquet and we'll have the best shark fin money can buy.'

'If you want my address, then you've really got me there!' laughs Peach-flower Woman. 'When we get to Chungking, I won't have an address until I've found my man!'

'Don't you have his address?'

'No.'

'Didn't he write you?'

'He wrote his mother.'

'Are you married to him?'

'Yes, I'm his wife. When I went to his house, I was really young. He's seven years younger than I am. I raised him. He went to Chungking to study. I stayed at home taking care of his mother, raising his son, working in the fields, weaving, picking tea leaves, gathering firewood. I can take anything, even his mother's cursing, as long as he's around. But someone came back from Chungking and said he had another woman. I can't stand that. I told his mother I wanted to go to Chungking. She wouldn't allow me to go. She wouldn't even let me go out on the street So I just picked up my baby, got together a few clothes, and took off. All I know is that he is studying at Chang-shou, Szechuan. When I get there I'm going to look for him. When I find him and if he's faithful, we're man and wife forever. But if he isn't, then he'll go his way, and I'll go mine.'

'Is the boy his?' asks the old man.

'Well, if he isn't my husband's, he certainly isn't yours, either.' She laughs, and lifts the baby up to the old man. 'Baby, say grandpa, say grandpa.'

'Grandpa!' The old man pulls at his greying beard with two fingers. 'I'm not that old yet!' He coughs and turns to Refugee student. 'If it's an address you want, that's hard for me to produce as well. In June 1937, I left Peiping, my home, and went to visit friends in Shanghai. July 7, 1937, the war broke out, and by the 28th, Peiping had fallen. So these past few years, I've been fleeing east and west with my friends. When will this war end? I couldn't stay with my friends forever, so I left them. I intend to do a little business between Chungking and Pa-tung. I don't know where I'll live when I get to Chungking.'

'My address is the air raid shelter in Chungking,' says Lao-shih coldly.

'You're kidding!' says Refugee Student.

'She's not kidding,' I interrupt. 'Her mother died when she was young. She escaped with her father from the Japanese-occupied area. She went to En-shih to study at the Provincial High School; he went to

33

Chungking on business. In 1941, the Japanese bombed Chungking and more than ten thousand people suffocated in the air raid shelter. Her father was one of them.'

'That's right. The famous air raid shelter suffocation tragedy!' The old man talks as if Lao-shih's father became famous because of that.

Refugee Student looks at me.

'I don't have an address either! My home is in En-shih. I ran away.'

'No place like home.' The old man takes a gold pocket watch out of the pocket of his jacket and looks at the time. He replaces it in his pocket, and suddenly I remember the jade griffin on my father's watch chain and think of great-grandfather, clutching the jade in his hands as he lay in the coffin. The old man stares at me. 'I have a daughter about your age. After I left Peiping my wife died. Right now I don't even know if my own daughter is dead or alive. Everyone has roots. The past is part of your roots, and your family, and your parents. But in this war, all our roots have been yanked out of the ground. You are lucky you still have a home, and roots. You must go back! I'm going to inform your father, tell him to come get you and take you home.'

'You don't know my family's address!' I sit on the bunk, one hand propping up my chin and smile at him.

The old man begins to cough again, and points his finger at me. 'You young people nowadays. You young people.'

'You sound like my father,' laughs Refugee Student. 'My father had seven wives. My mother was his legal wife. Father treated his seven wives equally: all under martial law. He calls them Number Two, Number Three, Number Four, . . . according to whoever entered the household first. Number Two was once one of our maids. She is five years younger than Number Seven. They got thirty dollars spending money per month and, every spring, summer, fall and winter, some new clothes. Once a month they all went to a hotel to have a bath and play mahjong. The seven women plus himself made exactly two tables. He took turns spending the night in their seven bedrooms, each woman one night, which made exactly one week. They had more than forty children; he himself can't keep straight which child belongs to which woman. The seven women called each other Sister, in such a friendly way, never squabbling among themselves, because they were all united against that man. Their seven bedrooms were all next to one another, dark and gloomy, shaded by tall trees on all sides. When the Japanese bombed Nanking, a bomb fell right in the middle of the house, and blasted out a crater as big as a courtyard. When the bomb hit, it was the first time those rooms were exposed to sunlight. My

34

mother was killed in that bombing. The six women cried. My father didn't even shed a single tear. When the Japanese occupied the area my father collaborated. I called him a traitor and he cursed me as an ungrateful son. Actually, I don't have an address myself.'

We hear muffled thunder in the distance. It might rain. We look at each other, our faces brighten.

Third Day Aground.

'There's thunder but no rain. The Dragon King has locked the Dragon Gate,' says the captain. 'From now on each person gets only one glass of fresh water a day. We only have two small pieces of alum left to purify the water.'

Fourth Day Aground.

Rain. Rain. Rain. We talk about rain, dream about rain, pray for rain. When it rains, the water will rise and the boat will float out from the gash between the teeth.

'I'm so thirsty.'

When people say they're thirsty it makes me even thirstier. Here at the bottom of the gorge, the sun blazes overhead for a few minutes, yet we're still so thirsty. No wonder the legendary hunter tried to end the drought by shooting down nine of the ten suns.

The old man proposes to divine by the ancient method of sandwriting.

Refugee Student says he doesn't believe in that kind of nonsense.

Peach-flower Woman says divining is a lot of fun: a T-shaped frame is placed in a box of sand. Two people hold the ends of the frame. If you think about the spirit of some dead person, that spirit will come. The frame will write words all by itself in the sand, tell people's fortunes, write prescriptions, resolve grudges, reward favours, even write poems. When the spirit leaves, the frame stops moving.

Lao-shih and I are very excited about the sandwriting and fight over who gets to hold the frame and write for the ghost. The old man says he must be the one to hold the frame because only sincere people can summon spirits.

Instead of sand, we use ashes from the cooking fire and put them in a basin. Then we tie the two fire sticks together and make a T shape. The old man and I hold the ends of the stick. He closes his eyes and works his mouth up and down. The stick moves faster and faster. My hands move with the stick. These are the words written in the ashes:

35

DEEDS RENOWNED IN THREE-KINGDOMS FAME ACHIEVED FOR EIGHTFOLD ARRAY

'That's his poem!' The old man slaps his thigh and shouts. 'It's the poet Tu Fu. I was silently reciting Tu Fu and he came. Tu Fu spent three years in this area and wrote three hundred and sixty-one poems here. Every plant and tree in this region became part of his poetry. I knew Tu Fu would come if I called him.' Then he addressed the ashes: 'Mr Tu, you were devoted to your emperor and cared about the fate of the country. You were talented, but had no opportunity to serve your country. You rushed here and there in your travels. Our fate is not unlike your own. Today all of us here on the boat wish to consult you. Is it auspicious or inauspicious that we are stranded on these rocks?'

MORE INAUSPICIOUS THAN AUSPICIOUS

'Will we get out?'

CANNOT TELL

'Are we going to die?'

CANNOT TELL

'Whether we live or die, how much longer are we going to be stranded here?'

TENTH MONTH TENTH DAY

'Horrible, we'll be stranded here until the Double Tenth Festival. When will it rain?'

NO RAIN

The stick stops moving in the basin.
'Tu Fu has gone. Tu Fu was a poet. What does he know? This time let's summon a military man. We're stranded here in this historically famous strategic pass. We should only believe the words of a military man.' The old man shuts his eyes again and works his mouth up and down. We hold the stick and draw in the ashes.

36

DEVOTED SLAVE TO THE COUNTRY
ONLY DEATH STOPS MY DEVOTION

'Good. Chuko Liang has come. I knew his heroic spirit would be here in the Chü-t'ang region. Not too far from here, Chuko Liang demonstrated his military strategy, the Design of the Eightfold Array.' The old man concentrates on the ashes. 'Mr Chuko, you were a hero. Your one desire was to recover the central part of China for the ruler of the Han Dynasty. Today China is also a country of three kingdoms: The National government in Chungking, the Communist government in Yenan, and the Japanese puppet government in Nanking. All of us here on the boat are going to Chungking; we are going there because we are concerned about the country. Now, instead, here we all are stranded in this rapids in a place not far from the Eightfold Array. Is it inauspicious or auspicious?'

VERY AUSPICIOUS

'Good, we won't die stranded here?'

NO

'Good! Can we reach Chungking?'

YES

'How long are we going to be stranded here?'

ONE DAY

'How will we get out of this place alive?'

HEAVEN HELPS THE LUCKY PERSON

'When will it rain?'

ONE DAY

'Mr Chuko, when we get to Chungking, we will all go on foot to your temple and offer incense to you.'
The sticks stop moving.

37

The old man stares at the ashes. After a long time, he returns from his reverie. 'We're stranded in the midst of history! The City of the White Emperor, the Labyrinth of Stone called the Eightfold Array, Thundering Drum Terrace, Meng-liang Ladder, Iron Lock Pass. All around us are landmarks left by the great heroes and geniuses of China. Do you know what Iron Lock Pass was? Iron Lock Pass had seven chains more than two thousand feet long crossing the river. Emperors and bandits in the past used those iron chains to close off the river and lock in the Szechuan Province. The Yangtze River has been flowing for thousands of years, these things are still here. This country of ours is too old, too old.'

'Sir, this is not the time to become intoxicated by our thousands of years of history!' says Refugee Student. 'We want to get out of here alive.'

'I'm sure it will rain tomorrow. When it rains, the waters will rise.'

'Do you really believe in sandwriting?' I ask. 'Was it you writing with the sticks or was it really Tu Fu and Chuko?'

'You young people these days!' He strokes his beard. 'Here I am, an old gentleman, would I try to deceive you?' He pauses. 'I really believe that heaven cares about us and answers prayers. Let me tell you a story from the *Chronicle of Devoted Sons*. There was a man called Yü Tzu-yü who was accompanying his father's coffin through the Chü-t'ang Gorge. In June the waters rose and the boat which was supposed to carry the coffin couldn't sail. Yü Tzu-yü burned incense and prayed to the Dragon King to make the waters recede. And the waters receded. After Yü Tzu-yü escorted the coffin through Chü-t'ang Gorge, the waters rose again.'

'Who's the devoted son aboard this boat?' asks Peach-flower Woman with a laugh.

No one answers.

'How long have we been stranded here?'
    'Has it been five days?'
    'No, seven.'
    'Six days.'
    'Well, anyway, it's been a long, long time.'
    'The moon has risen.'
    'Ummm.'
    'What time is it?'
    'If the moon is overhead, it must be midnight. Do you have a watch?'
    'Yes. It's stopped. I forgot to wind it. Who else has a watch?'

38

'I do, but I can't see what time it is. It's too dark.'

'It's so quiet. Only the sound of water on the rocks.'

'Is everyone asleep?'

'No.'

'No.'

'Then why don't you say something?'

'I'm so hungry and thirsty.'

'There went a big wave.'

'How can you tell? You can't see them from here.'

'I can hear them. It's very quiet, then suddenly there's a loud splash and then everything's quiet again.'

'Can you hear anything else?'

'No.'

'Are they still fighting?'

'Who?'

'Those people on the bank.'

'Oh, they won't come down here to fight. Mountains on both sides, water below, sky above.'

'Hey, everyone, say something. OK? If nobody speaks, it's like you're all dead.'

'What shall we say?'

'Anything.'

'When it's quiet like this and nobody is speaking, it's really scary. But when you talk it's also scary, like a ghost talking.'

'Well, I'll play my flute, then.'

'Good idea. I'll tell a story while you play the flute.'

'I'm going to play "The Woman and the Great Wall".'

'It was a moonlit night. Quiet like this. He woke up smelling gunpowder . . .'

'Who is "he".'

'The "he" in the story. He woke up smelling gunpowder. There were ashes everywhere. Even the moon was the colour of ash. When he woke up, he was lying under a large tree on a mountainside. The slope faced the Chialing River. Thick black columns of smoke arose from Chungking on the opposite bank. Reflected in the waters of the river, the black pillars of smoke looked like they were propping up the sky. Between the columns of smoke everything was grey as lead, as if all the ashes in Chungking had been stirred up.

'He stood up, shaking ashes and dust off his clothes. He had just woken up. He had been hiding in the air raid shelter dug into the mountain for seven days and nights. The Japanese bombers had come

39

squadron after squadron, bombing Chungking for more than one hundred fifty hours. More than two hundred people had hid in the shelter. Eating, drinking, defecating, urinating, all inside the shelter. He couldn't stand it anymore and had gone outside. Another squadron of bombers appeared, and he didn't have time to run back to the shelter. He heard an ear-splitting crash and sand scattered in all directions. When he awoke, he saw someone digging at the entrance of the shelter. A bomb had destroyed the shelter. He took to his heels, afraid he might be dragged back by the dead inside the shelter. He ran and ran. He didn't know where he was running to. Only by running could he be safe. Suddenly he heard a voice calling out, "Let me go, let me go!" '

'Hey, keep on playing the flute, don't stop.'

'You want me to keep on playing the same song over and over?'

'Yeah. Go on with the story.'

'All right. The voice kept repeating. "Let me go. Let me go." He stopped, looked all around. There was no one in sight, only some graves. There weren't even any tombstones. He walked to the right. The voice came from the left. He walked to the left. Then the voice came from the right. He walked straight ahead. The voice was behind him. He turned and walked back. The voice was silent. He couldn't keep walking in the opposite direction. That direction would take him back to the shelter that was full of dead bodies. He had to keep going forwards. He heard the voice again. "Let me go, let me go." The voice seemed to come from under his feet. He stopped. It was coming from the right. He walked to the right and the voice got louder. He saw an empty grave. The coffin had probably been removed recently. A woman was lying in the grave, her head sticking out of the grave, her eyes closed, repeatedly mumbling, "Let me go." He dragged her out of the pit. Then he recognised that she had been among the people hiding in the shelter. He couldn't tell if she was the ghost of someone killed in an explosion, or a living person who had escaped the bombing. He had a canteen with him. He poured some water down her throat. She regained consciousness. He asked her how she got out of the shelter and into the grave. She stared at him, as if she hadn't heard. She said, "Tzu-jao, can't you run faster than that?" He told her his name was Po-fu. The woman said, "Don't try to fool me. Has the soldier gone?" He said, "The bombers have gone." She became impatient and repeated over and over, "I mean the Japanese soldier who tried to rape me. Has he gone?" The man said, "There are no Japanese soldiers in Chungking." '

'The flute sounds especially nice tonight. That poor lonely woman looking for her husband and crying at the Great Wall. What about the woman?'

'Which woman? The woman at the Great Wall or the woman in the grave?'

'The one in the grave. Hurry up and tell us the rest of the story. It's like a modern-day Gothic.'

'OK. The woman sat down, beating the ground with her fist over and over. "This isn't Chungking. This is Nanking. We've just gotten married. The Japanese have just invaded the city." The man groped for his watch in his pocket, struck a match, and showed her the name Po-fu engraved on the watch. The woman said, "Don't try to fool me, Tzu-jao! This is a matter of life and death. Run quick. The Japanese are combing Nanking for Chinese soldiers. They think that anyone with calluses on his hands is a soldier: rickshaw pullers, carpenters, coolies. Yesterday in one day they took away one thousand three hundred people. The dogs in Nanking are getting fat, there are so many corpses to feed on." The woman looked around and asked, "Has the soldier gone?" He could only reply, "Yes, he's gone." The woman pointed to the river. "It was on that road through the bamboo thicket. I was walking in front. He was walking behind me. You know, Tzu-jao, we have been married more than a week and you still haven't been able to touch me. You called me a stone girl." '

'What do you mean, "stone girl"?'

'Stone girl. It means a girl who can't have sex.'

'Go on, you're just getting to the best part.'

'The woman kept on talking like that. She said, "It happened on that road through the bamboo thicket. I was walking in front. He was walking behind me. In full daylight, he stripped off his clothes as he followed me, throwing his uniform, boots, pants, underwear down at the side of the road. He stripped naked, leaving only his bayonet hanging by his side. When he was wearing his uniform, he seemed so much taller. Naked he looked shorter, even shorter than I am. He ripped off my clothes. He tossed me about like a doll. He threw down his bayonet. Just then, Tzu-jao, you came running up. Don't you remember? You ran out of Nanking, but you came back into the city. That Japanese was a head shorter than you. When he saw you, he jumped on your back, two hands gripping your neck. He was biting the back of your neck with his teeth. You reached back and cut his back with your fingernails. He screamed. Some people from the International Relief Committee came running up. The head of the

41

committee was a German. He ordered the Japanese soldier to leave. But the soldier kept biting your neck. Finally the German put out his arm and the Japanese saw his Nazi insignia. He slipped off your back and ran. He didn't even pick up his clothes or his bayonet." '

'What a good story. Then what happened to her?'

'When? After the rape incident in Nanking? Or after the bombing in Chungking?'

'After the bombing.'

'Her husband and son were looking for her. Just before the bombers hit, her two-year-old son started crying in the shelter. The people in the shelter cursed him and wanted to beat him to death. The father had to take the child outside. The mother was too anxious to stay in the shelter. She went outside to look for her husband and son. Then the bombers hit and bombed the shelter. After the bombing was over, she didn't know how she got into the grave. She didn't remember anything. She thought she was in Nanking and was reliving the past. Her husband had gone with their child to the police station to look at the list of the dead. I took her to the police station. She was still suffering from shell-shock and didn't recognise her husband and child. She said she had just gotten married and didn't have any children. She still believed she was in Nanking and was reliving the slaughter. When I saw that she was reunited with her husband and child, I left.'

'You? Are you telling us a story, or is that something that really happened to you?'

'It really happened to me. We've been stranded here so long that it seems like a story from a former life,' says the old man.

Refugee Student is still playing 'The Woman and the Great Wall' on his flute.

> With the New Year comes the spring
> Every house lights red lanterns
> Other husbands go home to their families
> My husband builds the Great Wall

A big wave passes with a crash. Then it's quiet. Another crash, then it's quiet. Human heads are bobbing in the water, their eyes wide open and staring at the sky. Everything is silent.

A large eagle flies overhead. It circles the heads and flaps its huge black wings. It is beautiful. It is dancing.

Suddenly the old man and Lao-shih are sitting on the eagle's wings,

42

each sitting on one side, like on a seesaw. The eagle wheels in the air. They wave at me.

Refugee Student suddenly appears, riding on the eagle's back. He begins to play his flute to the rhythm of the eagle's dance.

The eagle carries them off down the river.

The human heads float downstream.

I call to the eagle, begging them to stop. I want to fly away on the eagle, too.

Peach-flower Woman, her breasts exposed, appears, riding the crest of a wave. She waves at me. She wants me to join her on the waves.

The sound of the flute gets louder.

I wake up. The flute is coming from the stern. Lao-shih, the old man, and Peach-flower Woman are all asleep. Peach-flower Woman hugs her child to her bare breasts.

I sit up.

The sound of the flute suddenly stops.

I go out of the cabin and walk around the bales of cotton which are piled in the stern.

Refugee Student, bare-chested, is lying on the deck.

The gorge is black. He reaches up to me. I lie down beside him. We don't say anything.

My virgin blood trickles down his legs. He wipes it off with spit.

The Sixth Day Aground.

There is shouting on the river.

We run out. A ship tilts down over the crest of a wave. It spins around in the whirlpool. The people on the ship scream, women and children cry as it spins faster and faster, like a top.

White foam bubbles around the lip of the whirlpool. The foam churns up into a wall of water, separating us from the spinning ship. Then the wall collapses with a roar. The ship splits open like a watermelon. Everyone on board is tossed into the water.

Another huge wave rolls by. Everyone in the water has disappeared.

Silence.

The river rushes on. The sun dazzles overhead.

The beating of the drum begins.

Refugee Student, his shirt off, thick black hair bristling in his armpits and above his lip, is pounding on the drum, every muscle straining, teeth clenched. He raises the drumsticks over his head and pounds on the drum with all his strength. He isn't beating the drum. He is beating the mountains, the heavens, the waters.

43

The mountains, the heavens, the waters explode with each beat.

'Don't stop, don't stop. A victory song,' shouts the old man.

A crow flies toward our boat.

Refugee Student throws down the drumsticks and glares at the crow.

'Black crow overhead, that means if disaster doesn't strike misfortune will,' Peach-flower Woman says as she holds her child.

I pick up an empty bottle and throw it at the crow. 'I'll kill you, you stupid bird.' The bottle shatters on a rock.

Lao-shih picks up a bowl and hurls it at the crow. 'You bastard. Get out of here!' The bowl shatters on a rock.

The crow circles overhead.

The old man shakes his fist at the crow. His face turns purple. 'You think you can scare us, don't you? You think I'll just die stranded here, don't you? When the warlords were fighting, I didn't die. When the Japanese were fighting, I didn't die. Do you think I'm going to die now, on this pile of rocks? Hah!' He spits at the crow.

'Goddam mother fucker,' shouts Refugee Student, leaping at the crow. 'You can't scare me. Just wait and see. I won't die. I'll survive and I'll raise hell, that'll show you. Mountains, waters, animals, crows! Can you destroy the human race? You can destroy a man's body, but you can't destroy his spirit. Ships capsize, people drown, mountains are still mountains and water is still water. Millions of people are being born, millions of people have survived these rapids. The world belongs to the young. Don't you know that, you bastard? People won't die out. Don't you know that? They won't die out.'

The old man claps his hands. 'Attention, please. Everybody. This is a matter of life and death. I have something to say that I can't hold back any longer. I think the captain has been playing a game with our lives. This gorge is even more dangerous than Hundred Cage Pass. Of course he knows this danger. He's been sailing these gorges all his life. This boat should only carry freight; they shouldn't allow passengers. He certainly shouldn't take our money before we arrive safely at our destination. The ticket for this old wooden boat costs as much as a paddlewheel. But since he has taken passengers and taken our money, he is responsible. First, he ought to ensure our safety; next, he ought to take care of feeding us. When we cracked up on New Landslide Rapids, we were delayed four days in Tai-hsi. We trusted the captain. We didn't ask him to return our money. We got back on the boat. Then the tow-line broke at Yellow Dragon Rapids. We've been stranded here since then. The Yangtze River, several thousand miles long, is the greatest river in Asia, and we have to ration drinking water. What a joke. From that day on, he took no emergency measures. Not only that, but when we were screaming for help at the top of our lungs, he made sarcastic remarks. The captain and the crew know how to handle boats. In case anything happens, they'll know what to do and how to escape. We don't know what to do. The passengers and the crew make thirteen people, but there are only six of us, and we are all either too old or women and children. We're outnumbered and we can't fight them. And so, I want to stand up and be counted and speak out for justice. I represent the six passengers, including the baby, and I demand that the captain do something.'

The oarsmen and the passengers are silent.

The captain, squatting on deck, blank expression, sucks the empty pipe in his mouth. 'You people just don't understand the difficulties in sailing these Gorges. We boatmen make our living by relying on the water and Heaven. If it doesn't rain, the water won't rise and there's nothing we can do about it. Whether it's sailing the river or riding a horse, there's always danger involved. There's a slippery stone slab in front of everyone's door. No one can guarantee you won't slip on it and crack your skull. For human beings there is life and death, for things there is damage and destruction. It all depends on the will of Heaven. If you want someone to die, the person won't die. But if Heaven commands it, he will die. All I can do now is ask that you passengers calm down and wait patiently a while longer.'

'God, wait for how long?'

'If we have to wait, we at least ought to have food to eat and water to drink!'

'There's plenty of water in the river, and plenty of fish.' says the captain. 'If there's no more firewood, then eat raw fish. If there's no more alum, then drink muddy water. We boatmen can live like that. Can't you?' He sucks hard on his pipe. 'When our tobacco is gone, we smoke the dregs; when that's gone, we smoke the residue.' He reaches down and strikes the drum. 'Those who can't eat raw fish can chew the leather on this drum.'

Refugee Student spits at the captain. 'I'll chew on you.'

The captain throws his head back and laughs. 'Go ahead and chew. Go ahead and slice me up. Kill me. What good will that do? When the water rises and the ship floats up, you will need someone at the rudder.'

'Dice!' I yell as I cross the aisle into the 'Boys' Dormitory'. The old man is sitting on his bunk, rolling three cubes of dice around in his hand. I snatch them away and cast them on the bunk. 'Come on, let's gamble. Everybody, come here.'

'Just what I was thinking!' As soon as the old man gets excited, he starts coughing. 'You should live each day as it comes. I still have four bottles of liquor in my suitcase. I was going to give it to friends in Chungking. To hell with them, let's drink now.' He opens a bottle, gulps down a few swallows and strips off his coarse cotton jacket. He bares his chest. A few hairs stick out of his armpits.

The five of us crowd together in a circle. Lao-shih has ignored me all day. I wanted to sit next to her on the bunk, but I also want to sit beside Refugee Student. In the end I squeeze in between them. We pass the bottle around the circle. I've never drunk liquor before. I gulp down several swallows in one breath. My face burns. My heart pounds. My left hand rests on Lao-shih's shoulder and my right on Refugee Student's shoulder.

We put the dice in a porcelain bowl in the middle of the circle.

I raise my hand and shout, 'I'll be the dealer!'

'I'll be the dealer.'

'I'll be the dealer.'

'I'll be the dealer.'

'I'll be the dealer.'

'Let's decide by the finger-guessing game. Two people play; the winner gets a drink; then plays the next person. The last one to win gets to be dealer!'

'Let's begin. Two sweethearts!'

'Four season's wealth!'

'Six in a row!'

'Lucky seven!'

'Pair of treasures!'

'Four season's wealth!'

'Three sworn brothers.'

'Pair of treasures!'

'Eight immortals!'

'Six in a row!'

'One tall peak!'

'Four season's wealth!'

'Lucky seven!'

'All accounted for!'

'Three sworn brothers!'

'Six in a row!'

'Pair of treasures!'

'Eight immortals!'

'Lucky seven!'

'I win, I win,' yells Peach-flower Woman. 'I'm the dealer. Place your bets.'

'OK. Fifty dollars!'

'Sixty!'

'Seventy!'

'Eighty!'

'Another seventy!'

'Another eighty!'

Peach-flower Woman laughs. 'You just bet more and more. I haven't got that kind of money. If I win, I get to be the dealer again. If I lose, I'll give up. I get first crack at this!' She grabs the dice and throws them into the bowl with a flourish.

They spin in the bowl.

I take a drink. I see several dice spinning crazily in the bowl.

'Five points! The dealer has got five points!'

'I only want six points, not a single point more!' The old man cups the dice in his hands, blows on them, and then his hands open slowly like a mussel shell opening.

The dice spin in the bowl.

He bends over, glaring at the dice and yelling, 'Six points, six points! Six points! Six points . . . oh, three points.' He lifts Peach-flower Woman's hand and sticks the bottle in it. She takes a drink. She's still holding the bottle and he lifts her hand and puts the bottle in his mouth. He pulls her toward him with his free arm and presses her face against his naked chest. He strokes her face. He finishes off the liquor with one gulp and sucks on the empty bottle like a baby.

'Sir, men and women should not mix. The booze is all gone. I don't have anything for you either. You are supposed to be respectable. You shouldn't touch a woman's body like this,' laughs Peach-flower Woman as she struggles out of his embrace and straightens up. Her chignon comes undone and hair straggles across her chest. The buttons of her blouse pop open, exposing most of her breasts.

The dice click as they spin.

'Six points! Six points! Six points! I only want six points!' Lao-shih yells, rolling on the bunk.

I roll next to her, turn over and climb on her back, as if riding a horse, bumping up and down as if keeping time. I yell with her: 'Six points! Six points! Six points! Six points! Six points! If you keep on ignoring me, I won't let you go. Six points! Six points!'

She suddenly stops yelling, yanks me off and rolls over on the bunk and grabs me. Our faces press together, legs curl round each other, rolling this way and that. She mumbles. 'If you ignore me, I won't let you go. If you ignore me, I won't let you go.'

'Four points,' yells Peach-flower Woman. 'You got four points, Lao-shih! OK, Mulberry, it's your turn.'

I struggle out of Lao-shih's embrace, roll over to the circle and stuff the dice in my mouth. I spit them out into the bowl. 'Six points, come on, six points! Six points! Six points!' Refugee Student is sprawled beside me on the bunk. I pound on his hip with my fist. 'Six points! Six, six, six, six points. How many? How many did I get?'

'Five points. The dealer also got five. The dealer wins!' Another bottle of liquor is passed around.

Refugee Student sits up, grasps the dice with his toes and tosses them into the bowl. He looks at me and begins singing in a flirtatious way. The dice, as if minding their own business, clatter in the bowl.

> Wind blows through the window
> My body is cool
> The willow tree whistles in the wind
> Lovers behind the gauze curtain
> I have a husband, but we're not in love
> Ai-ya-ya-erh-oh!
> Ai-ya-ya-erh-oh!

'Too bad, you lose. You only got three points.' Peach-flower Woman smiles at Refugee Student. With one sweep she rakes in the money.

She beat all of us.

We place larger and larger bets. In the end, we take out all our money and valuables and place them down. Lao-shih and I share our money. We have only two hundred dollars left in our purse. I put down the two hundred dollars. She puts down the purse. The old man bets his gold watch. Refugee Student bets his flute.

We lose again. Refugee Student wins twenty dollars, the price of the flute. He proposes that we change dealers. The three losers all agree. Of course, he gets to be the dealer. In any case, since he's won once already, he's probably the only one who can beat Peach-flower Woman. But the three of us losers don't have anything else to bet.

'I have an idea,' says Refugee Student. 'We play only one more game. This time it will be a game of life or death. Everyone take out his

most prized possession. If you don't have anything, then be
I'm the dealer. If I win, I'll take things, if there are any. If no
people!'

'And what if you lose?'

'All I've got is myself, you can do what you want with my body, cut it
in two, chop it up, lick it, kiss it, fuck it.'

'Good Heavens!' laughs Peach-flower Woman, as she looks at her
baby asleep on the bunk. 'My most valuable possession is my son.'

Refugee Student leans over to her and says in a low voice, which
everyone can overhear: 'Your most valuable possession is your body.'

The old man chuckles. 'What you say sounds reasonable. I'll bet my
house in Peiping. If you win, you can go back and take possession. I
hope to retire there once the war is over.'

'I'll bet my family heirloom!' I yell as I step over to the 'Girls'
Dormitory' and fish out the jade griffin from the little leather case by
my pillow and return to the 'Boys' Dormitory'. 'Hey, everybody, this is
my family heirloom.'

The old man's eyes suddenly light up. He tries to take it out of my
hand. Refugee Student snatches it first and holds out his hand, staring
at me. 'Are you going to bet this piece of junk?'

'Yeah.'

'I'd rather have you! A sixteen-year-old virgin!'

Lao-shih jerks me behind her and thrusts out her chest. 'Hey,
Refugee Student, I'll make a deal with you. I'll bet this person here! If I
win, you get out of my way! If you win, I'll get out of your way. You
know what you did.'

'What did I do?'

'Mulberry, did you hear what he just said.'

'I heard. So what did I do?'

'Did you hear what she said, Miss Shih?' Refugee Student says. 'Two
negatives make a positive. They cancel each other out. OK, everybody,
back to your places. I won't steal your precious treasure. So what are
you going to bet? Speak up!'

'I don't have anything. I have only myself.'

'OK, if I win, I'll know what to do to you,' Refugee Student leans
over to Lao-shih and stares greedily into her eyes.

'Drink up! Come on and drink. It's the last half bottle.' The old man
raises the bottle to his lips.

We pass the bottle around. The liquor is gone. The dice click.
We shout.

'One, two, three.'

'One, two, three.'

'Four, five, six.'

'Four, five, six.'

'One, two, three.'

'One point!'

'OK, it's one point.'

'Come on, be good, be good, another one!'

'Be good, be good, don't listen to him. Let's have a two.'

'OK, four points, great, the dealer got only four points.'

The dice click again.

'Five points! Five points! Five points. Hey, you little beauties, did you hear me, I only want one more point than that bastard. Keep my house in Peiping for myself. Five points. Five points, please, five points . . . Ah! You fuckin' dice, you did it, you did it! Five points!'

The dice click again.

'Five points, five points, five points, I don't want any more, don't want any less, just give me five points. Good Heavens, let me win just this once in my life. Just this once. Only five points, only five points. Have they stopped? How many did I get? Six points, six points, thank Heavens.'

Everything is floating in front of my eyes. I feel the boat floating underfoot, everyone, everything is floating. The jade griffin is floating. It's my turn, they tell me. I grab the dice and throw them in the bowl. I get a six. They tell me I only picked up two dice and want me to throw again. Lao-shih stuffs the cubes in my hand. I can't hold on to them, they slip from my hand into the bowl. I hear Lao-shih moaning, 'It's over, it's over.'

Dealer, Refugee Student:	Four points
Old Man:	Five points
Lao-shih:	Six points
Mulberry:	Three points
Peach-Flower Woman:	Four points

'Dealer, I beat you by one point!' says the old man. 'You little punk, I want you to kneel before me and bow three times and kowtow nine times. Nine loud thumps of your head.'

Refugee Student kneels down on the bunk.

'No, no,' says the old man, crossing his legs on the bunk like a bodhisattva statuette. 'Haven't you ever seen your old man pray to his ancestor? Did he ever kneel on a bunk and kowtow to his ancestors that way? Humph. You have to kneel properly on the floor. Knock your head against the floor so I can hear it!'

Refugee Student jumps down from the bunk into the aisle and bends down.

'Hey, you punk, just slow down a little. Have you ever seen anyone kowtowing half-naked? Go put your clothes on!'

Refugee Student grinds his teeth.

Lao-shih, Peach-flower Woman and I burst into laughter.

He puts on his shirt, squeezes down in the narrow aisle between the two rows of bunks.

The old man sits erect on the bunk, strokes his beard and raises his voice like a master of ceremonies, 'First kowtow, second kowtow, third kowtow.'

Refugee Student stands up, bends and bows with uplifted hands, then kneels back down. 'Fourth kowtow, fifth kowtow, sixth kowtow!' He gets up again and bows and kneels back down. 'Seventh kowtow, eighth kowtow, ninth kowtow. Ceremony finished.'

Refugee Student scrambles to his feet and points at me. 'I beat you by one point. It's time to settle with you.'

'That's easy. You won, take the jade griffin.' I pick it up and give it to him.

He doesn't take it and just looks at me. 'What would I do with that? I'm a wanderer. All I want is a pair of straw sandals, a bag of dried food, and a flute. This jade griffin is nothing but a burden. Anyway,' his voice becomes oddly tender, 'I owe you something. I'll repay you by giving back your jade griffin.'

'You don't owe me anything. You said yourself, "two negatives make a positive." I don't owe you anything either.' As I'm talking, I try to put the jade griffin in his hand. I'm sure I'm holding it securely, but when I raise my hand, it slips through my fingers and falls. I let out a cry.

The griffin breaks in two on the floor.

The old man picks up the two halves and fits them together. It looks as if they're still one piece.

'All right, we'll do it this way. You take one half, I'll take the other,' Refugee Student says and stuffs one half into my hand.

'OK, problem solved,' Lao-shih rubs her palms together and noisily grinds her teeth. 'Now, I get to settle with the dealer. I'm the real winner; I beat the dealer by two points. I only wanted the satisfaction of beating you. I won't cut you in two or chop you up. I won't chew on you. I only want you to dress up like a girl and sing the Flower Drum Song.'

51

'Good idea.' I also want to get even with him. I toss my half of the jade griffin into the opposite bunk.

The three of us, Lao-shih, Peach-flower Woman and myself, strip off his clothes, leaving only his underpants. I remember when he lay naked on the deck, his weight on my body, headhanging over my shoulder, my thighs wet and sticky. I'm still a little sore there. I couldn't stop caressing his body, like a rock in the sun, so smooth, warm, hard. So a man's body was that nice. I wished I could stroke him forever, but when he used all his strength to push into my body, it hurt. How could Peach-flower Woman sleep with her man every night? And even have a baby? I don't see how she could bear the pain.

We dress him in Peach-flower Woman's clothes. He wears the peach flower blouse, blue print pants, a turban of a blue-flowered print wound around his head, two red spots painted on his cheeks, his masculine eyebrows thick and black.

He daintily folds his muscular hands and curtsies. He picks up Peach-flower Woman's red handkerchief and dances with it like a woman, twisting, turning and singing.

> You say life is hard
> My life is hard
> Looking for a good husband all my life
> Other girls marry rich men
> My husband can only play the flower drum.

The old man, sitting on the bunk, laughs until he has a coughing fit. Lao-shih, Peach-flower Woman and I roll with laughter on the bunk.

Suddenly Refugee Student leaps on the bunk and jumps on Lao-shih. 'If you ignore me, I won't let you go! I'm your girl. You have to give me a kiss!' He presses his mouth to hers and strokes all over her body. Lao-shih begins choking and can't speak.

I tackle him to save Lao-shih. 'Good, I've got you both!' He turns over and grabs us both, one on each side, arms locked around our necks, holding us down. 'You come here, too,' he says to Peach-flower Woman. 'I can put you on my chest.' Lao-shih and I beat on his chest with our fists.

He suddenly lets go and rolls over to Peach-flower Woman. He stretches up his hands to her, fingers curled like claws and moves closer and closer to her, saying. 'Now, I am going to settle with you!'

She laughs, her blouse still unbuttoned, straggling hair on her breasts. 'What do you want? Take all the money I've won?'

'Me? I want you!'

She points a finger at him. 'Let me ask you, are you man enough to deal with me?'

'If he isn't, I am,' chuckles the old man.

Refugee Student doesn't say anything. He rips open her blouse and jumps on her, grabs one of her breasts and begins to suck on it. The old man jumps over and grabs her other breast.

She laughs, her full breasts shaking. 'Do anything you want with my poor old body. Just don't take away my baby's food. My milk is almost gone!'

The baby on the bunk starts to cry.

She shoves them aside and goes to pick up the baby.

'I have an idea. I still have two cigarettes. Be my guest.' Refugee Student gropes in his pocket and pulls out two cigarettes – The Dog with a Human Head brand – and steps over to Peach-flower Woman.

She is lying on the bunk nursing her child. Refugee Student lights a cigarette, grabs Peach-flower Woman's right foot and sticks it between her toes. He presses his face against her sole and smokes, his two hands holding her foot.

The old man does the same with her left foot.

She lies flat on her back, her limbs flung out as the child clutches her breast and sucks loudly and the two men hold her feet and suck on the cigarettes.

She laughs and jerks back and forth. 'You devils, you're tickling me. You sex fiends. When you die, you'll get what's coming to you.

'Listen, listen. The bombers are coming back.' I hear the droning of aircraft.

We sit up stiffly in our bunks.

The roar comes toward us.

It's twilight in the Gorge, the time when day can't be distinguished from night, or clear dusk from a cloudy day.

The captain and the crew are in the bow.

'Hey, the bombers are coming. Come and hide in the cabin. Don't endanger everybody's lives!' shouts the old man.

No response.

'Look at that,' says the captain, 'three planes in each formation. Nine altogether.'

'Mother fuckers, those traitors. Only traitors aren't scared of bombers.' Refugee Student gnashes his teeth.

53

A boat comes downstream. People on board are yelling. Gongs are crashing.

The bombers are overhead. We sprawl on the bunks. I cover my head with the quilt, the rest of my body exposed.

The yelling, the gong, the roar of the planes get louder.

'I can't hear you,' the captain is shouting to the people on the other boat, 'say it again.'

Shouting, gongs, bombers.

'The Japanese have surrendered!' the captain finally yells.

We rush to the bow. A flame shoots up in the sky, bursting into colourful fireworks. A huge lotus flower opens above the Gorge.

The airplane sprinkles coloured confetti and flies off down the river.

The boat, separated from us by the churning rapids, glides downstream to the sound of cheering and gongs.

'Victory, victory, vic . . . tory . . . tory . . .'

The echoes of their cheers, the confetti swirl around us and disappear into the river.

'There are thunderheads on those mountains,' shouts the captain. 'It's going to rain. We'll float away.'

Dark clouds appear overhead.

Refugee Student, still dressed as the flower drum girl, snatches up a drumstick and pounds on the drum. The drum is thundering.

PART II

PART II

ONE

Peach's Second Letter to the Man from the USA Immigration Service

2 February 1970

CHARACTERS

PEACH, she tells the Immigration Service agent the story of cannibalism among a group of pioneers trapped in a snow storm for six months by Donner Lake in the Sierra Nevada mountains. With her letter she encloses the notebook Mulberry kept in Peiping in 1949 when the city was under siege by the Communists.
THE MAN FROM THE IMMIGRATION SERVICE.

Dear Sir:

I'm heading west on Interstate 80, just leaving Wyoming's Little America. I found a ride in a camper going to Donner Lake when I was in the gas station diner. The owner of the camper, Mr Smith, just got back from Vietnam. As soon as he got back, he got married. The newlyweds are going to Donner Lake for their honeymoon.

This is the newest model camper trailer. It's a moveable house: living room, bedroom, kitchen. It has every kind of electrical appliance imaginable: refrigerator, stove, air conditioner, heater, TV, radio, stereo, vacuum cleaner. The camper is full of second-hand store antiques: Victorian armchairs with torn satin covers, cracked Chinese vases (made in the reign of the Ch'ien-lung Emperor in the Ch'ing Dynasty), filthy sheepkin wine bags from Spain, fuzzily engraved silver platters from Iran, rusty Turkish swords, chipped Indian powder horns. A picture of a naked woman wearing a man's tophat is painted

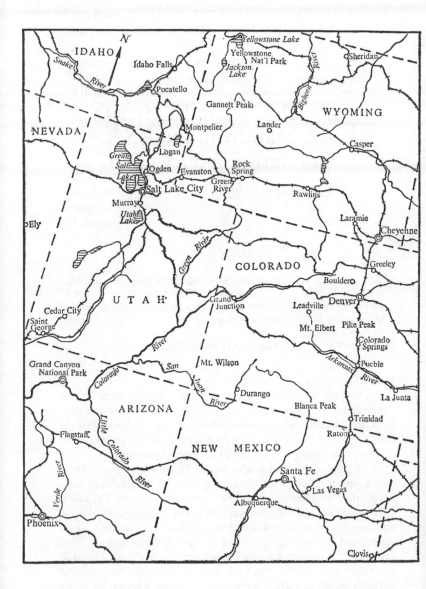

on the outside of the camper. She is kneeling with her back turned, head to one side looking over her shoulder, smiling. Her body is mapped in different coloured sections, labelled like a butcher's chart: ribs, loin, rump, soup, bone, chuck, shank.

Here I am, Peach, sitting in this honeymoon trailer writing you a letter. Mr Dark, you can see this trailer from far away. I'm sending you a map, too, to show you where I've been and where I'm going. If you want to chase me, then come on.

There are too many roads to explore. There are too many interesting things to tell you: changing scenery, changing climate, different animals (Wyoming's mountain goats, Utah's deer, wolves on the plains, foxes, jack rabbits . . .), so many different people. The further west you go, the friendlier the people get. In the East, not even little children will pay attention to you, but in the West, even policemen wave! (Mulberry, who is scared to death of the police, would faint at that!) In New York, you're only another worn-out foreigner, like thousands of others.

I've found out that I'm not the only hitchhiker. All along the highway, many lonely people are standing by the roadside, trying to thumb a ride. Some cars stop for you, some keep right on going. If you catch a driver's eye, he'll wave (they always wave at miniskirted girls on motorcycles, or bored children in backseats about to fall asleep), lightly lifting his hand from the steering wheel, waving, then lowering his hand; drivers always wave that way: solemn and self-assured.

Of course, it's dangerous. Someone in Colorado said to me, 'A woman hitchhiking alone! Didn't you see the newspaper yesterday? Several girls hitchhiking were killed; the murderer cut out their hearts and ate them, and then threw their bodies over a cliff. And then there was the male hitchhiker who disappeared; they found his clothes floating in the river, but they never his body. There were some young people hitchhiking and . . .' I've heard a lot of those stories.

I just got a ride in Rock Springs, Wyoming during a blizzard with a very strange man. After I got in the car, he couldn't stop laughing. 'Aren't you afraid of me, uh, Little Woman? Ha, ha, ha!' (He was even shorter than I am!) When he wasn't laughing, he was making strange noises: 'Wu–wu–wu–', like a yelping coyote. Then he would slide next to me and say, 'Do you know how porcupines have sex? Uh, Little Woman? Do you know how porcupines have sex? Wu–wu–.' The only time he stopped laughing was when the road got icy. Then he concentrated on driving. Waves of swirling snow billowed in front of us. His expression became serious. 'I can't hear the tyres hitting the pavement. That means black ice has formed on the road. This road will be the death of someone yet.' We struggled over that road all the way to Little America. From the distance we could see the huge billboard–

FOOD AND GAS

Before the car came to a complete stop, I jumped out and waved good-bye to the little porcupine. There was a nice diner at the gas station. The owner used to be a truck driver and had been stranded there in a blizzard many years ago. So he opened a rest stop on the very place. People passing through stop to eat and get gas. Inside the diner was all red; red walls, red lights, red carpet. But the tables were black. Blonde waitresses wove back and forth among the black tables. I sat down at an empty table near the door. A young couple at the table next to mine smiled at me; perhaps they smiled because I was a foreigner. We began to chat. They told me they were going to Donner Lake for their honeymoon. As soon as he started talking about Donner Lake, Mr Smith got excited, as if it were the most beautiful place in the world. Before he was sent to Vietnam, he went ice-skating every winter at Donner Lake.

He told me that Donner Lake is an important point between California and Nevada. Transcontinental highways pass through there. You can also get there by train. The trains have special equipment which protect them from being buried by avalanches. Or, if you want, you can abandon modern machines and get there on horseback, taking trails through the mountains to the lake.

Donner Lake lies in the basin of a valley. It's surrounded by mountains several thousand metres high. In the summer the lake is a green mirror reflecting forests of willow and pine. Quail, grouse, and antelope live there. The pure lake water reflects mountains capped with glittering snow, brooks, wild-flowers, and granite slabs. In the winter, Donner Lake is the West's largest skating rink. The mountains echo with bells from the ski lift and with the skaters' laughter on the lake. Everyone there is relaxed and carefree, looking for a good time.

It was getting dark. The snow fell harder; gust after gust of whistling wind and swirling snow. Someone in the diner put a quarter in the juke box and several young people started singing along with the Beatles' 'Blackbird'.

> Blackbird singing in the dead of night
> Take these broken wings and learn to fly.

60

All your life you were only waiting
For this moment to be free.
Blackbird singing in the dead of night . . .

Mr Smith said that the wind and snow reminded him of the story about the Donner Party. I asked him what the Donner Party was. He explained that it was a group of California-bound pioneers who were stranded, snowbound by the lake for six months. After that, the lake was called Donner Lake.

This is the story: In 1846, 'California Ho!' was a catchy phrase. The Gold Rush hadn't started yet and there was no overland route west. About one hundred people from the Midwest formed a group to go to California and Mr Donner was elected leader of the party. They started out in the spring, crossing valleys and deserts where there were no roads, pushing on through settlements of hostile Indians. When they reached Donner Lake it was the end of October. They found themselves facing towering cliffs. Winter set in earlier than usual that year. The oxen slowed down as they pulled the wagons, looking for grass under the snow. They could see that the pine forests on the mountains in the distance had already turned white. A blizzard was coming. They abandoned the wagons. They left the cattle to fend for themselves. They went on foot with the children and horses, trying to get through the mountain pass. It was hard for them to throw away the things they had brought with them. A tin of tobacco, a bolt of cloth: it took a long time to decide what to get rid of. They needed to rest. Then they started to climb the mountain in the snow. By evening they weren't far from the top. But it was too cold and they were too tired and they couldn't go on. They finally got a fire started and nothing could make them leave the fireside. They lay in the snow and fell asleep. While sleeping one of the men felt a weight pressing so heavily on his chest that he couldn't breathe. He woke and discovered he was buried in the snow. The people and the animals had vanished; around him was a vast expanse of whiteness. He yelled. Heads poked up through the snow. The animals were scattered. Snow blocked the pass.

They climbed down to the valley and built several small huts beside the lake. Again and again they struggled to cross the mountain and when they failed, they would climb back down. When the food supply ran out, they ate wild animals. Later they couldn't even find wild animals to eat. Blizzard followed blizzard. They were starving and didn't have the energy to gather firewood. After one month, the snow was piled up eight feet high, as tall as their huts. The winter had just begun. Some of them collapsed from hunger and cold. Some died. They tried to think of ways to escape. They used the U-shaped ox yokes to make snow shoes. Whether they tried to escape or whether they remained there, death was certain. Those who tried to escape struggled with fate. Those who remained were resigned to the will of heaven. Their fate was the same, but they responded differently. Some gave in and some didn't.

Ten men, five women, and two boys set out wearing the ox-yoke snow shoes. They spent several days climbing the mountain. Wind and snow kept coming and they were snowbound again. Later the place where they were stranded was called the Death Camp. Bitter cold, exhaustion, hunger. They lay in the snow beside the fire. Those who fell asleep had their hands burnt to a crisp. Several people died. Those who survived starved for five days. Then someone chopped off the legs and arms of the corpses and roasted them over the fire. As they ate, they turned their heads aside and cried. After two days, even those who had refused to eat human flesh in the beginning were eating it. There was only one rule: they wouldn't eat the flesh of their own kin. One girl stared wide-eyed at her little brother's heart which was stuck on a twig, roasting over the fire. A wife agreed that the others could eat her husband's corpse in order to save them from starvation. They cut off as much flesh as they could eat; the rest was made into jerky. Two men discovered deer tracks in the snow and they knelt down and wept and prayed, although they really weren't religious. They killed the deer and lay on top of its body, lapping up its blood. They sucked the deer dry and their faces were smeared with blood. (Too bad that Mulberry, who is scared by the sight of blood, couldn't have heard this story!) After thirty-three days, they finally reached safety. Only two men and five women were left.

Back by the lake, more people were dying. Others tried to escape. One mother set out alone so that her child could have her share of the food. They lived in the snowpit, subsisting on animal skins, bones, and rats. The children slurped spoonfuls of snow from fine porcelain teacups and pretended it was pudding. Everyone lay in his own little hut. Going to others' huts became an important affair.

A man named Boone kept a diary. He referred to the people in the other huts as strangers. The rescue team finally reached them in February. One woman, crying, asked if they had fallen down from heaven. Snow blocked the mountain pass and was still falling. A group of women and children, the sick and the weak, went with a rescue team.

Two men, three women, and twelve children remained at the lake. They didn't have the strength to leave.

When the remaining survivors at Donner Lake had eaten the last animal skin, they dug up the corpses of those who had died of starvation and ate them. In March, a second rescue team arrived. As the rescue team approached, they saw a man carrying a human leg. When the man saw them coming, he threw the leg down into a pit in the snow. At the bottom of the pit lay several heads so frozen that their faces were not distorted, torsos with legs and arms missing, chests ripped open, hollow where the hearts were dug out. Outside Donner's tent several children were sitting on logs, blood smeared on their mouths and chests. They were holding their father's heart, tearing off pieces to eat. They did not respond when they saw the rescue party. Around the fire were strewn bones, hair, and pieces of the limbs. The children's mother was lying in the hut. To save the children she told them to eat anything they could. But as for herself, she wouldn't eat her husband's flesh even if it meant she would starve to death.

In April the last of the survivors were rescued. Only half the people in the Donner party had survived.

Mr Smith finished telling the story. He asked me where I wanted to go.

'Donner Lake!'

He laughed. 'I've got a new recruit.'

> He's a real nowhere man,
> Sitting in his Nowhere Land
> Making all his nowhere plans for nobody . . .

The Beatles sang on. More people got up to dance.

'Nowhere Man, can you see me at all?' Mr Smith was singing along with the Beatles. He stood up, bowed to his bride, and stretching out his hand, swept her close to him and they began to dance. His hand was stainless steel.

Peach
2 February 1970

P.S. I am enclosing Mulberry's Peiping diary.

TWO

Mulberry's Notebook
Peiping, The Besieged City

(December 1948–March 1949)

CHARACTERS

MULBERRY, she flies north to Peiping, surrounded by the Communists. She is the only passenger on a one-way plane. She left her home at Nanking, because she was afraid of being arrested by the Nationalist government, which was still in power in the South of China, for her connections with some young people suspected of being Communist. In addition, she could not bear living at home: her brother had run away to the Communist-occupied area, her father had committed suicide, her mother is still having an affair with the family butler. In besieged Peiping, she stays with the Shens, an old, traditional family in decay. The Communists have taken most of the country.

AUNT SHEN, (in her sixties), she has been bedridden several years, covered with a red satin quilt embroidered with gold love birds. Joy, the slave maid, massages her paralysed legs. For many years after her marriage, she had no child. It was one of the most important Confucian values for any family to have a son who would carry on the family name. She 'promoted' one of the young slave maids to be concubine for her husband, and thought that she would take over the boy if the concubine bore one. The concubine bore a son, Chia-ch'ing. But Mrs Shen found that she could not control her when she was more favoured by the husband and became more and more powerful in the family. When the concubine became pregnant again, Mrs Shen murdered her with poison (more sons meant more favour and power). Mrs Shen represents the traditional order in its dying throes.

CHIA-KANG, (in his twenties), Mrs Shen's son. He represents the bourgeois class in traditional China. He has leisure, fine tastes and delicate fingers with long nails. He sings Peking Opera, flirts with girls. He is fondled, indulged and possessed by his mother. He wants to marry Mulberry to assert himself as a *man*.

HSING-HSING, (in her twenties), a lively, seductive girl. She lives with her mother, and grandfather on her father's side. Her father is an official working for the Nationalist government in Nanking and lives with his concubine. Hsing-hsing was in love with Chia-ch'ing before he left home and became a Communist. She expects the Communists to come and the world to change.

JOY, (in her twenties), Mrs Shen's slave maid. She is always smiling. She has waited on Mrs Shen many years, sitting on the edge of her bed and massaging her legs. When the Communists approach Peiping, Mrs Shen sends her to Hsing-hsing's grandfather as concubine.

MR WAN, Hsing-hsing's grandfather.

AMAH CHIEN, Aunt Shen's maid.

I'm the only passenger on the plane.

At the airport in Nanking as I was boarding, an airline official repeated to me, 'The Communists have already surrounded Peiping. Everyone is fleeing south.'

And I repeated to him: I understand the situation completely, but I have decided to go on to Peiping.

We are flying above the clouds.

Beneath the clouds Nanking slips by: strikes, hoarded rice, suspended classes, marches, demonstrations, bloody riots.

My past disappears under the clouds.

The only thing I've brought with me is the broken jade griffin.

Peiping is a square inside a square, shaped like the Chinese character: 回

The Forbidden City.

The Inner City.

The Outer City.

The Communists are outside the city.

In the alleys and lanes the hawkers are crying out:

> Sweet apples
> Fresh dates
> Popcorn.
> Who will buy my altar flowers?
> God of Wealth for sale.

65

The Shens live in the western part of the city, in a house with two courtyards.

The Main Gate.

The Gate of the Dangling Flowers.

The Gate at the Entrance of the courtyard.

The central part of the house is divided into three rooms.

The centre room is the parlour. Aunt Shen and her son Chia-kang live in the two rooms off the parlour. It was just a year ago, when the situation in the North deteriorated that Chia-kang moved from the west wing to the central part of the house and dismissed the cook and the chauffeur.

The tenants in the east and west wings come and go in an endless stream. They arrive here, having fled from the area beyond the Great Wall: from Shantung, and Shansi, from Honan, Hopei and other parts of the country. They usually stay less than two months, then flee south. Since September, the Communists have occupied the whole of the North-east and war has erupted again in Hsüchou and around Peiping and Tientsin. The east and west wings are hard to rent out. If they are left empty, army units or refugees will probably take them over. The east wing is now rented by the Chengs, who, born and bred in Peiping, swear they will never leave. They sold their own house. Their monthly rent is ten dollars. In November ten dollars could still buy twenty packs of cigarettes. In December it only bought ten packs. Amah Ch'ien and the maid, Joy (mentally retarded), live in the west wing. The two rooms in the south section of the house, beyond the Gate of the Dangling Flowers, are occupied by a group of more than twenty students who fled from T'ai-yuan in Shansi. T'ai-yuan has been surrounded by Communist forces for half a year now. I live in a small room off the corner courtyard. It was Chia-kang's father's study when he was alive. It is isolated from the rest of the house and has a cobblestone patio.

The sky is black and silent. In the central courtyard the old acacia tree, bent and blacker than the sky, its blossoms shed, stretches its branches upwards.

Two low explosions sound in the south horizon. The south sky reddens suddenly. Red sparks sprinkle down. Above the acacia branches the dark sky begins to glow.

Chia-kang and I race to the central part of the house to see his sick mother, Aunt Shen. She is lying on the brick *k'ang* facing the wall. A thin knot of ash-coloured hair sticks out from the thick red silk quilt.

Amah Ch'ien has just finished styling Aunt Shen's hair. She goes to get the spittoon. Joy is sitting on the edge of the *k'ang* massaging Aunt Shen's legs.

'Chia-kang,' she says, still turned to the wall. 'Was that the Eighth Army?'

'Mother, the Eighth Army is still a long way away. They wouldn't just fire two shots. It's probably some local explosion.'

'Do you think the Eighth Army is responsible?'

'The Eighth Army took over the airport the day after I arrived,' I say.

'Mulberry, that's only a rumour. It's not certain. There are rumours everywhere these days; that the Eighth Army has occupied the Summer Palace, that the Tower of Treasures has collapsed, that the glass arch in front of the Confucian Temple was smashed. That the ancient cypress grove by the Temple of Heaven was chopped down, that the golden Buddha of Yung-ho Palace was stolen! That the Temple of the Reclining Buddha. . .'

'All right, all right, Chia-kang. That's enough. Don't say any more. What you don't know won't hurt you.'

'Mother, don't worry. Peiping has always been an imperial city. It has a way of turning disaster into good fortune. The Mongols, Manchus, the Allied Army, the Japanese, none of them could swallow her; it's Peiping that swallowed them up.'

'Well, that cheers me up a little, Chia-kang.'

'Mother, if you stop worrying, you'll get better.'

'And when will that happen? I've seen doctors, I've gone on, I've drawn lots, made vows, it's all useless.'

I look at Joy. 'Since I've been in Peiping, Joy is the only person I've seen who is still smiling.'

Aunt Shen glances at her. 'I wish I were an idiot girl, with no responsibility except massaging someone's legs. If the sky fell, I'd still be massaging and grinning from ear to ear.'

'And I'd like to be a nightsoil collector,' says Chia-kang. 'I'd carry a large barrel on my back and take a long iron shovel in my hand and scoop it up from the ground and toss it into the barrel on my back, all the while humming lines from the opera.'

'Joy,' Aunt Shen cries out, still facing the wall.

'Hai,' she answers.

'Your day has arrived. You're going to have a better life from now on. But what about me? There will be no one to massage my legs. You better be good to old Mr Wan.'

'Hai.' Joy nods vigorously.

'Joy, do you really like that old guy?' asks Chia-kang with a smirk.

'L-l-luv bim.' She stutters.

'What about "bim" do you "luv"?'

'I l-l-uv bim.' Joy is still grinning.

' "Luv" to sleep with "bim"?'

'L-l-uv bim.'

'Chia-kang,' laughs Aunt Shen, 'I won't let you intimidate her.'

'What's wrong with a little joke? Nothing else to do in Peiping. There are soldiers and refugees all over, you can't go anywhere.'

'Go make fun of someone else then. It wasn't easy to find a master for her. If it doesn't work out this time I'll marry her off to you. Mulberry!' Aunt Shen suddenly turns to face me, 'Do you still have that little gold chain I gave you when you were little?'

I unbutton my collar and take out the necklace. 'I wear it all the time. After the war was over and I left Chungking and went back to Nanking, Mother gave it to me.'

'I gave it to you before the war. Was it '36? I took Chia-kang with me to Nanking and we stayed at your house. You were only six or seven then. Chia-kang was ten. You two played so happily together. I gave you that little gold chain for your birthday. Your mother laughed and pointed at you, "Twenty gold ingots. I'll sell her to you for that!" she said. In the wink of an eye twelve years have passed. Your father, Chia-kang's father, those two sworn brothers have both passed away . . .'

'Mother, all those years Mulberry's family has been in the South. We've been in the North. Just think, it was only after the end of the war with Japan that we got in touch again. Mulberry said that it was the strength of that little gold chain that brought her to Peiping.'

'Now that you are here, there's no way to leave, Mulberry. The railroad from Peiping to Tientsin has been cut. Thousands of people have made plane reservations, but you have to pay gold. We aren't able to do that.' Aunt Shen pauses, then suddenly cries out. 'Chia-kang! Chia-kang, I've got a cramp in my foot!'

Chia-kang runs over and shoves Joy aside. He pulls back the red silk quilt embroidered with mandarin ducks. He uncovers her small foot, no longer bound, pointed and wrinkled, the toes twisted.

'Ai-ya! Ai-ya! It hurts!'

'Mother, I'll massage it for you. Every time I do it, you get better,' says Chia-kang, cradling the small foot in his hands, massaging the muscles along the top of the foot with his thumbs.

'Good, that's good. Chia-kang, don't stop!'

Chia-kang cradles the calf of her leg as he massages. He presses his thumbs along the top of her foot. 'Mother, is it better? Is it better now, Mother?' he says over and over.

She doesn't answer. She stares at the foot in her son's hand. Then she says, 'Chia-kang, dig into it with your fingernails.'

Chia-kang presses his long nails into the top and arch of her foot.

'Chia-kang, harder. That's good, there . . .'

'Mother, I've pinched so hard that you're bleeding. Does it hurt?'

'If only I could feel pain. When I saw that foot in your hand, I was shocked. It wasn't my foot anymore.'

'If it's not yours, then whose is it?' Chia-kang laughs.

'I've been sick too long, Chia-kang. I'm in a daze all the time. Sometimes when your face suddenly flashes before my eyes, I even think it's your father.' She withdraws her foot from his hands and wiggles her toes at him, laughing. 'Look, it's alive again.'

Joy, still grinning, returns to her place on the *k'ang* and begins massaging Aunt Shen's legs.

The oil lamp on the table sputters and almost goes out. We haven't had electricity or water for two days. Now the fire in the stove is dying down.

Chia-kang opens the door to the stove and throws in a shovelful of coal. The fire flares up again, the flames licking higher and higher, about to leap out of the stove. He hurriedly slams the door shut. The shadow of the acacia tree, with its branches stretching up to the sky, appears etched in the paper window.

Suddenly the clamour of shouts and a dog's barking come toward us. The noise moves from the main gate to the Gate of the Dangling Flowers. The barking comes into the main courtyard. The howls lengthen into low muffled whimpers.

Aunt Shen turns to face the wall. 'Dogs cry at funerals. Chia-kang, get that dog out of here.'

I go with Chia-kang to the courtyard. Ice has formed on the ground. The sky is dark. Seven or eight of the students are beating a black shadow by the wall with clubs and poles. The shadow darts from corner to corner, whimpering. The rest of the students stand aside, cheering.

I ask them why they are beating the dog. 'There's nothing to eat in this city. When you're hungry, you want to eat meat!' replies one of the students, grinding his teeth.

'Mulberry, last night I dreamed you were at the Temple of Heaven.'

'I've never, ever been there, Chia-kang.'

'Maybe that's just as well. The Temple of Heaven, the Imperial Park, the Imperial Temple, the Confucian Temple, Yung-ho Palace, now they're all overrun by refugees. The holy grounds of the sacred temples of the past are now contaminated, but when I dreamed about the Temple of Heaven, there was one tiny part untouched.

'You know, the Temple of Heaven is the place where the Ming and Ch'ing emperors sacrificed to Heaven and prayed for a good harvest. All around, as far as you can see, are old cypress trees. The Hall of Prayer, the Imperial Circular Hall, and the Altar of Heaven are all located at the Temple of Heaven. The Hall of Prayer is where the emperors prayed for a good harvest. It's a huge round triple-roofed hall with double eaves. The ceiling of the dome is decorated with golden dragons and phoenixes, glazed blue tiles; there are no beams. The three roofs and the double eaves are supported solely by twenty-eight giant pillars. The Imperial Circular Hall houses the memorial tablets of the emperors. It's a small circular shrine with a golden roof, glazed blue tiles, red walls, and glazed doors. The Altar of Heaven is where the emperors sacrificed to heaven. It's a three-tiered circular terrace built of white marble. The centre of the altar is a round stone encircled by nine rings of marble. Each ring consists of marble slabs arranged in multiples of nine. The rings radiate from the centre like ripples on a pond. When you stand there, you feel like you've touched heaven. If you whisper in the centre of the altar, you can hear a loud echo.

'The Temple of Heaven I dreamed about wasn't like that at all. The Hall of Prayer, the Imperial Circular Hall, the Altar of Heaven were crowded with refugees' straw mats, quilts, and sheets. Ragged pants were hanging out to dry in the sun on the white marble balustrades. The memorial tablets of the emperors had been thrown down to the ground, and the Hall of Prayer was full of excrement.

'The old cypress trees had been cut down.

'Only the shrine of the Altar of Heaven was still clean: white marble stones. The sky above the shrine was still clear blue. Mulberry, I dreamed you were lying in the centre of the altar, naked, looking up at the sky. You were so clean and pure.'

He gently pushes me down on the sofa in my room and begins stripping off my clothes.

I suddenly sit up. 'No, Chia-kang, you must respect me.'

'I know you're a pure, clean girl. I want to marry you right away.

70

Even if we sleep together now, it's all right because we're going to get married.'

'Even if I sleep with my own husband, it's still dirty.'

The parlour door opens. Large flakes of snow whirl around the doorsill. Tiny icicles dangle from the acacia branches. A crow, immobile, sits on a branch, a black statue in ice.

Hsing-hsing hurries in, removes the red scarf from around her head and brushes the snow from her clothes. Her long pigtails swish back and forth. She goes into Aunt Shen's room, saying, 'A bomb went off at the airport, killing and wounding more than forty people!'

'Who did it?' asks Chia-kang.

'Someone said that the Nationalists did it as they were retreating from the airport. Someone else said the Eighth Army did it as they were seizing the airport . . .'

'Then the Eighth Army is really going to fight its way into Peiping.'

'Second Master Shen, the Eighth Army is already at the base of the city wall. Grain and vegetables can't get into the city. The city's food supply is almost gone. My mother hoarded up twenty sacks of flour and forty heads of cabbage. The Nationalist government just released a lot of prisoners in order to save food, but the prisoners didn't want to leave the prison. No one would feed them if they left. The guards forced them out with bayonets. The government has declared a general amnesty. They have even released traitors from the Japanese occupation and a lot of students who had been jailed for demonstrating. Five or six students from our university were released. Some people say that Nationalist Commander Fu Tso-i is talking peace with the Eighth Army, and that he wants to form a coalition government with them. Other people say that Fu Tso-i is withdrawing to the Northwest to join forces with Ma Hung-k'uei. Anyway, Peiping will never be the same. Someone else said . . .'

'Hsing-hsing, stop it, don't go on!' says Aunt Shen lying on the *k'ang* with her face to the wall.

'Hsing-hsing,' laughs Chia-kang. 'Tell us some good news, not bad news. We're just doing fine here, and then you come bursting in like a firecracker with all this bad news. May I ask where you got all these rumours?'

'Rumours? Things are changing out there. You are still shut up at home playing Second Master Shen. There are all sorts of reports on the bulletin board at school. We don't even go to class anymore. Everyone

71

is wriggling and dancing to the Rice-sprout Song.'

'Hsing-hsing, are you happy that the Eighth Army is coming?'

'Why should I be happy? I'm just not afraid, that's all.'

'Do you think that once the Eighth Army arrives, your family will have an easy time? Your grandfather was a wealthy landlord and your father is an official in Nanking!'

'That has nothing to do with me. My mother and I are victims of the old society. My father hasn't paid any attention to my mother for more than ten years. He took his concubine and her children to the South to live in luxury. We never had any part of it. My mother stayed home and took care of his parents. When the old lady died, she was the one who had to find someone for the old man. Joy!'

'Hai!' Joy is still sitting on the *k'ang*, massaging Aunt Shen's legs. She is still grinning.

'Joy, my grandfather has your new room all ready for you. He has even bought the flowers you'll wear!'

'White lilies.'

Hsing-hsing laughs. 'Silly girl, even if it were summer now, you couldn't find white lilies in Peiping. No fresh flowers or vegetables can come into the city. You have to pay gold for cabbages. Aunt, I came today about Joy . . .'

'Has the old gentleman changed his mind?' says Aunt Shen, suddenly turning over.

'He won't change his mind! He wants her to come earlier. He says that things are getting worse and worse. When the Eighth Army enters the city, he won't be able to marry Joy.

'He had wanted to invite enough guests to fill two tables at the wedding banquet. Now the guests can't come. Some suddenly left for the South. Others are moving to smaller houses. Some have set up stalls in Tung-tan selling things. Others are trying to get plane reservations to escape. The old gentleman asked me to come over and ask Auntie if Joy could come over tomorrow.'

'How can I bear to see Joy leave? For the past few years, I have had to have my legs massaged day and night. These days you have to give up whoever wants to leave and whatever you have to throw away. Come and get her tomorrow.'

'Joy!'

'Hai!'

'Pack up your things. I'll come get you early tomorrow.'

'Hai!' Joy's grin widens.

'Lately the old gentleman has been very cheerful, even praising my

72

mother for being a good daughter-in-law. Things are getting worse and worse. All the scrolls in the house have been taken down and packed away. He took out a painting of the sun rising in the East above the ocean and hung it in the parlour. He said it had a double meaning: it's supposed to bring good luck and decorate the room, but it also could welcome the Red Army. Mulberry,' Hsing-hsing suddenly turns to me, 'I really envy you. You came up here to the North all by yourself. The South really is more open-minded. I've never been to the South, but I really want to go. When I think of the South, I think of willow trees.'

'I've wanted to go to the South for a long time, but I couldn't get away,' says Chia-kang looking at his mother's tiny, flower-like chignon of grey hair. 'To me the South is an endless rampart of stone, an old monk, bent over, tugging on the rope to ring the bell at the Temple of the Crowing Cock, his whole life spent like that, just ringing the bell.'

'To me Peiping is grey cranes flying over the Gate of Heavenly Peace, it's mansions of the Manchu Monarchs, lots of gates, secluded courtyards. It's houses haunted by fox spirits,' I say.

Chia-kang laughs. 'So you escaped to Peiping. Hsing-hsing and I want to escape to the South.'

'But now both North and South are in chaos.'

'Did you hear that? Did you hear that, Chia-kang?' says Aunt Shen, still facing the wall. She raises her arm and shakes her finger in the air, 'The North and South are both in chaos. You better listen to me and stay at home.'

' "Inside Peking there's a big circle. In the big circle is a smaller circle. In the smaller circle is the imperial yellow circle where I live." ' Chia-kang begins to sing the role of the disguised emperor in the opera *The Town of Mei-lung*.

Hsing-hsing immediately takes up the role of the flirtatious innkeeper who does not recognise him.

' "I recognise you now."

"Whom do you recognise me to be?"

"You're my brother's . . ."

"Eh?"

"Brother-in-law."

"Ai, nonsense!"

"You military clerks aren't polite. You shouldn't flirt with women of good breeding."

"Good woman, good woman, you shouldn't wear begonias in your

73

hair. You wiggle delightfully. But most bewitching are your begonia flowers."

"Begonias, begonias. You are making fun of me. I make haste to throw these flowers on the ground. Throw them down, crush them underfoot. Never again will I wear begonia flowers."

"You, my lady, aren't being polite. You should not crush these begonia flowers. I, in all my dignity, shall retrieve them. I shall place, place, place these begonia flowers in your hair." '. Chia-kang throws the red scarf over Hsing-hsing's head.

' "You're nothing special!" ' Hsing-hsing brushes off the scarf and eyes Chia-kang flirtatiously, her taunting expression about to crinkle into a smile. 'Second Master Shen, return to your imperial yellow circle. Come on, Mulberry, sing a part.'

'How could a girl from the South know how to sing Peking Opera?' answers Aunt Shen.

'Do you know how to make dumplings, Mulberry?' asks Hsing-hsing.

'Sure I know. I roll out the dough really thin and then use the mouth of a glass to cut out the dumpling skins.'

Aunt Shen, Chia-kang, and Hsing-hsing laugh at my method. Joy, seeing them laugh, also chortles.

'Paper cutouts for windows!'

I don't know what they're selling outside.

'It's almost New Year's. We ought to put up fresh window paper. Well, we'll forget about it this year,' says Aunt Shen. 'Hsing-hsing, since you've been here, I feel a little better. Don't go. Stay and sleep on my bed. There aren't many good times left. That way you won't have to come again tomorrow. You can take Joy away early in the morning.'

I'm still an outsider at the Shen's.

Joy giggles as she goes out the door with her bags.

Mr Cheng, who has been staying in the east wing pays a visit to the Shens. He announces that his family is leaving tomorrow to fly to Nanking. He has a friend in Nanking named K'ung who wants to bring his whole family by plane to Peiping. The Chengs will live in the K'ung's house in Nanking. The K'ungs will come to stay in the Cheng's place in Peiping. He asks Aunt Shen if it's all right for the K'ungs to live in the east wing.

Aunt Shen says, 'As long as they are decent people, anybody can come live here free. It's better than having it occupied by troops or refugees. What's the use of fleeing south, though? Mulberry just came from there. The South is as chaotic as Peiping.'

I look at Mr Cheng and nod. 'Hsü-chou has been taken. The Communists will cross the Yangtze River any moment now. I just fled from Nanking to come here.'

Chia-kang says, 'Well, I'm not going to run away. In the last war we fought the Japanese. If you saw a short "devil" you could tell it was Japanese. But now it's Chinese fighting Chinese. You can't tell the people from the "devils". They are all Chinese.'

Mr Cheng chuckles ironically. 'Escape today, add one more day to your life. We've sold everything. And already bought plane tickets. We'll first go to Nanking, then on to Shanghai and Canton, and if we have to, we'll go to Taiwan as a last resort.' He continues to chat about 'meeting again sometime in the future' and other polite topics of conversation. Finally he asks Aunt Shen if we could keep a trunk of antiques and a trunk of scrolls for him, all priceless heirlooms.

Aunt Shen, lying on the *k'ang*, waves her hand. 'Do us a favour, Mr Cheng. Get those things out of here as quickly as possible. When the Eighth Army comes, they'll think they are ours. We have a roomful of our own furniture, furs and antiques that we haven't thrown out yet.'

A loud cracking noise comes from the courtyard.

Mr Cheng laughs. 'Don't worry. The students in the south section of the house are helping out. They're chopping up your furniture for firewood.'

Explosions.

The city gates are closed.

All connections with the outside world have been cut off: railroads, telephone lines, air routes.

'. . . Those of you living in the areas controlled by Chiang Kai-shek, please listen carefully: The Chinese People's Liberation Army is about to liberate the whole country. Please don't try to flee. Please remain where you are and take all steps necessary to protect people's lives, property, buildings and provisions. Please don't try to flee. Wherever you go, the People's Liberation Army will follow. The Liao-Shen campaign has already ended victoriously. The Huai-Hai campaign is in the last, decisive stages of victory. The People's Liberation Army is ready to cross the Yangtze River. The Peiping-Tientsin campaign is in the last decisive stages of victory: The People's Liberation Army has already completely cut off and surrounded enemy forces in Peiping,

75

Tientsin, Chang-chia-k'ou, Hsin Pao-an, and T'ang-ku, five isolated areas, and cut off the enemy's escape south and west . . .'

'. . . *As she listened, the ghost became afraid. Most honoured King of Hell, please listen to my plea. It was my parents' cruel hearts, they should not have sold me to the lane of mist and flowers. At twelve or thirteen I learned to sing and play the zither. At fourteen or fifteen I began receiving men. Chang San comes when he wants me; Li Ssu comes when he wants me. The money I earned went to make the old Procuress happy.* Yee-hsia! *If I didn't earn money, she would beat me and whip me.* Yee-hsia-hsia! . . .'

'. . . the Communist rebels, unconcerned about the lives and property of the people in Peiping have been savagely bombing Peiping since December thirteenth. Commander-in-Chief of the Extermination Campaign Against the Communist Rebels in North China, Fu Tso-i, has announced that he has utmost confidence in wiping out the rebels. He will fight to the finish. The six hundred thousand troops under Fu Tso-i's command have already undertaken rapid measures to protect Peiping and Tientsin. Several thousand workers are working around the clock to construct temporary landing strips at Tung-tan and the Temple of Heaven. The cypress groves at the Temple of Heaven have been completely uprooted. . . .'

'. . . *I, the commander, am mounted on my horse, and I am busy looking for signs of movement. Chuko Liang sits drinking in the watchtower playing his lute. Two servants are at his side. The old, worn-out soldiers are cleaning the street. I should send down the order to take the city. Kill, kill, but no. . . .*' Chia-kang keeps moving the radio dial back and forth.

The radio blares all day long in the parlour. Chia-kang and I sit by the radio for hours, and listen to the news of the war. The radio is our only connection with the outside world.

Shells whiz above the courtyard.

'Hey, why don't we take over those rooms,' the students are shouting in the courtyard. 'The east wing is empty. There's no one living there now.'

'You students, you have no respect for the law,' shouts Chia-kang from the doorway. 'You took over the south section and now you want the east wing. The government has declared that anyone taking over residences by force will be severely punished!'

'Listen, there are more than two hundred thousand troops in Peiping. Three or four hundred prisoners have just been released. The days that one family can occupy a whole house are over!'

'You rebels! The east wing has already been rented to a family from the South. They should arrive any day now.'

'I'm sorry, but from now on no one can get in or get out of this city.'

'Hey, what are you doing with those trunks? They belong to the Chengs. Hey, there are valuable things in those trunks . . .'

'Sorry, mister, it's cold and we need a fire.'

The students begin carrying their belongings into the east wing.

Broken antiques and torn scrolls litter the courtyard; a shredded picture of the Yangtze River, a cracked bamboo brush holder, a green gourd shaped vase split in half. Bits and shreds of mud-splattered scrolls, calligraphy copybooks, and classical texts are strewn everywhere. The only thing intact is a statue of the folk hero, The Foolish Old Man Who Moved the Mountain, lying in the corner of the courtyard. The Foolish Old Man is wearing a yellow robe and straw sandals. There's a pack lashed to his waist. He is holding a black axe in his right hand and with his left hand he strokes his long white beard. A boy, dressed in a white robe, blue pants and red smock, stands at his side, shouldering a yellow basket. The old man and the boy are standing on a cliff looking up.

The artillery booms. There's an explosion and the main gate blows open. Wind and sand whirl in around us.

Scraps of the Yangtze River flutter in the courtyard.

The Shens are dismissing Amah Ch'ien. They give her three months' wages. Amah Ch'ien mentions her mistress's jewelry. Aunt Shen gives her a gold bracelet. Amah Ch'ien continues: She is old, the mistress has suddenly dismissed her. Where is she supposed to go? She has waited on the same mistress for twenty years, and although she may not have been an exceptional servant, she did work hard. She deserves something more. In addition she is given a sheepskin jacket.

Amah Ch'ien leaves, the students take over the west wing. To celebrate, they kill another dog in the courtyard.

'Chia-kang, it's dark all of a sudden. Light the lamp.'

'There's no oil, Mother.'

'Well, then let's sit together and wait until it gets light outside.'

'Mother, are you better today?'

'I get worse every day.'

'Auntie, let me massage your legs.'

'All right, Mulberry, massage my legs. Chia-kang, come sit on the k'ang with me. It'll be warmer if the three of us crowd together.'

77

'OK.'

'Chia-kang, the jewelry box is beside my pillow. I want to go through it and put my jewelry in order, then you can bury the box under the floor boards.'

'Mother, can you find everything in the dark?'

'Eh. Right now I'm feeling the brocade pouch.'

'You mean the black, blue and pink brocade one? Don't forget the belt braided with blue and pink silk floss.'

'That's right, Chia-kang, you remember it exactly. All my prize possessions are in this pouch. Now I can feel the gold locket.'

'Mulberry, you've got to see how Mother looks in the photograph inside the locket.'

'Too bad we don't have any electricity.'

'You don't need light to see it, Mulberry. I can describe it for you. Mother had her hair in a chignon, with a magnolia flower tucked in it, hangs on her forehead. She is wearing a black satin dress with bell sleeves, a high mandarin collar, and high slits on the sides, white silk scarf and gold-rimmed glasses. She is holding a deluxe edition of a foreign book and she is posing by a small bridge over a stream, standing with one foot on tip-toe as if she is about to take a step, but can't.'

'Chia-kang, you remember so clearly how I looked. The next thing will be more difficult to guess. Guess what I'm holding in my hand now?'

'The jade bracelet?'

'You're wrong. It's the Jade Buddha that you played with when you were one year old. I bought it at the market outside Hartman city gate. I sewed it to your hat and you wore it for a picture. In the picture you were naked, sitting on a prayer mat, and giggling like a little laughing Buddha.'

'Mulberry, why are you so silent?'

'I'm looking and listening, Chia-kang.'

'It's so dark you can't even see your own hand. What can you see?'

'I can see everything you and Auntie are describing.'

'Chia-kang, now I'm holding the white jade bracelet. In the spring of 1933, there was a festival at the Shrine of the Fire God. There were many pearl and jade stalls set up there. I saw this white jade bracelet at the jade stall there. A lot of things happened that year. Your grandmother died, your grandfather died. Phoenix, your father's concubine, had a miscarriage and died. At that time we still had two maids, Ch'un-hsiang and Ch'un-hsia.'

78

'Mother, does Chia-ch'ing know he is Phoenix's son?'

'How could he not know? He just pretends not to know because Phoenix was a maid. Chia-ch'ing ran away from home in the summer of '39. Some people said he went to Yenan to join the Communists. If he comes back with the Eighth Army, we'll have a little protection.'

'Mother, Father is dead. You aren't his real mother. I'm afraid he might cause trouble for us.'

'It's not my fault his mother died.'

'That's not what I mean. I mean, he might come and carry on about class struggle and throw people out of their home and things like that.'

'Live each day as it comes, Chia-kang, don't talk about troubling things. Mulberry, can you see this wedding crown in my hand?'

'I can't see anything but a black shadow.'

'It's a red phoenix with two little black pearl eyes, wings outstretched with a string of red tassels in its tiny pointed beak. When I was carried into the Shen's house on a flower-decked brocade sedan-chair, I was wearing this crown and a pink silk cloak.'

'Mother, what about the jade frog ring?'

'It's in here somewhere. Here, I've found it. This was part of my dowry.'

'Auntie, your whole youth is in that pouch.'

'You're absolutely right, Mulberry. What I'm touching are the most splendid days of my life. Now I'm just an old, broken kite, unable to fly.'

'Mother, we ought to bury this jewelry immediately. I've been thinking, that jade frog ring . . .'

'Chia-kang, the fire is going out. Go and try to find a little coal.'

'All right.'

'Mulberry, don't massage me anymore. Just sit and talk to me. The whole country is fighting and here you are in Peiping. You don't know how happy that makes me. When I saw you in Nanking, such a tiny little thing, I loved you so much. I said to your mother "Let's hope our two families will be united in marriage." That's why I gave you that little gold chain. After all these years of war and fighting, you and Chia-kang are together again. Everything is decided by fate. I'm old now. I'm anxious to get a daughter-in-law and hold a grandson in my arms. There's only Chia-kang left in this branch of the family. Chia-ch'ing has become a Communist. He doesn't count any longer as a Shen family heir. Chia-Kang told me he wants to marry you immediately. No one knows a son like his mother. I have something I have to make clear to you. My Chia-kang is happy with his life, a loyal and generous person, but he has been spoiled. He has never had to struggle. If you marry him, you've got to give in to him in certain ways. He has only one fault, the same as his father. He likes to play around with girls. The best maids I had were ruined by his father. Later I bought this idiot maid, Joy. I had to be careful about the father and then I had to watch the son. It was like a mute taking medicine, can't even say it's bitter. Do you know why Hsing-hsing comes to visit so often?'

'I know. I realised that a long time ago.'

'That young girl is all right, but she is just fickle. When Chia-ch'ing was at home, she led him on. Now she and Chia-kang are having an affair. Did you know that?'

'Why doesn't he marry her?'

'Because I don't approve. There are only two sons in our family, if there were three, four, five, six or seven, she could have all the others. I'm telling you this so you'll be prepared. If you marry Chia-kang and he behaves himself, you're lucky. If he doesn't, you'll be prepared for it and it won't be so bad. I know what that kind of bitterness is like. It happened to me. I . . .'

'Mother, we don't have much coal left.' Chia-kang comes into the room.

'Don't waste it then. We don't know how long this siege is going to last. Chia-kang, I was just talking to Mulberry about the two of you getting married.'

'Mulberry, let's get married on New Year's. Today is the twentieth of the twelfth lunar month. Oh, no, wait a minute, we can't get married on New Year's. Ever since the city has been surrounded, there have been more and more wedding announcements in the paper. Everyone gets married on New Year's. There probably won't be an empty banquet hall we could rent. Let's get married on New Year's Eve. The sooner the better. Mother, do you think that's all right?'

'Of course it is. I've got the ring all ready for you. Here, Chia-kang, take it.'

'Oh, the glittering green frog. I can even see it in the dark. Mulberry, let me put the ring on your finger. Give me your hand.'

'Chia-kang, I want to go back to the South.'

'It's getting dark, Chia-kang, will you bury my jewelry box under the floor now?'

Chia-kang has found a second-hand dealer. The redwood furniture, furs, silks and satins, painting and scrolls . . . Aunt Shen and the dealer settle on a price. The money she gets is exactly enough to buy four sacks of flour and twenty cabbages.

It's getting dark. The second-hand dealer carts the things away.

'. . . The People's Liberation Army recaptured Chang-chia-k'ou on December 24. Fifty-four thousand enemy troops were wiped out . . . *Wild geese fly over the sand flats, frost on the road, landscape of the barbarian North* . . . Fu Tso-i, Commander-in-Chief of the Extermination Campaign Against the Communist Rebels in North China, announced that Peiping's defence is secure. The Communist rebels do not dare make any reckless moves . . . *Hand in hand, we climb into the gauze-curtained bed. I unbutton your gown, I will put on my sleeping slippers. Tonight, I will stay by your side and do my best to serve you. If they kill me, my head will fall to the ground* . . . An authoritative spokesman for the Chinese Communist Party has announced the names of the forty-three most wanted Kuomintang war criminals. On January 1, Chiang Kai-shek announced that he is seeking peace negotiations. He outlined three conditions under which he would consider negotiations with the Communists: maintaining the bogus constitution, the bogus constituted authority, and the Nationalist armed forces . . .'

'The Wall of Nine Dragons is falling down. The Wall of Nine Dragons is falling down! The Wall of Nine Dragons! Falling down! Falling down!' Aunt Shen murmurs unconsciously, lying on the *k'ang* with her face to the wall.

She has not eaten for two days.

The artillery fire becomes more frequent. The windows to the courtyard rattle with each explosion. The main gate keeps banging open. The sandy wind blows stronger.

I walk into Chia-kang's room and discover him and Hsing-hsing squeezed together on a chair. Hsing-hsing is sitting on his lap. His hand is inside her blouse. They stand up suddenly.

I run outside and hail a pedicab and hurry to the Peking Hotel to inquire about the airplanes. The airline has managed successful landings at the temporary landing strip at the Temple of Heaven. Because of the fuel shortage, there are only two flights a week. I make a reservation. I'm number eight thousand and twenty one, scheduled to depart in three months. The solar New Year has just began.

I walk through blowing sand to the lake, Pei Hai, which has just recently been opened to the public.

Golden Turtle and Jade Frog.

Double-Rainbow Pavilion.

Hall of the Serene Way.

Hall of Rippling Waters.

Five-Dragon Pavilion.

I approach the Wall of Nine Dragons. Nine colourful dragons are prancing between the blue heavens and the green waters, playing with their golden dragon pearls and their tongues of fire. The dragons, the sky, the water, the pearls, the tongues of fire are a mosaic of glittering glazed tile. The Wall of Nine Dragons stands more than twenty feet high. It has been standing here for seven or eight hundred years, since the Yuan Dynasty.

I go home, back to my room off the corner courtyard. Chia-kang is waiting for me there. He tells me that I'm the one he loves and that Hsing-hsing is really in love with his brother Chia-ch'ing. When they are together, he always hopes I will walk in and discover them because she is really thinking about Chia-ch'ing.

I tell him I've already made a reservation to go south and that his mother had already told me how things were.

'My mother! My mother! She is going to make me kill myself,' says Chia-kang stamping his foot. 'Mulberry, if you want to go away, then let's go away together.'

When he comes back from his mother's room, there are red marks on his face.

'. . . New China News Agency cable, 14 January: Mao Tse-tung, Chairman of the Central Committee of the Chinese Communist Party, has already rejected Chiang Kai-shek's January I request for peace negotiations. Comrade Mao Tse-tung announced the eight conditions under which peace negotiations can be held. (1) Punish all war criminals; (2) Abolish the bogus 'constituted authority'; (3) Abolish the bogus constitution; (4) Reorganise all counter-revolutionary armed forces according to democratic principles; (5) Confiscate bureaucrat-capital; (6) Reform the land system; (7) Abrogate treasonable treaties; (8) Convene a political consultative conference of all non-counter-revolutionary parties, and establish a democratic coalition government.

'The People's Liberation Army Broadcasting Station announced from Tientsin: The People's Liberation Army liberated Tientsin today, and took the puppet mayor of Tientsin, Tu Chien-shih and the Nationalist Party Garrison Commander Ch'en Ch'ang-chieh and others, captive. More than ten villages in the suburbs of Tientsin are still burning . . .' The students cut out the wire from the doorbell to repair their radio.

The Shen doorbell is now mute.

The Communists are shelling the centre of the city.

The landing strip at the Temple of Heaven is closed.

The gates to the city have been opened and the refugees who fled into the city are now pouring out. Daily there are four or five thousand people waiting by the gates to get out.

Amah Ch'ien and her son come to the Shens and demand that half the house be given to them. The Shens only offer her one ounce of gold.

She sews the gold into her belt and wraps it around her waist. She stands in the long line waiting for the guard to check her before leaving the city. The sun is setting. The gates will be closed before dark. When it is Amah Chi'en's turn to be inspected, a donkey pulling a cart of nightsoil passes by. The donkey, excited by the crowd, starts galloping. The guards chase the donkey and manure splatters all over the ground. When the donkey is finally subdued the gates have been closed and no one can leave the city. Suddenly an artillery shell falls on Amah Ch'ien's head. The donkey, excited again, gallops off.

Amah Ch'ien's son comes to tell us about her death and demands that the Shens pay for the coffin.

A loud thump comes from Aunt Shen's room.

Chia-kang and I run from the parlour into her room. She is sprawled on the floor. She stares at us, her eyes unnaturally bright. But she really doesn't see us.

She is no longer here in the house with us.

Chia-kang goes to lift her to the bed. She waves him away with her hand.

'Don't touch me. I have something to say. Your father and Phoenix have returned. I have been talking with them for a long time. I've told lies my whole life and I've heard lies all my life. Now I can tell the truth. Chia-kang, I haven't treated you fairly. I have suffocated you. I didn't want you to be a success. I only wanted you to spend your whole life quietly here with me. I held you back on purpose, telling you that you were too soft that you couldn't take it. I encouraged you to play around with the maids, even sleep with Hsing-hsing. I know you don't

83

really care about them. I let your father have Phoenix so I could keep him under my control. But now you are serious about Mulberry. When the two of you are together laughing and talking, I lie here crying alone. I said bad things about you in front of Mulberry. You want me to let you go. You told me that you can't spend your whole life with me. And I said to you that I have remained a widow my whole life for your sake. After your father died, there were men that were interested in me. You said you wanted me to remarry. I slapped you. You went to Mulberry's room. I held the jacket you had left in my room and cried the whole night. I pinched my feet, the way you used to pinch them, the way your father used to pinch them . . .'

'Mother . . .'

'Don't interrupt me.'

'Mother, I only have one question. Father always had other women. How could you stand it?'

She rolls on the floor laughing. 'I had one precious possession: a good body. It committed so many sins! Your father and I are even on that account. But not you. Chia-kang, I was a widow all these years for your sake. You . . .'

'Mother . . .'

'Don't interrupt me. I must say this: Chia-kang, you're not a true son of the Shen family. Chia-ch'ing, the runaway, is the only legitimate son!'

'Then whose son am I?'

'You were given to me by the gods at the White Cloud Temple . . .'

'Mother . . .'

'Listen to me. Phoenix was the maid who came with me when I married. I couldn't have children. I thought I could raise the sons she bore. But once she had a son, she became too haughty. Whoever bore sons had power in the Shen household. I was frantic. I went to see doctors – useless. I prayed and made vows – useless. I just couldn't get pregnant. The eighteenth of the first lunar month in 1925, I made a trip to the White Cloud Temple with some of the women that I used to play mahjong with. That evening the festival of the Immortals was celebrated at the White Cloud Temple. Late in the evening, two or three hundred male and female devotees chanted Taoist sutras in the great hall. There was chanting and chanting, the painted lanterns glowed, and cymbals and drums clashed as the Immortals descended to earth: there was the Primordial Heavenly Master, the Secluded Holy One, the Master of Penetrating Heaven, the Emperor of Dark Heaven, the Immortal of the Golden Cap, the Black Cloud Immortal, the

Golden Light Immortal, the Youths of the White Crane, the Youths of Fire and Water . . . all the important and unimportant immortals appeared. The Immortal of the Golden Cap told me that if I wanted a son I would have to borrow an embryo. He took me to the Hall of Four Emperors to steal a porcelain baby-image, and then he led me to the store house behind the great hall and taught me how to use it to borrow an embryo. Nine months later I gave birth to you, Chia-kang. I could have shared the glory with Phoenix. But who could have known she was pregnant again? . . . I took some arrowroot dug up in the dead of winter, made it into powder and put it in her tea. She drank it and had a miscarriage and died from hemorrhaging. Now, Chia-kang, everything I have kept secret has been said. Go ahead and curse me. The burden has been lifted from me.'

She turns suddenly and points at me. 'Mulberry, I have something to say to you, too. When you first came to Peiping, I didn't like you the minute I saw you. Your eyes are too watery. You're a girl who dreams wild and ridiculous dreams. You try to seem clean and pure, but in your heart, you're like a snake or a scorpion. You're an evil star – a jinx on your father, mother, husband and children! Chia-kang, do you still want to marry Mulberry?'

'If she is willing.'

'You are aware of all her faults?'

'Yes.'

'Chia-kang, why do you want to marry her?'

'Because she is different from girls from the North. I've been in Peiping too long.'

'Mulberry, do you want to marry Chia-kang?'

'Yes.'

'Chia-kang, are you really sure you want to marry her?'

'I decided that a long time ago.'

'My son. You're being a real man. You played around with the maids and Hsing-hsing because you wanted to be a man. But you couldn't escape your mother's clutches. Now you're a real man . . . You . . .'

'Mother, it's too cold on the floor. Mulberry and I will lift you back up to the *k'ang*.'

'Only on one condition: I can still go on talking when I'm back on the *k'ang* and you won't interrupt me. If I stop, the Wall of the Dragons will fall on me.'

'Go on and talk, Mother, you don't have to stop.'

The ideogram for double happiness, written in gold, hangs in the middle of the wall, between two scrolls with auspicious sayings. A red felt tablecloth has been spread out on the long table on which sit two burning red tapers. The Shens' parlour is the ceremonial hall.

There are thirteen guests: Hsing-hsing, her mother, her grandfather old Mr Wan, and his bride Joy – the whole family has come. Joy is pregnant.

My wedding dress, flowered velvet, is borrowed from Hsing-hsing. Hsing-hsing is styling my hair: long curls hanging down to my shoulders. She says that this hairstyle is worn by European aristocrats and that it brings out my classic features. The small notch in my right earlobe is covered by the curls. The mole below my right eye looks darker after I put on my makeup. Hsing-hsing leads me from the room near the garden into the ceremonial hall.

The groom is waiting. He stands between the tall red tapers, and facing old Mr Wan, the legal witness. The others lead his mother into the hall. She sits in the seat of honour at the long table. (She didn't stop talking for two days and nights, but she has calmed down.)

Artillery fire sputters over the roof.

'*President Chiang, due to reasons not yet disclosed, has announced that he will resign. . .*' The students' radio blares from the courtyard.

They come and go in front of the parlour and peer in at the ceremony.

I am standing beside the groom.

The master of ceremonies announces: 'Let the ceremony begin.'

The legal witness, old Mr Wan, delivers a speech: '. . . This modest gentleman and this fine and charming lady are a true match made in heaven. We Chinese value virtue above everything else in this world. If one must choose between a man of talent or a man of virtue, how much better it is to choose the gentleman of virtue . . .'

'. . . *The Headquarters of the Extermination Campaign Against the Communist Rebels in North China has announced that forces of more than fifty thousand soldiers have already safely withdrawn to T'ang-ku . . .*'

'. . . From ancient times, many treacherous ministers of state and dissipate sons have had great talent, but have lacked virtue. Those who have wrecked the state and ruined their families are too numerous to count. Thus, Chia-kang's virtue is especially precious in these troubled times. And his virtue is due to the efforts of his wise and saintly mother.'

'. . . *After eight years of the War of Resistance Against Japan, there followed three years of civil war. Not only has this destroyed the only thread of hope that survived the victorious war of resistance, but slaughtered by the tens of thousands . . .*'

86

'The first commandment in *The Way to Manage a Household* is: Do not listen to the words of women and do not treat your parents ungenerously. Then the household will be at peace and although there may be chaos in the world outside, one will find refuge in the joy of family love . . .'

'*Our armed forces have safely retreated from Peng-p'u and Ho-fei and have destroyed the main bridge over the Huai River* . . .'

'. . . For generations the Sangs have been a family of distinguished scholars. Mulberry Sang herself is a virtuous and capable woman. I will quote from *The Classic for Girls* the following words of advice: "A woman must submit to her husband. A wife should serve her husband's parents with the same attention with which she would hold an overflowing cup and cultivate herself as carefully as if she were treading on ice." Finally, I wish that the new bride and groom be as harmonious together as the lute and zither. May your sons and grandsons be without end.'

'. . . *Fu Tso-i and the Communists are holding peace talks in the Western Hills. Two bombs exploded in the house of one of the negotiators, the former mayor* . . .' Several students stand talking in the doorway.

Next the appointed matchmaker makes a speech. He first solemnly announces that he was forced up on the platform at the last minute and made to play the role of the matchmaker. When he gets to the word 'platform' he looks all around and adds in a low voice: 'There is no platform. In these troubled times, everything must be simplified.'

There are two loud blasts of artillery. The door to the ceremonial hall swings open and shut.

The matchmaker clears his throat and says that his virtue is his brevity. He doesn't want to delay the bride and groom's enjoyment of this happy occasion. 'The scenery was of mountains collapsing, the earth cracking open, bright and dazzling, revealing the golden light. Branches, leaves, flowers, and fruit too: a peach with a hard, solid seed wrapped in tender flesh.' He tells two more jokes and finally finishes by warning the new bride and groom, 'On the wedding night you must watch out for spies and be careful not to divulge your secrets. The city must be protected or else everything will be disrupted.'

My room off the corner courtyard becomes the wedding chamber. In the room there is a bed, a desk, and a wardrobe. The rest of the furniture was sold to the junk dealer. Chia-kang's father used to work at the long desk. His things are still arranged on it: a large marble brush stand, two rows of bamboo brush holders holding twelve unused brushes of different sizes. In the white flower-embossed ink box are two pieces of white silk wadding. There's a stack of writing paper with a red inscription 'The Room of Retreat'.

Two large red candles are burning on the desk. In the stove the fire is burning briskly. Chia-kang ran around the whole afternoon looking for a basket of coal to buy especially for the wedding.

The artillery suddenly stops.

Chia-kang takes the flashlight and examines every corner of the room, even under the bed, and then goes out to inspect the courtyard.

He comes in, closes the door, and locks it.

I am sitting on the edge of the bed.

He motions to me, pointing first at me and then at the bed.

I don't move.

He tugs at my dress.

I still don't move.

He paces up and down. He must not say anything. If the groom speaks first he will be the first to die. His shadow leaps from the wall to the ceiling. Then it suddenly looms larger and jumps down at me from the ceiling.

He walks over to me and sits down and begins to unbutton my dress. As soon as he undoes a button, I quickly fasten it up again.

He pushes me down on the bed and strips off all my clothes. Then he takes off all his clothes. Our clothes lie in a heap on the floor.

I slip under the embroidered quilt. He lifts the quilt and falls on top of me. Suddenly I start itching. I wriggle underneath him and try to scratch. He cocks his head and pouts at me. I pick up his hand and bring it near the candlelight. I can't see anything in the dark. My scalp and the soles of my feet begin to itch. I shove him aside and begin scratching wildly.

He begins scratching himself.

The two of us scratch on the bed: scratch lying down, sitting up, rolling over.

He gets out of bed and picks up one of the candles, still scratching himself.

Some sort of furry substance has been spread all over the bed.

We don't understand who would play a joke like this on our wedding night.

We brush ourselves off and then brush off the bed.

As soon as we get back into bed, a dog starts barking. Then we hear voices and a gong.

88

'Kill that beast,' the students are yelling.

The sound of the dog, the voices and the gong rush from the main gate through the Gate of Dangling Flowers into the courtyard.

An oil lamp is hung on the courtyard gate. Shadows of men with clubs in their hands appear on the paper window.

The dog is still barking.

The shadows vanish.

A gong sounds.

Six shadow puppets appear on the paper window. Six heads on six sticks nod and bow towards the barking dog.

Voices come from under the window. 'Congratulations to the bride and groom. Today is a happy occasion for the Shen family. If you don't make merry, you won't prosper. We are shadow puppets gathered together from all corners of the world: Pigsy, Monkey, Cripple Li, Chung Li, the God of Thunder, the Fox Spirit, and White Snake Spirit. We have heads but no bodies. You people have bodies but no heads.'

Two voices mimic the voices of clowns, an old man and a woman:

> Chao Ch'ien Sun Li (*Old Man*)
> Next door threshing rice (*Female Clown*)
>
> Chou Wu Cheng Wang (*Old Man*)
> Steal rice and take sugar (*Female Clown*)
>
> Feng Chen Chu Wei (*Old Man*)
> Dog climbs up God's altar (*Female Clown*)
>
> Chiang Shen Han Yang (*Old Man*)
> Eat the child and be silent (*Female Clown*)

The gong sounds again. The two voices begin to improvise nonsense variations on the Confucian text, *The Great Learning*:

> The way to great learning (*Old Man*)
> is to knock down Teacher (*Female Clown*)
>
> To understand enlightened virtue (*Old Man*)
> is to pick up Teacher (*Female Clown*)
>
> To be close to the people (*Old Man*)
> is to carry Teacher out the door (*Female Clown*)

To achieve great goodness (*Old Man*)
is to bury Teacher in a muddy hole (*Female Clown*)

The flickering shadow-clowns on the window sing to us. Chia-kang and I roll on the bed, scratching ourselves wildly. The shadows lurch towards the dog and the dog howls. The shadows swing toward us and we freeze on the bed. Their voices begin counting, the male and female clowns alternating the count:

One two (*Male Clown*)
Two one (*Female Clown*)

One two three (*Male Clown*)
Three two one (*Female Clown*)

One two three four (*Male Clown*)
Four three two one (*Female Clown*)

One two three four five (*Male Clown*)
Five four three two one (*Female Clown*)

One two three four five six (*Male Clown*)
Six five four three two one (*Female Clown*)

One two three four five six seven (*Male Clown*)
Seven six five four three two one (*Female Clown*)

One two three four five six seven eight (*Male Clown*)
Eight seven six five four three two one (*Female Clown*)

One two three four five six seven eight nine (*Male Clown*)
Kill! (*Male and Female Clowns*)

Suddenly the heads plunge towards the dog. Then all we hear is the crashing of sticks against the wall.

The dog howls and the door to our room bursts open. The dog darts into the room.

It rushes from corner to corner and finally scrambles under the bed. It yelps hysterically and its back thumps against the mattress as it twists and turns. It rubs against the furry substance that litters the floor.

The students stand in the doorway. They hold the sticks with the puppet heads, and they laugh at us: the two of us on the bed and the dog under the bed.

Chia-kang and I throw off the quilt and get out of bed.

They clap and cheer.

I stand in the corner naked. Chia-kang, also naked, picks up the mattress and the dog chases madly in a circle under the bed frame, barking.

The students drive the dog out with their sticks.

Chia-kang shuts the door.

The dog howls in the courtyard.

There is a loud thumping of sticks and the dog stops barking. It is dead.

Chia-kang and I lie on the bed and listen to the sound of fur rubbing against the stone slabs. They are dragging the dog's carcass away. I curl up into a ball.

Chia-kang turns over and straddles my body.

'Mulberry, you're not a virgin!' He pushes into my body and blurts out the first words of the wedding night. Then he clenches his teeth. He is the first one to speak tonight.

'Peace has been restored to Peiping. Fu Tso-i has announced a peace communique. From 22 January on, more than two hundred thousand troops under his command will be garrisoned outside Peiping to await reorganisation by the People's Liberation Army. The Peiping-Tientsin campaign has finally ended . . .'

Suddenly the shelling stops. The lights come back on.

The hawkers begin yelling in the lanes again.

'Sweet apples!'

'Fresh dates!'

'Popcorn!'

It is snowing. Powdery snow flutters in the air. It's one of the few times it has snowed since I arrived in Peiping.

Chia-kang sprawls on top of me, his head dangling over my shoulder. Suddenly he collapses.

He makes me tell him about Refugee Student in Chü-t'ang Gorge. I tell him that I have forgotten what happened in the past. I tell him that the night I married him I made up my mind: even if he had to roll down the Mountain of Knives I would roll down with him and if he died, I would be a widow all of my life. He says I shouldn't have thought about being a widow on our wedding night. It's an unlucky omen. He rolls off my body and stretches out beside me.

The winter sun shines on the window paper.

91

'It's New Year's. God of Wealth for Sale.' A hawker selling paper images of the God of Wealth yells from The Gate of Dangling Flowers.

'It's getting windy. Don't let the flame go out. Chia-kang, hold it carefully . . . At last, here we are, the five branches of the Shen family together again. Dozens of burning flames, like little flowers. Look, the flames of great-grandfather and great-grandmother are arranged in the first row. The flames of the sons and daughters-in-law and grandchildren and the flames of the concubines all arranged in order in front of the altar. See how they stretch across three courtyards to the entrance of Li-shih Lane. Pass the lighted flames along, hold them carefully. Chia-kang, be careful. It's getting windy . . .'

'Mother,' Chia-kang is standing beside the *k'ang*. 'Mother, are you awake? The Eighth Army has entered the city. There is going to be a huge parade today. Mulberry, Hsing-hsing and I want to go watch it from the Gate of Heavenly Peace.'

'Oh, have all the flames gone out?' She turns over on the *k'ang*. 'Chia-kang, where is my flame?'

'This is no time to think about flames, Mother. The Eighth Army has entered the city.'

'Oh, I thought we were at our old house on Li-shih Lane.'

'That was twenty years ago, Mother. Today is 3 February 1949. Eighth Army has entered the city. We're going to the Gate of Heavenly Peace to see what they look like.'

'Don't go. Be careful. You might run into Chia-ch'ing.' She stares hard at us for a while. 'Chia-kang, Mulberry, Hsing-hsing, are you all here in this room with me?'

'Yes, Mother, we're all here. You have been lying in bed too long. When you get better we'll go out for a walk with you.'

'Good. Just like before, in the spring when we went to see the black peonies at the Temple of Reverence. They are the same flowers for which Empress Wu held a ceremony to make them bloom faster, but it didn't work. But *I* saw them in bloom.' She laughs and turns back to face the wall.

'That's right, Mother. You even saw the hortensia bloom in the imperial garden. In all of Peiping, there is only one hortensia flower and it only blooms once a year. The peony is the flower of wealth and nobility and the hortensia flower is the flower of peace. And you have seen them both.'

'Yes, Chia-kang, I am one of the lucky ones. Chia-kang, with all this fighting, we didn't really celebrate the New Year. All we did to celebrate was to paste up the Gods of the Door. Next year we really have to do things right.'

'That's right, Mother. I'll go with you to do the New Year shopping. We'll buy New Year pictures at the flower market: "Fortune and Longevity", "Three-fold Happiness", "Good Fortune as One Wishes", "Wealth and High Rank Overflowing", "Plump Pig Bows at the Gate", "Summon Wealth and Gather Treasures", we'll buy them all. We'll buy some pretty lanterns and hang them in the courtyard, in the house, everywhere. We'll buy some long strings of firecrackers and set them off and scraps of red paper will fly all over the courtyard. And I'll buy you some pretty velvet flowers, red and green, to wear in your hair.'

'You want to dress me up to look like a coquette,' laughs Aunt Shen. 'There are many different festivals for the New Year. One the eve of the twenty-third of the twelfth month, there is the offering to the Kitchen God. On the night of the thirtieth, you must welcome back the Kitchen God and the God of Happiness. The second day of the New Year, you make offerings to the God of Wealth. The eighth day of the New Year, you pass around lighted flames to thank the ancestors for their protection and blessings in keeping our family healthy and safe. From the thirteenth to the seventeenth is the Lantern Festival. We'll buy a glazed glass lotus-flower lantern to hang at the Main Gate . . .'

'Those students tore off one side of the Main Gate for firewood,' Hsing-hsing says to me in a low voice. 'If she goes on talking like this, we'll miss the parade.'

'Chia-kang, Mulberry, Hsing-hsing, sit down and chat with me. A little conversation cheers me up. You know what? I've been walking all over the main streets and the alleys. I went back to all the places I had been before: The White Cloud Temple, the Peach Palace, Yung-ho Palace, the Temple of Exalted Wealth, the Temple of the Fire God . . . all the festivals at those temples. The Wen-ming Tea House where T'an Hsin-pei, Yang Hsiao-lou, and Yu Shu-yen sang opera. The Chi-hsiang Tea House where the great opera singers Mei Lan-fang and Yang Hsiao-lou sang. The tiger stalls at Tung-an Market and Hsi-tan Market. The Old Imperial Palace, the Pavilion of Sudden Rain, the Summer Palace. I visited the First Balcony overlooking the river in the northern part of the city and ate sesame biscuits and listened to the eunuchs of the Ch'ing Dynasty telling stories. And I saw all the imperial parks. And the Wall of Nine Dragons still hasn't fallen down. And . . .'

'Mother, we really have to go now. If we don't go now, we'll miss the parade.'

93

'Chia-kang, what you don't see can't hurt you. Why do you want to go see the Communists?'

'Everyone's going, Auntie,' says Hsing-hsing.

'Chia-kang, what if you run into Chia-ch'ing?'

'If Chia-ch'ing is there, there'll be a big family reunion, won't there?' says Hsing-hsing.

No one answers. Chia-kang reaches over and turns on the radio.

'. . . *I serve in the camp of the Hegemon of Western Ch'u. I am Yü-chi. I was well versed in the classics and in swordsmanship at an early age. Ever since that time I have followed my lord to campaigns and battles east and west. There have been hardships and difficulties. When will peace come . . .'*

'OK, you may go,' the old lady says. 'I'll listen to Mei Lan-fang sing *The Hegemon Bids Farewell to His Concubine!*'

A strong wind full of sand and grit swirls along the ground. Eventually, everything, everyone crumbles into sand at the touch of a finger. Peiping has turned to sand. The streets in front of the Gate of Heavenly Peace, Kung-an Street, Ch'i-p'an Street, Ministry of Justice Street and East and West Ch'ang-an Street are filled with shadowy figures, moving through the sand.

'Can you see the Gate of Heavenly Peace?' Chia-kang asks me.

We are walking on West Ch'ang-an Street toward the Gate of Heavenly Peace.

'I can't see anything. The sand it too thick.'

Chia-kang and Hsing-hsing compete with each other to tell me, the outsider, about the Gate of Heavenly Peace.

The Gate of Heavenly Peace is the main gate into the Imperial City. Inside the Imperial City, there's a moat. The Forbidden City lies across the moat. Inside the Forbidden City are the Imperial Palaces. Each palace is surrounded by a high wall. The Gate of Heavenly Peace is a many-tiered tower on the city gate which sits on a white marble pedestal. The roof is covered with glazed yellow tile. The walls and the pillars are red. Inside and outside of the Gate of Heavenly Peace statues of beasts and dragons are standing. Prancing along the edge of the roof are dragons, phoenixes, lions, horses, seahorses, fish, fire-eating unicorns, and one Immortal. On each end is a beast with a dragon head, with a sword stuck in his back to keep him from escaping. There are also strange beasts whose tails stir up waves to make rain. The River of Gold Water runs in front of the Gate of Heavenly Peace. Seven stone bridges straddle the river and on each bridge a pair of white marble pillars stand propping up the heavens. A plate has been placed on top of each pillar to gather dew. On each plate a dragon-headed wolf squats, facing south, watching for the emperor's return. A dragon curls around each pillar, his four five-clawed feet dance in the folds of the encircling clouds. Two stone lions squat in front of the Gate of Heavenly Peace. They have broad foreheads, curly manes. They lift their heads up and grin. Their plump glistening bodies are draped with fringed harnesses and bells. The lion on the left is playing with an embroidered ball with his right paw. The lioness on the right plays with a lion cub with her left paw. All these beasts and dragons protect the Imperial Palaces. There is a lance wound on the lioness' stomach. At the end of the Ming Dynasty the rebel, Li Chih-chen, fought his way into Peking as far as the Gate of Heavenly Peace. The stone lioness came to life and leaped at him. He lunged at her with his lance and she became stone again. Even now, when it rains, blood flows from the wound on her stomach.

'We welcome the People's Liberation Army to Peiping,' shouts from the distance the woman announcer with a precise, distinct voice.

The Gate of Heavenly Peace is in front of us. We are standing beside the wounded lioness. Red flags, a huge portrait of Mao Tse-tung and banners with slogans are hung on the Gate of Heavenly Peace. 'The Gate of Heavenly Peace is the sacred ground of the people's liberation!' 'Celebration of the Liberation of Peiping!' 'At the Gate of Heavenly Peace burns the eternal flame of struggle!' A whirlwind of sand beats against the flags, the portrait, the banners.

The onlookers move through the vast expanse of the square and approach the Gate of Heavenly Peace.

'. . . We welcome the strong, the victorious People's Liberation Army. The People's Liberation Army is the defender of peace in our fatherland! And the builder of socialism in our fatherland . . .'

The voice gets louder. The parade is still invisible in the sandstorm. There is only the voice.

'. . . The liberation of Peiping is in accord with the eight conditions for peace which were laid down by the Chinese Communist Party and this is the first good example of ending the war by peaceful means. The liberation of Peiping hastens the victorious conclusion of the War of People's Liberation . . .' A procession of shadows is passing by in the sandstorm.

A giant portrait of Mao Tse-tung appears out of the sand and wind and is hoisted above the heads of a crowd of young men riding in the broadcast truck.

'Long live Mao Tse-tung!'

'Safeguard Chairman Mao's eight conditions of peace! Punish the war criminals! Abolish the bogus constitution! Abolish the bogus constituted authority . . .'

The cries swirl away in the sandstorm.

Workers.

Students.

Children.

Civil servants.

Groups of people shouting slogans and waving banners in the blowing sand file past the Gate of Heavenly Peace.

Suddenly comes the noise of drums, cymbals, trumpets, and whistles. Children on stilts dressed in loose robes with wide sleeves appear, waving coloured fans and dancing with their instruments to the Rice Sprout Song.

The People's Liberation Army emerges from the sandstorm.

Infantry.

Cavalry.

Armoured Corps.

Tanks equipped with machine guns and mortars are followed by ambulances and jeeps. Hundreds of vehicles, all US-made, rumble past the Gate of Heavenly Peace. Soldiers, dressed in full uniform, their faces wrinkled and expressionless, very young yet very old, stare straight ahead as they march – six abreast, past the soaring, circling dragons and beasts which protect the Gate of Heavenly Peace. They vanish into the blowing sand. Rows and rows of soldiers emerge from the sand and wind.

'Look, it goes on and on,' an onlooker in the silent crowd remarks as we watch from the Gate of Heavenly Peace.

'That's him!' Hsing-hsing grabs my arm.

'Who?' asks Chia-kang.

'. . .'

'Who, Hsing-hsing?'

'Your brother!'

'Where?'

'There! The one in uniform, back to us, leading the troops in shouting slogans.'

The three of us stand on tiptoe to see, but we can only make out half his face. A gust of sand and wind whirls around us. When

96

we open our eyes again, he has vanished in the sandstorm.

The God of the Door that we pasted up for New Year is still there on the half of the main gate that remains. He is dressed in colourful armour. His chest is stuck out and his stomach protrudes. He has two swords. He leans on one sword and brandishes the other.

Some of the students come out of the house and tear the God of the Door off the gate. They rip him apart and throw the pieces on the icy ground.

They paste up a slogan in his place on the ruined gate:

PROTECTING THE PEOPLE'S PROPERTY IS THE NUMBER ONE DUTY!

Through the gap in the main gate another slogan can be seen on the Gate of the Dangling Flowers:

THE FRESH BLOOD OF REVOLUTION BRINGS FORTH BEAUTIFUL FRUIT.

'Phoenix, your son has returned. You have come back too. Good, you have both come to settle accounts with me . . .' I enter the room and hear the old lady talking to herself as she lies on the *k'ang*. 'Phoenix, your son has become a Communist and you're acting too proud . . . you have come to take me to the Western Heaven. But I know I am not allowed to go there. "When the Goddess of Mercy was engaged in the deep course of wisdom, she beheld the Five Substances and saw that these substances in their self-nature were empty. O Sariputra, here form is emptiness and emptiness is form . . ." The Wall of Nine Dragons is falling down. It's falling on top of me. I can't get out from under it. Phoenix, help me. Phoenix, Phoenix . . .'

'It's not Phoenix. It's Mulberry.' I sit on the edge of the *k'ang* and massage her legs.

'Ah, Phoenix isn't here.' She is still facing the wall. 'Is Chia-ch'ing here?'

'No, he has never been here.'

'Didn't you see him at the Gate of Heavenly Peace?'

'We could only see half his face, and we couldn't really tell if it was him or not.'

'If only Phoenix were still alive. Chia-ch'ing wouldn't do anything to us in front of his own mother.'

97

'Maybe he hasn't come to Peiping yet. Don't try to think too much.'

'My brain won't listen to me. I don't want to think, but it keeps on thinking, what I owe to other people, how I deceived others. I remember it all. Mulberry, do you hate me?'

'No, not anymore.'

'Mulberry, I have something to tell you.'

'All right.'

'That year when I couldn't get pregnant, I went to the Divine Astrologer of the Imperial Polarity at the festival of the Fire God to have my fortune told. My horoscope said that if I were to conceive the child would be famous, but since there have always been few males born into the Shen family, I would have to be careful with the child. He meant that the Shen family line was about to end.'

'I'm pregnant.'

She suddenly turns over and takes my hand. 'Mulberry, you're pregnant? Then I won't worry about it anymore. I don't care about money or position, all I want is a big bunch of grandchildren around me. No, no, enough grandchildren to fill the whole main hall, each holding a flower flame – a long line of burning flames like a huge fire dragon.'

'That day will come for you. I want a lot of children.'

She presses my hand and laughs.

'. . . Fox fur . . . The People's . . . Communists . . .' The refugee students are discussing something in the courtyard.

'Mulberry, don't go out there, it's dangerous.'

There are footsteps in the main hall.

'Chia-kang?'

'He went to the barber shop on the alley to get his hair cut,' I lie. I don't want her to know that he is at the People's Court.

'Someone's coming. He has come back already.'

Hsing-hsing comes into the room. 'Auntie, I came especially to tell you something, to prepare you for it. I saw it with my own eyes, on Wang-fu-ching Boulevard. The Nationalist slogans that used to be there are now all changed to Communist slogans. They were making a well-dressed woman in a fox fur coat crawl on the ground. A group of students surrounded her singing the Rice Sprout Song and taunting her, saying, "People in New China don't wear fur coats, only animals wear fur coats." Auntie, I know you have a lot of furs. By all means, don't wear them. The students in the courtyard are saying that they won't let anyone wear a fur coat in this courtyard.'

'I sold some of my furs. The rest I gave away. The only thing I have left is my fox fur jacket. It's hanging over there by the bed. When I get up I always put it on. Hsing-hsing, what should I do with it?'

'If you try to give it away now, no one would want it.'

Chia-kang comes into the room. Hsing-hsing repeats the story again and imitates the woman in the fox fur coat crawling on the ground.

Chia-kang throws the fur jacket on the floor and stamps on it. 'What kind of world is this anyway? If I knew things would turn out like this, I would have gone South even if I had to be a beggar.'

Hsing-hsing laughs, 'Second Master Shen, the South is about to fall, too. The executive government has already moved from Nanking to Canton. The Nationalist representatives are at the peace talks: Shao Li-tzu, Chang Shih-chao and three others have already arrived in Peiping.'

'Hsing-hsing,' Chia-kang stares at her. 'How do you know so much about what's going on outside? Are you . . .'

'Chia-kang, I'm not a Communist,' Hsing-hsing says, staring back, curling her lip in a smile. 'I couldn't be one even if I wanted to. I wasn't born in the right class. But the world is changing and we have to learn things all over again, learn how to be new, different people or else we can't go on living. The Peiping Military Control Committee of the People's Liberation Army has already been established. All sorts of discussion groups have been set up, too. There are discussion groups, demonstrations, speeches every day. Yesterday two hundred thousand people held a meeting at the Gate of Heavenly Peace. Now everybody is busy: workers, students, peasants, merchants, and here you are, Second Master Shen, still at home clutching an old fur jacket and you are not able to decide what to do with it!'

'Throw it in the outhouse!' Chia-kang picks up the fur jacket, signals to me, and heads for the door.

I follow him into the main hall.

'From now on, you've got to be careful about Hsing-hsing,' he says in a low voice as he caresses the fox fur. 'Maybe she's a spy for the Communists.'

'What happened at the People's Court?'

'Amah Ch'ien's son sued us saying we exploited her and tormented her to death. He wants half of the house as well as the expenses for her burial.'

'What did the court decide?'

'The house belongs to the people. It's not the Shen's nor the Ch'ien's. We'll have to give him more money to settle it. One of these

99

days, we're going to get kicked out of here. You stay inside and don't go out. Those students are getting pushy.'

Chia-kang wraps the jacket up. When it's dark, he takes the package and steals past the students dancing the Rice Sprout Dance in the courtyard.

When he returns, Hsing-hsing is laughing as she tell us about her grandfather and Joy. Joy's belly is swelling. The old man had his fortune told: Joy will certainly have an outstanding son. The old man was delighted and strutted around joyfully. 'Marriage at sixty, a grand birthday celebration at eighty. There are twenty good years left to enjoy.'

After Hsing-hsing leaves, the old lady calls Chia-kang to the *k'ang*. She faces the wall and says listlessly, 'Chia-kang, remember this: no matter what happens, the Shen family line must not be broken. Mulberry is pregnant. You two must get away to the South.'

It's spring. A narrow coffin is carried out of the courtyard. Chia-kang and I aren't dressed in mourning. We bury the old lady outside the City Gate in the paupers' graveyard, the Muddy Hole.

Chia-kang and I take a train for the South.

Peiping. Tientsin. Ching-hai. Ch'ing County. Ts'ang County. Tung-kuang. Te County. P'ing-yüan. Yü-ch'eng. Chi-nan. Chang-ch'iu. Ch'ing-chou. Chu-liu-tien.

Everyone has to get off at each stop where we are inspected by Communist guards.

We took the freight train. The Peiping-Tientsin railroad already has their passenger trains running. Between Tientsin and P'u-kou, there are only freight trains. I left my wedding ring and the broken jade griffin in Peiping.

We come to another station. Wei County is the last stop in the Communist-controlled area. Beyond Wei County is no man's land; the trains can't connect the two sides. Beyond the no man's land lies Nationalist-held Ch'ing-tao.

Twelve men and women have been travelling in the same car since Tientsin. Now each of us picks up his own luggage and walks to the Inn. There's a sign in big black characters on the mud wall at the Inn:

> EVERYONE ALLOCATED LAND MUST
> JOIN THE ARMY
> ANYONE NOT JOINING THE ARMY IS
> REACTIONARY

100

The twelve of us, strangers, sleep on a large communal *k'ang*. I lie next to the wall, beside Chia-kang. We are silent, all twelve of us. I haven't said a word for six days. Now I have to say something. I take Chia-kang's hand out from under the covers and write on his palm with my finger. We talk on his palm.

CAN'T SLEEP
COME HERE I'LL ROCK YOU TO SLEEP
NO
?
AFRAID
SLEEP DON'T BE AFRAID
FIRST, SAFETY
SAFETY WHERE
CH'ING-TAO
COMMUNISTS ALMOST THERE
NANKING
COMMUNISTS ALMOST THERE TOO
RETURN PEIPING
CAN'T RETURN
MUST KEEP GOING
UNTIL WHEN
UNTIL GOOD PLACE FOR CHILD
TAIWAN
BEAUTIFUL ISLAND
I WANT A SON
I WANT A DAUGHTER
SON CALLED YAO-TSU
DAUGHTER CALLED SANG-WA

No man's land.

The sun is setting. Only a few more miles to Ts'ai Village. No sign of the village in sight. The twelve people on the narrow path are silent. We are still strangers. We have to hurry. Wheelbarrows piled with luggage creak over the dry, cracked earth. Dust rises in veils, separating each of us from the others. Each figure is blurred, hidden in a tent of dust. The faster we walk, the quicker our hands swing: clenched fists poking through the swirling tents of dust. Wherever we go, the tent of dust whirls around us, no matter how fast or how far we walk.

It's growing dark. Still a couple of miles. The twelve of us are lined up on the narrow path. Chia-kang and I are at the end.

101

At the front a lantern is lit.

Ah, we all murmur. Someone coughs, spits loudly; another stumbles on a rock, and curses.

The lantern is held up, lighting the path for those at the back.

'Mulberry, I still want a son,' says Chia-kang in a low voice, leaning forward.

'And I still want a daughter.'

'Only sons, no daughters allowed,' he says and punches me playfully on the back.

Ahead of us a man from Shantung chuckles, 'I could tell all the time that you two were married.'

The lantern goes out.

Ah, we all murmur again.

'Excuse me, anyone have a match?' asks the one carrying the lantern.

'Here!' Chia-kang yells.

The man stops and lets the people behind him pass. 'Watch out, sir. A pit. Be careful, folks, there's a pit. Be careful, ma'am.' He stands in the dark and helps people across.

Chia-kang walks up and hands him the matches.

The lantern is lit again.

'Thanks, sir.' He hands the matches back to Chia-kang.

'Keep them, man, you have to hold the lantern.' Chia-kang thrusts the matches back into the man's hand.

There are several cottages at Ts'ai Village. All empty. On the slope stands a temple with a broken signboard above its entrance. The name of the temple is in fading gold characters.

The twelve of us relax in the main hall. The Buddha with a thousand arms lies on its back on the mud floor. The child in the Goddess of Mercy's arms is headless. Only the Laughing Buddha is intact, still laughing. We light the altar lamp, untie our luggage and sit on our bedrolls and eat our dry food. The main hall comes to life.

'Well, now!' someone suddenly yells. 'Let me sing you a passage from *Beat the Drum and Condemn Ts'ao Ts'ao*.

> Although you serve as Prime Minister
> You can't tell the virtuous from the stupid
> Your thief's eyes are impure
> You can't take good advice
> Your thief's ears are impure

You don't study the classics
Your thief's mouth is impure
You cherish thoughts of usurping the throne
Your thief's heart is impure.'

Someone else chimes in:

'Beyond the mountains are beautiful lands
Where people toil dawn to dusk
To eat, you must work with your own hands
No one serves as another man's slave

'. . .Hearing that, Huang Chung gets on his horse. He points his sword and shouts, "Master Kuan," the Great Han Army has been defeated. From the four corners of the empire gallant men rise up in the chaos . . .

'. . . Suddenly something jumped out at me. And you know what it was? A tiger. Where did that tiger come from? He was living in a remote valley on South Peak.'

Look, there's a dragon on my head
a dragon on my body
on my left side is a dragon
on my right side is a dragon
there's a dragon in front of me
and a dragon behind me
nine dragons all around me
golden dragons with five claws . . .

'Hey, all you opera singers, storytellers and folk singers. Stop all that noise and listen to my ghost story.'

The singing and chanting stop. Only the voice telling the story is heard:

'Yü and the girl in the green dress finish making love. Yü asks the girl to sing him a song. She laughs and says that she doesn't dare. Yü caresses her tenderly and repeats his request. The girl in green says that she doesn't mean to be inhospitable, but she is afraid someone might overhear. She lowers the gauze curtain and leans against the bedpost and softly begins to sing:

The Han River ceases its flow
Birds soar high
Where will they land
Here and there they fly
Tall peaks not so low
As city walls nearby.

She finishes her song and gets down from the bed. She looks out the window, looks in the corners, inspects the room. Yü laughs at her timidity and coaxes her back to bed. He begins to make love to her again, but the girl in green remains passive and melancholy, unwilling to make love. Yü entreats her and finally succeeds once more. At dawn, she gets dressed and climbs down from the bed, walks to the door, hesitates and returns to his side, quite frightened. Yü accompanies her to the door and watches as she vanishes down the corridor. Suddenly he hears her scream for help. He races over but sees no one, only hears a faint moan under the eaves. Looking closely, he sees a spider web under the eaves. The moan appears to come from the web. Looking again he sees a big spider with something in its grip. He tears down the web. A large green honey bee falls to the ground.'

'Hey, I'd like to meet a bee like that!'

'Does anybody know if the Communists have crossed the Yangtze yet?'

'Hey, you motherfuckers, still talking about the war. Look, see how beautiful the moon is, feel how soft the spring breeze is. The trees on the hill outside the temple are sprouting green leaves.'

'Hey, old man, thanks for carrying the lantern for us. What's your name?'

'Don't ask me my name. And don't ask where I'm going. I'll stay here in this dilapidated temple and take the first name in the *Book of the Hundred Names*; just call me Chao, as in Chao Emperor of the Sung Dynasty.'

'Master Chao, may I ask where Madame Chao is?'

'That's something I haven't thought about yet. I'm still a bachelor.'

Chia-kang glances left and right, looks at my stomach and laughs. 'I'm the one who is going to be the ancestor of later generations. My wife is pregnant. I'll take the next name in the *Book of the Hundred Names*. Call me Ch'ien.'

'If you're going to be the ancestor of later generations, you better

104

take care of your wife. On the road, you really tried to fool us. You avoided your woman as if she were a locust. But I knew a long time ago that you two were together.'

'We'll take the third name in the book,' a young man who looks like a student takes the hand of the girl sitting next to him.

'You too? Now that I couldn't tell.'

'We have just gotten engaged.'

'Get married tonight,' Master Chao jumps up. 'The main hall will be the wedding chamber. The mud floor the wedding bed. You can roll around and turn somersaults on the floor. Make love in front of the Buddha. The god of heaven, the god of earth, the god of man, none will bother you. No need for a minister, the witnesses or a matchmaker. The hell with them all.'

'Good idea!'

'No ceremony whatsoever. All you do is get into bed, no, get down on the ground to sleep.'

'What could be a better ceremony?'

The student and the girl look at each other. He pinches her. She pinches him. They lean against each other and laugh.

Chia-kang runs over and beats the drum in the hall three times. The wedding ceremony begins.

We all retreat to the courtyard. The bride and groom are the only ones left in the hall.

In a woodshed in the corner of the courtyard, we find a huge butterfly kite and a small red lantern.

A half moon shines on the hill. A soft breeze. We light the lantern and tie it to the kite with some string. The kite flutters upwards. The wings spread wide. As it goes higher, the lantern becomes a tiny point of light. We run; the string whispers in the wind. We race on the hill toward the mountain top. The kite soars higher, flickering like a firefly off the darkness. Suddenly the kite catches fire, blazes red above the village.

PART III

ONE

Peach's Third Letter to the Man from the USA Immigration Service

(22 February 1970)

CHARACTERS

PEACH, she lives with a tree cutter, a Polish Jew, in an abandoned water tower in Mid-west of America; they call it 'The Womb'. With her letter, Peach encloses Mulberry's diary kept during her life in the attic in Taiwan.
THE MAN FROM THE IMMIGRATION SERVICE.

Dear Sir:

I'm living with a lumberjack in a water tower in an open field south of Des Moines. The water tower is a round wooden tank supported by three legs, like the Eagle space capsule that landed on the moon. It stands in the middle of a vast expanse of corn and from the highway you can see it a long way away. If you want to chase me, then come on. I'll be sending you reports all along the way because I want to convince you that I'm not Mulberry.

I was hitchiking in Des Moines when I saw a very muscular man pulling a thick rope. The rope was tied around a huge termite-eaten elm tree; there was a semi-circle cut deep into the trunk and a large saw lay beside the tree on the ground. It was cold and dry outside. The man's face was bathed in sweat. He gritted his teeth as he pulled. The elm cracked and the gash opened wider. He suddenly jumped aside and the huge tree crashed to the earth.

I was standing by the roadside, watching him fell the huge tree.

109

He straddled his motorcycle and was about to start it up, when he suddenly turned around and looked at me.

'I'm waiting for a ride.'

'Where are you going?'

'Anywhere is fine with me.'

'Let's go get a drink.'

'OK.'

I climbed onto the back of his motorcycle and clutched him around the waist. The motorcycle moved like wind, like lightning. We rode up and down the undulating backroads of the Midwest, rising and falling, rising and falling. Dry flecks of fine snow were suspended in the sun.

The motorcycle stopped at the water tower. All around the earth was black and frozen. The grass around the water tower was very tall and the weeds had been hacked down unevenly. A large scythe was sunk in the grass. I was half-buried by the weeds.

'I'll make a path for you. This is where I live.' He picked up the scythe, hacking at the weeds with one hand, pulling them aside with the other, each stroke harder than the one before. 'Where are you from?'

'I'm a foreigner.'

'I could tell. I am, too. This is the age of the foreigner. People drift around everywhere. I'm a Polish Jew.'

'I'm an Asian Jew,' I joked.

He bent over, gripping the scythe and cut a path open through the weeds, all the way from the road to the foot of the water tower.

I climbed up into the water tower from that newly cut path. He had made the furniture in the tower from logs all by himself. We drank gin. He said that when he was thirteen he had been in Auschwitz. The Nazis had used his father, mother and older sister for bacteriological experiments, and they had died in the camp. After he got out, he became a drifter. He makes a living by cutting down termite-infested trees. By chance he discovered this abandoned water tower. He felt very safe there. No one could harm him there. During the time of the Indians, the water tower had supplied water to the soldiers. But now it's the space age. Who would want such a broken-down wooden tank? Deer, antelope, squirrels, and rabbits live around here, but no people. When he was small, he dreamed of having a zoo when he grew up, a zoo without tigers. When he was four he was almost eaten by a tiger. His father had taken him to the circus. They sat by the gate where the animals enter the ring. The tiger was supposed to come out and jump through hoops of fire. When he saw the tiger coming out, shaking its head and swishing its tail back and forth, he jumped up excitedly. The

110

tiger suddenly turned and clamped his head in its teeth. He heard the crowd's startled screams. He wasn't frightened but his neck hurt a little. He couldn't see anything; the tiger's mouth was a black cave. Then the trainer came and prised the tiger's mouth open. The teeth left holes in his head and neck, and its claws had ripped the skin on his shoulders. As he felt the blood dripping from his head, he told his father that he wanted to grow up in a hurry. He wanted to be as big as Tarzan so he could kill tigers.

I like boys who want to kill tigers, so I have settled down in this water tower.

I'm sending you Mulberry's diary written in the attic in Taipei, the T'ang poems and the Diamond Sutra which she copied out by hand, and Shen Chia-kang's pile of newspaper clippings.

Peach
22 February 1970

TWO
Mulberry's Notebook
An Attic in Taiwan

(Summer 1957–Summer 1959)

CHARACTERS

MULBERRY, she is now 28. She and her husband and child have lived in Taiwan since 1949. They are now hiding out from the Nationalist police in an attic. Her shattered past, her guilt, and life in the attic begin to wear away at her sanity. She begins to show signs of schizophrenia.

CHIA-KANG, is now in his 30s. He is wanted by the police for embezzling. Never very strong or independent he has become more and more self-pitying and bitter.

SANG-WA, their daughter, born in Taiwan.

MR TS'AI, an old friend of Mulberry's father who allows them to hide in an attic in his storage shed.

AUNT TS'AI, his wife, dying of cancer.

(A) Summer, 1957

The noise on the attic roof has started up again. It's like rotting ceiling beams splitting apart, or like rats gnawing on bones, gnawing their way slowly from the corner all along the eaves, stopping just above the place where I am lying. Gnawing overhead from my toes to my forehead, then back down again. Gnawing up and down, finally stopping at my breasts. Gnawing my nipples. Two rows of tiny, sharp rat teeth.

I am sleeping on my *tatami* mat.

Chia-kang is sleeping on his *tatami* mat.

Sang-wa is sleeping on her *tatami* mat.

Clothes are piled on half of the remaining *tatami* mat. The moon shines down on a small patch of the *tatami* mat where the clock sits. It's twelve thirteen.

Overhead the rat stops and gnaws at my nipples. Chia-kang writes something on my palm with his index finger. We talk on my palm.

SOMEONE ON ROOF
RAT
MAN
WHO
SOMEONE IS FOLLOWING US
WHAT SHOULD WE DO
WAIT
FOR WHAT
WAIT TILL HE LEAVES
SHOULDN'T HAVE RUN AWAY
BUT YOU'D BE IN JAIL
NO WAY OUT EITHER WAY
IT'S GNAWING MY HEART

Chia-kang reaches over to feel my heart, then continues writing on my palm.

I LET YOU DOWN
I CHOSE THIS
YOU'RE NOT A CRIMINAL
I AM
WHAT CRIME?
HARD TO SAY
MAYBE SPEND WHOLE LIFE HERE
THAT'S OK
WHY
CLEAN CONSCIENCE
HOW ABOUT SANG-WA
SHE HAS NO CHOICE
HE'S GONE
HOW DO YOU KNOW
HE'S GNAWING MY HEAD
MY HEAD
NO, *MINE*
CAN'T HEAR IT

GNAWING MY NOSE
CAN'T HEAR IT
GNAWING MY STOMACH
CAN'T HEAR IT
HE'S LEAVING
HOW DO YOU KNOW
NOT GNAWING ANYMORE
HAS HE GONE
YES
ALIVE AGAIN
SLEEP WELL

Taiwan is a green eye floating alone on the sea.

To the east is the eyelid.

To the south is a corner of the eye.

To the west another eyelid.

To the north, the other corner of the eye.

The sea surrounds the eyelids and the corners of the eye.

It's now typhoon season.

The little attic window looks out over the street. Peering out from the left side of the window, we can see the roof and the fence of the house at Number Three. Peering out from the right side we can see the roof and fence of the house at Number Five. Crows fly above the rooftops. Directly across from the window is the blackened chimney of a crematorium. We don't dare stand in front of the window for fear someone might see us.

The attic and the Ts'ai's house are enclosed by the same wall. Underneath the attic is a shed where the Ts'ais store junk.

The attic is the size of four *tatami* mats. The ceiling slants low over our heads. We can't stand up straight; we have to crawl on all fours on the *tatami* mats. Eight-year-old Sang-wa can stand up. But she doesn't want to. She wants to imitate the grown-ups crawling on the floor.

I sit on my *tatami* mat and read old newspapers. Old Wang, the Ts'ai family servant, piles the old newspapers for us at the foot of the attic stairs. Every day I go down to pick them up. Chia-kang crawls over to read them with me. He wants to read the international news. I want to read the police news, and we both want to see who is on the wanted list. I imagine how the story would appear:

At-large: Shen Chia-kang. While acting as Director of Accounting

114

of the Public Transportation Service, Shen Chia-kang embezzled 140,000 Taiwan dollars and fled with his wife and daughter. A warrant is now out for his arrest.

I also look to see if there is any news about Chao T'ien-k'ai. I imagine that the story would be written like this:

Chao T'ien-k'ai has been found guilty of collaborating with the Communist rebels. While attempting to flee the country, he was captured. Before his attempted escape, he was seen in the Little Moonlight Cafe with a mysterious woman. The police are now trying to find out the identity of this mysterious woman.

I arrange kitchen matches in the shapes of ideograms on the *tatami* mat, three characters:

LITTLE MOONLIGHT CAFE

Chia-kang also takes some matches and writes:

HAVE YOU GONE THERE?
TWICE
WHY
THIRSTY
BAD PLACE
I WAS THIRSTY
BE CAREFUL
CAN'T GO NOW
I'LL GIVE MYSELF UP
NO
WHY NOT
SINCE WE'RE HERE, ACCEPT IT
IF I GIVE MYSELF UP, WHAT WILL YOU DO
WAIT
HOW LONG
UNTIL YOU GET OUT
GOOD WOMAN
BAD
BAD GOOD WOMAN

I raise my head to look at Chia-kang. He opens his mouth in a silent

115

laugh. There's a big grin on his face.

He turns over and tries to repair the broken clock.

I take a pair of rusty scissors. I pick up handfuls of my long hair and begin snipping it off.

We have a big box of kitchen matches. They help pass the time. We use matches to talk and to play with our child. It's like playing with blocks. Sang-wa loves to play the word-making game. I write the easiest words for her.

THE WORLD IS AT PEACE

She scrambles the matches with her hand. She says that easy words aren't any fun. She wants harder ones. She copies complicated characters from the newspapers. She arranges them one by one, then scrambles up our matches, content, giggling.

COUNTRY
KILL
WARFARE
THIEF
ESCAPE
CRIME
POLICE
DRAGNET
UNDERGROUND
HIDE
CHEAT
DRUGS
DEFORMED
RIFLE
WOUND
CONFUSION
DESTROY
DIFFICULT
DREAM
INSANE
BURN
DEATH
PSEUDO

116

```
ANIMAL
PAIN
PRISON
INVASION
LOVE
MONEY
SEARCH
FOOD
HAPPY
GRIEF
CHANCE
```

On the roof the gnawing is beginning again. This time it's daylight outside. The noise starts in the corner and gnaws along the eaves. It gnaws as far as my head and stops. I am sitting on my *tatami* mat. The rat's sharp, tiny teeth gnaw into my head.

Chia-kang sits on his *tatami* mat, repairing the clock.

The time on the clock is still twelve thirteen.

He is working with a small drill. I take a pencil and write in the margin of an old newspaper:

```
DON'T FIX IT
I HAVE TO
NO USE FOR TIME HERE
CLOCK STOPS, THE WORLD STOPS
WORLD WON'T STOP. CLOCK WILL
JUST GO IN CIRCLES. DOESN'T
MATTER IF IT STOPS
```

Chia-kang continues working with the drill.

The rat teeth on the roof gnaw into my body. They gnaw into my heart and liver. They gnaw into my vagina.

I recite the Heart Sutra silently.

Newspaper clippings are piled beside Chia-kang's pillow, all cut out from the old newspapers he has read in the attic.

MASTER SAN-FENG'S TECHNIQUE
TO PRESERVE POTENCY

This technique is based on secret manual handed down from the

Taoist master, Chang San-feng. It enhances conjugal bliss in the bedroom. It cures impotency and premature ejaculation. Immediate results. May heaven and earth destroy us if any deceit or fraud is intended. Write for information. Include self-addressed stamped envelope. Mail to P.O. Box 14859, Taipei.

DREAM OF GOLD IN DESERTED MOUNTAIN

More than a thousand tons of gold are thought to be buried in the remote mountains of Hsin-yi Village in Nantou County. The gold was allegedly buried there when the Japanese army withdrew after World War II. Kao Wan-liang went bankrupt after spending three years digging for the treasure. It is said that the gold buried there is worth three hundred billion Taiwan dollars. At present, the government has only twenty-six billion dollars of currency in circulation. The government has already signed an agreement with Mr Kao. Ninety per cent of the treasure will go into the government treasury. Ten per cent will be awarded to the finder of the treasure.

DIGGING FOR TREASURE OR DIGGING A GRAVE?

Kao Wan-liang is digging for the treasure with a group of workmen. Fifty metres under, traces of dynamite used when burying the treasure were discovered. The workmen diggers were elated and speeded up the digging until the earth was piled high in the tunnel, narrowing the entrance to the tunnel to only six feet wide. There was no way to remove the earth. At this time, the diggers have been trapped in the poorly ventilated tunnel for three days. It is not known if they are still alive.

REALITY OR DREAM?

Kao Wan-liang and the other treasure hunters are still trapped in the tunnel. Informed sources are now expressing doubts concerning the possibility of buried treasure in these remote mountains. The road from Hsin-yi to the excavation site is steep and hazardous. It takes two hours to get there by car. During the Japanese occupation of Taiwan, there was no road and travelling by automobile was impossible. Transporting the gold, which weighed more than 1,000 tons, into the deep mountains on foot would have been virtually impossible.

Chia-kang also has a pile of clippings about a British cabinet official's affair with a model. Included is a photograph of the model lying in an empty bathtub with a wash cloth covering her vulva.

There is also a pile of clippings about a dismembered corpse. Included are photos of the body, head, and each of the arms and legs.

There is a pile of clippings of scenes of Old Peking. Wedding and funeral ceremonies. The flower market. The morning market. The night market. The ghost market. Opera theatres. Streetcars with bells. Mutton shops. Wine vats. Barber tents. Rickshaw pullers. The ruins of the Manchu palaces.

Chia-kang never tires of reading these clippings.

I've already copied out two books of the Diamond Sutra by hand, and two books of classical poetry. I keep copying and copying. I don't even know what I'm writing . . .

> The woman of Shang-yang Palace. Lady of Shang-yang
>   Palace.
> Her fresh face slowly fading, hair suddenly white.
> Prison guards in green watch at the palace gate.
> How many springs has the palace been closed?
> Chosen at the end of Emperor Hsüan-tsung's reign,
> She was only 16 then, but sixty now.
> More than one hundred were chosen then.
> Alone, the years pass, wilted by time.
> She recalls how she accepted her sorrow and bid farewell
>   to her family.
> She was helped into the chariot daring not to weep.
> Everyone said that she would be the emperor's favourite.
> Her face like hibiscus, her breasts like jade.
> But before the emperor met her
> Jealous Consort Yang ordered her sent away.
> All her life sleeping in an empty room, sleeping in an
>   empty room sleeping in an empty room sleeping in an
>   empty room empty room

Tonight there is no gnawing on the roof. Everything is black, inside and outside. The only light comes from the house at Number Three across the way. Chia-kang is asleep on his *tatami* mat. The clock, which is still being repaired, sits beside his pillow. In the dark I can't see what time the clock says.

Sang-wa is asleep on her *tatami* mat.

I lie wide awake on my *tatami* mat, waiting for the gnawing noise to begin on the roof.

Suddenly someone bangs at the gate, shouting, 'House check.' The police often use the pretext of a census check in order to search for fugitives.

I sit up with a start.

The main gate is opening. Someone comes into the courtyard. He shouts at Old Wang. He is ordering him to wake up everyone in the house. Tell them to get out their census papers and identification cards.

Chia-kang suddenly turns over and sits up. He lies down again and then sits up.

They've come? They've come? Have they finally come? He can't stop mumbling.

I nod and motion for him to be quiet.

We sit side by side. Each sitting on our separate *tatami* mats. Backs against the wall. Holding hands.

I hear them go into the Ts'ais' house.

Chia-kang writes on my palm:

> TS'AI WILL TURN US IN
> NO, MY FATHER SAVED HIS LIFE
> OLD WANG?
> NO
> I DON'T TRUST HIM
> HE HAS BEEN WITH THE TS'AIS
>   MORE THAN 20 YEARS
> THE TS'AIS HAVE SAVED OUR LIVES
> YES
> THEY'RE QUESTIONING HIM
> MAYBE
> THEY'LL SHOW HIM THE WARRANT
> MAYBE
> THEY ARE COMING UP TO THE ATTIC
> I'M READY
> I'LL GIVE MYSELF UP
> NO

120

```
WHY NOT
PERHAPS WE CAN ESCAPE
THEY'LL COME SOONER OR LATER
I'LL GO WITH YOU
YOU SHOULD BE FREE
FREEDOM WHERE
THEY'RE COMING
I'M LISTENING
IN THE COURTYARD
SOMEONE IS LAUGHING
LAUGHING AT WHAT
WHO KNOWS
ARE THEY COMING
WHO KNOWS
```

Hey, Old Wang, the inspection is over. Go on back to bed. They talk loudly as they walk out the gate. The gate is closing. Sound of boots on the stones in the alley. They knock on the gate to Number Three. In Number Three the lights go on one by one.

Chia-kang lies back down. I am still sitting by the window. He reaches out and tries to pull me over to his *tatami* mat. I can't move.

He wants to sleep. He wants to forget. It will be all right when the night is over. He mumbles and writhes under the blanket. I pull aside the blanket and lie down beside him.

Finally he falls asleep.

The noise on the roof starts up again. It gnaws from the corner along the eaves. I suddenly remember that there's a woodpecker that lives on the roof. Old Wang told me about it before we moved into the attic.

(B) Summer, 1958

The time on the clock in the attic is still twelve thirteen. It makes no difference if it's midnight or noon. The humidity and the heat are the same. The dampness seeps into the marrow of my bones and mildews there.

Chia-kang doesn't try to repair the clock anymore. We have our own time.

Sang-wa's *tatami* mat is near the window. The sun is shining down on her. Nine o'clock in the morning.

The sun is licking her body. Licking. Licking. Suddenly I look up. The sun has disappeared. Twelve o'clock noon.

The man who sharpens knives comes by, banging his iron rattle. Two in the afternoon.

In the distance the train whistles. Three in the afternoon.

The government commuter bus stops at the intersection. Civil servants in twos and threes walk down the lane. Five in the afternoon.

The woman who sings in the local street opera suddenly bursts into tears over a lover's quarrel on some nearby street. Seven in the evening.

The blind masseuse is blowing her whistle in the dark alley. Midnight.

For a long time there have been no house checks after midnight.

Chia-kang sits on his *tatami* mat telling his fortune over and over with a deck of cards, three cards are fanned out in his hand. He hunches over and studies them, mouthing words.

Three sworn brothers.

He motions to himself in a gesture of victory. He peers into the small mirror in the corner of the room and nods his head and laughs silently.

My hair has grown long again. I don't bother to cut or brush it. I let it flow over my shoulders.

I spend most of my time on the *tatami* mat writing the story of 'Her Life'. I no longer copy the Diamond Sutra out by hand.

She is an imaginary woman. I describe the important and unimportant events of her life. A collection of odd, disjointed fragments. She marries a man who once raped her. She is frigid.

When I'm not writing, I look at old newspapers. First I read stories about people running away. There are all sorts of escape stories in the newspaper.

There's a story about someone who goes to prison in place of her husband. Lai Su-chu's husband was a merchant who went bankrupt before he died. He used her name to write bad cheques. Lai Su-chu didn't have the money to cover them. She was sentenced to six months in prison. She took her two-year-old son with her and served out sentence in the prison.

I cut out the picture of this woman embracing her child in prison and stick it up on the attic wall.

Sang-wa is sitting on her *tatami* mat drawing. She draws the *Adventures of Little Dot* on the margins of old newspapers.

122

1. Little Dot

2. Little Dot, Papa and Mama
live on their *tatami* mats

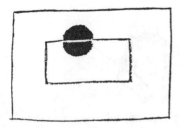

3. Little Dot wants to go away

4. Mama gets angry

5. Little Dot goes away

6. Little Dot wants the horse
to take her away

7. The horse takes Little Dot
to play on the sea

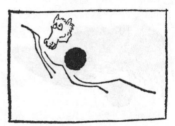

8. The horse carries Little Dot
to play on the mountains

9. Little Dot pats the horse and says she is happy

10. Little Dot goes back to her *tatami* mat. Papa and Mama are very angry

11. The horse tells Little Dot to fly out the window and marry him

12. Papa kills the horse with an arrow

13. The horse's hide is hung up to dry in the sun

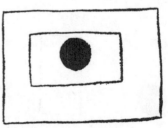

14. Little Dot looks out the window

15. The horse's hide rushes to hug Little Dot

16. Little Dot changes into a silkworm with a horse's head

I look out the window at the world outside. The world is covered with dust and cobwebs.

A white cat is dragging its black tail across the opposite rooftop.

Uncle Ts'ai and several friends come into the courtyard. They gesture and move their mouths. I quickly dodge to one side. Sang-wa crawls over to the window. I tell her not to look. However, I return to the window. The little window isn't big enough for two people to look out. I push her head down below the window sill.

Why can those people in the courtyard come and go as they please, Sang-wa asks me. Sometimes she presses her face to the window.

I explain. They can't go wherever they want to, either. There's a wall around the yard. Beyond the wall is the sea. Beyond the sea is the edge of the earth. The earth is a huge attic. The huge attic is divided into millions of little attics, just like ours. I want Sang-wa to understand that the other people in this world live just like us.

Chia-kang lies on his *tatami* mat mumbling to himself. His heart is pounding, it's about to burst. He has heart disease. He wants to die in the attic. He embezzled from public funds only for his family. If he were single, he would be innocent. Even if he has commited a crime, he could get out of the country. He could go to America or South America. Become a foreigner, just like that. His voice grows fainter and fainter. Finally he is just babbling and moving his mouth up and down. Whether his voice is loud or soft doesn't make any difference. Sang-wa and I ignore him completely. Besides, we aren't afraid of speaking in the attic anymore. We haven't used palm writing or writing with kitchen matches to converse for a long time.

Sang-wa sits on her *tatami* mat singing 'The Woman and the Great Wall' over and over in a small voice.

She sings and draws on the newspaper. One whole page is devoted to the important events in the history of modern China beginning with the founding of the Republic 47 years ago on January 1 when Sun Yat-sen took office as provisional president in Nanking, all the way to the present, to the Communist shelling of the Straits of Taiwan. In between there were the wars against the warlords, the war of resistance against Japan, and the Civil War. Sang-wa scrawls thick, crooked lines of ink all over those important events with her writing brush. Under the lines she draws little circles. Every circle has two eyes and a nose. She makes an ink blot on the thick line. She writes a caption:

Little Dot Plays on the Great Wall

She sings 'The Woman and the Great Wall' over and over.

I tell her not to sing anymore. That song is too old.

She says that it's the first song I taught her to sing. If Papa can talk to himself, then she can sing to herself. She keeps on singing the song.

> With the New Year comes the spring
> Every house lights red lanterns
> Other husbands go home to their families
> My husband builds the Great Wall.

Suddenly she stops singing. Suddenly Chia-kang stops talking. They turn. They glare at me.

I have put my hand on the window.

I tell them I want to open the window. But I don't open it.

The people in the yard have left. A fan made of palm fronds has been left on the grass.

It's twilight again.

The sun sets behind the attic. We can see only a few rays of red and purple light spreading through the sky. The further the rays of light extend, the fainter they become. Finally they blend with the darkening sky outside the attic window.

There are people in the courtyard.

This time I open the window. Just a crack. Now, not only can I see them, I can also hear their voices.

Uncle Ts'ai throws his head back in laughter. That's a good sign: as soon as I open the window, there is the sound of laughter.

They are speaking in Shanghai dialect. Peking dialect. Nanking dialect. Hu-nan dialect. Different voices. Different dialects. All tell the same story.

They are talking about a ghoul that eats people alive.

It happened on Lin Huo-t'u's thirtieth birthday in a village in the south of Taiwan. He invited three friends to his home to drink *t'ai-pai*. The four of them drank themselves into a stupor.

The next morning a monk walked into the yard of Pao-tz'u Temple. He saw a man lying under the palm tree. The monk carried him on his back into the temple and poured ginger water down his throat. When he came to, he said his name was Lin Huo-t'u.

Lin went home. At home he found his three friends dead. They were

126

lying in pools of water and they stank. The families of the dead men objected to the idea of having the coroner do autopsies. Instead, they held a ceremony to invoke the Ma-tsu Goddess to come. Speaking for the Goddess, the exorcist announced that an evil spirit was lurking in the tomb beside Pao-tz'u Temple. The coffin would have to be moved. Only then could the people of the village avoid calamity.

A girl, Pan Chin-chiao, was buried in the tomb. Six years before she had left the village to go to Taipei. Someone from the village had run into her when she was working as a prostitute in the red light district. She was beautiful and clever. She had acquired quite a reputation for herself in the district. Then, four years ago, Pan suddenly killed herself. There were only two sentences in her suicide note:

> This time I die just for fun
> To see what death is like

The people of the village moved Pan's coffin, but it was still buried in the same grave.

The third day, just as Lin was waking up, his own dog that he had had for three years, suddenly leaped at him. He fell to the ground and expired. In rapid succession, three young men between twenty and thirty died in the village.

After Lin's death, a story began circulating in the village. On Lin's birthday, the four drunk men had fallen asleep in their chairs. Dazed, Lin heard silk rustling. He opened his eyes and saw a girl in a red dress and hat. She had a lovely face and long hair; waves of cold came from her body. He pretended to be asleep. The girl in red breathed into the faces of the three other men. Lin jumped out of his chair and ran away. The girl in red chased him. He saw the lights of Pao-tz'u Temple. He thought to himself: Inside the temple, the gods will protect me. He ran up and pounded on the gate. There was no answer. The girl in red caught up with him. Lin grabbed hold of a cypress tree outside the temple to protect himself. The girl in red reached her arms around the tree and tried to grab him. He ducked left and right to get away from her. Her fingernails were like hooks and sank deep into the cypress bark. She couldn't pull them out. Lin jumped over the temple wall and rolled under the palm tree. Then he passed out. The next day the monk from Pao-tz'u Temple revived him. On the cypress tree there were four fingernail cuts each a foot deep. A trail of blood went from the gate to the temple all the way to Pan's grave.

... The ghoul devours people. Another young man died. The people of the village went to find the monk from Pao-tz'u Temple to have him verify the traces of blood left by the corpse. The monk had disappeared. It was rumoured that he did not keep his vows of chastity. It was said that he kept a woman from a good family at the temple. The district magistrate wanted to punish him according to the law, but the monk had run away. Someone found part of a corpse in a clump of straw in the mountains behind the village. All that remained were the thigh bones, pelvis, fingers, and head. His spine was missing. The coroner could not establish the cause of death. He guessed that the dead person had died while sitting in the clump of straw. It was sitting, facing south, looking at the village at the foot of the mountain. The people of the village claimed that it was the monk of Pao-tz'u Temple. He was sitting in the lotus position in the clump of straw when the ghoul found him. The girl in red ate human spines.

Two more people died in the village, both under strange circumstances. The people of the village went to Pao-tz'u Temple to ask for help from the gods. The exorcist said that Pan's body had not yet decomposed, so she had become a ghoul who ate human flesh. Though at first, she was only eating men, later she would eat women. In two months she would eat all the people in the village. In six months she would eat all the people in the city. In a year, she would finish off all the people on the island and not even the fishermen would be spared. Taiwan would become a deserted island. The people of the village must burn her body.

On the next day the exorcist died.

On the third day the statues of the gods in the temple disappeared.

The people of the village decided not to disturb the corpse.

Then the people in the village began to attribute calamities to a different spirit – the spirit of the 11th century Judge Pao, who returned to avenge secret crimes and reward good deeds. Sometimes he inhabited the body of the victims; other times he appeared in the flesh. It was said that he had two black horns on his head.

A seventy-two-year-old carpenter quarrelled with his wife over an egg. Suddenly he lost consciousness. When he came to, his wife was lying in a puddle of blood. He was holding a bloody cleaver in his own hand.

A woman dreamed that a man with two black horns on his head wanted to take her to heaven. From then on she saw that man with black horns during the day. She burned incense and lit candles to seek his forgiveness. But the man with black horns did not spare her. She hanged herself.

128

A woman visited her mother's house. When she saw her younger brother, she grabbed his hand and shouted for the Goddess of Mercy to save them from disaster. The two shouted as they raced toward the pond. When the family got there, the brother and sister had already drowned in the pond. Before their death, neither had shown any signs of depression. The sister had been married for ten years and had four children. The younger brother had just gotten married. The two were both happy, optimistic people, and not the least bit insane.

The people of the village decided that those people were all guilty of some secret crime and that was why Judge Pao had settled with each of them. Within one month, fourteen people died in the village. It had become a village of death. Every house kept the main gate shut. Pao-tz'u Temple was a temple without statues of the gods. No one chanted sutras. No one went there to ask the gods for help. The grave where the corpse lay became a taboo area. No one dared to go near it. When people from the outside walked past the grave they could hear the villagers' loud curses from far away. The more they cursed, the more impassioned their voices became, as if their cursing could appease the ghoul and they would escape death. No one dared to mention the ghoul. They would just say that 'the Granddaddy' was back which meant that the ghoul was out eating people again. Everyone was terrified. They all felt they were guilty of secret crimes. They lived waiting for death. Every time someone died, they didn't need to tell each other. They immediately smelled the odour of death. Then every household would hurriedly burn incense and chant sutras. They weren't paying homage to the gods. They were begging 'the Granddaddy' to spare their lives.

Ch'ing, who returned to the village from Taipei, didn't believe in evil spirits. He wanted to help the people of the village. He advocated cremating the corpse. But no one dared to remove a handful of dirt from the grave where the corpse lay buried. No one dared carry the corpse to the crematorium. Ch'ing took a shovel and knocked down the gravestone. He broke into the grave. He opened up the coffin. She was a sleeping beauty, looking very much alive. Dressed in a pink gown flecked with gold. Long, black hair. Sleek, supple arms. Eyes wide open, staring at the sky. Ch'ing sprinkled gasoline over the corpse and coffin. The fire burned from early morning until midnight. In the evening Ch'ing dug out her intestines with a stick. They were dripping with blood. The blood spattered on the grass of the grave. The odour of the smoke mingled with the smell of blood and fresh grass. A slight breeze carried the odour throughout the village.

The people of the village recognised the smell, that's what it smelled like when the ghoul was out eating people.

Four days after the corpse was cremated, Ch'ing died suddenly.

Twilight again. I open the window. No one is in the yard. A heavy rain mixed with hot air presses in the window.

A truck with a loudspeaker drives down the lane, warning that a typhoon has hit the northeast coast.

The people are asked to inspect their roofs, doors, and windows to make sure they are secured. They should collect flashlights, candles, and matches in case the electricity goes off. They should store drinking water in case the water supply is cut off. They must be careful with burners and stoves to prevent fires.

I speak to Chia-kang about leaving the attic. We have already gone through half of the ten thousand dollars that he embezzled from the government treasury when we fled. We can't depend on the Ts'ais for left-overs for the rest of our lives. He should give himself up. He can still get a reduced sentence. He can still get his freedom back someday.

He turns over suddenly and sits up. He says life in the attic is imprisonment. If he leaves, he'll just go to another prison. He simply won't flee anymore. He asks if I plan to escape alone. He wants to know that.

I say even if it came to rolling down the Mountain of Knives, I would roll down with him. But Sang-wa is an innocent child who should not suffer.

'I'm sorry. She was born at the wrong time.' When Chia-kang says this, he looks at Sang-wa and grits his teeth.

Over the past year I have unconsciously collected a lot of newspaper clippings about escapes. There's a large pile of newspaper clippings on my *tatami* mat.

NO WAY OUT FOR OUTLAW
ESCAPE ATTEMPT UNSUCCESSFUL
KITE FLIES FAR, BUT STRING IS
    LONG
END OF THE ROAD FOR RUNAWAY
HOODLUM SURRENDERS
BIG DRUG SMUGGLER AT LARGE
SEARCH THROUGHOUT PROVINCE
CRIMINAL CAUGHT

Chia-kang says that all those fugitives were extraordinarily clever. But they were all caught and sent back to prison. What's the use of trying to escape? With one finger he lifts the pile of clippings and weighs them.

It's late at night. The typhoon snarls above the green eye. The green eye is still open wide.

Downstairs I hear the sound of chiselling at the shed door.

They have really come for us.

The door is creaking open. The attic shudders with the wind and rain.

It is absolutely silent. I can see Chia-kang's eyes open wide, staring at the ceiling.

I am sitting on my *tatami* mat. He is lying on his *tatami* mat. They could come up for us at any time.

We wait out the night.

By morning the gale winds have died down. Downstairs Old Wang coughs when he comes to get some coal. I open the door to the stairway. He says that a burglar broke into a house on the lane during the storm. He was discovered when the owner returned. The burglar killed the owner with an iron, then fled. Old Wang discovered footprints leading from the wall to the door in the shed that goes up to the attic.

Did he get away? Did he get away? Chia-kang and I shout in unison from where we lie at the top of the stairs.

The three of us escape from the attic.

We are climbing a mountain a thousand metres high. Sang-wa climbs to the top without stopping to catch her breath. So she can really walk, after all.

We can't stop anywhere for long. If we stop we must report our place of residence to the police station. If we report our residence, we must show our identification cards. Our identification cards will give us away as fugitives. At night we stop in caves in the mountains to sleep. During the day we climb. We steal sweet potatoes and fruit. We drink water from ponds.

Sang-wa sees our reflections in the pond. She says there's an attic made of water in the pond. In the water attic there are three people made of water. Their faces are covered with dirt, their eyes open wide in fright. The water people change shape when the wind blows. Their bodies gleam and sparkle. She throws in a pebble. The three water people shatter. The

131

shards toss about on the ripples, then are reassembled into people again.

Look, there's somebody. Sang-wa points halfway down the mountain. Two people have climbed midway up the path. They look up and see us.

From then on we are on the run, we hide in the mountains. We find a wanted poster lying in the road. The police have notified the mountain people to be on the lookout for fugitives. In a single day, we see people five times. Twice, they are passers-by. Three times they are policemen, combing the area in a search. We evade them all.

Finally we find our way into a virgin forest. Red cypress. Hemlock spruce. Japanese cypress. Trees a thousand years old. The forest is dark and endless. No sign of human beings. We climb to the top of a tree and hide among the leaves. They can't see us here. Bullets can't reach us here.

More and more people are searching for us. Waves of people encircle the whole forest.

On the mountain, a bullhorn screams.

ATTENTION, Shen Chia-kang and Mulberry. You cannot hold out anymore. We all know you are hiding in the forest. This mountain is shaped like a sack. Several hundred policemen are surrounding the mouth of the sack. We have cut you off. There's no way you can escape. You can't last in the mountain. There's no food in the forest. You will all starve to death. When winter comes you'll freeze to death. You are not murderers. You are ordinary criminals. Many people have committed your crime. If you give yourselves up now, you can still get lighter sentences. Your attempt to escape is endangering the safety of all the people on this mountain. If you try to get away, we have orders to shoot. We will set the dogs after you. It is pointless to try to escape. Shen Chia-kang and Mulberry, come out now and give yourselves up.

There is no one on the beach. Not a boat on the sea. Beyond the beach rows and rows of pine trees have been planted to break the wind. The tongue of the beach stretches out into the sea. There are two large trees near the shore. A straw hut is built between the trees.

The three of us are hiding in the hut. Ah Pu-la is here with us. He has arranged for us to slip out of the island. We are all looking out to sea.

A grey dot appears on the horizon. It gets larger. It turns into a fishing boat. The boat fires a white signal flare. Ah Pu-la drags the bamboo raft from the hut down to the water. The three of us file out of the hut. The four of us climb onto the raft from a sandbar in the shallow water. We paddle toward the fishing boat. The fishing boat stops. The raft approaches it. We crawl aboard.

Ah Pu-la climbs aboard with us.

The captain of the boat informs the two sailors that they're smuggling us to Hong Kong. When the boat reaches Hong Kong, each of them will receive five thousand Taiwan dollars as a reward. We set out as though we were setting out to fish.

The captain hoists the nationalist flag.

As the flag reaches the top of the mast, one of the sailors hands Ah Pu-la a note. He asks him to take the note to his wife. He has decided not to come back. He asks her to take good care of their four children, his crippled mother, and his widowed sister-in-law. He wants Ah Pu-la to tell her the news. There's nothing he can do about it.

The other sailor scribbles several sentences on the back of the note. He asks Ah Pu-la to tell his wife that he's not going to come back either. He asks her take care of their five children and his blind elder brother. He is sorry that he has let her down, but he has to leave.

Ah Pu-la says that his family is a heavy burden. His wife is dead. They have three children and a seventy-year-old father. The family of five is supported solely by his fishing. He wants to go somewhere else. He doesn't intend to return either.

The captain orders the sailors to set sail at full speed. The name of the ship is Heaven Number One. It's an old fishing vessel weighing more than ten tons. More than twenty feet long, more than five feet wide. The helm is in the centre of the boat. Behind it is a small cabin. We spend the day hiding in the cabin. We're afraid of running into patrol boats who might search the boat and find us. The cabin is the size of two tatami mats and has a low ceiling. We still can't stand up.

A salty sun shines inside the cabin. We lie in that sun for two days. In three days we'll be in Hong Kong. When we get to Hong Kong, we'll be safe.

From the bow the captain announces that the wind is changing direction. A high cloud, shaped like a fishtail, appears on the horizon. A typhoon is approaching. They turn on the radio for the weather forecast.

The water gets rougher. On the radio an opera singer begins to weep. She finishes weeping. Then there is an announcement:

Attention: Fishing vessel Heaven Number One is attempting to smuggle Shen Chia-kang out of Taiwan. The authorities have already cabled the International Police Organisation to arrest Shen and the others at the moment they debark. They will soon be taken into custody and return to our country where they will be punished for their crimes. He

133

is wanted for embezzling government funds. Attention: Shen Chia-kang.
It is useless to try to escape. The navy patrol boats are in close pursuit.
Every port of entry in the surrounding waters has been alerted. Turn the
boat around and give yourselves up.

The blind masseuse is blowing her whistle again as she walks past the
attic.

I write page after page of escape stories. Getting away to the
mountains, getting away to the coast. How else could we escape?

(C) Summer, 1959

Aunt Ts'ai is ill. The Ts'ai family has saved our lives. I must leave the
attic to go and see her.

The most important consideration is his safety, says Chia-kang. It
isn't time to repay them for what they have done for us. Anyway, Mr
Ts'ai is a notorious sex fiend. As soon as I set foot outside the attic, I'll
fall into his clutches. That old sex fiend has hidden us in his attic
because he's got his eye on me. If he, Chia-kang, is caught and sent to
prison, how will Sang-wa and I survive? He is lying on his *tatami* mat.
He talks on and on. Beside his pillow is a spittoon. The spittoon is full
of his urine.

It's dark out. I want to take the spittoon outside.

He grabs hold of my hair. It has now grown down to my waist. He
tells me not to try to find excuses to go outside. He likes that pungent
smell. It reminds him of sex.

I go downstairs to the door. The courtyard is completely dark. A white
cat with a black tail is squatting on the wall.

I go back to the attic.

I go downstairs, out the door. Someone knocks on the main gate. I go
up to the attic again.

I go out into the yard. In the lane a policeman speeds by on a bicycle.

I go back to the attic again.

I approach one of the windows at the Ts'ais' house. There's a light on.
Uncle Ts'ai is sitting by his wife's bed. She is propped up on the bed.
They are talking.

He says he can't get out of the island now. Earlier, before the Communists crossed the Yangtze River, they had proposed peace negotiations. He had written editorials in which he advocated continuing the war. The Communists branded him as a war criminal. Now in Taiwan, he is advocating free elections. The Nationalists also consider him ideologically suspect. A pedicab is always parked at the intersection. The driver is always napping in his cab. That driver must be watching him.

Aunt Ts'ai says the driver is really watching the people who are hiding out in the attic. She doesn't understand why he is taking the risk of concealing a family of criminals. He should convince us to turn ourselves in to the police. He should tell us to leave the attic. He should remain silent. He should cut off his ties with the outside world. He should do this, he should do that. A lot of 'shoulds'.

I go back to the attic.

Aunt Ts'ai has cancer of the liver. I will risk everything to go see her.

Evening. Chia-kang and Sang-wa are asleep. At last I go out.

Uncle Ts'ai is alone in his study. I halt in the doorway when I see the mirror on the wall. It's a cheap mirror that warps its image. The farther away you stand, the more distorted your face becomes. He also sees the distorted face of the woman in the mirror. He turns in terror and stares at me. He tells me to come in. I don't know how to walk anymore. Hands. Feet. Body. All out of place. He tells me to sit down. My mouth moves up and down several times. I can't make a sound. I sit on the sofa, just like people outside the attic sit. I am three crooked sections. My torso rests on the back of the couch. My buttocks sit on the cushion of the couch. My feet rest on the floor. Each has its own part. The parts that should curve, do curve. The parts that should be straight, are straight.

He says he is pleased that I have come out of the attic. He has been thinking about advising us to leave the attic for a long time. But you can't tell other people what to do. They must decide things for themselves. Chia-kang should turn himself in to the police. Even if he has to serve a prison sentence, it would be for a limited term. Living in the attic is a sentence for life. Completely meaningless.

I explain. I am used to life in the attic. In the attic, all greed, anger, craving and love disappear. It would be traumatic if I changed my life. I'm afraid of changing. I have only come out to repay him for saving our lives. I want to help them in their time of difficulty. I will risk coming here every day to help them. I am speaking very slowly and softly. Sometimes I have to pause awhile before going on. As soon as I finish speaking I stand up.

He wants me to sit a little longer. He has just sent Aunt Ts'ai to the hospital and he needs to talk to someone.

The blind masseuse's whistle is shrieking again.

I go back to the attic before midnight. It's safer there.

It's dark.

I am walking down the road. One, two. One, two. One, two. My feet touch ground, one step after another. I pick up a pebble. The pebble rubs against my palm. I go on walking like that. Walking. Walking. Walking.

I pass the pedicab at the intersection. The police station. The funeral parlour.

I pass an obstetrician's clinic. A white sign with black characters hangs over the door. CONTRACEPTIVE INOCULATION. SCIENTIFIC CONTRACEPTION. FREE CONTRACEPTION ADVICE. MISCARRIAGE TREAT-MENT. RECONSTRUCTED BIRTH CANAL.

I pass a drug store. There's an ad in the window showing two Westerners talking on the telephone. The Westerner with black hair calls out wryly, 'Hey, old Chang, ha-ha, you know this Male 10 stuff has male hormones in it.' The white-haired Westerner, his eyes wide open, replies, 'Really? Then I'll buy a bottle and replenish my strength.'

I pass a newspaper stand. The headline is 'VICTORY SOON IN OUR STRUGGLE WITH THE COMMUNISTS FOR THE MAINLAND.'

I pass a school. The sign says: ADVANCE TO HIGH SCHOOL. ADVANCE TO THE UNIVERSITY. HUMANITIES, SCIENCE, MEDICAL SCHOOL, AGRI-CULTURAL SCHOOL. EXPERIMENTAL CLASSES, ADVANCED CLASSES, SPECIALISED CLASSES. TEST OF ENGLISH AS A FOREIGN LANGUAGE FOR STUDY ABROAD.

I pass an airline office. A yellow airplane hangs in the window. The nose of the plane slants toward the corner of the window. Black letters are painted on the body of the plane. The airplane's passenger service extends to major cities all over the world. Fast and Safe. Courteous Service.

I pass the intersection. OPEN YOUR HEART TO THE HOLY SPIRIT, black characters on a white dress flash past me. A woman's head sticks out from a white collar. A missionary. She smiles and hands a leaflet to me. SIN AND REDEMPTION. Please come hear the holy word. Please believe in the Lord.

136

A hand grabs my arm. On the wrist is a huge round watch with a luminous dial. The time on the watch is 8:20. A policeman is holding me by the arm. A train thunders past in front of me. Characters painted on the box cars, 'Beware of Communist Spies' flash by. The railroad crossing bar has been lowered in front of me. I duck under the bar and try to scurry across the tracks. The policeman says that the crossing bar is lowered to warn pedestrians and cars that a train is coming. Next time, remember that. Don't play around with your life.

A bizarre world.

I am walking down the long hospital corridor. The lights are glaring. At the end of the corridor is the morgue. I walk halfway down the corridor and then turn right. Past the patients' rooms. In a window of the building opposite a woman is crying.

I am standing in the doorway of Room Number Four. Aunt Ts'ai is propped up in bed. I am calling to her. She doesn't answer. She stares at me as though she is looking at a ghost.

I pick up a brush from the table next to the bed and brush her hair. I smooth down her hair with my hand. I braid her sparse hair into a pigtail.

She reaches out to feel my face. Arm. Hand.

She says she can feel me, so I must be real. As she says this, she squeezes my finger hard.

I tell her it really hurts.

My life splits in half. Daytime in the attic. Night-time at the hospital.

Chia-kang is lying on his *tatami* mat. His heart is racing. Head aching. He has a pain in his side. Back hurts. All his muscles are sore. Constipated. He says he's not going to make it.

He wants me to give him an enema. He squats over the spittoon. He wants me to look between his legs at his bottom. Has it come out? Has it come out yet? He is asking over and over. I want to turn around and vomit. He wants me to stick it in again. Stick it in. Stick it in. He shouts at me.

He blames me for destroying his whole life. I wasn't a virgin, he married 'a broken jar'. His illusions about me have been shattered. His illusions about everyone in the world have been shattered. That lousy bastard Ts'ai has hidden us in his attic, just so he can make believe he is God. Then Chia-kang brings up the subject of Refugee Student in Chü-t'ang Gorge.

Sang-wa wants to know who he's talking about.

That son of a bitch who raped your mother, says Chia-kang.

SANG-WA'S DIARY

Papa and Mama both have identity cards. Mama says that an identity card proves that you are a legal person. I'm already ten, but I still don't have one yet. Mama says that people in attics don't need identity cards. Only people on the outside need them. If they don't have identity cards, they will go to jail. I hate it when Mama goes outside every night. Papa says she goes to look for men. She wants to get rid of us. I want to tear up her identity card.

I hate my stepmother . . . She buys new dresses for her own daughter but I have to wear dresses made from grey flour sacks. I run away, Papa will beat her to death. Papa is an ugly old sick man. He lies on the tatami mat and always wants to hit us. I hate him, too. People on the outside hang their identity cards around their necks and let them swing back and forth on the chains. That's really neat. One chain for each person's identity card. Even cats and dogs have identity card chains. I don't have one and I'm afraid. I don't want to go to jail. I run back home. Papa and Stepmother are dead. I'm an orphan. I'm sorry, I shouldn't have run away.

Little Dot has an identity card. She is legal so she can go outside. She comes back and tells me lots of funny stories. People on the outside who have identity cards can even eat people. They grab pretty girls and plug up their butts and stick water hoses into their mouths. Their stomachs blow up like watermelons. Then they eat them. A watermelon that breaks open by itself tastes better than one cut with a knife. I lick my lips and say 'How sweet.'

Mama goes outside every night. Papa says, 'Oh that woman. She goes out to eat men.' I ask him if she eats someone so she can get his identity card chain. Papa doesn't understand what I mean. Mama brings back a whole trunk full of identity card chains. I make lots of dolls out of the grey flour sacks. Each doll has an identity card chain. When Mama finishes eating all the people on the outside, she'll eat Papa and me. But I'm not a boy so maybe she won't eat me. I want to run away and elope with someone. I don't want to eat anyone. Little Dot says people's meat is like

138

watermelon, red and sweet, but I think people's meat tastes bad. I bite my own finger and it's salty.

Mama says Aunt Ts'ai is dying. I don't know where people go when they die. She says they go to paradise when they die. People are very happy there. They aren't afraid. Whatever they want they can have. When offerings of paper servants and paper coins are burned, they go to heaven and become real. I ask if paradise has attics. She says no. I ask if people in paradise wear identity cards. She says no. I ask if people in paradise eat people. She says no. I don't believe her. Papa says Mama tells lies.

Aunt Ts'ai is dead. When it gets dark Uncle Ts'ai and I take her burial clothes to the Ecstasy Funeral Parlour.

A white curtain hangs in the morgue. Outside the curtain is an altar with two burning white candles. There's a strong pungent smell of antiseptic.

He pulls open the curtain. His wife is lying on the stone table. A gauze bedspread is hanging on the wall. We stand on either side of the stone table.

Her eyes are wide open. He closes the eyelids. The eyes are still wide open.

He suddenly chuckles. He says they slept together for more than thirty years, but only now does he realise that she doesn't have any eyebrows. She painted her eyebrows on when she was alive.

The mortician comes into the morgue. He drops a bundle of burial clothes on the legs of the corpse. He picks up one shroud after another and places them inside each other. Red. Yellow. Green. Blue. Purple. He removes the white sheet which covers the corpse.

The nylon rustles as it glides over the naked corpse. Her hair has fallen out, except for a little tuft of pubic hair between her thighs. I look at Uncle Ts'ai. He is looking at the gauze bedspread on the wall. The mortician wipes the corpse with a large towel. The breasts quiver.

Uncle Ts'ai walks out of the morgue. He chats with some people from the funeral parlour in the yard.

The mortician throws the towel in a corner. Some yellow pyjamas with black lace are piled in the corner. A dragonfly buzzes over and lands on them. The mortician lifts the upper half of the body to dress her in the burial clothes. The body is stiff. The clothes make a ripping sound. The seams of the sleeves are splitting.

Uncle Ts'ai walks in and says the burial cap should have a few pearls on it. He wants to go home to get them. He asks the mortician to wait awhile.

The mortician lets go of the body. It falls back on the stone table with a thud.

Forget it, he says. Anyway, the body is going to be cremated.

No, no, no, says Uncle Ts'ai. Not cremation. Burial. The coffin will be taken back to our old home on the mainland someday.

All right. The mortician's mouth twitches in a smile. I'll wait.

Someone lifts up the curtain and asks when the corpse will be taken out. A child has died. There aren't any empty tables. They're waiting to bring the child inside.

The mortician looks up at Uncle Ts'ai. Uncle Ts'ai motions to him to continue. The pearls aren't necessary.

The mortician slaps creme haphazardly over the face. Then powders it. Finally, he draws two thin lines for eyebrows and puts on the cap without pearls.

Fine. It's finished. Do you want that pile of clothes? He points to the lemon yellow pyjamas with black lace in the corner.

No, says Uncle Ts'ai.

The mortician picks them up and goes out.

We leave. We are silent all the way home.

I tell Uncle Ts'ai that I would like to live a normal life: going out during the day, coming home at night. Coming home to the attic.

He says it's not feasible. If I go out during the day, I am a threat to everyone I meet. I'm the wife of a criminal.

But it's only fair, I tell him. I live all my days threatened like that. They should feel threatened, too.

He asks me, am I innocent or guilty.

Both, I say. And neither. You could call me an innocent criminal.

He says he doesn't understand that. An innocent person should live outside the attic entirely. A criminal should hide during the day and go out at night. Then he told me a story about a criminal.

A murderer named Chu escaped from the prison. During the day he hid in a cemetery. At night he went out begging. No one noticed him. He hid in the cemetery for twenty days. But he couldn't go on hiding there. One night he went to a gambling joint. He won lots of money. He went to Taipei and rented a room.

He was a master of disguise. He passed as a policeman, a scholar, a business manager, a reporter, air force pilot, university professor, American Ph.D. graduate. He swaggered into dance halls and bars.

Finally, pretending to be a writer he began living with a bar girl. He wouldn't allow her to go back to the bar. She wanted to marry him, but he didn't want to. She got pregnant. He wanted her to get an abortion. She didn't want to. They had a fight. Then he wanted to go to bed with her. She didn't want to do that either. He beat her up and went out gambling. She took an overdose of sleeping pills and killed herself. In her room the police found a photo of him wearing a doctoral mortarboard. It was the man on the wanted list: Chu.

Chu won some more money at the gambling den. He felt the others were cheating him. He pulled out a gun. No one was frightened. He fired at the sky. Still no one was frightened. He fired at the window. Someone happened to be walking by the window. The bullet hit him in the chest. When the police arrived, Chu had already gotten away.

These two incidents were added to his record. The police put several detectives on the case.

Chu fled to T'ai-p'ing Mountain. He hid in the mountain for two weeks. He saw fireworks in the sky. He wanted to celebrate New Year too. He wanted to play some mahjong. He went back to Taipei. During the Spring Festival, every family was playing several games of mahjong. He pretended to have gone by mistake to the wrong house for a New Year's celebration. He was admitted into a house on Nan-ch'ang Street. He pretended to be an overseas Chinese just returned and played dominoes with the housewives. He went there for three days. An undercover policeman in the area became suspicious. On the fourth day the policeman recognised him from a photo. They frisked him and found a knife.

Uncle Ts'ai says that Chu's mistake after escaping from prison was that he forgot he was a fugitive. He had tried to live like an innocent man, but he just set a deeper trap for himself.

I say that my situation isn't the same. I'm not a criminal, and I don't carry around weapons to murder people with. I don't go on explaining. I just want him to know the facts and I want to prove to him I can live a normal life outside the attic. But at night I will stay in the attic to hide from house checks.

Uncle Ts'ai is having a few guests over for a party. I disguise myself as a servant, the kind that is resigned but still proud. I invent a good story. My husband was a government official. I escaped from the mainland to Taiwan with my four children. He is still trapped on the mainland. I am working as a maid to support my four children.

I hesitate for a long time in the kitchen before I make my entrance to the sitting room. Right now they are discussing the case of a certain Communist spy.

Three years ago a passenger jet crashed en route to the south of Taiwan from Taipei. All thirty-four passengers died. One of them was an overseas Chinese leader who had gone to Taiwan to talk with government officials about financing an attempt to reconquer the mainland.

A week earlier, Ying-ying, a singer at the Central Hotel, had disappeared after singing her last song on the programme. It was rumoured that she was caught and shot by the Security Police. She was the leader of a Communist spy ring. The crash was her doing. While accompanying the Chinese leader to the airport, she put a bomb in his luggage. A Mr Yin, who had lived with her for three years, reported her to the Security Agency. After she was shot he died in a car accident.

The guests are discussing the rumours. What was Ying-ying really? No one could say. They supposed she was a Communist. Then who was Mr Yin? There were several possibilities.

The first: Mr Yin was a Nationalist spy. The Security Agency sent him to live with Ying-ying. After he reported on Ying-ying's work as a Communist spy, the Security Agency ran over him with an army jeep to keep him from talking.

The second: Mr Yin was a Communist spy. Ying-ying had fallen in love with a Nationalist. Mr Yin reported to the Security Agency that Ying-ying had revealed his identity, so he committed suicide by running out in front of a car.

The third: Mr Yin did not belong either to the Nationalist or the Communist party. He was simply a jealous lover. Ying-ying had another lover, so he reported to the Security Agency that she was a Communist spy. Afterwards, he felt such remorse that he lost his mind. He died in a car wreck.

There are still other possibilites. No one knows for sure who he really was.

At that moment I step into the sitting room. Uncle Ts'ai is surprised. It is the first time I have shown myself to so many people at once. I ask him, Sir, when do you wish to eat. He immediately informs the guests that I am Mrs Chiang, just arrived. One of the guests asks me where I'm from. I say Szechuan. We begin to chat.

I say that my husband, before his death, was deeply in debt. I took my daughter to prison with me and served in his stead. My poor daughter died in prison. When I got out I came to work for the Ts'ais. I say whatever comes to my head with great confidence. It's completely different from the story I had prepared beforehand.

He introduces himself to me as Chiang. My name is also Chiang. He says I look familiar. My eyes and eyebrows remind him of his father's concubine. He says his father died in the war. The concubine became a Buddhist nun.

I burst out laughing. Mr Chiang, you are really confusing me. Which war are you talking about? The campaign against the warlords, the war of resistance against Japan, or the war between the Nationalists and Communists?

He doesn't answer, just stares at me as if in a daze.

Oh, Mr Chiang, I gesture toward him, don't stare at me so. If you keep staring at me like that, I'll turn into a Buddhist nun. If you go on staring at me, I'll turn into that concubine. Monkey could transform himself eighteen times. I really believe such magic exists.

All the guests laugh.

Chiang asks me when I left the mainland.

April 1949.

Where on the mainland.

Peiping.

Chiang claps his hands. He also escaped from Peiping in April 1949. Maybe we met on the way.

I murmur, uh. Was it possible? So many people were trying to escape then. Like ants in a hot frying pan, scurrying in all directions, not knowing which way to turn. I came from Peiping, Tientsin, Chi-nan, Wei County, through no man's land.

Chiang claps his hands again. That's right. That's right. He escaped from Peiping, Tientsin, Chi-nan, Wei County through no man's land.

Please have a cigarette, I interrupt and offer him a Long Life cigarette.

I light it for him.

Uncle Ts'ai says I should win an Oscar for the best performance by an actress. The name of the motion picture is *The Woman in the Attic*; the role is Mother Chiang.

I begin a new life. I go out during the day. Back to the attic at night. Uncle Ts'ai gets used to it.

Chia-kang sleeps twenty hours a day.

He bitches four hours a day.

When he isn't bitching, he masturbates under the covers.

SANG-WA'S DIARY

Mama goes out every day to eat people. When they get someone they first smoke him with nice-smelling grasses, then smear pig's blood over his body and barbecue him. The fire is burning hot. A big fire is burning all around the attic. They want to roast me and eat me, too. I have a way to get out. I draw lots of bird feathers on my flour sack dress. I look pretty in bird clothes. They are down below and laugh when they see the fire in the attic. They say I can't get out. The attic is on fire. The fire is so hot. I stand in the window and flap my wings at the sky. I turn into a bird. I fly away from the window.

The sun is so hot and burning. They want to use the sun to roast me and then eat me. I turn into lots of little bugs and fly in the sky. The little gold spirits in the sky come to help me. They all turn into little bugs flying in the sky and cover up the big sun. The sky becomes dark. The sun goes out. It can't roast the attic anymore.

The typhoon is coming. It is raining so hard. They want to hurt the attic with the wind and rain. They'll turn me into a wet chicken. They want to drink soup with people's meat in it. I draw a dragon on my flour sack. I wear dragon clothes then turn into a dragon girl. The typhoon breaks the attic window. Rain comes in. When the rain hits me I become a dragon and swim out the window. The more it rains, the happier I am. I give out silver rays as I swim in the sky. They lose again.

The sun roasts our attic every day. It's so unfair. I'll bet it's the people who eat people who do it. They tie the sun on the roof of the sky. The sun can't move. The little gold spirits help me. They make a branch come down from the sky. It dances in the window like a snake. I grab the branch and climb up on it and go up into the sky, then cut the rope off. The sun falls down with a boom. It turns into a big ball of fire. The earth catches on fire. The people who eat people all burn up and die. Ha, ha, ha. I laugh up at the sky. I pick up the rope with the sun tied on it and drop it into the sea. The sun goes out. I kick the sun like a rubber ball.

The people who eat people are all dead. Papa and Mama are also dead. I am left alone. I cry and walk to the sea shore. There is a big footprint on the beach. I don't know whose foot it is. I step on it with my foot to see

*how big it is. It is bigger than my foot. I faint and fall down. When I
wake up I have a big belly. I'm so scared I cry. I don't want to have a baby.
A big round ball of meat comes out from inside of me. I cut the ball of
meat into little balls and wrap them all up in pieces of paper. The wind
blows and breaks the paper. The little balls of meat fly through the sky.
When they fall to the ground they turn into stones. I look and the stones
move, float and turn into clouds. The clouds float away and turn into
white birds. The white birds circle in the sky and turn into snakes with
heads like people. The snakes with people heads are playing in the sky. A
black cloud sucks the snakes with people heads in and they turn into rain.
It's raining outside the attic.*

I must go back to the attic in the evening. I don't want to go back. I
want Uncle Ts'ai to take me out; I want to have fun for a while.

We go to the circus. The trapeze act has just ended. The ringmaster
on stage is announcing the next act.

Beauty and the Bear.

The Bear's name is Ah Ke. He is from South Africa. Four feet tall.
Two inches of black fur cover his body. Weight 220 pounds. A rare
animal in the world. He can roll a ball. Leap through a fiery hoop.
Walk on rolling barrels. Play the harmonica. Walk on his forepaws.
Dance the mambo.

Ah Ke is in his cage getting ready to make his appearance.

The gong sounds.

The ringmaster cracks his whip three times. Then shouts:

Hey. Ah Ke, come out.

Silence.

The whip cracks three more times. The ringmaster motions to the
audience. Hurray. Thundering applause.

Silence.

Ah Ke is temperamental. In Singapore, Bangkok, or Manila, he
refused to come out. In Saigon he came out only once. In Calcutta, he
came out twice. Ah Ke is happy in Taiwan. He will come out for sure.
He will come out for every performance here. The audience must be
patient. The ringmaster chats with the audience as he paces up and
down the stage. He's wearing a fancy flowered shirt that animal
trainers wear. He is holding his whip.

Hey. Ah Ke.

Another shout and more thundering applause.

The bear definitely won't come out, I whisper to Uncle Ts'ai. He
asks why. I say because the bear has seen a ghost in the audience. Uncle

145

Ts'ai laughs, that's just a circus superstition; we shouldn't believe it.

The whip cracks.

More shouts and applause.

More silence.

The audience begins whistling.

Don't get upset, I whisper to Uncle Ts'ai, wait till the bear forgets there's a ghost in the audience, then it will come lumbering out. Uncle Ts'ai says he doesn't believe in ghosts. I say there really are ghosts in the world, for example, ghouls who eat people alive.

The audience is screaming for a refund. Some people are standing up to leave.

Hey. Ah Ke, come out, shouts the ringmaster as he snaps his whip.

The ringmaster should put down his whip, I say to Uncle Ts'ai. The bear will come out on his own. No wild animal likes to be shut up in a cage. Uncle Ts'ai laughs. He says I have become an expert on training animals. The ringmaster's whip isn't just for taming the animals. It's also to give himself courage.

The ringmaster is strutting up and down the stage. He snaps the whip faster and faster. The audience is screaming for a refund. Some people have already left their seats.

Hey. Ah Ke is coming out. The ringmaster suddenly leaps on stage and yells.

The bear lumbers out from back stage.

Applause.

A large barrel comes rolling out.

The ringmaster stops the barrel. The bear climbs up on it. The ringmaster lets go and the barrel rolls away.

The bear spins on the barrel. The barrel spins under the bear. Spins and rolls. Rolls and spins. Faster, faster. It's as though the bear and the barrel were under a spell. Rolling, rolling. The audience is clapping. Flash bulbs are blinking. Reporters are snapping pictures.

A slender young woman steps out on stage in a skin-tight, flesh-coloured leotard. It's Beauty. The bear jumps down from the barrel. Beauty pats the bear. The bear rubs his face against her body. Beauty tells Ah Ke to kiss her. The bear stands up on his hind legs. He clasps her neck with his front paws. He licks her face. She tells him to kiss her neck. The bear licks her neck. Beauty turns her profile to the audience. She moves her face toward the bear. The bear embraces her and licks her on the lips.

Beauty murmurs with pleasure.

The audience claps. Flash bulbs blink. Reporters snap pictures.

Beauty smiles. The bear stands aside. She asks for someone in the audience to come up and meet Ah Ke.

Silence.

Two or three hands hesitate and wave.

Suddenly Uncle Ts'ai stands up. He climbs up to the stage. Beauty leads the bear over to meet him. He steps back a few paces. Laughter from the audience. Beauty tells him to come over and shake hands with Ah Ke. He doesn't move. Beauty laughs and calls him a coward. She signals to the bear. The bear gets up on his hind legs and walks over to Uncle Ts'ai. He leans back and then retreats. People are yelling for him. He can't move.

The audience is laughing.

Beauty points her finger at him. This is only the beginning. The best is yet to come, she says as she and the bear walk over to him. Ah Ke stretches out a front paw. Beauty takes Uncle Ts'ai's hand and gives it to the bear to shake. Uncle Ts'ai nods at the audience and laughs. Beauty says the bear wants to kiss his face. No, no, no, he quickly says. Bears never kiss men on the face. Beauty says it is a Western custom. She leads Ah Ke over to another part of the stage. The man and the bear are standing on opposite ends of the stage. Beauty signals to Ah Ke. The bear thrusts out his stomach and lumbers over to Uncle Ts'ai. Uncle Ts'ai stands there, leaning forward slightly, rubbing his hands together. His eyes are glued on the bear, waiting for it to attack at any time.

The people are cheering.

The bear walks to centre stage. Uncle Ts'ai comes to life. His feet start moving. At first he is hunched over and takes tiny steps. Then he straightens up and takes bigger steps.

The man and the bear stand staring at each other, face to face.

People are getting up.

The bear stretches out a forepaw and puts it on Uncle Ts'ai's shoulder.

I get up.

Uncle Ts'ai looks up. The bear draws close and licks his face.

Everyone is standing up. People in the back yell for the people in front to sit down. People are whistling at the man and the bear.

The bear is licking the man's face.

People leap and cheer. Flash bulbs blink. Reporters snap pictures.

The bear draws back.

The man and bear stand staring at each other, face to face.

Beauty takes Ah Ke's paw and bows to the audience.

Uncle Ts'ai stands there very stiffly. Staring in front of him, smiling.

A little girl comes out onto the stage and pins a yellow carnation on his lapel.

The audience is still screaming and clapping.

Frightened. Frightened, but with a strange sexual excitement, Uncle Ts'ai tells me after he leaves the stage. He laughs with satisfaction.

Chia-kang is sleeping. Sang-wa and I talk on paper:

> I'LL TAKE YOU OUTSIDE
> NO
> WHY NOT
> I DON'T HAVE AN IDENTITY CARD
> IF YOU GO OUT, YOU CAN GET ONE
> I'M AFRAID OF THE SUN
> WE'LL GO OUT AT NIGHT
> I'M AFRAID OF PEOPLE
> THERE'S NO ONE IN THE YARD AT
>   MIDNIGHT
> IT'S TOO DARK
> IT'S PRETTY WHEN IT'S DARK, EVERY-
>   THING GLITTERS
> WHAT MAKES IT GLITTER?
> THE SKY LIGHT
> I'M AFRAID OF DOGS AND CATS
> ANIMALS ARE AFRAID OF PEOPLE
> I'M A PERSON
> RIGHT
> DOGS AND CATS ARE AFRAID OF ME
>   TOO
> RIGHT
> REALLY?
> REALLY
> I WANT TO GO OUT AND SCARE THEM
> LET'S GO OUT TOGETHER

Sang-wa is so happy that she hugs her pillow and rolls over and over on the *tatami* mat. I look over at Chia-kang sleeping. She calms down suddenly. She knows Chia-kang won't let me take her outside.

Evening. I go back to the attic. Chia-kang and Sang-wa are asleep. I tap Sang-wa on the shoulder. She opens her eyes. I point out the

148

window. A full moon. She scrambles up, rubs her eyes. I point out the window again. She nods.

I pull her up on her feet. She hesitates. She ducks her head when she stands up because she is taller than the ceiling. I walk down the stairs ahead of her. She stops at the head of the stairs. I pull her hand. She walks halfway down the stairs, then turns around to go back to the attic. I jerk her hand again.

Finally she is standing on the ground in the yard. She is still hunched over. I tap her on the shoulder and she straightens up.

She stands there looking surprised. Her eyes linger a long time on each thing before they move to something else. She softly says the names of the things she sees:

> GRASS
> LEAVES
> STONES
> VINE
> JASMINE FLOWERS
> MOON
> STARS
> CLOUDS
> BUGS
> FIREFLIES
> LIGHT ON THE CORNER OF THE
>   WALL
> CAT: WHITE BODY, BLACK TAIL

Sang-wa grabs my hand. The cat hisses and jumps to the top of the wall. It squats there, its pupils two gleaming discs. I pat her hands. She doesn't move. The cat jumps down the other side of the wall. She looks up at me and smiles.

She says being outside the attic makes her tired. She has never stood straight up like this on the ground before.

I take her back to the attic.

It's very late at night.

Someone is knocking on the door, yelling, House Check. A light flashes across the window.

Sang-wa isn't in the attic.

I crawl over to the window. Sang-wa is standing in the yard holding the white cat with the black tail in her arms. Two flashlight beams are

149

riveted on the girl and the cat. Several other lights sweep in the air over her head.

Two policemen bend over to talk with Sang-wa. She is pointing at the attic. All the lights sweep over and shine on the attic.

I'm sitting by the window.

A flash of light nails me from behind. I turn. The white cat with the black tail is squatting on the *tatami* mat. Sang-wa is sitting behind the cat.

She says angrily:

'PEOPLE!'

She raises her hand and points at the attic stairs. A policeman's torso and another policeman's head emerge from the stairs.

House Check. Take out your identity cards, says the policeman whose torso is showing.

We took them to the Buddhist Lotus Society to get welfare rice, Chia-kang answers from his *tatami* mat.

Then take out your household registration papers, says the half-bodied policeman and he rummages through a file in his hand. The file has a copy of everyone's household registration paper.

I take my identity card out from under my pillow. Taipei, number 8271.

There's no stamp on the identity card. This woman has not reported to the police station yet, says the half-bodied policeman as he turns my card over and over. It's illegal not to report to the police station. According to the card, your spouse's name is Shen Chia-kang. He says the name; then suddenly pauses.

Right, his name is Shen Chia-kang, I repeat.

Chia-kang glares at me.

The clock in the attic still reads twelve thirteen.

PART IV

PART IV

ONE

Peach's Fourth Letter to the Man from the USA Immigration Service

(21 March 1970)

CHARACTERS

PEACH, she informs the Immigration Agent that the area residents felt threatened by Peach and the woodcutter because the ruined water tower where they live was declared unfit for habitation. This threatened woman, who even seems a threat to others, starts out again on her endless flight, in search of a place to have her baby. With the letter she encloses Mulberry's USA diary.

THE MAN FROM THE IMMIGRATION SERVICE.

Dear Sir:

I'm on the road again. I'm roaming around these places on the map.

I couldn't find any peace of mind in the water tower either. First the lumberjack's big saw disappeared. Next, my mud-splattered snow boots disappeared. Many people came to look at the strange couple living in the ruined wooden tank. The people living nearby reported us to the police saying that we were of questionable background and identity. Since we lived in such a broken-down wooden tank – that obviously meant something strange was going on; perhaps we had escaped from prison; or perhaps we were lunatics who had escaped from an insane asylum; they felt that their lives were threatened. Two policemen came to the water tower. The lumberjack and I were sitting nude in the water tower, discussing the baby's birth. After asking us a lot of questions, they discovered that we were only two wandering

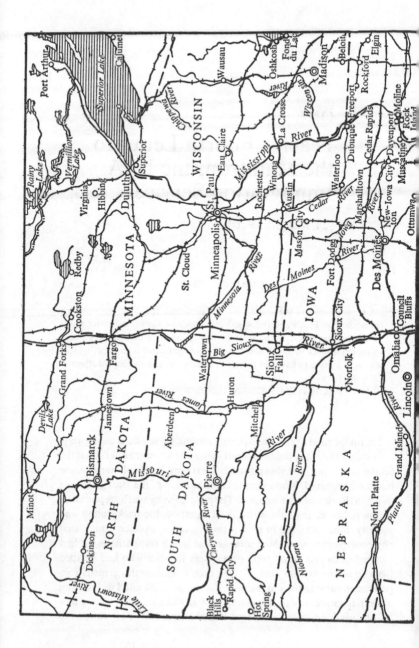

foreigners. We hadn't committed any crimes, and seemed very peaceable. We just wanted to live off the land naturally; we weren't threatening anybody. But they discovered that the dilapidated water tower was unfit for habitation. There were no sanitary facilities. The wood was rotten, and there was the danger that it would collapse at any time. Reporters came to interview us and take photos. We became newspaper headlines. They called us 'the people in the water tower'.

Finally, the police found the owner of the water tower, Mrs James. She had moved to California a long time ago. Her lawyer announced:

'Mrs James strove to preserve the water tower because it was a historic monument. But she doesn't want the water tower to endanger anyone's life. She has now decided to tear the water tower down.'

The lumberjack and I left the water tower. We hadn't planned on living there for the rest of our lives. He wanted to go east. I wanted to go west. We split up. He planned to cut down trees for people as he went, to save money to buy a camper to go to California. I told him the story about Donner Lake. He said he'd certainly pass through Donner Lake on the way to California. Now I'm alone again.

When I left the water tower I hung a wooden plaque on the iron legs with the following words, imitating what was written on the plaque that the astronauts left on the moon:

A WOMAN WHO CAME FROM AN UNKNOWN PLANET
ONCE LIVED IN THE WATER TOWER
22 FEBRUARY 1970–21 MARCH 1970
I CAME IN PEACE FOR ALL MANKIND.

Peach
21 March 1970

P.S. I enclose Mulberry's diary in America, several letters from Chiang I-po, several letters Mulberry wrote in New York but didn't mail, and several letters from Sang-wa in Taiwan: she has fallen in love with a middle-aged married man. His wife is expecting their fifth child.

TWO
Mulberry's Notebook
Lone Tree, America

(July 1969–January 1970)

CHARACTERS

MULBERRY, she is now 41. She has applied for permanent residency in the USA. Everything in her life has been destroyed: her past, her traditional values, and her ethics have been shattered. She is schizophrenic.

PEACH, Mulberry's other personality, who plunges Mulberry into a life of promiscuity and adventure.

CHIANG I-PO, a Chinese professor. He cannot commit himself to anything and cannot choose between Mulberry and his wife. He lives in China's past and is neither Chinese nor American.

TENG, (in his 30s), a Chinese college student. He represents some young Chinese intellectuals in the USA.

BETTY CHIANG, (in her 50s), Chiang's bored, crazy wife.

TAN-HUNG, (in her 40s), Teng's older sister. Married with no children.

JERRY, (in his 40s), Tan-hung's husband, an American born Chinese, a stock broker in New York. He is in love with machines, especially cameras, and is remote and indifferent to Chinese problems.

I'm in Room 81 of the Immigration Service. I sit facing the window. The window is shut. The row of windows opposite me, in the tall grey office building, is also shut. The investigator from the Immigration Service is sitting across from me; we are separated by a grey steel desk. He is bald with a sharp chin, and a pencil moustache. He is wearing dark glasses. A red-lipped secretary is sitting behind another grey steel desk. On the desk is an electric typewriter. The man in dark glasses pulls a thick folder out the file cabinet. In the corner of the folder is my alien registration number: (Alien) 89–785–462. He opens the folder, and pulls out a stack of forms and asks me to look them over.

Name: Helen Mulberry Shen
Sex: Female
Place of birth: Nanking
Date of birth: 16 October, 1929
Nationality: Chinese
Present address: Apartment 5, 33 Second Street, Lone Tree
Permanent address: None
Occupation: Chinese teacher
Employer: Holy Conception High School, Lone Tree
Marital status: Widow
Name of spouse: Chia-kang Shen (deceased)
Name of children: Sang-wa Shen (presently in Taiwan)
Have you ever joined any political party? No
Passport Number: Taiwan 53–28895
Date issued: 2 September 1966
Place issued: Foreign Ministry, Republic of China
Type of visa issued: Exchange visit
Purpose of application: Permanent residency
Date of application: 8 December 1968
Previous residences (from 16 years of age): . . .

So many dates, so many addresses. I don't read it all the way through. I pass the form back to the man in dark glasses. He opens the folder and replaces the form. Inside the folder are many more forms. He presses the folder shut with his two hands and shrugs. 'Helen, are there any mistakes in the form?'

'My name is Mulberry. I haven't used the name Helen for a long time.'

'Mulberry – foreign names sure sound funny. Now, let's get back to business.'

He opens the folder, studies the contents, then shuts it again. 'This is the information we obtained from our investigation of you. If you want to apply for permanent residency, you must go through an investigation. We still don't know the result of the investigation. We want to continue investigating. Now we want a deposition from you.' He motions to the secretary. She immediately poises her hands on the typewriter keyboard.

157

'Helen, please raise your right hand and repeat the oath after me.'

I raise my right hand.

'I, Helen Mulberry Shen, on July 17, 1969, do solemnly swear . . .'

'I, Helen Mulberry Shen, on July 17, 1969, do solemnly swear . . .'

'That what I am about to say is the truth, the whole truth and nothing but the truth . . .'

'That what I am about to say is the truth, the whole truth and nothing but the truth . . .'

'So help me God.'

'So help me God.'

'Or else I will fully submit to punishment by American Law.'

'Or else I will fully submit to punishment by American law.'

Da-da-da. The typewriter types each word.

'Now, I want to ask you some questions. What is your name?'

'Mulberry Shen.'

'I'm sorry. Please use the name Helen Mulberry Shen. What is your nationality?'

'Chinese.'

'When were you born?'

'October 16, 1929.'

'What is your father's name?'

'Sang Wan-fu.'

'When did he commit suicide?'

'October 7, 1948.'

'Why did he commit suicide?'

'I don't know.'

'Was he a Communist?'

'I don't think so.'

'What is your mother's name?'

'Sang Chin-chih.'

'Where is she now?'

'Mainland China.'

'Is she a Communist?'

'She wasn't a Communist when I left the mainland. After that, I don't know.'

'What did she do before she married your father?'

'She was a prostitute.'

'Are you in contact with her?'

'In the beginning, we wrote several times. Later, we stopped.'

'What is your younger brother's name?'

'Sang Pao-tz'u.'

158

'When did he leave Nanking to go to the Communist areas?'

'October 6, 1948, the day before my father committed suicide.'

'Is he a Communist?'

'When he was in Nanking, I don't think he was a Communist.'

'Why did he go to the Communist areas?'

'He couldn't survive at home.'

'Are you in contact with him?'

'No. He died in the Korean War.'

'When did you leave Nanking to go to Peking?'

'December 1948. It was after my father died. I don't remember the exact date.'

'At that time did you know Peking was encircled by the Communists?'

'Yes.'

'Were you a Communist at that time?'

'No.'

'Did you go to Peking to work for the Communists?'

'No.'

'Why did you flee to an encircled city?'

'I couldn't survive in Nanking. My only way out was Peking.'

'What's your husband's name?'

'Shen Chia-kang.'

'Was he a Communist?'

'I don't think so.'

'What did the Taiwan police want him for?'

'He embezzled government funds.'

'Why did you hide in the attic as well?'

'To be with him.'

'Were you guilty?'

'I wasn't guilty of any crime I know of.'

'Do you know a person by the name of Chao T'ien-k'ai?'

'Yes.'

'Is he a Communist?'

'When he was on the mainland, some people said he was a Nationalist. When he got to Taiwan, the Nationalists said he was a Communist. I really don't know which he was.'

'Why was he sent to prison?'

'I don't know.'

'Did you help him?'

'No.'

'Someone said you saw him the day before he was arrested.'

'Yes.'

'Where did you meet?'

'In the Little Moonlight Cafe in Taipei.'

'Why did you see him?'

'We were classmates from Nanking, and went together for a while. I ran into him on the street in Taipei, and we went to the Little Moonlight Cafe for a cup of coffee.'

'Did you commit adultery with him?'

'No.'

'Have you ever participated in any anti-American activity?'

'No.'

'Are you now a Communist?'

'No.'

'Are you a leftist?'

'No.'

'Are you loyal to the American government?'

'I'm Chinese.'

'But you're applying for permanent residency in America. Are you loyal to the American government?'

'Yes.'

'Is there anything else you would like to explain?'

'No.'

The man in the dark glasses signals with his hands. The electric typewriter stops.

'OK. The Immigration Service must continue its investigation. You'll have to await the final decision.'

'When will that be?'

'I don't know. The investigative process must go through related Chinese and American channels. We still have to interview many different kinds of people, and gather information on you from various sources. Only then can we reach a decision: permanent residency or deportation.'

'Whom are you interviewing?'

'Some are your friends. Some are people you don't know.'

'Even if they are friends, they don't necessarily know me.'

'That doesn't make any difference. What we want to investigate isn't your state of mind, your emotions, or your motivations. I'll say it again: what we want to investigate is your behaviour. And that can be observed by anybody. Now please make a fingerprint on the deposition.'

I make a fingerprint with my thumb on the deposition.

160

'Excuse me. I'll have to have you sign this as well.'

I sign 'Helen Mulberry Shen' on the deposition.

'Good luck, Helen.' The man in dark glasses stands up and thrusts his hand across the grey steel desk to shake hands.

I am running on top of the stone wall in Nanking. The sun is about to set over the lake. Rocks are strewn at the base of the city wall. On each rock perches a white cat with black tail. The city wall is crumbling about to fall, about to fall – about to fall down on top of all those white cats with black tails. I turn and run toward the Temple of the Crowing Cock. Where is the Temple? And where is the old monk who rings the bell? A man in dark glasses chases me on the stone city wall. First one, then two, then three, then four, then five ... close behind me, a file of men in dark glasses – all bald, with pointed chins and wearing dark suits. I turn around again and run toward the lake. The stone wall is about to fall down on the cats' backs. The cats glare at me. The men in dark glasses point at me shouting, '(Alien) 89–785–462, if you want to run, you'd better step on the cats' backs!' The stone wall collapses, the cats with the white bodies and black tails disappear. Corpses lie in heaps under the stone. My father, my brother, Chia-kang, my mother. Did mother die, too? Uncle Ts'ai? Did he die, too? He just married a young girl in Taiwan. He can't die! I step on the naked corpses as I run, leaving an imprint of my foot on each soft and pliant body and I babble, 'I treated you badly when you were alive and now you're dead and I still step on you. But I can't help it – I have to get away!' As I step on Chia-kang's body, he suddenly sits up. He doesn't speak but just looks at me laughing silently. Sang-wa stands far off to the side and points at my naked body yelling, 'Prostitute. The prostitute is going to give birth to a bastard!' 'I'm your mother. Come over here! We'll start a new life together.' I am screaming but no sound comes out. I look up to see Chiang I-po in a little boat on the lake. I call out, 'I-po! I-po! Come over here and take me back!' I still can't make any sound. I must already be dead. Only the dead can't make any sound. I'm already dead – dead – dead ...

Last night I took too many sleeping pills, and had a nightmare. Now, I'm still dazed; I grope my way into the bathtub. As I sink down into the water, I become a new woman – my headache, all my pains vanish. All feelings of suspicion, fear, and guilt disappear. The water warms my whole body. I am translucent as the water.

It is wonderful to be alive. The elm, the rays of the sun and the squirrels outside the window are also alive. The water laps against my breasts.

After getting out of the tub I open all the windows, doors, turn on the lights, the stereo and the TV. The whole world comes to me.

'The commander of the space capsule for the moon landing requests that everyone, no matter who you are or where in the world you are, remain silent for one moment, to meditate on the events of the last few hours and in your own way express the gratitude in your heart . . . those words were just spoken by astronaut Aldrin on the surface of the moon. Now the astronauts are preparing for the moonwalk . . .'

> '. . . the birds singing wildly
> the flowers dizzily bloom
> You, what a happy, happy feeling . . .'

The astronauts are ready to descend. The singer on the record croons along merrily. Carrying a small overnight bag, Chiang I-po tiptoes through the open door of my apartment. There's a movie screen tucked under his arm. He closes the door gently. Braced in the doorway he stares at me without speaking. After a moment he says: 'What's happened to you? You're not acting like yourself!'

'Professor, what's happened to you?' I am standing naked in the middle of the room, right under the light, facing a painting on the wall: a large lion embracing a naked woman in its paws – the woman, her legs slightly bent, lies on her back looking up at the sky; the lion rubs her breast with his ear.

'I'm fine. This morning, I went to church. In the afternoon I played tennis for a while and beat a young guy!'

'I think there's something really wrong with you, Professor.'

'What's that? I have a physical every July 7th on my birthday. My blood pressure and heart are both normal. Not only that, but this year when more mentally ill Chinese than ever are jumping off buildings committing suicide, here I am totally sane!'

'What? There's a woman in front of you and you're sitting there talking about mental health? Isn't that a little bit weird?'

I-po laughs. 'What's the hurry. Anyway, you won't escape from Monkey's grasp tonight!' He switches to English, '*I've got a surprise for you.*' He points to the screen on the floor.

'. . . Sea of Tranquility basecamp, Sea of Tranquility basecamp, this is Houston Control Center. Aldrin, please tell us, at this moment what is your exact position on the surface? . . .'

> '. . . I don't want this mad, mad world,

this mad, mad, mad, mad world . . .'

A police siren begins to shriek.

I-po switches off the TV and turns up the volume of the stereo. 'We're Chinese. What do Americans on the moon have to do with us? Let's listen to Golden Voice sing. When I left the mainland she was really popular . . .'

> Here the morning is free
> Here the morning is good
> Rice vendors far away
> Fruit hawkers far away . . .

He sings along in falsetto with Golden Voice as he sets up the screen. He takes the projector out of the bag and fishes around for the movie reel. He lowers his voice. 'The only people who live in this apartment house are either widows or old maids. Every time I come to see you, I feel as if they are all watching me. As I was carrying this stuff up the back stairs I ran into your landlady. She looked at the stairs and then at what I was carrying. I felt foolish going on, but I couldn't turn around, so I just kept on walking toward your apartment with my back to her. When I turned around finally, I saw her standing in her doorway, glaring at me. Her TV was on and behind her on the screen I saw a close up of a black woman's face, her mouth wide open as if she were pleading for help, but there was no sound, the volume had been turned off. The landlady stood at her end of the corridor and I stood at the other end. She stared at me and I stared at the black woman who couldn't make a sound. Boy, that was weird. I suddenly started laughing and she waved and said, "Have a good time, Professor," I took off my hat and replied, "Thank you, madam!" and strutted in here with these porn flicks.'

I pour him some gin and fix myself a Bloody Mary. I sit next to him on the sofa. His eyes are riveted on the porn flick, and he doesn't notice that I am drinking. I have never drunk before. It is as if he doesn't know there is a woman by his side. The Golden Voice is singing about a pair of phoenixes flying up to heaven.

The red light atop the police car flickers onto the window like blood splattering.

I-po kissed me. I spill my Bloody Mary on myself. He licks my neck with his tongue. 'Hey, bloody woman, why are you drinking today?'

I struggle out of his embrace and throw the empty glass to the floor. I run into the bathroom and turn on the faucet in the tub. The night breeze blows in the window. I stretch out in the tub. I-po walks in. He bends over me; he is breathing hard.

'I'm pregnant.'

He suddenly stood up. 'You're kidding.'

'The doctor's already verified it.'

'That's impossible. You'll have to get an abortion immediately!'

'That's illegal.'

'You'll have to get an abortion immediately!'

'The Immigration Service is investigating you.'

'What for? I've been an American citizen for a long time!'

'They're investigating you because we committed adultery.' I tell him about the Immigration Service's questioning me.

'It's better that we don't see each other.'

'You're in my bathroom right now, Professor!'

He laughs. 'You are my weakness: I can't do without you!'

'Then move in with me!'

'I can't do that. Betty and I are Catholics. We can't get a divorce; I have to protect my teaching position. Anyway, I'm too used to my freedom. I must retain some *dignity* in front of my friends. You know I wouldn't do anything rash.'

'I've decided to keep the child.'

'No, that won't do,' he frowns. 'You've got to get an abortion. New York. You can go to New York for the abortion. New York's changed the law: abortion is legal there. I'll pay for everything: travel expenses, medical expenses, all your expenses in New York.'

I suddenly leap out of the tub.

I turn on the TV. The astronauts are speaking.

'. . . I'm climbing down the ladder. The feet of the Eagle only sink one or two inches into the moon's surface. Getting closer, you can see that the moon's surface is made up of very fine dust, like powder, very, very fine. Now I'm going to leave the Eagle . . . That's one small step for man, one giant leap forward for mankind . . .' Armstrong, moving slowly one step at a time, explores the surface of the moon. He is hunched over like an exhausted ape man.

I mix another Bloody Mary.

Again footsteps echo in the corridor. The sound of decisive boots, boots with cleats like policemen wear, approaching my door. I lock the door. The siren on the police car whines they're going to break down the door and get in I'm going to jump out the window. No, no it's not the police siren. It's the kettle on the stove whistling.

The footsteps stop knock on my door. The landlady watched I-po walk into my room and secretly listened to I-po and me on the telephone. She's definitely the one who reported me to the Immigration Service. One evening I called I-po more than ten times I told him that I felt ashamed about the incident in the tub that evening, he's a good person I shouldn't torment him like that – I've decided to do as he said and go to New York to get an abortion, I shouldn't make problems for him I shouldn't leave proof of guilt for the Immigration Service, for the time being we won't see each other, then the Immigration Service can't accuse me of any more bad behaviour, not seeing him is a matter of life and death, I need him if I don't see him I will have nothing at all.

The knocking on the door gets more insistent as soon as I open the door I will see two large black lenses I've never seen his eyes.

As soon as I open the door two eyes fix on me they're the listless eyes of an old man. He asks me if I want to buy an evangelical pamphlet 'Guide to the Truth of Eternal Life'. He says this world doesn't have any god we should bring god back, very cheap only twenty-five cents will bring god back. I buy the 'Guide to the Truth of Eternal Life' for twenty-five cents. I close the door lock the door lock the old man's eyes outside the door. I leaf through the truth pamphlet in it is written 'The Dead May Hope for Resurrection' perhaps I should keep the child because of that hope I shouldn't harm a single life. I've hurt so many people. Keeping the child is my only chance for redemption. Sang-wa hasn't written for a long time. She hates me she despises me she won't live with me.

I see that red bird again with the blue breast and yellow eyes it's perched on my father's fresh grave. I pick up a stone and throw it at the bird the bird is pecking at the dirt on the fresh grave. I burn paper money before the grave the bird flies into the room I go into my father's study the bird flies in the door. It jumps around bobbing and bowing on my father's red yoga cushion. I ask the bird are you my father's incarnation it nods. I light three sticks of incense in front of the bird confessing that I stole the jade griffin ran away from home I seduced many men I threw away many men I stole Mama's gold locket gave it to my younger brother so he could run away from home I must change and become a new person I want to start a new life. The bird flies out the window.

The hospital in Nanking. The civil war. I am lying in a sick bed Chao T'ien-k'ai stamps into the room wearing tall US army boots his eyes are blood-shot a stubble of beard crawling all over his face. He tells me he hasn't slept for three days. There was a riot at the student anti-hunger demonstration and the Nationalist police arrested a truckload of students his two roommates were taken away people say that the Nationalists put the rioters in hemp bags and threw them into the Yangtze River, someone found Lao-shih, my best friend, lying on a path on campus her body covered with blood they don't know who beat her up like that, some people say it was the leftists who beat her up because she was a reactionary other people say it was the rightists who beat her up because she was a leftish. Other people say she is just sex-starved and helps the leftish student cause so the leftists will sleep with her and then helps the rightists so they will sleep with her and when her lovers found out they beat her up, Chao T'ien-k'ai isn't sure what she really is he doesn't even know what he himself is, some people says he's a reactionary, some people say he's on the left, he only knows one thing: he must think of a way to rescue his friends who were arrested . . . Chao T'ien-k'ai goes on talking without stopping. I lie on the bed looking at his stubble of beard my arm neck and part of my chest stick out from the covers. I tell him to calm down rest awhile. When the nurse comes in Chao T'ien-k'ai is lying under the covers beside me.

A large scar covers half of Lao-shih's face one eye stares blankly at me.

All that happened so long ago I've completely forgotten I hope I won't see those things before my eyes again.

Fifty, sixty, seventy mph. The car goes faster and faster. Red lights, yellow lights, black mud, red barns, white centre line, green trees, blue cars, brown turkeys rush past. A summer breeze sweeps in the window. I feel renewed.

Snow floats in the little crystal paperweight, floating above the Great Wall. Keeping one hand on the steering wheel, Teng picks up the glass paperweight from the dashboard and shakes it vigorously a few times.

The snow floats up in the paperweight, drifts over the Great Wall again.

'Where to?' I ask Teng.

'Don't know.'

He picks up the paperweight again and shakes it vigorously.

I laugh. 'Looks like you're mad at that paperweight.'

'I'm mad at myself. I've been thinking. It took me the strength of nine bulls and two tigers to escape from the mainland to Taiwan, and the strength of nine more bulls and two more tigers to escape from there to America. Once in America, I scrubbed toilets as a janitor, waited on tables. I have only a few more months until I get my Ph.D.

166

But once I get it, then what? Go back to Taiwan? I couldn't stand it! Go back to the mainland? I can't do that, either. Stay here? I'm nobody! Today I went to work at the university library. I was five minutes late. John Chang that son of a bitch bawled me out in English, yelling at me that I couldn't show up late, couldn't leave early, Chinese in America didn't come to pan for gold, everyone, no matter who, had to work hard. I said to him, "Hey, Chang, are you a Chinese? Speak in Chinese!" He pointed at me and said, "Just what are you? *You are fired*!" I walked out of there with my head held high, only saw him turn around and show the book of colour photos that just arrived, *Magnificent China*, to an American professor in the history department. "*It's a wonderful country, isn't it?*" As soon as I left the library I picked up an American girl.'

'And then what?'

Teng laughs. 'Mulberry, you don't need to ask what happened next. Then, well, you know. Really coarse skin. Just to have somebody to do it with. She even started to cry in bed, saying she'd never been so happy.' Teng steps on the gas as he says 'happy'.

Ninety miles an hour.

'Good!' I look at the headlights in front of us, like two eyes staring at us. Behind us are two more eyes staring at us. I'm not afraid of bright lights anymore.

'Help! My car had a breakdown. Could you please help me?' A head suddenly pokes out of a car at the side of the road, looks at us desperately and yells.

We zoom by. The car behind us catches up and is about to cross the yellow line. Teng steps on the gas again: one hundred miles an hour.

The two cars race side by side down the highway.

'You crossed the yellow line!' Teng sticks his head out the window and yells.

'You're speeding!'

'So are you!'

'You didn't stop to help!'

'You didn't either!'

'I couldn't stop!'

'I couldn't either!'

'You're crazy!'

'You're the one who's crazy!'

'No, you're the one who's crazy!'

'I'll kill you!' Teng picks up the paperweight, and is about to throw it at that car. Suddenly he withdraws his hand. 'Mother-fuckers, it's not worth it to throw the Great Wall at those white devils!'

The paperweight rolls on the seat.

The snow floats in the paperweight.

The other car falls back, about to turn at the intersection. Teng pulls a sailor's knife out of his pocket, snaps the blade in position, points it at the people in that car and yells:

'Good luck!'

Teng folds the knife and puts it back in his pocket, his two hands firmly holding the steering wheel, his eyes blankly staring at the road ahead, his short chunky body sitting up tall.

'Teng, you've suddenly become a man!'

'You've suddenly become a young girl!'

'You thought I was too old before!' I eye him and laugh, as I light up a cigarette.

'I didn't mean that. I only meant, you're so radiant today, and seem suddenly younger!'

I blow smoke in his face.

'You smoke?'

'Uh.'

'Since when?'

'Today.' I blow more smoke in his face.

'You're making me itch all over, Mulberry! Damn! We've gone the wrong way!' He looks at the sign at the side of the road, slows the car down. 'Highway 5! I've never heard of a Highway 5! I'm muddled because of that smoke!'

'Just keep on going down the highway, we're sure to come across the right road.'

'That's true. Let's just keep going.'

The car follows the curving highway awhile. Highway 7. Highway 12. No more highway. No more road signs. The car races along the gravel road. Speeds through a little town with no sign.

'This is just like a labyrinth!' Before Teng even finishes speaking, the car makes a strange whine, and suddenly stops.

Out of gas.

We are stopped by an auto graveyard. Junked Fords, Dodges, Chevrolets, and Pontiacs are piled in the yard. Most are twisted, empty shells, smashed up in wrecks. Beyond the graveyard is a street lined with grey houses with black windows. An empty gas station on the corner. No sign of anyone. It's a ghost town. It was once a booming town, then the young people left to make their way in the world and the old people all died off.

168

'What'll we do?'

'Wait.'

'For what?'

'Wait till someone drives through and we can ask for some gas.'

'Who'd come to this creepy place?'

'What else can we do except wait? It's too quiet! Let's have a little noise!' Teng turns around and switches on the tape recorder in the back seat.

'. . . To tell the truth, our Action Committee still has not taken a position. We're only a bunch of free Chinese who have banded together. We not only have freedom of thought, we also have freedom of action. But the desire for freedom is like smoking pot, the more you smoke, the more you want it. Once you're addicted the trouble begins. What the Action Committee advocates is "action". Some people say we're people without roots in a world without faith, worth or purpose. But it's better this way! Then we can have true freedom to create by our action a life of worth and purpose, even create a God. What kind of action? How to take action? I hope everyone will think about that when he's finished work for the day, finished writing his thesis or finished helping his wife with the dishes . . .*

'I propose organising a "Committee to Defend Human Rights" to protest against incidents which threaten human rights!*

'We must first get to know ourselves. Get to know each other, be frank with each other. How to act as Chinese, this is the most important thing. So . . . I suggest that we first take action, to understand through our actions, so . . . What you said is not right. I think . . .*

I laugh. 'We're stranded here in this ghost town listening to Chinese debate how to take action.'

'OK, here's concrete action! Listen to a recording of hog butchering in a packinghouse. "Killing" should be a course of action!' Teng turns around and presses a button on the tape recorder in the back seat, adjusts the tape, then presses the button again. He turns around, picks up the little glass paperweight and shakes it.

The snow floats up in the paperweight. All around is pitch black. The snow on the Great Wall is white.

The sound of machines, people – deafening clatter from the tape recorder.

The clatter stops.

'Our slaughterhouse slaughters 450 hogs an hour. The method we use is highly effective, the result of a combination of man working with machines.

'But we also strive to make it as humane as possible.

169

'Now, all of you who have come for hog butchering, please come with me. I'll explain every step in the slaughtering process. Over there is a small gate. Those hogs over there in front of the gate, raising up their snouts and looking at us, it's really funny, isn't it? They're ready to enter the slaughterhouse. First a number has to be stamped on the hog's body. That little gate only allows one hog to enter at a time. Beside the gate is a board which blocks from sight the man who wields the club. On the head of the club are many tiny needles; those tiny needles, when dipped in ink, make up the numbers. When each hog goes by, the man behind the board stamps him with the club with needles on it, a number is thus stamped on the hog's body. That number is stamped on its skin beneath the bristles. When the bristles are removed, by hot water, the number remains imprinted on the hog's body. This is what we consider our most efficient point.'

The sound of machines, people – deafening clatter.

The clatter stops.

'Now, these little fellas are going to take a hot bath. There's a pool with hot water. The hogs soak in it, the bristles soften up and then are pulled out. Then the preparation before entering the slaughterhouse has been completed.'

The sound of machines, people – deafening clatter.

The clatter stops.

'Now these little fellas are ready to enter the slaughterhouse. The method we use lessens the animals' pain as much as possible. The hog is on that slope. We use a pair of electric tongs like the curling irons women used to use to curl their hair a long time ago. You poke them in the hog's body. The hog is given an electric shock and it immediately blacks out and collapses. Someone above it lowers a hook, catches one of the hog's feet on the hook and lifts the hog up.'

The sound of machines, people – deafening clatter.

The clatter stops.

'Then a butcher raises a butcher's knife and skillfully pierces the hog's throat. He cuts right into the hog's heart. The hog's heart is very close to its throat. You could say the hog's an animal without a throat. (Laughter.) That one stroke, you could say, is quick of sight, quick of hand, beautiful and solemn, just like a religious ceremony.'

The sound of machines, people – deafening clatter.

The clatter stops.

'Now, the hog is hanging high in the air. The blood gushes down on the steel-ribbed, cement floor. The blood's bright red; it's very beautiful. That man standing on the high counter, wearing rubber boots, uses that thing in his hand, it looks like a broom, to sweep the blood into a gutter.

170

He stands in the blood all day long doing that. He's been doing it for twenty-six years. When the blood flows out the gutter, it coagulates. Man can use coagulated blood to make all kinds of food products. The Scots like to eat pudding made from hog's blood. The Chinese eat bean curd simmered with hog's blood.' The sound of machines and people combine into a deafening din, as if it will never stop . . .

'Look! Teng!' I point to the fields in front of us. After our car stops, the headlights have remained on, shining into the field. 'There are many dots of light like lanterns in the distance. Do you see them? There, over there, they're moving! They're coming toward us! One, two, three, four, five, six, more than ten! There, there're some more!'

We get out of the car and run toward the moving lights. They disperse, scatter in all directions.

'Deer! The light's from their eyes!' I call out.

The deer race back into the trees on the hillside.

Teng and I walk into the graveyard. A statue of a black angel, wings outstretched, bends over protecting a grave. Teng strikes a match to light up the inscription on the tombstone:

'Nicholai Vandefield 1805–1861'

The grass on the grave is tall, a little red flower has been placed on the grave.

The black silhouette of a barn looms on the horizon.

Teng and I lie down on the grass of the grave.

How could I have done such a shameless thing with that nice young man, Teng? I probably was insane I don't even recognise myself!

I hear my brain talking again, it seems like there's another brain inside my brain. The two brains are separate, one talks the other listens. I'm very frightened I sing loudly to suppress the voice in my brain but it still goes on talking I don't know what it's saying. The voice is unclear, it's as if it's ridiculing me now I can hear it. It says: 'You can't get an abortion!'

I-po didn't come. I called him over and over but no answer. Once it was Betty who answered I hung up. I want to tell him I don't want to get an abortion. I must not sin again.

> *'From the first to the fifteenth when the moon is full,*
> *Spring breezes sway the willow, the willow turns green . . .'*

I hear again our family servant singing a folksong in his soft voice. I ride on his shoulders to watch the monkey circus. We walk in wide-open fields. A beggar carrying a broken basket searches for burnt coal in the garbage.

The field in front of us is crowded with people Li suddenly stops singing, points saying Little Mulberry let's go see the execution. I ask are they executing good people or bad people Li says they're executing Communists. I ask are Communists good or bad, Li says whoever gives the common people food to eat is a good person whoever lets the common people starve is a bad person. A volley of gunfire. Li runs over carrying me on his back. The people who have been shot are lying on the ground in a pool of blood a thin stream of blood trickles down the hill. A skinny old woman kneels by the side crying and burning paper money scattering water and rice over the ashes. A scrawny yellow dog is sniffing at the trickling blood . . .

When I see the blood my whole body turns to ice, I curl up into a ball. I want to talk with someone I call Teng I want to tell him that I'm a bad woman, when he and I were together I was already pregnant with I-po's child. But I can only utter one word to him: 'blood!'

The train is rushing over the Pearl River Bridge in Canton refugees cling to the roof of the train many heads are sticking out the windows. A telephone wire scrapes along the roof of the train. One two three people drop with a splash into the river. Someone standing on the roof of the last car is pissing in the river as he sees the people falling into the river. The people at the window say that on such a sunny day it's raining but the rain smells a little strange. People at another window say the Communists have already crossed the Yangtze River and will take over China. The heads of the people in the river come up several times then vanish.

One instrument that establishes contact between people is the body, another is the telephone. My Friday night pastime is making telephone calls.

351–7789. 'Hello!'

'Helen!'

'How did you know it was Helen?'

'You have a foreign accent.'

'I haven't used the name Helen for a long time.'

'I'm sorry. I can't pronounce foreign names. I can't even pronounce my own husband's name, I-po. I call him *Bill*. What does Mulberry mean in Chinese?'

'Mulberry is a holy tree, Chinese people consider it the chief of the tree family, it can feed silkworms, silkworms can produce silk, silk can be woven into silk and satin material. The mulberry tree is green, the colour of spring . . .'

'Helen, don't stop, go on talking, go on, it's coming, that magical feeling is coming, crawling all over my body! Crawling all over my eyes! Crawling into my brain! I can see the silkworms, silver, twisting, curling, spitting out silk, wrapping it all around their bodies, the multi-coloured silk, delicate and luminous, wrapped around the bodies of the silkworms, their heads emerging from the strands of silk, no they're human heads . . .'

'Betty! You're hallucinating again, you've been smoking dope again . . .'

'The water of the Nile is flowing, flowing, look, it's flowing right there, do you see it? Helen, believe what I say, it's all true. I've even seen many, many people, many different worlds, they're all surging forth! They're all real people, real worlds . . .'

'I don't understand anything you're saying! Betty! The thing that's most real to me is the child in my womb, it's I-po's and my child.'

I hang up.

353–1876. No answer.

351–9466. The telephone buzzes. Busy.

338–2457. No answer.

338–0060. 'This is a recording. The number you have dialled is no longer in service.'

351–9063. 'Hello.'

'Hello. I want to speak with Teng.'

'You've got the wrong number!'

'What's your number?'

'I won't tell you. What number do you want?'

'351–9063.'

'I'll say it again: You've got the wrong number!'

I hang up.

351–9063. 'Hello.'

'It's you again! Wrong number! Please don't bother me, I want to sleep!'

'Good night.' I hang up again.

351–9063. 'Hello.'

'It's you again – it's that woman! What's the matter with you anyway?'

'You listen, lady. Just what's your problem? You . . .' The woman at the other end hasn't finished speaking when the man takes the phone and yells: 'We're just having a hell of a good time in bed! If you bother us again I'll kill you!'

'Are you committing adultery?'

173

'None of your business!' Slams the phone down.

351–9063. 'Hello.'

I laugh loudly. 'I'm sorry. I've interrupted again.'

'I WILL KILL YOU!' Slams the phone down.

351–9063. 'Hi!'

'Hi! Teng! You've finally wiggled your way out from under the bed!'

'What are you talking about? I just wiggled my way out of the lab. I killed another cat.'

'Killing a cat in the middle of the night!'

'I have to finish my experiment. It was a pregnant cat. I raised her awhile, waiting until she bore the kittens before killing her. When I slit open the cat's stomach, guess what I was thinking about?'

'Thinking about the new-born animals.'

'Thinking about you!'

'My stomach has to be cut open, too. I'll have to have a Caesarean.'

'What? I don't understand what you're saying!'

'I'm pregnant.'

'We'll get married immediately.'

'It's I-po's child.'

'Oh. Well, then he should take the responsibility.'

'I'm through with him. I'll take the responsibility myself.'

'You want the child?'

'Eh. It's a life, too.'

'I agree with you. We kill too many living things. In the beginning it was only people killing other people; now people use machines to kill. I had a strange feeling: when I was killing the cat, for a while it seemed as if I were that cat, one stroke, another stroke cutting the cat's body, was cutting into my own body as well. Do you really want the child?'

'No doubt about it!'

'I admire your nerve. But, but, in your situation perhaps it isn't wise for you to have an illegitimate child. I still haven't told you: The man from the Immigration Service came to see me and ask about you. I said in my whole life I've admired only two women, one is my mother, the other is you. In my eyes you two represent all the good womanly virtues.'

'What did he say?'

'He didn't say anything, only copied down what I said. That reminds me. About your child, I have a plan. My sister's been married twice and has never gotten pregnant. You know, my sister's husband is a second generation overseas Chinese, working in New York as a stock broker, quite well off. All my sister does is go to concerts, travel in Europe, vacation by the ocean, buy works of art, buy designer clothes – several hundred dresses, twenty or thirty pairs of shoes. She also writes poetry, but it's only a pastime. She's been to Taiwan once, but her life style didn't change when she returned. There's no purpose at all. If she had a child, perhaps her life would change. Before school starts I want to go to New York, in order to apply for jobs and meet the people in the firms, also for the "Action Committee", you know. We can drive there together and talk to my sister about this. You're old schoolmates, you can talk easily about anything. You can have a good time in New York. You . . .'

'You don't need to go on. I decided a long time ago to go to New York, not to talk to your sister about the child, but to see the Empire State Building.'

'Can I go over to see you now?'

'There's no Empire State Building here!'

'The hell with the Empire State Building!'

We hang up. The phone rings immediately.

'Hello.'

'Hi! Mulberry . . .'

'Professor, Mulberry's already dead.'

'Don't joke with me! Betty's dead!'

'You're kidding! I just talked to her on the phone!'

'When I came back, the room was really dark; there was a strange odour. Like the smell of drugs. I turned on the light, Betty was lying on the living room floor, an empty wine bottle beside her. Her mouth was open, fluid trickling from her mouth. I called to her, shook her, but no response. I was terrified. It's a sudden heart attack and she's dead! I felt her forehead, it was icy cold! I felt her nostrils, no air being exhaled. She died just like that!'

'Hurry up and call the police!'

'First I have to find something.'

'Find what?'

'Find the letters you sent me. What about your going to New York?'

'I've decided to go next week.'

'In fact, you needn't . . .'

'I have to go open my door. Teng's here!'

'What's he doing going to your apartment in the middle of the night?'

'Didn't you come in the middle of the night, too?'

'Is the child in your belly his?'

'No. It's yours. Sorry. He's knocking!' I hang up.

I open the door the man in dark glasses stands in the doorway behind him

175

is a long narrow corridor. He wants me to go to the Police Station at one o'clock to have a talk. I invite him inside to talk he says he wants to use the facilities at the Police Station. Is he going to use the lie detector? Is he going to torture me? Is he going to put me in prison?

I want to escape I don't dare meet the man in dark glasses. Since last time when he questioned me, he's certainly found out about a lot more of my crimes: my relationship with I-po my pregnancy my relationship with Teng Betty's death. Perhaps my being pregnant provoked her to commit suicide or perhaps she died of a stroke, perhaps I-po murdered his wife in order to keep his child. Although I didn't kill her I'm to blame. I call I-po on the phone no answer. Perhaps he went to the funeral parlour perhaps he was taken for questioning by the police. I call Teng on the phone no answer. I'm the only one left in the whole wide world I walk in circles around the room walking walking walking walking.

The police take me into a room shut the door and leave me there. The fluorescent lights in the room are all lit up the man in dark glasses sits behind a grey steel desk like the one at the Immigration Service. On the desk is a folder on the top is my alien registration number (Alien) 89–785–462 and an electric typewriter. He stands up and shakes my hand asks me to sit down. He says he came to this area to investigate a lot of aliens who are applying for permanent residency he'll take advantage of this opportunity to once again ask me some important questions. They are this careful with every case.

He suddenly asks me if I did or did not commit adultery with Chiang I-po I say we don't see each other anymore. He pulls a pile of papers from the file words crawl over the page, he says that is the information he found out since my first interrogation, all evidence in regard to my behaviour, some are the result of his questioning people some are the result of people reporting to him. He leafs through to a page that says according to the Landlady's report on the evening of 20 July, the very evening that the astronauts landed on the moon, Chiang I-po entered my apartment by way of the fire escape.

He says he still must continue investigating my case if they decide I am an undesirable alien they must deport me, where do I want to go? I say I don't know. He says he doesn't know what's the matter with Chinese all the Chinese people he's investigated answer the same way, the Chinese are foreigners who haven't any place to be deported to, this is a difficulty he's never encountered in investigating other aliens. I ask when they will decide he says he doesn't know. He tells me to wait wait wait wait . . .

My finger tips hurt suddenly I realise that the cigarette I'm holding is

burning my fingers my shoes are splattered with mud on the table beside
the bed there's a half-drunk Bloody Mary. What's happened to me. I
never touched alcohol cigarettes or mud. The calendar on the wall reads
2 September I only remember 30 August when the man in dark glasses
questioned me at the Police Station everything after that where I was and
what I did I don't remember at all.

My god there are some words scrawled in red on the mirror. Mulberry
is dead I hate Mulberry.

I wipe out these words. Who made this joke.

It was my joke. You were dead, Mulberry. I have come to life. I've been alive all along. But now I have broken free. You don't know me, but I know you. I'm completely different from you. We are temporarily inhabiting the same body. How unfortunate. We often do the opposite things. And if we do the same thing, our reasons are different. For instance. You want to keep the child because you want to redeem yourself. I want to keep the child because I want to preserve a new life. You don't see Chiang I-po anymore because you are scared of the Immigration Service agent; I ignore him because I despise him. When you're with Teng you feel guilty, when I'm with him I feel happy. You and I threaten each other like the world's two superpowers. Sometimes you are stronger; sometimes I am. When I'm stronger I can make you do things you don't want to do, for example the evening the astronauts landed on the moon, you teased and tormented I-po, when you acted like a slut with Teng in the ghost town graveyard. After those things happened you felt you were even more guilty – I like to do mischief with you like that. Because you limit my freedom. Now, you're dead, I hope you won't come back, then I'll be completely free! Do you know what happened after you died? I thought Betty was dead. I walked up to the Chiang house. Betty opened the door!

'I'm really happy that you're alive again! Betty!' I said to her.

She motioned to me to go around the yard and come in the back door. She was waiting for me at the back door. We went down to the basement. All I could hear was I-po and several people in the front living room competing to call out the names of old alleys in Peking.

'Goldfish Alley!'
'Emerald Flower Alley!'
'Lilac Alley!'
'Rouge Alley!'
'Sesame Wang Alley!'
'Master Ma Alley!'

'Pocket Alley!'

'Magpie Alley!'

'Fresh Alley!'

'Slender Reed Alley!'

'Ladder Alley!'

'Candlewick Alley!'

'Bean Sprout Alley!'

'White Temple Alley!'

'Cotton Alley!'

'Pa-ta Alley!' I-po was shouting.

'The professor isn't thinking of Pa-ta Alley. He's thinking of the courtesans who lived there.'

I-po laughed. 'That's right.'

> The east is red
> The morning sun rises
> In China Mao Tse-tung appears
> He works for the happiness of the people . . .

'Communist spy! You're playing a Communist record!' A girl's voice.

'Revolution, revolution!' Chiang I-po's voice. 'This young lady is going to turn in her old friend. Hsiao-Chuan, do you believe it? I even went to Taiwan last year and Chiang Kai-Shek's own son shook my hand.'

'You're putting me on. I don't believe it!'

The basement was one long room. Clothes, newspapers, magazines, cigarette boxes, and empty liquor bottles were strewn everywhere. There was a kitchenette in the corner, all sorts of things piled on the filthy stove. The only furniture in the room was a large colour TV and a box spring mattress studded with cigarette burns. The room smelled of marijuana. A boy with long hair was lying on the mattress watching television. He was wearing only jockey shorts. When he saw Betty and me he gave an unfriendly grunt. The news announcer looked out into the emptiness and began speaking in a monotonous voice: '. . . *A bomb from the Second World War was discovered today by a cleaning lady in Carpenterville, Illinois. The police have warned the residents in the vicinity to be on guard for an explosion, and they de-activated the bomb. But a young professor maintained that the bomb would not explode, it was only a new toy left over from the war, he had picked it up in a junk yard in Chicago to use for a room decoration . . .*'

178

'This is my territory! I feel at ease here. And have everything: booze, sex, entertainment, dope, even violence!' Betty laughed, pointed to the confrontation of the police and rioters on the TV screen.

'. . . *A federal grand jury charged five political activists with inciting a riot. The five have been charged with planning and inciting the bloody riot at the August 1968 Democratic National Convention in Chicago . . .*'

Upstairs, I-po roared with laughter. The Golden Voice was singing a love song.

> He closed the door I had to go,
> Their two hearts entwine as one,
> Madame, if you can leave them alone, then do,
> Why pursue the matter any further?

'*Bill's* never been down here in the basement. I call him the upstairs Chinese; he calls me the underground American,' Betty said.

'I call him the empty man,' I said.

Betty smiled darkly and drew closer. 'That is why he can't leave me: I give him freedom to live his vacuum life. If he were willing to leave me, he would have left a long time ago. When I met him, he was working hard on his Ph.D. At that time he wasn't interested in anything Chinese, he didn't even have Chinese friends. But now, it's just the opposite! Anything Chinese is good! Chinese culture, Chinese literature, Chinese food, Chinese style clothes, Chinese women! He especially likes young Chinese women.' Betty got up to open a cupboard, took out a pile of letters and threw them in my lap. 'These are all love letters Chinese girls have written him! I won't mention anything before, but when he went to Taiwan to visit he added quite a few more! You know, you yourself wrote him a lot of letters, when the man from the Immigration Service came to ask about you, he asked if I had any material to give them, so I gave him your letters.'

'I couldn't care less!' I picked up that bunch of the girls' letters and weighed them in my hand, then threw them back at Betty. 'Are you jealous?'

She shrugged. 'We're very fair, he has his life and I have mine.' She pointed to the half-naked man lying on the mattress watching television.

'All these letters, and yours, he gave to me, to show his faithfulness to me.' Betty laughed. 'Last night, he thought I was dead; I was lying

179

on the floor, in a daze. I thought I saw him walk in, I kept on thinking: I want to die once, I want to die once, I want to die once to scare him. I was thinking and thinking and didn't know where I was. I was floating in the clouds. The wind was blowing, the clouds floating, the flowers were swaying. I swayed along with those white round flowers, swaying, swaying. I suddenly understood why the wind blows in such a way, why clouds float along like they do, why the flowers sway like they do, that's the dance style of the wind, clouds, and flowers. I have my own dance style, too. We're each an independent life, and when we're together we dance differently to the same rhythms. I got up off the floor and went down to the basement, I came across *Bill* down there, that's the only time he's ever come down to my basement. He was holding a bunch of letters and looking through them, probably looking for the letters you wrote to him. "I've already given the letters you're looking for to the Immigration Service. I also know Helen's going to have a child, your child," I said standing in the doorway. He jumped. I laughed and said, "I'm not dead." He started laughing too. He said that bunch of letters was meaningless, he wanted to burn them. I said I still hadn't finished looking at them, I don't know Chinese, but those different characters look like different pictures. He said, well, then, save them for you as a pastime. *Bill* and I have been together for more than twenty years, our children are already married, and I still don't understand Chinese people. But I can communicate with you. We're very frank with each other. Now, I want to ask you a question. Do you want to keep the child?'

'And if I don't?'

'I can raise your child. I need a little something in my life.'

'Thanks, Betty. I want my child for myself.'

The people upstairs began singing Peking Opera. It seemed they were competing to remember opera verses – a line here, a line there, everyone scrambled to sing it first, intermixed with the singing was a girl's laughter.

'. . . Who was your first love?'

'At sixteen I slept with that King . . .'

'The feudal lords do not cooperate, with sword and lance they contend. Day and night I dream a thousand plots. I want to sweep the wolf out with the smoke, so peace will reign within the four seas like in the time of T'ang Yao . . .'

'Yo ya ya ya. But wait! On all sides are the songs of Ch'u. Can it be that Liu Pang – he, he, he's already captured the land of Ch'u?'

'Ah, great king, do not be alarmed. Send someone out to investigate, then you can make your plans.'

'Can it be my son is insane?'

'When I hear it said I'm mad I get so happy I just play along with it. I lie down in the dust and babble nonsense.'

'My son. Are you really mad?'

'What do you call it?'

'Mad.'

'Ha ha ha . . .' Chiang I-po laughed in a woman's voice then suddenly stopped.

I was standing in the doorway to the upstairs living room.

Who is that? I don't recognise her. She must be a ghost attaching itself to my body she frightens me she embarrasses me. How can I explain to people how can I make people understand that she isn't me? Since I barged into I-po's house since Betty and I criticised him I haven't the nerve to see I-po again, no matter how close we used to be I still need him with all my life the child in my womb is his. I call him and tell him I'm thinking of giving the child to Teng's sister, Tan-hung. That would solve two problems: Tan-hung will have a child and my child will be safe. He says that's a good idea he tells me to go to New York immediately to talk it over with Tan-hung. He wants to buy my plane ticket I say that's not necessary Teng and I are driving there together we'll stay at Tan-hung's place. As soon as I mention Teng he stops talking. I tell him Teng's sister, Tan-hung, and I are old classmates he's always treated me like an elder sister, he's almost finished with his Ph.D. and already got a job at a New York hospital, he wants to marry a very attractive girl, Chin, as soon as possible. I-po hangs up. I don't know why I wanted to lie to him.

New York. The Ford Building. I'm on Forty-Third Street.

The Ford Building is a huge glass tank, divided into smaller glass tanks. There's a person in every tank. Each person has a telephone by his side. There's a courtyard in the middle of the tank where flowers of all seasons bloom.

A blind man walks past the tank, led by a large fat dog.

Suddenly the blind man begins running and yelling in a frightened voice: 'The Ford Building is falling. The Ford Building is falling! My dog, where's my dog?'

I'm the only one who looks at him. I laugh.

It's drizzling, a good day for a funeral. There's a long long procession

181

of anti-war protestors on Fifth Avenue. White, black, yellow, one by one, streaming from Greenwich Village, past Washington Square, the Empire State Building, Rockefeller Center, St. Patrick's Cathedral (a sign hangs on the door: please come in and rest and pray), the Metropolitan Museum of Art, streaming toward Central Park.

Not a single pedestrian turns to look at them. The pedestrians are pushed along in the mob, pushed into the entrances to the iron ribbed, concrete buildings.

Only one person follows the demonstrators. His body jerks up and down, his head rolls backwards, he stretches out a crippled hand and waves at the protestors, laughing, 'Hello, hello, can you hear me? Hello! I have something to tell you: a monster from outer space has invaded New York. It's taken over the Empire State Building. Hello . . . Did you hear me? A monster from outer space has taken over the Empire State Building. Did you hear me?'

The demonstrators don't listen to him. The pedestrians don't listen either.

I approach him. I'm listening, I tell him. He invites me to the Red Onion for a Bloody Mary.

Mulberry, I'm glad I'm the one who came to New York, not you. I'm having a wonderful time. I'll be certain to write down everything interesting that happens. If you show up by chance, you will know what's been happening. Look, I'll cooperate with you if you won't spoil all the fun.

I don't know how long I disappeared or what happened then. I'm really scared. Where am I? There's a black wall with a large water colour scroll. The furniture is so black it makes me panic. The people? Where is everyone?

Tan-hung walks in led by a Pekinese dog on a leash the Pekinese runs right toward me. From the sofa I climb onto the table and stand there as the Pekinese leaps up at the table. Tan-hung laughs and says she knows I don't like dogs but she didn't know I was that scared of dogs my face has turned green. She calls the dog A-king, A-king. The dog races over and buries itself in her breast she sits on the sofa with the dog in her lap and rubs her face against his fur, its tongue licks her arm slowly, methodically, relentlessly, licking, licking.

I get down from the table and sit in a chair in the far corner. I don't know how to begin talking with Tan-hung I can't remember anything I ask what day is it where did Teng go? Tan-hung laughs and says I look like someone who just fell down here from the moon I don't know anything at all, today is 9 September, Saturday Teng and I went out together in the morning, I came back alone in the afternoon. She says he came to New York to apply for jobs but he doesn't seem to care a bit about that, every day he's holding 'Action Meetings' with a bunch of people those people are radicals, her father was killed by the Communists she and her brother must never side with the people who killed their father. Perhaps one day she'll go to Taiwan again. She wrote some poems just for fun and to her surprise they got published in Taiwan. Finally, after a pause, she laughs and says she can tell I'm really close to her brother. I say I'm a jinx whoever comes in contact with me is in for trouble, that's not fair to Teng, I've decided not to see him anymore after we go back. Tan-hung asks whether I still want to keep the child? (She seems to know everything, how does she know? Did I tell her?) I say I want to give the child to her. Her eyes light up. She says the other day I firmly stated that I wouldn't give the child to anyone. She hopes it's a boy she even talks about how she will decorate the child's room she wants to hang pictures of the holy child all over the room, but, but . . . She suddenly stops.

It's getting dark I turn on the lamp on the coffee table. The Pekinese dog has disappeared. Tan-hung walks over to her bedroom door, looks inside and grins then waves at me to come over. I walk over and see the dog sprawled on her bed asleep. She whispers in my ear that A-king is her boy.

I absolutely refuse to let you give the child to Tan-hung.

Teng and I go out sightseeing all day in New York. We go out at night. We go see a Broadway play. The people in the audience go up on stage, strip off their clothes and dance; the cast goes down and sits in the audience. They throw fruit peels at the people on stage. Teng explains that in that kind of play every person in the audience takes part. We don't tell Tan-hung about the play. She's too genteel to understand.

Suddenly I find myself lying in the bathtub and the bathroom door is open. Tan-hung's husband Jerry is standing in the doorway. His face is red.

I don't know what has happened. How did I get into the tub I must be insane. I wish I were dead.

I'll tell you what happened.

Jerry and I were in the living room with the black walls. Tan-hung and her Chinese friends had gone to the Chinese-American Friendship

Association to sing Peking Opera. Teng was at a meeting. Jerry's face was the colour of steel. Even when Tan-hung calls him Jerry darling his face remains the colour of steel. He was sitting at the table playing with his cameras. All in all he has fourteen different cameras, varying in size from a large box camera to a tiny match box. Recently he bought the latest German model, the one that fits into a match box, so the unlucky number thirteen became fourteen.

I sat on the sofa watching television: a girl in a long blond wig, blinked her long false eyelashes, thrust out her pointed breasts (perhaps, they're false, too!) and held up a Cralow electric mirror, her lips kept turning from pale white to pink to purple: '... All the mirrors of today reflect your face from only one source of light. In fact, there are many different light sources in the world. For this reason, Cralow Company has invented the Cralow True Light Mirror, all you need to do is press a button on the mirror and you can see your face in the various lights of sunlight, lamplight, and fluorescent light . . .'

'Pretty soon they'll be creating electric children,' Jerry said in English. 'Electric children would have one merit: they'd never grow up; they'd forever be in the state of infancy, then the world wouldn't have any more wars. Now we can use test tubes to make babies; the baby's sex and personality can all be decided beforehand, scientifically.' He was still playing with the cameras on the table.

I looked at his wristwatch: under the round glass shell were small cog wheels – the most recently invented toy. The knees of his tight pants were zipped closed with zippers. 'Tan-hung likes kids, you can make a baby in a test tube.' I was speaking in Chinese. I can't speak English to yellow faces.

'I don't like kids. I'd rather let Mary keep a dog.' He's never called her Tan-hung.

'Why?'

'People are more dangerous than dogs. If the world only had one-tenth the population it has now, it wouldn't be so chaotic. People create the chaos. Machines create order. It's best to interact with machines.'

The telephone rang. He went over to answer it, he listened a while, then said one sentence: 'Yao-hua, you must get hold of yourself.' Then he hung up, returned to the table and dusted the cameras with a soft cloth.

A-king ran over and tried to crawl up his legs, pawing at the zipper on his knees.

'Pete, don't move!'

'Pete?' I begin to laugh. 'Tan-hung calls him A-king; you call him Pete! Now which one is his name?'

'Both of them. Anyone can give him a name. You can call him John, too. This is the good point of keeping a dog: he doesn't protest. Mary calls him A-king. She says that name sounds like Peking, I can't pronounce Chinese names, so I call him Pete.'

The telephone rang again. He walked over to answer it, listened a while then again said only one sentence, 'Yao-hua, what you need is a good night's sleep.' Then he hung up. A-king leaped up at him. He picked him up, put him in the bedroom, closed the door. A-king scraped at the door.

The telephone rang again. He went over to answer, listened a while: 'OK, Mary, I'll bring Pete to the phone.' He opened the bedroom door, carried the dog over to the phone. It barked into the phone. He said into the phone receiver: 'Mary, hurry back. If you don't come back, Pete won't behave.' He hung up.

The telephone immediately rang. He picked up the phone and said: 'Hello. It's you again. Yao-hua.' He listened a while. 'You're not going to kill yourself. Get a good night's sleep and you'll be alright.' He hung up, walked back and sat down by the table.

The telephone rang again.

He shook his head and said: 'I can't stand it. Crazy.'

I laughed. 'Now you know machines can also be crazy.'

'I mean that person who's calling. That's Mary's cousin Yao-hua. He came from Taiwan several years ago. Mary doesn't like him. Dirty and muddle-headed. He studied philosophy at the University of Philadelphia. His English isn't any good. He hired someone to write his thesis. When the professor saw it, he asked him if he had hired someone to write it. He said yes. He was expelled. He worked as a waiter in a restaurant for three days then the boss fired him. Now, he calls several times a day, yelling that he's going to kill himself. Every Chinese has something wrong with him.'

The telephone started ringing.

He continued, 'Now they can use a scientific method to freeze people, you know that? Like freezing beef, freeze them for as long as you want, say a hundred years. For those one hundred years, he'd automatically defrost and he'd start living again from the age he was when he was frozen.'

'Then the present can be cancelled?'

'Right, cancelled; just live for the future.'

'After one hundred years, when you're defrosted, if there weren't

185

people anymore, only mechanical people on all the planets, who would you make love with?'

Jerry laughed. 'The mechanical people can take care of that, too.'

The telephone stopped ringing.

I wanted to play a joke on Jerry. I went into the bathroom and filled the tub. I stripped off my clothes. I lay in the bath water. I didn't close the door.

Mulberry, just at that time you reappeared. You saw his face turn red. You had to take over just at that moment, didn't you? I'll get even with you.

Teng and I are in the living room with black walls (Tan-hung's interior decorating is certainly unique!). Jerry went to Wall Street. Tan-hung took A-king to Fifth Avenue.

The telephone rings. Teng answers it. 'Hello . . . Yao-hua? . . . Please speak louder, I can't hear you . . . Yao-hua, you mustn't think about killing yourself, you're a man, you can take action, do anything you want as long as it's meaningful to you. The only way out is to die? OK! Then go find a way to do it. Go back to Taiwan! Use your actions to kill yourself; but for heaven's sake don't kill yourself with your own hand . . . hello, hello, Yao-hua, say something . . .'

The telephone rings. Teng answers it. 'Hello . . . Wang? If Yao-hua's locked the door then you must pry it open! He could try to kill himself . . . Ah, the police are coming . . . Yao-hua is coming up by the stairs! . . . What! He ran when he saw the police! . . . Do you think he's been smoking dope? . . . Please find him by all means. I'll wait for word from you. I can't come. If I were to drive it'd take at least two hours. Please keep me informed about Yao-hua. Thanks.'

The telephone rings. I answer the phone. 'Hello.'

'This is Yao-hua. I didn't die. I just came from the apartment of a Puerto Rican girl. I was having a little fun there. You could say she's an old "flame". I saw her once before. The first time I met her in a bar on 86th Street. We went to her apartment. I said I was hungry. She said all she had were some eggs. I said let's eat fried eggs then! After we ate the fried eggs we went to bed, slept a while, were hungry again, ate some more fried eggs, went to bed again, slept a while, were hungry again! Ate some more fried eggs. By that time it was already getting light outside. We had just finished eating a dozen eggs. Today I ran into her on 42nd Street. I didn't even have any money to buy peanuts. I said her fried eggs were really good. She said then eat some more. I just ate two fried eggs; when I left she said she liked me. Tan-hung, don't you think

that's wonderful? Tan-hung . . . can you lend me a little more money . . .
I know, I've borrowed too much already, and haven't paid back a cent.
But I'll pay you back someday. If I don't pay you back I would never
forgive myself. Tan-hung, why don't you say anything? Are you Tan-
hung? You won't lend me money, right? The hell with you! I'll show
you! Goodbye!'

I hang up. The telephone rings again. Teng answers. 'Hello . . .
Wang! Yao-hua just called. Wants to borrow some money, probably
trying to get a fix, doesn't seem like he's going to kill himself . . .
Luckily he still has friends like you; everyone's busy, no one has time to
look after anyone else – OK, goodbye.'

Two hours later, the phone rings. I answer it. 'Hello!'

'A Chinese jumped to his death from the 35th floor of Rockefeller
Center. We've found out the dead person's name is Jim Chang. We
don't know if it's Chang Yao-hua or not.'

'I don't know either,' I say.

*They're in the living room talking about Yao-hua's death I'm thinking
about the child in my womb. Tan-hung still can't decide if she wants to
raise the child as she talks she feeds A-king milk. When I think of the
child's fate after birth – an illegitimate child with no roots I don't have the
courage to keep it. If Tan-hung raises the child I won't ever worry about
it.*

*The train roars past I suddenly discover I am standing in the subway
tunnel from behind me shoes pounding the cement. It's probably the man
in the dark glasses who's coming! I begin to run in the tunnel the tunnel so
black, so dark I can't see the end in front of me appears a policeman.
There's no way out! He's coming toward me! The shoes on the cement
behind me stop I also stop the policeman also stops. Three people stand
far apart from each other no one can grab anyone, no one can escape –
there's no exit in the tunnel. I don't dare look around only hear the man
behind me yell: 'Hello! Have you heard? A monster from outer space has
invaded New York! It's taken over the Empire State Building! Did you
hear about it? Did you hear?'*

When Tan-hung goes out, Teng and I put the dog in a picnic basket
and take him away. Teng says Tan-hung doesn't know what to do with
her life, if she doesn't have the dog then she will want to raise a child, so
we'll simply get rid of the dog. But I don't want her to raise my child, I
only think killing the dog is something new to do.

187

We go by subway to the hospital, and we're going to give the dog to the hospital for their experimental research.

I like to travel back and forth in the subway network. I've never taken the wrong train. I know which train goes where. Some people jump into a car and ask in a foreign accent: 'Is this train going uptown or downtown?' I reply, 'This is the shuttle, it runs from Grand Central Station to Times Square and connects with the eastbound and westbound trains.' In New York, giving such definite answers to passengers is one of the happiest things in the world.

The subway is very colourful: skin colour, clothes, the advertisements. Miss Subway shows her white teeth as she smiles down from the blown-up photograph, her name, address and resumé are printed under her picture. 'College graduate, stenographer, likes to eat steak and pickles, hopes to find an ideal man and have five children. Sports: swimming, dancing. Her older brother died in Vietnam. Her younger brother is there now.'

That's what the colours are like.

On the subway Teng tells me how to kill a dog: first anaesthetise it and put it to sleep, give it an electrical shock in the cerebral cortex to keep it alive for a few days, then anaesthetise it again, slit open the chest, stain the cerebral cortex with a special dye and slice it into pieces. Then you can observe changes in the brain cells. When he finishes explaining the process, he changes his mind: we'll go throw the dog off the Washington Bridge into the Hudson River. Of course I agree.

We squeeze our way out of the subway, buy some strong rope, put a few rocks in the basket and seal the lid with some sticks. The dog desperately paws inside the basket, just like he pawed at Tan-hung's bedroom door.

We ride a bus past Central Park, riding along the river, we can see from the distance the high arch of lights on Washington Bridge. The dog thrusts himself against the basket. The basket is propped up against my legs. I can feel the dog's strength and warmth on my legs. The little body in my womb begins moving. Only three months now.

Teng and I are standing on Washington Bridge. The dark waters of the Hudson flow on below. I pick up the basket and weigh it in my hand; it's very heavy. 'Good-bye, little Peking,' I say. We let the rope out a little at a time and lower the basket to the water. The rope jerks in my hand, as it reaches the water it jerks more violently, then slowly grows lax and then is quiet.

Tan-hung has discovered that the dog is missing. She sits silently on the

188

sofa. Occasional noises outside make her sit up and she calls, 'A-king? You've come back. A-king, A-king.'

Her husband says he'll buy her another dog. She says, 'Don't bother.'

Does this face in the mirror belong to me? I want to cry but the face in the mirror is smiling. I'm grinning ear to ear just like a clown.

I write a note to Tan-hung, I killed your A-king, I don't know why I did such a thing I wish I were dead. Mulberry. I tape the note to her bedroom door.

The note is gone she probably read it and tore it up. I can't face her again, but I need her to raise my child.

I tore up the note, Mulberry. You mind your own business. I killed the dog. Tan-hung is not going to raise your child, so don't think about it.

I really have gone crazy. I'm afraid of that other self, her only purpose is to destroy me.

Suddenly I find myself walking between two rows of grey buildings on Wall Street. A strip of sky above. I don't know how I got here and I don't know where I'm going. Wall Street is crowded with men, most of them dressed in dark blue suits and carrying attaché cases. The man in dark glasses is hidden among them as soon as I see him I run away.

The man in dark glasses is walking toward me on the sidewalk I run into the stock exchange and squeeze into an elevator. The man in dark glasses is in the elevator. I can't escape! But he doesn't see me he's only looking at the buttons in the elevator. As soon as the elevator stops I dash out. He is there in the corridor. The man in dark glasses is everywhere. The only way I can get away is to find the women's restroom. I run through the stock exchange but I can't find the women's restroom upstairs I barge into a corridor, from that corridor you can see the world of stocks separated from you by glass: There in that enormous room people wave their hands some look like they are shouting some look like they are making speeches others move their lips some stand face to face opening and closing their mouths, someone else paces studying things he is writing in a notebook some throw scraps of paper on the floor and stamp on them. People run wildly around the room, they all seem drunk and they all look at the wall where an automated sign flashes countless symbols and numbers, right and left, flashing, changing continuously.

There's the man in the dark glasses. I run down to the basement. A policeman walks over and asks blandly what am I doing. I stammer that I have to go to the bathroom. I'm sorry there are no women's toilets, he says and takes the bunch of keys dangling from his waist, selects a key and unlocks a door for me. He tells me this isn't a public toilet but he will let me use it. With another key he opens another door to let a man in a grey suit go inside.

I am safe in the toilet I don't want to leave. The policeman knocks on the door saying I've been in here an hour and now I must come out I don't answer. Then there's a click and the door opens the policeman is standing there in the doorway of the toilet. I thought you went bankrupt playing the market and killed yourself he says.

I was the one who went to Wall Street, but you were the one who returned.

Tan-hung and I left together. She went to Wall Street to see her husband. I went to explore Wall Street. We took the bus.

'He killed A-king,' Tan-hung said suddenly.

'Who?' I asked.

'Jerry.'

'How do you know?'

'He's jealous. But he's so cold he won't even show jealousy. But I know he did something to A-king. Jerry is just the opposite of Lu, my first husband. Lu was very loving and sensitive when he was young. When the Communists took over he came to America. I followed him from the mainland to America.' Tan-hung smiled wanly. 'We were married. When the Communists took over the mainland, he panicked. His source of income was cut off. He didn't work and didn't study hard, just loafed around; he wanted to organise some kind of a third power. After I got my Master's, I found work in New York. He refused to come to New York; he didn't want me to support him. We were separated more than a year. When I saw him again, his features had completely changed; his face distorted by bitterness. He cursed the world, cursed the times, cursed the Communists, cursed the Nationalists, cursed everybody. Of course he also cursed me. He suspected that I'd slept with every man – my boss, my colleagues, even the doorman! He threatened that he'd destroy me. I almost lost my life. After that I've been afraid of men who get emotional. I married Jerry only because he was so cold. He's a second-generation overseas Chinese, you know. He seems to have transcended problems of the Chinese. The first time we met was at La Guardia Airport. I was sitting in the boarding lounge waiting for a plane. He walked over and asked

190

me if I wasn't Chinese. He pulled a pile of drafts out of his bag. He said they were articles his father had written. Because they were in Chinese, he didn't understand them. Before, he had opposed his father because he was too stubborn, too arbitrary, conservative. He couldn't stand it. But after his father died, he then discovered he himself had his father's character. He suddenly wanted to know what his father was like; he had been looking everywhere for someone to translate his father's articles into English; he could get to know his father from his writings. He hoped I could help. That was the only time in all these years I ever saw him get emotional. That's how we met and got married.' Tan-hung paused: 'I hadn't been able to decide about raising the child. Now, I've made a decision.'

I looked at her.

'I've decided I don't want the child.'

'I never thought to give the child to anyone.'

She looked at me strangely. 'I've decided to leave Jerry.'

'Because of A-king?'

'No. A-king's death only helped me decide. Jerry and I have always had problems. Right now I'm going to Wall Street to meet him for lunch and talk about it.'

The bus stopped at Wall Street.

I call more than twenty places from a list in a magazine of New York city doctors who perform abortions before finally getting ahold of a Dr Beasley. He says he has a long waiting list of people waiting to get an abortion, he can't see me for two weeks. I say getting an abortion is a matter of life or death for me I beg him to find a way to see me earlier he laughs and says women wanting abortions all say that. He suddenly asks me what nationality I am. I say Chinese. He pauses and says he'll do the best he can to see me within three days, he will first perform an examination at his clinic then perform the surgery the next day at a nearby hospital. He will reserve a hospital bed for me. The total cost will be four hundred dollars.

I call I-po he is very happy that everything has been arranged. He insists on paying all the costs he says he's never loved a woman like this before.

I tell Teng I have decided not to get an abortion. He says I should be completely free to make my own decision. No matter what I decide, he'll support it.

We talk about Tan-hung and her husband's separation. We decide not to tell her about killing the dog. That incident helped Tan-hung make a courageous decision. He says that sacrificing a dog's life to save a human life is very humane. He thinks that constant change keeps us alive. A person changes by his own choice. He also has a decision to make. After he tells me that he becomes silent. I tell him how I teased Jerry and made him blush. He laughs and says he didn't think that Jerry was capable of blushing.

I am suddenly standing by the doorway to Number 34 of a large building the sign by the door says 'OBSTETRICIAN – DR BEASLEY'. I push the door open and walk in, the waiting room is packed with women more than half are young women they happily talk about the birth of their child. In addition are several young girls sitting in a corner not saying anything looking very nervous very shy. They're probably only sixteen or seventeen years old just the age I was when I ran away from home and had the adventure in the Yangtze River Gorges. I fill out my medical history form at the nurse's desk and walk over to sit in the corner with those girls. A cat walks over to me.

I see Sang-wa again she is sitting on the ground in the courtyard holding the white cat with a black tail, a strong light shines on her body I can't even open my eyes . . .

I don't know what happened after that.

But I know!

I only went to see Dr Beasley out of curiosity. He looked at my medical history form; examined me; discovered I was already three months pregnant, he couldn't perform the regular method of scraping the womb, he must employ injection of a saline solution. He explained that the special saline solution was injected into the womb, after forty-eight hours the embryo would automatically miscarry. That's a dangerous operation, it's no light undertaking to perform it; not only that, the hospitals in New York City which performed that operation didn't have any empty beds, there were too many people waiting to get abortions, I have to wait another month. In the state of Pennsylvania alone every two hours an illegitimate child is born; he could give me a list of doctors in the suburbs, if I'm lucky, perhaps I could find a suburban doctor who would perform the saline solution injection for abortion.

'I'm sorry! I've already done my best to see you within three days, because you're Chinese. During the war . . .'

'Doctor, which war?' I asked.

'The Second World War. I was a doctor for the army in Burma. I served the Chinese army. With my own eyes I saw so many, so many Chinese die.'

'I want to keep the Chinese in my womb!' I said, smiling. 'I'm happy I'm already past the safety period for getting an abortion. I don't plan to look for another doctor.'

'*Hen hao* – very good.' He spoke in Chinese. 'You're the only person I've seen who is happy because you weren't able to get an abortion. Good luck to China!'

I make more than forty long distance phone calls to doctors on the list Dr Beasley gave me. I'm sorry the doctor is on vacation I'm sorry the doctor does not perform abortions by saline injection I'm sorry there are too many people waiting for an abortion I'm sorry the doctor is too busy I'm sorry I'm sorry I'm sorry . . .

I have to go back in three days. I came to New York to see a huge pile of steel, glass and people – my trip wasn't a waste.

Teng is going back with me. His job at the hospital is all set, salary at $15,000 per year. But he's become very silent, only saying 'his heart is in turmoil'.

I call I-po, tell him I couldn't get an abortion. He stammers and can't say anything, finally says, 'Please wait a minute. I want to go to the toilet.' I hang up, laughing.

Tan-hung and Jerry are sitting in the living room discussing hiring a lawyer to prepare the divorce papers. Next week Tan-hung will go to Taiwan for a vacation. Perhaps she won't come back, she says. Jerry gives her a going-away gift, looks like a tube of lipstick, it turns out to be a new kind of camera. Tan-hung can use it on her trip, he says. They even talk about scenery in Japan.

I again make innumerable phone calls. The Family Planning Information Center finally found me a doctor in Worchester, New York. Besides performing abortions in hospitals he also performs saline solution injection abortions at his own clinic every day there are more than ten people who go to his clinic, he doesn't know when he can fit me in he tells me to wait for his call.

I wait by the phone all day.

In the evening I call I-po he tells me not to worry about the cost one thousand two thousand he can pay . . . I cry over the phone he says:

Dear, I love you very very much.

193

I have only two days left in New York, I must get out and see the sights. I wander around between the steel and glass. Every time I come out of the subway I encounter a new surprise: Radio City, Times Square, Metropolitan Museum, Empire State Building, Greenwich Village, Broadway theatres . . . I've come back to Wall Street!

I come out of the exit of the subway and run into a man. There were bags around his eyes. When you look at him, he doesn't see you at all. Even if a pretty girl walks by, he doesn't see her, either. I smile at him, no response. He is coming out of the New York Stock Exchange and walking along Wall Street. His head lowered, he walks very slowly, amidst the hurrying people he appears very odd. I am curious about him, so I follow him to the end of Wall Street.

I follow him into a cemetery. He sits on a cracked tombstone. It's drizzling. I stroll between the tombs. The words carved on the tombstones are already faded. This is the only quiet place in New York. I circle around the cemetery. The man suddenly stands up. 'What about it!' He suddenly speaks, then looks up at the sky. He turns around, looks at me. I walk over. He says his name is Goldberg. I say he can call me anything. He laughs and invites me to dinner.

We drink in the Oak Room of the Fifth Avenue Plaza Hotel, a trio stops at our table to play the violin. He suddenly 'livens' up, calls me Miura Ayako. He says in his eyes all Oriental women are Miura Ayako. During the Korean War he was fighting in Korea, he went on leave in Tokyo, he had a Japanese woman called Miura Ayako. I say during the Korean War I was a waitress at the Imperial Hotel in Tokyo, my sole desire was to be a movie star. I fell in love with an American G.I.; his name was David. I go on making up stories. He raises his glass and calls me Miura Ayako. I raise my glass and call him David. We click glasses.

When we finish eating, he says I'm an interesting woman. He picks a rose from the vase on our table and gives it to me, kisses me on the cheek saying, 'I lost a million and a half dollars today.'

Dr Johnson in Worchester calls. He says I can go to his clinic tomorrow night at six o'clock, that's his supper time, he must charge double, altogether eight hundred dollars. I say, 'I'm sorry, dear doctor, I want to keep my child. I'm not coming.'

I call Dr Johnson and beg him to see me tomorrow night at six. I'm willing to pay triple the cost I'm an alien with no way out I must get an abortion, he coldly says all right but don't change your mind again.

I ask Teng to drive to Worchester, then drive back home. He agrees.
I call I-po. He is very happy, he says he's been thinking of the way I
looked soaking in the tub.

All right, let's see what's happening in Worchester.

Teng and I drive there. All along the way, sunny skies, black clouds, rain, fog, the weather keeps changing. The water flows, the wind flows, the light flows. The leaves are all turning red.

The car races down a slope. On two sides are dense forests. I smell a whiff of smoke, mixed with the fragrance of blood, mud, and fresh-cut grass. I don't know where it's coming from. Teng also smells it. When the car gets closer to the bottom of the hill, the smell of the fragrant smoke gets thicker. We drive to the front of a run-down gate, the smoke is drifting over from the other side of the wooden gate.

Teng and I get out of the car.

The wooden gate is open. Hanging on it is a rusty padlock. Teng and I walk in. The smoke drifts along the path. Several leaves float down, they float down, brush my face, wet and cool. I take off my shoes and walk in the mud; I breathe in deeply the fragrant smoke. Teng says I look so striking. It's getting dark. The smoke gets thicker.

The path turns and reaches the bottom of the valley. Thick columns of smoke shoot upwards; beneath the columns of smoke are mounds of mud; beneath the mud are burning branches; beneath the branches are pigs being roasted. Shadows bob up and down. Are they people or smoke? We can't tell. We stand still, then see they are people; then we see it's a large clearing, to the side are several small wooden huts. A strong beam of light shines from the corner of the clearing, the people are enveloped in the light. The light revolves, light and darkness alternating on the people's bodies like a slithering snake entwining itself around them, twisting and turning, the people begin to gyrate, too. All bright, then plunged into darkness. The people and the shadows sing 'Nothing Is Real'. Teng and I begin to dance along.

Suddenly a gunshot. The people and the shadows are still dancing in the slithering light. The smoke covers the entire mountain valley.

Another gunshot.

Someone says the gunshot came from the other mountain valley. Some people walk up the mountain path. Teng and I follow them, cross the low mountain, and descend into another valley. There is a river in the valley. There is a dense mist over the river. Several policemen and a woman are standing by the river. A strong beam of light shines into the small wooden hut on the opposite shore.

The strong light blinds me I can't open my eyes I see again Sang-wa sitting on the ground and holding the white cat with a black tail. The half-bodied policeman says house check take out your identity cards!

Suddenly a gun fires the bullet whizzes and disappears into the mist. Again the gun fires blindly in the mist. There is no god there is no god there is no god! A desperate voice cries out from the mist. George George don't shoot! I'm here your wife is here! George I love you come home with me! The woman on the bank shouts across the river into the mist. George shouts I have no home I have no home! Gunshots again. George don't shoot anyone put the gun down come home with me! Don't shoot anyone! George! I won't kill anyone I just want to kill myself I can't go on living there's nothing worth living for! George put the gun down come outside the house! I can't see you the mist is too thick! George I love you! George ... George ... come on home ... George ...

Teng drives slowly and steadily. He gives the glass ball on the seat a few shakes. Snow in the glass ball begins to fall floating above the Great Wall the land near the Great Wall is my homeland. I suddenly think of the abortion. Did I go to the doctor's? Did I kill my child? I talk to myself. Teng pats me on the shoulder and tells me to calm down. He says I've suffered so much he didn't know what to do, but now he knows. I don't need to go to see the doctor anymore, when he says that he stops, then picks up the glass ball again and shakes it saying Mulberry, I want to marry you, we can return to the mainland together, we can work together for the country, we can raise our children there together, our children should be raised on their own land. I stammer and can't say a word we both look at the Great Wall in the snow at last I say: Teng, you're still young you can't marry a woman who's already dead you must not see me again.

When I get home I call I-po. I call all day long but there's no one home. I hope to tell him immediately that I didn't go through with the abortion, I will take all the responsibility.

I call him the next day at noon.

'Hello.' His voice is very soft.

'I'm back! I've kept the child.'

'...'

'Hello, are you there?'

'Betty's dead. I need you.'

'Did she really die this time?'

'She really died. Heart attack. Just like that – gone. Now at the funeral parlour. The funeral's tomorrow morning. I'll come over to see you.'

'That's not necessary.'

'Why not? Our problem is solved! I'm happy you kept the child.'

'The child has nothing to do with you.'

'I want my child!'

'Then make one in a test tube!' I hang up.

I call Teng. No answer.

I call Teng no answer. I want to tell him he is my only strength, my reason to go on living, but he shouldn't marry a woman like me. I already owe him so much so much. I try all night to call him but no answer. Where did he go suddenly I am afraid.

I go to Betty's funeral from the entrance to the cemetery I can see I-po standing there. Yellow leaves drift all over the graveyard . . .

I didn't enter the cemetery, but went to Teng's place. His room was locked. His name wasn't on the mailbox anymore. No matter where he goes, he will take it as it comes. In his heart he's found freedom. Because he has decided his own course of action.

I get a phone call from the man in dark glasses. He says next Monday he'll be passing by my area he must question me once again because he has discovered some new problems with my case, before they make the final decision. He must make sure everything is clear . . .

(LONE TREE, IOWA) LAST NIGHT A FREAK ACCIDENT OCCURRED ON A ONE WAY STREET IN LONE TREE. AN EMPTY CAR CRASHED INTO A TREE AND BURNED. A WOMAN WAS FOUND LYING BY THE ROADSIDE A THOUSAND YARDS AWAY. SHE WAS UNCONSCIOUS, BUT DID NOT SUFFER ANY SERIOUS INJURY. SHE IS NOW RECOVERING IN MERCY HOSPITAL. THE CAUSE OF THE ACCIDENT IS NOT KNOWN. THE WOMAN'S IDENTITY IS NOT KNOWN.

I find the news story at the newsstand, I buy a copy for a souvenir after I escape from Mercy Hospital.

EPILOGUE

Princess Bird and the Sea

One day Nu-wa, daughter of Yen-ti the sungod, sets sail to the East Sea in a small boat. There's a storm and the boat capsizes. Nu-wa drowns, but she refuses to die.

She turns into a bird with a blue head, white beak and red claws. She is called Princess Bird and goes to live on Ring Dove Mountain.

Princess Bird wants to fill in the sea and turn it into solid ground.

Carrying in her beak a tiny pebble from Ring Dove Mountain, she flies to the East Sea, then drops the pebble in the water. She flies back and forth, day and night; each trip she takes another pebble.

The Sea roars, 'Forget it, little bird. Don't think that you can fill me in even if you take thousands and millions of years.'

Princess Bird drops another pebble into the sea and says, 'I will do it if it takes me billions and trillions of years, until the end of the world. I will fill you in.'

The East Sea bursts out laughing. 'Go ahead, you silly bird!'

Princess Bird flies back to Ring Dove Mountain, takes another pebble, flies back to the East Sea, and drops it in the water.

To this day, Princess Bird is flying back and forth between the Sea and the Mountain.

The Women's Press is a feminist publishing house. We aim to publish a wide range of lively, provocative books by women, chiefly in the areas of fiction, literary and art history, physical and mental health and politics.

To receive our complete list of titles, please send a stamped addressed envelope. We can supply books direct to readers. Orders must be pre-paid with 60p added per title for postage and packing. We do, however, prefer you to support our efforts to have our books available in all bookshops.

The Women's Press, 34 Great Sutton Street, London EC1V 0DX

BRUSSELS

BRUGES, GHENT & ANTWERP

BRUSSELS

BRUGES, GHENT & ANTWERP

DK

LONDON, NEW YORK,
MELBOURNE, MUNICH AND DELHI
www.dk.com

Produced by Duncan Baird Publishers
London, England

MANAGING EDITOR Rebecca Miles
MANAGING ART EDITOR Vanessa Marsh
EDITORS Georgina Harris, Michelle de Larrabeiti
DESIGNERS Dawn Davies-Cook, Ian Midson
DESIGN ASSISTANTS Rosie Laing, Kelvin Mullins
VISUALIZER Gary Cross
PICTURE RESEARCH Victoria Peel, Ellen Root
DTP DESIGNER Sarah Williams

Dorling Kindersley Limited
PROJECT EDITOR Paul Hines
ART EDITOR Jane Ewart
MAP CO-ORDINATOR David Pugh

CONTRIBUTORS
Zoë Hewetson, Philip Lee, Zoë Ross,
Sarah Wolff, Timothy Wright, Julia Zyrianova

PHOTOGRAPHERS
Demetrio Carrasco, Paul Kenward

ILLUSTRATORS
Gary Cross, Richard Draper, Eugene Fleury,
Paul Guest, Claire Littlejohn, Robbie Polley,
Kevin Robinson, John Woodcock

Reproduced by Colourscan (Singapore)
Printed and bound by South China Printing Co. Ltd., China

First published in Great Britain in 2000
by Dorling Kindersley Limited
80 Strand, London WC2R 0RL

Reprinted with revisions 2003

Copyright 2000, 2003 © Dorling Kindersley Limited, London
A Penguin Company

FLOORS ARE REFERRED TO THROUGHOUT IN ACCORDANCE WITH EUROPEAN
USAGE; IE THE "FIRST FLOOR" IS THE FLOOR ABOVE GROUND LEVEL.

**The information in this
Dorling Kindersley Travel Guide is checked regularly.**
Every effort has been made to ensure that this book is as
up-to-date as possible at the time of going to press. Some details,
however, such as telephone numbers, opening hours, prices,
gallery hanging arrangements and travel information are liable to
change. The publishers cannot accept responsibility for any consequences arising from the use of this book, nor for any material
on third party websites, and cannot guarantee that any website
address in this book will be a suitable source of travel information.
We value the views and suggestions of our readers very highly.
Please write to: Publisher, DK Eyewitness Travel Guides,
Dorling Kindersley, 80 Strand, London WC2R 0RL, Great Britain.

◁ **The Grand Place, centre of the Lower Town, at night**

CONTENTS

INTRODUCING BRUSSELS

PUTTING BRUSSELS
ON THE MAP *8*

Belgian heroes Tintin and Snowy

A PORTRAIT OF
BRUSSELS *12*

BRUSSELS THROUGH
THE YEAR *24*

THE HISTORY OF
BRUSSELS *28*

Revellers in colourful costume at a
festival in the Grand Place

Vista of a tree-lined path in the Parc du Cinquantenaire

Belgian oysters

Gilt statue on façade of a Guildhouse in Antwerp

Basilique National du Sacré-Coeur

Artist's impression of Cathédrale Sts Michel et Gudule in Brussels

INTRODUCING BRUSSELS

Putting Brussels on the Map

Brussels is the capital of Belgium and the centre of government for the European Union. Although Belgium is one of Europe's smallest countries, covering 30,500 sq km (11,580 sq miles), it has one of the continent's highest population densities, with 10 million inhabitants (300 people for every square kilometre). Belgium is a bilingual country (Flemish and French). Although Brussels falls geographically in the Flemish half, it is largely French-speaking. Belgium's largest city, with almost one million inhabitants, Brussels is also the most visited, receiving some six million visitors a year, although 70 per cent of these come for business. Today, Brussels' excellent communications make it an ideal place from which to explore historic Belgian cities such as Antwerp, Ghent and Bruges.

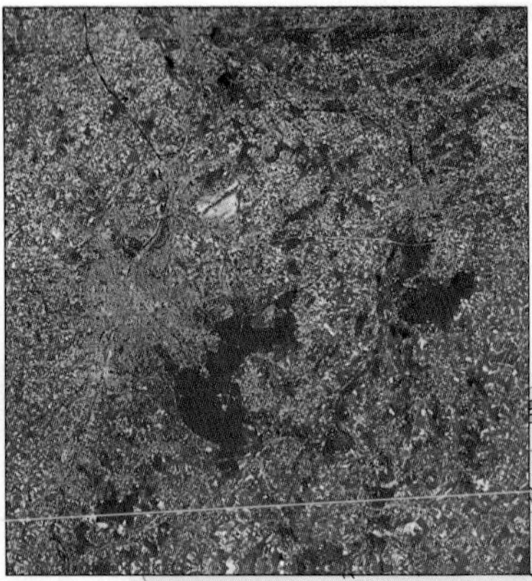

Satellite photograph of Brussels: buildings appear as light blue, red represents green vegetation

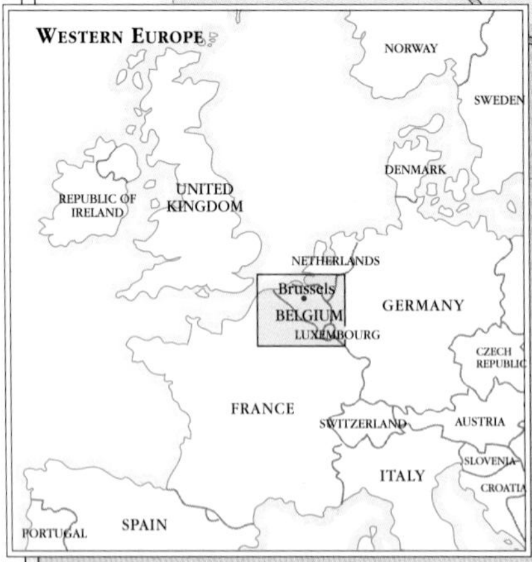

WESTERN EUROPE
NORWAY
SWEDEN
DENMARK
REPUBLIC OF IRELAND
UNITED KINGDOM
NETHERLANDS
Brussels
BELGIUM
LUXEMBOURG
GERMANY
CZECH REPUBLIC
FRANCE
SWITZERLAND
AUSTRIA
SLOVENIA
ITALY
CROATIA
PORTUGAL
SPAIN

Western Europe

Brussels is known for its efficient road and rail systems, linking the city to the Netherlands Germany, France and the United Kingdom.

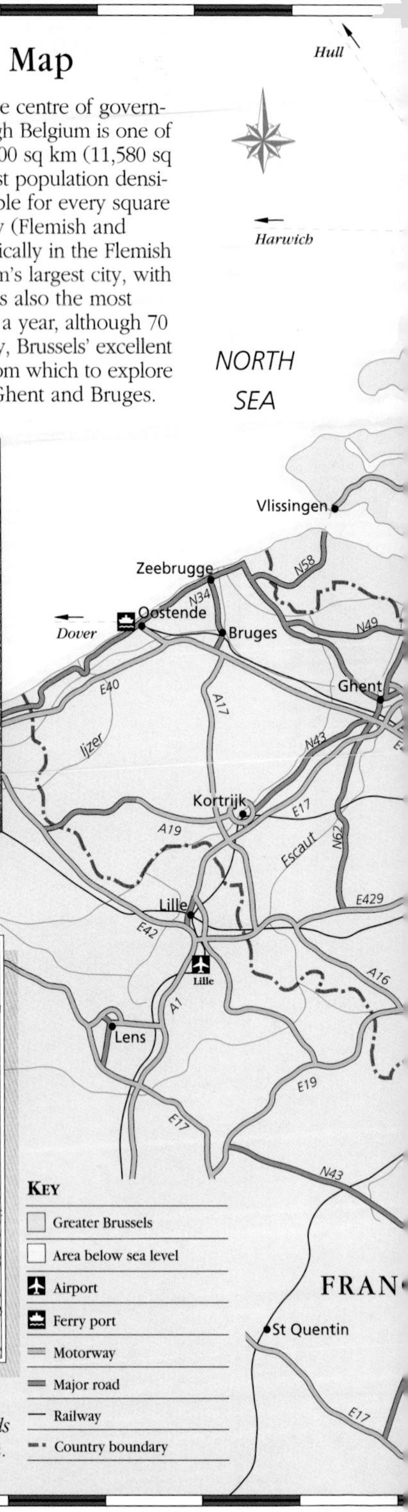

Hull
Harwich
NORTH SEA
Vlissingen
Zeebrugge
N58
N34
Oostende
Dover
Bruges
N49
Ghent
E40
A17
Ijzer
N43
Kortrijk
E17
A19
Escaut
N62
Lille
E429
A26
E42
Lille
A16
A1
Lens
E19
E17
N43
FRAN
St Quentin
E17
KEY
Greater Brussels
Area below sea level
Airport
Ferry port
Motorway
Major road
Railway
Country boundary

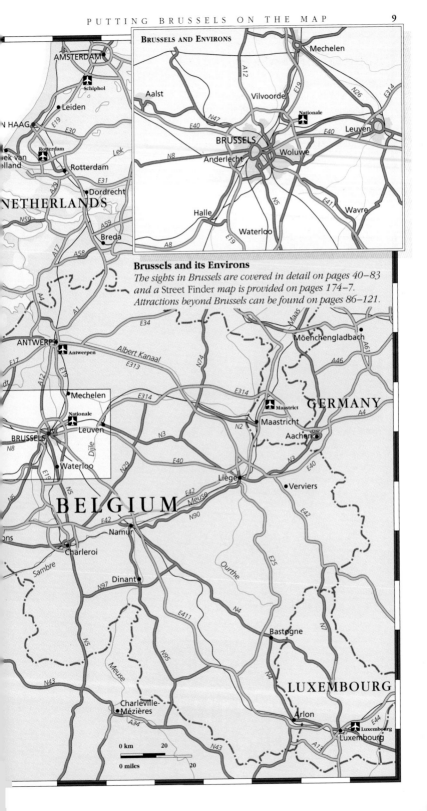

BRUSSELS AND ENVIRONS

Mechelen

Aalst

Vilvoorde

Nationale

Leuven

BRUSSELS

Anderlecht

Woluwe

Halle

Wavre

Waterloo

Brussels and its Environs

*The sights in Brussels are covered in detail on pages 40–83
and a Street Finder map is provided on pages 174–7.
Attractions beyond Brussels can be found on pages 86–121.*

AMSTERDAM

Schiphol

Leiden

DEN HAAG

Hoek van
Holland

Rotterdam

Dordrecht

NETHERLANDS

Breda

Möenchengladbach

ANTWERP

Antwerpen

Albert Kanaal

GERMANY

Maastrict

Mechelen

Maastricht

Nationale

Leuven

Aachen

BRUSSELS

Dijle

Waterloo

Liège

Verviers

BELGIUM

Meuse

Namur

Charleroi

Sambre

Dinant

Ourthe

Bastogne

LUXEMBOURG

Charleville-
Mézières

Arlon

Luxembourg
Luxembourg

0 km   20

0 miles   20

Central Brussels

CENTRAL BRUSSELS is divided into two main areas, each of which has its own chapter in the guide. Historically the poorer area where workers and immigrants lived, the Lower Town contains the exceptional 17th-century heart of the city, the Grand Place, as well as the cosmopolitan Place de Brouckère, and the historic workers' district, the Marolles. The Upper Town, traditional home of the aristocracy, is an elegant area which encircles the city's green oasis, the Parc de Bruxelles. Running up through the area is Rue Royale, which ends in the 18th-century Place Royale, home to the city's finest art museums.

Hôtel de Ville
The focus of the Grand Place, Brussels' historic Town Hall dates from the early 15th century. Its Gothic tracery façade features the famous needle-like crooked spire (see pp44–5).

KEY

- Major sight
- Place of interest
- Other building
- **P** Parking
- Tourist information
- Police station
- Hospital
- Bus terminus
- Tram stop
- Train station
- **M** Metro station
- Church

La Bourse façade
Overlooking the city from busy Boulevard Anspach in the Lower Town, Brussels' Stock Exchange was built in 1873 in ornate style (see p47).

Place du Petit Sablon
*This square is a jewel
of the Upper Town.
Originally a horse market,
the central area became
a flower garden in 1890,
surrounded by wrought-
iron railings decorated
with stone statuettes.
Each figure represents a
medieval trade or craft
that brought prosperity to
the capital (see p68–9).*

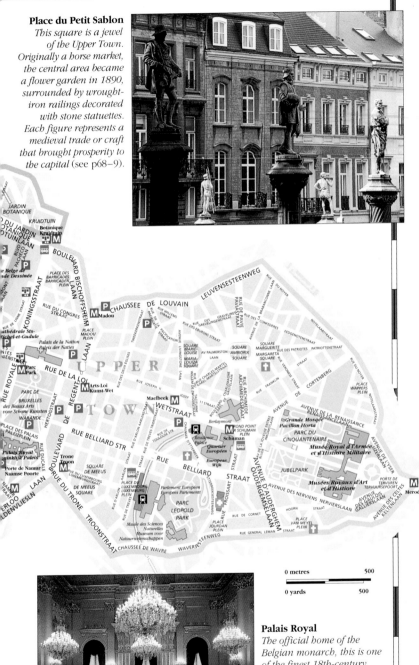

Palais Royal
*The official home of the
Belgian monarch, this is one
of the finest 18th-century
buildings in the Upper Town.
A highlight of Neo-Classical
architecture, it overlooks Parc
de Bruxelles (see pp58–9).*

0 metres 500

0 yards 500

Brussels' Best: Architecture

REFLECTING Brussels' importance in the history of northern Europe, the city's architecture ranges from grand medieval towers to the glittering post-modern structures of European institutions. With a few examples of medieval Brabant Gothic still on show, the capital of Europe has the best Flemish Renaissance architecture in the world in the Baroque splendour of the Grand Place, as well as elegant Neo-Classical churches and houses. The quantity and quality of Art Nouveau *(see pp16–17)*, with its exquisite interiors and handmade features, are highlights of 19th- and 20th-century residential building. The cutting-edge designs in the Parliament Quarter, planned by committees of European architects, take the tour up to date.

Basilique du Sacré-Coeur
Begun in 1904 and only completed in 1970, this huge Art Deco edifice is the world's fifth-largest church (see p81).

BASILIQUE DU
SACRÉ-COEUR

Grand Place
Almost entirely rebuilt by merchants after French bombardment in 1695, this cobbled square is one of the world's best Baroque ensembles (see pp42–3).

Palais de Justice
Bigger in area than St Peter's in Rome, the city's law courts were built in Neo-Classical style using the profits of colonialism, and completed in 1883 (see p69).

Lower Town

Porte de Hal
This imposing 14th-century tower is the only remaining trace of the city's solid, thick second perimeter wall. It owes its survival to its use as an 18th-century prison and latterly as a museum (see p79).

0 metres   500

0 yards   500

Cathédrale Sts Michel et Gudule
The white stone façade from 1250 is an outstanding example of Brabant Gothic style (see pp70–71).

Palais de la Nation
The home of the Belgian Parliament since the country's independence in 1830, this magnificent building was constructed in the late 18th century by the Neo-Classical architect Guimard, who also designed the expansive stone façade and many of the surrounding state buildings.

Upper Town

Palais d'Egmont
This 18th-century ducal mansion bears the name of a Flemish count executed for defending his countrymen's civil rights in 1568.

European Parliament
Named "Les Caprices des Dieux" ("The Whims of the Gods"), this glassy postmodern construction serves 626 politicians.

Belgian Artists

BELGIAN ART ROSE to the fore when the region came under Burgundian rule in the 15th century. Renaissance painters produced strong works in oil, characterized by intricate detail and lifelike, unidealized portraiture. The quest for realism and clarity of light was heavily influenced by the new Dutch schools of art. Yet, in contrast, Belgium's second golden artistic age, in the 20th century, moved away from these goals, abandoning reality for surrealism in the challenging work of artists such as René Magritte.

Belgium is justifiably proud of its long artistic tradition. Rubenshuis in Antwerp *(see pp96–7)*, Brussels' Musée Wiertz *(see p72)* and Musées Royaux des Beaux-Arts *(see pp62–7)* are fine examples of the respect Belgium shows to its artists' homes and their works.

Portrait of Laurent Froimont
by Rogier van der Weyden

THE FLEMISH PRIMITIVES

ART IN BRUSSELS and Flanders first attracted European attention at the end of the Middle Ages. **Jan van Eyck** (c.1400–41) is considered to be responsible for the major revolution in Flemish art. Widely credited as the creator of oil painting, van Eyck was the first artist to use the oil medium to fix longer-lasting glazes and to mix colour pigments for wood and canvas. As works could now be rendered more permanent, the innovation spread the Renaissance fashion for panel paintings. However, van Eyck was more than just a practical innovator, and can be seen as the forefather of the Flemish Primitive school

with his lively depictions of human existence in an animated manner. Van Eyck is also responsible, with his brother, for the striking polyptych altarpiece *Adoration of the Holy Lamb*, displayed in Ghent Cathedral *(see p110)*.

The trademarks of the Flemish Primitives are a lifelike vitality, enhanced by realism in portraiture, texture of clothes and furnishings and a clarity of light. The greatest interpreter of the style was Rogier de la Pasture (c.1400–64), better known as **Rogier van der Weyden**, the town painter of Brussels, who combined van Eyck's light and realism with work of religious intensity, as in *Lamentation (see p66)*.

Many in Belgium and across Europe were schooled and inspired by his work, continuing and expanding the new techniques. **Dieric Bouts** (1415–75) extended

the style. With his studies of bustling 15th-century Bruges, **Hans Memling** (c.1433–94) is considered the last Flemish Primitive. Moving towards the 16th century, landscape artist **Joachim Patinier** (c.1475–1524) produced the first European industrial scenes.

THE BRUEGHEL DYNASTY

IN THE EARLY years of the 16th century, Belgian art was strongly influenced by the Italians. Trained in Rome, **Jan Gossaert** (c.1478–1533) brought mythological themes to the art commissioned by the ruling Dukes of Brabant.

But it was the prolific Brueghel family who had the most influence on Flemish art throughout the 16th and 17th centuries. **Pieter Brueghel the Elder** (c.1525–69), one of the greatest Flemish artists, settled in Brussels in 1563. His earthy rustic landscapes of village life, peopled with comic peasants, are a social study of medieval life and remain his best-known work. **Pieter Brueghel the Younger** (1564–1638) produced religious works such as *The Enrolment of Bethlehem* (1610). In contrast, **Jan Brueghel the Elder** (1568–1625) painted intricate floral still lifes with a draped velvet backdrop, becoming known as "Velvet Brueghel". His son, **Jan Brueghel the Younger** (1601–78) also became a court painter in Brussels and a fine landscape artist of note.

The Fall of Icarus **by Pieter Brueghel the Elder**

Self-portrait by Rubens, one of many from his lifetime

THE ANTWERP ARTISTS

IN THE 17TH century, the main centre of Belgian art moved from the social capital, Brussels, to Antwerp, in the heart of Flanders. This move was largely influenced by **Pieter Paul Rubens** (1577–1640), who lived in Antwerp. He was one of the first Flemish artists to become known through Europe and Russia. A court painter, Rubens was also an accomplished landscape artist and interpreter of mythology, but is best known for his depiction of plump women, proud of their figures. Rubens was so popular in his own time that his bold and large-scale works were translated by Flemish weavers into series of tapestries.

Anthony van Dyck (1599–1641), a pupil of Rubens and court portraitist, was the second Antwerp artist to gain world renown. The Brueghel dynasty continued to produce notable figures: Jan Brueghel the Elder eventually settled in Antwerp to produce art with Rubens, while his son-in-law, **David Teniers II** (1610–90) founded the Antwerp Academy of Art in 1665.

THE EUROPEAN INFLUENCE

THE INFLUENCE OF Rubens was so great that little innovation took place in the Flemish art scene in the 18th century. In the early years of

the 19th century, Belgian art was largely dominated by the influence of other European schools. **François-Joseph Navez** (1787–1869) introduced Neo-Classicism to Flemish art. Realism took off with **Constantin Meunier** (1831–1905) and Impressionism with **Guillaume Vogels** (1836–96). The Brussels-based **Antoine Wiertz** (1806–65) was considered a Romantic, but his distorted and occasionally disturbing works, such as *Inhumation précipitée* (c.1830) seem to have early surrealist leanings. **Fernand Khnopff** (1858–1921) was influenced by the German Romantic Gustav Klimt. An early exponent of Belgian Symbolism, Khnopff's work is notable for his portraits of menacing and ambiguous women. Also on a journey from naturalism to surrealism, **James Ensor** (1860–1949) often used eerie skeletons in his work, reminiscent of Bosch. Between 1884 and 1894, the artists' cooperative **Les XX (Les Vingt)** reinvigorated the Brussels art scene with exhibitions of famous foreign and avant garde painters.

SURREALISM

THE 20TH CENTURY began with the emergence of Fauvism led by **Rik Wouters** (1882–1916), whose bright sun-filled landscapes show the influence of Cézanne.

Surrealism began in Brussels in the mid-1920s, dominated from the start by **René Magritte** (1898–1967). The movement had its roots back in the 16th century, with the phantasmagoria of Bosch and Pieter Brueghel the Elder. Fuelled by the chaos of World War I, much of which took place on Flemish battlefields, Magritte defined his disorientating surrealism as "[restoring] the familiar to the strange". More ostentatious and emotional, **Paul Delvaux** (1897–1989) produced elegant, freakish interiors occupied by ghostly figures. In 1948 the **COBRA Movement** promoted abstract art, which gave way in the 1960s to conceptual art, led by installationist **Marcel Broodthaers** (1924–76), who used daily objects, such as a casserole dish full of mussels, for his own interpretation.

Sculpture by Rik Wouters

UNDERGROUND ART

Notre Temps (1976) by Expressionist Roger Somville at Hankar station

Some 58 Brussels metro stations have been decorated with a combination of murals, sculptures and architecture by 54 Belgian artists. Although none but the most devoted visitor to the city is likely to see them all, there are several notable examples.

Annessens was decorated by the Belgian COBRA artists, Dotremont and Alechinsky. In the **Bourse**, surrealist Paul Delvaux's *Nos Vieux Trams Bruxellois* is still on show with *Moving Ceiling*, a series of 75 tubes that move in the breeze by sculptor Pol Bury. At **Horta** station, Art Nouveau wrought ironwork from Victor Horta's now destroyed People's Palace is displayed, and **Stockel** is a tribute to Hergé and his boy hero, Tintin *(see pp18–19)*.

Brussels' Best: Art Nouveau

A MONG EUROPE'S most important architectural movements at the start of the 20th century, Art Nouveau in Belgium was led by Brussels architect Victor Horta (1861–1947) and the Antwerp-born interior designer Henry van de Velde (1863–1957). The style evolved from the Arts and Crafts Movement in England and the fashion for Japanese simplicity, and is characterized by its sinuous decorative lines, stained glass, carved stone curves, floral frescoes and elaborately curled and twisted metalwork. As new suburbs rose up in the 1890s, over 2,000 new houses were built in the style. Although many were demolished, details can still be seen in almost every Brussels street.

Hôtel Métropole
The high-vaulted lobby and bar of this luxurious 1894 hotel recall the city's fin-de-siècle heyday (see p49).

Old England
This former department store uses glass and steel rather than brick, with large windows and twisted metal turrets (see p60).

Hôtel Ciamberlani
Architect Paul Hankar designed this redbrick house in rue Defacqz for the sgraffiti artist Albert Ciamberlani, with whom he worked.

The Lower Town

Musée Horta
Curved window frames and elaborate metal balconies mark this out as the home and studio of Art Nouveau's best-known architect (see p78).

Hôtel Hannon
This stylish 1902 townhouse was built by Jules Brunfaut (1852–1942). One of its metal-framed windows has striking stained-glass panes (see p79).

Maison Cauchie
Restored in 1989, architect Paul Cauchie's home in rue des Francs has examples of sgraffiti, a technique in which designs are incised onto wet plaster to reveal another colour beneath.

Maison Saint Cyr
Horta's disciple Gustave Strauven was keen to outdo his mentor with this intricate façade, only 4 m (14 ft) wide (see p72).

The Upper Town

0 metres	500
0 yards	500

Hôtel Solvay
An early Horta creation of 1894, this home was built for a wealthy family. Horta designed every element of the building, from the ochre and yellow cast-iron façade columns and glass front door to the decorative but functional doorknobs (see p79).

Belgian Comic Strip Art

Tintin's dog Snowy

BELGIAN COMIC STRIP art is as famous a part of Belgian culture as chocolates and beer. The seeds of this great passion were sown when the US comic strip Little Nemo was published in French in 1908 to huge popular acclaim in Belgium. The country's reputation for producing some of the best comic strip art in Europe was established after World War II. Before the war, Europe was awash with American comics, but the Nazis called a halt to the supply. Local artists took over, and found that there was a large audience who preferred homegrown comic heroes. This explosion in comic strip art was led by perhaps the most famous Belgian creation ever, Tintin, who, with his dog Snowy, is as recognizable across Europe as Mickey Mouse.

Hergé at work in his studio

HERGÉ AND TINTIN

TINTIN'S CREATOR, Hergé, was born Georges Remi in Brussels in 1907. He began using his pen name (a phonetic spelling of his initials in reverse) in 1924. At the young age of 15, his drawings were published in the *Boy Scout Journal*. He became the protégé of a priest, Abbot Norbert Wallez, who also managed the Catholic journal *Le XXe Siècle*, and was swiftly given the

responsibility of the children's supplement, *Le petit Vingtième*. Eager to invent an original comic strip, Hergé came up with the character of Tintin the reporter, who first appeared in the story *Tintin au Pays des Soviets* on 10 January 1929. Over the next 10 years the character developed and grew in popularity. Book-length stories began to appear from 1930.

During the Nazi occupation in the 1940s *Tintin* continued to be published, with political references carefully omitted, in an approved paper *Le Soir*. This led to Hergé being accused of collaboration at the end of the war. He was called in for questioning but released later the same day without charge. Hergé's innocence was amply

demonstrated by his work before and during the war, where he expressed a strong sense of justice in such stories as *King Ottakar's Sceptre*, where a fascist army attempts to seize control of a central European state. Hergé took great care in researching his stories; for *Le Lotus Bleu* in 1934, which was set in China, he wrote: "I started... showing a real interest in the people and countries I was sending Tintin off to, concerned by a sense of honesty to my readers."

Spirou cover

POST-WAR BOOM

BELGIUM'S OLDEST comic strip journal *Spirou* was launched in April 1938 and, alongside the weekly *Journal de Tintin* begun in 1946, became a hothouse for the artistic talent that was to flourish during the post-war years. Many of the country's best-loved characters were first seen in *Spirou*, and most of them are still in print. Artists such as Morris, Jijé, Peyo and Roba worked on the journal. Morris (b.1923) introduced the cowboy parody, *Lucky Luke* in *Spirou* in 1947, a character who went on to feature in several live-action films and many US television cartoons.

Statue of Tintin and Snowy

COMIC STRIP CHARACTERS
Some of the world's best-loved comic strip characters originated in Belgium. *Tintin* is the most famous, but *Lucky Luke* the cowboy, the cheeky children *Suske en Wiske* and *The Smurfs* have also been published worldwide, while modern artists such as Schueten break new ground.

Tintin by Hergé

Lucky Luke by Morris

During the 1960s, the idea of the comic strip being the Ninth Art (after the seventh and eighth, film and television) expanded to include adult themes in the form of the comic-strip graphic novel.

PEYO AND THE SMURFS

BEST KNOWN for *The Smurfs*, Peyo (1928–92) was also a member of the team behind the *Spirou* journal which published his poetic medieval series *Johan et Pirlouit*, in 1952. *The Smurfs* first appeared as characters here – tiny blue people whose humorous foibles soon eclipsed any interest in the strip's supposed main characters. Reacting to their popularity, Peyo created a strip solely about them. Set in the Smurf village, the stories were infused with satirical social comment. *The Smurfs* were a popular craze between 1983 and 1985, featuring in advertising and merchandising of every type. They spawned a feature-length film, TV cartoons and popular music, and had several hit records in the 1980s.

Modern cover by Marvano

WILLY VANDERSTEEN

WHILE SPIROU and *Tintin* were French-language journals, Willy Vandersteen (1913–90) dominated the Flemish market. His popular creation, *Suske en Wiske* has

been translated into English and appears as *Bob and Bobette* in the UK, and *Willy and Wanda* in the US. The main characters are a pair of "ordinary" kids aged between 10 and 14 who have extraordinary adventures all over the world, as well as travelling back and forth in time. Today, Vandersteen's books sell in their millions.

COMIC STRIP ART TODAY

COMIC STRIPS, known as *bandes dessinées* or *beeldverhaal*, continue to be published in Belgium in all their forms. In newspapers, children's comics and graphic novels the Ninth Art remains one of the country's biggest exports. The high standards and imaginative scope of a new generation of artists, such as Schueten and Marvano, have fed growing consumer demand for comic books. Both French and Flemish publishers issue

Contemporary comic-strip artists at work in their studio

over 22 million comic books each year. Today, Belgian cartoons are sold in more than 30 countries, including the US.

Larger-than-life cartoon by Frank Pé adorns a Brussels building

STREET ART

THERE ARE currently 18 large comic strip images decorating the sides of buildings around Brussels' city centre. This outdoor exhibition is known as the Comic Strip Route and is organized by the Centre Belge de la Bande Dessineé (the Belgian Centre for Comic Strip Art) *(see pp50–51)* and the city of Brussels. Begun in 1991 as a tribute to Belgium's talent for comic strip art, this street art project continues to grow. A free map of the route is available from tourist information offices, as well as from the comic museum itself.

uske en Wiske by Vandersteen

The Smurfs by Peyo

Contemporary cartoon strip by Schueten

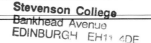

Tapestry and Lace

Lacemaker's studio sign

FOR OVER SIX CENTURIES, Belgian lace and tapestry have been highly prized luxury crafts. Originating in Flanders in the 12th century, tapestry has since been handmade in the centres of Tournai, Brussels, Arras, Mechelen and Oudenaarde, while the lace trade was practised from the 1500s onwards in all the Belgian provinces, with Bruges and Brussels particularly renowned for their delicate work. The makers often had aristocratic patrons; intricate lace and fine tapestries were status symbols of the nobility and staple exports throughout Europe from the 15th to 18th centuries. Today Belgium remains home to the very best tapestry and lace studios in the world.

Tapestry weavers numbered over 50,000 in Flanders from 1450–1550. With the ruling Dukes of Burgundy as patrons, weavers prospered, and hangings grew more elaborate.

Tapestry designs involve weaver and artist working closely together. Painters, including Rubens, produced drawings for a series of weavings of six or more on grand themes (detail shown).

The texture of the weave was the finest ever achieved; often 12 threads to the inch (5 per cm).

Weavers working today still use medieval techniques to produce contemporary tapestry, woven in Mechelen and Tournai to modern designs.

TAPESTRY

By 1200, the Flemish towns of Arras (now in France) and Tournai were Europe-wide known centres of weaving. Prized by the nobility, tapestries were portable and could be moved with the court as rulers travelled their estates. As trade grew, techniques were refined; real gold and silver were threaded into the fine wool, again increasing the value. Blending Italian idealism with Flemish realism, Bernard van Orley (1492–1542) revolutionized tapestry designs, as seen above in *The Battle of Pavia 1525,* the first of a series. Flemish weavers were eventually lured across Europe, where ironically their skill led to the success of the Gobelins factory in Paris that finally stole Flanders' crown in the late 1700s.

The lace trade *rose to the fore during the early Renaissance. Emperor Charles V decreed that lace-making should be a compulsory skill for girls in convents and béguinages (see p53) throughout Flanders. Lace became fashionable on collars and cuffs for both sexes. Trade reached a peak in the 18th century.*

Classical myths were popular themes for tapestry series.

Lace makers *are traditionally women. Although their numbers are dwindling, many craftswomen still work in Bruges and Brussels, centres of bobbin lace, creating intricate work by hand.*

Victorian Lace *heralded a revival of the craft after its decline in the austere Neo-Classical period. Although men no longer wore it, the growth of the status of lace as a ladies' accessory and its use in soft furnishing led to its renewed popularity.*

Belgian Lace *is bought today mainly as a souvenir, but despite the rise in machine-made lace from other countries, the quality here still remains as fine as it was in the Renaissance.*

Brussels: Political Capital of Europe

Manneken Pis statue

HOME TO MOST of the European Union's institutions and the headquarters of NATO, Brussels is one of Europe's most important political and business centres. Since the 1950s, the sense of Brussels as an international powerhouse has drawn an influx of people from around the world. The city has proved itself a fine host to the thousands of Eurocrats and business people that both visit and live here, with its celebrated hotels and restaurants, as well as with its cultural heritage, reflected in its historic buildings and museums. The people of Brussels are proud of their role in the new Europe. Despite the intricate and separatist-torn nature of Belgian politics, the country is unified in its support for a united Europe.

The signing of the European Common Market Treaty, Rome, 1957

HISTORICAL BEGINNINGS

THE EUROPEAN Union has its origins in the aftermath of World War II. The spirit of postwar reconciliation led France and West Germany to join forces to create the European Coal and Steel Community (ECSC). The project to continue the consolidation of Europe as a single political and financial entity began with the signing of the Treaty of Rome in 1957. This inaugurated the creation of a common market, the European Economic Community (EEC). Initially, six countries joined the EEC *(see opposite)* and the organization came into being on January 1, 1958.

The EEC was made up of two bodies, the Council of Ministers and the Commission, and coexisted with the ECSC and the atomic energy commission, Euratom. In 1967, however, these three groups merged, later becoming known as the European Community (EC). By this time the economic benefits of membership were evident, with intra-Community trade increasing by almost 30 per cent each year. The six founder members had also made an agreement on a common agricultural policy (CAP), which fixed prices and offered grants to EEC farmers. With economic improvement came calls for political union. As early as 1961, member states discussed the possibility of collaborative government. The larger states were less enthusiastic than smaller countries, and obstructed agreements over union.

Euro coin

The UK, Denmark and Ireland joined the EC in 1973, increasing its population by 25 per cent. The expectation of a return to profitable trade was crushed by the world recession of the mid-1970s which brought economic hardship to each of the member states.

Nonetheless this decade saw two important innovations: the creation of the European Regional Development Fund, which offers aid to the poorest areas of the EC, including major beneficiary, Ireland, and the European Monetary System (EMS), established in 1979. Otherwise known as the Exchange Rate Mechanism or ERM, this system was designed to protect member states from the vicissitudes of world markets. The European Currency Unit or ECU, a forerunner to the single currency (the Euro), was also initiated, despite the problem of a budget deficit in the 1980s.

MAASTRICHT

AFTER THE BUDGET issue was resolved in 1988 by the then Commission President Frenchman Jacques Delors, the 12 member states began to discuss the creation of a single European currency. The foundations were laid by the Maastricht Treaty of 1992, which changed the EC into the European Union (EU) and which set out a detailed timetable for economic and monetary union (EMU). The treaty imposed stringent economic criteria on states which wanted to participate. At the 1992 summit held in Edinburgh, Brussels' position as the focus city of the EU was also confirmed.

Denmark and Britain were among those reluctant to commit themselves to the single currency, a situation reflecting Britain's great wariness of the far-reaching consequences of the idea and its ambivalence towards the European project in general. This was further illustrated by the fact that Britain is one of only two European Community countries (the other being Ireland) not to have signed up to the EU's Schengen Agreement, under which border controls between EU member states have been removed. This means that travellers can now journey around all of the other member states without once showing their passports.

THE FUTURE

THE EU HAS developed throughout the 1990s, with the arrival of Sweden, Finland and Austria in 1995 and, on January 1, 1999, the establishment of a single European currency in 11 of the EU's member states. Despite this, criticism of the EU escalated in the 1990s. Its bureaucracy was seen as a source of irritation by many of its 375 million citizens. The EU's executive body, the Commission has also been the focus of resentment. EU President Jacques Santer was forced to resign in 1999 after allegations of mismanagement, incompetence and fraud.

Former Italian Prime Minister Romano Prodi replaced Jacques Santer in 1999. Debate continues about the accession of central and eastern European states, as well as the long-term goal of increased political unity.

THE EUROPEAN COMMISSION

THE COMMISSION is the EU's executive arm, responsible for formulating policies which are then ratified or rejected by the Council of Ministers. There are twenty Commissioners, including the President, each with a specific area of responsibility ranging from transport to technology. The Commission

is responsible for ensuring that policies are carried out, and that member states do not violate EC law.

Once based in the star-shaped Berlaymont building, the Commissioners have been rehoused while asbestos is removed from the building.

THE COUNCIL OF MINISTERS

THE COUNCIL of Ministers is composed of representatives of each member state: each nation has a block of votes depending on its size. The Council must approve all legislation for the EU, often a difficult task to accomplish given that most Europe-wide laws will seldom be to the liking of every state; most laws require a "qualified majority" of 62 out of 87 votes before they are passed. The Council of Ministers meets behind closed doors, and its members are answerable only to their national governments, which has led to calls for reform.

THE EUROPEAN PARLIAMENT

THE EUROPEAN Parliament is responsible for approving the EU's annual budget, as well as monitoring the Commission's performance.

The Parliament is the only European institution subject to election by the general public. There are 626 MEPs, elected by proportional

representation. The Parliament sits in Brussels, Strasbourg and Luxembourg. In Brussels, the glass-and-steel Parliament building on Rue Wiertz is nicknamed *Le Caprice des Dieux* (The Whims of the Gods) (*see p73*).

BRUSSELS' POLITICS

BELGIUM'S system of government is complex as regional interests are powerful. The country is divided into three federal regions, Flanders Wallonia and Brussels, and conflict between separatist Walloon and Fleming factions threatens Belgian unity.

The Brussels' regional government oversees the city's 19 communes. Each one has its own powers, including a police force. Separate French and Flemish organizations rule on cultural matters.

Contemporary geometric bridge in Brussels' Quartier Européen

BRUSSELS THROUGH THE YEAR

THE TEMPERATE climate of Brussels is typical of Northern Europe and means that a range of activities throughout the year take place both inside and out. Mild damp winters and gentle summers allow the city's strong artistic life to flourish in historic buildings and modern stadiums alike. The Belgians make the most of their seasonal changes. Theatre, dance and film start their season in January, with evening venues

Revellers at Ommegang

that range from ancient abbeys lit by the setting sun to drive-in cinemas. The city's flower festival launches the summer in highly colourful style, with the Grand Place literally carpeted in millions of blooms every other August. Through the year, festivals in Brussels range from energetic, exuberant historic processions that have taken place yearly since medieval times, to innovative European experimental art.

SPRING

BRUSSELS' LIVELY cultural life takes off as the crisp spring days lengthen and visitors begin to arrive in the city. Music festivals take place in a wide variety of open-air venues. As the city's parks burst into bloom, the world-famous tropical greenhouses at Laeken are opened to the public and Brussels' chocolatiers produce delicious creations for Easter.

MARCH

International Fantasy Film Festival *(middle fortnight)*. Lovers of the weird and wonderful will find new and vintage work here in cinemas all over the city.
Ars Musica *(mid-Mar to early Apr)*. This celebration of modern music is one of Europe's finest festivals, boasting famous performers and beautiful venues, often the Musée d'art ancien *(see pp62–3)*. The festival is now a must for connoisseurs of the contemporary music world.
Eurantica *(last week)*. The Baudouin Stadium at Heysel plays host to hundreds of traders and members of the public anxious for bargains in the world of antiques.
Easter *(Easter Sunday)*. The annual Easter Egg hunt, with eggs allegedly hidden by the bells of churches in Rome. Over 1,000 brightly coloured

The Royal Glasshouse at Laeken, famed for its rare exotic orchids

Easter eggs are hidden by adults in the Parc Royal, and Belgian children gather to forage among the flowerbeds.

APRIL

Sablon Baroque Spring *(third week)*. The Place du Grand Sablon hosts new classical ensembles in a gathering of young Belgian talent performing 17th-century music.
The Royal Greenhouses at Laeken *(12 days, dates vary)*. The private greenhouses of the Belgian Royal family are opened to the public as their numerous exotic plants and cacti start to flower. Breathtaking 19th-century glass and wrought ironwork shelters hundreds of rare species *(see pp82–3)*.
Flanders Festival *(mid-Apr to October)*. A celebration of all things musical, this

classical medley offers more than 120 performances by internationally renowned choirs and orchestras.
Scenes d'Ecran *(third weekend)*. Over 100 new European films draw crowds in cinemas across the city.

MAY

Europe Day Festivities *(7–9 May)*. As the capital of Europe, Brussels celebrates its role in the European Union – even Manneken

Runners taking part in the Brussels twenty-kilometre race

AVERAGE DAILY HOURS OF SUNSHINE

Hours

10
8
6
4
2
0

Jan Feb Mar Apr May Jun Jul Aug Sep Oct Nov Dec

Climate
Belgium has a fairly temperate Northern European climate. Although not often freezing, winters are chilly and a heavy coat is required. Summers are warmer and much brighter, though you will still need a jersey for the evenings. Rainwear is always a necessity.

Pis is dressed as a Euro-supporter, in a suit of blue, decorated with yellow stars.

Kunsten FESTIVAL des Arts *(9–31 May)*. This innovative festival covers theatre and dance and is the forum for much exciting new talent.

Queen Elisabeth Music Contest *(May to mid-June)*. Classical fans will flock to the prestigious musical competition, now in its fifth decade. Young singers, violinists and pianists gather in front of well-known conductors and soloists to determine the champion among Europe's finest student players.

Brussels Twenty-Kilometre Race *(last Sunday)*. As many as 20,000 keen professional and amateur runners race round the city, taking in its major landmarks.

Jazz Marathon *(last weekend)*. Bistros and cafés are the venues for myriad small jazz bands, with some well-known artists playing anonymously.

SUMMER

THE SEASON OF pageantry arrives with Ommegang in July, one of Europe's oldest and best-known processions, which takes place in the Grand Place and the surrounding streets. Multi-cultural music runs throughout the summer, with classical, jazz and avant-garde US and European performers playing in venues ranging from tiny beer cafés to the great King Baudouin stadium in Heysel. Independence is celebrated

on Belgian National Day. Families enjoy the Foire du Midi, the huge fairground over 2 km square (1 sq mile) covered with rides and stalls.

JUNE

City of Brussels Summer Festival *(early June to Sep)*. Classical concerts take place in some of the city's best-known ancient buildings.

Festival of Wallonia *(Jun–Oct)*. Covering Brussels and Flanders, this series of gala concerts showcases the best in young Belgian classical orchestral and soloist talent.

Couleur Café Festival *(last weekend)*. Spread over three summer evenings in the Tour et Taxis renovated warehouse, the fashionable and funky programme includes salsa, African drummers, acid jazz and multicultural music.

Fête de la Musique *(last weekend)*. Two days of concerts and recitals featuring world music take place in the halls and museums of the city.

African drummer performing at the Couleur Café Festival

JULY

Ommegang *(first weekend in July)*. This festival has been celebrated in Brussels since 1549, and now draws crowds from around the world. Translated as "a tour", the procession revolves around the Grand Place and the surrounding streets. Over 2,000 participants dress up and become members of a Renaissance town; jesters, courtiers, nobles and soldiers; they go on to parade before Belgian dignitaries. Tickets have to be booked months in advance.

The Ommegang pausing in front of dignitaries in the Grand Place

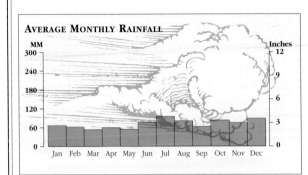

AVERAGE MONTHLY RAINFALL

Rainfall chart
On the whole Belgium is rather a rainy country, with Brussels experiencing constant low rainfall throughout the year. Spring is the driest season, but summers can be damp. In winter, rain may turn to snow and sleet.

Brosella Folk and Jazz Festival *(second weekend)*. Musicians from all over Europe play informal gigs in the Parc d'Osseghem in the shadow of the Atomium.

Festival d'Eté de Bruxelles *(Jul–Aug)*. Classical concerts take place through the high summer in venues around the Upper and Lower Town.

Foire du Midi *(mid-Jul–mid-Aug)*. Brussels' main station, Gare du Midi, is host to this month-long funfair, which attracts people in their thousands. Especially popular with children, it is one of the biggest fairs in Europe, and includes an enormous Ferris wheel.

Belgian National Day *(21 Jul)*. The 1831 declaration of independence is commemorated annually with a military parade followed by a firework display in the Parc de Bruxelles.

Palais Royal Open Days *(last week in Jul–second week of Sep)*. The official residence of the Belgian Royal family, the opulent staterooms of the Palais Royal, including the huge throne room, are open to the public for six weeks during the summer *(see pp58–9)*.

AUGUST

Plantation du Meiboom *(9 Aug)*. This traditional festival dates from 1213. Parading crowds dressed in huge puppet costumes parade around the Lower Town and finally reach the Grand Place where a maypole is planted as a celebration of summer.

Costumed revellers at the Plantation of the Meiboom

Tapis des Fleurs *(mid-Aug, biannually, for four days)*. Taking place on even-numbered years, this colourful celebration pays tribute to Brussels' long-established flower industry. The Grand Place is carpeted with millions of fresh flowers in patterns echoing historical scenes. The beautiful flower carpet measures 2,000 sq m (21,000 sq ft).

AUTUMN

FRESH AUTUMN days are the cue for many indoor events; innovative jazz is performed in the city's cafés and the French cultural centre in Le Botanique. Architecture is celebrated in the heritage weekend where the public can tour many private houses and personal art collections.

SEPTEMBER

The Birthday of Manneken Pis *(last weekend)*. Brussels' celebrated mascot is clothed in a new suit by a chosen dignitary from abroad.

Lucky Town Festival *(first weekend)*. Sixty concerts take place in over 30 of some of Brussels' best-known and atmospheric cafés.

Les Nuits Botaniques *(last week)*. Held in the former greenhouses of the Botanical gardens, now the French cultural centre, this series of musical events is a delight.

The Grand Place, carpeted in millions of fresh flowers

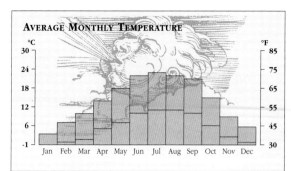

Average Monthly Temperature

Temperature chart
This chart gives the average maximum and minimum temperatures for Brussels. Generally mild, Brussels' climate does produce chilly weather and cold winters from October to March. Spring sees milder temperatures and is followed by a warm summer.

Journées du Patrimoine/ Heritage Days *(second or third weekend)*. Private homes, listed buildings and art collections are opened for a rare public viewing to celebrate the city's architecture.

OCTOBER

Audi Jazz Festival *(mid-Oct–mid-Nov)*. All over Belgium informal jazz concerts bring autumnal cheer to country towns and the capital. Performers are mainly local, but some European stars fly in for performances in Brussels' Palais des Beaux-Arts. Ray Charles and Herbie Hancock have appeared in past years.

WINTER

SNOW AND RAIN typify Brussels' winter weather, and attractions move indoors. Art galleries launch world-class exhibitions and the Brussels Film Festival showcases new and established talent. As the festive season approaches, the ancient Lower Town is brightly lit and families gather for Christmas with traditional Belgian cuisine.

NOVEMBER

Nocturnes des Sablons *(last weekend)*. Shops and galleries stay open until 11pm around the Place du Grand Sablon. Horse-drawn carriages transport shoppers around the area, with mulled wine on offer in the festively decorated main square.

DECEMBER

Fête de Saint Nicolas *(6 Dec)*. The original Santa Claus, the patron saint of Christmas, is alleged to arrive in the city on this day. Children throughout the country are given their presents, sweetmeats and chocolate.
Reveillon/Fête de Noel *(24–25 Dec)*. In common with the rest of mainland Europe, Christmas is celebrated over a feast on the evening of 24 December. Gifts are given by adults on this day, and 25 December is traditionally for visiting extended family. The city's Christmas decorations provide a lively sight until 6 January.

JANUARY

Fête des Rois *(6 Jan)*. Epiphany is celebrated with almond cake, the *galette des rois*, and the search for the bean inside that declares its finder king for the night.
Brussels Film Festival *(mid–late Jan)*. Premières and film stars are adding weight to this European film showcase.

FEBRUARY

Antiques Fair *(middle fortnight)*. Brussels' crossroads location is useful here as international dealers

Christmas market in the Grand Place around the traditional Christmas Pine

gather in the historic Palais des Beaux-Arts *(see p60)*.
International Comic strip and Cartoon Festival *(middle fortnight)*. Artists and authors, both new and established, arrive for lectures and screenings in this city with its comic strip heritage.

PUBLIC HOLIDAYS

New Year's Day (1 Jan)
Easter Sunday (variable)
Easter Monday (variable)
Labour Day (1 May)
Ascension Day (variable)
Whit Sunday (variable)
Whit Monday (variable)
Belgian National Day (21 July)
Assumption Day (15 Aug)
All Saints' Day (1 Nov)
Armistice Day (11 Nov)
Christmas Day (25 Dec)

THE HISTORY OF BRUSSELS

AS THE CULTURAL AND CIVIC *heart of Belgium since the Middle Ages, Brussels has been the focus of much political upheaval over the centuries. But, from the battles of the 17th century to the warfare of the 20th century, it has always managed to re-create itself with vigour. Now, at the start of a new millennium, Belgium's capital is prospering as the political and economic centre of Europe.*

When Julius Caesar set out to conquer the Gauls of northern Europe in 58 BC, he encountered a fierce tribe known as the Belgae (the origins of the 19th-century name "Belgium"). Roman victory led to the establishment of the region they called Gallia Belgica. The earliest mention of Brussels itself is as "Broucsella", or "settlement in the marshes" and dates from a 7th-century manuscript.

15th-century Flemish tapestry showing the stars

Following the collapse of the Roman Empire in the 5th century, a Germanic race known as the Franks came to rule the region and established the Merovingian dynasty of kings, based in their capital at Tournai. They were followed by the Carolingian dynasty, which produced one of the most important figures of the Middle Ages – Charlemagne (AD 768–814). His noted military expertise ensured that invaders such as the Northern Saxons and the Lombards of Italy were repelled. He was also credited with establishing Christianity as the major religion across western Europe. The pope rewarded him by crowning him Emperor of the West in AD 800; effectively he was the first Holy Roman

Emperor, ruling a vast area extending from Denmark to Italy. By the 10th century, the inheritance laws of the Franks meant that the empire was divided up among Charlemagne's grandsons, Louis, Charles the Bald and Lothair. Lothair's fortress, founded in 979, marks the official founding of Brussels. The period had brought a measure of stability to the area's volatile feudal fiefdoms, leading to a trading boom in the new towns of the low countries.

INDUSTRIAL BEGINNINGS

At the start of the 12th century, commerce became the guiding force in western Europe and the centres of trade quickly grew into powerful cities. Rivers and canals were the key to the growth of the area's trading towns. Ghent, Ypres, Antwerp and Bruges became the focus of the cloth trade plied across the North Sea between France, Germany, Italy and England. Brussels, with its skilled craftsmen, became a trade centre, and impressive buildings such as the Cathédrale Sts Michel et Gudule *(see pp 70–71)*, built in 1225, demonstrated its stature.

TIMELINE

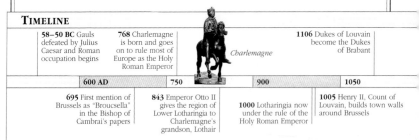

58–50 BC Gauls defeated by Julius Caesar and Roman occupation begins

768 Charlemagne is born and goes on to rule most of Europe as the Holy Roman Emperor

Charlemagne

1106 Dukes of Louvain become the Dukes of Brabant

600 AD	750	900	1050

695 First mention of Brussels as "Broucsella" in the Bishop of Cambrai's papers

843 Emperor Otto II gives the region of Lower Lotharingia to Charlemagne's grandson, Lothair

1000 Lotharingia now under the rule of the Holy Roman Emperor

1005 Henry II, Count of Louvain, builds town walls around Brussels

◁ *Philip the Good*, **Duke of Burgundy (c.1500) by Rogier van der Weyden**

Nineteenth-century painting of the Battle of the Golden Spurs

THE CRAFTSMEN'S REBELLION

Over the next two hundred years Brussels became one of the foremost towns of the Duchy of Brabant. Trade here specialized in fine fabrics that were exported to lucrative markets in France, Italy and England. A handful of merchants became rich and exercised political power over the towns. However, conflict grew between the merchants, who wanted to maintain good relations with England, and their autocratic French rulers who relied upon tax revenue from the towns.

The 14th century witnessed a series of rebellions by the craftsmen of Bruges and Brussels against what they saw as the tyranny of the French lords. In May 1302, Flemish craftsmen, armed only with spears, defeated the French at the Battle of the Golden Spurs, named for the humiliating theft of the cavalry's spurs. Encouraged by this success, the Brussels craftsmen revolted against the aristocracy who controlled their trading economy in 1356. They were also angered by the Hundred Years' War between England and France, which began in 1337. The war threatened wool supplies from England which were crucial to their cloth-based economy. The subsequent depression marked the beginning of decades of conflict between the craftsmen and merchant classes. In 1356, Jeanne, Duchess of Louvain, gained control over Brussels, and instituted the workers' Charter of Liberties. Craftsmen were finally given some political powers in the city. Trade resumed, attracting new people to Brussels. As the population grew, new streets were built outside the city walls to accommodate them. Between 1357 and 1379 a second town wall was constructed around these new districts.

THE HOUSE OF BURGUNDY

The new town walls were also built in reply to the invasion of Brussels by the Count of Flanders. However, in 1369 Philip, Duke of Burgundy, married the daughter of the Count of Flanders, and when the count died in 1384 the Low Countries and eastern France came under the couple's Burgundian rule.

In the 1430s Brussels became the capital of Burgundy, a situation that was to change the city forever. Brussels

Richly detailed Brussels tapestries such as this *Allegory of Hope* (1525) were prized commodities

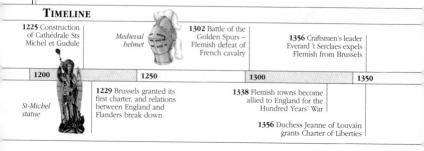

TIMELINE

1225 Construction of Cathédrale Sts Michel et Gudule	*Medieval helmet*	**1302** Battle of the Golden Spurs – Flemish defeat of French cavalry	**1356** Craftsmen's leader Everard 't Serclaes expels Flemish from Brussels
1200	**1250**	**1300**	**1350**
St-Michel statue	**1229** Brussels granted its first charter, and relations between England and Flanders break down	**1338** Flemish towns become allied to England for the Hundred Years' War **1356** Duchess Jeanne of Louvain grants Charter of Liberties	

Painting of the family of the Hapsburg King of Austria, Maximillian I and Mary of Burgundy

was now an administrative and cultural centre, famous for its grand architecture, in the form of mansions and churches, and its luxury crafts trade.

THE HAPSBURG DYNASTY

In 1477 Mary of Burgundy, the last heir to the duchy, married Maximillian of Austria. Mary died in 1482, leaving Maximillian and the Hapsburg dynasty rulers of the city at a time when Brussels was experiencing serious economic depression. In 1488 Brussels and the rest of Flanders rebelled against this new power which had reinstated relations with France. The Austrians held on to power largely because of the plague of 1490 which halved Brussels' population. Maximillian passed his rule of the Low Countries to his son, Philip the Handsome in 1494 the year after he became Holy Roman Emperor. When

Portrait of Charles V, Holy Roman Emperor

Maximillian died, his daughter, Regent Empress Margaret of Austria, moved the capital of Burgundy from Brussels to Mechelen, where she educated her nephew, the future emperor Charles V.

SPANISH RULE

In 1515, at the age of 15, Charles became Sovereign of Burgundy. The following year he inherited the Spanish throne and, in 1519, became the Holy Roman Emperor. As he was born in Ghent, and considered Flanders his real home, he restored Brussels as the capital of Burgundy. Dutch officials arrived to run the three government councils that were now based here.

For the first time the city had a court. Both aristocratic families and immigrants, eager to cash in on the city's expansion, were drawn to the heady mix of tolerance, intellectual sophistication and business. Brussels quickly emerged as the most powerful city in Flanders, overtaking its long-standing rivals Bruges and Antwerp.

However, the Reformation, begun in Germany by Martin Luther, was to usher in a period of religious conflict. When Charles V abdicated in 1555, he fractured the empire's unity by leaving the Holy Roman Empire to his brother Ferdinand and all other dominions to his devoutly Catholic son, Philip II of Spain. His persecution of the Protestant movement finally sparked the Revolt of the Netherlands led by the House of Orange. Brussels' Protestant rulers surrendered to Philip in 1585. His power ended when the English defeated the Spanish Armada in 1588, by which time 8,000 Protestants had been put to death.

1400	1450	1500	1550

1419 Philip the Good succeeds as Count of Burgundy

1430 Under Burgundian control, Brussels becomes the major administrative centre of the region

1506 Margaret of Austria moves the Burgundian capital from Brussels to Mechelen

1490 Plague decimates the city

1488 Civil war – Brussels joins Flanders against Maximillian of Austria

1515 Charles Hapsburg becomes Sovereign of Burgundy

Count Egmont

1555 Catholic Philip II succeeds Charles V as religious reformation comes to Brussels

1566 Conseil des Troubles set up by Duke d'Alba. Prominent Counts Egmont and Hornes executed

The armies of Louis XIV, the Sun King, bombard Brussels' city walls

THE COUNTER-REFORMATION

From 1598 Archduchess Isabella and Archduke Albert were the Catholic rulers of the Spanish Netherlands, installing a Hapsburg governor in Brussels. They continued to persecute Protestants: all non-Catholics were barred from working. Thousands of skilled workers moved to the Netherlands. But such new trades as lace-making, diamond-cutting and silk-weaving flourished. Isabella and Albert were great patrons of the arts, and supported Rubens in Antwerp *(see pp96–7).*

Protestant prisoners paraded in Brussels during the Counter-Reformation under Albert and Isabella

INVASION OF THE SUN KING

The 17th century was a time of of religious and political struggle all over Europe. The Thirty Years War (1618–48) divided western Europe along Catholic and Protestant lines. After 1648, France's Sun King, Louis XIV, was determined to add Flanders to his territory.

By 1633 both Albert and Isabella were dead and Philip IV of Spain, passed control of the Spanish Netherlands to his weak brother, the Cardinal-Infant Ferdinand. Keen to pursue his ambitions, Louis XIV besieged Maastricht in the 1670s and took Luxembourg. Having failed to win the nearby enclave of Namur, the piqued Sun King moved his army to Brussels, whose defences were weaker.

On August 13, 1695, the French bombarded Brussels from a hill outside the city walls, destroying the Grand Place *(see pp42–3)* and much of its environs. The French withdrew, but their desire to rule the region was to cause conflict over subsequent decades.

A PHOENIX FROM THE ASHES

Despite the destruction incurred by the bombardment, Brussels was quick to recover. The guilds ensured that the Grand Place was rebuilt in a matter of years, with new guildhouses as a testament to the on-going success of the city's economic life and craftsmanship.

The building of the Willebroek canal during the 17th century gave Brussels access to the Rupel and Scheldt rivers, and thus to Antwerp and the North Sea. Large industries began to replace local market trading. Factories and mills grew up around the city's harbour, and Brussels became an export centre.

TIMELINE

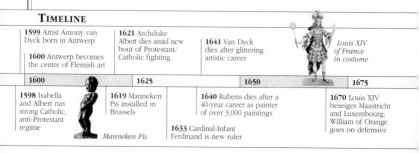

1599 Artist Antony van Dyck born in Antwerp

1600 Antwerp becomes the centre of Flemish art

1621 Archduke Albert dies amid new bout of Protestant/Catholic fighting

1641 Van Dyck dies after glittering artistic career

Louis XIV of France in costume

1600   **1625**   **1650**   **1675**

1598 Isabella and Albert run strong Catholic, anti-Protestant regime

Manneken Pis

1619 Manneken Pis installed in Brussels

1640 Rubens dies after a 40-year career as painter of over 3,000 paintings

1633 Cardinal-Infant Ferdinand is new ruler

1670 Louis XIV beseiges Maastricht and Luxembourg; William of Orange goes on defensive

AUSTRIAN SUCCESSION

Subsequent decades were dogged by war as Austria and England sought to stave off French ambitions. When Philip of Anjou succeeded to the Spanish throne, it looked as if the combined threat of Spain and France would overwhelm the rest of Europe. Emperor Leopold I of Austria, together with England and many German states, declared war on France. The resulting 14-year War of the Spanish Succession ended with the Treaty of Utrecht in 1713, which ceded the Netherlands, including Brussels, to Austria.

Governor of Brussels, Duke Charles of Lorraine

The treaty did not end the conflict. Emperor Charles VI of Austria ruled after Leopold, but failed to produce a male heir. His death in 1731 sparked another 17 years of war – The War of the Austrian Succession over whether his daughter Maria Theresa should be allowed to inherit the crown. It was not until 1748, with the signing of the Treaty of Aix-la-Chapelle, that Maria Theresa gained control.

THE BOOM PERIOD

The endless fighting took its toll, and Brussels, along with the rest of Belgium, was impoverished. Despite the sophistication of the aristocratic elite, the majority of the population were still ruled by feudal laws: they could not change jobs or move home without permission; and only three per cent of the population was literate.

In the 1750s Empress Maria Theresa of Austria installed her brother, Charles of Lorraine, in Brussels. Under the influence of the Enlightenment, his court attracted European artists and intellectuals, and Brussels became the most glamorous city in Europe. Industry also boomed with the construction of new roads and waterways. Brussels was transformed as the Place Royale and Parc de Bruxelles were laid out.

THE WORKERS' REVOLT

While the aristocracy and new middle-classes flourished, Brussels' workers were suffering. As the city's population grew there were more workers than jobs: wages plummeted and factory conditions were harsh.

When Joseph II succeeded Maria Theresa in 1780, he enforced a series of reforms including freedom of religion. However, he also cancelled the 500-year-old Charter of Liberties.

Influenced by the ideas of the French Revolution of 1789, the Belgians now demanded reform. Their rebellion was to result in an independent state.

French prince Philip of Anjou became Philip V of Spain, sparking the War of the Spanish Succession

595 French ombardment ` Brussels	**1713–14** Treaties of Utrecht and Rastadt mark beginning of Austrian period	*Ceramic Delft plate*	**1760s** Brussels is cultural and artistic centre of Europe	**1788** Joseph II cancels Charter of Liberties which results in liberal opposition
1700	**1725**		**1750**	**1775**
697 Willebroek Canal completed, nks Brussels to the ea via Antwerp	**1731** Beginning of the 17-year-long war against Austrian rule	**1748** Treaty of Aix-la-Chapelle restores the Netherlands to Austrian rule	**1753** New roads and canals constructed, which boosts industry in Brussels	**1789** Belgian revolt for independence fired by French Revolution

The Fight for Independence

BELGIUM WAS AGAIN occupied by foreign powers between 1794 and 1830. First, by the French Republican armies, then, after Napoleon's defeat at Waterloo in 1815, by the Dutch. French radical reforms included the abolition of the guild system and fairer taxation laws. Although French rule was unpopular, their liberal ideas were to influence the Belgian drive for independence. William I of Orange was appointed King of the Netherlands (which included Belgium) after 1815. His autocratic style, together with a series of anti-Catholic measures, bred discontent, especially in Brussels and among the French-speaking Walloons in the south. The south was also angered when William refused to introduce tariffs to protect their trade – it was the last straw. The uprising of 1830 began in Brussels and Léopold I became king of the newly independent nation.

King William I of Orange
William's rule as King of the Netherlands after 1815 was unpopular.

A Cultural Revolution in Brussels
French ideas not only influenced the revolution, but also Belgian culture. Under Napoleon the city walls were demolished and replaced by tree-lined boulevards.

Liberals joined workers already protesting in the square outside.

The Battle of Waterloo
Napoleon's influence came to an end after the battle of Waterloo on 18 June, 1815. A Prussian army came to Wellington's aid, and by 5:30pm Napoleon faced his final defeat. This led to Dutch rule over Belgium.

Agricultural workers
Harsh weather in the winter of 1829 caused hardship for both farmers and agricultural labourers, who also joined the protest.

The Revolution in Industry
Unemployment, low wages and factory closures during the early decades of the 19th century sparked unrest in 1830.

La Théâtre de la Monnaie
A patriotic song, L'Amour Sacré de la Patrie led the audience in the theatre on the night of 25 August, 1830, to join demonstrators outside.

BELGIAN REVOLUTION

High unemployment, poor wages and a bad winter in 1829 provoked protests about living and working conditions. The revolution was ignited by a patriotic and radical opera at the Brussels' opera house, and the largely liberal audience rushed out into the street, raising the Brabant flag. Ten thousand troops were sent by William to quash the rebels, but the Belgian soldiers deserted and the Dutch were finally driven out of Belgium.

The initial list of demands asked for administrative independence from the Dutch, and for freedom of press.

This symbolic illustration of the revolution shows both liberals and workers ready to die for their country.

King of Belgium, Léopold I
The crowning of German prince, Léopold of Saxe-Coburg, in Brussels in 1831 finally established Belgium's independence.

TIMELINE

1790 Republic of United Belgian States formed. Temporary end of Austrian rule	**1799** Emperor Napoleon rules France	*Wellington*	**1815** Battle of Waterloo. Napoleon defeated by army led by the Duke of Wellington	**1830** Rebellion begins at the Théâtre de la Monnaie in Brussels
1790	**1800**	**1810**	**1820**	**1830**
	1794 Brussels loses its importance to The Hague	**1815** Belgium, allied with Holland under the United Kingdom of the Netherlands, is ruled by William I of Orange. Brussels becomes second capital	**1831** State of Belgium formed on 21 July. Treaty of London grants independence	
1790 War between France and Austria			**1835** Continental railway built from Brussels to Mechelen	

THE FLEMISH AND THE WALLOONS: THE BELGIAN COMPROMISE

Linguistically and culturally, Belgium is divided. In the north, the Flemish have their roots in the Netherlands and Germany. In the south are the Walloons, the French-speaking Belgians, culturally connected to France. The "Linguistic Divide" of 1962 officially sanctioned this situation, dividing Belgium into Flemish- and French-speaking zones. The exception is Brussels, an officially bilingual city since the formation of Bruxelles-Capitale in 1963, and a national region by 1989 when it came to comprise 19 outlying districts. Conflicts still erupt over the issue, but the majority of Belgians seem to be in favour of a united country.

Bilingual road signs

CONSOLIDATING THE NEW STATE

During its early days as an independent nation, Brussels was a haven for free-thinkers, including the libertarian poet Baudelaire, and a refuge for exiles, such as Karl Marx and Victor Hugo. Belgium's industries also continued to expand throughout the 19th century.

By 1870 there were no less than four main railway stations in Brussels able to export goods all over Europe. However, the population of Brussels had almost doubled, resulting in poor-quality housing and working conditions. Towards the end of the reign of Belgium's second monarch, Léopold II (r.1865–1909), industrial unrest led to new legislation which improved conditions, and all men over 25 gained the right to vote in 1893. But the king's principal concern was his colonialist policy in the Congo in Central Africa.

THE GERMAN OCCUPATIONS

Albert I succeeded Léopold II as Belgium's new king. He encouraged the nation's artists and architects, and was a keen supporter of Art Nouveau *(see pp16–17)*. All of this ended as the country entered its bleakest period.

Despite its neutral status, Belgium was invaded by the German army in the summer of 1914. All of the country, except for the northern De Panne region, was occupied by the Germans. Some of the bloodiest battles of World War I were staged on Belgian soil. Flanders was the scene of brutal trench warfare, including the introduction of poison gas at Ypres *(see p107)*. Today, Belgium contains several vast graveyards, which include the resting places of the tens of thousands of soldiers who died on the Western Front.

The Belgians conducted resistance from their stronghold in De Panne, cutting telephone wires and destroying train tracks. The Germans responded by confiscating property, deporting Belgians to German labour camps

King Léopold III visits a goldmine in the Congo in Africa

TIMELINE

1840	1870	1900	1925
1847 Opening of Europe's first shopping mall, the Galéries St Hubert	**1871** Under Léopold II, the River Senne is reclaimed, and new districts built to cope with the growing city	**1898** Flemish language given equal status to French in law	**1914–18** World War I. Germany occupies Belgium
The Belgian Congo	**1884** Léopold II is granted sovereignty over the Congo	**1910** World Fair in Brussels promotes Belgium's industrial boom. Art Nouveau flourishes	**1929–31** Great Depression and reduction in foreign trade
1839 Treaty of London grants neutrality to Belgium			

German troops raising the German flag at the Royal Castle at Laeken, near Brussels

INTERNATIONAL STATUS

Belgium's history in the latter half of the 20th century has been dominated by the ongoing language debate between the Flemish and the French-speaking Walloons. From 1970 to 1994 the constitution was redrawn, creating a federal state with three separate regions; the Flemish north, the Walloon south and bilingual Brussels. While this smoothed over conflicts, cultural divisions run deep. Today, all parliamentary speeches have to be delivered in both French and Flemish.

Like most of Europe, Belgium went from economic boom in the 1960s to recession and retrenchment in the 1970s and 1980s. Throughout these decades Brussels' stature at the heart of Europe was consolidated. In 1958, the city became the headquarters for the European Economic Community (EEC), later the European Union. In 1967 NATO also moved to Brussels.

and murdering random hostages. Belgium remained under German occupation until the last day of the war, 11 November, 1918.

The 1919 Treaty of Versailles granted Belgium control of Eupen-Malmédy, the German-speaking area in the southeast. But by 1940 the country was again invaded by the Germans under Hitler. In May of that year, King Léopold III surrendered.

Despite national resistance to the Occupation, the King was interned at Laeken until 1944, after which he was moved to Germany until the end of the war. Rumours that Léopold had collaborated with the Nazis led to his abdication in 1951, in favour of his 20-year-old son, Baudouin.

THE EUROPEAN CAPITAL

Modern Brussels is a multilingual and cosmopolitan city at the forefront of Europe. This historically industrial city now prospers as a base for many large corporations such as ICI and Mitsubishi.

Despite its flourishing status, the city has had its fair share of disasters, including the deaths of 38 Italian football supporters at the Heysel stadium in 1985. Also, two tragic paedophile murder cases in the 1990s led many Belgians to protest against what they considered to be an incompetent police system. However, Brussels' future as a city of world importance seems certain as the centre of the EU's new European Monetary Union.

The European Parliament, Brussels

1939–45 World War II. Germany again occupies Belgium | **1951** Abdication of Léopold III; Baudouin I succeeds — *Baudouin I* | **1962** The Belgian Congo is granted independence — *European flag* | **1993** King Baudouin I dies; Albert II succeeds | **2002** The euro becomes legal tender

1950 | **1975** | **2000**

1944 Benelux Unions with Holland and Luxembourg formed | **1967** Brussels is new NATO HQ | **1985** Heysel Stadium disaster | **1989** Brussels is officially a bilingual city with 19 outlying districts | **2001** Crown Prince Philippe and Princess Mathilde have a daughter, Elisabeth

1934 Albert I is killed in a climbing accident

BRUSSELS
AREA BY AREA

THE LOWER TOWN

OST VISITS TO Brussels begin with a stroll around the Lower Town, the ancient heart of the city and home to its most famous area, the Grand Place. The original settlement of the city

Maison du Cygne, Grand Place

was here; most of the streets surrounding this huge market square date from as far back as the Middle Ages up to the 18th century. The architecture is an eclectic blend of Gothic, Baroque and Flemish Renaissance.

In and around the Place de Brouckère and the busy Boulevard Anspach are the more recent additions to the city's history. These appeared in the 19th century when the slums around the River Senne were cleared to make way for ornate constructions such as the financial centre, La Bourse, and Europe's first shopping arcade, Galéries St-Hubert. With its many restaurants and cafés, the Lower Town is also popular at night.

SIGHTS AT A GLANCE

Historic Buildings and Monuments
Hôtel de Ville see pp44–45 ②
Manneken Pis ③
La Bourse ⑦

Museums and Galleries
Musée du Costume et de la Dentelle ①
Bruxella 1238 ⑧
Centre Belge de la Bande Dessinée see pp50–51 ⑭
Maison de la Bellone ㉑

Churches
Notre-Dame de la Chapelle ④
Eglise St-Nicolas ⑨
Eglise St-Jean-Baptiste ⑲
Eglise Ste-Catherine ㉒

Shopping
Galeries St-Hubert ⑩
Rue Neuve ⑯

Streets and Squares
Rue des Bouchers ⑪
Place de Brouckère ⑱

Theatres
Théâtre Marionnettes de Toone ⑫
Théâtre Royal de la Monnaie ⑬
Théâtre Flamand ⑳

Cultural Centres
Le Botanique ⑮

Historic Districts
Quartier Marolles ⑤
Halles St-Géry ⑥

Hotels
Hôtel Métropole ⑰

KEY

🚊	Tram stop
Ⓜ	Metro station
🚌	Bus terminus
ℹ	Tourist information
P	Parking

GETTING AROUND

The area is well served by trams which encircle the old town. However, the tiny streets are often pedestrianized, and usually the quickest and most enjoyable means of transport for short distances is on foot. Otherwise metro stations are well placed.

0 metres	500
0 yards	500

◁ Detail of the façade of the Hôtel de Ville in the Grand Place – centre of the Lower Town

The Grand Place

THE GEOGRAPHICAL, HISTORICAL and commercial heart of the city, the Grand Place is the first port of call for most visitors to Brussels. This bustling cobblestone square remains the civic centre, centuries after its creation, and offers the finest surviving example in one area of Belgium's ornate 17th-century architecture. Open-air markets took place on or near this site as early as the 11th century, but by the end of the 14th century Brussels' town hall, the Hôtel de Ville, was built, and city traders added individual guildhouses in a medley of styles. In 1695, however, two days of cannon fire by the French destroyed all but the town hall and two guild façades. Trade guilds were urged to rebuild their halls to styles approved by the Town Council, producing the harmonious unity of Flemish Renaissance buildings here today.

The morning flower market in bloom in the Grand Place

The Maison du Roi was first built in 1536 but redesigned in 1873. Once the residence of ruling Spanish monarchs, it is now home to the Musée de la Ville, which includes 16th-century paintings, tapestries, and the 400 tiny outfits of Manneken Pis.

① NORTHEAST CORNER

② MAISON DU ROI

The Hôtel de Ville occupies the entire southwest side of the square. Still a functioning civic building, Brussels' town hall is the architectural masterpiece of the Grand Place (see pp44–5).

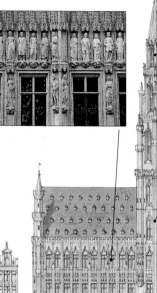

Ornate stone carvings

The spire was built by Jan van Ruysbroeck in 1449 and stands 96 m (315 ft) high; it is slightly crooked.

Everard 't Serclaes was murdered defending Brussels in the 14th century; touching the bronze arm of his statue is said to bring luck.

⑤ EVERARD 'T SERCLAES

Le Pigeon was home to Victor Hugo, the exiled French novelist who chose the house as his Belgian residence in 1852. Some of the most complimentary comments about Brussels emerged later from his pen.

LOCATOR MAP
See Brussels street finder, map 2

La Maison des Ducs de Brabant is a group of six guildhouses. Designed by the Controller of Public Works, Guillaume de Bruyn, the group is Neo-Classical with Flemish additions.

Stone busts of the ducal line along the façade gave this group of houses their name.

③ LE PIGEON

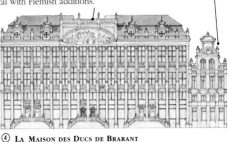

④ LA MAISON DES DUCS DE BRARANT

Le Renard was built in the 1690s as the guildhouse of the haberdashers by the Flemish architects Marc de Vos and van Nerum. Façade details show St Nicolas, patron saint of merchants, and cherubs playing with haberdashery ribbons.

Le Cornet displays Italianate Flemish style. This Boatmen's Guildhouse (1697) is most notable for its gable, which is constructed in the form of a 17th-century frigate's bow.

La Maison des Boulangers, also known as "Le Roi d'Espagne", was a showpiece built by the wealthy and powerful guild of bakers. The 1676 octagonal copper dome is topped by a dancing golden figure.

Le Roi d'Espagne now houses the Grand Place's finest bar with a view of the bustling square and its splendours above ground level. *(see p154)*. The gilt bust over the front entrance represents Saint Aubert, patron saint of bakers. A vast bust of Charles II of Spain sits in stone drapery on the third floor.

⑦ LE RENARD, LE CORNET AND LE ROI D'ESPAGNE

Musée du Costume et de la Dentelle ❶

Rue de Violette 6, 1000 BRU.
Map 2 D3. 📞 *(02) 512 7709.*
Ⓜ *Bourse, de Brouckère.*
🕐 *10am–12:30pm, 1:30–5pm Mon, Tue, Thu, Fri; 2–4:30pm Sat, Sun.* ⬤ *Wed.*
🖼 ♿ ✔ *on request.*

FOUND WITHIN two 18th-century gabled houses is the museum dedicated to one of Brussels' most successful exports, Belgian lace *(see pp20–21)*. The intricate skill employed by Belgian lace-makers has contributed a vital economic role in the city since the 12th century, and the

A wedding dress at the Musée du Costume et de la Dentelle

collection explains and displays the history of the craft. On the ground floor costumes from the 18th to the 20th centuries are displayed

on mannequins, demon-strating how lace has adorned fashions of every era. The second floor houses a collection of antique lace, carefully stored in drawers and demonstrating the various schools of lacemaking in France, Flanders and Italy.

Manneken Pis ❸

Rues de l'Etuve & du Chêne, 1000 BRU. **Map** 1 C3. 🚌 *34, 48.* 🚋 *23, 52, 55, 56, 81.* Ⓜ *Bourse.*

AN UNLIKELY ATTRACTION, this tiny statue of a young boy barely 30 cm (1 ft) high reliev-ing himself into a small pool is as much a part of Brussels as

Hôtel de Ville ❷

Stone gargoyle

THE IDEA OF having a town hall to reflect Brussels' growth as a major European trading centre had been under consideration since the end of the 13th century. It was not until 1401 that the first foundation stone was laid and the building was finally completed in 1459, emerging as the finest civic building in the country, a stature it still enjoys.

Jacques van Thienen was commissioned to design the left wing and belfry of the building, where he used orn-ate columns, sculptures, turrets and arcades. The tower and spire begun in 1449 by Jan van Ruysbroeck helped seal its reputation. In 1995, the 1455 statue of the city's patron saint, Michael, was restored and returned to its famous position on top of the tower in 1997, where it is used as a weather vane. Tours are available of the interior, which contains 15th-century tapestries and works of art.

A detail of the delicately carved façade with stone statues

137 statues adorn walls and many mullioned windows.

★ **Aldermen's Room**
Still in use today for the meetings of the aldermen and mayor of Brussels, this council chamber contains a series of 18th-century tapestries depicting the history of 6th-century King Clovis.

STAR SIGHTS

★ **Conference Room Council Chamber**

★ **Aldermen's Room**

the Trevi Fountain is part of Rome or Trafalgar Square's reclining lions are of London.

The original bronze statue by Jérôme Duquesnoy the Elder, was first placed on the site in 1619, the tongue-in-cheek design reflecting a genuine need for fresh drinking water in the area. Its popularity led, in 1770, to the addition of an ornate stone niche, giving more prominence to the small figure. Several attempts to steal the statue were made during the 18th century, notably by the French and then British armies in 1745, but it was the theft in

1817 by a former convict, Antoine Licas, which caused the most alarm – the robber smashed the bronze figure shortly after procuring it. A replica of the statue was cast the following year and returned to its revered site, and it is this copy that is seen today. In 1698 governor Maximilian-Emmanuel donated a suit of clothing with which to dress the statue. It was to be the beginning of a tradition that continues to this day. Visiting heads of state to Brussels donate miniature versions of their national costume for the boy, and now 400 outfits, including an Elvis suit, are housed in the Musée de la Ville *(see p42).*

(see p42).

THE LEGENDS OF MANNEKEN PIS

The inspiration for this famous statue remains unknown, but the mystery only lends itself to rumour and fable and increases the little boy's charm. One theory claims that in the 12th century the son of a duke was caught urinating against a tree in the midst of a battle and was thus commemorated in bronze as a symbol of the country's military courage.

The belfry was built by architect Jan van Ruysbroeck. A statue of St Michael tops the 96 m (315 ft) spire.

Aldermen's Room

The gabled roof, like much of the town hall, was fully restored in 1837, and cleaned in the 1990s.

Cabinets des Echevins

Ornamental stone balcony staircase

VISITORS' CHECKLIST

Grand Place, 1000 BRU. **Map** 2 D3. [(02) 279 4365. 🚍 29, 34, 47, 48, 60, 63, 65, 66, 71, 95, 96. 🚊 23, 52, 55, 56, 81. M *Bourse, Gare Centrale.* **Museum** ⬜ 10am–5pm Tue–Sun (to 1pm Sat & Sun). ⬤ *pub hols, election days.* 🖼 🎫 11:30am & 3:15pm Tue, 12:15pm Sun (call for details).

★ **Conference Room Council Chamber**
The most splendid of all the public rooms, ancient tapestries and gilt mirrors line the walls above an inlaid floor.

Wedding Room
A Neo-Gothic style dominates this civil marriage office, with its many ornate carved timbers, including ancient ebony and mahogany.

Notre-Dame de la Chapelle ❹

Place de la Chapelle 1, 1000 BRU.
Map 1 C4. 🄲 *(02) 513 5348.*
🚌 *34, 95, 96.* 🚊 *91, 92, 93, 94.*
🅼 *Porte de Namur.* 🄾 *5:30pm
Mon – Sat; Mass 6:30pm daily.*

IN 1134 KING Godefroid I
decided to build a chapel
outside the city walls. It quickly
became a market church, serving the many craftsmen living
nearby. In 1210 its popularity
was such that it was made a
parish church, but it became
really famous in 1250, when a
royal donation of five pieces
of the True Cross turned the
church into a pilgrimage site.
  Originally built in Romanesque style, the majority of the
church was destroyed by fire
in 1405. Rebuilding began in
1421 in a Gothic style typical
of 15th-century Brabant architecture, including gables decorated with finials and interior
capitals decorated with cabbage leaves at the base. The
Bishop of Cambrai consecrated
the new church in 1434.
  One of the most striking
features of the exterior are the
monstrously lifelike gargoyles
which peer down on the community – a representation of
evil outside the sacred interior.
The Baroque belltower was
added after the 1695 bombardment by the French *(see p32)*.
Another moving feature is the
carved stone memorial to the
16th-century Belgian artist
Pieter Brueghel the Elder
(see p14), who is buried here.

Rue Haute in the Quartier Marolles, with old-style shops and cafés

Quartier Marolles ❺

Map 1 C5. 🚌 *20, 48.* 🚊 *91.*
🅼 *Louise, Porte de Hal.*

KNOWN COLLOQUIALLY as "Les
Marolles", this quarter of
Brussels is traditionally working
class. Situated between the two
city walls, the area was home
to weavers and craftsmen.
Street names of the district,
such as Rue des Brodeurs
(Embroiderers' St) and Rue des
Charpentiers (Carpenters' St),
reflect its artisanal history.
  Today the area is best known
for its fine daily flea market,
held in the **Place du Jeu de
Balle**. The flea market has
been held on this site since
1640. Between 7am and 2pm,
with the biggest and best markets on Thursday and Sunday,
almost anything from junk to
pre-war collector's items can
be found among the stalls.
  Shopping of a different kind
is on offer on nearby Rue
Haute, an ancient Roman road.
A shopping district since the
19th century, it is still popular
with arty types with its specialist stores, interior and
antique shops. The street has
a long artistic history, too –
the elegant red-brick house at
No. 132 was home to Pieter
Brueghel the Elder and the
sculptor Auguste Rodin had a
studio at No. 224. No. 132
now houses the small **Maison
de Brueghel**, dedicated to the
16th-century painter.
  At the southern end of Rue
Haute is **Porte de Hal**, the
stone gateway of the now-
demolished outer city walls.
Looming over the Marolles is

the imposing Palais de Justice
(see p69), which has hilltop
views of the area west of the
city, including the 1958 Atomium *(see p83)* and the Basilique
Sacré-Coeur *(see p81)*.

🏛 Maison de Brueghel
Rue Haute 132, 1000 BRU.
🄾 *May–Sep: Wed & Sun pm
(groups with written permission only).*
🄲 *Oct–Apr.* 🈸

Busy restaurants and cafés
outside Halles St-Géry

Halles St-Géry ❻

Place St-Géry, 1000 BRU. **Map** 1 C2.
🚌 *47.* 🚊 *23, 52, 55, 56, 81.*
🅼 *de Brouckère.*

IN MANY WAYS, St-Géry can be
considered the birthplace of
the city. A chapel to Saint Géry
was built in the 6th century,
then in AD 977 a fortress took
over the site. A 16th-century
church followed and occu-
pied the location until the
18th century. In 1881 a

The cool, elegant interior of
Notre-Dame de la Chapelle

covered meat market was erected in Neo-Renaissance style. The glass and intricate ironwork was renovated in 1985, and the hall now serves as a cultural centre with an exhibition on local history.

La Bourse ❼

Palais de la Bourse, 1000 BRU.
Map 1 C2. *(02) 509 1211.*
47. *23, 52, 55, 56, 81.*
Bourse. *10am daily, by appointment.* *Sat & Sun, public hols.* *of the exchange market.*

BRUSSELS' Stock Exchange, La Bourse, is one of the city's most impressive buildings, dominating the square of the same name. Designed in Palladian style by architect Léon Suys, it was constructed from 1867 to 1873. Among the building's most notable features are the façade's ornate carvings. The great French sculptor, Auguste Rodin, is thought to have crafted the groups representing Africa and Asia, as well as four caryatids inside. Beneath the colonnade, two beautifully detailed winged figures representing Good and Evil were carved by sculptor Jacques de Haen.

Detail of a Rodin statue, La Bourse

Some areas of the building are open to the public, but a screen divides visitors from the frantic bidding and trading that takes place on weekdays on the trading floor.

Bruxella 1238 ❽

Rue de la Bourse, 1000 BRU. **Map** 1 C3. *(02) 279 4350.* *34, 48, 95, 96.* *23, 52, 55, 56, 81.*
Bourse, de Brouckère. *10:15am, 11:15am, 1:45pm, 2:30pm, 3:15pm, Wed.* *obligatory, starts from Maison du Roi, Grand Place.*

ONCE HOME to a church and 13th-century Franciscan convent, in the early 19th century this site became a Butter Market until the building of the Bourse commenced in 1867. In 1988 municipal roadworks began alongside the

Place de la Bourse. Medieval history must have been far from the minds of the city authorities but, in the course of working on the foundations for the Bourse, important relics were found, including 13th-century bones, pottery and the 1294 grave of Duke John I of Brabant. Visitors can now see these and other pieces of Burgundian history in a small museum built on the site.

Eglise St-Nicolas ❾

Rue au Beurre 1, 1000 BRU. **Map** 1 C2. *(02) 513 8022.* *34, 48, 95, 96.* *23, 52, 55, 56, 81.*
Bourse, de Brouckère. *10am–4pm daily, except during services.*

AT THE END of the 12th century a market church was constructed on this site, but, like much of the Lower Town, it was damaged in the 1695 French Bombardment. A cannon ball lodged itself directly into an interior pillar and the belltower finally collapsed in 1714. Many restoration projects were planned but none came to fruition until as late as 1956, when the west side of the building was given a new, Gothic-style façade. Named after St Nicolas, the patron saint of merchants, the church contains choir stalls dating from 1381 which display detailed medallions telling St Nicolas' story. Another interesting feature is the chapel, constructed at an angle, reputedly to avoid the flow of an old stream. Inside the church, works of art by Bernard van Orley and Peter Paul Rubens are well worth seeing.

The 19th-century domed glass roof of Galéries St-Hubert

Galeries St-Hubert ❿

Rue des Bouchers, 1000 BRU. **Map** 2 D2. *29, 38, 60, 63, 65, 66, 71.*
Gare Centrale.

SIXTEEN YEARS after ascending the throne as the first king of Belgium, Léopold I inaugurated the opening of these grand arcades in 1847.

St-Hubert has the distinction of being the first shopping arcade in Europe, and one of the most elegant. Designed in Neo-Renaissance style by Jean-Pierre Cluysenaar, the vaulted glass roof covers its three sections, Galerie du Roi, Galerie de la Reine and Galerie des Princes, which house a range of luxury shops. The ornate interior and expensive goods on sale soon turned the galleries into a fashionable meeting place for 19th-century society, including resident literati – Victor Hugo and Alexandre Dumas attended lectures here. The arcades remain a popular venue, with shops, a cinema, theatre, cafés and restaurants.

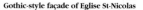

Gothic-style façade of Eglise St-Nicolas

Pavement displays of restaurants along Rue des Bouchers

Rue des Bouchers ⓫

Map 2 D2. 🚌 *29, 60, 63, 65, 66, 71.* 🚊 *23, 52, 55, 56, 81, 90.* Ⓜ *Gare Centrale, Bourse.*

Like many streets in this area of the city, Rue des Bouchers retains its medieval name, reminiscent of the time when this meandering, cobblestoned street was home to the butchers' trade. Aware of its historic importance and heeding the concerns of the public, the city council declared this area the Ilot Sacré (sacred islet) in 1960, forbidding any of the architectural façades to be altered or destroyed, and commanding those surviving to be restored. Hence Rue des Bouchers abounds with 17th-century stepped gables and decorated doorways.

Today, this pedestrianized thoroughfare is best known as the "belly of Brussels", a reference to its plethora of cafés and restaurants. Many cuisines are on offer here, including Chinese, Greek, Italian and Indian. But the most impressive sights during an evening stroll along the street are the lavish pavement displays of seafood, piled high on mounds of ice, all romantically lit by an amber glow from the streetlamps.

At the end of the street, at the Impasse de la Fidélité, is a recent acknowledgement of sexual equality. Erected in 1987, Jeanneke Pis is a coy, cheeky female version of her "brother", the more famous Manneken Pis *(see p45)*.

Théâtre Marionettes de Toone ⓬

Impasse Schuddeveld 6, off the Petite Rue des Bouchers, 1000 BRU. **Map** 2 D2. 🅒 *(02) 511 7137.* 🚌 *29, 34, 48, 60, 63, 65, 66, 71, 95, 96.* 🚊 *23, 52, 55, 56, 81.* Ⓜ *Bourse, Gare Centrale.* ⭘ *bar: noon–midnight daily; theatre: performance times (8:30pm Tue–Sat).* ⬤ *Sun, pub hols.* 📷 ✉ *on request, for tour reservations* 🅒 *(02) 217 2753.* **Museum** ⭘ *intervals.*

A popular pub by day, at night the top floor of this tavern is home to a puppet theatre. During the time of the Spanish Netherlands *(see p32)*, all theatres were closed because of the satirical performances by actors aimed at their Latin rulers. This began a fashion for puppet shows, the vicious dialogue more easily forgiveable from inanimate dolls. In 1830, Antoine Toone opened his own theatre and it has been run by

Harlequin puppet

the Toone family ever since; the owner is the seventh generation, Toone VII. The classics are enacted by these wooden marionettes in the local Bruxellois dialect, and occasionally in French, English, German or Dutch.

Théâtre Royal de la Monnaie ⓭

Place de la Monnaie, 1000 BRU. **Map** 2 D2. 🅒 *(02) 229 1211.* 🚌 *29, 60, 65, 66.* 🚊 *23, 52, 55, 56, 81.* Ⓜ *de Brouckère, Bourse.* ⭘ *performance times, Mon–Sat; box office: 11am–6pm Tue–Sat.* ⬤ *Sun, public hols.* 📷 ✉ *noon Sat only.*

This theatre was first built in 1817 on the site of a 15th-century mint (Hôtel des Monnaies) but, following a fire in 1855, only the front and pediment of the original Neo-Classical building remain. After the fire, the theatre was redesigned by the architect, Joseph Poelaert, also responsible for the imposing Palais de Justice *(see p69)*.

The original theatre was to make its historical mark before its destruction, however, when on 25 August, 1830, a performance of *La Muette de Portici* (*The Mute Girl*) began a national rebellion. As the tenor began to sing the nationalist *Amour Sacré de la Patrie* (*Sacred love of the homeland*), his words incited an already discontented city, fired by the libertarianism of the revolutions taking place in France, into revolt. Members of the audience ran out into the street in a rampage that developed into the

The original Neo-Classical façade of Théâtre Royal de la Monnaie

The 19th-century glasshouse of Le Botanique in summer

Similar to London's Oxford Street, but now pedestrianized, this is the heart of commercial shopping. It houses well-known international chainstores and shopping malls, such as **City 2**, which has shops, cafés and the media store Fnac all under one roof. Inno department store was designed by Horta *(see p78),* but after a fire in 1967 was entirely rebuilt.

To the east of Rue Neuve is Place des Martyrs, a peaceful square where a monument pays tribute to the 450 citizens killed during the 1830 uprising.

City 2
Rue Neuve 123, 1000 BRU. (02) 211 4060. 10am–7pm Mon–Thu & Sat, 10am–8pm Fri. Sun, public hols.

September Uprising *(see p34–5).* The theatre today remains the centre of Belgian performing arts; major renovations took place during the 1980s. The auditorium was raised 4 m (13 ft) to accommodate the elaborate stage designs, but the luxurious Louis XIV-style decor was carefully retained and blended with the new additions. The central dome is decorated with an allegory of Belgian arts.

Centre Belge de la Bande Dessinée 14

See pp50–51.

Le Botanique 15

Rue Royale 236, 1210 BRU. **Map** 2 E1. (02) 226 1211. 38, 58, 61. 92, 93, 94. Botanique. 10am–8pm daily.

IN 1797, THE CITY of Brussels created a botanical garden in the grounds of the Palais de Lorraine as a source of reference for botany students. The garden closed in 1826, and new gardens were relocated in Meise, 13 km (9 miles) from Brussels.

A grand glass-and-iron rotunda was designed at the centre of the gardens by the French architect Gineste. This

iron glasshouse still stands, as does much of the 19th-century statuary by Constantin Meunier *(see p15),* including depictions of the Four Seasons. The glasshouse is now home to the French Community Cultural Centre and offers plays, concerts and exhibitions.

Rue Neuve 16

Map 2 D2. 29, 60, 63, 65, 66, 71. 23, 52, 55, 56, 81, 90. Bourse, de Brouckère, Rogier.

BRUSSELS shoppers have been flocking to the busy Rue Neuve since the 19th century for its reasonably priced goods and well-located stores.

Rue Neuve, the longest pedestrian shopping street in the city

Hôtel Métropole 17

Place de Brouckère 31, 1000 BRU. **Map** 2 D2. (02) 217 2300. 29, 60, 65, 66. 23, 52, 55, 56, 81. de Brouckère.

THE AREA lying between Place Rogier and Place de Brouckère is known as the hotel district of Brussels, and one of the oldest and grandest hotels in the area is the Métropole.

In 1891 the Wielemans Brewery bought the building and commissioned the architect Alban Chambon to redesign the interior, with money no object. The result was a fine Art Nouveau hotel which opened for business in 1894 and has since accommodated numerous acclaimed visitors to the city, including actress Sarah Bernhardt. In 1911 the hotel was the location of the science conference Conseil Physique Solvay, attended by the great scientists Marie Curie and Albert Einstein.

The Hôtel Métropole continues to welcome guests from all walks of life, at surprisingly reasonable cost given its beauty, history and location. It is particularly popular for drinks in its café and heated pavement terrace, which are both open to non-residents to enjoy cocktails and cappuccinos in elegant surroundings.

Centre Belge de la Bande Dessinée ⓮

Affectionately known as *cébébédé*, the Museum of Comic Strip Art pays tribute to the Belgian passion for comic strips or *bandes dessinées* and to many world-famous comic strip artists from Belgium and abroad.

Arranged over three levels, the collection is housed in a Horta-designed Art Nouveau building. One of the most popular permanent exhibitions is a tour of the great comic strip heroes, from *Tintin* to *The Smurfs*, both of whose creators were Belgian. Other displays detail the stages of putting together a comic strip, from examples of initial ideas and pencil sketches through to final publication. The museum regularly holds major exhibitions featuring the work of famous cartoonists and studios, and also houses some 6,000 original plates, displayed in rotation, as well as a valuable archive of photographs and artifacts.

The famous Tintin rocket

Three Comic Figures
Tintin, Professor Calculus and Captain Haddock greet visitors on the 1st floor.

The Smurfs
These tiny blue characters first appeared in the Spirou *journal in 1958. By the 1980s they had their own TV show and hit records.*

A Suivre
Founded in 1978, A Suivre expanded the comic strip genre, and led to the new form of graphic novels: adult stories in cartoon form.

★ **Life-size Cartoon Sets**
A series of authentic comic scenes encourages children to enter the world of their favourite comic strip characters.

STAR SIGHTS

★ **Entrance Hall**

★ **Life-size Cartoon sets**

VISITORS' CHECKLIST

20 rue des Sables, 1000 BRU.
Map 2 E2. (02) 219 1980.
38, 58, 61. 56, 81, 90.
Botanique, Rogier, Centrale.
10am–6pm Tue–Sun. Mon,
1 Jan, 25 Dec.

★ **Entrance Hall**
This airy space designed by Victor Horta features stained glass and wrought-ironwork.

Comic Library
The museum library doubles as a study centre for both art students and enthusiasts of all ages. This unique collection includes a catalogue of hundreds of old comic strips, artists' equipment, biographies, comic novels and photographs.

A HORTA-DESIGNED BUILDING

This beautiful building was constructed between 1903 and 1906 to the design of the Belgian Art-Nouveau architect Victor Horta. Originally built as a fabric warehouse, and known as the Waucquez Building, it was one in a series of department stores and warehouses in the city designed by him. Saved from demolition by the French Cultural Commission of Brussels, in 1989 the building re-opened as a museum dedicated to the comic strip, Belgium's so-called Ninth Art *(see pp18–19)*. Carefully restored, the building has many classic features of Art Nouveau design, including the use of curves on structural iron pillars. In the impressive entrance hall is a display of Horta's architectural drawings for the building, and on the right the Brasserie Horta serves traditional Belgian dishes in a charming glass and marble Art Nouveau setting.

Cast-iron pillar

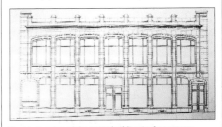

Horta's drawing of the CBBD building in the museum

THE CHANGING FACE OF HERGÉ'S TINTIN

Perhaps the best-known Belgian comic character, *Tintin* made his debut in a children's paper in 1929. He began life as a simple black line drawing, featuring the famous quiff, but no mouth. By 1930 Hergé began to produce *Tintin* in book-form and gave him both a mouth and a more complex character suggested by a greater range of facial expressions. By the 1940s *Tintin* was appearing in colour, alongside such new characters as Captain Haddock, the Thompsons and Professor Calculus.

Nineteenth-century building in Place de Brouckère

Place de Brouckère ⑱

Map 2 D2. 🚌 29, 60, 63, 65, 66, 71. 🚋 23, 52, 55, 56, 81, 90. Ⓜ de Brouckère, Bourse.

Iᴺ 1872 ᴀ ᴅᴇsɪɢɴ competition was held to encourage the construction of buildings of architectural interest in de Brouckère. Twenty winning applicants were selected and commissioned to give prominence to this Brussels junction. The Parisian contractor Jean-Baptiste Mosnier was responsible for taking the original plans through to completion.

The French influence of Mosnier and his workers is still evident on the square. Many of the buildings were erected in stone, common in France at the end of the 19th century, whereas brickwork was more usual in Brussels. Several original façades survive today, including the 1874 Hôtel Continental by Eugene Carpentier.

One of the great hotels of Brussels, the Hôtel Métropole (*see p49*) is situated on the south side of the square. The 1900–10 interior is splendidly gilded and can be seen either through the doorway or by pretending to be a guest. Café Métropole next door is, however, open to the public; here the lavishly ornate surroundings date from around 1890.

In the 20th century, architectural style was still at a premium in the district. In 1933 a Neo-Classical cinema was erected with an impressive Art Deco interior. During the 1960s, two imposing glass buildings blended the contemporary with the classical. Today, the varied historic architecture of Place de Brouckère enhances one of the city's busiest squares, despite recent additions of advertising hoardings.

Eglise St-Jean-Baptiste-au-Béguinage ⑲

Place du Béguinage, 1000 BRU. **Map** 1 C1. 🄲 (02) 217 8742. 🚌 47. Ⓜ Ste-Cathérine. ◻ 9am–5pm Tue–Sat, 9:30am–noon Sun. ⬤ Mon. ♿

Tʜɪs sᴛᴏɴᴇ-ᴄʟᴀᴅ church was consecrated in 1676 around the long-standing and largest béguine community in the country, established in 1250. Fields and orchards around the site contained cottages and houses for up to 1,200 béguine women, members of a lay religious order who took up charitable work and enclosed living after widowhood or failed marriages. In medieval times the béguines ran a laundry, hospital and windmill for the people of the city. Still a popular place of worship, the church is also notable for its Flemish Baroque details from the 17th century, especially the onion-shaped turrets and ornamental walls. The nave is also Baroque, decorated with ornate winged cherubs, angels and scrolls. The confessionals are carved with allegorical figures and saints. A more unusual feature are the aisles, which have been widened to allow more light in. In the apse is a statue of St John the Baptist. The 1757 pulpit is a fine example of Baroque woodcarving, showing St Dominic and a heretic.

Théâtre Flamand ⑳

Rue de Laeken 146, 1000 BRU. **Map** 1 C1. 🚌 47. 🚋 18. Ⓜ Yser. ⬤ for renovations. 🆆 www.kvs.be

Tʜᴇ ғᴏʀᴍᴇʀ Qᴜᴀʏ area of Brussels, on the banks of the old River Senne, still survives as a reminder that the city was once a thriving port. In 1882, architect Jean Baes was commissioned to enlarge one of the former waterfront warehouses and then turn it into a theatre but was instructed to retain the original 1780 façade. Baes solved this problem ingeniously by placing the façade directly behind the frontage of the new building. The

The ornate façade of Eglise St-Jean-Baptiste-au-Béguinage

Théâtre Flamand has other interesting design features peculiar to the late 19th century. The four exterior metal terraces and a staircase leading to the ground were built for audience evacuation in the event of fire. The theatre is now undergoing restoration, due to finish in 2004. For the duration, the resident Flemish theatre company are staging productions nearby in rue de Launoy (call 02 412 7040).

The 19th-century interior staircase of Théâtre Flamand

Maison de la Bellone 𝟚𝟙

Rue de Flandre 46, 1000 BRU.
Map 1 C2. ☎ (02) 513 3333. 🚌 63.
Ⓜ Ste-Catherine. ◯ 10am–6pm
Tue–Fri (exhibition centre open noon–6pm). ⬤ Sat–Mon, Jul.

THIS 17TH-CENTURY aristocratic residence, now shielded under a glass roof and no longer visible from the street, was once the headquarters of the Ommegang procession (see p25). The original façade is notable for its decoration. There is a statue of Bellona (goddess of war), after whom the house is named, above the central arch, and the window ledges have medallions of Roman emperors.

Stonework on the Maison de la Bellone

Today the house, its exhibition centre and once-private theatre are open for dance and cinema shows, and temporary exhibitions of art and furniture.

THE BÉGUINE MOVEMENT

The béguine lifestyle swept across Western Europe from the 12th century, and Brussels once had a community of over 1,200 béguine women. The religious order is believed to have begun among widows of the Crusaders, who resorted to a pious life of sisterhood on the death of their husbands. The women were lay nuns, who opted for a secluded existence devoted to charitable deeds, but not bound by strict religious vows. Most béguine convents disappeared during the Protestant Reformation in

Béguine lay nun at prayer in a Brussels béguinage

much of Europe during the 16th century, but begijnhofs (béguinages) continued to thrive in Flanders. The grounds generally consisted of a church, a courtyard, communal rooms, homes for the women and extra rooms for work. The movement dissolved as female emancipation spread during the early 1800s, although 20 convents remain, including those in Bruges (see p117) and Ghent.

Eglise Ste-Catherine 𝟚𝟚

Place Ste-Catherine 50, 1000 BRU.
Map 1 C2. ☎ (02) 513 3481. 🚌 47. 🚋 23, 52, 55, 56, 81, 90.
Ⓜ Ste-Catherine, De Brouckère. ◯ 8:30am–5:30pm daily. ♿ on request.

SADLY, THE ONLY remnant of the first church here, built in the 15th century, is its Baroque tower, added in 1629. Inspired by the Eglise St-Eustache in Paris, the present church was redesigned in 1854–59 by Joseph Poelaert in a variety of styles. Notable features of the interior include a 14th-century statue of the Black Madonna and a portrait of St Catherine herself. A typically Flemish pulpit was installed at some stage; it may have come from the parish of Mechelen. Two impressive tombs were carved by Gilles-Lambert Godecharle. To the east of the church is the Tour Noire (Black Tower), a surviving remnant of the 12th-century stone city walls.

Although this area has been dedicated to the saint since the 13th century, the square

of Place Ste-Catherine was only laid in front of this large church after the basin once here was filled in. Paved in 1870, the square contrasts the peacefulness of the religious building with today's vigorous trade in good fish restaurants.

The central square was once the city's main fish market, and this is still the best place to indulge in a dish or two of Brussels' famous seafood, but prices are generally high. Flanking the square, Quai aux Briques and Quai au Bois à Brûler (Brick Quay and Timber Quay, named after their industrial past), contain lively parades of fish restaurants.

Eglise Ste-Catherine showing the spacious Victorian interior

THE UPPER TOWN

BRUSSELS' UPPER TOWN is separated from the lower part of the city by an escarpment that runs roughly north-south from the far end of Rue Royale to the Palais de Justice. Modern developments are now scattered across the whole city, and the difference between the two areas is less distinct than in the past; traditionally the Lower Town was mainly Flemish-speaking and a bustling centre

Peter Pan statue in Palais d'Egmont

for trade, while the Upper Town was home to French-speaking aristocrats and royalty. Today the Upper Town is known for its beautiful Gothic churches, modern architecture and fine museums. The late 18th-century elegance of the Parc de Bruxelles and Place Royale is complemented by Emperor Leopold II's sweeping 19th-century boulevards that connect the Parc du Cinquantenaire to the city centre.

SIGHTS AT A GLANCE

Historic Streets and Buildings
Hôtel Ravenstein **6**
Palais de Charles
  de Lorraine **8**
Palais d'Egmont **14**
Palais de Justice **15**
Palais Royal pp58–9 **2**
Parliament Quarter **22**
Place du Grand Sablon **11**
Place du Petit Sablon **13**
Place Royale **4**
Square Ambiorix **19**

Parks and Gardens
*Parc du Cinquantenaire
  pp74–5* **25**
Parc Léopold **24**

Museums and Galleries
Institut Royal des Sciences
  Naturelles **23**
Musée Charlier **9**
Musée de la Dynastie **1**
Musée Instrumental **7**
Musée Wiertz **21**
*Musées Royaux des Beaux-
  Arts pp62–7* **10**

Churches and Cathedrals
*Cathédrale Sts Michel et Gudule
  pp70–71* **17**

Chapelle de la Madeleine **18**
Eglise St-Jacques-sur-
  Coudenberg **3**
Notre-Dame du Sablon **12**

Theatres and Concert Halls
Palais des Beaux-Arts **5**

Modern Architecture
Quartier Européen **20**

Shopping
Galérie Bortier **16**

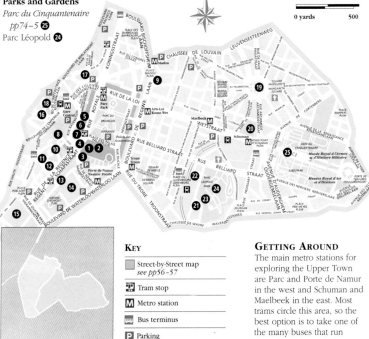

0 metres 500
0 yards 500

KEY

Street-by-Street map
see pp56–57

🚊 Tram stop

Ⓜ Metro station

🚌 Bus terminus

🅿 Parking

GETTING AROUND
The main metro stations for exploring the Upper Town are Parc and Porte de Namur in the west and Schuman and Maelbeek in the east. Most trams circle this area, so the best option is to take one of the many buses that run through the Upper Town.

◁ **Detail of a façade in a terrace of Art Nouveau houses in Square Ambiorix**

Street-by-Street: Quartier Royal

THE QUARTIER ROYAL has traditionally been home to Brussels' nobility and rulers. Chosen because the air was purer on the hill than it was in the Lower Town, the area once known as Coudenberg Hill was occupied by the 15th-century Coudenberg Palace, home to the Dukes of Brabant and Renaissance rulers. In 1731, the palace was destroyed in just six hours by a fire. Slowly rebuilt during the 18th and 19th centuries, four new palaces and much of the park were designed in Neo-Classical style chosen by Charles de Lorraine *(see p33).* Today the Royal Quarter presents a peaceful elegance, with some of Europe's finest 18th-century buildings framing the tree-lined paths and fountains of Parc de Bruxelles.

Fountain in park

Rue Royale runs for 2 km (1 mile) from the Quartier Royal to Jardin Botanique. In contrast to the 18th-century Neo-Classicism of its beginnings, along its route many fine examples of Victorian and Art Nouveau architecture stand out.

Eglise St-Jacques-sur-Coudenberg
One of Brussels' prettiest churches, St-Jacques' 18th-century façade was modelled exactly on a classical temple. The barrel-vaulted nave and half-domed apse are sprinkled with floral plasterwork and contain several fine Neo-Classical paintings ❸

★ **Place Royale**
In the centre of this attractive, symmetrical square is a statue of Godefroi of Bouillon, a Brabant soldier who fought the first Catholic Crusades and died in Palestine ❹

RUE ROYALE

PLACE ROYALE

KEY

– – – Suggested route

STAR SIGHTS

★ **Palais Royal**

★ **Parc de Bruxelles**

★ **Place Royale**

Place des Palais divides Palais Royal and the park. In French, "Palais" refers to any large stately building, and does not have royal connotations.

0 metres   100

0 yards   100

★ Parc de Bruxelles
On the site of medieval hunting grounds once used by the dukes of Brabant, the park was redesigned in the 1770s with fountains, statues and tree-lined walks.

LOCATOR MAP
See Streetfinder Map 2

RUE DE LA LOI

RUE DUCALE

CE DES PALAIS

Palais de la Nation
Designed by French architect Barnabé Guimard, the Palais de la Nation was built in 1783 and restored in 1883 after a fire. Since 1831, it has been the home of both chambers of the Belgian Parliament.

★ Palais Royal
The largest of the palaces, the low-rise Palais Royal is the official home of the Belgian monarch and family. A flag flies to indicate when the king is in the country ❷

Palais des Académies
Built in 1823 as the residence of the Crown Prince, this has been the private premises of the Académie Royale de Belgique since 1876.

Musée de la Dynastie ❶

Place des Palais 7, 1000 BRU.
Map 2 E4. 📞 *(02) 511 5578.*
🚌 *20, 34, 38, 54, 60, 71, 95, 96.*
🚊 *92, 93, 94.* Ⓜ *Trone, Parc.*
🕐 *10am–5pm Tue–Sun.* ● *Mon,*
1 Jan, 21 Jul, 25 Dec.

THE MUSÉE de la Dynastie contains a broad collection of paintings, documents and other royal memorabilia charting the history of the Belgian monarchy from independence in 1830 to the present day. Since 1992 it has been housed in the former Hôtel Bellevue, an 18th-century Neo-Classical building lying adjacent to the Palais Royal, which was annexed to the palace in 1902. A permanent exhibition in honour of the late, immensely popular, King Baudouin (r.1951–1993) was added in

The Neo-Classical façade of the Musée de la Dynastie

1998. As well as official portraits, informal photographs are on display which give a fascinating insight into the private lives of the Belgian royal family. The collection is displayed in chronological order in a series of rooms with a bust of the sovereign to which it is devoted at the entrance to each one.

Eglise St-Jacques-sur-Coudenberg ❸

Place Royale, 1000 BRU. **Map** 2 E4. 📞 *(02) 511 7836.* 🚌 *95, 96.* 🚊 *92, 93, 94.* Ⓜ *Trone, Parc.* 🕐 *3–5pm Mon, 10am–6pm Tue–Sat, 9am–noon Sun.*

THE PRETTIEST building in the Place Royale, St-Jacques-sur-Coudenberg is the latest in a series of churches to have occupied this site. There has been a chapel here since the 12th century, when one was built to serve the dukes of Brabant. On construction of the Coudenberg Palace in the 13th century, it became the ducal chapel. The chapel suffered over the years: it was ransacked in 1579 during conflict between Catholics and Protestants, and was so badly damaged in the fire of 1731 that destroyed the Coudenberg Palace that it

Palais Royal ❷

THE PALAIS ROYAL is the most important of the palaces around the Parc de Bruxelles. An official residence of the Belgian monarchy, construction of the modern palace began in the 1820s on the site of the old Coudenberg Palace. Work continued under Léopold II (r.1865–1909), when much of the exterior was completed. Throughout the 20th century the palace underwent interior improvements and restoration of its older sections. It is open only from July to September, but this is a fine opportunity to tour Belgium's lavish state reception rooms.

The Field Marshal's Room contains a portrait of the first Belgian king, Léopold I, after Winterhalter's 1843 original.

STAR SIGHTS

★ **Throne Room**

★ **Hall of Mirrors**

★ **Throne Room**
One of Brussels' original state-rooms, the huge throne room is decorated in grand style, with huge pilastered columns, 11 large candelabras and 28 wall-mounted chandeliers.

The 19th-century cupola of Eglise St-Jacques-sur-Coudenberg

was demolished soon after. The present church was built on the same site in the Neo-Classical style of the rest of the area and was consecrated in 1787, although it served several years as a Temple of Reason and Law during the French Revolution, returning to the Catholic Church in 1802. The cupola was completed in 1849. The interior is simple and elegant, with two large paintings by Jan Portaels on either side of the transept, and a royal pew.

Place Royale ❹

Map 2 E4. 38, 60, 71, 95, 96. 92, 93, 94. Ⓜ Trone, Parc.

THE INFLUENCE of Charles de Lorraine is still keenly felt in the Place Royale. As Governor of Brussels from 1749 to 1780 he redeveloped the site once occupied by the Coudenberg Palace along Neo-Classical lines reminiscent of Vienna, a city he greatly admired.

When the area was being worked on, the ruins of the burnt-down palace were demolished and the entire site was rebuilt as two squares.

However, in 1995, excavation work uncovered ruins of the 15th-century Aula Magna, the Great Hall of the former palace. This was part of the extension of the palace started under the dukes of Brabant in the early 13th century and then developed under the rule of the dukes of Burgundy, in particular Philip the Good. It was in this room that the Hapsburg emperor Charles V abdicated in favour of his son, Philip II. The ruins can now be seen in a corner of the Place Royale.

Although criss-crossed by tramlines and traffic, the Place Royale maintains a feeling of dignity with its tall, elegant, cream buildings symmetrically set around a cobbled square. Visitors can tour the area on foot, admiring the stateliness of Brussels' parade of exceptional Neo-Classical buildings.

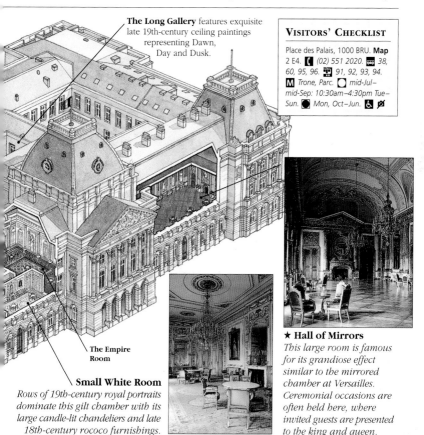

The Long Gallery features exquisite late 19th-century ceiling paintings representing Dawn, Day and Dusk.

VISITORS' CHECKLIST

Place des Palais, 1000 BRU. **Map** 2 E4. 【 (02) 551 2020. 38, 60, 95, 96. 91, 92, 93, 94. Ⓜ Trone, Parc. ◻ mid-Jul–mid-Sep: 10:30am–4:30pm Tue–Sun. ● Mon, Oct–Jun. ♿ 🚫

The Empire Room

Small White Room
Rows of 19th-century royal portraits dominate this gilt chamber with its large candle-lit chandeliers and late 18th-century rococo furnishings.

★ Hall of Mirrors
This large room is famous for its grandiose effect similar to the mirrored chamber at Versailles. Ceremonial occasions are often held here, where invited guests are presented to the king and queen.

The Victor Horta-designed façade of the Palais des Beaux-Arts

Palais des Beaux-Arts **❺**

Rue Ravenstein 23, 1000 BRU.
Map 2 E3. **[** (02) 507 8200,
511 3433. **🚌** 20, 71, 60, 95, 96.
🚋 92, 93, 94. **Ⓜ** Centrale.
◯ 11am – 7pm daily. **●** public hols.
◙ ▯

THE PALAIS des Beaux-Arts
owes its existence to Henri
Le Boeuf, a music-loving finan-
cier who gave his name to the
main auditorium. In 1922 he
commissioned the architect
Victor Horta (see p78) to
design a cultural centre which
would house concert halls
and exhibition areas open
to all visitors and embracing
the artistic fields of music,
theatre, cinema and art. The
construction took seven years
as the building was on a
slope but could not be so tall
as to block the view of the
town from the Palais Royal:
Horta had to revise his plans
six times. The centre was the
first of its kind in Europe.

The complex has a fine
reputation and has played a
key role in the cultural life of
Brussels for over 70 years. It
is the focus for the city's music
and dance, and is home to
the Belgian National Orchestra.

The complex also houses the
Musée du Cinema, set up in
1962, with its fine archive and
exhibition of old cameras and
lenses. Its main activity is the
daily screening of classic films.

🏛 Musée du Cinema

Rue Baron Horta 9, 1000 BRU.
[(02) 507 8370. **◯** 5:30 – 10:30pm
daily. **▨**

Hôtel Ravenstein **❻**

Rue Ravenstein 3, 1000 BRU.
Map 2 E3. **🚌** 20, 95, 96. **🚋** 92,
93, 94. **Ⓜ** Parc. **◯** restaurant only.

OVER THE centuries the
Hôtel Ravenstein has
been the home of patrician
families, soldiers and court
officials, and, for the past 100
years, the Royal Society of
Engineers. The building was
designed at the end of
the 15th century for
Adolphe and Philip
Cleves-Ravenstein;
in 1515 it became
the birthplace of
Anne of Cleves.
Consisting of two
parts, joined by
gardens and
stables, it is the last
remaining example
of a Burgundian-
style manor house. The Hôtel
Ravenstein was acquired by
the town in 1896 and used to
store artworks. Sadly, it fell
into disrepair and renovation

The pretty open courtyard of the
Hôtel Ravenstein

took place in 1934. One half is
now a Belgian restaurant, the
other the Royal Society of
Engineers' private HQ. However, the pretty, original inner
courtyard which links the two
elegant gabled red-brick
buildings can still be seen.

Musée Instrumental **❼**

Rue Montagne de la Cour 2, 1000
BRU. **Map** 2 E4. **[** (02) 545 0130.
◯ 9:30am–5pm Tue–Fri (to 8pm
Thu), 10am–5pm Sat & Sun. **🚌** 20,
95, 96. **🚋** 92, 93, 94. **Ⓜ** Parc. **▨**
◙ ▯ ▯ �&

ONCE A department store, the
building known as Old
England is a striking showpiece
of Art Nouveau architecture
located by the Place Royale.

Architect Paul Saintenoy
gave full rein to his imagination when he designed these
shop premises for the Old
England company in 1899.
The façade is made entirely of
glass and elaborate
wrought iron. There is
a domed gazebo on
the roof, and a turret
to one side.
Surprisingly, it was
only in the 1990s
that a listed
buildings policy
was adopted in
Brussels, which
has secured treas-
ures such as this.
Much preservation work is
now taking place. Old England
is one of the buildings that
has undergone extensive
renovation work, having been
used until recently as a temporary exhibition space. The
building is now home to the
Musée Instrumental, moved
from the Sablon. Meanwhile,
the Old England company is
still flourishing, with its premises now at No. 419 in the
fashionable Avenue Louise.

The collection of the Musée
Instrumental began in the 19th
century when the state bought
80 ancient and exotic instruments. It was doubled in 1876
when King Léopold II don-
ated a gift of 97 Indian musical
instruments presented to him
by a maharajah. A museum
displaying all of these artifacts

Old England, home to
the Musée Instrumental

opened in 1877, and by 1924 the museum boasted 3,300 pieces and was recognized as a leader in its field. Today the collection contains more than 6,000 items and includes many fine examples of wind, string and keyboard instruments from medieval times to the present. Chief attractions include a collection of proto-type instruments by Adolphe Sax, the Belgian inventor of the saxophone, mini violins favoured by street musicians and a faithful reproduction of a violin maker's studio. In June 2000 the museum moved to its specially designed home in the newly renovated Old England building, where there is much more room in which to display this world-class collection.

Antique violin

Palais de Charles de Lorraine ➑

Place du Musée 1, 1000 BRU. **Map** 2 D4. ☎ (02) 519 5371. 🚌 20, 95, 96. 🚋 92, 93, 94. Ⓜ Parc. ◑ 1–5pm Mon–Tue, Thu–Fri. ● pub hols, last two weeks in Aug, 25 Dec–1 Jan. ☑ for details ☎ (02) 519 5786.

H IDDEN BEHIND this Neo-Classical façade are the few rooms that remain of the palace of Charles de Lorraine,

The state room with marble floor at the Palais de Charles de Lorraine

Governor of Brussels during the mid-18th century. He was a keen patron of the arts, and the young Mozart is believed to have performed here. Few original features remain, as the palace was ransacked by marauding French troops in 1794. Extensive renovations were recently completed. The bas-reliefs at the top of the stairway, representing air, earth, fire and water, reflect Charles de Lorraine's keen interest in alchemy. Most spectacular of all the original features is the 28-point star set in the floor of the circular drawing room. Each of the points is made of a different Belgian marble, a much sought-after material which was used in the construction of Versailles, and St Peter's Basilica in Rome.

Musée Charlier ➒

Avenue des Arts 16, 1210 BRU. **Map** 2 F2. ☎ (02) 218 5382, 220 2690. 🚌 23, 63, 65, 66. Ⓜ Madou, Arts-Loi. ◑ 1:30–5pm Mon–Fri (by appointment). ● Sat–Sun. 🖼 ☑

T HIS QUIET MUSEUM was once the home of Henri van Cutsem, a wealthy collector and patron of the arts. In 1890 he asked the young architect Victor Horta to re-design his house as an exhibition space for his extensive collections. Van Cutsem died, and his friend, the sculptor Charlier, installed his own art collection in the house. Charlier commissioned Horta to build another museum, at Tournai in southern Belgium, to house van Cutsem's collection. On Charlier's death in 1925 the house and contents were left to the city as a museum.

The Musée Charlier opened in 1928. It contains paintings by a number of different artists, including portraits by Antoine Wiertz (see p72) and early landscapes by James Ensor. The collection also includes sculptures by Charlier, and the ground floor contains collections of glassware, porcelain, chinoiserie and silverware. Of special note are the tapestries, some from the Paris studios of Aubusson, on the staircases and the first floor, and the displays of Louis XV- and Louis XVI-style furniture on the first and second floors.

Musée Charlier, home to one of Belgium's finest individual collections of art and furnishings

Musées Royaux des Beaux-Arts: Musée d'art ancien ❿

JOINTLY KNOWN AS the Musées Royaux des Beaux-Arts, The Musée d'art ancien and Musée d'art moderne are Brussels' premier art museums. The museums' buildings, adjacent to the Place Royale, are home to exhibits from two eras, *ancien* (15th–18th century) and *moderne* (19th century–present day). Housed in a Neo-Classical building designed by Alphonse Balat between 1874 and 1880, the Musée d'art ancien is the larger of the two sections.

Hercules Sculpture

The art collection dates back to the 18th century when it consisted of the few valuable works left behind by the French Republican army, which had stolen many of Brussels' treasures and taken them back to Paris. This small collection was initially exhibited in the Palais de Charles de Lorraine (*see p61*), but donations, patronage and the recovery of some pieces from the French, enlarged the collection. The present gallery opened in 1887. The Musée d'art ancien is best known for the finest collection of Flemish art in the world, and many Old Masters, including van Dyck and Rubens, are also well represented.

Façade of museum
Corinthian columns and busts of Flemish painters adorn the entrance.

★ The Assumption of the Virgin (*c.1610*)
Pieter Paul Rubens (1577–1640) was the leading exponent of Baroque art in Europe, combining Flemish precision with Italian flair. Here, Rubens suppresses background colours to emphasize the Virgin's blue robes.

Ground level

Interior of the Main Hall
Founded by Napoleon in 1801 to relieve the packed Louvre in Paris, these are the oldest museums in Belgium. More than 2,500 works are exhibited in the museums' buildings.

Entrance

Entrance to Musée d'art moderne

Lower level

STAR EXHIBITS

★ **The Assumption of the Virgin by Rubens**

★ **The Annunciation by the Master of Flémalle**

Upper level

VISITORS' CHECKLIST

Rue de la Régence 3, 1000 BRU.
Map 2 D4. *(02) 508 3211.*
25, 95, 96. 91, 92, 93, 94.
M *Gare Centrale.* 10am–
noon, 1–5pm Tue–Sun. Mon,
public hols.
W www.fine-arts-museum.be

The Census at Bethlehem *(1610)*
*Pieter Brueghel the Younger (c.1564–1638) produced
a version of this subject some 40 years after the original
by his father. Shown together, the two works illustrate
the development of Flemish painting in its peak period.*

**Madonna with Saint Anne
and a Franciscan donor** *(1470)*
*Hugo van der Goes (c.1440–82) was
commissioned to paint this symbolic
work for the monk shown on the
right for his personal devotional use.*

★ **The Annunciation** *(c.1406–7)*
*The Master of Flémalle (c.1378–1444) sets the
holy scene of the Archangel Gabriel announcing the impending birth of the Messiah in a
homely, contemporary setting, with daily objects
an apparent contrast to the momentous event.*

KEY

☐ 15th–16th century (blue route)

☐ 17th–18th century (brown route)

☐ Sculpture gallery

☐ Temporary exhibitions

☐ Non-exhibition space

GALLERY GUIDE

*In the gallery different coloured signs are
used to lead the visitor through different
eras of art (see pp66–7). On the first floor,
in rooms 10 to 34, the blue route covers the
15th and 16th centuries. The brown route is
in rooms 50 to 62 and covers the 17th and
18th centuries. The sculpture gallery is
housed on the lower ground floor.*

Musées Royaux des Beaux-Arts: Musée d'art moderne

O PENED IN 1984, the Musée d'art moderne is situated in a unique setting: eight levels of the building are underground, but a lightwell allows many of the works to be seen by natural daylight filtering in from the Place du Musée. The top three levels above ground are temporary exhibition space. As is the case for the Musee d'art ancien, the collection of works is wide and varied, displayed in chronological order. Many well-known 20th-century artists from 1900 to the present day are included, but the most popular paintings are those of the Belgian Surrealists.

Skeletons Fighting over a Pickled Herring (1891)
Moving from a naturalistic style, James Ensor became the leading light of the Belgian Surrealist artists. His uneasy preoccupation with death and the macabre is shown in this witty, disturbing oil.

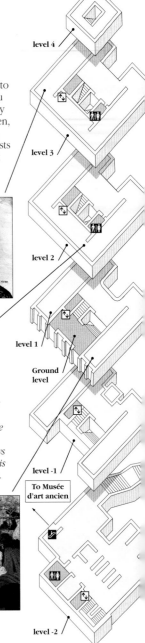

View of London (1917)
Heavily influenced by Monet's work, Emile Claus developed a variant of Impressionism with fellow artists called "Luminism". The Belgian Claus was a refugee to London, and his Luminist interest in light effects is shown through the damp fog of this London twilight. The painting shows a clarity of definition that is almost realist in technique.

The Orange Market at Blidah (1898)
Henri Evenepoel is known for his use of raw colour and tone; here, the market bustle is secondary to the arrangement of the shades in the traders' bright robes.

STAR EXHIBITS

★ **Woman in a Blue Dress by Rik Wouters**

★ **The Domain of Arnheim by René Magritte**

GALLERY GUIDE

The yellow route, in rooms 69–91, is dedicated to the 19th century. Level -4 covers work from the first quarter of the 20th century and its various art movements, such as Fauvism and Cubism. Level -5 contains the Surrealist collection. Level -6 includes the Magritte exhibition, the Jeune Peinture Belge and COBRA schools. Levels -7 and -8 exhibit works from the 1960s to the present day. Levels 2, 3 and 4 contain temporary exhibitions that are changed regularly.

Composition (1921)
(detail shown)
Two stylized human
figures form the centre
of this work by Belgian
painter Pierre-Louis
Flouquet, combining
Futurism and Cubism
in a "plastic" style.

★ **Woman in a Blue
Dress in front of a
Mirror** (1914)
Rik Wouters was a
Fauvist painter
whose fascination
with colour led him
to innovative spatula
painting techniques,
as seen here.

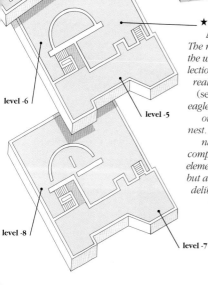

level -4

level -3

**Draped Woman on
Steps** (1957–8)
The prolific British
artist Henry Moore
is the world's most
exhibited sculptor.
This piece reveals
his characteristic
fluidity of line,
together with
tension in
the waiting
figure.

level -6

level -5

★ **The Domain of
Arnheim** (1962)
The museum contains
the world's largest col-
lection of work by sur-
realist René Magritte
(see p15). Here, an
eagle-mountain rears
over a small bird's
nest. The inexplicable
nature of the eerie
composition draws its
elements into question,
but answers are made
deliberately difficult.

level -8

level -7

KEY

☐	19th century (yellow route)
☐	20th century (green route)
▨	Non-exhibition space

Exploring the Musées Royaux des Beaux-Arts

SIX CENTURIES OF ART, both Belgian and international, are displayed in the two museums that make up the Musées Royaux des Beaux-Arts. The combination of the two museums contains works from many artistic styles, from the religious paintings of the 15th-century Flemish Primitives to the graphic art of the 1960s and 1970s. The Musée d'art moderne also stages regular temporary exhibitions. The museums are very well set out, guiding the visitor easily through the full collection or, if time is short, directly to the art era of special interest. Each section is highly accessible, as both museums are divided into different coloured routes which relate to the art of each century, taking the visitor through galleries representing the varied schools of art by period.

Flemish still life, *Vase of Flowers* (1704) by Rachel Ruysch

THE BLUE ROUTE

THIS ROUTE leads visitors through a large display of works dating mostly from the 15th and 16th centuries. In the first few rooms are works by the renowned Flemish Primitive School (*see p14*). As is the case with much painting of the Middle Ages, the pictures are chiefly religious in nature and depict a variety of biblical scenes and details from the lives of saints. A work of particular note is *The Annunciation* by the Master of Flémalle, which shows the Archangel Gabriel appearing to the Virgin Mary as she sits at her fireside in a typically Flemish parlour. Also on display are a number of pictures by Rogier van der Weyden, the most famous of all the Flemish Primitive artists and city painter to Brussels during the mid-15th century; of note is his version of the

Lamentation. The work of Bruges artist Hans Memling is mostly shown in his native city, but his *The Martyrdom of Saint Sebastian* is found here.

The most important works in this collection are the paintings by the Brueghels, father and son. Both were renowned for their scenes of peasant life, and on display are *The Bird Trap* (1565) by Pieter Brueghel the Elder, and *The Village Wedding* (1607) by his son, Pieter.

Also on view are beautiful tapestries and the Delporte Collection, which groups sculpture, paintings and *objets d'art* from around the world.

THE BROWN ROUTE

THE SECOND route wends its way through the works of the 17th and 18th centuries. The rooms are wider and taller here in order to house the larger canvases of that time.

A highlight of the route is the world-famous collection of works by Pieter Paul Rubens (1557–1640), which affords a fine overview of the artist's work. As well as key examples of his religious works, there are some excellent portraits, such as *Hélène Fourment*, a portrait of his young wife. Of special interest are the sketches and paintings made in preparation for Rubens' larger works, such as *Four Negro Heads*, a work made in preparation of the 1620 *Adoration of the Magi*.

Other works of note in this section are the paintings by Old Masters such as van Dyck's *Portrait of a Genoese Lady with her Daughter* of the 1620s and Frans Hals' *Three Children with Goatcart*, as well as several paintings by representatives of later Flemish schools, including Jacob Jordaens and his depiction of myths, such as *Pan and Syrinx* (c.1645) and *Satyr and Peasant*. Baroque and Flemish art are all well represented on the tour, a journey through the best painting of the time.

Also on display are some small sculptures which were studies of larger works by Laurent Delvaux, a leading sculptor of the 18th century, particularly *Hercules and Erymanthian Boar*, a study for the sculpture by the staircase in the Palais de Charles de Lorraine (*see p61*).

Works of the Italian, Spanish and French schools of this era are also represented, notably a depiction by Claude Le Lorrain in 1672 of the classical poetic scene *Aeneas hunting the Stag on the Coast of Libya*.

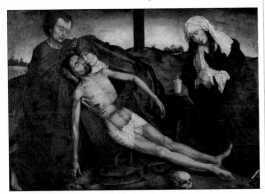

Lamentation (c. 1420–50) by Rogier van der Weyden

THE YELLOW ROUTE

Tᴴɪꜱ ꜱᴇᴄᴛɪᴏɴ covers the 19th century and is closer to the contemporary collection both in position and period. It is an informed introduction to the cutting-edge displays nearby.

The works along the yellow route vary greatly in style and subject matter, from Romanticism, exemplified by David, and Neo-Classicism, to Realism and Symbolism. There are, as in the other sections, examples of work by artists from outside Belgium, including Pierre Bonnard's *Nude against the Light* (1907), Edouard Vuillard's *Two Schoolchildren* (1894) and Monet's *Sunset at Etretat* (1885), but once again most emphasis is on Belgian artists.

Social realist artist Constantin Meunier (1831–1905) is represented by many of his sculptures, including *Firedamp* (1888). Much of the work of James Ensor (1890–1949) remains in his native city Ostend, but many of his macabre works are displayed here, such as *Scandalized Masks* (1883) and *Two Skeletons Fighting over a Pickled Herring* (1891). This section also offers the chance to see pictures by artists who are less well known outside Belgium, such as Henri Evenepoel (1872–99) whose lively Arab scene *Orange Market at Blidah* (1898) provides a contrast to the stark works of painters such as Ensor. The work of Impressionist Emile Claus is of value to followers of the movement. Of local interest is the landscape of Brussels by van Moer, painted in 1868,

Le Joueur Secret (1927) by Magritte

which clearly shows the River Senne before it was covered over for hygiene reasons. Moving from the passion of Romanticism to grim industrial realism and gentle Impressionism, this survey is definitive.

The underground Sculpture Gallery, with carvings and bronzes

THE ORANGE ROUTE

Aɴʏᴏɴᴇ ᴡɪᴛʜ an interest in sculpture should follow this route down to the lower ground level in the Musée d'art ancien. Here, 18th- and 19th-century stone, marble and bronze Belgian sculpture is displayed alongside an exhibition explaining various methods behind many of the works on show, from carving to casting and burnishing in the materials of past centuries. There is also access to a sculpture terrace from outside the entrance of the Musée d'art ancien.

THE GREEN ROUTE

Tʜᴇ ᴄᴏʟʟᴇᴄᴛɪᴏɴ of modern art is wide and varied and includes works by well-known 20th-century painters from Belgium and around the world. There is no clearly defined route to follow within this section, nor are the exhibits strictly grouped by period or movement, so it is best to wander through the collection, stopping at areas of interest.

There are a number of works by the leading Belgian artists of the 20th century, such as Fauvist painter Rik Wouters' (1882–1916) *The Flautist* (1914). International artists include Matisse, Paul Klee and Chagall. But the real draw for most people is the collection of pictures by the Belgian Surrealists, in particular René Magritte (1898–1967). His best-known paintings, including *The Domain of Arnheim* (1962), are on display here. Another noted Surrealist, Paul Delvaux, is also well represented with works such as *Evening Train* (1957) and *Pygmalion* (1939).

Belgian art of the 20th century tends to be severe and stark, but the postwar *Jeune Peinture Belge* school reintroduced colour in an abstract way and is represented in works such as Marc Mendelson's 1950s *Toccata et fugue*.

Sculpture highlights in this section include Ossip Zadkine's totem pole-like *Diana* (1937) and Henry Moore's *Draped Woman on Steps* (1957–8).

Death of Marat (1793) by David, a leading work on the yellow route

Busy café scene at Place du Grand Sablon

Place du Grand Sablon ⓫

Map 2 D4. 🚌 *34, 48, 96.* 🚊 *92, 93, 94.* Ⓜ *Gare Centrale, Louise.*

Situated on the slope of the escarpment that divides Brussels in two, the Place du Grand Sablon is like a stepping stone between the upper and lower halves of the city. The name "sablon" derives from the French "*sable*" (sand) and the square is so-called because this old route down to the city centre once passed through sandy marshes.

Today the picture is very different. The square, more of a triangle in shape, stretches from a 1751 fountain by Jacques Berge at its base uphill to the Gothic church of Notre-Dame du Sablon. This is a chic, wealthy and busy part of Brussels, an area of up-market antiques dealers, fashionable restaurants and trendy bars, which come into their own in warm weather when people stay drinking outside until the early hours. Wittamer, at No. 12, is a justifiably well-known *patisserie* and chocolate shop which also has a tea room on the first floor.

Every weekend the area near the church plays host to a lively and thriving, if rather expensive, antiques market. At No. 40 the old **Musée des postes et des telécommunications** houses a vast collection of letterboxes, uniforms and antique telephones. Set up in 1516 by the Tour et Taxis family, the postal service was useful for its political power, and later became Europe's first international postal service.

🏛 Musée des postes et des télécommunications
Place du Grand Sablon 40, 1000 BRU. 📞 *(02) 511 7740.* ⏰ *10am–4:30pm Tue–Sat, 11am–4pm Sun.* ⬤ *Mon, public hols.* 📷

Notre-Dame au Sablon ⓬

Rue Bodenbroeck 6, 1000 BRU. **Map** 2 D4. 📞 *(02) 511 5741.* 🚊 *92, 93, 94.* Ⓜ *Gare Centrale, Louise.* ⏰ *8am–6pm Mon–Fri, 10am–7pm Sat & Sun.* ♿ 📷 *on request.*

Along with the Cathédrale Sts Michel et Gudule (*see p70–71*), this lovely church is one of the finest remaining examples of Brabant Gothic architecture in Belgium.

A church was first erected here when the guild of cross-bowmen was granted permission to build a chapel to Our Lady on this sandy hill. Legend has it that a young girl in Antwerp had a vision of the Virgin Mary who instructed her to take her statue to Brussels. The girl carried the statue of the Virgin to Brussels down the Senne river by boat and gave it to the crossbowmen's chapel, which rapidly became a place of pilgrimage. Work to enlarge the church began

Notre-Dame du Sablon window

around 1400 but, due to lack of funds, was not actually completed until 1550.

The interior of the church is simple but beautifully proportioned, with inter-connecting side chapels and an impressive pulpit dating from 1697. Of particular interest, however, are the 11 magnificent stained-glass windows, 14 m (45 ft) high, which dominate the inside of the church. As the church is lit from the inside, they shine out at night across the Rue de la Régence like welcoming beacons. Also worth a visit is the chapel of the Tour et Taxis family, whose mansion once stood near the Place du Petit Sablon. In 1517 the family had tapestries commissioned to commemorate the legend that led to the chapel becoming a place of pilgrimage. Some now hang in the Musées Royaux d'art et d'histoire in Parc du Cinquantenaire (*see p75*), but others were stolen by the French Revolutionary army in the 1790s.

The magnificent interior of the church of Notre-Dame du Sablon

Place du Petit Sablon ⓭

Map 2 D4. 🚌 *20, 34, 48, 96.* 🚊 *92, 93, 94.* Ⓜ *Gare Centrale, Louise.*

These pretty, formal gardens were laid out in 1890 and are a charming spot to stop for a rest. On top of the railings that enclose the gardens are 48 bronze statuettes by Art Nouveau artist Paul Hankar, each one representing a different medieval guild of the city.

One of the lavish fountains in the gardens of Petit Sablon

At the back of the gardens is a fountain built to commemorate Counts Egmont and Hornes, the martyrs who led a Dutch uprising against the tyrannical rule of the Spanish under Philip II, and were beheaded in the Grand Place in 1568 (*see p31*). On either side of the fountain are 12 further statues of 15th- and 16th-century figures, including Bernard van Orley, whose stained-glass windows grace the city's cathedral. Gerhard Mercator, the Flemish geographer and mapmaker, whose 16th-century projection of the world forms the basis of most modern maps, is also featured.

Statue of Peter Pan in Palais d'Egmont gardens

has twice been rebuilt, in 1750 and again in 1891, following a fire. Today it belongs to the Belgian Foreign Ministry. It was here that Great Britain, Denmark and Ireland signed as members of the EEC in 1972.

Though the palace itself is closed to the public, the gardens, whose entrances are on the Rue du Grand Cerf and the Boulevard de Waterloo, are open. There is a statue of Peter Pan, a copy of one found in Kensington Gardens, in London. Many of the gardens' buildings are now run down, and plans have started to restore the ancient orangery and the disused ice house.

Palais d'Egmont ⑭

Rue aux Laines, 1000 BRU. **Map** 2 E4. ▩ *34.* ▦ *91, 92, 93, 94.* Ⓜ *Louise.* ♿

THE PALAIS d'Egmont (also known as the Palais d'Arenberg) was originally built in the mid-16th century for Françoise of Luxembourg, mother of the 16th-century leader of the city's rebels, Count Egmont. This palace

Palais de Justice ⑮

Place Poelaert 1, 1000 BRU. **Map** 1 C5. Ⓒ *(02) 508 6111.* ▩ *34.* ▦ *91, 92, 93, 94.* Ⓜ *Louise.* ◐ *9am– noon, 1:30–4pm Mon–Fri.* ● *Sat & Sun, public hols.* ♿ ✔ *on request.*

THE PALAIS DE JUSTICE rules the Brussels skyline and can be seen from almost any vantage point in the city. Of all the ambitious projects of King Léopold II, this was perhaps the grandest. It occupies an area larger than St Peter's Basilica in Rome, and was one of the world's most impressive 19th-century buildings. It was built between 1866 and 1883 by architect Joseph Poelaert who looked for inspiration in classical temples, but sadly died mid-construction in 1879. The Palais de Justice is still home to the city's law courts.

Detail of a cornice at the Palais de Justice

Galerie Bortier ⑯

Rue de la Madeleine 55, 1000 BRU. **Map** 2 D3. 🚌 20, 38. 🚋 92, 93, 94. Ⓜ *Gare Centrale*. ◯ *9am–6pm Mon–Sat*. ⬤ *Sun, public hols*. ♿

GALERIE BORTIER is the only shopping arcade in the city dedicated solely to book and map shops, and it has become the haunt of students, enthusiasts and researchers looking for secondhand French books and antiquarian finds.

The land on which the gallery stands was originally owned by a Monsieur Bortier, whose idea it was to have a covered arcade lined with shops on either side. He put 160,000 francs of his own money into the project, quite a considerable sum in the 1840s. The 65-m (210-ft) long Galérie Bortier was built in 1848 and was designed by Jean-Pierre Cluysenaar, the architect of the Galéries St-Hubert nearby (*see p47*). The Galérie Bortier opened along with the then-adjacent Marché de la Madeleine, but the latter was unfortunately destroyed by developers in 1958.

A complete restoration of Galérie Bortier was ordered by the Ville de Bruxelles in 1974. The new architects kept strictly to Cluysenaar's plans and installed a replacement glass and wrought-iron roof made to the original 19th-century Parisian style. The Rue de la Madeleine itself also offers plenty of browsing material for bibliophiles and art lovers.

Crammed interior of a bookshop at the Galérie Bortier

Cathédrale Sts Michel et Gudule ⑰

THE CATHEDRALE Sts Michel et Gudule is the national church of Belgium, although it was only granted cathedral status in 1962. It is the finest surviving example of Brabant Gothic architecture. There has been a church on the site of the cathedral since at least the 11th century. Work began on the Gothic cathedral in 1226 under Henry I, Duke of Brabant, and continued over a period of 300 years. It was finally completed with the construction of two front towers at the beginning of the 16th century under Charles V. The cathedral is made of a sandy limestone, brought from local quarries. The interior is very bare; this is due to Protestant iconoclast ransacking in 1579–80 and thefts by French revolutionists in 1783. It was fully restored and cleaned in the 1990s and now reveals its splendour.

The twin towers rise above the city. Unusually, they were designed as a pair in the 1400s; Brabant architecture typically has only one.

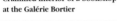

★ Last Judgement window
At the front of the cathedral, facing the altar, is a magnificent stained-glass window of 1528 depicting Christ awaiting saved souls. Its vivid reds, blues and yellows place it in the 16th-century style. The Renaissance panes are surrounded by later Baroque garlands of flowers.

Romanesque remains of the first church here, dating from 1047, were discovered during renovation work. They can be seen and toured in the crypt.

STAR SIGHTS

★ **Last Judgement window**

★ **Baroque pulpit**

Chapelle de la Madeleine ⑱

Rue de la Madeleine, 1000 BRU.
Map 2 D3. ☎ (02) 511 2845.
🚌 20, 38. 🚃 92, 93, 94. Ⓜ Gare
Centrale. ⏰ 7am–7pm Mon–Sat;
7am–noon, 5pm–8pm Sun. ♿

A view of the Chapelle de la Madeleine with restored brickwork

THIS LITTLE church once stood on the site now occupied by the Gare Centrale, but it was moved, stone by stone, further down the hill to make way for the construction of the Art Deco-style station and its car park during the early 1950s.

The 17th-century façade of the church has been restored. The original 15th-century interior has been replaced by a plain, modest decor, with simple stone pillars and modern stained-glass windows. Off the regular tourist track, the chapel is used by people as a quiet place for worship. The Baroque chapel which was once attached has now gone.

The transept
windows represent the rulers of Belgium in 1538. Jan Haeck made the designs after Bernard van Orley's sketches.

Sainte Gudule
This 7th-century saint is very dear to the people of Brussels. Her relics were scattered to the winds by ransacking Protestants in 1579, but this only served to reinforce her cult.

VISITORS' CHECKLIST

Parvis Ste-Gudule, 1000 BRU.
Map 2 E2. ☎ (02) 217 8345,
219 1170. 🚌 65, 66. 🚃 92,
93, 94. Ⓜ Gare Centrale. ⏰
8am–6pm daily. 💰 to crypt.
✝ regular services throughout
the day. ♿ on request.

The Statue of St Michael is the cathedral's symbol of its links with the city. While the gilded plaster statue is not itself historically exceptional, its long heritage is; the patron saint of Brussels, the Archangel St Michael is shown killing the dragon, symbolic of his protection of the city.

The Lectern

★ **Baroque pulpit**
The flamboyantly carved pulpit in the central aisle is the work of an Antwerp-born sculptor, Henri-François Verbruggen. Designed in 1699, it was finally installed in 1776.

The Art Nouveau façade of No. 11 Square Ambiorix

Square Ambiorix ⑲

Map 3 B2. 🚍 *54, 63.* Ⓜ *Schuman.*

CLOSE TO THE EU district, but totally different in style and spirit, lies the beautiful Square Ambiorix. Together with the Avenue Palmerston and the Square Marie-Louise below that, this marshland was transformed in the 1870s into one of the loveliest residential parts of Brussels, with a large central area of gardens, ponds and fountains.

The elegant houses, some Art Nouveau, some older, have made this one of the truly sought-after suburbs in the city. The most spectacular Art Nouveau example is at No. 11. Known as the Maison St Cyr after the painter

whose home it once was, this wonderfully ornate house, with its curved wrought-iron balustrades and balconies, is a fine architectural feat considering that the man who designed it, Gustave Strauven, was only 22 years old when it was built at the turn of the 20th century.

Quartier Européen ⑳

Map 3 B3. 🚍 *20, 54.* Ⓜ *Maelbeek.*

THE AREA at the top of the Rue de la Loi and around the Schuman roundabout is where the main buildings of the European Union's administration are found.

The most recognizable of all the EU seats is the star-shaped Berlaymont building, now nearing completion following the removal of large quantities of poisonous asbestos discovered in its structure. The Berlaymont, formerly the headquarters of the European Commission, will continue to be modernized and refurbished until further notice. The commission workers (the civil servants of the EU) are at present dotted around the area. The Council of Ministers, which comprises representatives of member-states' governments, now meets in the sprawling pink granite block across the road from the Berlaymont, known as Justus Lipsius, after a Flemish philosopher. Further down the road from the Justus Lipsius building is the Résidence Palace, a luxury 1920s housing complex that boasts a theatre, a pool and a roof garden as well as several floors of private flats. It

now houses the International Press Centre. Only the theatre is now open to the public, but EU officials are allowed into the Art Deco swimming pool.

This area is naturally full of life and bustle during the day, but much quieter in the evenings and can feel almost deserted at weekends. What is pleasant for both workers and visitors, though, is the close proximity of the city's green spaces including Parc Léopold, Parc du Cinquantenaire (*see pp74–5*) and the verdant Square Ambiorix.

Paintings and sculpture on show in the Musée Wiertz gallery

Musée Wiertz ㉑

Rue Vautier 62, 1000 BRU. **Map** 3 A4.
📞 *(02) 648 1718.* 🚍 *34, 80.*
Ⓜ *Maelbeek, Schuman, Trone.*
🕐 *10am– noon, 1–5pm Tue –Fri; every 2nd weekend.* ⬤ *Mon, weekends Jul–Aug, public hols.*

MUSEE WIERTZ houses some 160 works, including oil paintings, drawings and sculptures, that form the main body of Antoine Wiertz's (1806–65) artistic output. The collection fills the studio built for Wiertz by the Belgian state, where he lived and worked from 1850 until his death in 1865, when the studio became a museum.

The huge main room contains Wiertz's largest paintings, many depicting biblical and Homeric scenes, some in the style of Rubens. Also on display are sculptures and his death mask. The last of the six rooms contains two of his more gruesome efforts, one a scene of poverty entitled *Madness, Hunger and Crime.*

The Justus Lipsius, the pink granite EU Council building

A tall European parliament building rising up behind the trees of Parc Léopold in the Parliament Quarter

Parliament Quarter ㉒

Map 3 A4. 🚌 20, 54, 80.
Ⓜ *Maelbeek, Schuman.*

THE VAST, MODERN, steel-and-glass complex, situated just behind Quartier Léopold train station, is one of three homes of the European Parliament, the elected body of the EU. Its permanent seat is in Strasbourg, France, where the plenary sessions are held once a month. The administrative centre is in Luxembourg and the committee meetings are held in Brussels.

This gleaming state-of-the-art building has many admirers, not least the parliamentary workers and MEPs themselves, who were proud of what was at one point the largest building site in Europe. But it also has its critics: the huge domed structure housing the hemicycle that seats the 600-plus MEPs has been dubbed the "*caprices des dieux*" ("whims of the gods"), which refers both to the shape of the building which is similar to a French cheese of the same name, and to its lofty aspirations. Many people also regret that, to make room for the new complex, a large part of Quartier Léopold has been lost. Though there are still plenty of restaurants and bars, a lot of the charm has gone. When the MEPs are absent, the building is often used for meetings of European Union committees.

Institut Royal des Sciences Naturelles ㉓

Rue Vautier 29, 1000 BRU. **Map** 3 A4.
📞 *(02) 627 4238.* 🚌 *34, 80.*
Ⓜ *Maelbeek, Schuman.* 🕙 *9:30am–4:45pm Tue–Fri, 10am–6pm Sat & Sun.* ⬤ *Mon, 1 Jan, 1 May, 25 Dec.*
📷 🎫 ♿ 🏪 🚻

THE INSTITUT Royal des Sciences Naturelles is best known for its fine collection of iguanadon skeletons dating back 250 million years. The museum also contains interactive and educational displays covering all aspects and evolutionary eras of natural history.

Parc Léopold ㉔

Rue Belliard. **Map** 3 B4. 🚌 20, 59.
Ⓜ *Maelbeek.*

PARC LEOPOLD occupies part of the grounds of an old estate and a walk around its lake follows the old path of the Maelbeek river which was covered over in the 19th-century for reasons of hygiene.

At the end of the 19th century, scientist and industrialist Ernest Solvay put forward the idea of a science park development. Solvay was given the Parc Léopold, the site of a zoo since 1847, and set up five university centres here. Leading figures including Marie Curie and Albert Einstein met here to discuss new scientific issues. The park is still home to many scientific institutes, as well as a haven of peace in the heart of this busy political area.

Whale skeleton inside the Institut Royal des Sciences Naturelles

Parc du Cinquantenaire ㉕

Musée de l'Armée gun

THE FINEST OF LEOPOLD II's grand projects, the Parc and Palais du Cinquantenaire were built for the Golden Jubilee celebrations of Belgian independence in 1880. The park was laid out on unused town marshes. The palace, at its entrance, was to comprise a triumphal arch and two large exhibition areas, but by the time of the 1880 Art and Industry Expo, only the two side exhibition areas had been completed. Further funds were eventually found, and work continued for 50 years. Before being converted into museums, the large halls on either side of the central archway were used to hold trade fairs, the last of which was in 1935. They have also been used for horse races and to store homing pigeons. During World War II, the grounds of the park were used to grow vegetables to feed the Brussels people.

★ Musée de l'Armée
Opened in 1923, the museum covers all aspects of Belgium's military history, and exhibits over 200 years of militaria. Historic aircraft are on display in the hall next door.

View of Park with Arch
Based on the Arc de Triomphe in Paris, the arch was not completed in time for the 50th Anniversary celebrations but was finished in 1905.

The Grand Mosque was built in Arabic style as a folly in 1880. It became a mosque in 1978.

Tree-lined Avenue
In part formal garden, part forested walks, many of the plantations of elms and plane trees date from 1880.

Pavillon Horta

Underpass

STAR SIGHTS
★ Musées Royaux d'Art et d'Histoire
★ Musée de l'Armée

0 metres   100

0 yards   100

The Central Archway
*Conceived as a gateway into
the city, the arch is crowned
by the symbolic bronze sculpture* Brabant Raising the
National Flag.

VISITORS' CHECKLIST

Ave de Tervuren, 1040 BRU. **Map**
3 C3. 28, 36, 67. 81, 82.
Schuman, Mérode.
Autoworld: (02) 736 4165.
10am–5pm daily (Apr–Sep:
to 6pm). 1 Jan, 25 Dec.
The Grand Mosque:
(02) 735 2173. 10am–6pm
daily. Please dress with respect.

Autoworld
*Housed in the south wing
of the Cinquantenaire
Palace, Autoworld is
one of the best collec-
tions of automobiles
in the world. There
are some 300 cars,
including an 1886
motor, and a
1924 Model-T
Ford that still runs.*

The park is
popular with
Brussels' Eurocrats
and families at lunch-
times and weekends.

★ Musées Royaux d'Art et d'Histoire
*Belgian architect Bordiau's plans for the two
exhibition halls, later permanent showcases,
were partly modelled on London's Victorian
museums. The use of iron and glass in their
construction was inspired by the Crystal Palace.*

Musées Royaux d'Art et d'Histoire

Parc du Cinquantenaire 10. (02)
741 7211. 9:30am–5pm Tue–Sun
(from 10am Sun and pub hols). 1
Jan, 1 May, 1 & 11 Nov, 25 Dec.

Also known as the Musée du
Cinquantenaire, this excellent
museum has occupied its present site since the early 1900s,
but the history of the collections goes back as far as the
15th century, and the quantity
of exhibits is vast. Sections on
ancient civilizations include
Egypt and Greece, and also
Persia and the Near East. Other
displays feature Byzantium and
Islam, China and the Indian
Subcontinent, and the Pre-
Columbian civilizations of the
Americas. There are decorative
arts from all ages, with glassware, silverware and porcelain
as well as a fine collection of
lace and tapestries. Religious
sculptures and stained glass are
displayed around a courtyard
in the style of church cloisters.

**The aircraft display at the Musée
Royal de l'Armée**

Musée Royal de l'Armée et d'Histoire Militaire

Parc du Cinquantenaire 3.
(02) 737 7811. 9am–noon,
1–4:30pm Tue–Sun. Mon, 1 Jan,
1 May, 1 Nov, 25 Dec.
Together with the section on
aviation, displays cover the
Belgian Army and its history
from the late 1700s to today,
including weapons, uniforms,
decorations and paintings.
There is a section covering
the 1830 struggle for
independence (see p34–5).
Two new sections show both
World Wars, including the
activities of the Resistance.

GREATER BRUSSELS

PAST THE heart-shaped ring-road of Brussels city centre lie 19 suburbs (*communes*) which form the Bruxelles-Capitale region. While many are residential, a handful are definitely worth the short ride to sample outlying treasures of Brussels' fascinating history. For fans of early 20th-century architecture, the suburb of St-Gilles offers numerous original examples of striking Art Nouveau buildings including Musée Horta. In Koekelberg and visible from the Upper Town is the huge Sacré-Coeur basilica, started

Detail from annexe of Chinese Pavilion, Laeken

in 1904. To the north, Heysel offers attractions whose modernity contrasts with the historical city centre. The 1958 Atomium, now restored, stands next to the Bruparck theme park. To the east, the Central Africa Museum reflects Belgium's colonial past in the Congo, and the tram museum takes a journey through Brussels' urban past. Peace and tranquillity can be found close to the metropolis, in the orderly landscape of Royal Laeken and the lush open spaces of the Bois de la Cambre and the Fôret de Soignes.

SIGHTS AT A GLANCE

Churches and Cathedrals
Basilique Nationale du Sacré-Coeur **8**

Historic Monuments, Buildings and Districts
Anderlecht **7**
Avenue Louise **2**
Ixelles **4**
St-Gilles **3**
Uccle **6**

Parks and Gardens
Bruparck **13**
Domaine de Laeken see pp82–3 **11**
Fôret de Soignes **5**

Museums and Exhibition Areas
The Atomium **12**
Musée Horta see p78 **1**
Musée du Tram **9**

Musée Royal de l'Afrique Centrale **10**

KEY

▨	Central Brussels
□	Greater Brussels
✈	Airport
▬	Major Road
▨	Minor Road

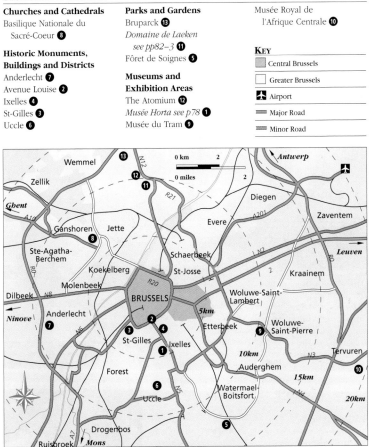

◁ **The Atomium towering over Mini-Europe in the Bruparck**

Musée Horta ❶

VISITORS' CHECKLIST

Rue Américaine 23–25, 1060
BRU. **(** (02) 543 0490. **54.**
81, 82, 91, 92. M Albert,
Louise. **○** 2–5:30pm Tue–Sun.
● Mon, public hols.

ARCHITECT VICTOR HORTA (1861–1947) is considered by many to be the father of Art Nouveau, and his impact on Brussels architecture is unrivalled by any other designer of his time. A museum dedicated to his unique style is today housed in his restored family home, which he designed from 1898 to 1901. His skill lay not only in his grand, overall vision but in his equal talent as an interior designer, blending themes and materials into each detail. The airy interior of the building displays trademarks of the architect's style – iron, glass and curves – in every detail, while retaining a functional approach.

Art Nouveau candelabra

★ **Central Staircase**
Decorated with curved wrought iron, the stairs are enhanced further by mirrors and glass, bringing natural light into the house.

The bedroom
features Art Nouveau furniture, including a wardrobe inlaid with pale and dark wood.

★ **Dining Room**
White enamel tiles line the walls, rising to an ornate ceiling, decorated with the scrolled metalwork used in other rooms.

Madame Horta's sitting-room features blue-and-cream wool rugs woven to Horta's design, and a marble fireplace.

Front Entrance

STAR FEATURES

★ Central Staircase

★ Dining Room

Living Room
The detail of Horta's work can be best seen here, from sculpted bannister ends to finely wrought door handles that echo larger forms.

Exclusive boutique in the chic Avenue Louise

Avenue Louise ❷

Map 2 D5. 🚋 34, 54. 🚌 93, 94.
Ⓜ Louise.

Most visitors to Brussels travelling by car will come across this busy thoroughfare, its various underpasses constructed in the 1950s and 1960s to link up the city centre with its suburbs. In fact, the avenue was constructed in 1864 to join the centre with the suburb of Ixelles. However, the north end of the avenue retains a chic atmosphere; by the Porte de Namur, fans of designer labels can indulge themselves in Gucci and Versace, as well as investigating the less expensive but no less chic boutiques.

The avenue also has its architectural treasures. The **Hôtel Solvay** at No. 224 was built by Victor Horta in 1894 for the industrialist Solvay family. Its ornate doorway, columns and balconies are a fine example of Art Nouveau style (see p16–17). The house is still a private home. At No. 346, **Hôtel Max Hallet** is one of Horta's masterpieces, built in 1903. Continuing south leads to the peaceful atmosphere of Ixelles and its parkland.

St-Gilles ❸

🚋 20, 48. 🚌 23, 55, 90.
Ⓜ Porte de Hal, Parvis St-Gilles.

Named after the patron saint of this district's main church, St-Gilles is traditionally one of Brussels' poorer areas. However, amid the low-quality functional housing are architectural survivors which make the suburb well worth a visit. Art Nouveau and sgraffiti gems (see p17) can be found in streets such as Avenue Jean Volders and Rue Vanderschrick. The **Hôtel Hannon** (1902), now a photography gallery, remains one of the city's most spectacular Art Nouveau structures. Restored in 1985, it has a stained-glass window and ornate statuary that take this architectural style to its peak (see p16).

Art Nouveau details can be seen in the nearby streets, particularly in Rue Felix Delhasse and Rue Africaine.

One of the most striking features of St-Gilles is the **Porte de Hal**. Brussels' second set of town walls, built in the 14th century, originally included seven gateways, of which Porte de Hal is the only survivor (see p12). Used as a prison from the 16th to 18th centuries, it escaped the modernizing influence of the Austrian Emperor Joseph. Restored in 1870, it is now a small museum of folk art, including a collection of 19th-century toys.

Art Nouveau detail on façade in Rue Africaine

⚕ Hôtel Hannon
Ave de la Jonction 1, BRU 1060.
📞 (02) 538 4220. Ⓜ Albert.
🏛 Porte de Hal
Blvds de Midi & de Waterloo, BRU 1000. 📞 (02) 534 1518.
⬤ for renovation until further notice.

Ixelles ❹

🚋 54, 71, 95, 96. 🚌 81, 82, 93, 94.
Ⓜ Porte de Namur.

Although one of Brussels' largest suburbs and a busy transport junction, the heart of Ixelles remains a peaceful oasis of lakes and woodland.

The idyllic **Abbaye de la Cambre** was founded in 1201, achieving fame and a degree of fortune in 1242, when Saint Boniface chose the site for his retirement. The abbey then endured a troubled history in the wars of religion during the 16th and 17th centuries. It finally closed as an operational abbey in 1796 and now houses a school of architecture. The abbey's pretty Gothic church can be toured and its grassy grounds and courtyards offer a peaceful walk.

South of the abbey, the Bois de la Cambre remains one of the city's most popular public parks. Created in 1860, it achieved popularity almost immediately when royalty promenaded its main route. Lakes, bridges and lush grass make it a favoured picnic site.

The **Musée Communal d'Ixelles** nearby has a fine collection of posters by 19th- and 20th-century greats, such as Toulouse Lautrec and Magritte, as well as sculptures by Rodin. The former home of one of Belgium's finest sculptors is now **Musée Constantin Meunier**, with 170 sculptures and 120 paintings by the artist, and his studio preserved in its turn-of-the-century style.

⚕ Abbaye de la Cambre
Ave de Général de Gaulle, BRU 1050.
📞 (02) 648 1121. ⬤ 9am–noon, 3–6:30pm daily. ⬤ public hols.
🏛 Musée Communal d'Ixelles
Rue J Van Volsem 71, BRU 1050.
📞 (02) 511 0984. ⬤ 1–6:30pm Tue–Fri, 10am–5pm Sat–Sun.
⬤ Mon, public hols.
🏛 Musée Constantin Meunier
Rue de l'Abbaye 59, BRU 1050.
📞 (02) 648 4449. ⬤ 10am–noon, 1–5pm Tue–Sun. ⬤ Mon, public hols.

The Forêt de Soignes, once a royal hunting ground and now a park

Forêt de Soignes ❺

🚊 71, 72. 🚋 23, 90. Ⓜ Demey, Hermann Debroux. 🔵 Thu, Sun.
☎ (02) 215 1740.

THE LARGE FORESTED area to the southeast of Brussels' city centre has a long history: thought to have had prehistoric beginnings, it was also here that the Gallic citizens suffered their defeat by the Romans (see p29). However, the forest really gained renown in the 12th century when wild boar roamed the landscape, and local dukes enjoyed hunting trips in the woodland.

The density of the landscape has provided tranquillity over the ages. In the 14th and 15th centuries it became a favoured location for monasteries and abbeys. Few have survived, but Abbaye de Rouge-Cloître is a rare example from this era.

In a former 18th-century priory is the **Groenendaal Arboretum**, in which more than 400 forest plants are housed, many of which are extinct elsewhere. The most common sight, however, is the locals enjoying a stroll.

🌼 **Groenendaal Arboretum**
Duboislaan 14, 1560 BRU.
☎ (02) 657 0386.
🔵 8:30am–5pm, Mon–Fri.

Uccle ❻

🚊 49, 50. 🚋 18, 52.

UCCLE IS A smart residential district, nestling in its tree-lined avenues. Not immediately a tourist destination, it is worthwhile taking a trip to the

Musée David et Alice Buuren. The 1920s residence of this Dutch couple is now a small private museum, displaying their eclectic acquisitions. Amid the Dutch Delft-ware and French Lalique lamps are great finds, such as original sketches by Van Gogh. Visitors will enjoy the modern landscaped gardens at the rear.

🏛 **Musée David et Alice Buuren**
Ave Léo Errera 41, 1180 BRU. ☎ (02) 343 4851. 🔵 1–5:45pm Sun, 2–5:45pm Mon. Group visits by appointment. ⚫ 24–31 Dec.

Anderlecht ❼

🚊 63, 89. 🚋 82. Ⓜ Bizet, Clemenceau.

CONSIDERED to be Brussels' first genuine suburb (archaeological digs have uncovered remnants of Roman housing), Anderlecht is now best known

Mirò-style drawings, Anderlecht

as an industrial area, for its meat market, and its successful football club of the same name. Despite this, the Modernist Spanish painter Joan Mirò added a unique artistic contribution inspiring bright cartoon-like murals on Rue Porcelaine.

Although only a few pockets of the suburb are now residential, during the 15th century this was a popular place of abode and some houses remain from that era. **Maison Erasme**, built in 1468, is now named after the great scholar and religious reformer, Erasmus (1466–1536), who lived here for five months in 1521. The house was restored in the 1930s. Now a museum dedicated to the most respected thinker of his generation, it displays a collection of 16th-century furniture and portraits of the great humanist by Holbein and van der Weyden.

Nearby is the huge edifice of **Eglise Sts-Pierre-et-Guidon**. This 14th-century Gothic church, completed with the addition of a tower in 1517, is notable for its sheer size and exterior gables, typical of Brabant architecture. The life of St Guidon, patron saint of peasants, is depicted on interior wall murals.

Illustrating a more recent history, the **Musée Gueuze** is an operational family brewery that has opened its doors to the public to witness the production of classic Belgian beers such as lambic, gueuze and kriek (see pp142–3).

Maison Erasme in Anderlecht, with its courtyard and fountain

The Basilique Nationale du Sacré-Coeur rising over the city

🏛 Maison Erasme

Rue du Chapitre 31, 1070 BRU.
📞 (02) 521 1383. 🕐 10am–5pm
Tue–Sun. ● Mon, 1 Jan, 25 Dec. ♿

⛪ Eglise Sts-Pierre-et-Guidon

Place de la Vaillance, 1070 BRU.
🕐 9am–noon, 2:30–6pm Mon–Fri.
● Sat & Sun.

🏛 Musée Gueuze

Rue Gheude 56, 1070 BRU.
📞 (02) 521 4928. 🕐 8:30am–5pm
Mon–Fri, 10am–5pm Sat.
● Sun, public hols. ♿ including 1
free beer.

Basilique Nationale du Sacré-Coeur ❽

Parvis de la Basilique 1, Koekelberg,
1083 BRU. 📞 (02) 425 8822.
Ⓜ Simonis. 🚌 87. 🚊 19. 🕐 9am–
4pm (5pm summer), daily.
♿ by appointment.

ALTHOUGH A small and popular suburb among Brussels' residents, there is little for the visitor to see in Koekelberg other than the striking Basilique Nationale du Sacré-Coeur, but this does make the journey worthwhile for those interested in the best of Art Deco.

King Léopold II was keen to build a church in the city which could accommodate vast congregations to reflect the burgeoning population of early 20th-century Brussels.

He commissioned the church in 1904, although the building was not finished until 1970. Originally designed by Pierre Langerock, the final construction, which uses sandstone and terracotta, was the less expensive adaptation by Albert van Huffel. Very much a 20th-century church, in contrast to the many medieval religious buildings in the city centre, it is dedicated to those who died for Belgium, in particular the thousands of Belgian soldiers who were never to return from the two world wars, killed in battles fought on their own terrain.

The most dominating feature of the church is the vast green copper dome, rising 90 m (295 ft) above ground. For those who do not manage to visit the church itself, it is this central dome that is visible from many points in the city, including the Palais de Justice.

Musée du Tram ❾

Ave de Tervuren 364b, BRU 1150. 📞
(02) 515 3108. 🚊 39, 44. 🕐 Apr–
Sep: 1:30pm–7pm Sat & Sun, pub hols.
Group tours possible. Every Sun and
pub hol, the museum organizes a tour
to Heysel (9:45am). ● Oct–Mar. ♿

THIS MUSEUM traces the history of public transport in Belgium, with marvellous displays of heritage machinery. Horse-drawn trams are available to transport visitors round the site, which features fully-working early versions of the electric tram, buses and plenty of interactive exhibits.

Musée Royal de l'Afrique Centrale ❿

Leuvensesteenweg 13, Tervuren 3080.
📞 (02) 769 5211. 🕐 10am–
5pm Tue–Fri, 10am–6pm, Sat & Sun.
● Mon, public hols. ♿

IN THE 19th century, the colony of the Belgian Congo was Belgium's only territorial possession. It was handed back to self-government in 1960 and eventually renamed Zaire (now the Democratic Republic of Congo). This museum, opened in 1899, is a collection gleaned from over 100 years of colonial rule. Galleries show ceremonial African dress and masks, and displays on colonial life.

Dugout canoes, pagan idols, weapons and stuffed wildlife, feature heavily. There is a horrifying collection of conserved giant African insects, much beloved by children. The museum has been adding constantly to its collection and is now a memento to a past way of life in the Congo.

The Musée Royal de l'Afrique Centrale façade in Tervuren

Domaine de Laeken ⓫

IN THE 11TH CENTURY Laeken became popular among pilgrims after reported sightings of the Virgin Mary. Since the 19th century, however, it has been firmly etched in the minds of all Belgians as the residence of the nation's monarchy. A walk around the sedate and peaceful area reveals impressive buildings constructed in honour of the royal location, not least the sovereign's official residence and its beautifully landscaped parkland. More surprising is the sudden Oriental influence. The great builder, King Léopold II, wanted to create an architectural world tour; the Chinese and Japanese towers are the only two buildings that came to fruition, but show the scope of one monarch's vision.

★ Pavillon Chinois
Architect Alexandre Marcel designed this elaborate building in 1909; inside are examples of Oriental porcelain.

Tour Japonais

Parc de Laeken

Villa Belvedere
was once the residence of the Royal Family, and is now home to the heir to the throne.

Monument Léopold
stands as the focus of the park complex and layout. It honours Léopold I, first king of the Belgians. Built in Neo-Gothic style, it has a filigree cast-iron canopy and tracery around the base.

Place de la Dynastie
is part of the attractive park that was once the Royal Family's private hunting ground.

★ Serres Royales
These late 19th-century glasshouses are home to exotic trees, palms and camellias. Open to the public annually in April, they are the King's private property.

Château Royal
The Belgian royal residence, in the heart of the 160-ha (395-acre) estate, was heavily restored in 1890, with a façade by architect Poelaert covering the 18th-century original.

**Domaine Royale de
Laeken** is the royal estate,
adjacent to the Parc de
Laeken in the city district
of Laeken; the woodland
features old magnolias
and blooming hawthorns.

The Atomium rising 100 m (325 ft) over the Bruparck at dusk

The Atomium ⑫

Boulevard du Centenaire, 1020 BRU.
📞 *(02) 474 8977.* Ⓜ *Heysel.*
⬤ *Apr–Aug: 9am–7:30pm;
Sep–Mar: 10am–5.30pm.* 📷

BUILT FOR THE 1958 World
Fair *(see p37)*, the Atomium
is probably the most identifi-
able symbol of Brussels, as
recognizable as the Eiffel
Tower of Paris or the Colis-
eum in Rome. As the world
moved into a new age of
science and space travel at
the end of the 1950s, so the
design by André Waterkeyn
reflected this with a structure
of an iron atom, magnified
165 billion times. Now a
small museum, each of
the nine spheres that
make up the "atom" are
18 m (60 ft) in diameter,
and linked by escalators.

Bruparck ⑬

Boulevard du Centenaire, 1020 BRU.
📞 *(02) 474 8377.* 🚃 *84, 89.* 🚋
23, 81. Ⓜ *Heysel.* **Mini-Europe
& Océade** 📞 *(02) 478 0550 (Mini-
Europe); (02) 478 4220 (Océade).*
⬤ *Apr–Sep: 9:30am–6pm daily
(Jul–Aug: to midnight); Oct–mid-Jan:
10am–5pm daily.* ⬤ *end Jan–Mar.*
📷 **Kinepolis** 📞 *(02) 474 2600.* ⬤
performances. 📷 *for film screenings.*

ALTHOUGH NOWHERE near as
large or as grand as many
of the world's theme parks,
Bruparck's sights and range of
fast-food restaurants are always
a popular family destination.
The first and favourite port
of call for most visitors is Mini-

Europe, where more than 300
miniature reconstructions take
you around the landscapes of
the European Union. Built at
a scale of 1:25, the collection
displays buildings of social or
cultural importance, such as
the Acropolis in Athens, the
Brandenburg Gate of Berlin
and the Houses of Parliament
from London. Even at this
scale the detail is such that it
can be second only to visiting
the sights themselves.

For film fans, Kinepolis
cannot be beaten. Large
auditoriums show a range of
popular films from different
countries on 29 screens. The
IMAX cinema features surround
sound and a semi-circular 600
sq m (6,456 sq ft) widescreen.

If warmth and relaxation
are what you are looking for,
Océade is a tropically heated
water park, complete with
giant slides, wave machines,
bars, cafés and even realistic
re-created sandy beaches.

0 metres   250

0 yards   250

London's Houses of Parliament in
small scale at Mini-Europe

BEYOND BRUSSELS

BEYOND BRUSSELS

BRUSSELS IS AT THE HEART *not only of Belgium, but also of Europe. The city marks the divide between the Flemish north and the French-speaking Walloon south. Its central position makes Brussels an ideal base for visitors: within easy reach are the ancient Flemish towns of Antwerp, Ghent and Bruges, each with their exquisite medieval architecture, superb museums and excellent restaurants.*

Although Belgium is a small country, it has one of the highest population densities in Europe. An incredibly efficient road and rail network also means that large numbers of people move around the country every day, with around half the population employed in industry, particularly in textiles, metallurgy and chemicals. Despite this, parts of Belgium are still farmed. Stretching south from the defences of the North Sea is the plain of Flanders, a low-lying area which, like the Netherlands, has reclaimed land or *polders*, whose fertile soil is intensively cultivated with wheat and sugar beet. Bordering the Netherlands is the Kempenland, a sparsely populated area of peat moors, which in the 19th century was mined for coal.

There are small farms here today which cultivate mainly oats, rye and potatoes. Northeast Belgium also contains the large port of Antwerp, a major centre of European industry, with its ship-building yards, oil-refineries and car factories. The towns of Leuven, Lier and Mechelen are noted for their medieval town centres, while Oudenaarde produces exceptionally fine tapestries in a trade dating back to the 13th century.

Brussels itself is surrounded by both Flemish and Walloon Brabant, a fertile region famous for its wheat and beet farms and pasture for cows. Just a few kilometres south of the capital is Waterloo, the most visited battlefield in the world, where Napoleon was defeated by Wellington in 1815.

Brussels

Visitors sail under the Blinde Ezelstraat Bridge on a tour of Bruges

◁ **The Brabo Fountain in Antwerp's Grote Markt**

Exploring Beyond Brussels

BELGIUM OCCUPIES one of the most densely populated parts of Europe, with a concentration of towns and villages across the flat landscapes of the Flemish plain. Along the North Sea coast there are fewer settlements, set among fertile farmland. To the north and west of Brussels are the three easy-to-reach towns of Antwerp, Ghent and Bruges which, with their ancient buildings and vibrant cultural life, are attractive destinations. East of Brussels is the charming university town of Leuven, and further on is the open-air museum of Bokrijk, whose restored buildings focus on the the history of the Flemish people.

Bronze statue of Silvius Brabo in Antwerp's Grote Markt

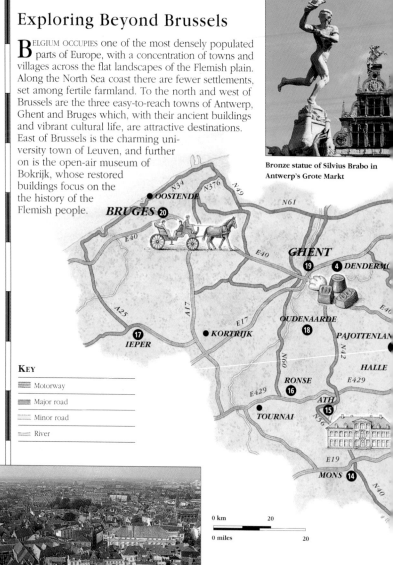

KEY

▦	Motorway
▦	Major road
▦	Minor road
▦	River

0 km   20

0 miles   20

View over Bruges from the Belfort

SIGHTS AT A GLANCE

GETTING AROUND

In Belgium distances are short, with a wide choice of routes – even the tiniest village is easily reached. Brussels sits at the hub of several major highways such as the E19 and the E40 (which link the capital to the country's principal towns). The fully integrated public transport system has frequent train services and a comprehensive bus network.

Namur's Citadel from the River Meuse

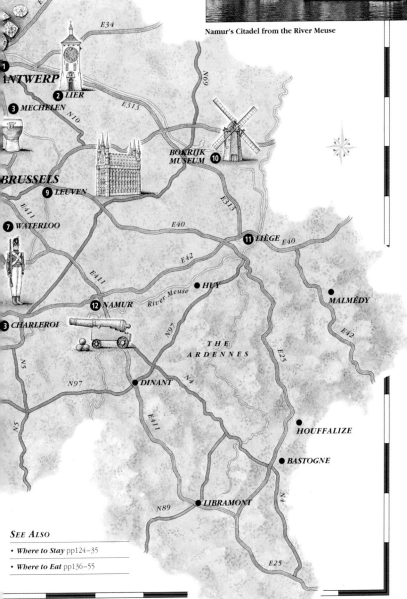

Street-by-Street: Antwerp ❶

FANNING OUT FROM the east bank of the River Scheldt, Antwerp is Belgium's second-largest city. It is also the centre of the international diamond trade, which is run from the unassuming buildings that line the streets near Centraal Station. Today, the city's industries lie away from its medieval core whose narrow streets and fine buildings cluster around the cathedral and the Grote Markt. Most sites of interest are within easy walking distance of the Grote Markt whose surrounding streets house museums, shops and exuberant cafés and bars.

Gilt statue on guildhouse

Nationaal Scheepvaart-museum
This model of an 18th-century armed merchant ship is in Antwerp's Maritime Museum.

To Koninklijk
Museum voor
Schone Kunsten

The Vleeshuis
Occupied by the Butcher's Guild for three centuries, this beautiful 1504 building has striking layers of brick and stone that look like alternating strips of fat and lean meat.

The Ethnografisch Museum has artifacts from around the world.

Stadhuis

The Brabo Fountain
This statue, in the centre of the Grote Markt, depicts the fearless soldier, Silvius Brabo. Said to be the nephew of Julius Caesar, Brabo is shown throwing the hand of the mythical giant, Antigonius into the River Scheldt.

KEY

– – – Suggested route

STAR SIGHTS

★ **Grote Markt**

★ **Kathedraal**

Sint Pauluskerk
This imposing church was built in 1517, but has a magnificent Baroque gate and spire dating from the late 17th century. Inside, there is a noted collection of paintings, including one especially fine work by Rubens.

★ Grote Markt
Antwerp's golden age of trade in the 16th century is reflected in the square's cosmopolitan 1565 town hall, built by architects from all over Europe.

★ Onze Lieve Vrouwe Kathedraal
The largest Gothic cathedral in Belgium, this building occupies a 1-ha (2.5-acre) site in Antwerp's centre. Work began on this elegant church, noted for its spire, in 1352 and took two centuries to complete.

→ To Centraal Station

→ To Rubenshuis

Groenplaats
The Groenplaats or Green Square is a pleasant open space with trees and flower beds. Lined with cafés, bars and restaurants, the square is a popular spot with both locals and visitors for a peaceful stroll or meal.

0 metres 50

0 yards 50

ZIRKSTRAAT

SMIDSTRAAT

Exploring Antwerp

THERE HAS BEEN a settlement here, on the banks of the River Scheldt, since the 2nd century. The city of Antwerp grew up and became part of the Duchy of Brabant in 1106. Within 200 years it was a thriving hub of the European cloth industry and Brabant's main port. Today, Antwerp is the principal city of Flemish-speaking Belgium. It is a large metropolis whose port and older residential areas surround a compact centre packed with evidence of its rich history. There are exquisite guild-houses, where the medieval merchants once traded, and imposing churches and several museums, where collections of paintings by the city's most famous son, Pieter Paul Rubens (1577–1640), are also to be found. Antwerp also has many contemporary attractions, such as excellent restaurants, busy nightclubs and bars. Thanks to the Antwerp Six, a group of adventurous designers, the city also has a reputation for cutting-edge fashion.

Visitors tour Antwerp on an historic horse-drawn bus

Getting Around
The best way to get around Antwerp is by using the public transport system. The excellent bus and tram network is focused on Centraal Station, where most visitors arrive. Fast and frequent trams and buses travel from here to the centre. Most of the city's main sights are within walking distance of the Grote Markt.

🏛 Grote Markt
Grote Markt. 📞 *(03) 232 0103.* ⚐
Antwerp's central square, or Grote Markt, is flanked by the ornately gabled Stadhuis (town hall), which was built in 1565 by the architect and sculptor Cornelis Floris. Its interior was restored in the 19th century and houses a series of paintings which celebrate the city's history. The north side of the square has a series of guild-houses, each of which is decorated with gilded figures. The tallest of these is the House of the Crossbowmen at number seven, on top of which is a statue of St George and the dragon. The Brabo fountain in the middle of the square is one of Antwerp's noted landmarks.

Carvings above the cathedral door depict the Last Judgement

🔒 Onze Lieve Vrouwe Kathedraal
Groenplaats 21 or Handschoenmarkt. 📞 *(03) 213 9940.* ⚐ *10am–5pm Mon–Fri, 10am–3pm Sat, 1–4pm Sun.* 🎫 ⚐
The building of Antwerp's Onze Lieve Vrouwe Kathedraal (Cathedral of Our Lady) took almost two centuries, from 1352 to 1521. This magnificent structure has a graceful tiered spire that rises 123 m (404 ft) above the winding streets of the medieval city centre. Inside, the impression of light and space owes much to its seven-aisled nave and vaulted ceiling. The collection of paintings and sculpture includes three works by Rubens, of which two are triptychs – the *Raising of the Cross* (1610) and the *Descent from the Cross* (1612).

🔒 Sint Pauluskerk
St-Paulusstraat 22 or Veemarkt 14. 📞 *(03) 231 3321.* ⚐ *Easter Sat–Sep: 2–5pm daily.* 🎫 *3pm Sun & pub hols.*
Completed in the early 17th century, this splendid church is distinguished by its combination of both Gothic and Baroque features. The exterior dates from about 1517, and has an added elaborate Baroque gateway. The interior is noted for its intricately carved wooden choir stalls. St Paulus also possesses an outstanding series of paintings illustrating the Fifteen Mysteries of the Rosary, one of which, *The Scourging of the Pillar*, is an exquisite canvas by Rubens. There are also paintings by van Dyck and Jordaens.

Fresco paintings of the dukes of Brabant adorn the Stadhuis walls

Vleeshuis

Vleeshouwersstraat 38–40. ☎ (03) 233 6404. ○ 10am–4:45pm Tue–Sun, Easter Mon. ● 1 & 2 Jan, 1 May, Ascension, 1 & 2 Nov, 25 & 26 Dec.

The Vleeshuis (Meat Hall) was completed in 1504 to a design by Herman de Waghemakere. The structure features slender towers with five hexagonal turrets and rising gables, all built in alternate strips of stone and brick – giving it a streaky bacon-like appearance.

Inside, there is an impressive collection of medieval wood-carvings and old musical instruments. In the 17th century, Antwerp was renowned for its manufacture of instruments, including the eccentrically shaped harpsichords and clavichords on display here. There are also paintings, but the highlight is the retable (altarpiece), depicting Christ's Entombment, Crucifixion and Ascent to Heaven, which was carved in wood by Jacob van Cothem in 1514.

Statue of an ogre outside the Maritime Museum

Nationaal Scheepvaartmuseum

Steenplein 1. ☎ (03) 232 0850. ○ 10am–5pm Tue–Sun. ● Mon.

The Maritime Museum is located in the gatehouse of Antwerp's original fortress, or Steen, the oldest building in the city. Built from the 10th to 16th centuries, it was used in medieval times as a prison. Today, this restored building has 12 rooms devoted to the history of all things nautical, from fearsome Viking ships' heads to the small but elegant gondola built for the visit of Napoleon to the city in 1808. Outside, moored along the riverside, is a selection of old canal tugs and barges.

Rubenshuis

See pp96–7.

Sint Jacobskerk

Lange Nieuwstraat 73–75, Eikenstraat. ☎ (03) 225 0414. ○ Apr–Oct: 2–5pm Mon–Sat; Nov–Mar: 9am–noon, Mon–Sat; Sun services only.

Noted as Rubens' burial place, this sandstone chuch, built over three centuries from 1491 to 1656, occupies the site of a chapel which lay along the pilgrimage route of St James of Compostella. The rich interior contains the tombs of several other notable Antwerp families, as well as much 17th-century art, including sculptures by Hendrik Verbruggen, and paintings by van Dyck, Otto Venius (Rubens' first master) and Jacob Jordaens. When Rubens died, in 1640, he was buried in his family chapel, located in the ambulatory directly behind the high altar. The chapel altar is where one of Rubens' last paintings, *Our Lady Surrounded by Saints* (1634), is displayed.

Koninklijk Museum voor Schone Kunsten

See pp94–5.

Modenatie

Nationalestraat 28. ☎ (03) 226 1447. ○ call for details.

The Fashion Museum houses the Flanders Fashion Institute, the Fashion Department of Antwerp's Royal Academy and a museum of fashion (MOMU).

Provincial Diamond Museum

Koningin Astridplein 19–24. ☎ (03) 202 4890. ○ call for details.

This museum is a celebration of diamonds, one of Antwerp's best-known attributes.

Late 16th-century printing press in the Museum Plantin-Moretus

Museum Plantin-Moretus

Vrijdagmarkt 22–23. ☎ (03) 221 1450. ○ 10am–5pm Tue–Sun, Easter Mon. ● Mon, 1 & 2 Jan, 1 May, Ascension, 1 & 2 Nov, 25 & 26 Dec.

This fascinating museum occupies a large 16th-century house that belonged to the printer Christopher Plantin, who moved here in 1576. The house is built around a court-yard, and its ancient rooms and narrow corridors resemble the types of interiors painted by Flemish and Dutch masters. The museum is devoted to the early years of printing, when Plantin and others began to produce books that bore no resemblance to earlier, illuminated medieval manuscripts.

Antwerp was a centre for printing in the 15th and 16th centuries, and Plantin was its most successful printer. Today, his workshop displays several historic printing presses, as well as woodcuts and copper plates. Plantin's library is also on show and includes an array of beautifully made volumes, ranging from medical books to French literature. One of the gems here is a Gutenberg Bible – the first book to be printed using moveable type, a new technique invented by Johannes Gutenberg in 1455.

View of the Vleeshuis' striking façade

Koninklijk Museum voor Schone Kunsten

Aᴺᵀᵂᴇʀᴘ'ˢ ʟᴀʀɢᴇˢᵀ and most impressive fine art
collection is exhibited in the Museum voor Schone
Kunsten, which occupies a massive late 19th-century Neo-
Classical building almost 2 km (1 mile) to the south of the
Grote Markt. The permanent collection contains both
ancient and modern works. The earlier collection on the
upper floor begins with medieval Flemish painting and
continues through the 17th century, with the 'Antwerp
Trio' of Rubens, van Dyck and Jordaens well represented.
At ground level, modern exhibits include the work of
Belgian artists such as René Magritte, James Ensor and
Paul Delvaux, as well as an important collection of work
by Rik Wouters, a Fauvist influenced by Matisse. Tissot
and van Gogh are among the foreign artists on show.

First Floor

Façade of Gallery
*Building began on
this imposing struc-
ture in 1884. The
Neo-Classical façade
with its vast pillars
has carved women
charioteers atop
each side. It was
opened in 1890.*

★ **Saint Barbara** *(1437)*
*Jan van Eyck's painting of
Saint Barbara in several
tones of grey shows the
saint sitting in front
of a huge Gothic
cathedral tower
still under
construction,
while a prayer
book lies open
on her lap.*

**Main
Entrance**

STAR PAINTINGS

★ **Saint Barbara
by Jan van Eyck**

★ **Adoration of
the Magi by Pieter
Paul Rubens**

★ **Woman Ironing
by Rik Wouters**

★ **Woman Ironing** *(1912)*
*This peaceful domestic scene by
Rik Wouters employs the muted
colours of Impressionism. This was
a productive period for Wouters
who painted 60 canvases in 1912.*

**GALLERY
GUIDE**
*The gallery is divided
into two floors. Flemish
Old Masters are housed
on the first floor of the
museum, and the ground
floor focuses on the 19th
and 20th centuries. Each
room is lettered and vis-
itors may view exhibits
chronologically, starting
with the de Keyser series
in the entrance hall.*

★ **Adoration of the Magi** (1624)
One of Rubens' master-pieces, this painting displays a remarkable freedom of composition.

As the Old Sang, the Young Play Pipes (1638)
Jacob Jordaens' (1593–1678) joyous celebration of life in this painting of a family enjoying a musical evening contrasts with his religious paintings.

Pink Bows (1936)
Paul Delvaux's dream-like style clearly shows the influence of Sigmund Freud's psycho-analytic theories on Surrealist painting.

Madame Récamier (1967)
René Magritte's macabre version of the original painting by David is a classic Surrealist work.

KEY

☐	15th-century paintings
☐	16th-century paintings
☐	17th-century paintings
☐	17th century in Holland
☐	Re-creation of a 17th-century Art Gallery
☐	19th century
☐	19th-century salon
☐	20th century
☐	Temporary exhibitions
☐	Non-exhibition space

Ground Floor

Rubenshuis

Statue of Neptune

RUBENSHUIS, ON Wapper Square, was Pieter Paul Rubens' home and studio for the last thirty years of his life, from 1610 to 1640. The city bought the premises just before World War II, but by then the house was little more than a ruin, and what can be seen today is the result of careful restoration. It is divided into two sections. To the left of the entrance are the narrow rooms of the artist's living quarters, equipped with period furniture. Behind this part of the house is the kunstkamer, or art gallery, where Rubens exhibited both his own and other artists' work, and entertained his friends and wealthy patrons, such as the Archduke Albert and the Infanta Isabella. To the right of the entrance lies the main studio, a spacious salon where Rubens worked on – and showed – his works. A signposted route guides visitors through the house.

Façade of Rubenshuis
The older Flemish part of the house sits next to the later house, whose elegant early Baroque façade was designed by Rubens.

Formal Gardens
The small garden is laid out formally and its charming pavilion dates from Rubens' time. He was influenced by such architects of the Italian Renaissance as Vitruvius when he built the Italian Baroque addition to his house in the 1620s.

★ Rubens' Studio
It is estimated that Rubens produced some 2,500 paintings in this large, high-ceilinged room. In the Renaissance manner, Rubens designed the work which was usually completed by a team of other artists employed in his studio.

STAR SIGHTS

★ **Kunstkamer**

★ **Rubens' Studio**

Bedroom

The Rubens family lived in the Flemish section of the house, with its small rooms and narrow passages. The portrait by the bed is said to be of Rubens' second wife, Helena Fourment.

The Familia Kamer, or family sitting room, is cosy and has a pretty tiled floor. It overlooks Wapper Square.

VISITORS' CHECKLIST

Wapper 9–11. ☎ (03) 201 1555.
🚌 1, 9, 19. 🚊 2, 15. ⏰ 10am–
5pm Tue–Sun, Easter Mon. ● 1 &
2 Jan, 1 & 2 Nov, 25 & 26 Dec. ♿

Dining Room

Intricately fashioned leather panels line the walls of this room, which also displays a noted work by Frans Snyders.

★ Kunstkamer

This art gallery contains a series of painted sketches by Rubens. At the far end is a semi-circular dome, modelled on Rome's Pantheon, displaying a number of marble busts.

Chequered mosaic tiled floor

Baroque Portico

One of the few remaining original features, this portico was designed by Rubens, and links the older house with the Baroque section. It is adorned with a frieze showing scenes from Greek mythology.

The Centenary Clock on Lier's Zimmertoren or watchtower

Lier ❷

🏛 30,000. 🚊 🚌 ℹ Grote Markt 57, (03) 491 1393. ⓦ www.lier.be

LIER IS AN attractive small town, just 20 km (12 miles) southeast of Antwerp. The Grote Markt is a spacious cobbled square framed by handsome historic buildings. The Stadhuis (town hall) was built in 1740, and its elegant dimensions contrast strongly with the square, turreted 14th-century Belfort (belfry) adjoining. Nearby is the **Stedelijk Museum Wuyts**, with its collection of paintings by Flemish masters including Jan Steen, Brueghel and Rubens. East of here the church of St Gummaruserk, with its soaring stone pillars and vaulted roof, evokes medieval times, and the carved altarpiece is notable for the intricate detail of its biblical scenes. The stained-glass windows are among the finest in Belgium and were a gift from Emperor Maximillian I in 1516.

One of Lier's highlights is the **Zimmertoren**, a 14th-century watchtower that now houses the clocks of Lodewijk Zimmer (1888–1970). This Lier merchant wanted to share his knowledge of timepieces.

🏛 **Stedelijk Museum Wuyts**
Florent van Cauwen straat 14.
📞 (03) 491 1396. 🕐 Apr–Oct: Wed–Sun. 🎫
🏰 **Zimmertoren**
Zimmerplein18. 📞 (03) 491 1395.
🕐 daily. 🎫

Mechelen ❸

🏛 75,000. 🚊 🚌 ℹ Stadhuis 21, Grote Markt, (015) 29 7655.

THE SEAT of the Catholic Archbishop of Belgium, Mechelen was the administrative capital of the country under the Burgundian prince, Charles the Bold, in 1473. Today, it is an appealing town whose expansive main square is flanked by pleasant cafés and bars. To the west of the square is the main attraction, **St Romboutskathedraal**, a huge cathedral that took some 300 years to complete. The building might never have been finished but for a deal with the Vatican: the cathedral was allowed to sell special indulgences (which absolved the purchaser of their sins) to raise funds, on condition that the pope received a percentage. Completed in 1546, the cathedral's tower has Belgium's finest carillon, a set of 49 bells, whose peals ring out at weekends and on public holidays. The church also contains *The Crucifixion* by Antony van Dyck (1599–1641).

Less well-known in Mechelen are three 16th-century houses by the River Dilje. They are not open to visitors, but their exteriors are delightful. The "House of the Little Devils" is adorned with carved demons.

Mechelen is famous for its local beers, and visitors should try the Gouden Carolus, a dark brew, which is said to have been the favourite tipple of the Emperor Charles V.

🏛 **St Romboutskathedraal**
St Romboutskerkhof. 📞 (015) 29 7655. 🎫 obligatory. Easter–Sep: 2pm Sat, Sun & pub hols; Jun–mid-Sep: 7pm Mon (Jul & Aug: also 2pm). Tours depart from the Tourist Office.

Mechelen's main square, the Grote Markt, on market day

Dendermonde ❹

🏛 40,000. 🚊 🚌 ℹ Stadhuis, Grote Markt, (052) 21 3956.

A QUIET, INDUSTRIAL town, Dendermonde is about 20 km (12 miles) southeast of Ghent. Its strategic position, at the confluence of the Scheldt and Dender rivers, has attracted the attention of a string of invaders

Vleeshuis façade on the Grote Markt in Dendermonde

Wood panelled walls and paintings adorn the hall at Gaasbeek Castle

over the centuries, including the Germans who shelled Dendermonde in 1914. But the town is perhaps best-known as the site of the Steed Bayard, a carnival held every ten years at the end of August.

Today, the town's spacious main square is framed by the quaint turrets and towers of the the Vleeshuis or Meat Hall. The Town Hall is an elegant 14th-century building which was extensively restored in 1920. Dendermonde also possesses two exquisite early religious paintings by Anthony van Dyck which are on display in the Onze Lieve Vrouwekerk (Church of Our Lady).

Pajottenland ⑤

🏛 111,700. 🛈 Toerisme Pajotten-land en Zennevalaaei, (02) 356 4259.
🖥 www.toerismevlaanderen.be

THE PAJOTTENLAND forms part of the Brabant province to the southwest of Brussels, and is bordered in the west by the Dender River. The gentle rolling hills of the landscape contain many farms, some of which date back to the 17th century. The village of Onze Lieve Vrouw Lombeek, just 12 km (7 miles) west of Brussels, is named after its church, an outstanding example of 14th-century Gothic architecture.

Just a few kilometres south of the village lies the area's main attraction, the castle and grounds of **Gaasbeek**. The

castle was remodelled in the 19th century, but actually dates from the 13th century, and boasts a moat and a thick curtain wall, strengthened by huge semi-circular towers. The castle's interior holds an excellent collection of fine and applied arts. Among the treasures are rich tapestries, 15th-century alabaster reliefs from England, silverware and a delightful ivory and copper hunting horn which belonged to the Protestant martyr Count Egmont in the 16th century. The Pajottenland is also known

for its beers, especially lambic and gueuze. Lambic is one of the most popular types of beer in Belgium (see pp142–3).

🏰 **Gaasbeek**
Kasteelstraat 40. 📞 (02) 532 4372.
🕐 Apr–Nov: Tue–Thu, Sat & Sun (Jul & Aug: also on Mon).
⬤ Dec–Mar. 🈲

Halle ⑥

🏛 30,000. 🚉 🚌 🛈 Stadhuis, Grote Markt, (02) 356 4259. 🖥 www.halle.be

LOCATED ON THE outskirts of Brussels, in the province of Brabant, Halle is a peaceful little town. It has been a major religious centre since the 13th century because of the cult of the Black Virgin, an effigy in the Onze Lieve Vrouwebasiliek, the town's main church. The holy statue's blackness is due to its stained colour, which is said to have occurred through contact with gunpowder during the religious wars of the 17th century.

The virgin has long been one of Belgium's most venerated icons and each year, on Whit Sunday, the statue is paraded through the town.

THE STEED BAYARD

Dendermonde's famous carnival of the Steed Bayard occurs every ten years at the end of August. The focus of the festival is a horse, the Steed Bayard itself, represented in the carnival by a giant model. It takes 34 bearers to carry the horse which weighs 700 kg (1,540 lb) and is 5.8 m (19 ft) high. A procession of locals dressed in medieval costume re-enact the Steed Bayard legend – a complex tale of chivalry and treachery, family loyalty and betrayal. The four Aymon brothers (who were said to be the nephews of Emperor Charlemagne) ride the horse, and it is their behaviour towards the animal which serves to demonstrate their moral worth.

Waterloo

Death mask of Napoleon

THE BATTLE OF WATERLOO was fought on 18 June, 1815. It pitted Napoleon and his French army against the Duke of Wellington, who was in command of troops mostly drawn from Britain, Germany and the Netherlands. The two armies met outside the insignificant hamlet of Waterloo, to the south of Brussels. The result was decisive. The battle began at 11:30am and just nine hours later the French were in full retreat. Napoleon abdicated and was subsequently exiled to the island of St Helena, where he died in mysterious circumstances six years later.

Despite its importance, the battlefield has not been conserved, and part of it has been dug up for a highway. However, enough remains to give a general sense of the battle. The best place to start a visit here is at the Musée Wellington, some 3 km (2 miles) from the battlefield.

predates the battle, after which it was extended, with the newer portions containing dozens of memorial plaques and flagstones dedicated to those British soldiers who died at Waterloo. Several of these plaques were paid for by voluntary contributions from ordinary soldiers in honour of their officers.

The Butte de Lion viewed from the Waterloo battlefield

⬥ Musée Wellington
Chaussée de Bruxelles 147. **(** (02) 354 7806. ◯ daily. ● 1 Jan, 25 Dec. ▨ Ⓦ www.waterloo.be
The Waterloo inn where Wellington spent the night before the battle has been turned into the Musée Wellington, its narrow rooms packed with curios alongside plans and models of the battle. One curiosity is the artificial leg of Lord Uxbridge, one of Wellington's commanders. His leg was blown off by a cannon ball during the

battle and buried in Waterloo. After his death, the leg was sent to join the rest of him in England and, as recompense, his relatives sent his artificial one back to Waterloo.

⬥ Eglise St-Joseph
Chaussée de Bruxelles.
((02) 354 0011.
Across the road from the Musée Wellington is the tiny church of St-Joseph, which was built as a royal chapel at the end of the 17th century. Its dainty, elegant cupola

⬥ Butte de Lion
149 Chaussée de Bruxelles, N5, 3km (2 miles) S of Waterloo.
((02) 354 9910. ◯ daily. ▨
Dating from 1826, the Butte de Lion is a 45-m (148-ft) high earthen mound built on the

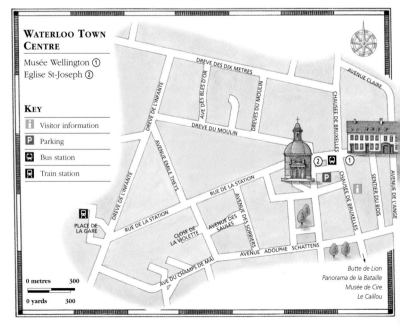

WATERLOO TOWN CENTRE

Musée Wellington ①
Eglise St-Joseph ②

KEY

ℹ	Visitor information
🅿	Parking
🚌	Bus station
🚉	Train station

0 metres   300
0 yards   300

DREVE DES DIX METRES
AVENUE CLAIRE
DREVE DE L'INFANTE
AVE DES BLES D'OR
DREVES DU MOULIN
CHAUSSEE DE BRUXELLES
DREVE DU MOULIN
AVENUE EMILE THEYS
DREVE DE L'INFANTE
RUE DE LA STATION
RUE DE LA STATION
AVENUE DES SORBIERS
SENTIER DU BOIS
AVENUE DE L'ANGE
CHAUSSEE DE BRUXELLES
PLACE DE LA GARE
CLOSE DE LA VIOLETTE
AVENUE DES SAULES
AVE DU CHAMPS DE MAI
AVENUE ADOLPHE SCHATTENS

Butte de Lion
Panorama de la Bataille
Musée de Cire
Le Caillou

spot where one of Wellington's Dutch generals, the Prince of Orange, was wounded during the battle. Steps lead to the top, which is guarded by a huge cast-iron lion, and from here there is a great view over the battlefield. The French army approached from the south and fought up the slope across farmland that became increasingly marshy as the day went on, while their opponents had the drier ridge at the foot of the mound. A plan of the battle is displayed at the top.

🏛 Panorama de la Bataille
252–254 Route du Lion, Braine-L'Alleud. N5, 3 km (2 miles) S of Waterloo. **C** (02) 385 1912. ☐ daily. 🖼
This is perhaps the most fascinating of the several attractions located beneath the Butte de Lion. This circular painting of the battle by artist Louis Demoulin was erected in 1912. It is 110 m (360 ft) long and stretches right round a circular, purpose-built gallery. Panoramic, circular paintings came to be very popular in the late 19th century; this is one of the few works that remain intact.

🏛 Musée de Cire
315–317 Route du Lion, N5, 3 km (2 miles) S of Waterloo. **C** (02) 384 6740. ☐ Apr–Oct: daily; Nov–Mar: pub hols, Sat & Sun. 🖼
The Musée de Cire is a wax museum where pride of place goes to the models of soldiers dressed in the military regalia of 1815. It seems strange today that the various armies dressed their men in such vivid colours, which made them easy targets. Indeed, many commanders paid for the uniforms of their men themselves, competing with each other for the most flamboyant design.

🏛 Napoleon's Last Headquarters
66 Chaussée de Waterloo, Vieux-Genappe, N5, 7 km (4.5 miles) S of Waterloo. **C** (02) 384 2424. ☐ Tue–Sun. ● 1 Jan, 25 Dec. 🖼
Napoleon spent the eve of the battle in a farmhouse, Le Caillou. This is now a museum containing some artifacts from Napoleon's army, a bronze death mask of the Emperor and his army-issue bed.

Southeast side of Nivelles' imposing church, Collégiale Ste-Gertrude

Nivelles ❽

🚶 20,000. 🚉 🚌 ℹ Waux-Hall, Place Albert I, (067) 88 2275.

Tucked away among the rolling hills of the province of Brabant, the little town of Nivelles was, for centuries, the site of one of the wealthiest and most powerful abbeys in the region. Earlier it was the cradle of the Carolingian dynasty, whose most celebrated ruler was the Emperor Charlemagne (747–814). The main sight today is the vast church, the Collégiale Ste-Gertrude, that dominates the town centre. Something of an architectural hotchpotch, the church dates back to the 10th century and is remarkable in that it has two imposing chancels – one each for the pope and the king.

Leuven ❾

See pp102–103.

Bokrijk Museum ❿

See pp104–105.

Liège ⓫

🚶 400,000. 🚉 🚌 ℹ En Féronstrée 92, (04) 221 9221.

Belgium's third-biggest city, Liège is a major river port and industrial conurbation at the confluence of the rivers Meuse and Ourthe. The city

has an unusual history in that it was an independent principality from the 10th to the 18th century, ruled by Prince Bishops. However, the church became widely despised and when the French Republican army arrived in 1794, they were welcomed by the local citizens with open arms.

Today, Liège possesses some notable attractions and highlights include the **Musée de la Vie Wallone** (Museum of Walloon Life), housed in an outstanding 17th-century mansion. The museum focuses on Walloon folklore and culture, which is depicted in a series of reconstructed interiors and craft workshops from the city's history.

🏛 Musée de la Vie Wallone
Cour des Mineurs. **C** (04) 223 6094. ☐ Tue–Sat. 🖼

Namur ⓬

🚶 100,000. 🚉 🚌 ⛴ ℹ Square Léopold, (081) 24 64 49.

French-speaking Namur is a friendly, attractive town whose narrow central streets boast several elegant mansions and fine old churches, as well as lots of lively bars and outstanding restaurants. Until the Belgian army left in 1978, Namur was also a military town. The soldiers were stationed within the Citadel, located on top of the steep hill on the south side of the centre, which remains the town's main attraction. An exploration of its bastions and subterranean galleries takes several hours.

Namur's ancient walls or Citadel seen from the River Meuse

Leuven **❾**

ITHIN EASY STRIKING distance of Brussels, the historic Flemish town of Leuven traces its origins to a fortified camp constructed here by Julius Caesar. In medieval times, the town became an important centre of the cloth trade, but it was as a seat of learning that it achieved international prominence. In 1425, Pope Martin V and Count John of Brabant founded Leuven's university, and by the mid-1500s it was one of Europe's most prestigious academic institutions, the home of such famous scholars as Erasmus and Mercator.

Font Sapienza

Even today, the university exercises a dominant influence over the town, and its students give Leuven a vibrant atmosphere. The bars and cafés flanking the Oude Markt, a large square in the centre of town, are especially popular. Adjoining the square is the Grote Markt, a triangular open space which boasts two fine medieval buildings, the Stadhuis and St Pieterskerk.

Lively café society in the Oude Markt

♜ Oude Markt

This handsome, cobblestoned square is flanked by a tasteful ensemble of high-gabled brick buildings. Some of these date from the 18th century; others are comparatively new. At ground level these buildings house the largest concentration of bars and cafés in town, and as such attract the town's university students in their droves.

♜ Stadhuis

Grote Markt. **(** *(016) 21 1539.* ◯ *daily.* 🖼️ 🎫 *obligatory. At 3pm daily (Apr–Sep: also at 11am Mon–Fri).*

Built between 1448 and 1463 from the profits of the cloth trade, Leuven's town hall, the Stadhuis, was designed to demonstrate the wealth of the city's merchants. This distinctive, tall building is renowned for its lavishly carved and decorated façade. A line of narrow windows rise up over three floors beneath a steeply pitched roof adorned with dormer windows and

pencil-thin turrets. It is, however, in the fine quality of its stonework that the building excels, with delicately carved tracery and detailed medieval figures beneath 300 niche bases. There are grotesques of every description as well as representations of folktales and biblical stories, all carved in exuberant late-Gothic style. Within the niche alcoves is a series of 19th-century statues depicting local dignitaries and politicians. Guided tours of the interior are available, and include three lavishly decorated reception rooms.

Stone carvings of medieval figures decorate the Stadhuis façade

Huge buttresses support the tower of the Church of Saint Peter

⛪ St Pieterskerk and Museum voor Religieuze Kunst

Grote Markt. **(** *(016) 29 5133.* ◯ *Mar–Oct: daily, Nov–Feb: Tue–Sun.* 🖼️ *to museum.*

Across the square from the Stadhuis rises St Pieterskerk, a massive church built over a period of two hundred years from the 1420s. The nave and aisles were completed first, but when the twin towers of the western façade were finally added in 1507, the foundations proved inadequate and they soon began to sink. With money in short supply, it was decided to remove the top sections of the towers – hence the truncated versions of today.

Inside the church, the sweeping lines of the nave are intercepted by an impressive 1499 rood screen and a Baroque wooden pulpit, depicting the conversion of Saint Norbert. Norbert was a wealthy but irreligious German noble, who was hit by lightning while riding. He was unhurt but his horse died under him, and this led to his devoting himself to the church.

The church also houses the Religious Art Museum which has three exquisite paintings by Dieric Bouts (1415–75). Born in the Netherlands, Bouts spent most of his working life in Leuven, where he became the town's official artist. In his *Last Supper* (1468), displayed here, Bouts painted Judas's face in shadow, emphasizing the mystery of Holy Communion rather than the betrayal.

🜨 Fochplein

Adjacent to the Grote Markt is the Fochplein, a narrow triangular square containing some of Leuven's most popular shops, selling everything from fashion to food. In the middle is the Font Sapienza, a modern fountain that shows a student pouring water through his empty head – a pithy view of the town's student population.

🏛 Museum Vander Kelen-Mertens

Savoyestraat 6. **C** (016) 22 6906.
◯ *Tue–Sun.* 🎟

The Museum Vander Kelen-Mertens has fair claim to be Leuven's most enjoyable museum, with its well-presented collection arranged over two floors. Once the home of the Vander Kelen-Mertens family, the rooms are furnished in a variety of historical styles, ranging from a Renaissance salon to a rococo dining room.

Much of the art on display is by the early Flemish masters, including the work of Quentin Metsys (1466–1550), who was born in Leuven and is noted for introducing Italian style to north European art. The collection also includes a beautiful *Holy Trinity* by Rogier van der Weyden (1400–1464). Fine art is located in the first-floor galleries where there is also an impressive display of 16th- and 17th-century embroidered vestments, stained glass and Oriental ceramics.

🔒 St Michielskerk

Naamsestraat.
◯ *Jun–Sep: Wed, Sat & Sun.*
One of Leuven's most impressive churches, St Michielskerk was built for the Jesuits in the middle of the 17th century. The church was badly damaged during World War II, but has since been carefully restored. Its graceful façade with its flowing lines is an excellent illustration of the Baroque style. The interior is regularly open to visitors for three afternoons during the summer months. The stunning 1660 carved woodwork around the altar and choir are well worth seeing.

🔒 Groot Begijnhof

Schapenstraat. ◯ *daily, for street access only.*
Founded around 1230, the Groot Begijnhof was once one of the largest béguinages in Belgium, home to several hundred béguines (*see p53*).

VISITORS' CHECKLIST

👥 85,000. 🚉 Bondgenoten-laan. 🚏 Grote Markt 9.
ℹ Vanderkelenstraat 30, 3000 Leuven, (016) 21 1540.

The complex of 72 charming red-brick cottages (dating mostly from the 17th century) is set around the grassy squares and cobbled streets near the River Dilje. Leuven university bought the complex in 1961 and converted the cottages into student accommodation.

The red-brick houses of Leuven's Groot Begijnhof

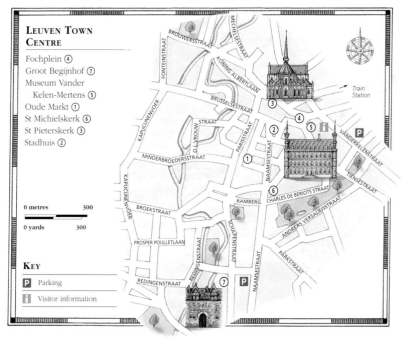

LEUVEN TOWN CENTRE

0 metres   300
0 yards   300

KEY

P   Parking

ℹ   Visitor information

Bokrijk Openluchtmuseum ❿

BOKRIJK VILLAGE CONTAINS an immensely popular open-air museum devoted to Flemish rural life before 1900. Set among the forest and rolling pasture of Limburg province, about 10 km (6 miles) northeast of the town of Hasselt, the open-air museum was established in 1953 by the provincial government. The land has been farmed since the Middle Ages, and in the early 20th century was used by the Belgian Farmer's Union for agricultural trials.

Bokrijk is made up several settlements which have been moved here and reconstructed, and has more than a hundred restored buildings. The collection is divided into three main sections, each representing a distinct geographical area. Manned by costumed guides, the farmhouses, barns and workshops offer various live demonstrations of an assortment of traditional crafts.

Costumed character
Characters such as this man, dressed in typical peasant's clothing of the 19th century, enhance the Bokrijk's authentic atmosphere.

Visitor riding historic bike
The museum offers the chance to participate in a range of activities from cycling and fishing to such traditional crafts as baking and even farming with antique tools.

The Old Town

Pigeon Tower
The pigeon nests in this 1634 tower were located in the upper part of the building, which was accessible only by ladder, to prevent the theft of the young birds.

Fertile Uplands: Brabant

Fertile Uplands: Limburg Haspengouw and the Maasland

★ **Interior features**
Most of the buildings here have original interior features. This 18th-century fireplace has Delft tiles that depict biblical scenes such as the birth of Christ.

The Fertile Lowlands: East and West Flanders

★ **Agricultural architecture**
This 16th-century farmhouse was built in Saxon style and has a fine thatched roof. The adjacent windmill dates from 1788 and was used to grind grain. It still contains the original millstones.

The Poor Heathlands, or the Kempen, is one of the principal geographical areas in the museum. It was an area of reclaimed land where villagers eked out a living from their farms.

Grain store
This elegant, timber-framed grain store, or spijker, dates from the 16th century. This building comes from Limburg province, where it probably formed part of a brewery.

Village priest
Many of the Bokrijk's costumed workers, such as this village priest, are on hand to explain what life was like in these pre-industrial rural areas.

tres   50

rds   50

STAR FEATURES

★ **Agricultural architecture**

★ **Interior features**

Charleroi ❸

🏛 *200,000.* ✈ 🚆 🚌 ℹ *Square de la Gare du Sud, (071) 31 8218.*

Wᴵᵀʜ ᴀ ᴘᴏᴘᴜʟᴀᴛᴵᴏɴ of more than 200,000, the industrial centre of Charleroi is one of the largest cities in French-speaking Belgium. Named after the Hapsburg king Charles II, who had the town fortified in 1666, it achieved prominence in the 1800s as the focus of a burgeoning coal-mining and steel area known as the Pays Noir (Black Country). Its busy centre fans out from the River Sambre, dividing into the Lower City, which is largely concerned with commerce and is of little interest to the casual visitor, and the Upper City, an older quarter around Place Charles II. The highlights are the **Photography Museum** and the **Musée du Verre** (Glass Museum), with its collection of glass ranging from Assyrian necklaces to contemporary glasswork. From Charleroi, it is around 20 km (12 miles) west to the little town of Binche, the site of one of Belgium's most famous carnivals. Every year in March, parties lead up to a Shrove Tuesday festival.

St Christophe's church in Charleroi's Upper City

🏛 **Photography Museum**
Avenue Paul Pastuur 11. 📞 *(071) 43 5810.* ⃝ *Tue–Sun.* ⬤ *Mon.* 📷

🏛 **Musée du Verre**
Blvd Defontaine 10. 📞 *(071) 31 0838.* ⃝ *Tue–Sun.* ⬤ *Mon.* 📷

Mons ❹

🏛 *90,000.* 🚆 🚌 ℹ *Grand Place 22, (065) 33 5580.*

Pᴇʀʜᴀᴘs ʙᴇsᴛ known for its association with both World Wars, Mons is actually an ancient town. The capital of the French-speaking province of Hainaut, Mons lies across the steep hill that first made

The summer drawing room in the 18th-century Chateau d'Attre, near Ath

it important. Natural strongpoints are rare in this part of the country and the Romans, observing the lay of the land, established a fortified camp here in the 1st century AD.

Today, Mons is a friendly town whose social life focuses around the Grand Place and its pavement cafés. Also overlooking the Grand Place is the 15th-century Hôtel de Ville, an imposing Gothic structure. A cast-iron monkey, known as the *Singe du Grand Garde*, sits on the outside wall near the main entrance, and is meant to bring good luck to those who stroke its head. Southwest of the Grand Place are the town's well-preserved medieval streets and the Collégiale Ste-Waudru, a late-Gothic church.

Mons' other important sights are the **Musée du Guerre**, which focuses on the role of Mons in both World Wars, and the **Musée du Vieux Namy**, with its collection of ceramics and Delftware.

🏛 **Musée du Guerre**
Rue Houdain 13.
📞 *(065) 33 5213.*
⃝ *Tue–Sun.*

🏛 **Musée du Vieux Namy**
Rue Mouzain 31, Namy.
📞 *(065) 36 0825.*
⃝ *May–Sep: Sat–Sun.*

Ath ❺

🏛 *11,700.* 🚆 🚌 ℹ *Rue de Pintamont 54, (068) 26 9230, 26 5170.*

Tʜᴵs ǫᴜᴵᴇᴛ ᴛᴏᴡɴ grew up around the River Dendre. Ath is known for its festival – the Ducasse – which occurs every year on the fourth weekend in August. Held over two days, it features the "Parade of the Giants", a procession of gaily decorated giant figures representing characters from local folklore and the Bible, such as the Aymon brothers and the Steed Bayard (*see p99*), as well as David, Goliath and Samson.

The surrounding country of gently rolling hills is dotted with hamlets and farms, as well as historical sights. A few kilometres north-east of Ath is one of the most popular attractions

The Gothic church Collégiale Ste-Waudru, Mons

in the region, the **Château d'Attre**. This handsome 18th-century palace was built in 1752 by the Count of Gomegnies, chamberlain to the Hapsburg Emperor Joseph II, and was a favourite haunt of the Hapsburg aristocracy. Its interior is opulent, with ornate plasterwork, parquet floors and paintings. The River Dendre crosses the delightful grounds.

♣ **Château d'Attre**
Attre. ☎ *(068) 45 4460.* 🚆 *to Attre.* ⏱ *Jul–Aug: Thu–Tue; Apr–Jun & Sep–Oct: Sat & Sun.* ● *Nov–Mar.*

The southeast entrance of the chapel of St Hermes, Ronse

Ronse ⑯

🚶 *25,000.* 🚆 🚌 ℹ️ *Stadhuis, Grote Markt, Oudenaarde, (05) 531 7251.*

SET AMONG the pretty hills of the Flemish Ardennes, Ronse is famous for its *Zotte Maandag*, or Crazy Monday festivities. Every year, on the second weekend in January, a boisterous procession of masked medieval characters parades through the town.

In medieval times, Ronse was where thousands of the mentally ill were taken to seek a cure. The object of the pilgrimage was a visit to the chapel of Hermes, a Roman saint thought to be an expert in exorcism. Today, the chapel retains three rusty iron rings that recall the days when the insane were chained up awaiting a miracle. A painting here depicts St Hermes on a horse, dragging a devil behind him.

Ieper ⑰

🚶 *35,000.* 🚆 🚌 ℹ️ *34 Market Square, (057) 22 8584.*

IEPER IS THE Flemish name of the town familiar to hundreds of thousands of British soldiers as Ypres – its French appellation. During World War I, this ancient town, which was once a centre of the medieval wool trade, was used as a supply depot for the British army fighting in the trenches just to the east.

The Germans shelled Ieper to pieces, but after the war the town was rebuilt to its earlier design, complete with an exact replica of its imposing, 13th-century Lakenhalle (cloth hall). The original building was located by the River Ieperlee (which now runs underground), and boats could unload their wares on site. Today, part of the interior has been turned into the excellent "In Flander's Fields" Museum, a thoughtfully laid-out series of displays that attempt to conjure the full horrors of World War I. There is a simulated gas attack, personal artifacts and an array of photographs.

Another reminder of war is the huge Menin Gate memorial (just east of the Grote Markt) inscribed with the names of over 50,000 British and Commonwealth troops who died in and around Ieper but have no known resting place. The last post is sounded here every evening at 8pm.

Weaving a tapestry at the Huis de Lalaing workshop, Oudenaarde

Oudenaarde ⑱

🚶 *30,000.* 🚆 🚌 ℹ️ *Stadhuis, Grote Markt, (05) 531 7251.*

STRATEGICALLY situated beside the River Scheldt, the little town of Oudenaarde has suffered at the hands of many invaders, and little remains of the old town. The 16th-century Stadhuis has survived, and is adorned with beautiful stonework. The interior is open to visitors and is famous for an exquisitely carved oak doorway and its outstanding collection of tapestries – one of the finest in the country.

Oudenaarde was once a centre of tapestry manufacture and its products were bought by monarchs across Europe. Today, visitors can see tapestries being made at the Huis de Lalaing, a workshop near the Grote Markt.

THE YPRES SALIENT

The Ypres Salient was the name given to a bulge in the line of trenches that both the German and British armies felt was a good place to break through each others' lines. This led to large concentrations of men and four major battles including Passchendaele in July 1917, in which hundreds of thousands of men died. Today, visitors can choose to view the site with its vast cemeteries and monuments by car or guided tour.

View of the battlefield at Passchendaele Ridge in 1917

Street-by-Street: Ghent ®

Bell on display in the Belfort

As a tourist destination, the Flemish city of Ghent has long been over-shadowed by its neighbour, Bruges. In part this reflects their divergent histories. The success of the cloth trade during the Middle Ages was followed by a period of stagnation for Bruges, while Ghent became a major industrial centre in the 18th and 19th centuries. The resulting pollution coated the city's antique buildings in layers of grime from its many factories. In the 1980s Ghent initiated a restoration programme. The city's medieval buildings were cleaned, industrial sites were tidied up and the canals were cleared. Today, it is the intricately carved stonework of its churches and antique buildings, as well as the city's excellent museums and stern, forbidding castle that give the centre its character.

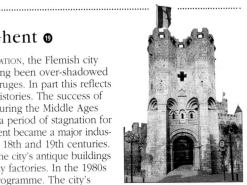

★ Het Gravensteen
Ghent's centre is dominated by the thick stone walls and imposing gatehouse of its ancient Castle of the Counts.

★ Museum voor Sierkunst
This elegant 19th-century dining room is just one of many charming period rooms in the decorative arts museum. The collection is housed in an 18th-century mansion and covers art and design from the 1600s to the present.

Graslei
One of Ghent's most picturesque streets, the Graslei overlooks the River Leie on the site of the city's medieval harbour. It is lined with perfectly preserved guildhouses; some date from the 12th century.

STAR SIGHTS

★ St Baafskathedraal

★ Het Gravensteen

★ Museum voor Sierkunst

To Ghent St-Pieters

Korenmarkt
This busy square was once the corn market; the commercial centre of the city since the Middle Ages. Today, it is lined with popular cafés.

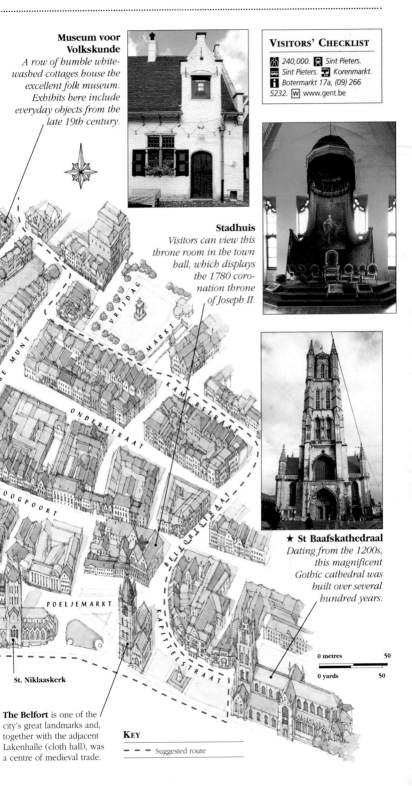

Museum voor Volkskunde
A row of humble white-washed cottages house the excellent folk museum. Exhibits here include everyday objects from the late 19th century.

VISITORS' CHECKLIST

240,000. Sint Pieters. Sint Pieters. Korenmarkt. Botermarkt 17a, (09) 266 5232. www.gent.be

Stadhuis
Visitors can view this throne room in the town hall, which displays the 1780 coronation throne of Joseph II.

★ St Baafskathedraal
Dating from the 1200s, this magnificent Gothic cathedral was built over several hundred years.

0 metres 50
0 yards 50

St. Niklaaskerk

The Belfort is one of the city's great landmarks and, together with the adjacent Lakenhalle (cloth hall), was a centre of medieval trade.

KEY
- - - Suggested route

Exploring Ghent

Charles V's coat of arms

T HE HEART OF Ghent's historic centre was originally built during the 13th and 14th centuries when the city prospered as a result of the cloth trade. Ghent was founded in the 9th century when Baldwin Iron-Arm, the first Count of Flanders, built a castle to protect two important abbeys from Viking raids. Despite constant religious and dynastic conflicts, Ghent continued to flourish throughout the 16th and early 17th centuries. After 1648, the Dutch sealed the Scheldt estuary near Antwerp, closing vital canal links, which led to a decline in the fortunes of both cities. By the 19th century there was a boom in cotton spinning, and the wide boulevards in the south of the city reflect the affluence of the factory owners. Today, textiles still form a big part of Ghent's industry.

The Gothic turrets of Sint-Niklaaskerk seen from St Michael's Bridge

Getting around

Ghent is a large city with an excellent bus and tram system. The main rail station, St Peters, adjoins the bus station from where several trams travel to the centre every few minutes. However, many of Ghent's main sights are within walking distance of each other. Canal boat trips are also available.

🅰 St Baafskathedraal

St Baafsplein. **[** (09) 225 1626.
◯ daily. **Adoration of the Mystic Lamb ◯** Apr–Oct: daily; Nov–Mar: Sun–Fri. 🈺
Built in several stages, St Baafskathedraal has features representing every phase of Gothic style, from the early chancel through to the later nave, which is the cathedral's architectural highlight. The cavernous nave is supported by slender columns and has a soft dappled light filtering through the windows. In a

small side chapel one of Europe's most remarkable paintings is on display, Jan van Eyck's polyptych *Adoration of the Mystic Lamb* (1432). Van Eyck is noted for his attention to detail, but is also universally respected as the first painter to master the art of working with oils. His use of colours and

tones is so realistic that even today, hundreds of years after the work was completed, the skin of his characters looks real enough to touch. The cover screens of this seminal work feature portraits of the donor – Joos Vijd – and his wife below an Annunciation scene. The inside is stunning. Here, God the Father, John the Baptist and the Virgin Mary are pictured on the upper level in radiant tones, while the Lamb, the symbol of Christ's sacrifice, is the centrepiece below.

🏛 Stadhuis

Botermarkt 1. **[** (09) 266 5211.
🈺 **[** May–Oct: 3pm Mon–Thu. Tours depart from the Tourist Office.
The Stadhuis façade displays two different architectural styles. Overlooking Hoogstraat, the older half dates from the early 16th century, its tracery in the elaborate Flamboyant Gothic style. The plainer, newer part, which flanks the Botermarkt, is a characteristic example of post-Reformation architecture. The statues in the niches on the façade were added in the 1890s. Among this group of figures it is possible to spot the original architect, Rombout Keldermans, who is shown studying his plans.

The building still serves as the city's administrative centre. Guided tours allow a glimpse at a series of large rooms. Perhaps the most fascinating of these is the Pacification Hall, which was once the Court of Justice and the site of the signing of the Pacification of Ghent (a treaty between Catholics and Protestants against Hapsburg rule) in 1576.

The tiled floor forms a maze in the Pacification Hall in Ghent's Stadhuis

Views of Graslei and 16th-century guildhouses along the River Leie

Graslei
The Graslei runs along the River Leie and is the eastern side of the Tussen Bruggen, once Ghent's main medieval harbour. The quay possesses a fine set of guildhouses. Among them, at No. 14, the sandstone façade of the Guildhouse of the Free Boatmen is decorated with finely detailed nautical scenes, while the late 17th-century Corn Measurers' guildhouse next door is adorned by bunches of fruit and cartouches. The earliest building here is the 12th-century *Spijker* (Staple House) at No. 10. This simple Romanesque structure stored the city's grain supply for several hundred years until a fire destroyed the interior.

Het Gravensteen
Sint-Veerleplein. (09) 225 9306, 269 3730. daily. 1 & 2 Jan, 25 & 26 Dec.
Once the seat of the counts of Flanders, the imposing stone walls of Het Gravensteen (or the Castle of the Counts) overlook the city centre. Parts of the castle date back to the late 1100s, but most are later additions. Up to the 14th century the castle was Ghent's main military stronghold, and from then until the late 1700s it was used as the city's jail. Later, it became a cotton mill.
From the gatehouse, a long and heavily fortified tunnel leads up to the courtyard, which is overseen by two large buildings, the count's medieval residence and the

earlier keep. Arrows guide visitors round the interior of both buildings, and in the upper rooms there is a spine-chilling collection of medieval torture instruments.

Museum voor Sierkunst
Jan Breydelstraat 5. (09) 267 9999. Tue–Sun.
This decorative arts museum has a wide-ranging collection contained within an elegant 18th-century townhouse. The displays are arranged in two sections, beginning at the front with a series of lavishly furnished period rooms that feature textiles, furniture, and artifacts from the 17th to the 19th centuries. At the back, an extension completed in 1992 focuses on modern design from Art Nouveau to contemporary works, and includes furniture by Victor Horta (*see p78*), Marcel Breuer and Ludwig Mies van der Rohe. One highlight is an Art Nouveau room designed by the noted Belgian artist Henry van der Velde.

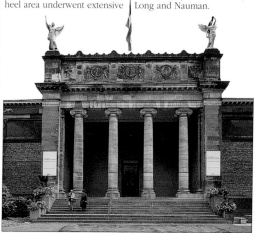
Sofa at Sierkunst Museum

The Patershol
North of the Kraanlei are the quaint little lanes and low brick houses of the Patershol, a district that developed in the 17th century to house the city's weavers. This once down-at-heel area underwent extensive

refurbishment in the 1980s and is now one of the trendiest parts of town, with upmarket restaurants, cafés and shops.

Museum voor Schone Kunsten
Citadelpark. (09) 222 1703. Tue–Sun.
Ghent's largest collection of fine art is displayed in this Neo-Classical building dating from 1902. Inside, a rotunda divides the collection, with the older works in a series of rooms on the right and 19th- and 20th-century art to the left. The medieval paintings include the *Bearing of the Cross* by Hieronymus Bosch (1450–1516). There are also works by Rubens (*see pp14–15*), Anthony van Dyck (1599–1641) and Jacob Jordaens (1593–1678).
The museum will close for renovations at the end of 2003. Some pieces will temporarily be rehoused at the Archeological Museum Van De Bijloke on Godshuizenlaan (tel: 09 225 1106).

Stedelijk Museum voor Actuele Kunst (SMAK)
Citadelpark. (09) 222 1703. www.smak.be.
This museum includes works by Belgian and international contemporary artists, such as Bacon, Beuys, Broodthaers, Long and Nauman.

The grand, Neo-Classical façade of the Museum voor Schone Kunsten

Street-by-Street: Bruges ⑳

Traditional organ grinder

WITH GOOD REASON, Bruges is one of the most popular tourist destinations in Belgium. An unspoilt medieval town, Bruges' winding streets pass by picturesque canals lined with fine buildings. The centre of Bruges is amazingly well preserved. The town's trade was badly affected when the River Zwin silted up at the end of the 15th century. It was never heavily industrialized and has retained most of its medieval buildings. As a further bonus Bruges also escaped major damage in both world wars.

Today, the streets are well maintained: there are no billboards or high rises, and traffic is heavily regulated. All the major attractions are located within the circle of boulevards that marks the line of the old medieval walls.

View of the River Dijver
A charming introduction to Bruges is provided by the boat trips along the city's canal network.

Onze Lieve Vrouwekerk
The massive Church of Our Lady employs many architectural styles. It took around 200 years to build, and its spire is Belgium's tallest.

Hans Memling Museum
Six of the artist's works are shown in the small chapel of the 12th-century St Janshospitaal, a city hospital that was still operating until 1976.

0 metres	100
0 yards	100

★ The Markt
Medieval gabled houses line this 13th-century market square at the heart of Bruges, which still holds a market each Saturday.

VISITORS' CHECKLIST

119,000. Stationsplein.
Stationsplein, Markt.
Burg 11, 8000 Bruges, (050)
44 8686. W www.brugge.be

Oude Griffie, or Old Recorder's House

BURG

WOLLESTRAAT

ROZENHOEDKAAI

Blind Donkey Alley
This narrow, arched alley leads from the Burg to the 18th-century Vismarkt.

Heilig Bloed Basiliek

DIJVER

★ Stadhuis
One of the oldest and finest town halls in Belgium, this was built between 1376 and 1420. Inside, the beautifully restored Gothic hall is noted for its 1385 vaulted ceiling.

Groeninge Museum
(see pp118–19)

Arentshuis Museum

Gruuthuse Museum
(see pp116–17)

KEY

– – – Suggested route

The Belfort
Built in the 13th century, the Belfort or Belfry is a stunning octagonal tower where the city's medieval charter of rights is held.

STAR SIGHTS

★ The Markt

★ Stadhuis

Exploring Central Bruges

BRUGES DEVELOPED around a 9th-century fortress, built to defend the coast against the Vikings. Despite the vagaries of successive invasions by the French, between the 14th and 16th centuries Bruges became one of northern Europe's most sophisticated cities. Today, it owes its pre-eminent position to the beauty of its historic centre, whose narrow cobbled lanes and meandering canals are lined by an ensemble of medieval buildings. These are mostly the legacy of the

Bell maker in market

town's heyday as a centre of the international cloth trade, which flourished for two hundred years from the 13th century. During this golden age, Bruges' merchants lavished their fortunes on fine mansions, churches and a set of civic buildings of such extravagance that they were the wonder of northern Europe.

Bruges' medieval buildings reflected in the River Dijver

Getting Around

The centre of Bruges is compact, and as most major sights are near each other, it is easiest to walk around. However, the bus service is useful for getting from the railway station to the centre. Half-hour boat trips along the canals leave from several jetties. From March to November, boats depart twice every hour.

The Vismarkt

Braambergstraat. ⬜ daily.

From the Burg an attractive arched path called the Alley of the Blind Donkey (Blinde Ezelstraat) leads to the open-air fish market with its elegant 18th-century colonnades. Fish is still sold here early each morning and business is brisk.

The Burg

The Burg, a pleasant cobbled square a few metres from the Markt, was once the political and religious focus of Bruges. It is also the site of the original fort around which the city grew. Some of the most imposing civic buildings are located here. The beautiful sandstone Stadhuis or town hall has a façade dating

from 1375, and is adorned with turrets and statues. In contrast, the Proostdij or Provost's House was built of grey stone in 1662 in the Baroque style and boasts an ornate entrance.

Stadhuis

Burg 12. ((050) 44 8111.
⬜ daily. 📷

The intricately carved façade of the Stadhuis was completed in 1375, but the niche statues are modern effigies of the counts and countesses of Flanders. These were added in the 1960s to replace those destroyed by the French army over a century before. The building is still used as a town hall. It is also a popular venue for Bruges weddings. Inside, a staircase leads up from the spacious foyer to the beautiful Gothic Hall, which is open to visitors year round. This magnificent parliamentary chamber was built around 1400. Immaculately restored, the ceiling boasts some lavish woodcarvings including 16 beautiful corbels (brackets) bearing representations of the seasons and the elements. A series of paintings around the hall was completed in 1895, each portraying a key event in the city's history.

In an adjacent building is the Renaissance Hall, which houses a massive wood, marble and alabaster chimney designed by Lanceloot Blondeel. The chimney is one of the best sculptural works of 16th-century Flanders.

Heilig Bloed Basiliek

Burg 10. ((050) 44 8111, 33 3767.
⬜ daily. ● Mon (in winter).

The Basilica of the Holy Blood holds one of the most sacred reliquaries in Europe. The basilica divides into two distinct sections, the lower part being the evocative St Basil's chapel with its plain stone-pillared entrance and arches. The upper chapel was rebuilt in the 19th century after the French destroyed it in the 1790s. Here, brightly coloured decorations surround a silver tabernacle of 1611 which houses a sacred phial, supposed to contain a few drops of blood and water washed from the body of Christ by Joseph of Arimathea. The phial was brought here from Jerusalem in 1150, and is still the object of great veneration. The church also has a museum that houses paintings, vestments and other artifacts.

⚜ The Markt

The Markt is Bruges' main square and marketplace (a market has been held on this site since the 10th century). It is an impressive open space lined with 17th-century houses and overlooked by the Belfort on one side. The oldest façade on the square (dating from the 15th century) belongs to the Huis Bouchotte, which was the home of Charles II of England during part of his exile from 1656–7.

In the middle is a statue of Pieter de Coninck and Jan Breidel, two 14th-century guildsmen who led a rebellion against the French in 1302. Known as the *Bruges Matin*, they led Flemish soldiers to attack the French at dawn on May 18, 1302, killing almost all of them. This bloody uprising paved the way for a form of independence for the Low Countries' major towns. Rights such as the freedom to trade were subsequently enshrined in the towns' charters until the 15th century.

⚜ The Belfort

Markt. ⬚ *daily.* 🖼
The Markt is dominated by the belfry, whose octagonal belltower rises 83 m (272 ft) above the square. Built between the 13th and 15th centuries, the belfry is Bruges' most celebrated landmark as it was used to store the town's charter, and is therefore a constant reminder of the city's past as a centre of trade. Inside the tower a winding staircase leads up, past the chamber where the town's rights and privileges were stored, to the roof, where the views across Bruges are delightful.

Bruges' Belfort or belltower overlooking the Markt

Groeninge Museum

See pp118–19.

🏛 Arentshuis Museum

Dijver 16. 📞 *(050) 44 8763.* ⬚ *Apr–Sep: daily; Oct–Mar: Wed–Mon.* 🖼
The Arentshuis Museum is housed in a genteel, 18th-century mansion overlooking the Dijver Canal. The interior is divided into two sections, with the ground floor devoted to a delightful selection of antique lace. Bruges was a centre of Belgian lace making and, although there were a few local factories, most of the work was done by women toiling in their own homes. The beautifully presented collection focuses on needlepoint and bobbin lace, with several fine examples of Bruges floral or Duchesse lace as well. Upstairs is the work of Frank Brangwyn (1867–1956), a painter and sculptor who was born in Bruges of Welsh parents. Most of Brangwyn's life was spent in Britain, but he bequeathed this collection to Bruges, as well as his drawings, furniture and carpets. Among his work, the dark and powerful canvases depicting industrial scenes are perhaps the most diverting.

Statue of Breidel and Pieter de Coninck

⚜ Concertgebouw

't Zand. 📞 *(050) 47 6999.*
Built as part of the celebrations for Bruges' European City of Culture, this terracotta concert hall features a 28-m (92-ft) tower that offers great views.

Gruuthuse Museum

See pp116–17.

🔒 Onze Lieve Vrouwekerk

Mariastraat. ⬚ *Apr–Sep: Sun–Fri; Oct–Mar: Mon–Sat.* 🖼 *mausoleum only.*
The Church of Our Lady took over two hundred years to build, starting in 1220, and incorporates a variety of styles. The interior, with its white walls, stark columns and black-and-white tiled floor has a medieval simplicity, while the side chapels and pulpit are lavishly decorated in the Baroque manner.

One of the church's artistic highlights is Michelangelo's sculpture *Madonna and Child* (1504–5), at the end of the southern aisle. This marble statue was imported by a Flemish merchant, and was the only one of the artist's works to leave Italy during his lifetime. In the choir there are fine paintings by Pieter Pourbus including a *Last Supper* (1562), and the carved mausoleums of the Burgundian prince Charles the Bold and his daughter Mary.

The soaring spire of the Church of Our Lady

Gruuthuse Museum

Facial fireguard

THE GRUUTHUSE MUSEUM occupies a large medieval mansion close to the Dijver Canal. In the 15th century, it was inhabited by the merchant (or Lord of the Gruuthuse) who had the exclusive right to levy a tax on the "Gruit", an imported mixture of herbs added to barley during the beer-brewing process. The mansion's labyrinthine rooms, with their ancient chimneypieces and wooden beams, have survived intact and nowadays hold a priceless collection of fine and applied arts. There are tapestries, wood carvings, furniture and even a medical section devoted to cures of everyday ailments such as haemorrhoids. The authentic kitchen and original 1472 chapel transport visitors back to medieval times.

2nd Floor

1st Floor

Façade of the Gruuthuis
The museum's Gothic façade, with its elegant tower, stepped gables and fine stone windows, was built in the 15th century.

Ground Floor

★ **Charles V**
This incredibly life-like terracotta and wood bust of Hapsburg king Charles V was carved in 1520 and is attributed to German sculptor Konrad Meit.

Entrance

STAR EXHIBITS
★ Charles V bust
★ Chapel

The Seven Free Arts
Dating from around 1675, this exquisite tapestry depicts the "free arts", which included music.

GALLERY GUIDE

Laid out over three floors, the
collection is organized into
types of object from glassware,
porcelain and ceramics to
medical instruments in a
series of 22 numbered rooms.
Visitors may view the rooms
in sequence from 1–22 and
get a good sense of the
original uses and layout of
the house in doing so.

★ Chapel
Built in 1472, this oak-
panelled chapel on the
museum's second floor
overlooks the high altar
of the church next door.

KEY

- ☐ Glassware, porcelain and ceramics
- ☐ Kitchen
- ☐ Chapel
- ☐ Musical instruments
- ☐ Coins
- ☐ Tapestries
- ☐ Tools, weights and measures
- ☐ Entrance hall
- ☐ Textiles and lace
- ☐ Household implements
- ☐ Renaissance works
- ☐ Baroque works
- ☐ Reliquary and furniture
- ☐ Medical instruments
- ☐ Great Hall
- ☐ Weaponry

House on the Southern Bridge at Minnewater

🏛 Hans Memling Museum

Mariastraat 38, 8000 Bruges.
☎ *(050) 44 8771.* ◯ *Tue–Sun.* 🖼.
This small museum (a former
13th-century hospital) contains
the works of Hans Memling
(1430–94), one of the most
talented painters of his era.
Among them, *The Mystical
Marriage of St. Catherine*
(1479), the central panel of a
triptych, is superb. The former
wards also house a collection
of paintings and furniture
related to the hospital's history.

⛪ Sint Salvator-Kathedraal

St Salvatorskof 1, 8000 Bruges.
☎ *(050) 33 61 88.* ◯ *Apr–Sep:*
daily. ● *1 Jan, 25 Dec.* 🖼.
Built as a parish church from
the 12th and 15th centuries,
this large, yellow-brick building became Bruges' cathedral
in 1788 when the French army
destroyed the existing one. The
interior is enormous and quite
plain except for a handsome
set of Brussels' tapestries hanging in the choir, and a 1682
organ adorned with angels.

**Pale brick tower of St Salvator-
Kathedraal in Bruges**

🌿 Minnewater

Just south of the Begijnhof,
Minnewater is a peaceful
park with a lake populated
by ducks and swans. Swans
have been here since 1448
when Maximilian of Austria
ordered they be kept in mem-
ory of his councillor, Pierre
Lanchais, who was beheaded
by the Bruges citizens.

Once this was a bustling
harbour which connected to
the canal network and the sea.
Today, Minnewater can be
visited by one of the tourist
barges that take visitors on a
tour of Bruges by canal. It is
also a popular spot for walkers
and picnickers who may view
the pretty 15th-century lock
gate and house and the 1398
tower (Poedertoren).

🏛 Begijnhof

Wijngaardplein 1, 8000 Bruges.
☎ *(050) 36 01 40.* ◯ *daily.*
Béguines were members of
a lay sisterhood founded in
1245. They lived and dressed
as nuns but did not take vows
and were therefore able to
return to the secular world
at will. The begijnhof or
béguinage is the walled complex in a town that housed
the béguines. In Bruges, this
is an area of quiet tree-lined
canals faced by white, gabled
houses, with a pleasant green
at its centre. Visitors and locals
enjoy strolling here and may
visit the small, simple church
which was built in 1602. The
nuns who live in the houses
are no longer béguines, but
Benedictine sisters who moved
here in the 1930s. One of the
houses is open to visitors and
displays simple rustic furniture
and artifacts that illustrate the
women's contemplative lives.

Groeninge Museum

BRUGES' PREMIER FINE ARTS museum, the Groeninge, holds a fabulous collection of early Flemish and Dutch masters, featuring artists such as the influential Rogier van der Weyden (1399–1464), Jan van Eyck (d.1441), and Hans Memling (1430–94). Hieronymous Bosch (1450–94), famous for the strange freakish creatures of his moral allegories, is well represented too, as are Gerard David (d.1523) and Pieter Brueghel the Younger (1564–1638). These early works are displayed in the first ten rooms of the museum and beyond is a collection of later Belgian painters, most notably Paul Delvaux (1897–1994), and René Magritte (1898–1967). Originally built between 1929 and 1930, the museum is small and displays its collection in rotation.

Serenity *(1970)*
This unusually representative work by Paul Delvaux was commissioned by the museum, and retains elements of the artist's surrealist style.

Last Judgement
Painted on three oak panels in the early 16th century, this detail from Hieronymous Bosch's famous tryptich depicts scenes of cruelty and torture. The strong moral tone of the work suggests that man's sinful nature has created a hell on earth.

★ **The Moreel Triptych** *(1484)*
This panel of the triptych, by German-born artist Hans Memling, was designed to adorn the altar in a Bruges church. It is said to be the first ever group portrait.

STAR PAINTINGS

* ★ Virgin and Child with Canon by Jan van Eyck

* ★ The Moreel Tryptich by Hans Memling

★ **Virgin and Child with Canon** *(1436)*
Jan van Eyck's richly detailed painting is noted for its realism. It shows van Eyck's patron, the canon, being presented to St Donatian by St George.

1st Floor

Ground Floor

VISITORS' CHECKLIST

Dijver 12, 8000 Bruges. ☎ (050) 44 7841. 🚌 Markt. ◷ 9:30am– 5pm Tue–Sun (tickets sold until 4:30pm). ● 1 Jan, 25 Dec. ♿

KEY

- ☐ 15th and 16th centuries
- ☐ 17th to 19th centuries
- ☐ 20th century
- ☐ Temporary exhibitions
- ▨ Non-exhibition space

GALLERY GUIDE

The Groeninge is arranged on one level with a two-storey extension. The main entrance leads to a series of rooms displaying the early Flemish masters and 20th-century art. Works from the 17th to the turn of the 20th century are exhibited in the extension which is reached through the back of the main gallery.

Portrait of Bruges family (1645)
Jacob van Oost the Elder's focus on the affluence of this family overlooking their beloved city shows why he was Bruges' most popular artist of the Baroque period.

Household Cares (1913)

Rik Wouters used his wife Nel as the model for this statue, cast in bronze. The work's Fauvist style (see p15), is reflected in the bold planes that enhance the figure's anxious stance.

Museum Façade and Entrance
Originally built in 1930, the gallery was extended in 1994 to a design by architect Joseph Viérin. The entrance is based on that of a Romanesque convent.

Main Entrance

Exploring Northeast Bruges

Statue of Jan van Eyck

IN THE HEIGHT OF THE summer and on holiday weekends, tourists pour into Bruges, and parts of the city centre often get too crowded for comfort. Fortunately, the narrow cobbled streets and picturesque canals to the north-east of the Markt never suffer from this, and this fascinating area remains one of the most delightful parts of Bruges. Streets of charming, medieval terraced houses are dotted with grand, yet elegant 18th-century mansions. The best approach is via Jan van Eyckplein, in medieval times the city's busiest harbour, from where it is a short stroll along Spinolarei and Potterierei streets to the many museums and churches that are found in this historic district.

The historic buildings and lovely canals of northeast Bruges

Lace-making skills on show at the Kantcentrum lace centre

⊕ Kantcentrum

Peperstraat 3. ⚹ (050) 33 0072. ⬡ Mon–Sat. ▨

The area from the white-washed cottages to the east of Potterierei Street is one of several old neighbourhoods where the city's lace workers plied their craft. Mostly, the women worked at home, receiving their raw materials from a supplier who also bought the finished product.

Lace-making skills are kept alive at the Kantcentrum, the Lace Centre at the foot of Balstraat, where local women (and a few men) fashion lace in a variety of styles, both modern and traditional. It is a busy place, and visitors can see the lace-making demon-strations held every afternoon during the summer. Some of the finished pieces are sold in the Kantcentrum shop at very reasonable prices.

🏛 Brugse Brouwerij-Mouterijmuseum

Verbrand Nieuwland 10. ⚹ (050) 33 2697. ⬡ daily. Call for details. ▨

Up to World War I there were 31 breweries operating in Bruges. This brewery museum,

housed in a malthouse built in 1902, lies south of the lace centre and the Jerzalemkerk. On display are artifacts and documents that tell the cen-turies-old story of beer and brewing in the city. Next door to the museum, De Gouden Boom is a working brewery founded in 1584 that produces the noted beer Brugse Tripel and the spicy wheat beer (known as *bière blanche*), Brugs Tarwebier.

🏠 Jeruzalemkerk

Peperstraat. ⬡ Mon–Sat. ▨

Next door to the Kantcentrum, the Jeruzalemkerk is Bruges' most unusual church. The present building dates from the 15th century, and was built on the site of a 13th-century chapel commis-sioned by a family of wealthy Italian merchants, the Adornes family, whose black marble tomb can be seen inside. Based on the design of the church of the Holy Sepulchre in Jerusalem, the structure possesses a striking tower with two tiers of wooden, polygon-shaped lan-terns topped by a tin orb. Inside, the lower level contains a macabre altarpiece, carved with skulls and assorted demons. Behind the altar is a smaller vaulted chapel; leading

from this is a narrow tunnel guarded by an iron grate. Along the tunnel, a lifelike model of Christ in the Tomb can be seen at close quarters.

⊕ The Kruispoort and the windmills

Medieval Bruges was heavily fortified. It was encircled by a city wall which was itself protected by a moat and strengthened by a series of massive gates. Most of the wall was knocked down in the 19th century, but the moat

The Jeruzalemkerk was built in 1497

has survived and so has one of the gates, the Kruispoort, a monumental structure dating from 1402 that guards the eastern approach to the city. The earthen bank stretching north of the Kruispoort marks the line of the old city wall, which was once dotted with some 20 windmills. Today, only three remain overlooking the canal. The first windmill, the Bonne Chieremolen, was brought here from a village in Flanders in 1911, but the second – St Janshuismolen – is original to the city, an immaculately restored structure erected in 1770. The northernmost mill of the three is De Nieuwe Papegai, an old oil mill that was relocated here in 1970.

The massive Kruispoort is all that remains of Bruges' old city walls

🔒 English Convent

Carmersstraat 85. **(** (050) 33 2424. ☐ Mon–Sat. ☑ obligatory.

The English Convent was where dozens of English Catholics sought asylum following the execution of Charles I in 1642, and during Oliver Cromwell's subsequent rule as Lord Protector. The conventual buildings are not open to the public, but the nuns provide a well-informed tour of their beautiful church, which was built in the Baroque style in the 1620s. The interior has a delightful sense of space, its elegant proportions enhanced by its cupola, but the highlight is the altar, a grand affair made of around 20 types of marble.

🏛 Museum voor Volkskunde

Rolweg 40. **(** (050) 33 0044. ☐ Tue–Sun. ☑

The Museum voor Volkskunde is one of the best folk museums in Flanders. It occupies

These 17th-century almshouses house the Museum voor Volkskunde

an attractive terrace of low, brick almshouses located behind an old neighbourhood café called the "Zwarte Kat" (Black Cat), which serves as the entrance. Each of the almshouses is dedicated to a different aspect of traditional Flemish life, with workshops displaying old tools. Several different crafts are represented here, such as a cobbler's and a blacksmith's, through to a series of typical historical domestic interiors.

🏹 Schuttersgilde St Sebastiaan

Carmersstraat 174. **(** (050) 33 1626. ☐ Tue–Thu & Sat (May–Sep: also open on Fri). ☑

The Archers' guild (the Schuttersgilde) was one of the most powerful of the militia guilds, and their 16th- and 17th-century red-brick guildhouse now houses a museum.

The commercial life of medieval Bruges was dominated by the guilds, each of which represented the interests

The St Sebastiaan guildhouse belonged to the archers

of a particular group of skilled workmen. The guilds guarded their privileges jealously and, among many rules and customs, marriage between children whose fathers were in different guilds was greatly frowned upon. The guild claimed the name St Sebastian after an early Christian martyr, who the Roman Emperor Diocletian had executed by his archers. The bowmen followed orders – and medieval painters often show Sebastian looking like a pincushion – but miraculously Sebastian's wounds healed and he had to be finished off by a band of club-wielding assassins. The guildhouse itself is notable for its collection of paintings of the guild's leading lights, gold and silver trinkets and guild emblems.

🏛 Museum Onze Lieve Vrouw van de Potterie

Potterierei 79. **(** (050) 44 8777 ☐ Tue–Sun. ☑

Located by the canal in one of the quietest parts of Bruges, the Museum Onze Lieve Vrouw van de Potterie (Our Lady of Pottery) occupies part of an old hospital that was founded in 1276 to care for elderly women. There is a 14th- and 15th-century cloister, and several of the old sick rooms are now used to display a modest collection of paintings, the best of which are some realistic 17th- and 18th-century portraits of leading aristocrats. The hospital church is in excellent condition, too; it is a warm, intimate place with fine stained-glass windows and a set of impressive Baroque altarpieces.

TRAVELLERS' NEEDS

WHERE TO STAY

F OR MOST OF the year, Brussels is primarily a business or political destination, and accommodation is often priced accordingly. The wide range of top hotels has one fine advantage for the visitor; weekend and summer deals make it possible even on a modest budget to stay in some of Europe's most luxurious establishments. The mid-range of hotels is also well represented

Métropole bellboy

in the city, with period houses turned into stylish family-run hotels and chain hotels. To keep accommodation costs to a minimum, choose from Brussels' abundance of youth hostels and bed-and-breakfast options. *Choosing a Hotel* on pp128–9 will help you find at a glance the best hotels to suit your needs. A more detailed description of each hotel is listed on pp130–35.

Hallway in the Hôtel Métropole on Place de Brouckère *(see p132)*

HOTEL LOCATIONS

W HILE BRUSSELS does not have a specific hotel area, there are clusters of hotels in various parts of the city. Centrally, the most fertile ground is between Place Rogier and Place de Brouckère, which is within walking distance of both the Upper and Lower Town and a short bus ride from most major sights. The streets to the west of the Grand Place are also well supplied for those who want to be in the historic centre of town, but road noise can be a problem at night. To the north, Place Ste-Catherine or the streets behind Avenue de la Toison d'Or also have plenty of options. Following the pattern of cities worldwide, hotels generally reduce in price the further they are from the centre. Bed-and-breakfast rooms are dispersed across the capital and can often be found in residential

districts at very good rates. When arriving in the city from abroad by train or plane, it is worth knowing that the Gare du Midi and the airport both have nearby hotel colonies, although the station surroundings are run down in places. The airport has principally attracted chain hotels, which often offer good value package deals with the national airlines, although sightseeing from here is inconvenient.

ROOM RATES

H OTELS AT THE TOP end of the market offer exceptional standards of comfort and convenience to their largely corporate clients, and their prices reflect this. In general, prices are higher than in the rest of Belgium, but on a par with other European capitals. For a night in a luxury hotel, expect to pay €250 to €300 for a double room; the price for a room in the city averages in the €150 to €175 bracket.

Façade of the Crowne Plaza Hotel, one of the hotel chain *(see p131)*

However, there are numerous discounts available *(see Special Rates, p126)*.

Single travellers can often find reasonable discounts on accommodation, although few places will offer rooms at half the price of a double. It is usual to be charged extra if you place additional guests in a double room. Travelling with children is not the financial burden it might be in this child-friendly society *(see p127)*. Youth hostels cater very well to the budget student traveller and some also have family rooms.

TAXES AND CHARGES

R OOM TAXES and sales taxes should be included in the cost of your room, so the price quoted should be what appears as the total. The price of car parking may be added. Some hotels offer free parking, others charge up to €17 a night. In hotels with no private car park, it is worth checking discounts for public parking facilities if these are located nearby. While many hotels are happy to allow pets, many will add a small nightly charge to the bill.

Breakfast is not always included in the price of a room, even in very expensive establishments. However, many hotels do offer excellent free breakfasts, so ask when you book. The fare usually consists of continental breakfasts, including good coffee, warm croissants and brioche rolls, preserves and fruit juice. Bear in mind that if the expensive place where you are staying is charging €20 for a morning meal, there will be plenty of places nearby offering equal quality for much less money. The usual price for a hotel breakfast ranges upwards from €2.50, but coffee and rolls are usually priced at around €6.20. Unusually, youth hostels also offer lunches and dinners at around €9.90 each.

Phone calls from hotel rooms can be extremely expensive, with unit charges of €.60 for even a local call not uncommon. To make a long-distance call, buying a phonecard and using the efficient public payphone service is several times less expensive. Hotel faxes or modem charges, when available, can also mount up.

Minibar charges are usually very high, although no more so than in any other western European city. Watching satellite or pay-TV stations can also be expensive. However, Belgium's advanced cable network and proximity to other countries means that there are usually more than 20 free channels to choose from including the BBC as well as French and German television.

FACILITIES

I N A CITY with so many luxury hotels, fierce competition has led to ever more sophisticated gadgets and services for businesspeople. Several private phone lines, screened calls, free internet access, automatic check-out services, 24-hour news via Reuters, secretarial services, free mobile phones and even executive suites designed expressly for women

A business traveller's room at the Hotel Alfa Sablon *(see p132)*

are all on offer. Most of the top hotels also house extensive fitness facilities, including saunas and full gymnasiums, although there are few large swimming pools.

Brussels' reputation as a centre for fine dining is significantly enhanced by the hotel trade, with major hotels often offering several options, from expert gastronomy to excellent brasserie dining. For snacks and drinks, Brussels' hotels are known for their old-style, entertaining bars with piano music for those guests who prefer not to venture into the city at night. A handful have nightclub facilities where lively crowds meet for cocktails and dancing.

As one of Europe's major centres for the convention trade, Brussels is not short of meeting and function rooms, with the big hotels offering dozens of spaces for anything from conferences to society weddings and even relatively modest hotels offering good-sized rooms for business seminars and the like. Many

more expensive hotels have serviced apartments on offer; these can be useful for the greater freedom they provide.

19th-century courtyard of the Conrad International *(see p135)*

HOW TO BOOK

R OOMS ARE available in Brussels at most times of the year, but you should book several days in advance to ensure that you get the place you want. In mid- and top-range hotels, a credit card is the usual way to book, giving card details as a deposit; in smaller hotels, bookings can often be made simply by giving your name and details of the day and time of arrival.

The **Tourist Office** offers a free, same-day reservation service on-site. It also publishes a practical guide to Brussels hotels, updated annually, which is available on request. For booking by telephone, **Belgian Tourist Reservations** is a free service for visitors and very helpful.

Bar of the Hotel Arenberg, decorated with a cartoon mural *(see p131)*

View of the Grand Place from a room at Auberge Saint-Michel *(see p130)*

SPECIAL RATES

BRUSSELS IS AN exceptional destination, in that relatively few people come for the weekend or in July and August, meaning that often remarkable deals can be acquired at these times.

The cost of staying in one of the top hotels over the weekend or at off-peak times can plummet by as much as 65 per cent (for example, from €300 to €100 for a double room), so checking before booking about any special deals may save a large sum of money. A few hotels also offer discounts for guests who eat in their restaurants.

Some reservation services charge a small fee, but they can usually find competitively priced accommodation. Any deposit given is deducted from the final hotel bill.

Many travel agents also offer packages for visiting Brussels or Belgium, with accommodation working out less expensively than a custom-booked break.

Another option worth looking into is to check with your airline about possible discounts through its reservation services, and to find out about frequent-flyer bargains for affiliated hotels.

Bellboy at the Conrad International

DISABLED TRAVELLERS

HOTELS IN Brussels and the rest of Belgium take the needs of disabled travellers seriously. Many have one or more rooms designed with wheelchair-bound guests in mind. Bear in mind that many hotel buildings in Brussels are historic and therefore may not be suitable. Most staff, however, will be helpful. It is wise to ask in advance whether the hotel can cater to travellers with special needs. Most hotels will allow the visually handicapped to bring a guide dog onto the premises, although again it is best to make sure that this is the case before you arrive.

YOUTH ACCOMMODATION

BRUSSELS HAS several central, excellent youth hostels, with modern facilities, reasonably priced food and more privacy than is usually associated with hostel stays. Perhaps the best are the **Jacques Brel**, close to Place Madou, and the **Sleep Well**, which has disabled access. A bed in a four-person room should cost in the region of €11.70, rising to around €17.40 for a single room. Breakfast is sometimes included or costs from €2.50, with lunch and dinner for a charge of around €9.90. If you are not a member of the International Youth Hostel Foundation, rates will rise by €2.50 extra per night; membership cards, priced €12.40, are available at most hostels.

DIRECTORY

RESERVATION AGENCIES

Belgian Tourist Reservations
Boulevard Anspach 111, Brussels 1000. **Map** 1 C3.
((02) 513 7484.

Tourist Information Board
Town Hall, Grand Place 1, Brussels 1000. **Map** 2 D3.
((02) 513 8940.
W www.tib.be

AUBERGES DE JEUNESSE/YOUTH HOSTELS:

Jacques Brel
Rue de la Sablonnière 30, Brussels 1000. **Map** 2 F1.
((02) 218 0187.

Jeugdherberg Bruegel
Rue du Saint-Esprit 2, Brussels 1000.
((02) 511 0436.

Generation Europe
Rue de l'Eléphant 4,
Brussels 1080. **Map** 1 A1.
((02) 410 3858.

New Sleep Well
Auberge du Marais, Rue du Damier 23, Brussels 1000.
Map 2 D1. **(** (02) 218 50 50. **W** www.sleepwell.be

BED AND BREAKFAST

Bed and Breakfast Taxi Stop
Rue du Fossé-aux-Loups 28, Brussels 1000. **Map** 2 D2. **(** (02) 223 2310.

New Windrose
Avenue Brugmann, Brussels 1060.
((02) 534 7191.

Bed & Brussels
Rue Kindermans 9, Brussels 1050. **(** (02) 646 0737.
W www.bnb-brussels.be

GAY AND LESBIAN ACCOMMODATION

Tels Quels
Rue du Marché au Charbon 81, Brussels 1000. **Map** 1 C3. **(** (02) 512 4587.

The Hilton Brussels, formerly the Albert Premier Rogier (see p130)

Joining is worthwhile when seeing the rest of Belgium, as there are over 30 hostels around the countryside.

GAY AND LESBIAN ACCOMMODATION

THERE ARE NO specifically gay or lesbian hotels in the city, but same-sex couples should have few problems finding welcoming accommodation. The **Tels Quels** association is the best source of information about suitable lodging, and also has a documentation centre covering most aspects of gay life in the city.

TRAVELLING WITH CHILDREN

CHILDREN ARE welcome at all hotels in Brussels. Most allow one or two under-12s to stay in their parents' room without extra charge; indeed, some hotels will extend this

principle to under-16s and under-18s. When travelling with children, it is worth reserving in advance as the hotel will find the room that best suits your needs. Families planning a long stay in Brussels should consider renting a suite or a self-catering apartment, which are economical.

SELF-CATERING APARTMENTS

THERE IS NO shortage of self-catering accommodation in Brussels, with many places available for a short stay as well as by the week or month. A few are attached to hotels as suites, with the rest run by private companies. Prices start at around €300 per week, for a fairly basic but furnished one- or two-bedroom apartment, to €990 or more for more luxurious lodgings. Contact the Belgian Tourist Reservations or visit the Tourist Office for a detailed list of suggestions.

BED-AND-BREAKFAST

BED-AND-BREAKFAST, also called *chambre d'hôte*, accommodation can be a very pleasant alternative to staying in a cheap hotel, and rooms can often be found even in the centre of town. You may come across a bargain by wandering the streets, but the easiest way to find bed-and-breakfast lodgings is through the Tourist Office or one of the capital's specialist agencies.

USING THE LISTINGS

Hotel listings are on pp128–35. Each hotel is listed according to area and price category. The symbols after each hotel summarize its facilities.

🛏 all rooms have bath and/or shower unless otherwise indicated
1 single-rate rooms available
🏢 rooms for more than two people available, or an extra bed can be put in a double room
24 24-hour room service
TV television in all rooms
Y mini-bar in all rooms
🚭 non-smoking rooms available
▤ air conditioning in all rooms
💪 gym/fitness facilities available in hotel
🏊 swimming pool in hotel
🗐 business facilities: these include message-taking service, fax service, desk and telephone in each room, and meeting room within the hotel
🧒 caters for children
♿ wheelchair access
🛗 lift
🐕 pets allowed in bedrooms
P hotel parking available
🌷 garden or grounds
Y bar
🍴 restaurant
💳 credit cards accepted:
AE American Express
DC Diners Club
MC Mastercard/Access
V Visa

Price categories for hotels are based on a standard double room per night in high season, including tax and service. As most hostel accommodation is dormitory-style, prices are based on the the cost of a single bed in a dormitory.

€ up to €62
€€ €62–112
€€€ €112–174
€€€€ €174–248
€€€€€ over €248

The interior of the George V hotel (see p130)

Choosing a Hotel

THE HOTELS AND HOSTELS on the following pages have all been inspected and assessed specifically for this guide. This chart highlights some of the factors that may affect your choice. During the week, Brussels is Europe's top business destination, and hotels with office facilities are included here; but sight-seeing travellers may find weekend discounts. For more information on each entry, see pp 130–35. They are listed by area and appear alphabetically within their price categories.

		Number of Rooms	Business Facilities	Restaurant	Garden	Quiet Location	Period Decor	Weekend Discounts
The Lower Town *(see pp130–32)*								
Barry	€	32						●
Les Eperonniers	€	21					■	
Auberge Saint-Michel	€€	15					■	●
George V	€€	16						
Hilton Brussels City	€€	285					■	
Ibis Brussels City	€€	236	■					
La Légende	€€	26				●	■	
La Madeleine	€€	52						●
Matignon	€€	37		●				
Mozart	€€	47					■	●
Noga	€€	19	●			●		
Orion	€€	169			■			●
Queen Anne	€€	60						
Welcome	€€	10		●			■	
Windsor	€€	24	■					●
Arenberg NH	€€€	155	■	●		●		
Art Hotel Siru	€€€	101	■	●			■	
Atlas	€€€	88	■					
Crowne Plaza	€€€	356		●		●	●	●
Dome	€€€	125	■	●			■	
Ibis off Grand Place	€€€	184			■			
Vendôme	€€€	106	■	●				●
Aris	€€€€	55						●
Bedford	€€€€	319	■	●				●
Novotel off Grand Place	€€€€	136	■	●				●
Amigo	€€€€€	182	■	●			■	●
Carrefour de L'Europe	€€€€€	63	■	●				●
Métropole	€€€€€	410	■	●	■		■	●
Plaza	€€€€€	193	■	●			■	●
Radisson SAS	€€€€€	281	■	●			■	●
Sheraton Towers	€€€€€	533	■	●	■			●
The Upper Town *(see pp132–33)*								
Les Bluets	€	10						
Argus	€€	41	■			●		●
Sabina	€€	24				●	■	
Alfa Sablon	€€€	32				●		●
Dixseptième	€€€	24	■		■	●	■	●
Hilton	€€€€	434	■	●				●
Sofitel	€€€€	175	■	●			■	●
Stanhope	€€€€	50	■	●	●	●		●
Astoria	€€€€€	118	■	●			■	●
Dorint	€€€€€	212	■	●	■			●
Jolly Grand Sablon	€€€€€	193	■	●			■	●
Méridien	€€€€€	224	■	●				●
Renaissance Brussels Hotel	€€€€€	257	■	●		●		●
Royal Windsor	€€€€€	266	■	●			■	●

Price categories for a double room (not per person), including service:

€ up to €62
€€ €62–112
€€€ €112–174
€€€€ €174–248
€€€€€ over €248

WEEKEND DISCOUNTS
Substantial drops in the room rate at weekends.

RESTAURANT
Hotel contains a dining room or restaurant serving lunch and dinner for hotel guests.

BUSINESS FACILITIES
Conference rooms, desks, fax, internet and computer service for guests.

PERIOD DECOR
Historic features, furniture and art decorate the public and private rooms.

QUIET LOCATION
Quiet residential neighbourhood or quiet street in a busy area.

	Price	NUMBER OF ROOMS	BUSINESS FACILITIES	RESTAURANT	GARDEN	QUIET LOCATION	PERIOD DECOR	WEEKEND DISCOUNTS
GREATER BRUSSELS (see pp 134–35)								
De Boeck's	€€	36			■	●		●
Les Tourelles	€€	21	■			●	■	
Sun	€€	22				●		
Abbey	€€€	47	■					
Alfa Louise	€€€	40			■			
Château Gravenhof	€€€	26	■		■	●	■	
Holiday Inn City Centre	€€€€	201	■	●				●
Hyatt Regency Barsey	€€€€	99	■				■	●
Manos Stéphanie	€€€€	55			■	●		●
NH Brussels City Centre	€€€€	246	■	●				●
President WTC	€€€€	302	■	●	■	●		●
Sofitel	€€€€	125	■	●	■	●		●
Bristol Stéphanie	€€€€€	142	■	●			■	●
Conrad International	€€€€€	269	■	●	■			●
Gresham Belson	€€€€€	135	■					●
Montgomery	€€€€€	63	■	●		●	■	●
Sheraton	€€€€€	304	■	●				●
ANTWERP (see p135)								
Firean	€€€	15		●				
Hilton	€€€€€	211		●				●
BRUGES (see p135)								
de Pauw	€€	8		●				
't Bourgoensch Hof	€€€	22		●				
Hotel de Tuilerieen	€€€€	45						
GHENT (see p135)								
Erasmus	€€	11						
Gravensteen	€€€	49						●

THE LOWER TOWN

Barry

Place Anneessens 25, 1000 Brussels.
[☎] (02) 511 2795. [FAX] (02) 514 1465.
[@] hotel.barry@skynet.be *Rooms:*
32. 🛏 1 ⊞ TV 🏊 🅿 AE,
DC, MC, V. €

Basic but comfortable hotel in an
early 20th-century building in a
slightly rundown square, south
of the Bourse and close by the
Anneessens metro station. Breakfast
is included in the already very low
prices. A 10 per cent discount
operates at weekends.

Les Eperonniers

Rue des Eperonniers 1, 1000 Brussels.
Map 2 D3. [☎] (02) 513 5366.
[FAX] (02) 511 3230. *Rooms: 21.*
🛏 1 TV 🅿 AE. €

The location, on a bustling street
near the Grand Place, is a great
bonus for this small and very basic
hotel. Low prices make it a
favourite with young travellers on
a budget. Many of the rooms have
showers, which for a small extra
fee are recommended. Breakfast is
not included.

Auberge Saint-Michel

Grand Place 15, 1000 Brussels.
Map 2 D3. [☎] (02) 511 0956. [FAX] (02)
511 4600. *Rooms: 15.* 🛏 1 TV 🅿
🅿 AE, DC, MC, V. €€€

This former ducal mansion has a
peerless Baroque façade and stunning views of the square and Town
Hall. Unfortunately, not all the
rooms face on to the Grand Place;
Room 22 has the best view. Service
is excellent, but the noise from the
square may be a little intrusive.

George V

Rue 't Kint 23, 1000 Brussels. **Map** 1
B3. [☎] (02) 513 5093. [FAX] (02) 513
4493. [@] reservations@george5.com
Rooms: 16. 🛏 1 ⊞ TV 🏊
🅿 AE. €€

One of the city's few examples of
English-inspired 19th-century architecture, the George V is just a short
stroll from the Bourse. The hotel
retains a degree of old-world charm.
Recent changes have made rooms
more comfortable, and those for
three and four people are among
the cheapest per person in Brussels.

Hilton Brussels Hotel

Place Rogier 20, 1000 Brussels. **Map**
2 D1. [☎] (02) 203 3125. [FAX] (02) 203
4331. [@] ras.brussels.city@hilton.com
Rooms: 285. 🛏 1 ⊞ TV Y 🏊
🅿 €€

Before World War II, this attractive
Art Deco establishment had ambitions to become one of Brussels'
best hotels. After the war, the hotel
suffered neglect from which it has
never fully recovered. Nonetheless
it remains comfortable, conveniently
situated and good value for budget
travellers. The hotel was taken
over in 2001 by the Hilton Group.

Ibis Brussels City

Rue Joseph Plateau 2, 1000 Brussels.
[☎] (02) 513 7620. [FAX] (02) 514 2214.
Rooms: 236. 🛏 1 TV 🏊 🅿 🅿
🅿 🅿 Y 🅿 AE, DC, MC, V.
€€

One of the major attractions of this
bland but good-value hostelry just
off Place Ste-Catherine was its proximity to the 12th-century Black
Tower, now built into the walls of
the new Novotel Brussels City next
door. The location is still convenient, and breakfast is included.

La Légende

Rue du Lombard 35, 1000 Brussels.
Map 1 C3. [☎] (02) 512 8290.
[FAX] (02) 512 3493. [W] www.hotella
legende.com *Rooms: 26.* 🛏 1
TV 🅿 🅿 🅿 AE, DC. €€

This reasonably priced and tourist-
friendly hotel is very close to the
Grand Place, and offers great value
in central Brussels. Its charmingly
dishevelled 18th-century buildings
are arranged around a pleasant
central courtyard. The rooms are
clean and functional, although costs
rise for rooms with bathrooms and
a TV. Breakfast is included.

La Madeleine

Rue de la Montagne 20–22, 1000
Brussels. **Map** 2 D3. [☎] (02) 513 2973.
[FAX] (02) 502 1350. *Rooms: 52.* 🛏 1
TV 🅿 🅿 🅿 AE, DC, MC, V. €€

This friendly, basic hotel, usefully
located near the Grand Place, is
fêted by many Belgians for its
Parisian charms. Slightly shabby
furniture and frumpy decor char-
acterize the modern public areas,
but the rooms are perfectly decent.

Matignon

Rue de la Bourse 10, 1000 Brussels.
Map 1 C2. [☎] (02) 511 0888. [FAX]
(02) 513 6927. *Rooms: 37.* 🛏 ⊞
1 TV 🅿 🅿 Y 🍴 🅿 AE, DC,
MC, V. €€

The beautiful, 19th-century Belle
Epoque façade conceals a recently
renovated, family-owned hotel in
an excellent location opposite the
Bourse. The spot is a noisy one, but
the rooms are comfortable. Five
multi-occupancy suites provide
great-value accommodation.

Mozart

Rue du Marché-aux-Fromages 23, 1000
Brussels. **Map** 2 D3. [☎] (02) 502 6661.
[FAX] (02) 502 7758. [@] hotel.mozart@
skynet.be *Rooms: 47.* 🛏 1 TV
🅿 AE, DC, MC, V. €€

On a street festooned with fast-food
outlets, this plain building has the
advantage of being a short walk
from the Grand Place. This hotel
is a decent option for those on a
budget, with pleasant oak-beamed
rooms, all with fridges. Breakfast is
included and service is helpful.

Noga

Rue du Béguinage 38, 1000 Brussels.
[☎] (02) 218 6763. [FAX] (02) 218 1603.
[@] info@nogahotel.com *Rooms: 19.*
🛏 Y 🅿 🅿 🅿 🅿 P 🅿 Y
AE, DC, V. €€

This smart hotel on a quiet street
in the Ste-Catherine area is at the
top end of the cut-price accommodation market. The modern rooms
are cosy and in excellent condition. A games room with billiard
table is also on site.

Orion

Quai aux Bois à Bruler 51, Brussels.
Map 1 C1. [☎] (02) 221 1411. [FAX] (02)
221 1599. [W] www.citadines.com
Rooms: 169. 🛏 1 ⊞ TV 🅿
🅿 P 🅿 🅿 AE, DC, V. €€

This apartment-hotel on Place
Ste-Catherine offers studios and
apartments at very competitive
prices. The stark modern exterior
is echoed in the functional decor.
There is a peaceful courtyard and
well-appointed rooms compensate
for the initial lack of homeliness.
The apartments are particularly
good for long-term visitors.

Queen Anne

Boulevard Emile Jacqmain 110, 1000
Brussels. **Map** 2 D1. [☎] (02) 217
1600. [FAX] (02) 217 1838. *Rooms: 60.*
🛏 1 TV 🅿 🅿 🅿 Y 🅿 AE, DC,
MC, V. €€

This family-run hotel on a main
road, a short walk from the city
centre is relaxed, friendly and very
good value for money. Once a
three-star hotel, the Queen Anne
has lost its accolade but little of its
charm, with sizeable rooms, a warm
welcome, a homely atmosphere and
a good night's sleep guaranteed.

Welcome

Rue du Peuplier 5, 1000 Brussels.
[☎] (02) 219 9546. [FAX] (02) 217
1887. [W] www.hotelwelcome.com
Rooms: 10. TV 🅿 🅿 P 🅿 Y
🅿 DC, MC, V. €€

The self-styled "smallest hotel in Brussels" offers simple but tasteful rooms in a sidestreet opposite Ste-Catherine metro station. The friendly owners keep their establishment in immaculate condition and offer guests a 5 per cent discount at the hotel's restaurant, the excellent Truite d'Argent *(see p153)*.

Windsor

Place Rouppe 13, 1000 Brussels. **Map** 1 C4. **(** (02) 511 2014. **FAX** (02) 514 0942. **Rooms:** 24. 1 TV AE, DC, MC, V. €€€

This is a cheerful and clean hotel about 15 minutes' walk from the town centre, with an appealing 19th-century stucco façade. Two people can stay here for two nights and still splash out on a meal at Comme Chez Soi, the Michelin three-star restaurant across the street, for the cost of a night in a mid-priced hotel *(see p149)*.

Arenberg NH

Rue d'Assaut 15, 1000 Brussels. **Map** 2 D2. **(** (02) 501 1616. **FAX** (02) 501 1818. **@** info@gtgrandplace. goldentulip.be **Rooms:** 155. 1 TV AE, DC, MC, V. €€€

Fans of Belgian comic strip art will love this hotel on a quiet street between the cathedral and Place de la Monnaie. The decor is loosely inspired by the country's classic cartoon heroes *(see pp18–19)*, while the bar-restaurant, L'Espadon, is a tribute to the Blake and Mortimer series.

Art Hotel Siru

Place Rogier 1, 1210 Brussels. **Map** 2 D1. **(** (02) 203 3580. **FAX** (02) 203 3303. **Rooms:** 101. **@** art.hotel.siru @skynet.be TV AE, DC, MC, V. €€€

Built on the site where 19th-century poets and lovers Paul Verlaine and Arthur Rimbaud once stayed, the Siru was transformed in the late 1980s into one of Brussels' most distinctive hotels. Over 100 Belgian artists were invited to refurbish it, turning every room into a mini art gallery. Some would say that the hotel offers a better survey of contemporary Belgian art than any of the city's museums.

Atlas

Rue du Vieux Marché-aux-Grains 30, 1000 Brussels. **Map** 1 C2. **(** (02) 502 6006. **FAX** (02) 502 6935. **@** info@ atlas-hotel.be **W** www.atlas-hotel.be **Rooms:** 88. 1 TV AE, DC, MC, V. €€€

This comfortable modern hotel is off the fashionable Rue Dansaert. Rooms are spacious if slightly lacking in character. The relaxed atmosphere makes this hotel popular with businesspeople who prefer a more intimate establishment.

Crowne Plaza

Rue Gineste 3, 1210 Brussels. **Map** 2 E1. **(** (02) 203 6200. **FAX** (02) 203 5555. **W** www.crowneplaza.com **Rooms:** 356. AE, DC, MC, V. €€€

Built by a disciple of Victor Horta in 1910, this elegant building near Place Rogier was Grace Kelly's hotel of choice when she stayed in Brussels. Art Nouveau still features strongly in the interior here. The hotel combines period elegance with modern convenience. Guests can visit the art gallery on the eighth floor, and 30 rooms are furnished in lavish Second Empire style. Expensive in high season.

Dome

Boulevard du Jardin Botanique 12–13, 1000 Brussels. **Map** 2 E1. **(** (02) 218 0680. **FAX** (02) 218 4112. **Rooms:** 125. AE, DC, MC, V. €€€

This elegant edifice is the work of architect Alban Chambon, who also designed the Métropole. Built in 1902, at the height of the Art Nouveau movement, the Dome failed to stand the test of time, closing in the 1960s. Its fortunes changed in 1990, with a launch combining the original Art Nouveau façade with a modern wing and minimalist decor. Each room is individually decorated and all are spacious and comfortable.

Ibis off Grand Place

Rue du Marché-aux-Herbes 100, 1000 Brussels. **Map** 2 D3. **(** (02) 514 4040. **FAX** (02) 514 5067. **Rooms:** 184. AE, DC, MC, V. €€€

This reliable, functional and professional chain hotel near the Grand Place has little to delight visitors but nothing to offend. With a sister hotel near Place Ste-Catherine, the chain is less expensive than similar hotels. Breakfast is not included.

Vendôme

Boulevard Adolphe Max 98, 1000 Brussels. **Map** 2 D1. **(** (02) 227 0300. **FAX** (02) 218 0683. **W** www.hotel-vendome.be **Rooms:** 106. AE, DC. €€€

The Vendôme is a comfortable modern hotel north of Place de Brouckère catering mainly to business people. Each generously sized and tasteful room comes with an en-suite bathroom. The hotel feels less anonymous than any similar establishment. Breakfast is not included in the tariff.

Aris

Rue du Marché-aux-Herbes 78–80, 1000 Brussels. **Map** 2 D3. **(** (02) 514 4300. **FAX** (02) 514 0119. **W** www.aris hotel.be **Rooms:** 55. 1 TV DC, MC, V. €€€€

Housed in a late 19th-century building with an attractive stone façade, this comfortable and efficient hotel is ideal for families. Situated right next to the Grand Place and only a few minutes' walk from the Ilôt Sacré with its many restaurants, it offers a duplex room for four people at very reasonable rates. Otherwise, prices are rather expensive, although breakfast is included. There are considerable discounts to be had for weekend bookings.

Bedford

Rue du Midi 135, 1000 Brussels. **Map** 1 C3. **(** (02) 512 7840. **FAX** (02) 507 0010. **@** hotelbedford@pophost. eunet.be **Rooms:** 319. 1 TV AE, DC, MC, V. €€€€

Incongruously situated towards the rundown end of central Brussels, the Bedford is an efficient hotel that does what all hotels should: it keeps on improving. The rooms are excellent and the service is impeccable. Although the weekday price seems a little high, there is a 50 per cent reduction at weekends. The Grand Place is just a short walk away.

Novotel off Grand Place

Rue du Marché-aux-Herbes 120, 1000 Brussels. **Map** 2 D3. **(** (02) 514 3333. **FAX** (02) 511 7723. **W** www. novotel.com **Rooms:** 136. TV AE, DC, MC, V. €€€€

This extremely successful mid-market chain hotel, a stone's throw from the Grand Place, is good for families and groups. A sofa bed is installed in each room and children under 16 have free accommodation. Breakfast is not included. There is a well-equipped children's play area next to the breakfast room. Single travellers should be aware that the room rate is not reduced.

Amigo

Rue de l'Amigo 1–3, 1000 Brussels.
Map 1 C3. 📞 (02) 547 4747.
FAX (02) 513 5277.
W www.hotelamigo.com
Rooms: 182.
AE, DC, MC, V. €€€€€

This elegant six-storey hotel
occupies the site of a 16th-century
prison, only a minute's stroll from
the Grand Place. The luxurious
rooms, recently renovated, are
decorated in the style of the
Spanish Renaissance, which was
popular during the reign of the
French king Louis XV. The Amigo
offers excellent facilities and an
extremely friendly, helpful service
in what is primarily a business
hotel. The marble bathrooms are
suavely charming if slightly
cramped. There is also a good
choice of restaurants. Breakfast
is included in the price of the
room. Rates from Friday through
Sunday nights inclusive are
reduced by half.

Carrefour de l'Europe

Rue du Marché-aux-Herbes 110,
1000 Brussels. **Map** 2 D3.
📞 (02) 504 9400. FAX (02) 504
9500. W www.carrefoureurope.net
Rooms: 63.
AE, DC, MC,
V. €€€€€

This business-oriented hotel is in
a modern building near the Grand
Place and the Gare Centrale. The
rooms are uniformly decorated
but comfortable; the triple glazing,
important in this busy city, ensures
that the worst of the city's noise is
kept at bay.

Métropole

Place de Brouckère 31, 1000 Brussels.
Map 1 D2. 📞 (02) 217 2300.
FAX (02) 218 0220.
W www.metropolehotel.be
Rooms: 410.
AE, DC, MC, V. €€€€€

Located on the busy, crowded
but central Place de Brouckère,
this Belle Epoque masterpiece
dates from 1895 and inside recalls
the city in its Art Nouveau heyday.
The period lift offers a wonderful
view of the richly decorated lobby
with its high ceilings, gilt cornices
and crystal chandeliers. The
modern rooms are comfortable
if a touch less characterful. The
bar is splendidly decorated with
Corinthian columns, palm plants
and roomy sofas. The room price
includes a good continental
breakfast.

Plaza

Boulevard Adolphe Max 118–126,
1000 Brussels. **Map** 2 D1. 📞 (02)
227 6740. FAX (02) 223 7929. W
www.leplaza-brussels.be **Rooms:** 193.
AE, DC, MC, V.
€€€€€

The quarters of choice for senior
German officers during World
War II, this classic 1930s building on
a rather downbeat street off Place
de Brouckère has been resurrected
after a 20-year closure. Combining
old-fashioned style with state-of-the-
art facilities, period features include
chandeliers and Murano glassware.
Several rooms are tailored to busi-
nesswomen, and have been decorated in a gently relaxing pastel
pale turquoise with hairdryers
and extra-special toiletries.

Radisson SAS Hotel

Rue du Fossé-aux-Loups 47, 1000
Brussels. **Map** 2 D2. 📞 (02) 219
2828. FAX (02) 219 6262.
W www. radisson.com **Rooms:** 281.
AE, DC,
MC, V. €€€€€

Built around a 12th-century
section of the city walls, this
Art Deco-inspired hotel near the
Galéries St-Hubert is among
the city's most impressive, with
comfortable rooms tastefully
decorated in Asian, Italian or
Scandinavian style. Services for
guests include a personal answer-
phone and free mobile phones.
Tours of the city, as well as golfing
trips, can be organized by the
hotel. The hotel's 2-star Michelin
Sea Grill restaurant is among
Brussels' finest (see p153).

Sheraton Towers

Place Rogier 3, 1210 Brussels. **Map** 2
D1. 📞 (02) 224 3111. FAX (02) 224
3456. W www.sheraton.com/brussels
Rooms: 533.
AE, DC, MC, V.
€€€€€

Even among the looming sky-
scrapers that rear over Place
Rogier, there is no mistaking the
twin towers of the capital's biggest
hotel. The emphasis here is firmly
on comfort, with large rooms decorated in understated brown and
deep red tones. This is a luxurious
and relaxing environment for
businesspeople to work, rest or
play with ease. Some rooms have
private offices, and all have well-
equipped work stations. The indoor
swimming-pool on the 30th floor
has spectacular views over the city.

THE UPPER TOWN

Les Bluets

Rue Berckmans 124, 1060 Brussels.
📞 (02) 534 3983. FAX (02) 543
0970. W www.geocities.com/
les_bluets/angl1/html **Rooms:** 10.
AE, DC, MC, V.

This charming late-19th-century
hotel is non-smoking throughout.
The decor features antique
furniture, lots of plants and caged
birds. Rooms are simply furnished
and breakfast is included in the
already reasonable price.

Argus

Rue Capitaine Crespel 6, 1050
Brussels. **Map** 2 D5. 📞 (02) 514
0770. FAX (02) 514 1222.
W www.hotel-argus.be **Rooms:** 41.
 AE, DC,
MC, V. €€

Handily placed between the
Porte de Namur and Place Louise,
this tasteful, quiet hotel makes
a good base for exploring the
whole city. The rooms are clean
and comfortable. Prices drop
further at weekends and throughout July and August.

Sabina

Rue du Nord 78, 1000 Brussels.
Map 2 F2. 📞 (02) 218 2637.
FAX (02) 219 3239. W www.hotel
sabina.be **Rooms:** 24.
AE, DC. €€€

This friendly and well-kept hotel
occupies an elegant 19th-century
building. Inside, authentic wood
panelling and fireplaces enhance
the peaceful atmosphere. The
hotel is located on a quiet street
in the residential area around
Place Madou. It is also close to
Brussels' main attractions and the
European government institutions.

Alfa Sablon

Rue de la Paille 2–8, 1000 Brussels.
📞 (02) 513 6040. FAX (02) 511
8141. W www.alfahotels.com
Rooms: 32.
AE, DC, MC, V.
€€€

This calm, refined hotel boasts a
great location near the Place du
Grand Sablon, which is noted for
its appealing antique shops and
enticing cafés. An attractive late
19th-century façade houses a light,
inviting contemporary interior.
There is a garden and a sauna,
and the four large, split-level
suites are particularly comfortable.

Dixseptième

Rue de la Madeleine 25, 1000 Brussels.
Map 2 D3. 【 *(02) 502 5744.* FAX *(02) 502 6424.* @ info@ledixseptieme.be
W www.ledixseptieme.be **Rooms:** 24.
AE, DC, MC, V. €€€€

Built in the 17th century as the home of the Spanish ambassador, this small, peaceful hotel offers a calming break from the bustling Ilôt Sacré. Each room is named after a Belgian artist, and enthusiasts can refresh their painting knowledge thanks to the art library in the lounge. Many of the rooms are authentically decorated in Baroque style with parquet flooring through-out, and flamboyant crystal chandeliers in the public areas. A splendid Louis XIV staircase connects some of the rooms, several of which look out over a private courtyard.

Hilton

Boulevard de Waterloo 38, 1000 Brussels. **Map** 2 E5. 【 *(02) 504 1111.* FAX *(02) 504 2111.* W www.hilton.com
Rooms: 434. AE, DC, MC, V. €€€€

In addition to the usual features – crisp service, business facilities and large, comfortable rooms – the Hilton offers personal security guards and such facilities for Japanese visitors as Japanese speakers, newspapers and kimonos. The lobby is decorated with a large golden frieze depicting the Grand Place. The hotel also houses the Michelin-starred restaurant Maison de Boeuf.

Sofitel

Avenue de la Toison d'Or 40, 1050 Brussels. **Map** 2 E5. 【 *(02) 514 2200.* FAX *(02) 514 5744.* W www.accorhotels.com **Rooms:** 175.
AE, DC, MC, V. €€€€

Dwarfed by the looming 1960s-built Hilton on the opposite side of the street, this relatively discreet branch of the upmarket French chain easily holds its own in terms of elegance. The most impressive features are the English-style bar and library with its comfortable leather chairs. It is also possible to escape from the bustle of the city in the Sofitel's beautiful garden, with its statues by Belgian sculptor Jean Cayette. Inside the rooms, king-size beds and a quiet, comfortable atmosphere attract plenty of admirers. The hotel does not have its own restaurant but is within five minutes' walk of a selection of Brussels' finest.

Stanhope

Rue du Commerce 9, 1000 Brussels.
Map 2 F4. 【 *(02) 506 9111.* FAX *(02) 512 1708.* W www.summit hotels. com **Rooms:** 50.
AE, DC, MC, V. €€€€

The Stanhope represents a luxurious Belgian vision of traditional upper-class historic British hospitality. The hotel has taken over three adjacent townhouses to deliver its elegant old-world service, which includes chauffeur-driven cars, afternoon tea and newspapers pushed under the door in the mornings. The rooms have marble bathrooms, handmade furniture and paintings on the walls. Breakfast is included. There are very good rates at weekends.

Astoria

Rue Royale 103, 1000 Brussels.
Map 2 E2. 【 *(02) 227 0505.* FAX *(02) 217 1150.* W www.sofitel.com
Rooms: 118. AE, DC, MC, V. €€€€€

This opulent Belle Epoque master-piece recalls the capital's glory days of the early 20th century, when such famous statesmen as Eisen-hower and Churchill were among its most distinguished guests. The lobby, staircase, wood-panelled lift and furnishings are all original. The recently renovated rooms retain their individual character, and each is triple-glazed. The Pullman bar is in a former Orient Express carriage.

Dorint

Boulevard Charlemagne 11–19, 1000 Brussels. **Map** 3 B2. 【 *(02) 231 0909.* FAX *(02) 231 3371.* W www.dorint.be
Rooms: 212. AE, DC, MC, V. €€€€

Situated near the European govern-ment complex, the Dorint is favoured by visiting journalists, diplomats and politicians. The hotel offers ISDN lines, translation cabins and a bar with a Reuters terminal updating news 24 hours a day. Try the fitness club with its Turkish bath, sauna and solarium, or take a stroll in the tranquil Oriental garden. For a taste of Brussels' culture, contemporary works by local photographers hang in the rooms.

Jolly Grand Sablon

Rue Boedenbroeck 2–4, 1000 Brussels.
Map 2 D4. 【 *(02) 512 8800.* FAX *(02) 512 6766.* W www.jollyhotels.it
Rooms: 193. AE, DC, MC, V. €€€€

With an unbeatable location on the southern edge of the Place du Grand Sablon, this Italian chain's flagship Brussels hotel offers impeccable service and grand rooms. The façade is an unobtru-sive addition to the wonderful Baroque masterpieces all around it. Good weekend rates.

Méridien

Carrefour de l' Europe 3, 1000 Brussels. 【 *(02) 548 4211.* FAX *(02) 548 4080.* W www.meridien.be
Rooms: 224.  AE, DC, MC, V. €€€€€

This luxurious modern hotel is very close to the Grand Place but is also opposite the Gare Centrale, which can be, to some tastes, a slightly seedy area. The hotel is decorated in modern style and has a plush lobby featuring a large brass chandelier; this is a popular meeting place with a comfortable atmosphere that is enhanced by a regular pianist. The rooms are furnished in English Victorian style. The hotel manages to cater to both business travellers and families, with corporate facilities such as multilingual staff.

Renaissance Brussels Hotel

Rue de Parnasse 19, 1050 Brussels.
【 *(02) 505 2929.* FAX *(02) 505 2555.* **Rooms:** 257.
AE, DC, MC, V. €€€€€

The first luxury hotel to establish itself near the European Parliament, just a few minutes from the Palais Royal, the former Archimède was taken over by Renaissance in 2001. Each bedroom is large and well equipped. Guests also have access to the world-class Academy Gym next door.

Royal Windsor

Rue Duquesnoy 5, 1000 Brussels.
Map 2 D3. 【 *(02) 505 5555.* FAX *(02) 505 5500.* W www.warwickhotels.com/brussels
Rooms: 266. AE, DC, MC, V. €€€€€

This charactenful deluxe hotel near the Grand Place has small but exquisite facilities. The sump-tuous French-styled bedrooms are reckoned to be Brussels' most expensive per square metre. However, the wonderful marble bathrooms make up for the lack of space. Other facilities include a restaurant with a glorious circular stained-glass window in its ceiling.

GREATER BRUSSELS

De Boeck's

Rue Veydt 40, 1050 Brussels. 【 (02) 537 4033. FAX (02) 534 4037. @ hotel. deboecks@euronet.be **Rooms:** 36. 🛏 1 🏫 TV ⇄ 🔒 *AE, DC.* €€

De Boeck's is a converted turn-of-the-century townhouse on a quiet street not far from Avenue Louise. The pleasant rooms have a family feel and many cared-for touches. Breakfast is included. The city centre is easily accessible by the 93 or 94 tram. At the weekend rooms can be had for just 50 per cent of the already very reasonable daily rate.

Les Tourelles

Avenue Winston Churchill 135, 1180 Brussels. 【 (02) 344 9573. FAX (02) 346 4270. @ les.tourelles@ skynet.be **Rooms:** 21. 🛏 1 TV 🔒 🐾 P 🔒 *AE, MC, V.* €€

Les Tourelles' fake medieval towers and rustic cottage façade stand out among the modern villas and stucco townhouses of Avenue Winston Churchill. Inside, the wood-heavy decor has an old-fashioned feel, while the hotel's atmosphere retains the personal idiosyncracies that hotel schools have, weirdly, done their best to stamp out. This family-friendly place also offers an evening babysitting service.

Sun

Rue du Berger 38, 1050 Brussels. **Map** 2 E5. 【 (02) 511 2119. FAX (02) 512 3271. @ sunhotel@ skynet.be **Rooms:** 22. 🛏 1 TV 🐾 P 🔒 *AE, DC, MC, V.* €€

If a firm mattress is essential to your slumber, then this comfortable, homely establishment near Porte de Namur will suit you. Although the quiet street on which it stands may be a little run down, this small hotel is spotlessly clean and popular, with light-green decor and a glass mural in the breakfast room.

Abbey

Kerkeblokstraat 5, 1850 Grimbergen. 【 (02) 270 0888. FAX (02) 270 8188. **Rooms:** 47. 🛏 1 🏫 TV 🔒 🔒 📊 🐾 P 🔒 *AE, DC, MC, V.* €€€

This modern, villa-style hotel just north of the city is a pleasant alternative to staying near the airport. It is popular with businesspeople in town for an event at the Heysel Exhibition Centre. The rooms are large and well appointed, with massage showers in the bathrooms.

Alfa Louise

Avenue Louise 212, 1050 Brussels. **Map** 2 D5. 【 (02) 644 2929. FAX (02) 644 1878. w www.alfa hotels.com **Rooms:** 40. 🛏 1 🔒 TV 🔒 📊 🔒 P 🔒 🔒 *AE, DC, MC, V.* €€€

All of the Alfa's rooms are extremely large, with a sizeable desk and a pleasant sitting area, while the bathrooms come with hairdryer and bathrobes. Many also have individual terraces. The city centre is a 10-minute tram-ride away (on the 93 or 94), and guests can take advantage of an unusual extra and make use of a nearby health centre, with gym and pool, at no extra charge.

Château Gravenhof

Alsembergsesteenweg 676, 1653 Dworp. 【 (02) 380 4499. FAX (02) 380 4060. w www. gravenhof.be **Rooms:** 26. 🛏 1 🔒 24 TV 🔒 🔒 📊 🐾 🔒 🐾 Y 🔒 *AE, DC, MC, V.* €€€

For those visitors to Brussels who prefer a quieter location, this 18th-century manor house is ideal. Located in handsome grounds in a leafy village, not far south of the city, the hotel is close to a golf course and equestrian facilities. Perhaps because it is not in the city proper, Château Gravenhof attracts more convention clients than overnight visitors, which may explain the relatively low prices on offer. Period fittings and furniture create an atmosphere of relaxed gentility, and the luxurious feel of the place represents extremely good value for money.

Holiday Inn City Centre

Chaussée de Charleroi 38, 1060 Brussels. 【 (02) 533 6666. FAX (02) 538 9014. w www. holidayinn.com/bru/cityctr **Rooms:** 201. 🛏 1 🔒 TV 🔒 Y 📊 🔒 🐾 🐾 P 🐾 🔒 *AE, DC, MC, V.* €€€€

The Holiday Inn's flagship Brussels branch is not exactly in the city centre, but it is close to Avenue Louise and the major sights are a short ride away on the 91 or 92 trams. The building is modern and the rooms have all the comforts of a business-oriented hotel, including a safe, room service and a trouser press. Triple-glazing makes the rooms surprisingly quiet, while the firm queen-size double beds (in some rooms) ensure a good night's sleep. The service is polite.

Hyatt Regency Barsey

Avenue Louise 381, 1050 Brussels. 【 (02) 649 9800. FAX (02) 640 1764. **Rooms:** 99. 🛏 1 24 TV 🔒 🔒 🔒 🐾 🔒 *AE, DC, MC, V.* €€€€

Awarded four stars by the Belgian authorities, the Mayfair has enlisted the services of top French interior designer Jacques Garcia to provide an opulent feel for its loyal visitors, who are mostly businessmen. The public rooms will be decorated in traditional English style, with 19th-century antique furniture and silk drapery. Many of the rooms have views out over a private garden.

Manos Stéphanie

Chaussée de Charleroi 28, 1060 Brussels. 【 (02) 539 0250. FAX (02) 537 5729. w www.manoshotel.com **Rooms:** 55. 🛏 1 🏫 TV 🔒 🔒 🔒 P 🔒 *AE, DC, MC, V.* €€€€

This charming, friendly hotel resides in a converted townhouse, whose Parisian flavour is popular with visiting actors and well-heeled French families. While all rooms are well-appointed and spacious, some are larger than others: the split-level room 103 is particularly enticing. Breakfast is included. There is no restaurant, but a chef is available every evening until 10:30pm for room service orders.

NH Brussels City Centre

Chaussée de Charleroi 17, 1060 Brussels. 【 (02) 539 0160. FAX (02) 537 9011. **Rooms:** 246. 🛏 1 TV 🔒 Y 🔒 🔒 🔒 🐾 P 🐾 🔒 *AE, DC, MC, V.* €€€€

This hotel has been recently refurbished, with the installation of a maritime-themed bar, Deck 17, the most obvious sign of restored pride. The rooms are all to three-star standard and the staff will make your stay as pleasant as possible.

President WTC

Boulevard du Roi Albert II 248, 1000 Brussels. **Map** 2 D1. 【 (02) 203 2020. FAX (02) 203 2440. @ info@president hotels.be **Rooms:** 302. 🛏 1 🏫 TV 🔒 Y 🔒 🐾 🔒 🔒 🔒 🔒 🐾 🔒 *AE, DC, MC, V.* €€€€

The best of the three President hotels in Brussels, this business-oriented establishment near the World Trade Centre is the hotel of choice for conference organizers. The sky-blue and white rooms are fresher than in most business hotels, and the Jacuzzi, sunbeds and table-tennis tables are added benefits for the traveller in need of relaxation.

Sofitel

Bessenveldstraat 15, 1831 Diegem.
[(02) 713 6666. FAX (02) 721 4345. @ ho548@accor-hotels.be
Rooms: 125.
AE, DC, MC, V. €€€€

This smart, professional establishment is part of an upmarket French chain. The lobby and public spaces are discreetly luxurious with deep comfortable armchairs and sofas. The rooms are large with inviting king-size double beds. Efficient triple-glazing excludes the noise from the nearby Brussels National Airport. The open-air swimming pool, surrounded by the hotel's gardens, is a rare treat.

Bristol Stéphanie

Avenue Louise 91–93, 1050 Brussels.
Map 2 D5. [(02) 543 3311.
FAX (02) 538 0307. W www.bristol.be
Rooms: 142.
AE, DC, MC, V. €€€€€

Norwegian entrepreneur Olav Thon turned the Bristol Stéphanie into a sophisticated homage to his native land. The large rooms and suites are decorated in chalet-style, with wooden floors, and some also have kitchen facilities. The hotel offers baby-sitting, as well as conference facilities and room service, and there is a heated indoor pool.

Conrad International

Avenue Louise 71, 1050 Brussels.
Map 2 D5. [(02) 542 4800. FAX (02) 542 4200. W www.brusselsconrad international.com **Rooms:** 269.
AE, DC, MC, V.
€€€€€

Combining old-fashioned elegance with business conveniences (such as multi-line phones, modem and fax in the room, and 12 meeting rooms), this palatial establishment is perhaps the best of Brussels' luxury hotels. Former US President Bill Clinton is among the hotel's many celebrity guests. Even the standard rooms are huge, often featuring a mezzanine, and all boasting sumptuous marble bathrooms. There are two good restaurants here: Café Wiltcher and the gourmet establishment La Maison de Maître.

Gresham Belson

Chaussée de Louvain 805, 1140 Brussels. [(02) 705 2030. FAX (02) 705 2043. W www.belson.be **Rooms:** 135.
AE, DC, MC, V.
€€€€€

This efficient hotel is conveniently located between Brussels National Airport and the Grand Place, and is only five minutes' drive from the EC headquarters. Facilities are especially good for business visitors, with fax and computer points in many rooms. Transport to and from the airport is included.

Montgomery

Avenue de Tervuren 134, 1150 Brussels.
Map 4 E4. [(02) 741 8511. FAX (02) 741 8500. @ hotel@montgomery.be
Rooms: 63.
AE, DC, MC, V. €€€€€

Despite the futuristic façade, this luxurious hotel near the European institutions has a resolutely old-fashioned atmosphere. The rooms are decorated in three themed styles: Oriental, English and New England. Each room has a well-equipped office area with internet and fax connections. The hotel is a member of the Leading Small Hotels of the World group.

Sheraton

Brussels National Airport, 1930 Zaventem. [(02) 725 1000. FAX (02) 710 8777. W www.sheraton.com/ brussels **Rooms:** 304.
AE, DC, MC, V. €€€€€

The Sheraton is the only hotel in Belgium to have its own airport, as Belgian critics never tire of joking. While the airport is not exclusively reserved for Sheraton guests, the hotel's on-site presence makes it improbably convenient for short-stay guests. A 24-hour business centre is available for those who want to work till departure.

ANTWERP

Firean

Karel Oomsstraat 6, 2018 Antwerp. [(03) 237 0260. FAX (03) 238 1168. W www.firean.com **Rooms:** 15.
AE, DC, MC, V. €€€

A small, family-run hotel with a warm atmosphere. Trams run from outside the hotel, housed in an Art Deco building in a residential neighbourhood, to the city centre. Breakfast is included.

Hilton

Groenplaats, 2000 Antwerp. [(03) 204 1212. FAX (03) 204 1213. W www. hilton.com **Rooms:** 211.
AE, DC, MC, V. €€€€€

Situated at the heart of the Old Town, behind a listed Baroque

façade, the Hilton has large, well-equipped rooms. Facilities include a sauna and a solarium.

BRUGES

de Pauw

Sint-Gilliskerkhof 8, 8000 Bruges.
[(050) 33 7118. FAX (050) 34 5140. W www.hoteldepauw.be
Rooms: 8. MC, V. €€

This family-run hotel, located in a quiet side street, offers great value for money and a warm, friendly service. All but two rooms have their own bathroom and TV.

't Bourgoensch Hof

Wollestraat 39, 8000 Bruges.
[(050) 33 1645. FAX (050) 34 6378. W www.bourgoensch-hof.be
Rooms: 15.
MC, V. €€€

The rooms at this cosy hotel in the heart of the city centre are decorated in Flemish style, and some have romantic views of the canal. Breakfast is included.

Hotel de Tuilerieen

Dijver 7, 8000 Bruges. [(050) 34 3691. FAX (050) 34 0400.
W www.hoteltuilerieen.com **Rooms:** 27.
AE, DC, MC, V. €€€€

This canalside hotel occupies a beautiful 15th-century mansion, close to some of the city's best museums and tourist attractions. The hotel also offers a heated swimming pool, sauna, jacuzzi and solarium. Childminding available.

GHENT

Erasmus

Poel 25, 9000 Ghent. [(09) 224 2195. FAX (09) 233 4241. @ hotel erasmus@proximedia.be **Rooms:** 11.
AE, MC, V. €€

An immaculate family-run hotel with a lovely wood-beamed lounge and rooms with stone fireplaces. There is also a small, private garden.

Gravensteen

Jan Breydelstraat 35, 9000 Ghent.
[(09) 225 1150. FAX (09) 225 1850. W www.gravensteen.be
Rooms: 49.
AE, MC, V. €€€

Housed in a 19th-century mansion, the Gravensteen has been refurbished in the Second Empire style. A buffet breakfast is included in the price of the room.

WHERE TO EAT

I T IS ALMOST impossible to eat badly in Brussels. Some say one can eat better here than in Paris, and even meals in the lower- to mid-price bracket are always carefully prepared and often innovative. Venues range from top gastronomic restaurants to unpretentious local taverns where you can find generous

Thai chef in Brussels

servings of local specialities. If you tire of Belgian fare, try the variety of excellent local seafood and the range of ethnic cuisine that reflects the city's lively cultural diversity. The listings on pp146–53 give a detailed description of all the selected restaurants and the key features of each restaurant are summarized on pp144–5.

Brasserie Horta in Centre Belge de la Bande Dessinée *(see p146)*

WHERE TO EAT

T HE BELGIAN love affair with dining out makes for an astonishing concentration of restaurants and eateries: a 10-minute stroll from almost anywhere in Brussels should bring you to a decent, and often almost undiscovered, tavern or brasserie. However, superb dining is to be had without leaving the Ilôt Sacré, the area around the central Grand Place, where many

very good and surprisingly reasonable restaurants abound. Beware the tourist traps around the Grand Place that make their living from gulling unwary visitors into spending far more than they intended to. The impressive displays of seafood adorning the pavements of Rue des Bouchers northwest of the Grand Place and Petite Rue des Bouchers can promote rather touristy restaurants, but those on pp146–7 are recommended.

TYPES OF CUISINE

E LSEWHERE IN the city centre is a wealth of quality fish restaurants, especially around the former fish market at Place Ste-Catherine, while the city's trendiest eateries can be found on Rue Dansaert and in the Place Saint-Géry district. If you are planning to explore other parts of Brussels, or if you are staying outside the city centre, you will find plenty of good Belgian fare on offer in the southern communes of Ixelles and Saint-Gilles, and in Etterbeek, where the European Commission buildings are

located. Ixelles also boasts the largest concentration of Vietnamese and Southeast Asian cuisine, especially around Chaussée de Boondael. This student area in the Matonge district is also home to several African restaurants, serving food from the Congo (formerly Zaire), Senegal and Rwanda.

North of the city centre, in the communes of Schaerbeek and Saint-Josse, Turkish and North African communities have sprung up, and excellent Moroccan and Tunisian cuisine is commonplace. There is also a growing trend for "designer couscous", with Belgian restaurateurs exploiting the popularity of North African food in spectacularly ornate venues, often featuring ethnic music in the evenings.

Spanish and Portuguese restaurants can be found in the Marolles district and in Saint-Gilles, reflecting the wave of immigration in the 1950s and 1960s when many southern Europeans chose to settle in Brussels. The city is also liberally sprinkled with Greek restaurants, although many veer on the over-touristy side. A better bet are the modern Latin American eateries.

VEGETARIANS

D ESPITE A MARKED upturn in recent years, Brussels is far from being a vegetarian-friendly city, since there are only a handful of specialist vegetarian restaurants *(see p153)*. However, those who eat fish will find mainstream restaurants cater generously to their needs; Brussels is very strong on fish and seafood. Also, the traditional dish, *stoemp*, mashed potatoes

Façade of the popular brasserie La Belle Epoque *(see p147)*

mixed with root vegetables, is a classic vegetarian speciality. North African restaurants usually offer vegetarian couscous options, and there are plenty of Italian options for cheese-eaters. Indian restaurants are few and far between, but most offer vegetable curries. Vegans may struggle, particularly in European restaurants.

HOW MUCH TO PAY

MOST RESTAURANTS, taverns and cafés display a menu in the window and the majority take credit cards. Prices usually include VAT (21 per cent) and service (16 per cent), although it is worth checking the latter before you tip. A meal at the city's most luxurious restaurants can cost up to €150 per head, but you can eat superbly for around €50 per head (including wine) and a hearty snack in a tavern should cost no more than €15. The mark-up level on wine can be very high, especially in most Mediterranean restaurants and in obviously touristic areas, but most taverns do a reasonable *vin maison* and serve myriad varieties of beer.

Service in all but the most expensive restaurants can be erratic by British and US standards. But beneath the sometimes grumpy exterior, you will often find warmth and an earthy, cheerfully self-deprecating sense of humour that is unique to Belgium. There are no hard and fast rules, but some diners leave an additional tip of up to 10 per cent if they are especially

The exotic interior of the Blue Elephant, Thai restaurant *(see p151)*

satisfied with the quality of the meal and the service. Note that some restaurants cannot take service on a credit card slip, and this, plus the tip, will have to be paid in cash, as do other gratuities in the city.

Stall selling freshly made snacks in Saint-Gilles at the weekend

DINING ON A BUDGET

MANY RESTAURANTS offer bargain, fixed-price or rapid lunchtime menus for under €12.50, plus reasonably priced dishes of the day. Even the city's most expensive

eateries have similar deals, meaning you can sample haute cuisine for less than €37. In the evening, look out for set menus with *vin compris* (wine included), which are often a way to save a large part of the dining bill.

At the other end of the scale, Brussels has most of the usual fast-food outlets, and sandwiches are sold at most butchers or delicatessens (*traiteurs*), usually with tuna, cheese or cold meat fillings. Some of the latter offer sit-down snacks too. Alternatively, take advantage of Belgium's national dish, *frites/frieten* (French fries, hand-cut and double-fried to ensure an even crispiness). There are *Friteries/Frituurs* all over town, serving enormous portions of French fries with mayonnaise and dozens of other sauces, plus *fricadelles* (sausages in batter), lamb kebabs, fish cakes or meat-balls. Inevitably, these establishments vary in quality; one sure bet is Maison Antoine on Place Jourdan in Etterbeek, where they have been frying for over half a century.

Brussels' sizeable Turkish community means that kebab, gyros and pitta restaurants are ubiquitous, especially in Saint-Josse and on the gaudy Rue du Marché aux Fromages, just off the Grand Place. Perhaps a better bet is the nearby L'Express, a Lebanese take-away specializing in chicken and felafel pittas, generously crammed with fresh salad.

Most cafés and taverns offer *petite restauration* (light meals) on top or instead of

Interior of Scheltema, a Belle Epoque brasserie *(see p153)*

Entrance of the historic tavern In 't Spinnekopke *(see p146)*

a regular menu. These simple, traditional snacks include croque monsieur, shrimp croquettes, chicory baked with ham and cheese, salads, spaghetti bolognaise and *américain* (raw minced beef with seasoning). Do not be fooled by the word "light" – most of these dishes will keep you going from lunchtime well into the evening.

Healthy breakfasts and light lunches with an emphasis on organic food are the staple of Le Pain Quotidien/Het Dagelijks Brood *(see p155)*, a fashionable Belgian chain where customers are seated all together around a large wooden table: trying this out is highly recommended if breakfast is not included in

your hotel accommodation. For snackers who are sweet-toothed, waffle stands or vans appear on almost every corner, while cafés and taverns offer a tempting variety of waffles (topped with jam, cream or chocolate). Pancakes *(crêpes)* are just as popular – and filling – although you can cut down the calories with a savoury wholewheat pancake at one of the city's crêperies.

Ethnic food can also work out at a very reasonable price; large portions of couscous, pizzas and African specialities are often to be found at good rates in student areas and at stands throughout the city.

Open-air tables outside fish restaurants in Rue des Bouchers

OPENING TIMES

SINCE time-consuming business lunches are still very much part of the culture in Belgium, most restaurants are open for lunch from noon until 2 or 3pm. Dinner is generally served from 7pm onwards and last orders are taken as late as 10pm. You are more likely to find late-night restaurants, serving until midnight, in the side streets of downtown Brussels; only a handful provide meals after 1am. Breakfast bars usually open around 7am. For details of café and bar opening times, see pp154–5.

MAKING A RESERVATION

WHEN VISITING one of the city's more celebrated restaurants, it is always wise to book in advance. The listings indicate where booking is advisable. If you are planning to go to the legendary Comme Chez Soi, you should reserve weeks ahead rather than hope for a last-minute cancellation. Trendy designer restaurants are often crowded in the evening, but usually take reservations well in advance.

READING THE MENU

MENUS AT most restaurants are written in French, sometimes in Flemish and French. Some, especially in tourist areas, may have explanations in English. Dishes of the day or suggestions are often illegibly scribbled on

The Art Nouveau interior of Comme Chez Soi, often praised as Brussels' best restaurant *(see p149)*

The 16th-century cellar of 't Kelderke in the Grand Place *(see p147)*

blackboards. Fortunately, most waiters speak at least a little English. You may find a food dictionary useful. For details of some of the most popular Belgian specialities, see pp140–41. The phrasebook on pp189–91 also gives translations of many menu items.

ETIQUETTE

BRUSSELS IS LESS relaxed than, say, Amsterdam and, although casual or smart-casual dress is acceptable in most restaurants, you will probably feel more at home dressing up for upmarket places. A few formal restaurants will insist on a jacket and tie for men. The dress code for women is more flexible, but smartness is appreciated.

CHILDREN

IN GENERAL, Brussels is family-oriented and child-friendly, perhaps because Belgian children tend to be restrained and well behaved in restaurants. Many establishments have children's menus, although they are not always a bargain, and several offer free meals for children under 12. High-chairs should be available on request, and some restaurants have inside play areas, including some of the big hotels, where children are usually welcome. On the outskirts of Brussels or near one of the city's many parks, eateries can offer extensive outside playgrounds. Ethnic restaurants, in particular Vietnamese, Greek and the

less formal Italian ones, tend to be especially accommodating. They do not always have children's menus, but are happy for adults to share their meal with youngsters. Children are usually allowed in cafés and in bars although they are forbidden to drink alcohol. Some restaurants may be too formal for children to feel comfortable.

SMOKING

BRUSSELS IS STILL very much a smokers' city. Although a new law requests all but the smallest establishments to provide non-smoking areas plus ventilation, many do not conform to this regulation. If you are truly averse to cigarette smoke, make sure you ask about arrangements when reserving, or before you take a seat. Many cafés and taverns can be very smoky, and some locals do not take kindly to

Place settings at the restaurant La Truffe Noire *(see p149)*

being asked to put out a cigarette. Smokers should know that most restaurants do not sell cigarettes.

DISABLED FACILITIES

FACILITIES FOR the disabled are poor in Brussels, although there have been some recent improvements. The cobbled streets and hilly areas may well be difficult to negotiate, but most people are very helpful and will go out of their way to help those with difficulty walking or in a wheelchair. There is a limited number of restaurants with ramps and ground-floor bathrooms, so do check the extent of the access before making a reservation or taking a seat. A list of restaurants and cafés with disabled facilities is published by a Flemish charity; contact AWIPH at Rue de la Rivelaine 21, 6061 Charleroi (071 205 711).

USING THE LISTINGS

Key to symbols in the listings on pp144–53:

❑❑❑❑ fixed price menu, either at lunch or for dinner.
V vegetarian dishes a speciality
♣ childrens' portions
♿ wheelchair access to all or part of the restaurant
▦ outdoor eating
❒ good wine list
♫ live music on some nights of the week
★ highly recommended
▨ credit cards accepted
AE American Express
DC Diners Club
MC Master Card/Access
V VISA

Price categories for a three-course meal for one, including cover charge, service and half a bottle of wine or other drinks:

€ up to €25
€€ €25–37
€€€ €37–50
€€€€ €50–62
€€€€€ over €62

A Glossary of Belgian Dishes

BELGIANS LOVE food, and the quality of their cooking is matched only by the vast size of their portions. The Flemish and the Walloons each have their own style of cooking, both readily available in Brussels. With its lively history of invasions from around Europe, the culinary traditions of Holland, Spain and Austria have occasionally filtered into both cuisines. Walloon (Belgian-French) food is similar to French provincial cuisine – hearty and spicy, with rich dishes throughout the menu. Flemish cuisine is often simpler, featuring some substantial stews and traditional cooking. Many regions of Belgium have their specialities, such as Ardennes pâté and Liège sausage, but Brussels is truly the culinary heart of the country, and the city contains many fine restaurants to suit every budget. Most menus in the tourist areas will offer explanations in English but if not, usually the waiter will try to assist.

French fries served with mayonnaise

Moules marinières, sweated in wine and onion, served in a tureen

Steaming waffles freshly made on a stand, a familiar scent in the city

SNACKS

SOME OF THE most famous Belgian food is snack food, and with the amount of chip vans and waffle stands dotted around Brussels, you need never go hungry. Perhaps not appealing to all taste buds, but authentically Belgian, are the *caricole* stands, offering steaming hot, ready to eat buttered sea snails.

Frites
Thinly cut potato chips (French fries) are twice-fried and usually served in a cardboard cone, accompanied by a dollop of mayonnaise.
Gaufres
Waffles made of sweet batter, "toasted" in a waffle iron and served with syrup, chocolate or dusted with icing sugar.
Speculoos
Sugared ginger biscuits, often baked in patron saint-shaped moulds, served with coffee.
Smoutebollen
Sugared doughnuts.

Caricoles
Salted, boiled and buttered sea snails wrapped in paper.
Pistolets
Round oval-shaped bread breakfast rolls, with a hard crust and fluffy white interior.

SOUPS

SOUP IN BELGIUM is often a hearty meal in itself, served in large tureens accompanied by freshly baked bread. Vegetable soups with a stock base are particularly common, using ingredients such as carrot, cauliflower, cabbage or green peas, often mixed. Vegetarians, however, should be warned; green pea soup often includes pork and spicy sausage as well as potatoes.
Waterzooi
A stew of chicken or fish simmered in their stock, with cream and often white wine, and served with puréed vegetables.
Bisque de homard
Lobster poached in reduced seafood stock with brandy.

FISH AND SEAFOOD

MOST OF THE FISH served in Brussels comes straight from the Ostend coast, which, on a direct route less than 90 km (55 miles) away, means that it is fresh every day. At the turn of the 20th century, the port of Brussels extended as far north as the Eglise Ste-Catherine, with a huge covered fish market behind the church. This area is still the centre of a bustling trade in seafood; although the market has long since vanished, the surrounding streets and alleys are filled with terraced fish restaurants.

The Belgians' love of seafood extends further than the national dish, *moules et frites*. Ostend sole, eels in green sauce, lobster in season and crispy shrimp croquettes are just some of the favourites. While the city's more formal establishments tend to be expensive, there are plenty of simple eateries offering the day's catch at very low prices.
Moules
Mussels, traditionally served in copper tureens, cooked in white wine and onions, with a side order of *frites*.

Marinated herring

Hareng
Herring, prepared in a variety of ways: roll-mop, fried, steamed, marinated in vinegar or smoked.
Langouste
Spiny lobster, brought in fresh from Ostend; when it is available much will be made of it in lavish seafood displays and on daily "specials" menu boards.
Huîtres
Oysters, swallowed raw or served *au gratin*; covered with breadcrumbs, bacon, herbs and cheese and grilled.
Anguilles au vert
Eels, commonly served with green herbs such as thyme or parsley, and cooked in butter.
Sole Ostendaise
Fresh sole fillet served with lemon and butter.

Meat

Although happy to use poultry in soups and lighter dishes, Belgians use their abundant supplies of red meat to create hearty main meals, often marinated in cream sauces or alcohol.

Choesels
Very fresh sweetbreads in cream sauces are a Brussels speciality.

Carbonnade of beef

Ragoût d'agneau
Lamb braised for hours with chicory, onions and herbs.

Gentse stoverij
Ghent's long-standing culinary legacy takes the form of a beer and beef stew with mustard.

Ardennes pâté
A coarse pork pâté often flavoured with garlic.

Bloedpens
Black pudding with chopped bacon.

Lapin
Rabbit will be seen in many guises, but it is most traditionally served with prunes soaked in brandy, or with beer and mustard.

Carbonnades flamandes
A popular Flemish dish for centuries, fillets of beef are braised very slowly in gueuze beer, or occasionally kriek, cherry fruit beer.

Faisan à la Brabançonne
Pheasant roasted with braised chicory, herbs and bacon.

Vegetables

Vegetables are often treated as accompaniments to the main meat or fish course, although some can be served as dishes in their own right.

Witloof*, chicory wrapped in ham and braised *au gratin

Choux de Bruxelles
The Brussels sprout is served young, fresh and dripping with crispy lardons and butter.

Witloof/Chicon
Chicory, a favourite vegetable all over Brussels, is often served with ham and cheese.

Jets de houblon
Young Belgian hop shoots are braised to make a tender side dish.

Stoemp
Coarse mash of potatoes and vegetables (usually carrots or cabbage) served with sausage.

Desserts

Almost any dessert wished for can be found in restaurants in Brussels, from chocolate cake, mousses and profiteroles, to the classic French dishes, *tarte tatin* (upside-down apple cake) and *crème caramel*. Second only to the reputation of Belgium's chocolatiers is that of its pastry- and cakemakers. Using the same fine ingredients, and techniques honed since the 18th century, pastry chefs create concoctions as breathtakingly good-looking as they are delicious to eat.

Profiteroles

Shelves of fresh cream and chocolate cakes in a pâtisserie

A common way to finish off a meal, however, is with cheese, served before or instead of dessert. Often mild and un-cured, local cheeses are made in the damp, fertile, cattle-grazing land of Wallonia and delivered fresh to the city.

Herve
A soft runny cheese, often served in bowls, with bread.

Tartine de fromage blanc
This soft cheese open sandwich is eaten with radishes.

Tarte tatin, upside-down apple cake made with fresh fruit

BELGIAN CHOCOLATE

Belgian chocolate is considered by many to be the finest in the world. The chocolate manufacturing industry took off during the 1880s, aided by the acquisition of the Belgian Congo (*see p36*), which meant easy access to Africa's cocoa plantations. Traditionally Belgian chocolates, known as *pralines*, are filled with cream, nuts or a high-quality rich dark chocolate and covered with milk or white chocolate. Plain chocolate has a high cocoa content, usually at least 70 per cent. Belgian chocolate houses have passed down their recipes over generations, the contents of which are highly guarded and secret. Some of the renowned *"grandes maisons de chocolat"* include Mary, Neuhaus, Godiva, Léonidas and Wittamer. Ideal for a gift, buying chocolates is a treat; individually picked, they are often packaged in crêpe tissue in a finely decorated box.

Belgian chocolates wrapped in a typical luxury gift box

Belgian Beer

Gambrinus, legendary Beer King

BELGIUM MAKES MORE beers, in a greater mix of styles and flavours, than any other country in the world. The Belgian citizen drinks on average 100 litres (200 pints) a year, and even small bars will stock at least 20 varieties. The nation's breweries produce over 400 different beers.

The cheerful peasants in Brueghel the Elder's 15th-century medieval village scenes would have been drinking beer from their local brewery, many of which had been active since the 11th century, as every small town and community produced its own beer. By 1900 there remained 3,000 private breweries throughout Belgium. Today, more than 100 still operate, with experts agreeing that even large industrial concerns produce a fine quality beer.

Detail from *The Wedding Dance* by Pieter Brueghel the Elder

TRAPPIST BEERS

Chimay label with authentic Trappist mark

Label for Westmalle Trappist beer

THE MOST REVERED of refreshments, Belgium's Trappist beers have been highly rated since the Middle Ages when monks began brewing them. The drink originated in Roman times when Belgium was a province of Gaul, Gallia Belgica. Beer was a private domestic product until the monasteries took over and introduced hops to the process. Today's production is still controlled solely by the five Trappist monasteries, although the brewers are mostly laymen. Trappist beers are characterized by their rich, yeasty flavour. They are very strong, ranging from 6.2 to 11 per cent in alcohol content by volume. The most celebrated of the 20 brands is Chimay, brewed at Belgium's largest monastic brewery in Hainaut. This delicate but potent bottled beer has three different strengths, and is best kept for many years before drinking. The strongest Trappist beer is Westvleteren, from Ypres.

Chimay served in its correct glass

LAMBIC BEERS

MADE FOR CENTURIES in the Senne Valley around Brussels, the unique family of lambic beers are made using yeasts naturally present in the air to ferment the beer, rather than being added separately to the water and grain mix. Containers of unfermented wort (water, wheat and barley) are left under a half-open roof in the brewery and wild airborne yeasts, only present in the atmosphere of this region of Belgium, descend to ferment it. Unlike the sterility of many breweries and officially exempt from EU hygiene regulations, lambic cellars are deliberately left dusty and uncleaned in order for the necessary fungal activity to thrive. Matured in untreated wooden casks for up to five years, the lambic is deliciously sour to drink, with a moderate strength of 5 per cent alcohol.

Lambic cherry beer

Young and old lambic beers are blended together to produce the variant of gueuze. A tiny bead, distinctive champagne mousse and a toasty, slightly acid flavour, are its main characteristics. Bars and restaurants lay down their gueuze for up to 2 years before it is drunk.

Brewer sampling beer from the vat at a brewery outside Brussels

SPECIALITY BELGIAN BEERS

Duvel

Chimay

Brugse Tripel

De Verboden Frucht

Kwak

SPECIALITY BEERS are common in Belgium, where the huge variety of brands includes unusual tastes and flavours. Fruit beers are a Brussels speciality but are available throughout the country. The most popular, kriek, is traditionally made with bitter cherries grown in the Brussels suburb of Schaerbeek; picked annually, these are added to the lambic and allowed to macerate, or steep. The distinctive almond tang comes from the cherry stone. Raspberries are also used to make a framboise beer, or frambozen.

For a characterful amber ale, Kwak is good choice. Strong beers are also popular; apart from the Trappist beers, of which Chimay is a popular variety, the pilseners De Verboden Frucht (meaning "forbidden fruit") and Duvel ("devil") are both as strong as red wine. Brugse Tripel, from Bruges, is also popular. Even Belgium's best-sellers, Jupiler and Stella Artois, are good quality beers.

Fruit beer mat of Chapeau brewery

The façade of a beer emporium in Brussels

BLANCHE BEERS

Hoegaarden

BELGIUM'S REFRESHING wheat beers are known as "blanche", or white beers, because of the cloudy sediment that forms when they ferment. Sour, crisp and light, they are relatively low in alcohol at 5 per cent. Blanche is produced in the western region of Hoegaarden, after which the best-known blanche is named. Many people now serve them with a slice of lemon to add to the refreshing taste, especially on warm summer evenings.

HOW TO DRINK BELGIAN BEER

THERE ARE NO snobbish distinctions made in Belgium between bottled and casked beer. Some of the most prestigious brews are served in bottles, and, as with casks, bottles are often laid down to mature. The choice of drinking glass, however, is a vital part of the beer-drinking ritual. Many beers must be drunk in a particular glass, which the bar-man will supply, ranging from goblets to long thin drinking tubes. Beers are often served with a com-plementary snack; cream cheese on rye bread and radishes are a popular accompaniment.

The traditional drinkers' snack of *fromage blanc* on rye bread

Choosing a Restaurant

THE RESTAURANTS IN THIS GUIDE have been selected for their good value, exceptional food and interesting location. This chart highlights some of the factors which may influence your choice. Entries are listed in alphabetical order within price category, starting with the least expensive. The more detailed listings on pp146–53 are arranged by type of cuisine. Information on cafés and bars is on pp154–55.

		PAGE	CREDIT CARDS	HIGHLY RECOMMENDED	TABLES OUTSIDE	CHARACTER SETTING	ETHNIC	FIXED-PRICE MENU	CHILD FRIENDLY
THE LOWER TOWN									
Brasserie Horta (Belgian)	€	146	●			■			●
Chez Léon (Belgian)	€	146	●		●			■	●
Chez Patrick (Belgian)	€	146	●	■		■			
El Papagayo (Latin American)	€	152			●		●	■	
La Grande Porte (Belgian)	€	146	●			■			
Le Petit Chou de Bruxelles (Belgian)	€	146			●	■			
Al Barmaki (Lebanese)	€€	151	●				●		
Auberge des Chapeliers (Belgian)	€€	146	●			■			
Aux Paves de Bruxelles (Belgian)	€€	146	●		●				
Bij den Boer (Seafood)	€€	153	●	■					●
Brasserie de la Roue d'Or (Belgian)	€€	146	●	■		■			
Cantina Cubana (Latin American)	€€	152	●	■		■	●		
Casa Manuel (Portuguese)	€€	152	●		●			■	
Domaine de Lintillac (French)	€€	148				■			
In't Spinnekopke (Belgian)	€€	146	●		●	■			
L'Achepot (Seafood)	€€	153	●		●				●
La Marée (Seafood)	€€	153	●	■					
La Rose Blanche (Belgian)	€€	147	●			●			
Rugantino (Italian)	€€	149	●	■		●			
't Kelderke (Belgian)	€€	147	●	■					
Aux Armes de Bruxelles (Belgian)	€€€	147	●			●		■	
Aux Marches de la Chapelle (French)	€€€	148	●			■		■	
Bonsoir Clara (French)	€€€	148	●			■			
La Taverne du Passage (Belgian)	€€€	147	●			●			
Le Pou qui Tousse (Sardinian)	€€€	150	●			■			
La Truite d'Argent (Seafood)	€€€€	153	●	■	●			■	
L'Ogenblik (French)	€€€€	149	●			●			
Scheltema (Seafood)	€€€€	153	●			●			
Comme Chez Soi (French)	€€€€€	149	●	■		■			●
Sea Grill (Seafood)	€€€€€	153	●	■					
THE UPPER TOWN									
La Pirogue (African)	€	150			●		●		
Le Dieu des Caprices (Belgian)	€	146	●		●	■		■	●
Entrée des Artistes (French)	€€	148	●		●	■		■	●
Au Vieux Saint-Martin (Belgian)	€€€	147	●						●
La Porte des Indes (Indian)	€€€	151	●	■		■	●	■	
L'Estrille du Vieux Bruxelles (Belgian)	€€€	147	●			■			
Chez Moi (Belgian)	€€€€	147	●		●			■	
L' Ecailler du Palais Royal (Seafood)	€€€€€	153	●	■					
GREATER BRUSSELS									
Dolma (Vegetarian)	€	153	●					■	●
Gri Gri (African)	€	150	●	■	●		●	■	●
Hông Hoa (Vietnamese)	€	150					■	●	●
La Cantonnaise (Chinese)	€	151			■			●	●
Le Pacifique (Vietnamese)	€	151	●	■			●		●

Price categories for a three-course meal for one, including cover charge, service and half a bottle of wine or other drinks:
€ up to €25
€€ €25–37
€€€ €37–50
€€€€ €50-62
€€€€€ Over €62

CREDIT CARDS
Establishment accepts a combination of major credit cards.

HIGHLY RECOMMENDED
The quality of the dishes, decor and service are especially highly commended.

TABLES OUTSIDE
Outdoor dining facilities and service in summer.

CHARACTER SETTING
Unusually attractive interior decor and/or street setting and atmosphere.

ETHNIC
Exotic world cuisine of a high standard from outside Europe.

Restaurant	Price	Page	Credit Cards	Highly Recommended	Tables Outside	Character Setting	Ethnic	Fixed-Price Menu	Child Friendly
L'Ouzerie (Greek)	€	151	●						
L'Ouzerie du Nouveau Monde (Greek)	€	151	●	●	●				
Poussières d'Etoiles (Vietnamese)	€	151			●		●	●	●
Shanti (Vegetarian)	€	153	●	●			●	●	
Tsampa (Vegetarian)	€	153				●			
Au Brabançon (Belgian)	€€	146	●	●					
Aux Anges (Italian)	€€	149	●			●	●		
El Yasmine (African)	€€	150	●				●	●	
Ile de Gorée (African)	€€	150				●	●		●
Kocharata (Bulgarian)	€€	152							
La Belle Epoque (Belgian)	€€	147	●			●		●	
La Citronnelle (Vietnamese)	€€	151	●			●	●	●	
La Danse des Paysans (Belgian)	€€	147	●	●	●				
Le Grain de Sel (French)	€€	148	●	●	●	●		●	
Les Ateliers de la Grande Ile (Russian)	€€	152	●						
La Maison de Thailande (Thai)	€€	151	●			●	●	●	
Medina (African)	€€	150	●				●	●	●
Mon Village (Belgian)	€€	147	●						●
Sahbaz (Turkish)	€€	151	●						
Tierra del Fuego (Latin American)	€€	152	●		●	●	●		
Amadeus (French)	€€€	148	●		●	●			●
A'mbriana (Italian)	€€€	149	●					●	
La Brouette (Belgian)	€€€	147	●					●	
La Fin de Siècle (Italian)	€€€	149	●	●	●				
La Scala (Italian)	€€€	149	●						
Le Doux Wazoo (French)	€€€	148	●					●	
Le Fils de Jules (French)	€€€	148	●		●	●			
Le Forcado (Spanish)	€€€	152	●	●	●			●	
Le Pain et le Vin (French)	€€€	148	●		●				
Les Amis du Cep (French)	€€€	149	●		●			●	
Les Brasseries Georges (French)	€€€	149	●	●	●				●
Les Jardins de Bagatelle (African)	€€€	150	●		●	●	●	●	
Osteria delle Stelle (Italian)	€€€	150	●	●		●		●	
Blue Elephant (Thai)	€€€€	151	●	●			●	●	
La Truffe Noire (French/Italian)	€€€€€	149	●		●	●		●	

ANTWERP

Restaurant	Price	Page	Credit Cards	Highly Recommended	Tables Outside	Character Setting	Ethnic	Fixed-Price Menu	Child Friendly
't Zolderke (French)	€€	148	●					●	
De Matelote (Seafood)	€€€€€	153	●					●	

BRUGES

Restaurant	Price	Page	Credit Cards	Highly Recommended	Tables Outside	Character Setting	Ethnic	Fixed-Price Menu	Child Friendly
Den Dyver (Belgian)	€€€	147	●	●	●			●	
de Karmeliet (Belgian)	€€€	147	●	●				●	
't Bourgoensche Hof (Belgian)	€€€	148	●	●	●			●	

GHENT

Restaurant	Price	Page	Credit Cards	Highly Recommended	Tables Outside	Character Setting	Ethnic	Fixed-Price Menu	Child Friendly
Pakhuis (French)	€€	148	●					●	
't Buikske Vol (Belgian)	€€€	147	●	●				●	

BELGIAN

Although Belgium is a relatively new European state, its culinary traditions date back to the Middle Ages, when the dukes of Burgundy ruled over the Low Countries. To this day Burgundian is a synonym for hearty extravagance, of which the Belgians are inordinately fond. Authentic Belgian cooking is very rooted in peasant traditions, including warming winter stews such as *waterzooi* (chicken or fish stewed with cream), or *carbonnades* (beef casseroled in beer) as well as the national vegetable, chicory. Slow cooking in beer is also an integral part of Belgian cuisine. Dieting is not, and never will be, compatible with rich Belgian food.

Most of the restaurants in this section offer authentic versions of Belgian dishes, usually at relatively affordable prices. While some pay great attention to presentation, lesser establishments are often more rewarding; this is a cuisine robust enough to cope with a few rough edges and dated decor.

Brasserie Horta

Rue des Sables 20. **Map** 2 E2.
((02) 217 7271. **⊘** AE, DC, MC, V.
◐ 10am–6pm daily. **⚘ ⚹ €**

The Comic Strip Centre's restaurant is worth a visit to see the airy, high-ceilinged Art Nouveau brasserie designed by Victor Horta. Admire the cartoons of Tintin, the Smurfs and Lucky Luke while sampling cheap, hearty portions of chicken-stuffed vol-au-vents, spicy meatballs, *waterzooi*, beef stewed in beer and home-made *frites*. The bar is open during restaurant hours.

Chez Léon

Rue des Bouchers 18. **Map** 2 D2. **(**
(02) 511 1415. **⊘** AE, DC, MC, V. **◐**
11:30am–11pm daily. **⚘ ▦ ¶⊙ €**

It may be more a fashionable factory-style diner than an intimate dining experience, but this casual haunt near the Grand Place provides unquestionable value for money in an expensive area (and has been doing so since 1893). It also offers a wide range of *moules-frites* dishes and a free menu for children under 12.

Chez Patrick

Rue des Chapeliers 6. **Map** 2 D3. **(**
(02) 511 9815. **★ ⊘** AE, DC, MC, V.
◐ noon–3pm, 6–10pm Tue–Sat. **⚹**
¶⊙ €

Despite its popularity with tourists and expats, the family-run Chez Patrick has remained quintessentially Bruxellois since it opened in 1931. Wooden benches and white tiles give the dining room a spartan, functional feel and the daily specials are scribbled on to mirrors on the walls. Beer cuisine figures large, but you can also tuck into *choucroute* (cabbage and sausage hotpot) or chicken *waterzooi*.

La Grande Porte

Rue Notre-Seigneur 9. **Map** 1 C4.
((02) 512 8998. **⊘** MC, V.
◐ noon–3pm, 6pm–2am Tue–Fri;
6pm–2am Sat. **⚹ €**

This late-night spot in the Marolles area combines French *chanson* background music and an artfully chaotic interior adorned with finds from the flea market on Place du Jeu de Balle. Enjoy quality versions of basic Belgian fare such as *stoemp*, meatballs in tomato sauce or the traditional chicory grilled with cheese and, in winter, onion soup.

Le Dieu des Caprices

Rue Archimède 51. **Map** 3 B2.
((02) 736 4116. **⊘** AE, DC, MC, V.
◐ noon–3pm, 6:30–11pm Mon–
Fri; 6:30–11pm Sat. **⚘ ▦ ¶⊙ €**

Nestling in the shadow of the European institutions, this traditional restaurant is going from strength to strength, thanks to a prize-winning young chef. The decor has an antiques market feel, and you can devour monkfish *waterzooi* and rabbit with plums and *foie gras* to the sound of 1960s background music.

Le Petit Chou de Bruxelles

Rue du Vieux-Marché-aux-Grains 2.
Map 1 C2. **(** (02) 502 6037.
◐ noon–10pm daily. **◑** Wed &
Thu in winter. **▦ €**

Despite the dingy glass-fronted interior and non-existent decor, this café near Place Ste-Catherine is well worth the visit, especially for a full meal outside normal eating hours. Old-fashioned cooking includes home-made pork rillettes and horse steaks. In summer, the renovated outdoor terrace is pleasant.

Auberge des Chapeliers

Rue des Chapeliers 3. **Map** 2 D3.
((02) 513 7338. **⊘** AE, DC, MC, V.
◐ noon–2pm, 6:30–11pm daily
(until midnight on Sat). **€€**

This 17th-century building near the Grand Place houses a cosy, split-level eatery with several dining sections and, unusually, a non-smoking area. The menu features sizeable helpings of classic Belgian dishes: mussels in a variety of preparations, black pudding Brussels-style (*boudin*), salmon steak cooked in white beer and marinated herring fillets.

Au Brabançon

Rue de la Commune 75. **Map** 3 A1.
((02) 217 7191. **★ ⊘** AE, MC, V.
◐ noon–2:30pm, 7–9:30pm
Mon–Sat. **◑** Sun. **¶⊙ €€**

This tiny St-Josse restaurant is a haven for lovers of authentic Belgian specialities. The formidable septuagenarian owner loves to cook offal, including brains and sweetbreads. The faint-hearted can opt for creamy chicken *waterzooi* or Marolles-style meatballs once they have deciphered the handwritten menu. As with much Belgian food, this is not an establishment for slimmers or vegetarians.

Aux Paves de Bruxelles

Rue Marché-aux-Fromages 1–3.
Map 2 D3. **(** (02) 502 0457.
⊘ AE, DC, MC, V. **◐** noon–2:30pm,
7–11pm Mon–Fri; 7pm–midnight Sat.
◑ Sun. **▦ €€**

At this old-fashioned eatery in a 17th-century house near the Grand Place, good prices and a sturdy emphasis on red meat keep the place packed for lunch and dinner. While Argentine steaks and spare ribs are house specialities, the mussel dishes should satisfy non-carnivores and fish-eating vegetarians.

Brasserie de la Roue d'Or

Rue des Chapeliers 26. **Map** 2 D3.
((02) 514 2554. **★ ⊘** AE, DC,
MC, V. **◐** noon–12.30am daily.
◑ mid-Jul–mid-Aug. **€€**

This upmarket Art Nouveau brasserie with Surrealist murals excels in modernism. The great-value menu blends Belgian and French cuisine: eel in mustard sauce, pig's trotter vinaigrette, prawn croquettes, snails in garlic butter and home-made *frites*. Pierre Wynants, the chef of Michelin three-star Brussels restaurant Comme Chez Soi, is an enthusiastic visitor.

In 't Spinnekopke

Place du Jardin aux Fleurs 1. **Map** 1
B2. **(** (02) 511 8695. **⊘** AE, DC,
MC, V. **◐** noon–3pm, 6–11pm Mon–
Fri; 6pm–midnight Sat. **⚹ ▦ €€€**

This former coaching inn at the end of Rue Chartreux is popular with canny tourists and local politicians alike. Enjoy Belgian fare and creative beer cuisine in 18th-century decor: the restaurant's name means "In the spider's head" and, while spider is not on the menu, exotic dishes include guinea-fowl in raspberry beer and calf's head with vinaigrette. There is a huge choice of small cottage-industry beers.

La Belle Epoque

Avenue Houba de Strooper 188. 📞
(02) 478 9647. 🅿 *AE, DC, MC, V.*
🕐 *noon–11pm Sun–Thu; noon–mid-night Fri & Sat.* 🎅 ♿ 🍷 🍴 €€€

One of the best restaurants near the Atomium, this hospitable 1920s brasserie offers French and Italian cuisine as well as Belgian classics. Dishes include eels in herbs, rabbit in gueuze beer, *osso bucco* (stewed veal in wine and tomatoes) and veal kidneys in cider. Wash it all down with a reasonably priced selection of New World wines.

La Danse des Paysans

Chaussée de Boondael 441. 📞 *(02) 649 8505.* ★ 🅿 *MC, V.* 🕐 *noon–3pm, 6:30–11:30pm Mon–Fri; 6:30–11:30pm Sat.* 🍷 €€€

In the heart of the university area, this rustic restaurant is a perfect spot to sample authentic beer cooking such as scampi stew with white beer and lamb in pastry with mint and the blanche beer Duvel.

La Rose Blanche/ De Witte Roos

Grand Place 11. **Map** 2 D3.
📞 *(02) 513 6479.* 🅿 *AE, DC, MC, V.* 🕐 *10am–11pm daily.* 🍷 €€€

One of the best places for tradi-tional Belgian beer cuisine, this Baroque tavern serves mussels in beer, roast salmon with Faro beer, chicken in kriek and even waffles with a Ardennes brew called La Chouffe. The popular three-course menu is centred around three dif-ferent types of beer, with a bottle of each included in the set price.

Mon Village

Rue Champ de la Couronne 6.
📞 *(02) 478 3579.* 🅿 *AE, DC, MC, V.* 🕐 *noon–3pm, 7–11:30pm Tue–Sat.* €€€

At this informal restaurant close to Parc de Laeken, the owner also does the cooking, and favourites include chicken cooked in strong Duvel beer and rillettes prepared with white beer.

't Kelderke

Grand Place 15. **Map** 2 D3. 📞 *(02) 513 7344.* ★ 🅿 *AE, DC, MC, V.* 🕐 *noon–2am daily.* €€€

This reasonably priced restaurant in a 17th-century cellar feels genuine despite its commercial location. Speedy waiters proffer huge pots of mussels and good-sized portions of traditional Belgian food. Waffles and whipped cream make a fine ending. No reservations are accep-ted, so queues are not uncommon.

Au Vieux Saint-Martin

Place du Grand Sablon 38. **Map** 2 D4.
📞 *(02) 512 6476.* 🅿 *MC, V.* 🕐 *noon–midnight daily.* 🎅 🍷 €€€

A truly professional establishment with crisp modern decor, swift and courteous waiters, this restaurant also boasts a contemporary art collection. The accomplished menu features regional specialities like *stoemp*, rabbit in kriek and *filet américain*, prepared to a recipe conceived by the restaurant's founder in the 1920s.

Aux Armes de Bruxelles

Rue des Bouchers 13. **Map 2** D2.
📞 *(02) 511 5550.* 🅿 *AE, DC, MC, V.* 🕐 *noon–11pm Tue–Sun.* ● *mid-Jun–mid-Jul.* 🍷 🍴 €€€

This friendly restaurant was a favourite of Belgian chanson legend Jacques Brel. Some critics complain that its charm has faded a little in recent years, but the restaurant still offers classic, high-quality cuisine including lobster, mussels, poached cod, veal and, in season, game. The freshly made shrimp croquettes are a must. It is important to reserve in advance.

Den Dyver

Dijver 5, Bruges. 📞 *(050) 33 6069.* ★
🅿 *AE, V.* 🕐 *noon–2pm, 6:30–9pm Thu–Tue.* ● *Thu lunch.* 🍽 🍴 €€€

This excellent restaurant, located close to the Markt, specializes in Flemish beer cooking. There is no drinks list, and diners are automatically served a glass of the beer that features in their dish.

La Brouette

Boulevard Prince de Liège 61, Anderlecht. 📞 *(02) 522 5169.*
🅿 *DC, MC, V.* 🕐 *noon–2:30pm, 7–9:30pm Tue–Sun.* ● *Sat lunch, Sun eve.* 🍷 🅿 *DC, MC, V.* 🍴 €€€

A restaurant with a well-deserved Michelin star, La Brouette is a jewel off the beaten track. Chef Hermann Dedapper, a top sommelier, provides gourmet food and an innovative menu in an unpretentious setting.

La Taverne du Passage

Galerie de la Reine 30. **Map** 2 D2.
(02) 512 3731. ★ 🅿 *AE, DC, MC, V.* 🕐 *noon–midnight daily.* ● *Jun–Jul: Wed & Thu.* 🍷 €€€

This Belgian brasserie has an alluring Art Deco interior and 70 years' worth of culinary expertise. Housed in the elegant

Galerie de la Reine, between Rue des Bouchers and Rue du Marché aux Herbes, it features roasts carved at your table, as well as shrimp croquettes, steak tartare and mussels. The waiters are helpful and efficient; this is a popular choice with families. Relax on the terrace in the arcade and watch the world go by under the Art Deco roof.

L'Estrille du Vieux Bruxelles

Rue de Rollebeek 7. **Map** 2 D4.
📞 *(02) 512 5857.* 🅿 *AE, DC, MC, V.* 🕐 *noon–2pm, 6:30–10pm Mon–Fri; noon–3pm, 6:30–10:30pm Sat & Sun.* ● *Sun lunch.* €€€

Just off the Place du Grand Sablon and housed in an elegant 16th-century building, this cosy tavern specializes in meat grilled over an open fire in the main room. Homely dishes include beef stew, rabbit with plums and gueuze beer, eel in herbs and, in season, game. The background music is usually classical or jazz.

't Buikske Vol

Kraanlei 17, Ghent. 📞 *(09) 225 1880.* 🅿 *AE, V.* 🕐 *noon–2pm, 7–9:30pm Mon, Tue, Thu; 7–9:30pm Fri & Sat.* 🍴 €€€

The trendy Patershol district is home to many upscale restaurants, and this is one of the best. The beautifully prepared dishes range from river fish *waterzooi* close to sweetbreads with rabbit.

Chez Moi

Rue du Luxembourg 66. 📞 *(02) 280 2666.* 🅿 *DC, MC, V.* 🕐 *noon–3pm, 7–10pm Mon–Fri.* 🍷 🍴 €€€

Close to the European Parliament, this welcoming restaurant is popular with Eurocrats at lunch, but quieter and more romantic in the evening. The menu offers fish and game with good vegetable side dishes.

de Karmeliet

Langestraat 19, Bruges. 📞 *(09) 33 8259.* ★ 🅿 *AE, DC, MC, V.* 🕐 *noon–2pm, 7–9:30pm Tue–Sun.* ● *Tue lunch, Sun eve.* 🍷 🍽
🍴 🎅 🍴 €€€ 📞

Impeccable service, lavish surroundings in the centre of town and exquisite Belgian/French cuisine have earned this restaurant in the heart of historical Bruges three Michelin stars. Try the rabbit with Rodenbach beer and the delicious thin omelettes.

't Bourgoensche Hof

Wollestraat 41, Bruges. ▌ (050) 33
7926. ★ ▣ AE, MC, V. ◯ noon–
2pm, 7–9:15pm Thu–Mon. ▤ ▦
▤ ▥ ▧ ▨ €€€€€

This 19th-century wooden building
is the ideal place for a romantic,
canalside meal. The perfect setting
is matched by superior cuisine,
especially the seafood dishes.

FRENCH

Perhaps unsurprisingly given its
proximity to France, Brussels has
a large number of extremely good
French restaurants, from grand
Parisian-style brasseries to modern
establishments serving nouvelle
cuisine. While the brasserie menus
sometimes overlap with their
Belgian counterparts, the nouvelle
cuisine places offer a lighter option
for those fed up with frites. Many
of the city's great French restaurants are expensive, but there are
plenty of bargains to be had,
especially at lunchtime or following
the set menus. Value for money is
almost universally guaranteed.

Domaine de Lintillac

Rue de Flandre 25. **Map** 1 B1.
▌ (02) 511 5123. ◯ noon–2pm,
7:30–10pm Tue–Sat. ▥ €€€

This small restaurant serves nothing
but duck: wine-soaked pâté, sliced
breasts, *rillettes* cooked in lard and
pounded to a fine paste, confit, as
well as the gourmet *foie gras*. Each
of the tables has a toaster to ensure
your pâté toast is cooked to per-
fection. The main courses include
a marvellous cassoulet, with duck,
pork and goose cooked for hours in
duck fat, a rich wine tomato sauce
and haricot beans. For dessert, try
the excellent crème brulée. The rich
fare is not for those on a diet, but
is delicious for a special occasion.

Entrée des Artistes

Place du Grand Sablon 42. **Map** 2 D4.
▌ (02) 502 3161. ▣ AE, MC, V. ◯
8am–2am daily. ▧ ▦ ▧ €€€

The Grand Sablon can be an
unsatisfyingly expensive place to
eat, but this unassumingly trendy
brasserie is a happy exception.
Cinema posters and licence plates
decorate the walls and the well-
judged brasserie fare includes
toast with mushrooms, salmon
steaks and lobster. A *plat du jour*
at lunchtime costs around €7.

Le Grain de Sel

Chaussée de Vleurgat 9. ▌ (02) 648
1858. ★ ◯ noon–3:15pm, 7:30–
10:30pm Tue–Fri; 7:30–10pm Sat.
▧ ▥ ▦ €€€

Tucked away in a townhouse
near Place Eugène Flagey in
Ixelles, this exquisite eatery is
one of Brussels' best-kept secrets.
Book in advance to ensure a spot
on the rambling rose-filled patio
at the back, then settle down to
a selection of light, fresh dishes:
cannelloni with goat's cheese and
spinach, scampi in creamy curry
sauce, crispy roast duck, pan-fried
beef with rocket and exquisite
home-made ice cream. The three-
course menu offers a wide selection of regular dishes as well as
daily suggestions.

Pakhuis

Schuurkensstraat 4, Ghent. ▌ (09)
223 5555. ▣ AE, DC, MC, V.
◯ noon–2:30pm, 6:30pm–midnight
Mon–Sat. ▥ ▤ ▧ ▧ €€

This popular brasserie occupies a
huge, early-19th-century converted
warehouse. Its special attractions
are the oyster bar and the fresh
shellfish served daily.

't Zolderke

Hoofdkerkstraat 7, Antwerp. ▌ (03)
233 8427. ★ ▣ MC, V. ◯ 6–11pm
Mon–Fri, noon–midnight Sat & Sun.
▧ ▤ ▥ ▧ ▧ €€

The menu at this light and airy
French restaurant features old
classics such as steak in
peppercorn and roquefort sauce
with fries, and meats such as boar
and deer when in season.

Amadeus

Rue Veydt 13. ▌ (02) 538 3427.
▣ AE, DC, MC, V. ◯ noon–3pm,
6:30pm–midnight Tue–Fri, Sun;
6pm–12:30am Mon & Sat. ▥ ▧
▦ ▧ €€€

Near the Place Stephanie, off
Chaussée de Charleroi, this romantic
candle-lit restaurant and wine bar
was once the studio of 19th-century
French sculptor Auguste Rodin.
Diners come more for the ornate
mirrors and intimate corners than
the brasserie fare, which is
adequate but unremarkable by
Brussels standards. The wine list,
however, is top quality, and the
view of the entrance hall alone is
worth the trip.

Aux Marches de la Chapelle

Place de la Chapelle 5. **Map** 1 C4.
▌ (02) 512 6891. ▣ AE, MC, DC, V.
◯ noon–2:30pm, 6–11pm Mon–Fri;
7pm–midnight Sat; noon–2:30pm,
7–10pm Sun. ▧ ▧ €€€

A Brussels institution, this stylish
restaurant with opulent Belle
Epoque decor and chandeliers is

a favoured gourmet haunt. Try the
excellent sauerkraut, poached egg
with grey shimps, or eel dishes.

Bonsoir Clara

Rue Antoine Dansaert 22. **Map** 1 B2.
▌ (02) 502 0990. ▣ AE, MC, V.
◯ noon–2:30pm, 7–11:30pm
Mon–Fri; 7–midnight Sat & Sun.
▧ ▧ €€€

Like most of the restaurants started
by young restaurateur Frederic
Nikolay, Bonsoir Clara is a great
place to eat in, rather than a great
place to eat. The city's fashionable
crowd are drawn by the prime
location on Brussels' trendiest
street, by the extravagant decor, a
confection of multicoloured quilt-
ing and garish mirror walls, and
by the chance to see and be seen.
The food is upmarket brasserie
cooking, with dishes including
seared tuna and caramelized duck
among the regular specialities.

Le Doux Wazoo

Rue du Relais 21. ▌ (02) 649 5852.
▣ AE, DC, MC, V. ◯ noon–2:30pm,
7–11pm Mon–Fri; 7–11:45pm Sat.
◯ Mon pm. ▧ ▧ ▧ €€€

A small, cheerful turn-of-the-
century bistro in the university
district, where the owners'
bohemian philosophy is applied
to the atmosphere rather than the
service. Confit of duck, roast lamb
with pepper purée or duck stew
are on the menu, all made with
quality local produce. The
restaurant's name translates as
"the sweet bird", although non-
natives might find this hard to
work out.

Le Fils de Jules

Rue du Page 35. ▌ (02) 534 0057.
▣ AE, DC, MC, V. ◯ noon–2:30pm,
7–11pm Mon–Fri; 7pm–midnight
Sat. ▦ ▧ ▧ €€€

Brussels' only Basque restaurant
offers rich, imaginative cuisine and
fine wines from southwest France
in a plum spot near Ixelles' busy
Place du Châtelain. Dishes include
spiced squid, *foie gras* with a
compote of figs, and duck breast in
walnut sauce. While the cooking is
clearly Mediterranean, the setting
is a stylishly minimal blend of Art
Deco and the French modernist
designer Philippe Starck, who has
designed many of Europe's top
restaurants including the London
Conran chain. Reserve in advance.

Le Pain et le Vin

Chaussée d'Alsemberg 812a. ▌ (02)
332 3774. ▣ AE, MC, V. ◯ noon–
2:30pm, 7–10:30pm Mon–Fri;
7–10:30pm Sat. ▦ ▧ €€€€

Eric Boschman is one of Belgium's most talented sommeliers, so it is no surprise that his restaurant on the southern tip of Brussels offers a splendid selection of French and New World wines at extremely reasonable prices. The good news is that it also offers light, imaginative French and modern Mediterranean cuisine, with an emphasis on fish, and a candle-lit garden.

Les Amis du Cep

Rue Theodore Decuyper 136. ☏ (02) 762 6295. ★ 🅴 *AE, MC, V.* ⏱ noon–2pm, 7–10pm Tue–Sat. 🍴 ❙❙ 🇪🇪🇪

This refined restaurant housed in a Thirties villa in the residential Woluwe-Saint-Lambert district offers classic and modern French food. Most people choose the four-course "surprise menu" for two, but some may prefer to stick to the à la carte menu, which includes quail stew with *foie gras*, and *scallop tartare*. The lunch menu is fantastic value.

Les Brasseries Georges

Ave Winston Churchill 259. ☏ (02) 347 2100. ★ 🅴 *AE, DC, MC, V.* ⏱ 11:30am–midnight Sun–Thu; 11:30am–1am Fri & Sat. 🍴 🇪🇪🇪

The first thing to notice here is the ostentatious pavement stall, piled high with tubs of oysters and lobsters. Inside, the brash, bustling brasserie has become one of southern Brussels' landmarks. The service is professional if a little brusque, which is understandable given the volume of custom. The extensive wine list includes several vintages by the glass, and menu staples vary from grilled tuna with herb butter to kidneys in mustard sauce, although the Georges' fame depends partly on the exquisitely fresh seafood platters.

L'Ogenblik

Galerie des Princes 1. **Map** 2 D2. ☏ (02) 511 6151. ★ 🅴 *AE, MC, DC, V.* ⏱ noon–2:30pm, 7pm–midnight Mon–Thu; 7pm–12:30am Fri & Sat. 🍴 🇪🇪🇪🇪

In a little side street off the Rue des Bouchers, this classy but informal establishment masks its quality behind artfully faded Parisian-style bistro decor. The creative dishes, among them fillet of sea bass with aubergine caviar and calf sweetbreads with cheese-topped courgette, are prepared with impeccably fresh ingredients. Despite the central location, the lively crowd is mostly composed of well-heeled locals.

Comme Chez Soi

23 Place Rouppe. **Map** 1 C4. ☏ (02) 512 2921. ★ 🅴 *AE, DC, MC, V.* ⏱ noon–1:30pm, 7–9:30pm Tue–Sat. 🍴 🍷 ❙❙ 🇪🇪🇪🇪🇪

Brussels' best restaurant works hard to maintain its three Michelin stars, with head chef Pierre Wynants continually creating adventurous market-based dishes for those not satisfied by his legendary sole fillet with Riesling mousse. The game, *foie gras* and caviar are superlative, as is the Art Nouveau decor, although the intimacy can border on the cramped. Tables must be booked weeks in advance.

La Truffe Noire

Boulevard de la Cambre 12. ☏ (02) 640 4422. 🅴 *AE, DC, MC, V.* ⏱ noon–2pm, 7–10pm Mon–Fri; 7–10pm Sat. 🍷 🍴 ❙❙ 🇪🇪🇪🇪🇪

This gourmet restaurant is seventh heaven for truffle-lovers. The location – a townhouse on a quiet street near Bois de la Cambre – has a discreetly exclusive feel, heightened by the fresh, modern interior and the classical background music. Indulge in truffle-stuffed pigeon, truffle carpaccio, truffle purée or the extravagant six-course menu, which takes in all aspects of this delicious fungus.

ITALIAN

Belgium has a sizeable Italian community, most of whom arrived in the 1950s to work in the mines of Wallonia. Many moved to Brussels, where they opened unpretentious trattorias or pizzerias. The bulk of the capital's Italian restaurants fall into this category, and are often unremarkable, though handy for those on a budget. Brussels also has several upmarket Italian restaurants, serving more accomplished and authentic food. These establishments tend to be rather formal, and booking is always advisable.

Aux Anges

Rue Diderich 33–35. ☏ (02) 539 3906. 🅴 *MC, V.* ⏱ noon–2pm Mon; noon–2pm, 7–11pm Tue–Sat. 🍴 🇪🇪

This small hideout in the backstreets of St-Gilles is a must for couples, not least because of the half-veiled corner niche designed especially for two. The decor features statuettes of angels and Raphael reproductions, while the menu offers modern, sophisticated pasta dishes such as penne with *foie gras* and truffle oil. Light modern cuisine is also represented in the use of grilled polenta and macerated olive oils.

Rugantino

Blvd Anspach 184–186. **Map** 1 C3. ☏ (02) 511 2195. ★ 🅴 *AE, MC, V.* ⏱ noon–3pm, 6:30pm–midnight Mon–Fri; 6:30–11:45pm Sat. 🇻 🇪🇪

A short walk from the Grand Place, this airy, high-ceilinged trattoria has cream-coloured walls and flamboyant Art Deco motifs. The owner is from Abruzzi in Italy and the menu reflects his origins, with signature dishes including beef topped with rocket and Parmesan, rosemary roast lamb and pasta with spinach and ricotta.

A'mbriana

Rue Edith Cavell 151. ☏ (02) 375 0156. 🅴 *AE, DC, MC, V.* ⏱ noon–2:30pm, 7–10:30pm Wed–Mon; 7–10:30pm Sat. 🇻 🍴 ❙❙ 🇪🇪🇪

Exquisite Italian food and wine and a warm welcome have earned this slick modern eatery near Parc Montjoie a fine reputation, helped by the low prices of the fixed and lunch-time menus. Classic dishes include *carpaccio* of swordfish, beef with rocket and black lasagne with seafood and leeks. Much favoured by Eurocrats, the menu changes often but manages to stay both fresh and modern. Booking in advance is recommended.

La Fin de Siècle

Avenue de l'Armée 3. **Map** 4 F4. ☏ (02) 732 7434. ★ 🇻. ⏱ noon–2:30pm, 7–10:30pm Mon–Sat. 🍴 🇪🇪🇪

Younger Eurocrats get business off their mind in this restfully Baroque restaurant, where candles and classical music ensure a harmonious ambiance. The creative, contemporary Italian menu includes linguine with scallops and truffle oil or smoked salmon with saffron and mascarpone. Its sister restaurant, Fin de Siècle, occupies a townhouse on Avenue Louise, with similar setting and dishes, but improved facilities for disabled travellers.

La Scala

Chaussée de Wavre 132. **Map** 2 F5. ☏ (02) 514 4945. 🅴 *AE, DC, MC, V.* ⏱ noon–2:30pm, 7–10pm Mon–Fri; 7–11pm Sat. 🎵 🇪🇪🇪

One of the best Italian deals in town, this upbeat eatery has a popular fixed menu, which includes wine and coffee. Classical dishes include veal kidneys, *foie gras* with wild mushrooms and duck ravioli. Candle light and the owner's occasional tinklings on the piano provide plenty of romantic atmosphere.

Le Pou qui Tousse

Vieille Halle aux Blés 49. **Map** 1 C3.
📞 *(02) 512 2871.* 💳 *AE, DC, MC, V.*
🕐 *noon–2pm, 6:30–10pm Mon,
Tue, Thu–Sat; noon–2pm Wed.*
🚫 *Sun.* €€€

Le Pou qui Tousse (the coughing
flea) is a pleasant, family-run
Sardinian restaurant just off Rue
de Lombard, where you can watch
the chefs prepare risotto with cut-
tlefish ink, grill Mediterranean fish
or toss seafood salad in an open-
plan kitchen. The walls are hung
with contemporary European art.

Osteria delle Stelle

Avenue L. Bertrand 53–61.
📞 *(02) 241 4808.* ★ 💳 *AE, DC,
MC, V.* 🕐 *noon–3pm, 7–11pm
Mon–Sat.* 🍴 €€€

A hundred years ago, the northern
commune of Schaerbeek was one
of Brussels' most elegant districts,
and the splendid Art Nouveau
interior of this Italian brasserie
provides a poignant reminder of
former glories. A delightful place
to dine, fresh octopus salad, or sea
bass caught on a line accompany
gorgonzola polenta on the wide
menu. The all-you-can-eat buffet
of antipasti costs around just €15.
It is wise to reserve.

NORTH AFRICAN AND CENTRAL AFRICAN

Whether the sharp, nutty tastes of
central Africa or a spicy couscous
from Morocco appeal, African
cooking is among the world's most
vibrant, and the sizeable communities from the Democratic Republic
of Congo and North Africa have
brought plenty of flavour to
Brussels' dining scene. The city's
more enterprising entrepreneurs
have opened lavishly decorated
"designer couscous" eateries,
although many feel these are not
entirely authentic. Central African
food can vary sharply, and
although the quality of the cooking is not always consistent, dishes
such as the peanut-based chicken
moambe and chicken yassa, made
with limes, are deliciously simple.
The relaxed atmosphere is great.

Gri Gri

Rue Basse 16. 📞 *(02) 375 8202.*
★ 💳 *AE, DC, MC, V.* 🕐 *6:30–
11pm Mon; noon–3pm, 6:30–11pm
Tue–Fri; 6:30–11pm Sat.* 🍴 €

South of the city centre in the
district of Uccle, this small, brightly
decorated restaurant is an education
for those unfamiliar with central

African cooking. The starters
include spicy cod croquettes and
crispy meat samusas (deep-fried
mince-filled filo parcels) with a
sweet sauce. Kenyan-style scampi
with sweet curry and crocodile,
chicken yassa (in a lime sauce) or
stuffed crab are among the main
courses. On occasion, the owner
plays the drums for his customers.

La Pirogue

Rue Sainte-Anne 18. **Map** 2 D4.
📞 *(02) 511 3525.* 🕐 *noon–2:30pm
7–10:30pm Tue–Sun.* €

If you find the cafés and restaurants on Place du Grand Sablon too
formal, then this is the perfect anti-
dote. Tucked away at the end of a
nearby quiet alley, it has an extensive and secluded outdoor seating
area where you can sip home-made
ginger beer or tamarind juice into
the early hours, or enjoy chicken
yassa (made with onions and lime),
spicy mutton chops or chicken in
peanut sauce. Given the location,
the prices are very low.

El Yasmine

Rue Defacqz 7. 📞 *(02) 647 5181.*
★ 💳 *AE, MC, V.* 🕐 *7–10:30pm
Mon–Sat.* €€€

This excellent restaurant specializes in refined Moroccan and
Tunisian cooking at reasonable
prices. The tent-like azure canopy
is reminiscent of Arabian legends,
and the eight-course gourmet
menu offers an excellent all-round
sample of authentic cuisine. The
quality of produce is much better
than in many of the city's couscous haunts, and the owner's
relaxed but attentive attitude –
not to mention his vast collection
of traditional music – create a
welcoming atmosphere.

Ile de Gorée

Rue Saint-Boniface 28. **Map** 2 E5.
📞 *(02) 513 5293.* 🕐 *noon–2:30pm,
4–11pm Mon–Sat.* €€€

One of the legacies of Belgium's
colonial occupation of central
Africa is an abundance of
Congolese, Senegalese and
Rwandan bars and eateries in
the capital. This upmarket, cosy
restaurant near Porte de Namur
boasts traditional music, decor and
cuisine, including smoked turkey
wings, generous portions of couscous and spicy lamb. The service
is leisurely and relaxed.

Medina

Avenue de la Couronne 2.
📞 *(02) 640 4328.* 💳 *AE, DC, MC, V.*
🕐 *noon–2:30pm, 6pm–10:30pm
Tue–Sun.* €€€

Moorish arches, high ceilings and
blue-and-white tiles give this popular Moroccan restaurant in Ixelles
a bright, airy feel. Lift the funnelled
clay tajine lid that arrives over your
food and the aroma of lemons,
onions and fruit floods out, adding
considerably to the appeal of the
couscous and tajines that are the
menu's mainstays. Other specialities include pigeon-stuffed
pastries and orange and cinnamon
salad. A belly-dancer performs at
the weekend, much to the delight
of local patrons and their families.

Les Jardins de Bagatelle

Rue du Berger 17. **Map** 2 E5. 📞 *(02)
512 1276.* 💳 *AE, DC, MC, V.*
🕐 *noon–2pm, 7–11:30pm Tue–Sat.*
🚫 *Sat lunch.* 🍴 €€€

A turn-of-the-century Ixelles
townhouse houses one of the
capital's most eclectic restaurants,
where the leopard-skin chairs and
tropical plants are offset by stately
English porcelain. Equally lively,
the kitchen bursts with flavours
from across the globe. African and
French influences predominate,
with Congolese chicken, Louisana-
style prawns or salmon tartare
with a creamy lemon sauce.

ASIAN AND PACIFIC RIM

Brussels has an enormous number
of both Chinese and Vietnamese
restaurants, ranging from drop-in
snack bars to veritable miniature
palaces. The Chaussée de Boondael
student area in Ixelles has the best
choice, with over 20 good restaurants. Lighter and more pungent
than Chinese cuisine, Vietnamese
food is simpler and more homely
than Thai. Its emphasis on spicy
soups and pancakes can be a
diversion in a city of such rich food.
Brussels' Chinese restaurants may
not be entirely exceptional, but the
city's Thai restaurants, especially
the more expensive ones, are of
high quality. Those keen on low-
priced Indian food may be disap-
pointed, but, again, the more lavish
dining locations are excellent.

Hông Hoa

Rue du Pont de la Carpe 10.
Map 1 C2. 📞 *(02) 502 8714.*
🕐 *noon–11pm daily.* 🍴 €

There are only eight tables in this
cosy, crimson-walled restaurant
near the Halles St-Géry. Service
is fast and friendly and the food
includes pancakes stuffed with
pork and prawns, diced beef with
onions and crispy duck with fresh
slices of ginger.

La Cantonnaise

Rue Tenbosch 110. 📞 (02) 344 7042.
🕐 11:30am–3pm, 7–11pm Mon–Fri;
5–11pm Sat & Sun. ★ 🈲 🍴 ♿ €

The owner of this deceptively plain
little restaurant off Chaussée de
Waterloo once ran a more formal
establishment, but realized that, by
reducing the number of tables and
dishes on offer, he could slash his
prices without compromising on
quality. The result is a restaurant
and take-away offering some of
the capital's tastiest Chinese food:
freshly cooked dim sum and spicy
beef and pork dishes are prepared
following recipes by the owner's
mother, who is a professional cook.

Le Pacifique

Boulevard du General Jacques 115.
📞 (02) 640 5259. ★ 🈲 MC, V.
🕐 noon–3pm, 6:30–11pm
Wed–Mon. 🈲 🍴 ♿ €

Le Pacifique is an unpretentious,
hospitable Vietnamese restaurant in
the bustling Chaussée de Boondael
area of Ixelles, near the university.
The prices are geared to the
student market, but the cooking is
subtle and makes considerable use
of fresh herbs. Try clear, spicy soup
with scampi and lemon, chicken
and beansprout salad with mint
or the restaurant's signature dish,
pork-and-scampi stuffed pancakes.

Poussières d'Etoiles

Chaussée de Boondael 437. 📞 (02)
640 7158. 🕐 noon–2:30pm, 6:30pm–
11:30 daily. 🈲 ♿ 🈲 🎵 🍴 ♿ €

Despite the kitschy decor – starry
skylights, twinkling twigs and
fluffy, feather-fringed lanterns – this
newish Vietnamese restaurant near
the university is a welcome addition
to the city's low-cost culinary
scene, attracting a trendy but laid-
back crowd. The range of dishes is
unusually small, with the emphasis
on quality produce rather than
diversity: fragrant seafood stew
with ginger and lime, caramelized
langoustines and chicken with
mushrooms and tangy ginger.
Portions are on the delicate side.

La Citronnelle

Chaussée de Wavre 1377. 📞 (02)
672 9843. 🈲 AE, DC, MC, V.
🕐 noon–2:30pm, 6:30–10:30pm
Tue–Fri & Sun; 6:30–10:30pm Sat.
🈲 🍴 ♿ €

This Vietnamese restaurant in
Auderghem oozes charm whether
you sit in the plant-filled interior
or the pretty garden. Traditional
music plays in the background, and
the delicate dishes include crispy
duck with ginger, grilled scampi
with lemongrass and braised beef.

La Maison de Thailande

Rue Middelbourg 22. 📞 (02) 672
2657. ★ 🈲 AE, DC, MC, V.
🕐 noon–2pm, 7–10:30pm Tue–Fri.
🕐 Tue lunch. 🍴 🈲 ♿€

Lauded for its refined, delicious
Thai cuisine, this restaurant in leafy
Watermael-Boitsfort is run by a
Thailand-obsessed Belgian photo-
grapher and his Thai wife. The
"discovery menu" offers five starters
and four main courses, offering a
surprising array of delicate dishes,
including fish and duck recipes.

La Porte des Indes

Avenue Louise 455. **Map** 2 D5. 📞
(02) 647 8651. ★ 🈲 AE, DC, MC, V.
🕐 noon–2:30pm, 7–10:30pm daily.
🕐 Sun lunch. 🍴 🈲 V ♿€€€

Brussels is something of a wilder-
ness for curry-lovers, but this
upmarket Indian eatery provides
considerable consolation. Lavishly
decorated with antiques collected
by owner Karl Steppe, who also
runs the Blue Elephant, La Porte
des Indes serves delicate traditional cuisine from the Pondicherry
region. Both exotic and traditional
dishes are on offer, including Parsee
fish with mint and coriander
wrapped in banana leaf parcels and
beef Pondicherry-style. Choose the
"Brass Plate" menu if you want to
sample several dishes. Traditional
drinks, including Indian beers, are
also on offer as well as the
ubiquitous sweet and sour lassi
and various native lager beers.

Blue Elephant

Chaussée de Waterloo 1120. 📞 (02)
374 4962. ★ 🈲 AE, DC, MC, V. 🕐
noon–2:30pm, 7–10:30pm Sun–Fri;
7–11:30pm Sat. 🍴 🈲 🈲 €€€€€

This high-dining experience at the
Bois de la Cambre end of Chaussée
de Waterloo shares an owner with
the famous British restaurant of the
same name; both are run by the
Belgian nomad and antiques collector Karl Steppe. Thai paraphernalia
and exotic plants fill the dining
room without cluttering it, and the
subtly spicy food has the same
admirable clarity, combining sweet,
hot, sour and bitter tastes without
blurring them. The lunch menu,
at around €13, is wonderful.

MEDITERRANEAN AND MIDDLE EASTERN

Like most European cities, Brussels
has some authentic Mediterranean
restaurants dotted about town.
Considering the size of the city's
Turkish population, Turkish restaurants have yet to make their mark,
but the number of good Lebanese

establishments is growing. Many
specialize in meze and Lebanese
kebabs, a quick way to eat well.
Greek restaurants have also had
a loyal following for decades.

L'Ouzerie

Chaussée d'Ixelles 235. **Map** 2 E5.
📞 (02) 646 4449. 🈲 AE, MC, V.
🕐 7pm–midnight, Mon–Sat. V ♿ €

This informal eatery stands out for
the quality of its dishes and service.
The decor is refreshingly simple, as
is the menu, which avoids clichéd
moussaka or grilled lamb, focusing
instead on such traditional dishes
as spinach and cheese stuffed pastries, grilled peppers and aubergine
salad. L'Ouzerie can get crowded,
so is worth booking in advance.

L'Ouzerie du Nouveau Monde

Chaussée de Boondael 290. 📞 (02)
649 8588. ★ 🈲 AE, DC, MC, V.
🕐 noon–3pm, 6pm–midnight Sun–
Fri; 6pm–1am Sat. V 🈲 €

Along with L'Ouzerie, this authentic
Greco-Cretan restaurant has
breathed fresh life into Brussels'
Greek restaurant scene, with low
prices, delightful food and a warm
welcome. The emphasis is on meze
starters: grilled pepper salad, char-
grilled ribs, stuffed vine leaves,
spicy sausages, and Cypriot goat's
cheese; around four per person
should satisfy most appetites.

Al Barmaki

Rue des Eperonniers 67. **Map** 2 D3.
📞 (02) 513 0834. 🈲 MC, V.
🕐 7pm–midnight Mon–Sat.
V 🍴 €€

A short walk from the Grand Place,
this cavernous eatery is probably
Brussels' best Lebanese restaurant.
Al Barmaki specializes in meze, an
assortment of small dishes that
include tabouleh (a pungent mint,
parsley and Bulgur wheat salad),
felafel and hummus, as well as
spicy sausages or chicken kebabs.

Sahbaz

Chaussée de Haecht 102–104. 📞 (02)
217 0277. 🈲 MC, V. 🕐 11:30–3pm,
6pm–midnight Mon–Tue, Thu–Sun.
V ♿ 🎵 €€

Brussels' oldest Turkish restaurant
opened in 1980, when a wave of
migrants from Turkey arrived in
the city. Now quite an institution,
a mixed crowd flocks to the little
restaurant to sample sheep's head
soup, oven-baked lamb, minced
meat in aubergine parcels and, for
vegetarians, crispy rolls stuffed
with sour goat's cheese. Turkish-
style omelettes and vegetable
pizzas are on offer for the more
budget-conscious.

SPANISH AND PORTUGUESE

Both Spanish and Portuguese cuisines adapt well to the Brussels food scene, as Belgium's fresh seafood and emphasis on quality ingredients reflect Mediterranean traditions. The Hapsburg dynasty ruled both Belgium and Spain for generations, and it was their diplomatic movements through the centuries that introduced these new schools of cookery to Brussels.

Casa Manuel

Grand Place 34. **Map** 2 D3.
((02) 511 4746. ⊠ AE, DC, MC, V. ◯ noon–2:30pm, 6:30–midnight daily. ▦ ♿ ♫ ¶♦¶ €€

A great place in the heart of town to escape the crowds, this unshowy restaurant has been serving Spanish and Portuguese specialities since 1960. Eat paella, smoked swordfish, and prawns in garlic as you are serenaded by a guitarist and, occasionally, the tuneful head waiter.

Le Forcado

Chaussée de Charleroi 192.
((02) 537 9220. ★ ⊠ AE, DC, MC, V. ◯ noon–2pm, 7–10pm Tue–Sat. ▦ ¶♦¶ €€€

The fado music, cool 18th-century tiles and Renaissance lanterns lend an authentic atmosphere to Brussels' best Portuguese restaurant. The food includes mushroom gratin with port, salt-cod croquettes, grilled red mullet and marinated pork with clams as well as the national dish, fish stew. For dessert, try thet home-made cakes and pastries, many flavoured with cinammon which can also be found on sale at the restaurant's shop just around the corner.

CENTRAL AND EASTERN EUROPE

Spicy, warming dishes are sometimes welcome in a city renowned for its haute cuisine. From blinis with smoked salmon and caviar to rich goulash and hearty casseroles, the range of Central and Eastern European authentic dishes is a wide one for such a small capital, and for the most part the dishes are very reasonably priced for the high quality on offer.

Kocharata

Avenue Parc 4. ((02) 537 4296.
◯ noon–1pm, 6pm–midnight Tue–Sun. €€

This simple restaurant, run by an elderly Bulgarian couple who amaible welcome belies a canny business sense, has turned out substantial and good-value food for 30 years. It is tucked away in the heart of Saint-Gilles and has a loyal and ebullient following among locals and the city's east European community. Specialities include meatballs, kebabs, beetroot soup and a mountain goat's cheese served like a fondue.

Les Ateliers de la Grande Ile

Rue de la Grande Ile 33. ((02) 512 8190. ⊠ AE, DC, MC, V. ◯ 7:30pm–2am Tue–Sun. €€

This Russian eaterie is popular with large parties whose top priority is having fun without being told to keep the noise down. Copious quqntities of speciality vodkas are next on the list, with the food a resolutre third. Chicken Kiev is a favourite, not bad considering the speed at which it arrives. Table-thumping and sing-songs are regular here. This is the place to go if you want to let your hair down, but watch out for the hangover-inducing quaffability of the vodkas.

LATIN AMERICAN

This exotic cuisine was brought to Brussels after World War II. Providing a light-hearted and less calorific cuisine to the native Belgian, South American restaurants are known for their warm, relaxed ambience and reasonable prices. Fresh ingredients and fine fillets of meat are priorities in the kitchens. The jazzy atmosphere is often accompanied by live salsa and pre-dinner cocktail menus can be innovative and sometimes seductively powerful.

El Papagayo

Place Rouppe 6. **Map** 1 C4. ((02) 514 5083. ◯ 4pm–2am Mon–Fri; 6pm–2am Sat & Sun. ▦ ¶♦¶ €

Across the road from the majestic Comme Chez Soi, this Latino restaurant compensates for its slightly less refined cuisine with a relaxed and intimate atmosphere, perfect for relaxing in after a hard day's sightseeing. There are three floors, each with two or three tiny dining areas. The walls are unpainted brick and the innovative tables are converted iron sewing-machine stands. The South American food includes raw fish with lime, chili con carne, spicy pork stew and a wide range of salads. The cocktail menu is terrific. Unusually for Brussels, freshly made cocktails are on offer; exotic fruit juices and fruit pulp are poured over crushed ice and mixed with a powerful variety of spirits and tequilas, including gold tequila and Mexican brandies.

Cantina Cubana

Rue des Grands-Carmes 6. **Map** 1 C3. ((02) 502 6540. ⊠ MC, V. ★ ◯ Jun–Sep: 8pm–midnight daily; Oct–May: 7–11:30pm daily. €€

In a little street across the way from Manneken Pis, this small Cuban diner has brought a welcome taste of the Caribbean to central Brussels. Sway to the sound of traditional guitar in the background while admiring the photographs on the white-washed walls and the daily menu chalked up on a blackboard. The emphasis is on chicken, fish and pork dishes – chicken with coconut sauce, cod with salsa verde, spare ribs and pork with sour black bean sauce – as well as exotic fruit drinks and cocktails. Tropical fruit dishes are on offer for dessert, including mango sorbet and fruit crème brulée. The service is very friendly.

Tierra del Fuego

Rue Berckmans 14. ((02) 537 4272. ⊠ MC, V. ◯ 7–11pm Mon–Fri; 6:30pm–2am Sat–Sun. ▦ €€

The bar-restaurant of Brussels' Latin-American cultural centre near Place Stéphanie is an accomplished blend of Old and New World cultures, with Spanish-style Moorish touches, offset by embossed ceiling stars and pictures of snow-capped peaks that recall South America's ancient Inca culture. The well-judged cuisine includes guacamole, marinated raw fish, burritos and Argentine beef, while you can relax after dinner with a Cuban cigar and South American coffees.

FISH AND SEAFOOD

The tradition of seafood in Belgium is a long and illustrious one. With more Michelin-starred restaurants in the country than France, the centuries-old refinement of recipes and dishes owes something to the exceptional quality of fresh produce available from the ports. Even today fresh fish and shellfish are delivered to Brussels within two hours of the catch; sole, plaice and cod among the regular deliveries, with baskets of shrimps caught by horseback riders on the coast ferried daily to market. Both French and Flemish schools influence the cooking, which includes historic favourites such as Ostend sole and grilled lobster.

Bij den Boer

Quai aux Briques 60. **Map** 1 C1.
📞 (02) 512 6122. ★ 💳 AE, DC,
MC, V. 🕐 noon–2:30pm, 6–
10:30pm Mon–Sat. ♿ 👶 🍴
€€€

This Flemish-run restaurant is
one of the most reasonably priced
and authentic brasseries on the
Vismarkt, or Old Fish Market.
The mirror panels and check
tablecloths give it a local, unpretentious feel, but the kitchen offers
accomplished versions of classic
fish dishes, including monkfish
with oysters.

L'Achepot

Place Ste-Catherine 1. **Map** 1 C2.
📞 (02) 511 6221. 💳 V.
🕐 noon–3pm, 6:30–10:30pm daily.
🖼 👶 €€

The best reason to visit this
earthy but nonetheless stylish
bistro-tavern near the Vismarkt
is to try the *poisson du jour* (fish
dish of the day), a cheap, fresh
and invariably delicious meal
such as whiting in lemon and
butter with plain boiled potatoes.
The menu also features traditional
brasserie fare, including chicken
breast with tarragon sauce, goat's
cheese parcels and spare ribs.

La Marée

Rue de Flandre 99. **Map** 1 B1.
📞 (02) 511 0040. ★ 💳 AE, DC,
MC, V. 🕐 noon–2:30pm, 6–11pm
Tue–Sat; noon–2:30pm Sun.
♿ €€

Simplicity is the hallmark of this
cosily unpretentious fish restaurant
located near Place Ste-Catherine.
The service is extremely professional and the pared-down, elegant
cooking puts many more expensive establishments to shame. Try
the fried cod with tartare sauce,
skate wings with butter or one of
eight varieties of stewed mussel
preparations. When in season,
plain grilled lobster is a highlight,
served with green herb sauce.

La Truite d'Argent

Quai au Bois à Bruler 23. **Map** 1 C1.
📞 (02) 219 9546. ★ 💳 AE, DC,
MC, V. 🕐 noon–2:30pm, 7–
11:30pm Mon–Fri; 7–11:30pm Sat.
🖼 🍴 €€€€

This opulent but intimate restaurant in a 19th-century townhouse
is among the best restaurants on
the Vismarkt. The fresh, inventive
and uncluttered cuisine includes
beautifully prepared millefeuille of
salmon, North Sea bouillabaisse,
six different preparations of
lobster, a splendidly nostalgic

prawn cocktail and steamed
monkfish with spinach. The
waiters go out of their way to
make you feel special, and the
wine list is varied and far from
overpriced.

Scheltema

Rue des Dominicains 7. **Map** 2 D2.
📞 (02) 512 2084. 💳 AE, MC.
🕐 11:30am–3pm, 6pm–11:30pm
Mon–Thu; 11:30am–3pm, 6pm–
12:30am Fri & Sat. 🖼 €€€€

This superb Belle Epoque brasserie off Rue des Bouchers in the
heart of Brussels is a place for a
celebration, with a cheery atmosphere and upmarket fish cuisine.
Although the prices undoubtedly
reflect the central location and the
proliferation of tourists, the food
is excellent and generous, with
prominence given to such delicacies
as sole and scallops in champagne
vinaigrette, fish soup, lobster and
salmon grilled with orange.

De Matelote

Haarstraat 9, Antwerp. 📞 (03) 231
3207. ★ 💳 AE, DC, MC, V.
🕐 noon–2pm, 7–10pm Mon–Sat.
🌑 Mon & Sat lunch, Jul. 📖 V
🍴 €€€€€€

Located in the old town, the cosy,
12-table De Matelote is reputed to
be Antwerp's best fish restaurant.
The menu varies daily and depending on the season, but typical
dishes include sea scallops cooked
with a stock of mushrooms and
sorrel and langoustines in a light
curry sauce. Reservations essential.

L'Ecailler du
Palais Royal

Rue Bodenbroeck 18. **Map** 2 D4.
📞 (02) 512 8751. ★ 💳 AE, DC,
MC, V. 🕐 noon–2:30pm, 7–10:30pm
Mon–Sat. ♿ 🍷 €€€€€

Despite its awesome reputation
and a star location on Place du
Grand Sablon, this unshowy restaurant is the epitome of elegant
discretion. It specializes in French-
influenced fish and seafood, with
produce whose high quality lends
itself to simple preparations: monkfish with herb butter, lobster ravioli
and heavenly prawn croquettes.
The excellence, however, is reflected in the pricing: even a lunchtime dish of the day will set you
back around €25.

Sea Grill

Rue du Fosse-aux-Loups 47. **Map** 2 D2.
📞 (02) 227 3120. ★ 💳 AE, DC,
MC, V. 🕐 noon–2:30pm, 7–10:30pm
Mon–Sat. 🌑 Sat lunch. ♿ 🍷
€€€€€

When the Swedish hotel group
Radisson SAS hired French chef
Yves Mattagne to run the restaurant
at their new Brussels hotel in 1991,
they could never have anticipated
his success. Before the end of the
century, he had won two Michelin
stars and a reputation as the best
fish cook in Belgium. Mattagne's
classic dishes include sea bass
roasted in sea salt, crab with olive
oil and thyme, Breton lobster and
sumptuous seafood platters,
although the daily suggestions are
usually also worth careful attention. The decor is modern and
functional, but service is superb.

VEGETARIAN

Because of the Belgian dedication
to red meat, Brussels is not a
haven for the vegetarian. Healthy
establishments, many located in
the student district of Chaussée
de Boondael, serve wholesome
dishes and often sell takeaways
and organic supplies.

Dolma

Chaussée d'Ixelles 329. **Map** 2 E5.
📞 (02) 649 8981. 💳 AE, DC, MC, V.
🕐 noon–2pm, 7–9pm Mon–Sat. V
👶 🍴 €

This eatery near Place Flagey
specializes in Tibetan dishes,
with a suitably ethnic decor. Its
hallmark is the reasonably priced
all-you-can-eat vegetarian buffet.
Snacks are on sale in the organic
shop just next door.

Shanti

Avenue A. Buyl 68. 📞 (02) 649 4096.
★ 💳 AE, DC, MC, V. 🕐 noon–
2pm, 7–10pm Tue–Sat. V 🍴 €€

This Ixelles eatery is one of
Brussels' most popular vegetarian
restaurants, albeit not against that
much competition. The atmosphere is relaxed, with classical
music at lunchtime and jazz in
the evening. Try fragrant rice,
aubergine or tandoori fish.

Tsampa

Rue de Livourne 109. 📞 (02) 647
0367. 🕐 noon–2pm, 7–9:30pm
Mon–Sat. V ♿ 🖼 🍴 €

This plant-filled restaurant has an
organic produce shop at the front
and an Asian-inspired menu
drawing on Thai and Indian cuisine
in the rear dining area. Organic
wines are served with curries and
basmati rice and Tibetan-style
ravioli and cheese dishes, such
as deep-fried pastries stuffed with
sheep's cheese. With a lively
crowd composed of students and
the city's youth, the restaurant has
a cheery, bohemian atmosphere.

Cafés and Bars

WITH A WATERING hole on almost every street offering world-famous quality ales, Brussels fully deserves its reputation as a paradise for beer-lovers. Taverns, cafés and bars all serve a range of at least twenty beers, as well as a handsome variety of continental coffees, herbal teas, fruit juice and spirits. Most establishments stay open from morning to midnight, and often later at weekends.

CLASSIC CAFES

A DRINK ON the Grand Place is an essential part of any visit to Brussels, although costs can be high. Perhaps the best, and one of the best priced, is **Le Roy d'Espagne** *(see p43)*, a huge two-tiered bar housed in the bakers' guildhouse with prime views from its terrace. The terraces at neighbouring La Brouette offer similar views, as does Le Cygne, where Karl Marx worked on *The Communist Manifesto* during the early 1840s.

Moments from the Grand Place lies **Au Bon Vieux Temps**, a quiet bar in a 17th-century building with the homely feel of an English pub. **Le Cirio**, near the Bourse, is a quintessential café from the 1900s, beloved by fans of Belle Epoque decor. Close by is **A la Mort Subite**, one of the capital's most celebrated establishments. Immense wooden tables, peeling mirrors and brusque service add to the appeal. Moving eastward to Place de Brouckère, the Hôtel Métropole contains a fabulous, opulent Belle Epoque bar, **The 19th**, as well as a heated outdoor terrace.

The Place du Grand Sablon is a favourite area for café-goers and those who want to catch the feel of the bustling city. The most upmarket spot here is **Au Vieux Saint-Martin**. **Les Salons du Sablon**, nearby, is a luxurious tea-room run by top chocolatiers Wittamer. This family-run business uses a century's worth of skill to create delicious confections.

SPECIALIST BEER BARS

B EER BUFFS should head to **Chez Moeder Lambic**, near the town hall in St-Gilles. A small and chaotic bar with a few tables tottering outside on the pavement, it serves over 1,000 beers. The choice covers most of Belgium's 400 or so varieties, as well as exotic brews from overseas, many customers cope with the choice by picking a letter from the alphabetized menu.

ART NOUVEAU

A FORMER haunt of Surrealist painter René Magritte, **Le Greenwich** is now the city's premier venue for chess enthusiasts; matches run around the clock. Also celebrated is **Les Fleurs en Papier Doré**, the meeting point for Belgian Surrealists in the late 1920s and still lively. **Café Falstaff**, opened in 1903 by the Bourse, has original Horta-designed furniture. South of Place du Grand Sablon, **Le Perroquet** attracts a young crowd, keen on its filled pittas. The best-known Art Nouveau bar, **De Ultieme Hallucinatie**, is nearby.

COSMOPOLITAN

B RUSSELS HAS a thriving social scene for the young and fashionable, most of which takes place around Place St-Géry in the Lower Town. Trendy, but not pretentious or stuffy, the clutch of bars here are mostly modernist in design, with some restored historic features. **Zebra** is a tastefully minimal bare brick and metal bar with a huge terrace that attracts crowds on warm evenings. Opposite Zebra is **Mappa Mundo**, a two-storey oak-panelled drinking spot which offers light meals and a good beer selection. Nearby the cavernous **Beurs Café** attracts the artistic crowd with its DJ sets and hip sounds. **L'Archiduc** boasts a breathtaking Art Deco interior and live jazz performances *(see p159)*.

DIRECTORY

CLASSIC

Le Roy d'Espagne
Grand Place 1. **Map** 2 D3.
☎ (02) 513 0807.

Au Bon Vieux Temps
Rue du Marché aux Herbes 12.
Map 2 D3. ☎ (02) 217 2626.

Le Cirio
Rue de la Bourse 18.
Map 1 C2. ☎ (02) 512 1395.

A la Mort Subite
Rue Montagne aux Herbes 7.
Map 2 D2. ☎ (02) 513 1318.

Au Vieux Saint-Martin
Place du Grand Sablon 38.
Map 2 D4. ☎ (02) 512 6476.

Les Salons du Sablon
Place du Grand Sablon 12.
Map 2 D4. ☎ (02) 512 3742.

SPECIALIST BEER BARS

Chez Moeder Lambic
Rue de Savoie 68.
☎ (02) 539 1419.

ART NOUVEAU

Le Greenwich
Rue des Chartreux 7.
Map 1 C2. ☎ (02) 511 4167.

La Fleurs en Papier Doré
Rue des Alexiens 55.
Map 1 C4. ☎ (02) 511 1659.

Café Falstaff
Rue Henri Maus 21.
☎ (02) 511 8789.

Le Perroquet
Rue Watteau 31. **Map** 2 D4.
☎ (02) 512 9922.

De Ultieme Hallucinatie
Rue Royale 316. **Map** 2 E2.
☎ (02) 217 0614.

COSMOPOLITAN

Zebra
Place St-Géry 33–35.
Map 1 C2. ☎ (02) 511 0901.

Mappa Mundo
Rue Pont de la Carpe 2–6.
☎ (02) 514 3555.

Beurs Café
Rue Auguste Orts 28.
☎ (02) 513 8290.

Light Meals and Snacks

BESIDES ITS TRADITIONAL taverns, luxurious patisseries and lively cafés, not to mention the celebrated chip and sticky waffle stands, Brussels is home to a growing number of fashionable quick lunch venues. Several ethnic restaurants also offer hearty, inexpensive snacks.

BREAKFASTS

BRUSSELS WAS the birthplace of Le Pain Quotidien, the designer breakfast phenomenon, which now boasts chic outlets in New York, Munich and Paris. Wholesome breakfasts and lunches, featuring organic yogurt and wholemeal breads, are served around communal wooden tables. Founded in 1829, speculoo biscuit specialist Dandoy is an institution, popular with locals and visitors alike for coffee and homemade waffles. La Maison de Paris has delicious croissants.

TAVERNS

THE TRADITIONAL refreshment of Belgian beer and shrimp or cheese croquettes can be found in the city's historic taverns. Le Paon Royal is an insight into true Brussels style. Plattesteen serves steaks and salads. Nearby Mokafe is an elegant café, perfect for a bowl of pasta or a croque monsieur.

CHIP AND WAFFLE SHOPS

THE WARM SMELL of frites and sweet waffles is part of Brussels life. Maison Antoine, whose clients have included Johnny Hallyday and the Rolling Stones, is the most renowned friterie. Fritland, near the Grand Place, is also something of an institution.

SANDWICHES AND SNACKS

MOST TAVERNS and butchers offer straightforward cheese, ham and salami sandwiches, but for tartines (British-style sandwiches) or baguettes (French bread), try the elegant Lunch Company. Belgian action star Jean-Claude van Damme favours the downtown Au Suisse, which has been in the business since 1873 and offers a large choice of fillings, plus its popular double hot-dog. The Flemish Cultural Centre, De Markten, sells filling and wholesome snacks.

TEA ROOMS

BELGIUM IS NOTED for top-quality pastries and cakes, which easily rival its celebrated chocolates. Au Flan Breton has been baking fruit-filled cream pastries for nearly a century. Uptown, Passiflore serves heavenly chocolate concoctions. Ice-cream enthusiasts should head south to Zizi's, a family-run, traditional parlour.

ETHNIC

MIDDLE EASTERN snacks and take-away food are very well priced at Orientalia. Lebanese L'Express is often lauded as the best pitta joint in Brussels. L'Orfeo has a good selection of pittas and fresh salads. Downtown, Chinese restaurant Chaochow City has a bargain lunch room. The Italian bistro Intermezzo serves excellent Italian pasta, with many non-meat sauces.

VEGETARIAN

THE DELICIOUS quiches and salads at Arcadi, near the Galéries Saint-Hubert, are largely vegetarian. For organic vegan fare, Den Teepot is recommended; it offers a good daily dish or soup of the day, and vegan fruit tarts.

DIRECTORY

BREAKFASTS

Dandoy
Rue Charles Buls 14–18.
(02) 512 6588.

La Maison de Paris
Rue de Namur 89. Map 2
E4. (02) 511 1195.

Le Pain Quotidien
Rue Antoine Dansaert 16.
Map 1 B1. (02) 502 2361.

TAVERNS

Mokafe
Galerie du Roi 9.
(02) 511 7870.

Le Paon Royal
Rue du Vieux Marché aux Grains 6. Map 1 C2.
(02) 513 0868.

Plattesteen
Rue du Marché au Charbon 41. Map 1 C3. (02) 512 8203.

CHIP AND WAFFLE SHOPS

Fritland
Rue Maus.

Maison Antoine
Place Jourdan 1. Map 3 B4. (02) 230 5456.

SANDWICHES AND SNACKS

Au Suisse
73-75 Blvd Anspach.
(02) 512 9589.

Orientalia
129 Ch de Mons. Map 1 A3. (02) 520 7575.

The Lunch Company
Rue de Namur 16. Map 2 E4. (02) 502 0976.

TEA ROOMS

Au Flan Breton
Chaussée d'Ixelles 54. Map 2 E5. (02) 511 8708.

Passiflore
Rue du Bailli 97.
(02) 538 4210.

Zizi's
Rue de la Mutualité 57a.
(02) 344 7081.

ETHNIC

Chaochow City
Boulevard Anspach 89.
Map 1 C3. (02) 512 8283.

De Markten
Passage du Marché aux Grains. (02) 512 3425.

L'Express
Rue des Chapeliers 8. Map 2 D3. (02) 512 8883.

Intermezzo
Rue des Princes 16.
(02) 218 0311.

L'Orfeo
Rue Haute 18. Map 1 C4.
(02) 512 6041.

VEGETARIAN

Arcadi
Rue d'Arenberg 1b. Map 2 D2. (02) 511 3343.

Den Teepot
Rue des Chartreux 66.
Map 1 C2. (02) 511 9402.

SHOPPING IN BRUSSELS

BRUSSELS IS an ideal place to shop for luxury goods, from its glorious chocolate shops to quirky market finds and cutting-edge fashion. Street markets are popular year round, or, if your tastes are more glitzy, head for Avenue Louise and Boulevard de Waterloo, where top designers are represented; for the original creations

Belgian chocolates

of the Antwerp Six and new-wave fashions, try Rue Antoine Dansaert. For specialist stores, including home decoration, go to rues Haute and Blaes. Many mainstream stores are located on Brussels' longest pedestrian shopping street, Rue Neuve. Other pockets of interest lie a short detour from downtown, in Uccle, St-Gilles and Ixelles.

A colourful designer fashion boutique on Rue Neuve

OPENING HOURS

THERE ARE NO set opening times in Brussels, but most places are open at least between 10am and 5pm.

Mainstream shops in arcades, malls and the Rue Neuve area typically open at 9.30am and close between 6 and 7pm. Late-night shopping runs at some places until 8pm on Friday. Otherwise it depends on where the shop is located and what it is selling.

Mondays and Wednesday or Saturday afternoons are the likeliest times for smaller shops to close (some shut for lunch daily), while many now open for part of Sunday (not supermarkets). For late-night purchases, the White Night chain stays open until 1am. From mid-July to mid-August, many specialist shops, cafés and restaurants close.

HOW TO PAY

CASH IS THE preferred method of payment, and a surprising number of shops will not accept credit cards, including most supermarkets and many smaller establishments.

At small shops discounts are sometimes given on the more expensive items when they are paid for in cash.

VAT EXEMPTION

NON-EU residents visiting Belgium are entitled to VAT refunds on purchases of over €124 spent in one store. Deducting VAT from the selling price gives a saving of 5.6 to 17.35 per cent. When shopping, look for the "Tax-Free Shopping" logo. After purchase ask for a Global Refund or Tax-Free Shopping Cheque. This will be stamped by customs on your way out of the EU, and refunds made on the spot at the airport. Customs often ask to see goods, so carry them as hand luggage.

SALES

SALES DATES IN Belgium are fixed by law. The summer sales run from July 1 to 31 and the January sales from the first weekday after New Year's Day until the end of the month. Discounts start at 10 per cent and gradually drop, reaching 40–50 per cent in the last week.

DEPARTMENT STORES AND SHOPPING ARCADES

THE MAIN department store in the city is **Inno**. It is not spectacular by British and American standards. Brussels' equivalent to Harrods toy department is Serneels on Place Louise, in the luxury Wiltshire shopping complex. Traditional men's outfitter Degand has recently started selling luxury gift items.

Rue Neuve contains mainstream stores, including popular Dutch stores – We for clothes and Blokker and Hema for household goods and toys – and French cutprice store Tati. There are three shopping malls at either end of the road: the Anspach and Monnaie Centres at Place de la Monnaie and City 2 at Place Rogier.

Window shopping in the city's numerous boutiques or arcades is a popular Sunday pastime. The best arcade is the recently renovated

Galéries Saint-Hubert historic 19th-century shopping arcade

Browsers enjoying the Place du Jeu de Balle market in the sunshine

Galéries Saint-Hubert which dates from 1847 (see p47). It houses several jewellers, and luxury leather bag maker Delvaux, as well as chocolate shops and smart boutiques, including popular women's fashion designer Kaat Tilley.

Less conservative is the **Galéries d'Ixelles** to the north of the city centre, where a bustling collection of cafés and tiny ethnic shops thrives in the city's trendy Matonge district. A stone's throw away, Galéries Toison d'Or and the adjacent Galéries Louise are mostly full of chain and adults' high-street European fashion boutiques.

Downtown towards the Grand Place is the quaint **Galérie Bortier**, the place to visit for collectors of antiquarian books and maps.

MARKETS

A TRIP TO Brussels must include the city's fabulous street markets, which offer anything from cheap flowers and food to second-hand bicycles and fine antiques.

Good for unusual fine antiques and a pleasant stroll is the weekend market on Place du Grand Sablon (from 9am, Saturday and Sunday). In the ancient Marolles district, the flea market on the Place du Jeu de Balle (daily, 7am to 1pm) is a colourful, eclectic affair.

Most spectacular is the huge vibrant market around Gare du Midi (Sundays, 6am to 1pm), with its mix of North African and home-grown delicacies.

It has a staggering blend of Moroccan and southern European treats, including oils, spices, and exotic herbs.

BEST BUYS AND SPECIALIST SHOPS

F OR CHOCOLATE, choose from **Pierre Marcolini**'s edible sculptures and gateaux, or the internationally known fine chocolatiers **Wittamer** and **Godiva**. Their flagship stores are in the Place du Grand Sablon. Fine biscuit specialist **Dandoy** can be found just behind the Grand Place.

Serious collectors of comic-strip memorabilia should visit **Little Nemo** and **La Bande des Six Nez**. At **Beer Mania**, speciality beers can be bought on the spot or delivered.

Elvis Pompilio's hats and bags

Milliner **Elvis Pompilio** produces hand-made hats at his pilot store. The best of Belgian fashion, including Dries Van Noten and Ann Demeulemeester, is on offer at upmarket store **Stijl**.

BOOKSHOPS AND MAGAZINES

A BRANCH OF English bookstore Waterstone's (see p163) sells English-language magazines, fiction and reference material. Nijinsky (15 Rue de Page) is great for secondhand English-language fiction. French store Fnac at the City 2 mall also has a good English-language section. For international papers, go to Librairie de Rome, 50 Avenue Louise.

DIRECTORY

DEPARTMENT STORES AND SHOPPING ARCADES

Inno
Rue Neuve 111. **Map** 2 D2.
Avenue Louise 12. **Map** 2 D5.
 (02) 211 2111.

Galéries d'Ixelles
Chaussée d'Ixelles. **Map** 2 E5.

Galérie Bortier
Rue de la Madeleine 17–19.
Map 2 D3.

BEER

Beer Mania
Chaussée de Wavre 174–178.
Map 2 E5.
 (02) 512 1788.

CHOCOLATE

Pierre Marcolini
Place du Grand Sablon 39.
Map 2 D4.
 (02) 514 1206.

Godiva
Grand Place 22.
Map 2 D3.
 (02) 511 2537.

Wittamer
Place du Grand Sablon 6–12.
Map 2 D4.
 (02) 512 3742.

Dandoy
Rue au Beurre 31. **Map** 2 D3.
 (02) 511 0326.

FASHION

Elvis Pompilio
Rue du Lombard 18. **Map** 1 C3.
 (02) 511 1188.

Stijl
Rue Antoine Dansaert 74.
Map 1 B2.
 (02) 512 0313.

CARTOONS

Little Nemo
Boulevard Lemonnier 25.
 (02) 514 6804.

La Bande des Six Nez
Chaussée de Wavre 179.
Map 2 E5.
 (02) 513 7258.

ENTERTAINMENT IN BRUSSELS

WITHIN EASY REACH of London, Paris and Amsterdam, Brussels is an established stop on the international touring circuit, with regular visits from the world's best orchestras, soloists, rock bands and dance troupes. It is also a great place to experience Belgium's thriving cultural scene, which is especially distinguished in the fields

**Ecran Total
Cinema poster**

of medieval music, jazz and contemporary dance. Brussels has several cinemas showing a wide range of films, including movies from the US and Europe (many in English). Professional theatre here is mostly performed in French or Flemish. Outside the city's major venues, the quality of entertainment can vary, but jazz and blues bars offer good free gigs.

The 19th-century interior of La Monnaie Opera House

OPERA, CLASSICAL MUSIC AND DANCE

BRUSSELS' OPERA HOUSE, **La Monnaie**, has a unique claim to fame: on August 25, 1830, an aria in Auber's opera *La Muette de Portici* provoked the capital's citizens into rioting against their Dutch rulers, setting the country on the road to independence *(see pp34–5)*. Now the house is among Europe's finest venues for opera. Its current artistic director Antonio Pappano will join London's Royal Opera House when his contract runs out in 2003. The season runs from September to June, with tickets starting at €7.50. Most productions are sold out many months in advance.

Designed by Victor Horta in 1928, the **Palais des Beaux-Arts** is the capital's flagship cultural venue, with an exhibition space, a theatre, film archives, a small cinema and Brussels' largest auditorium for classical music *(see p60)*. Following sustained criticism

of the accoustics, the Art Nouveau hall has recently been renovated. The venue is home to the Belgian National Orchestra, which has grown in stature under Russian conductor Yuri Simonov. Again, the season runs from September to June, with tickets costing from €7.50 to €75.

In March, the city hosts a trend-making contemporary classical festival, *Ars Musica*, with an emphasis on new works and an impressively avant-garde feel. In the holiday season, the Brussels' Summer

Festival offers concerts on the Grand Place as well as informal events in the Town Hall and the Palais des Beaux-Arts (see pp 62–7) nearby. In September and October, the Festival of Flanders is a gala-heavy event showcasing top Belgian artists as well as world-famous singers and conductors.

Over the past 15 years Belgium has won a reputation for being on the cutting edge of contemporary dance. Anne Teresa De Keersmaeker and her company Rosas put on regular performances, as do several other major Belgian companies, at the beautiful Art Deco **Kaaitheater** or the **Halles de Schaerbeek**, a 19th-century former market. Although Brussels has no ballet company of its own, it attracts major European touring companies including Jiri Kylian's outstanding Nederlands Dans Theater.

ROCK AND JAZZ

ANTWERP MAY be the centre of Belgium's alternative rock scene, but Brussels has several superb venues for rock gigs. Big names such as Aerosmith and Céline Dion

Le Botanique cultural centre in Brussels' Rue Royale

perform at **Forest-National**, a modern arena southeast of the city centre. The **Ancienne Belgique** downtown is a medium-sized venue hosting hip or up-and-coming guitar bands, folk, Latin and techno acts; **Le Botanique**, the French-speaking Community's cultural centre, has a strong if intermittent roster of rock and electronic music, including a marvellous ten-day festival, *Les Nuits Botanique*, held at the end of September.

The best places to catch good jazz acts are **Travers**, a cramped, intimate bar frequented by most of the country's top players, and **Sounds**, a larger venue which places an equal emphasis on blues music. On Saturday and Sunday afternoons, it is worth stopping by **L'Archiduc**, a refurbished Art Deco bar in the centre of town where you can find jazz musicians in relaxed, informal mood.

CINEMA

NORTH OF THE CITY, by the Heysel exhibition centre, the **Kinepolis** cinema is a state-of-the-art 28-screen multiplex which rivals US giants for consumer comfort. It screens all the Hollywood blockbusters and major French and British releases; one IMAX screen shows a selection of nature and adventure films. Parking is free.

In the centre of Brussels, the major cinema is **UGC/De Brouckère**, a modern 12-screen complex with a standard programme of mainstream releases. A second, smaller UGC is in Avenue de la Toison d'Or.

The **Arenberg/Galeries**, in the Galéries Saint-Hubert, is another quality cinema with comfortable auditoriums and an arthouse slant. From late June to September, it hosts "Ecran Total", a festival combining as yet unreleased films from around the world with established classics, often in remastered or "director's" versions. Perhaps the best of

Brussels' cinemas is the Musée du Cinema, part of the Palais des Beaux-Arts complex. Home to one of the world's largest film archives, the museum shows classics, from Chaplin to Tarantino, for just €2.30. Silent films are accompanied by live piano music.

Tickets for most cinemas are around €6.20. Visit www.cinebel.be to find out which film is playing where.

INFORMATION

THE PRINCIPAL source of entertainment information in English is *The Bulletin* magazine, which has comprehensive listings of forthcoming events in Brussels and the rest of Belgium. The magazine is published weekly and is available at newsstands throughout the country. Costing around €2.30, it has excellent coverage of news, travel ideas and a pot-pourri of information about life in the capital. The magazine's listings section, *What's On*, is also distributed free to hotels in the capital.

The company that publishes *The Bulletin* also owns an English-language website (www.xpats.com). The portal includes cultural information, news, weather reports and useful links for expats. The central **Tourist Information Office** (*see p162*) offers free maps, as well as information about arts and entertainment events, and publishes a calendar of major events. Advisors will assist in the booking of tickets.

French-speakers should try the monthly *Kiosque*, which offers capsule roundups of major arts events and a regular coupon with a variety of free ticket offers. Two daily papers, *Le Soir* and *La Libre Belgique*, publish cultural supplements on Wednesdays, with detailed arts and cinema listings. For Flemish-speakers, *Humo* or the daily newspaper *De Morgen*, also offer information on events and exhibitions.

Magazines on sale in Brussels

(*see p162*)

SURVIVAL
GUIDE

PRACTICAL INFORMATION

ALTHOUGH COMFORTABLE with its status as a major political and business centre, Brussels has sometimes struggled with its role as a tourist destination. It can be hard to find all but the most obvious sights: the same goes for inexpensive hotels. Both the Upper and Lower Town can easily be negotiated on foot, which might be a relief to those visitors reluctant to take

Guided tour walking group

on the challenging Belgian drivers and roads. Brussels is a very cosmopolitan city, and its residents, many of whom are foreigners themselves, are usually charming and friendly, with most speaking English. The tourist office goes out of its way to help travellers enjoy the city and provides help with everything from finding hidden sights to medical and financial information.

CUSTOMS AND IMMIGRATION

BELGIUM IS ONE of the 11 EU countries to have signed the 1985 Schengen agreement, which means travellers moving from one Schengen country to another are not subject to border controls. If you enter Belgium from France, Luxembourg, Germany or the Netherlands, you will not have to show your passport, although it is wise to carry it in case of trouble. Bear in mind that it is a legal requirement in Belgium to carry ID on the person at all times. Britain does not belong to Schengen, so travellers coming from the UK must present a valid passport and hold proof of onward passage when entering Belgium. This also applies to US, Australian, Canadian and other Commonwealth citizens.

British travellers no longer benefit from duty-free goods on their journey. Travellers from non-EU countries are still entitled to refunds of VAT (21 per cent on most products) if they spend more than €127 in a single transaction.

TOURIST INFORMATION

BRUSSELS IS RARELY crowded, so you should not expect to queue at major attractions and museums unless a special event or show is taking place. If you are planning to do extensive sightseeing, the one-day tram and bus pass (see pp168–9) is a must. Better still, pick up a "tourist passport" from the tourist office (see below). Drivers should avoid rush hour (Monday to Friday

from 8am to 9:30am and 5pm to 7pm), although public transport is manageable throughout the day. Many of the city's prestige hotels slash their rates at weekends, when business custom slacks off, so it can be worthwhile timing a short visit around this. Although Brussels' reputation as a rainy city is overplayed, bring a raincoat or waterproof jacket in summer and warm clothing for winter.

The Tourist and Information Office publishes a variety of maps, guides and suggested walks and tours. It offers a tourist passport for €7.44, which includes a one-day tram and bus pass, discounts on train tickets countrywide as well as reductions on museum daily admission prices worth over €50.

OPENING HOURS

MOST SHOPS AND businesses are open Mondays to Saturdays from 10am to 6pm, with some local shops closing for an hour during the day.

Supermarkets are usually open from 9am to 8pm. For late-night essentials and alcohol, "night shops" stay open to 1am or 2am. Banking hours usually run on weekdays from 9am to 1pm and 2 to 4pm. Most branches have 24-hour ATMs, and many have Visa or Euro points with Maestro, where foreign cashcards can be used. Many sights are closed on Mondays. Public museums are usually open on Tuesdays to Sundays from 10am to 5pm.

MUSEUM ADMISSION CHARGES

THERE WAS MUCH controversy when the city's major museums, including the Musées des Beaux-Arts and the Musées Royaux d'art et d'histoire introduced a €3.70 admission charge in the mid-1990s, but so far the money seems to have been well spent, with the Cinquantenaire Museum in particular undergoing much-needed layout improvements. Elsewhere, admission charges

The sculpture court in the Musées Royaux des Beaux-Arts in summer

Visitors taking a break from sightseeing in a pavement café

range from free entry to a daily tariff starting at €5. Reductions for students, children, the unemployed and senior citizens are always given.

TIPPING

A SERVICE CHARGE OF 16 per cent as well as VAT of 21 per cent are included in restaurant bills (this is marked on the menu as *"Service et TVA compris"*), but most diners round up the bill or add about 10 per cent if the service has been particularly good. Service is also included in taxi fares, although a 10 per cent tip is customary. Some theatre and cinema ushers expect €0.25 per person. You should pay nightclub doormen around €1 if you plan to go back. In hotels, a small tip for the chambermaid and porter should be given personally to them or left in your vacated room, and expect to pay railway porters €1 per bag. Finally, many public toilets – including those in bars, restaurants and even cinemas – have attendants who should be given €0.25.

DISABLED TRAVELLERS

B RUSSELS IS NOT the easiest city for the disabled traveller, but the authorities are beginning to recognize that there is room for improvement. Most of the more expensive hotels have some rooms designed for people with disabilities, and most metro stations have lifts.

There are designated parking spaces for disabled drivers, and newer trams have wheelchair access. The Tourist Office provides information and advice about facilities within the city.

Façade of the Sterling bookshop

NEWSPAPERS, TV AND RADIO

M OST BRITISH AND American daily newspapers produce international editions, which are on sale at major newsstands. The *Financial Times*, the *International Herald Tribune* and the *Wall Street Journal* are widely available. **Librairie de Rome, Waterstone's** or **Sterling Books** sell English magazines.

Belgium has one of the world's most advanced cable TV networks, with access to more than 40 channels, including BBC 1 and 2, CNN, NBC, MTV and Arte. Belgian channels include RTL and RTBF 1 and 2 (French-speaking) and VTM and Ketnet/Canvas (Flemish-speaking). TV listings are in the English-language magazine *The Bulletin*. Classical music stations include Musique 3 (91.2 FM), Studio Brussel (100.6 FM), or Radio 3.

DIRECTORY

TOURIST INFORMATION

Tourist and Information Office of Brussels
Grand Place 1, 1000 Brussels.
Map 2 D3. 〖 *(02) 513 8940.*
Ⓦ www.tib.be.
Hotel room reservation service.
Map 2 D3. 〖 *(02) 513 7484.*

UK Tourism Flanders
Ⓦ www.visitflanders.com

US Belgian Tourist Office
Ⓦ www.visitbelgium.com

BOOKSHOPS

Librairie de Rome
Avenue Louise 50.
Map 2 D5. 〖 *(02) 511 7937.*

Waterstone's
Boulevard Adolphe Max 71–75.
Map 2 D1. 〖 *(02) 219 2708.*

Sterling Books
Rue du Fossé-aux-Loups 38.
Map 2 D2. 〖 *(02) 223 6223.*

GUIDED TOURS

On foot:
Arau
Boulevard Adolphe Max 55.
Map 1 A2. 〖 *(02) 219 3345.*
Art Nouveau walks a speciality.

La Fonderie
Rue Ransfort 27. 〖 *(02) 410 1080.*
Industrial heritage, chocolate and beer walks.

Arcadia
Rue du Métal 38.
〖 *(02) 534 3819.*
Architectural walks.

By water:
Brussels by Water
2B Quai de Péniches.
〖 *(02) 203 6406.*
Cruises on the canal.

By cycle:
Pro vélo
Rue de Londres 15.
〖 *(02) 502 7355.*
Comic strip tours, Art Nouveau.

By coach:
Chatterbus
Rue des Thuyas 12. 〖 *(02) 673 1835.* 8am–7pm Mon–Sat. Individual and group tours.

Greylines
Rue de la Colline 8.
〖 *(02) 513 7744.*
Brussels city tours and excursions.

Personal Security and Health, Banking and Communications

B RUSSELS IS ONE OF Europe's safest capitals, with street crime against visitors a relatively rare occurrence. The poorer areas west and north of the city centre, including Anderlecht, Molenbeek and parts of Schaerbeek and St-Josse, have quite a bad reputation, but these areas are perfectly safe during the daytime for everyone except those who flaunt their wealth. After dark, it is sensible not to walk around on your own in these areas. Public transport is usually safe at all hours. Banking follows the European system and is straightforward. In addition, there are hundreds of 24-hour cashpoints located around the city.

LAW ENFORCEMENT

B ELGIUM HAS A complex policing system, whose overlapping and often contradictory mandates have been criticized in the past. Calls have been made to simplify the judicial structure, a process that is still slowly taking place. Major crimes and motorway offences are handled by the national gendarmerie. However, visitors are most likely to encounter the communal police, who are responsible for law and order in each of the capital's 19 administrative districts. All Brussels police officers must speak French and Flemish.

The main police station for central Brussels is on Rue du Marché au Charbon, close to the Grand Place. If stopped by the police visitors will be asked for identification, so carry your passport at all times. Belgian law classes as a vagrant anyone carrying less than €15 cash. Not using road crossings correctly is also illegal here.

Female police officer

SAFETY GUIDELINES

M OST OF Brussels' principal tourist attractions are located in safe areas where few precautions are necessary. When driving, make sure car doors are locked and any valuables are kept out of sight. If you are sightseeing on foot, limit the amount of cash you carry and never leave bags unattended. Women should wear handbags with the strap across the shoulder and the clasp facing towards the body. Wallets should be kept in a front, not back, pocket. Hotel guests should keep rooms and suitcases locked and avoid leaving cash or valuables lying around. Rooms often come with a safe; if not, there should be one at reception.

At night, avoid the city's parks, especially at Botanique and Parc Josaphat in Schaerbeek, both of which are favoured haunts of drug-dealers.

LOST PROPERTY

C HANCES OF retrieving property are minimal if it was lost in the street. However, it is worth contacting the police station for the commune in which the article disappeared. (If you are not sure where that is, contact the central police station on Rue du Marché au Charbon.) Public transport authority **STIB/MIVB** operates a lost-and-found service for the metro, trams and buses. Report items lost in a taxi to the police station nearest your point of departure; quote registration details and the taxi licence number.

TRAVEL AND HEALTH INSURANCE

T RAVELLERS FROM Britain and Ireland are entitled to free healthcare under reciprocal agreements within the EU. British citizens need an E111 form from a post office, which should be validated before their trip. Europeans should make it clear that they have state insurance, or they may end up with a large bill. While generous, state healthcare subsidies do not cover all problems and it is worth taking out full travel insurance. This can also cover lost property.

MEDICAL MATTERS

WHETHER OR not you have insurance, doctors in Belgium will usually expect you to settle the bill on the spot – and in cash. Arrange to make a payment by bank transfer (most doctors will accept this if you insist).

Pharmacies are generally open Mondays to Saturdays from 8:30am to 6:30pm, with each commune operating a rota system for late-night, Sunday and national holiday cover. All pharmacies display information about where to find a 24-hour chemist.

Assistants at pharmacies may not speak good English, so when receiving a prescription, make sure the doctor goes through the details before you leave the surgery.

EMERGENCIES

FOR EMERGENCIES requiring police assistance, call 101; for medical or fire services, phone 100. Hospitals with emergency departments include **Institut Edith Cavell** and **Hôpital Universitaire Saint-Luc**. The Community Help Service's (CHS) 24-hour English-language help line is for expatriates, but it may be able to assist tourists.

CURRENCY

BELGIUM, together with 11 other countries, has replaced its traditional currency with the euro. Austria, Finland, France, Germany, Greece, Ireland, Italy, Luxembourg, Netherlands, Portugal and Spain also chose to join the new currency.

The euro came into circulation in Belgium on 1 January 2002. A transition period has allowed euros and Belgian francs (BF) to be used together, with the franc phased out by mid-2002.

The Euro bank notes have seven denominations. The 5-euro note (grey) is the smallest, followed by the 10-euro note (pink), 20-euro note (blue), 50-euro note (orange), 100-euro note (green), 200-euro note (yellow) and the 500-euro note (purple). The euro has eight coin denominations: the 1 euro and 2 euros are both silver and gold in colour; the 50-, 20- and 10-cent coins are gold; and the 5-, 2- and 1-cent coins are bronze.

BANKING

MOST BANKS IN Brussels are open from 9am–1pm and 2–4pm; some open late on Friday until 4:30 or 5pm, and a few on Saturday mornings.

Banks often offer very competitive exchange rates, and most will happily serve non-clients. Many transactions (especially money transfers) are liable to banking fees, so ask in advance what these rates might be. Most banks will be able to cash traveller's cheques with the signatory's passport or other form of photographic identification. Visitors are usually able to exchange foreign currency, again with valid ID. Many bank attendants speak good English.

CREDIT CARDS

AMERICAN EXPRESS, Diners Club, Mastercard and Visa are widely accepted in Brussels, although it is wise to check in advance if booking a hotel or restaurant. Most hotels will accept a credit card booking. The cardholder may be asked for a credit card imprint at check-in.

BUREAUX DE CHANGE

IF YOU ARE unable to change money at a bank, you may be forced to rely on bureaux de change, which often charge commission of 3 to 4 per cent and may have uncompetitive exchange rates. There is a 24-hour automated exchange machine at Grand Place 7, while the streets around the square have several bureaux open until 7pm or later. There are also exchange booths at the city's major stations.

Travellers using currency from one of the countries which are members of the European single currency have a rate of exchange fixed at constant rates. Commission for transactions between them should be 1.5 per cent. If a bureau does not honour these conditions, go elsewhere.

ATM machine in Brussels

AUTOMATED TELLER MACHINES

MOST BANK branches have 24-hour cashpoint facilities, with a lobby reserved for bank members and an ATM on the wall outside. Most ATMs will accept cards belonging to the Cirrus, Maestro, Plus and Star systems, as well as MasterCard and Visa cards.

POST AND COMMUNICATIONS

BRUSSELS' PUBLIC payphones are run by former state operator Belgacom. Public phone booths are plentiful but the service information can be difficult to understand; the operator can be contacted by dialling 1380 or directory enquiries in English on 1405. Payphones accept Belgacom phonecards, and most will take collect and calling-card calls. Both €5 and €10 Belgacom cards are sold at newsagents, post offices and train stations. Payphones in metro stations accept cash.

When using the postal service, bear in mind that Belgium's service is automated, so addresses should be written in capital letters. A blue "A prior" sticker should ensure swifter delivery on international mail. Stamps are on sale in some supermarkets and post offices.

Red Belgian postbox

GETTING TO BRUSSELS

BRUSSELS IS WELL suited to both casual and business travellers, with abundant and excellent connections by air, rail and road. The increasing political significance of Brussels in its new role as the heart of Europe has led to greater competition between airlines, with many

High-speed Thalys train

operators offering a variety of discounted fares. The Eurostar and Thalys high-speed trains link the city with London, Paris, Amsterdam and Germany, and compare favourably with flying in terms of time. British travellers can use the Channel Tunnel to bring their car with them.

An aeroplane from Belgian carrier SN Brussels Airlines' fleet

ARRIVING BY AIR

SITUATED 14 KM (8¾ miles) northeast of the city centre, Brussels National Airport is in the Flemish commune of Zaventem (the name by which it is known to most citizens, including taxi drivers). A centre for Belgian carrier SN Brussels Airlines, which replaced the bankrupt airline Sabena, the airport is also served by major carriers such as British Airways, American Airlines, Air Canada, Delta, Lufthansa and Air France. Among the low-cost operators flying to and from Zaventem are Virgin Express (for London and Europe) and City Bird (for US destinations). A typical journey from London takes 45 minutes. Costs for UK flights range from £60 for a student flight to £270 for a scheduled return flight. Fares are lower out of season, but tend to rise at the weekend.

Reaching Brussels from the US can be more expensive than reaching other major European cities. Return flights

average US $700 for a charter return from New York. Prices from Canada are comparable.

The best-value flights from Australia and New Zealand include Alitalia, Lauda-air, and KLM, with fares from A$2,100.

Brussels South-Charleroi Airport has become a second important hub, since Ryanair has been operating scheduled flights from various European destinations, including the UK. It is 55 km (34 miles) from the centre of Brussels and can be reached by train or coach.

AIRPORT FACILITIES

BRUSSELS NATIONAL Airport has been extensively renovated over the past decade, with a new concourse for intra-EU travel due for completion by 2003. Brussels airport features baggage reclaim, customs, car-hire booths, tourist information and ground transport on the lower level. The departure lounge has check-in facilities, ticket and insurance counters and restaurants, bars and shops, before and after the security checkpoints. In addition, there are special lounges for busi-

ness or first-class SN Brussels Airlines passengers, and a corporate meeting centre. On arrival, passengers will also find ATMs, foreign exchange booths and coin- and card-operated payphones.

GETTING INTO TOWN

THE CHEAPEST way of getting from Zaventem to the city centre is the express train from the airport to Gare du Nord, Gare Centrale or Gare du Midi. Tickets (about €2.50) are on sale in the airport complex or, for a small supplementary fee, on the train itself. Three trains run each hour, between 5am and midnight; the journey to Gare Centrale takes 20 minutes.

There is a taxi rank outside the arrivals hall. A one-way fare to the centre of Brussels will cost €25–€30 and should take around 20 minutes (longer at rush hour). If you plan to return by taxi, ask the driver about deals as some companies offer discounts on return fares.

An SNCB/NMBS train runs from Charleroi to Gare du Midi. It takes about 45 minutes to/from the station.

ARRIVING BY TRAIN

BRUSSELS IS AT the heart of Europe's high-speed train networks, connected to London by the Eurostar service and to Paris, Amsterdam and Cologne by the Thalys network. These trains have a top speed of 300 kph (186 mph) and have slashed journey times between northern Europe's major cities, making them a challenge to the supremacy of the airlines.

Eurostar passengers should book their tickets at least a week in advance, especially to take advantage of reduced

SN Brussels Airlines

Logo for SN Brussels Airlines

fares; they should also arrive at the terminal at least 20 minutes before departure to go through check-in and customs before boarding. You may be refused access to the train if you arrive after this, although you can often be transferred to the next service at no extra charge.

Trains run hourly between London's Waterloo station and Brussels via the Channel Tunnel; the journey takes 2 hours 40 minutes, arriving at the Gare du Midi. Return fares start at around £70/€87. The trains are comfortable, with plenty of legroom, and have two buffet cars, one of which is licensed; first-class passengers receive a meal, free drinks and the day's international newspapers.

Many visitors to Brussels arrive from mainland Europe. The high-speed train company Thalys offers a comfortable journey, with Paris accessible in 1 hour 25 minutes, Amsterdam in around two hours and Cologne in under three.

Eurostar train arriving at the Gare du Midi, Brussels

ARRIVING BY SEA

BELGIUM CAN easily be reached from the UK several times daily. Hoverspeed operates a catamaran service, the SeaCat, from Dover to Ostend. The crossing takes around two hours. Cross-Channel ferries run frequently from Dover to Calais, Felixstowe to Ostend and Hull to Zeebrugge. Foot passengers do not usually need to book, but those with cars should always reserve a space and arrive promptly. Visitors with children should be aware that ferry companies have good child discounts, often with children under 14 years old travelling free.

ARRIVING BY CAR

THE OPENING of the Channel Tunnel has given drivers from Britain a new option for reaching mainland Europe: Le Shuttle. This is a car train that takes vehicles from the Tunnel entrance near Folkestone to Calais, with the journey taking around 35 minutes. From there, Brussels is a two-hour drive via the A16 motorway, which becomes the E40 when you cross the Franco-Belgian border. Follow signs to Brugge (Bruges), then Brussels. Those planning to ride Le Shuttle should book tickets in advance and try to arrive early. Three trains per hour run between 6:30am and midnight, with one train hourly from midnight to 6:30am. Standard fares start at £169 return per vehicle in low season, but rise for stays over five days and at popular times.

PASSPORTS AND ENTRY REQUIREMENTS

VISITORS FROM Britain will find that a passport is the only documentation required for a stay of up to 90 days. For a visit of the same length, European nationals should be prepared to produce their identity card. Travellers from the US and Canada need a full passport. All visitors should, if asked, be able to produce enough money, or proof of access to money, on arrival to pay for their entire stay as well as a return ticket to their home country.

DIRECTORY

BRUSSELS NATIONAL AIRPORT INFORMATION

(www.brusselsairport.be)

Flight Information
(02) 753 3913.

Disabled Travellers and Special Needs
(02) 723 6381.

Airport Police
(02) 753 7000.

Customs
(02) 753 4850.

AIRLINES

SN Brussels Airlines
(020) 8780 1444 (UK).
www.brussels-airlines.com

Air Canada
(0990) 247 226 (UK).

Air France
(0845) 084 5111 (UK).

American Airlines
(020) 8572 5555 (UK).
(1 800) 433 7300 (US).
www.americanair.com

British Airways
(020) 8759 5511 (UK).
www.britishairways.com

City Bird
(212) 947 1408 (US).

Delta
(0800) 414 767 (UK).
(404) 765 5000 (US).

Lufthansa
(0345) 737 747 (UK).

Ryanair
(08701) 569 569 (UK).

Swissair
(020) 7434 7300 (UK).

Virgin Express
(020) 7744 0004 (UK).

TRAIN AND BOAT INFORMATION

Belgian & International Railway Info
www.b-rail.be

Belgian Transport
(02) 515 2000.
www.stib.be

Eurostar
(0870) 578 6186 (UK).

Eurotunnel
(0990) 353 535 (UK).

Hoverspeed
(0870) 240 8070 (UK).

Thalys
(0900) 10366 (Belgium).

The Hoverspeed catamaran SeaCat crossing the Channel

Getting around Brussels

**Metro station
street sign**

ALTHOUGH ITS public transport system is clean, modern and efficient, Brussels is a city best explored on foot. Most of the key attractions for first-time visitors are within a short walk of the Grand Place, and the Art Nouveau architecture in Ixelles and Saint-Gilles is also best enjoyed on a leisurely stroll. For those anxious to see the main sights in limited time, the tram and metro network covers most of the city at speed, while buses are useful for reaching more out-of-the-way areas. Although expensive, taxis are recommended for late-night journeys. Cycling can be hazardous for the inexperienced.

PLANNING YOUR JOURNEY

IF YOU ARE seeing Brussels by car, avoid its major roads during rush hours, which run on weekdays from 8–9:30am and 5–7pm as well as Wednesday lunchtimes during the school year, when there is a half day. Tram and bus services run frequently at peak time and are usually not too crowded. However, the small size of Brussels means that walking is usually a viable option.

WALKING IN BRUSSELS

THE SHORT distance between sights and the interest in every corner make central Brussels easy to negotiate on foot. Outside the city centre, walking is the only way to appreciate the concentration of Art Nouveau buildings on and around Square Ambiorix, around the district of Ixelles and near St-Gilles Town Hall.

Drivers in Brussels have a bad reputation, and it is important to be alert to traffic while crossing roads. Until 1996, motorists were not obliged to stop at pedestrian crossings: the laws came into effect on April 1 of that year and many drivers still treat them as a seasonal pleasantry. At traffic lights, motorists turning right or left may ignore the walkers' priority. It is essential to be careful even in residential areas.

Blue or white street signs are placed on the walls of buildings at one corner of a street, and can be somewhat hard to locate. Street names

are always in French first, then Flemish, with the name in capital letters and the street type in small letters to the top left and bottom right corners (for example, Rue STEVIN straat).

**Mother and child seeing Brussels'
historic architecture by bicycle**

CYCLING

COMPARED TO THE cyclist-friendly cities of Flanders, Brussels can be a frustrating place for pushbike-riders. Car-free zones are few and far

between, and cycle lanes are rare. However, on a trip to the suburbs or the Fôret de Soignes, bicycles are the best option and can be cheaply hired from most railway stations (non-Belgians must leave a small deposit).

TRAVELLING BY BUS, TRAM AND METRO

THE AUTHORITY governing Brussels' public transport is the bilingual **STIB/MIVB**, which runs buses, trams and metro services in the capital. Tickets are valid on all three services, which run between 5:30am and 12:30am on weekdays with shorter hours on Sundays and public holidays.

A single ticket, which allows the passenger an unlimited number of changes within one hour (excluding the Nato-Brussels Airport line 12), costs €1.40. You can also buy a ten-ticket card at €9 or a one-day pass costing €3.59. The five-ticket card, for €6.20, is not competitively priced but it can be convenient for avoiding repeated queues. There are also combined "STIB/MIVB + Taxi" tickets, a single ticket that offers a reduction on taxi rides.

Single tickets can be bought on buses and trams, and should be stamped in the orange machines next to the exits; you must restamp your ticket if the journey involves a change. On the metro, tickets must be bought and stamped before you reach the platform. Metro ticket offices and most private newsagents sell 10-ticket cards and one-day passes.

Bus at a stop in Brussels city centre

A city tram travelling down Rue Royale towards the city centre

Most stops have clear, comprehensible maps of the city's public transport system, with metros in orange, trams in blue and buses in red *(see endpaper)*, and timetables mark all the stops on each route. Metro stations in the city centre have electronic displays showing where each train is in the system. Those unfamiliar with the tram system will notice the lack of on-board information; there is no indication of what the upcoming stop is, of which many are request stops. Request stops can be made by pressing the yellow buttons by each of the vehicle's exits. Ask the driver to call the relevant stop. Smoking is banned, as is playing music, although dogs are allowed on trams and buses.

One-day travel pass

A few bus services in the capital are run by the Walloon transport group (TEC) or the Flemish operator De Lijn. These services have lettered rather than numbered codes (for instance, the 60 bus is run by STIB/MIVB, the W by De Lijn), but most tickets are valid on all the services.

BRUSSELS BY CAR

I T MAY BE A small city, but Brussels has been known to reduce motorists to tears. The seemingly perverse one-way system in many sections of the city centre can swiftly confuse newcomers, while the network of tunnels that bisect the city are notoriously difficult to navigate even for city-dwellers. Belgian drivers, too, have been the butt of jokes from their fellow Europeans for decades. Nonetheless the city's systems are not difficult to learn, and a car is handy for planning day trips around the rest of Belgium.

Most international rental agencies have branches here, many at the National Airport in Zaventem or at the Gare du Midi, where the Eurostar and train services arrive.

Like the rest of mainland Europe, Belgium drives on the right, and the "priorité à droite" rule – which means that the driver coming from the right at junctions has absolute priority to pull out unless otherwise indicated – is enforced with sometimes startling regularity. Always watch for vehicles coming from the right, no matter how small the road; some drivers have been known to take their priority even though it means a crash, secure in the knowledge that they are legally correct. Verve and confidence are helpful when driving in a city where many motorists take a flexible approach to road rules. Essential safety precautions, however, should be adhered to at all times. Safety belts are obligatory in all seats, and children under 12 years old are not allowed in the front when other seats are free.

Cars and taxis threading their way through the main streets

Drink-driving is illegal (the limit in Belgium is currently 0.5g/l). Speed limits are 50 kph (30 mph) in built-up areas, 120 kph (75 mph) on motorways and dual carriageways and 90 kph (55 mph) on all other roads. Always give way to trams, who will ring their bells should a car be in the way. Street parking, usually by meter, is becoming increasingly difficult in the city centre.

TAKING A TAXI

B RUSSELS' TAXIS are among Europe's more expensive, but most journeys are short and cabs are the city's only 24-hour transport service. Service is generally efficient, with most drivers speaking at least a little English, although some people may be surprised at many drivers' lack of familiarity with sections of the city. All taxis have a rooftop sign which is illuminated when the vehicle is vacant. Most cars are either black or white, with Mercedes the make of choice for most companies. It is advisable to find a taxi rank or order a cab by phone, although occasionally drivers will stop if hailed on the street. Passengers ride in the back seat, with the fare meter on the dashboard or just behind the gear-stick. Fares should be posted inside the vehicle. Tips are included in the price, but an extra tip is usually expected.

To make a complaint, write to the **CCN-Service Regional des Taxis et Limousines**, Rue du Progrès 80, 1030 Brussels. Give the taxi's registration number, its make and colour when making the complaint.

DIRECTORY

USEFUL NUMBERS

STIB/MIVB
Avenue de la Toison d'Or 15
1050 Brussels. **Map** 2 D5. █
(02) 515 2000. W www.stib.be

CCN-Service Regional des Taxis et Limousines
Rue du Progrès 80,
1030 Brussels.
█ (02) 201 5100.

Getting around Belgium

As you might expect from a country that is small, modern and predominantly flat, Belgium is an extremely easy place in which to travel. The toll-free motorways compare favourably with any in France, train travel is swift and competitively priced and there are good bus services in those areas not covered by the railway network. Public transport is clean and efficient and the range of touring tickets allows a great deal of freedom and the ability to see the whole country inexpensively. In the level Flemish countryside to the north, hiking and cycling are highly pleasant ways to get around.

Cyclists on a tour of the scenery of Durbuy in the Ardennes

TRAVELLING BY CAR

After the rather enervating traffic in Brussels, driving in the rest of Belgium comes a something of a relief. The motorways are fast, reasonably well maintained and toll-free, while major roads are also excellent. Drivers in cities outside the capital tend to be more relaxed, although the trend in Flanders for car-free city centres can make navigation demanding. The only difficulty most drivers encounter is an occasional absence of clear signs for motorway exits and junctions, which can necessitate taking extra care when approaching junctions (in Flanders, many drivers are confused by signs for "Uitrit". It means exit).

The road rules detailed in the Getting Around Brussels section *(see p169)* hold good for the rest of the country, with speed limits at 50 kph (30 mph) in built-up areas, 120 kph (75 mph) on motorways and dual carriageways and 90 kph (55 mph) on other national roads.

If you break down, three motoring organizations should be able to provide assistance: **Touring Club de Belgique, Royal Automobile Club de Belgique** and **Vlaamse Automobilistenbond** in Flanders. It is worth getting breakdown coverage before you leave, and you must have a valid driving licence (from the EU, US, Australia or Canada) or an International Driving Licence on your person. It is also essential to have comprehensive insurance and/or a Green card, and visitors are expected to carry a first-aid kit and a warning triangle at all times.

All the major rental agencies operate in Belgium, although renting a car can be an expensive business. To rent a vehicle, you must be 21 or over, with a year's driving experience, and have a credit card. A week's rental with unlimited mileage will cost €370 or more but might be reduced on the regular special deals at the big firms. Local agencies may also be cheaper, but be sure to check the terms and conditions. Bicycle hire is available in most Flemish towns with a modest deposit of €15.

TRAVELLING BY TRAIN

Belgium's train network is a more than adequate means of getting to and from major towns and cities. From Brussels, there are direct links to Antwerp, Ghent, Bruges, Ostend, Liège, Mons, Namur and the Ardennes, and even journeys involving a change rarely take more than two hours in total.

Run by **Belgian National Railways** (Société Nationale Chemins de Fer Belges/ Belgische Spoorwegen), the system is clean, modern and efficient, although the quality of rolling stock varies somewhat: older carriages have a slightly drab feel, but new

FRENCH/FLEMISH PLACE NAMES

One of the most confusing aspects of travel in Belgium is the variation between French and Flemish spellings of town names. On road signs in Brussels, both names are given, while in Flanders only the Flemish and in Wallonia only the French are shown. The following list gives main towns:

French	Flemish	French	Flemish
Anvers	Antwerpen	Malines	Mechelen
Ath	Aat	Mons	Bergen
Bruges	Brugge	Namur	Namen
Bruxelles	Brussel	Ostende	Oostende
Courtrai	Kortrijk	Saint-Trond	Sint-Truiden
Gand	Gent	Tongrès	Tongeren
Liège	Luik	Tournai	Doornik
Louvain	Leuven	Ypres	Ieper

Train travelling through Belgium on a spring evening

models are spacious, very comfortable, and, typically Belgian, offer fine meals and light refreshments.

Fares for standard second-class tickets are calculated by distance, with 100 km (63 miles) costing around €9.40; first-class fares will set you back around 50 per cent more. Because distance is the determining factor in price, return tickets generally offer no saving and are valid only until midnight. Children aged under six travel free, with a maximum of four children allowed per adult, and those aged between six and 11 receive a 50 per cent discount. Several special tariffs are available, including discounts for young adults aged under 26, with weekend tickets and day returns

reducing the price by up to 40 per cent. The more people travelling, the larger the discount; family members may be eligible for discounts of up to 60 per cent.

A variety of rail passes are on offer for extensive travel. The Belgian Tourrail pass (approximately €52) allows unlimited travel on any five days within one month of purchase, while the Carte de reduction à prix fixe (at approximately €15) offers 50 per cent off all first- and second-class tickets for one month.

TRAVELLING BY BUS

WHILE SLOWER and less comfortable for travelling between major cities, buses come into their own in the more remote or rural areas of the rest of Belgium, as well as in city suburbs. In Flanders, buses are run by the **De Lijn** group; in Wallonia, the network is operated by **TEC**. Fares are calculated according to distance, and are bought from the driver. Bus stops and terminals are generally close to railway stations. Buses have priority on public roads, so journeys are often swift.

Train and motor tour logos

SPECIALIST TOURS

TOURING CAN BE be a journey full of cultural variety in both Brussels and the rest of the country. In the capital, the Tourist Information Centre

(see p162) runs a series of over 40 walking and car day tours that cover all the capital and its 19 districts with topics as diverse as "Humanist Brussels" and "Industrial Belgium". The focus is largely on the city's exceptional range of art and architecture, but many diverse themes are covered.

In each major regional city, detailed, multi-lingual private tours are available in the historic town centre; contact the town's main tourist booth for full information.

Away from cities, Belgium also offers hiking and cycling excursions, ranging from one-day adventures to five-day hikes. The Ardennes are a popular destination for hikers, who can appreciate the area's flora and fauna as well as its dramatic history. First Travel Management (02 716 1870) will arrange tours.

DIRECTORY

TRAINS AND BUSES

SNCB/BS (Belgian National Railways)
C (02) 555 2555, 555 2525.
w www.sncb.be

TEC
C (010) 235353.

De Lijn
C (02) 526 2828.

MOTORING ORGANIZATIONS

Police Road Information
w www.policefederale.be

Touring Club de Belgique
Rue de la Loi 44, 1040 Brussels.
Map 3 A2. C (02) 233 2211.

Royal Automobile Club de Belgique
Rue d'Arlon 53, 1040 Brussels.
Map 3 A3. C (02) 287 0911.

Vlaamse Automobilistenbond
Sint-Jacobsmarkt 45, Antwerp.
C (03) 234 3434.

CAR RENTAL

C Avis (02) 730 6211.
C Budget (02) 646 5130.
C Europcar (02) 640 9400.
C Hertz (02) 513 2886.

A coach full of passengers travelling on a main bus route in Belgium

BRUSSELS STREET FINDER

THE PAGE GRID superimposed on the area by area grid below shows which parts of Brussels are covered in this *Street Finder*. The central Upper and Lower Town areas are marked in the colours that are also the thumbtab colours throughout the book. The map references for all sights, hotels, restaurants, shopping and entertainment

Nymph in Parc de Bruxelles

venues described in this guide refer to the maps in this section. A street index follows on pp178–81. The key, set out below, indicates the scales of the maps and shows what other features are marked on them, including transport terminals, emergency services and information centres. All the major sights are clearly marked so they are easy to locate. The map on the inside back cover shows public transport routes.

KEY TO STREET FINDER

▢	Major sight
▢	Other sight
▢	Other building
Ⓜ	Metro station
🚇	Train station
🚊	Tram route
🚌	Bus station
🚕	Taxi rank
🅿	Parking
ℹ	Tourist information
✚	Hospital
👮	Police station
✝	Church
⊠	Post office
=	Railway line
	One-way street
	Pedestrian street

SCALE OF MAPS   **1:16,000**

0 metres	250
0 yards	250

1

GAND CHAUSSEE DE GENTSESTEENWEG

QUE DU COMMERCE

BOUL

Canal Bruxelles-Charleroi

CHAUSSEE DE MONS BERGENSE

BVD DU MIDI ZUID LAAN

RUE DE FRANCE FRANKRIJKSTRAAT

Lower Town

BOU

Façade of La Maison des Ducs de Brabant, Grand Place *(see pp42–3)*

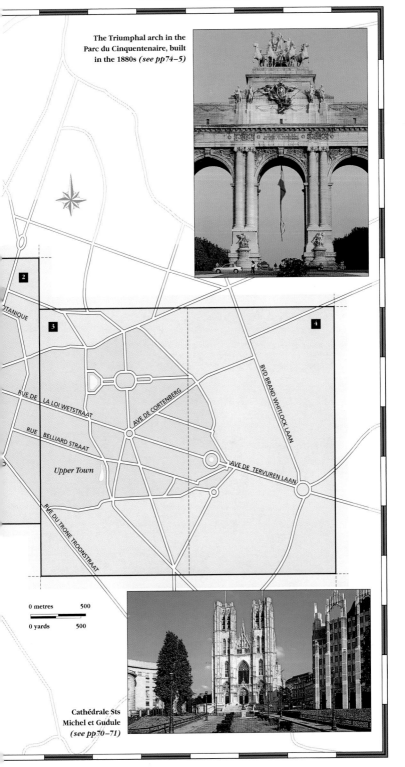

The Triumphal arch in the
Parc du Cinquentenaire, built
in the 1880s *(see pp74–5)*

2

3

4

BOTANIQUE

RUE DE LA LOI WETSTRAAT

RUE BELLIARD STRAAT

AVE DE CORTENBERG

BVD BRAND WHITLOCK LAAN

AVE DE TERVUREN LAAN

Upper Town

RUE DU TRONE TROONSTRAAT

0 metres 500

0 yards 500

Cathédrale Sts
Michel et Gudule
(see pp70–71)

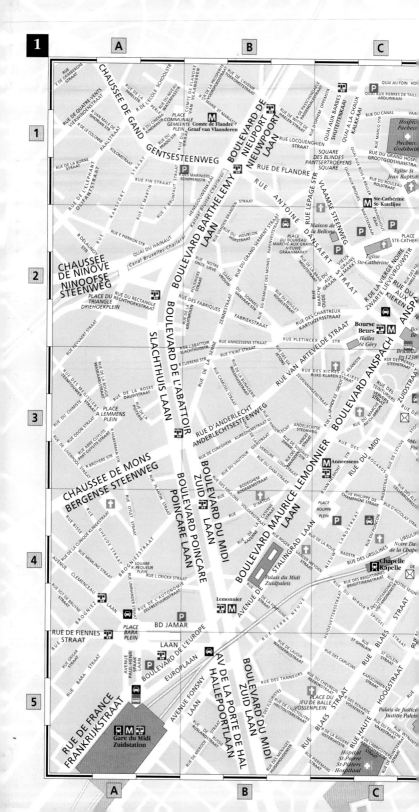

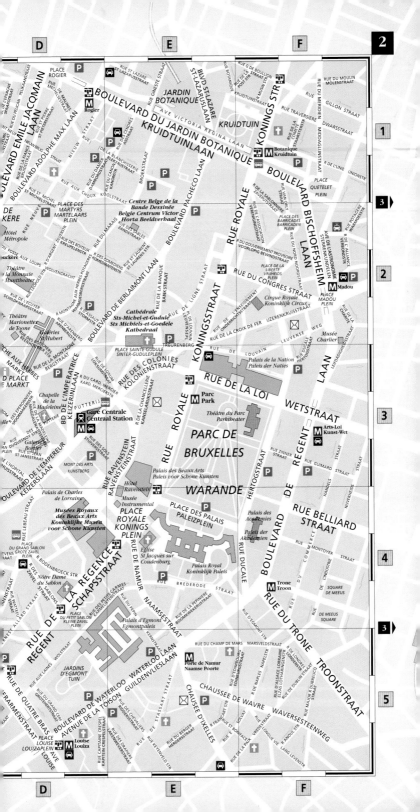

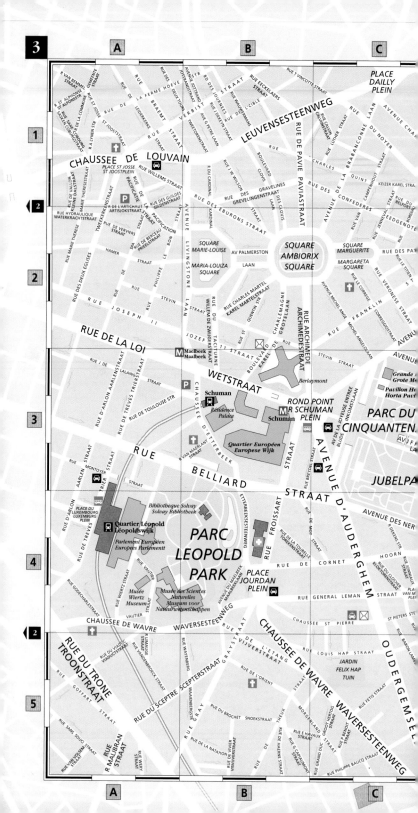

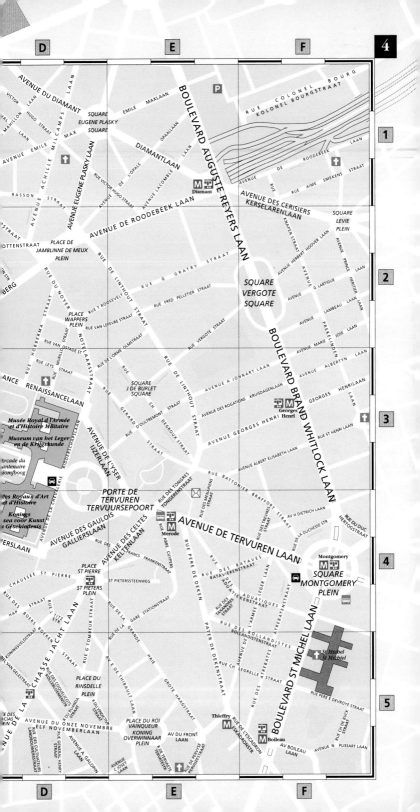

Street Finder Index

All entries are listed in French, with the Flemish variant following in Italics where applicable.

General Index

Page numbers in **bold** type refer to
main entries. Places are listed according to the Flemish or French name by
which they are referred to in the text
and are best known; for a list of translations of major towns, see page 170.

Acknowledgments

DORLING KINDERSLEY would like to thank the following people whose assistance contributed to the preparation of this book:

MAIN CONTRIBUTORS

ZOË HEWETSON is based in London but works in Brussels as a simultaneous translator for the European Commission. She is also a keen walker and has recently published a guide to walking in Turkey.

PHILIP LEE lives and works in Nottingham. A veteran travel writer, he has contributed to numerous *Rough Guide* and *Dorling Kindersley Travel Guide* publications, including the *Rough Guide to Belgium*. He frequently writes on travel for British newspapers and magazines.

ZOË ROSS is a London-based writer and editor. She has worked on several Dorling Kindersley travel guides, and is now a freelance author.

SARAH WOLFF has lived and worked in Brussels for several years. An editor and journalist, she is currently working for *The Bulletin*, Brussels' English-language newsweekly magazine.

TIMOTHY WRIGHT lived in Brussels for most of the 1990s. A successful journalist, he contributed to several English-language magazines published in Brussels and elsewhere in the Benelux countries.

JULIA ZYRIANOVA is a freelance journalist and translator. She lived in Brussels and Paris for several years and is now based in London.

FOR DORLING KINDERSLEY

Gillian Allan; Douglas Amrine; Louise Bostock Lang; Vivien Crump; Donald Greig; Marie Ingledew; Lee Redmond; Marisa Renzullo.

PROOFREADER

Sam Merrell.

INDEXER

Hilary Bird.

ADDITIONAL PHOTOGRAPHY

Steve Gorton, Ian O'Leary, Neil Mersh, David Murray, Tim Ridely, Jules Selmes, Clive Streeter, Matthew Ward.

SPECIAL ASSISTANCE

Many thanks for the invaluable help of the following individuals: Joanna at Belgo; Derek Blyth; Christiana Ceulemans at Institut Royal Du Patrimonie Artistique; Charles Dierick at Centre Belge de la Bande Dessinée; Anne at Gaspard de Wit; Elsge Ganssen and Georges Delcart at Rubenshuis; Doctor Janssens at the Domaine de Laeken; Leen de Jong at Koninklijk Museum Voor Schone Kunsten; Antwerpen; Noel at Leonidas; Chantal Pauwert at Stad Brugge Stedelijke Musea; Marie-Hélène van Schonbroek at Cathédrale Sts Michel et Gudule; Elaine de Wilde and Sophie van Vliet at Musées Royaux des Beaux-Arts.

PHOTOGRAPHY PERMISSIONS

Dorling Kindersley would like to thank all the cathedrals, churches, museums, hotels, restaurants, shops, galleries and sights too numerous to thank individually for their assistance and kind permission to photograph at their establishments.

Placement Key - t=top; tl=top left; tlc= top left centre; tc= top centre; trc= top right centre; tr= top right; cla= centre left above; ca= centre above; cra= centre right above; cl = centre left; c= centre; cr= centre right; clb= centre left below; cb = centre below; crb = centre right below; bl= bottom left; b= bottom; bc= bottom centre; bcl= bottom centre left; br= bottom right; d = detail.

Works of art have been produced with the permission of the following copyright holders: ©Casterman 19 br, Ted

Benoit Berceuse Electrique 50clb; ©DACS 2000 16bl, 51t/cra/crb/b, 78tr/cl/cr; ©Dupuis 1999 18tr, 19ca; Sofa Kandissy ©Alessandro Medini 111c; Lucky Luke Licensing ©MORRIS 18br; @Moulinsart SA 4, 18tl/cr/cl/bl, 50tl/tr/cra/crb, 51cla/clb; ©Peyo 1999 - Licensed through I.M.P.S. (Brussels) 19bc; 50cla;

The publishers would like to thank the following individuals, companies, and picture libraries for their kind permission to reproduce their photographs:

AKG, LONDON: 31b, 34t, 36b, 37bl, 37br, 142tr; Galleria Nazdi Cupodimonte 20-1; Erich Lessing 28, / Kunsthistoriches Museum 31t; Musée du Louvre 29b; Musée Royaux d'Arts et d'Histoire, Brussels 35c; Museo de Santa Cruz, Toledo 29t; Museum Deutsche Geschichte, Berlin 31c; Private Collection 142tl; Pushkin Museum 30c; Victoria and Albert Museum, London 32c.

DUNCAN BAIRD PUBLISHERS: Alan Williams 143br. CH. BASTIN & J. EVRARD: 16tr/cb/bc, 17tr/br, 82bl/br; 91t, 99t, 112b, 115br; BRIDGEMAN ART LIBRARY, LONDON: Christie's Images, London Peter Paul Rubens (1557–1640) *Self Portrait* 15t; Musée Crozatier, Le Puy-en-Velay, France designed by Berain (c.1725–1730) *Dawn*, Brussels lace 21bl; Private Collection/ Marie-Victoire Jaquotot (1778–1855) *Portrait of the Duke of Wellington* 35b./Max Silbert (b.1871) *The Lacemakers of Ghent* 1913 21t; Private Collection French School (19th century) Louis XIV (1638–1715) of *France in the costume of the Sun King in the ballet 'La Nuit' c.1665* (litho) 32br; Private Collection/Bonhams, London/Robert Alexander Hillingford (1825–1904) *The Turning Point at Waterloo* (oil on canvas) 34bl; STAD BRUGGE STEDELIJKE MUSEA: Groeninge-museum 118ca/cb/b, 119c/bl; Paul Delvaux *Serenity*, 1970 ©Foundation P. Delveaux – St Idesbald, Belgium 118t; Gruithuis 116t/cb/b, 117c; Gruuthusemuseum 30t.

CAFE COULEUR: 25t; CEPHAS: Nigel Blythe 122-3; TOP/A. Riviere-Lecoeur 142bl; CHIMAY: 142cr; DEMETRIO CARRASCO: 137b; ALAN COPSON: 13bl, 37c; CORBIS: David Bartruff 19cb, 140tr; Wolfgang Kaehler 167c; Patrick Ward 25b.

DAS PHOTO: 158c, 164c, 166t, 170.

ECRAN TOTAL©CINEDIT: 158t; ET ARCHIVE: Imperial War Museum, London 107b; EUROPEAN COMMISSION: 22b.

ROBERT HARDING PICTURE LIBRARY: Julian Pottage 77t, 169b; Roger Somvi 15b, 24t/c; HOVERSPEED: 167b; HULTON GETTY COLLECTION: 22c, 33t, 34c, 36c, 91b; Keytone 37t.

INSTITUT ROYAL DU PATRIMOINE ARTISTIQUE/KONINKLIJK INSTITUUT VOOR HET KUNSTPATRIMONIUM: 20tr, Sociéte des Expositions du Palais des Beaux-Arts de Bruxelles 53tr.

KONINKLIJK MUSEUM VOOR SCHONE KUNSTEN, ANTWERP: P. Delvaux *Pink's Bow* ©Foundation P. Delveaux – St Idesbald, Belgium/DACS, London 2000 95c; J. Jordaens *As the old sang, the young ones play pipes* 95tr; R. Magritte *Madame Recamier*©ADAGP, Paris and DACS, London 2000 95b; P.P. Rubens *Adoration of the Magi* 95tl; J. Van Eyck *Saint Barbara* 94c; R. Wouters *Woman Ironing* 94b.

MUSÉE DE L'ART WALLON DE LA VILLE DE LIÈGE: Legs M. Aristide Cralle (1884) 35tl; MUSÉES ROYAUX DES BEAUX-ARTS DE BELGICA, BRUXELLES-KONINKLIJK MUSEA VOOR SCHONE KUNSTEN VAN BELGIË, BRUSSEL: photo Cussac 6–7, 14t, 34–5, 62clb, 63crb/bl, 64c/b, 65tl/tr, 66t, 67b, /©ADAGP, Paris and DACS, London 2000 65br, /© The Henry Moore Foundation 65c; photo Speltdoorn 14b, 15c, 20c, 63cr, 66b,/©ADAGP, Paris James Ensor *Skeletons Fighting Over a Pickled Herring*, 1891 ©DACS 2000 64t; and DACS, London 2000 67t.

Document OPT: Alain Mathieu 171t.

Pictor: 89t; Robbie Polley: 112b, 116ca, 117b, 119br, 162t, 163c, 165t, 168c/b, 171b; Private Collection: 7, 34, 39, 85, 123, 161.

Rex Features: 22, 24b, 26c, Action Press 36t; Sipa Press/Vincent Kessler 23t.

Sabena: 166clb; Science Photo Library: CNES 1992 Distribution Spot Image 8; ©Standaard Strips: 19bl; Neil Setchfield: 20tl, 88t, 140c, 157t/c; Sundancer: © Moulinsart 18cl.

Telegraph Colour Library: Ian McKinnell 84-5; Archives du

Theatre Royal de la Monnaie: 35tr; Tony Stone Images: Richard Elliott 27; Hideo Kurihara 2–3; ©Toerisme Ooost-Vlaanderen: 99br; Service Relations Exterieures City of Tournai: 20b.

Roger Viollet: 32t; Musee San Martino, Naples 33b.

World Pictures: 26b, 101b.

All other images ©Dorling Kindersley.
For further information see: www.dkimages.com

Jacket: All special photography except Britsock: SEIP-BACH clb; Alan Copson: cra; Robert Harding Picture Library: Roy Rainford t; Sofa Kandissy ©Alessandro Medini crb.

DORLING KINDERSLEY SPECIAL EDITIONS

Dorling Kindersley books can be purchased in bulk quantities at discounted prices for use in promotions or as premiums. We are also able to offer special editions and personalized jackets, corporate imprints, and excerpts from all of our books, tailored specifically to meet your own needs.

To find out more, please contact:
(in the United Kingdom) – Special Sales, Dorling Kindersley Limited, 80 Strand, London WC2R ORL;

(in the United States) – Special Markets Dept., DK Publishing, Inc., 375 Hudson Street, New York, NY 10014.

Phrase Book

TIPS FOR PRONOUNCING FRENCH

French-speaking Belgians, or Walloons, have a throaty, deep accent noticeably different from French spoken in France. Despite this, there are few changes in the vocabulary used in spoken and written language.

Consonants at the end of words are mostly silent and not pronounced. *Ch* is pronounced *sh*; *th* is *t*; *w* is *v*; and *r* is rolled gutturally. *Ç* is pronounced *s*.

IN EMERGENCY

Help!	Au secours!	oh sek**oor**
Stop!	Arrêtez!	aret-**ay**
Call a doctor!	Appelez un medecin	apuh-**lay** uñ meds**añ**
Call the police!	Appelez la police	apuh-**lay** lah pol-**ees**
Call the fire brigade!	Appelez les pompiers	apuh-lay leh poñ-**peeyay**
Where is the nearest telephone?	Ou est le téléphone le plus proche	oo ay luh tehleh**fon** luh ploo **prosh**
Where is the nearest hospital?	Ou est l'hôpital le plus proche	oo ay l'**opeetal** luh ploo **prosh**

COMMUNICATION ESSENTIALS

Yes	Oui	wee
No	Non	noñ
Please	S'il vous plait	seel voo **play**
Thank you	Merci	mer-**see**
Excuse me	Excusez-moi	exkoo-**zay** mwah
Hello	Bonjour	boñz**hoor**
Goodbye	Au revoir	oh ruh-**vwar**
Good night	Bonne nuit	boñ-**swar**
morning	Le matin	mat**añ**
afternoon	L'apres-midi	l'apreh-**meedee**
evening	Le soir	swah
yesterday	Hier	eeyehr
today	Aujourd'hui	oh-zhoor-**dwee**
tomorrow	Demain	duhm**añ**
here	Ici	ee-**see**
there	Là bas	lah bah
What?	Quel/quelle?	kel, kel
When?	Quand?	koñ
Why?	Pourquoi?	poor-**kwah**
Where?	Où?	oo
How?	Comment?	kom-**moñ**

USEFUL PHRASES

How are you?	Comment allez vous?	kom-moñ tal**ay voo**
Very well, thank you.	Très bien, merci.	treh byañ, mer-**see**
How do you do?	Comment ça va?	kom-moñ sah **vah**
See you soon	A bientôt.	byañ-toh
That's fine	Ça va bien.	Sah vah byañ
Where is/are...?	Où est/sont...?	ooh ay/soñ
How far is it to...?	Combien de kilomètres d'ici à...?	kom-**byañ** duh keelo-**metr** d'ee-**see** ah
Which way to...?	Quelle est la direction pour...?	kel ay lah deer-ek-**syoñ** poor
Do you speak English?	Parlez-vous Anglais?	par-**lay** voo oñg-**lay**
I don't understand.	Je ne comprends pas.	zhuh nuh kom-proñ pah
Could you speak slowly?	Vous puissez parlez plus lentement?	voo pwee-say par-lay ploos **lon**tuh-moñ
I'm sorry.	Excusez-moi.	exkoo-**zay** mwah

USEFUL WORDS

big	grand	groñ
small	petit	puh-**tee**
hot	chaud	show
cold	froid	frwah
good	bon	boñ
bad	mauvais	moh-**veh**
enough	assez	assay
well	bien	byañ
open	ouvert	oo-**ver**
closed	fermé	fer-**meh**
left	gauche	gohsh
right	droite	drawh
straight on	tout droit	too drwah
near	près	preh
far	loin	lwañ
up	en haut	oñ oh
down	en bas	oñ **bah**
early	tôt	toh

late	tard	tar
entrance	l'entrée	l'on-**tray**
exit	la sortie	sor-**tee**
toilet	toilette	twah-let
occupied	occupé	o-koo-**pay**
free (vacant)	libre	leebr
free (no charge)	gratuit	grah-**twee**

MAKING A TELEPHONE CALL

I would like to place a long-distance telephone call	Je voudrais faire un interurbain	zhuh voo-dreh faire uñ añter-oorbañ
I'd like to call collect	Je voudrais faire un communication PCV	zhuh voo-**dreh** faire oon kom-oonikah-**syoñ** peh-seh-veh
I will try again later	Je vais essayer plus tard	zhuh vay ess-ay-eh ploo tar
Can I leave a message?	Est-ce que je peux laisser un message?	es-**keh** zhuh puh les-**say** uñ meh-sazh
Could you speak up a little please?	Pouvez-vous parler un peu plus fort?	poo-**vay** voo par-**lay** uñ puh ploo for
Local call	Communication local	komoonikah-**syoñ** low-**kal**

SHOPPING

How much does this cost?	C'est combien?	say kom-**byañ**
I would like....	Je voudrais	zhuh voo-**dray**
Do you have...	Est-ce que vous avez...	es-**kuh** voo zavay
I'm just looking	Je regarde seulement	zhuh ruhgar suhl-moñ
Do you take credit cards?	Est-ce que vous acceptez les cartes de crédit	es-**kuh** voo zaksept-**ay** leh kart duh kreh-**dee**
Do you take travellers' cheques?	Est-ce que vous acceptez les chèques de voyage	es-**kuh** voo zak-sept-**ay** lay shek duh vwayazh
What time do you open?	A quelle heure vous êtes ouvert	ah kel urr voo zet oo-**ver**
What time do you close?	A quelle heure vous êtes fermé	ah kel urr voo zet fer-**may**
This one	Celui-ci	suhl-wee **see**
That one	Celui-là	suhl-wee **lah**
expensive	cher	shehr
cheap	pas cher, bon marché	pah shehr, boñ mar-shay
size, clothes	la taille	tye
white	blanc	bloñ
black	noir	nwahr
red	rouge	roozh
yellow	jaune	zhownh
green	vert	vehr
blue	bleu	bluh

TYPES OF SHOPS

shop	le magasin	le maga-**zañ**
bakery	la boulangerie	booloñ-**zhuree**
bank	la banque	boñk
bookshop	la librairie	lee-**brehree**
butcher	la boucherie	boo-**shehree**
cake shop	la pâtisserie	patee-**sree**
chocolate shop	la chocolatier	shok-oh-lah-tyeh
chip stop/stand	la friterie	free-tuh-ree
chemist	la pharmacie	farmah-**see**
delicatessen	la charcuterie	shah-koo-tuh-**ree**
department store	le grand magasin	groñ maga-**zañ**
fishmonger	la poissonerie	pwasson-**ree**
greengrocer	le marchand des légumes	mar-**shoñ** duh lay-**goom**
hairdresser	le coiffeur	kwaf**uhr**
market	le marché	marsh **ay**
newsagent	le magasin de journaux/tabac	maga-**zañ** duh zhoor-**no**/ta-bak
post office	le bureau de poste	boo-**roh** duh pohst
supermarket	le supermarché	soo-pehr-**marshay**
travel agent	l'agence de voyage	azhons duh vwayazh

SIGHTSEEING

art gallery	le galérie d'art	galer-**ree** dart
bus station	la gare routière	gahr roo-tee-yehr

cathedral	la cathédrale	katay-**dral**
church	l'église	aygleez
closed on public holidays	fermeture jour ferié	fehrmeh-tur zhoor fehree-ay
garden	le jardin	zhah-**dañ**
library	la bibliothèque	beebleeo-tek
museum	le musée	moo-**zay**
railway station	la gare (SNCF)	gahr (es-en-say-ef)
tourist office	les informations	layz uñ-for-mah-syoñ
town hall	l'hôtel de ville	ohtel duh vil
train	le train	trañ

STAYING IN A HOTEL

Do you have a vacant room?	est-ce que vous avez une chambre?	es-kuh voo **zavay** oon shambr
double room with double bed	la chambre à deux personnes, avec un grand lit	la shambr uh duh per-**son** uh-vek uñ groñ lee
twin room	la chambre à deux lits	la shambr ah duh lee
single room	la chambre à une personne	la shambr ah oon pehr-**son**
room with a bath	la chambre avec salle de bain	shambr ah-vek sal duh bañ
shower	une douche	doosh
I have a reservation	J'ai fait une reservation	zhay fay oon ray-zehrva-**syoñ**

EATING OUT

Have you got a table?	Avez vous une table libre?	avay-**voo** oon tahbl leebr
I would like to reserve a table.	Je voudrais réserver une table.	zhuh voo-dray rayzehr-**vay** oon tahbl
The bill, please.	L'addition, s'il vous plait.	l'adee-**syoñ**, seel voo **play**
I am a vegetarian.	Je suis végétarien.	zhuh swee vezhay-**tehryañ**
waitress/waiter	Garçon, Mademoiselle	gah-sohn/ mad-uh-mwah-zel
menu	le menu	men-**oo**
cover charge	le couvert	luh koo-**vehr**
wine list	la carte des vins	lah **kart**-deh vañ
glass	verre	vehr
bottle	la bouteille	boo-**tay**
knife	le couteau	koo-**toh**
fork	la fourchette	for-**shet**
spoon	la cuillère	kwee-**yehr**
breakfast	le petit déjeuner	puh-**tee** day-zhuh-nay
lunch	le déjeuner	day-**zhuh-nay**
dinner	le dîner	dee-**nay**
main course	le grand plat	groñ plah
starter	l'hors d'oeuvres	or duhvr
dessert	la dessert	duh-zehrt
dish of the day	le plat du jour	plah doo joor
bar	le bar	bah
cafe	le café	ka-**fay**
rare	saignant	say-nyoñ
medium	à point	ah **pwañ**
well done	bien cuit	byañ **kwee**

NUMBERS

0	zero	zeh-**roh**
1	un	uñ, oon
2	deux	duh
3	trois	trwah
4	quatre	katr
5	cinq	sañk
6	six	sees
7	sept	set
8	huit	weet
9	neuf	nerf
10	dix	dees
11	onze	oñz
12	douze	dooz
13	treize	trehz
14	quatorze	katorz
15	quinze	kañz
16	seize	sehz
17	dix-sept	dees-**set**
18	dix-huit	dees-**zweet**
19	dix-neuf	dees-**znerf**
20	vingt	vañ
21	vingt-et-un	vañ ay uhn
30	trente	tront
40	quarante	karoñt
50	cinquante	sañkoñt

60	soixante	swahsoñt
70	soixante-dix	swahsoñt-dees
80	quatre-vingt	katr-vañ
90	quatre-vingt-dix/ nonante	katr vañ dees/ nonañ
100	cent	soñ
1000	mille	meel
1,000,000	million	miyoñ

TIME

What is the time?	Quelle heure?	kel uhr
one minute	une minute	oon mee-**noot**
one hour	une heure	oon uhr
half an hour	une demi-heure	oon **duh-mee** uhr
half past one	une heure et demi	uhr ay duh-mee
a day	un jour	zhuhr
a week	une semaine	suh-mehn
a month	un mois	mwah
a year	une année	annay
Monday	lundi	luñ-**dee**
Tuesday	mardi	mah-**dee**
Wednesday	mercredi	mehrkruh-**dee**
Thursday	jeudi	zhuh-**dee**
Friday	vendredi	voñdruh-**dee**
Saturday	samedi	sam-**dee**
Sunday	dimanche	dee-**moñsh**

BELGIAN BEER AND FOOD

fish	poisson	pwah-**ssoñ**
bass	bar/loup de mer	bah/loo duh mare
herring	hareng	ah-**roñ**
lobster	homard	oh-ma
monkfish	lotte	lot
mussel	moule	mool
oyster	huitre	weetr
pike	brochet	brosh-ay
salmon	saumon	soh-moñ
scallop	coquille Saint-Jacques	kok-eel sañ jak
sea bream	dorade/daurade	doh-rad
prawn	crevette	kreh-vet
skate	raie	ray
trout	truite	trweet
tuna	thon	toñ

MEAT

meat	viande	vee-**yand**
beef	boeuf	buhf
chicken	poulet	poo-**lay**
duck	canard	kanar
lamb	agneau	ahyoh
pheasant	faisant	feh-zoñ
pork	porc	por
veal	veau	voh
venison	cerf/chevreuil	surf/shev-roy

VEGETABLES

vegetables	légumes	lay-**goom**
asparagus	asperges	ahs-pehrj
Belgian endive /chicory	chicon	shee-koñ
Brussels sprouts	choux de bruxelles	shoo duh broocksell
garlic	ail	eye
green beans	haricots verts	arrykoh vehr
haricot beans	haricots	arrykoh
potatoes	pommes de terre	pom-duh **tehr**
spinach	epinard	aypeenar
truffle	truffe	troof

DESSERTS

pancake	crêpe	crayp
waffle	gauffre	gohfr
fruit	fruits	frwee

DRINKS

coffee	café	kah-**fay**
white coffee	café au lait	kah-**fay** oh lay
milky coffee	caffe latte	kah-**fay** lat-uh
hot chocolate	chocolat chaud	shok-oh-lah shoh
tea	thé	tay
water	l'eau	oh
mineral water	l'eau minérale	l'oh meenay-ral
lemonade	limonade	lee-moh-nad
orange juice	jus d'orange	zhoo doh-ronj
wine	le vin	vañ
house wine	vin maison	vañ may-sañ
beer	un bière	byahr

TIPS FOR PRONOUNCING FLEMISH

Flemish is a dialect of Dutch, with most of the language remaining the same, bar some regional differences. The language is pronounced in largely the same way as English, although many vowels, particularly double vowels, are pronounced as long sounds. *J* is the equivalent of the English *y*, *v* is pronounced *f*, and *w* is *v*.

IN EMERGENCY

Help!	**Help!**	help
Stop!	**Stop!**	stop
Call a doctor!	**Haal een dokter!**	Haal uhn **dok**-tur
Call the police!	**Roep de politie!**	Roop duh poe-**leet**-see
Call the fire brigade!	**Roep de brandweer!**	Roop duh **brahnt**-vheer
Where is the nearest telephone?	**Waar ist de dichtsbijzijnde telefoon?**	Vhaar iss duh **dikst**-baiy-zaiyn-duh-tay-luh-**foan**
Where is the nearest hospital?	**Waar ist het dichtsbijzijnde ziekenhuis**	Vhaar iss het **dikst**-baiy-zaiyn-duh **zee**-kuh-hows

COMMUNICATION ESSENTIALS

Yes	**Ja**	yaa
No	**Nee**	nay
Please	**Alstublieft**	ahls-tew-**bleeft**
Thank you	**Dank u or**	dhank-ew
Excuse me	**Pardon**	pahr-**don**
Hello	**Bedankt**	be-dunk
Goodbye	**Dag**	dahgh
Good night	**Slaap lekker**	slap **lek**-kah
morning	**Morgen**	**mor**-ghugh
afternoon	**Middag**	**mid**-dahgh
evening	**Avond**	**av**-vohnd
yesterday	**Gisteren**	**ghis**-tern
today	**Vandaag**	**van**-daagh
tomorrow	**Morgen**	**mor**-ghugh
here	**Hier**	heer
there	**Daar**	daar
What?	**Wat?**	vhat
When?	**Wanneer?**	vhan-**eer**
Why?	**Waarom?**	vhaar-**om**
Where?	**Waar?**	vhaar
How?	**Hoe?**	hoo

USEFUL PHRASES

How are you?	**Hoe gaat het ermee?**	Hoo ghaat het er-**may**
Very well, thank you	**Heel goed, dank u**	Hayl ghoot, dhank ew
How do you do?	**Hoe maakt u het?**	Hoo maakt ew het
See you soon	**Tot ziens**	Tot zeens
That's fine	**Prima**	**Pree**-mah
Where is/are...?	**Waar is/zijn...?**	vhaar iss/zayn
How far is it to...?	**Hoe ver is het naar...?**	Hoo vehr iss het nar
How do I get to...?	**Hoe kom ik naar...?**	Hoo kom ik nar
Do you speak English?	**Spreekt u engels?**	Spraykt uw **eng**-uhls
I don't understand	**Ik snap het niet**	Ik snahp het neet
Could you speak slowly?	**Kunt u langzamer praten?**	Kuhnt ew **lahng**-zarmer-praat-tuh
I'm sorry	**Sorry**	sorry

USEFUL WORDS

big	**groot**	ghroat
small	**klein**	klaiyn
hot	**warm**	vharm
cold	**koud**	khowt
good	**goed**	ghoot
bad	**slecht**	slekht
enough	**genoeg**	ghuh-**noohkh**
well	**goed**	ghoot
open	**open**	open
closed	**gesloten**	ghuh-**slow**-tuh
left	**links**	links
right	**rechts**	rekhts
straight on	**rechtdoor**	rehkht dohr
near	**dightbij**	dikht baiy
far	**ver weg**	vehr vhekh
up	**omhoog**	om-**hoakh**
down	**naar beneden**	naar buh **nay**-duh
early	**vroeg**	vrookh

late	**laat**	laat
entrance	**ingang**	**in**-ghang
exit	**uitgang**	**ouht**-ghang
toilet	**wc**	vhay-say
ocupied	**bezet**	buh-**zett**
free (vacant)	**vrij**	vraiy
free (no charge)	**gratis**	**ghraah**-tiss

MAKING A TELEPHONE CALL

I'd like to place a long-distance telephone call	**Ik wil graag interlokal telefoneren**	ik vhil ghraakh **inter**-loh-kaal tay-luh-foh-**neh**-ruh
I'd like to call "collect"	**Ik wil "collect call" bellen**	ik vhil "collect call" **bel**-luh
I will try again later	**Ik probeer het later nog wel eens**	ik pro-**beer** het laater nokh vhel ayns
Can I leave a message?	**Kunt u een boodschap doorgeven?**	kuhnt ew uhn **boat**-skhahp **dohr**-ghay-vuh
Could you speak up a little please?	**Wilt u vat harder praten?**	vhilt ew vhat **hahr**-der **praat**-ew
Local call	**Lokaal gesprek**	low-**kaahl** ghuh-**sprek**

SHOPPING

How much does this cost?	**Hoeveel kost dit?**	hoo-**vayl** kost dit
I would like...	**Ik wil graag...**	ik vhil ghraakh
Do you have...?	**Heeft u...?**	hayft ew
I'm just looking	**Ik kijk alleen even**	ik kaiyk alleyn **ay**-vuh
Do you take credit cards?	**Neemt u credit cards aan?**	naymt ew credit cards aan?
Do you take travellers' cheques?	**Neemt u reischeques aan?**	naymt ew **raiys**-sheks aan
What time do you open?	**Hoe laat gaat u open?**	hoo laat ghaat ew opuh
What time do you close?	**Hoe laat gaat u dicht?**	hoo laat ghaat ew dikht
This one	**Deze**	**day**-zuh
That one	**Die**	dee
expensive	**duur**	dewr
cheap	**goedkoop**	ghoot-**koap**
size	**maat**	maat
white	**wit**	vhit
black	**zwart**	zvhahrt
red	**rood**	roat
yellow	**geel**	ghayl
green	**groen**	ghroon
blue	**blauw**	blah-ew

TYPES OF SHOPS

antique shop	**antiekwinkel**	ahn-**teek**-vhin-kul
bakery	**bakker**	**bah**-ker
bank	**bank**	bahnk
bookshop	**boekwinkel**	**book**-vhin-kul
butcher	**slager**	slaakh-er
cake shop	**banketbakkerij**	bahnk-**et**-bahk-er-aiy
chip stop/stand	**patatzaak**	pah-**taht**-zak
chemist/drugstore	**apotheek**	ah-poe-**taiyk**
delicatessen	**delicatessen**	daylee-kah-**tes**-suh
department store	**warenhuis**	**vhaah**-uh-houws
fishmonger	**viswinkel**	**viss**-vhin-kul
greengrocer	**groenteboer**	**ghroon**-tuh-boor
hairdresser	**kapper**	**kah**-per
market	**markt**	mahrkt
newsagent	**krantenwinkel**	**krahn**-tuh-vhin-kul
post office	**postkantoor**	**pohst**-kahn-tor
supermarket	**supermarkt**	**sew**-per-mahrkt
tobacconist	**sigarenwinkel**	see-**ghaa**-ruh-vhin-kul
travel agent	**reisburo**	**raiys**-bew-roa

SIGHTSEEING

art gallery	**gallerie**	ghaller-ee
bus station	**busstation**	**buhs**-stah-shown
bus ticket	**strippenkaart**	**strip**-puh-kaart
cathedral	**kathedraal**	kah-tuh-**draal**
church	**kerk**	kehrk
closed on public holidays	**op feestdagen gesloten**	op **fayst**-daa-ghuh ghuh-slow-**tuh**
day return	**dagretour**	**dahgh**-ruh-tour
garden	**tuin**	touwn
library	**bibliotheek**	bee-bee-yo-**tayk**
museum	**museum**	mew-**zay**-um

railway station	**station**	stah-**shown**
return ticket	**retourtje**	ruh-**tour**-tyuh
single journey	**enkeltje**	**eng**-kuhl-tyuh
tourist information	**dienst voor tourisme**	deenst vor **tor**-ism
town hall	**stadhuis**	**staht**-houws
train	**trein**	traiyn

STAYING IN A HOTEL

Do you have a vacant room?	**Zijn er nog kamers vrij?**	zaiyn er nokh **kaa**-mers vray
double room with double bed	**een twees persoons-kamer met een twee persoonsbed**	uhn **tvhay** per-**soans**-ka-mer met uhn **tvhay** per-**soans** beht
twin room	**een kamer met een lits-jumeaux**	uhn **kaa**-mer met uhn lee-zjoo-**moh**
single room	**eenpersoons-kamer**	**ayn**-per-**soans** kaa-mer
room with a bath/shower	**kaamer met bad/ douche**	**kaa**-mer met baht/doosh
I have a reservation	**Ik heb gereserveerd**	ik hehp ghuh-ray-schr-**veert**

EATING OUT

Have you got a table?	**Is er een tafel vrij?**	iss ehr uhn **tah**-fuhl vraiy
I would like to reserve a table	**Ik wil een tafel reserveren**	ik vhil uhn **tah**-fel ray sehr-**veer**-uh
The bill, please	**Mag ik afrekenen**	muhk ik **ahf**-ray-kuh-nuh
I am a vegetarian	**Ik ben vegetariër**	ik ben fay-ghuh-**taahr**-ee-er
waitress/waiter	**serveerster/ober**	sehr-**veer**-ster/**oh**-ber
menu	**de kaart**	duh kaahrt
cover charge	**het couvert**	het koo-**vehr**
wine list	**de wijnkaart**	duh **vhaiyn**-kart
glass	**het glass**	het ghlahss
bottle	**de fles**	duh fless
knife	**het mes**	het mess
fork	**de vork**	duh fork
spoon	**de lepel**	duh **lay**-pul
breakfast	**het ontbijt**	het ont-**baiyt**
lunch	**de lunch**	duh lernsh
dinner	**het diner**	het dee-**nay**
main course	**het hoofdgerecht**	het **hoaft**-ghuh-rekht
starter, first course	**het voorgerecht**	het **vhor**-ghuh-rekht
dessert	**het nagerecht**	het **naa**-ghuh-rekht
dish of the day	**het dagmenu**	het **dahg**-munh-ew
bar	**het cafe**	het kaa-**fay**
café	**het eetcafe**	het **ayt**-kaa-**fay**
rare	**rare**	'rare'
medium	**medium**	'medium'
well done	**doorbakken**	door-**bah**-kuh

NUMBERS

1	**een**	ayn
2	**twee**	tvhay
3	**drie**	dree
4	**vier**	feer
5	**vijf**	faiyf
6	**zes**	zess
7	**zeven**	**zay**-vuh
8	**acht**	ahkht
9	**negen**	**nay**-guh
10	**tien**	teen
11	**elf**	elf
12	**twaalf**	tvhaalf
13	**dertien**	**dehr**-teen
14	**veertien**	**feer**-teen
15	**vijftien**	**faiyf**-teen
16	**zestien**	**zess**-teen
17	**zeventien**	**zayvuh**-teen
18	**achtien**	**ahkh**-teen
19	**negentien**	**nay-ghuh**-tien
20	**twintig**	**tvhin**-tukh
21	**eenentwintig**	**aynuh**-tvhin-tukh
30	**dertig**	**dehr**-tukh
40	**veertig**	**feer**-tukh
50	**vijftig**	**faiyf**-tukh
60	**zestig**	**zess**-tukh
70	**zeventig**	**zay**-vuh-tukh
80	**tachtig**	**tahkh**-tukh
90	**negentig**	**nayguh**-tukh

100	**honderd**	**hohn**-durt
1000	**duizend**	**douw**-zuhnt
1,000,000	**miljoen**	mill-**yoon**

TIME

one minute	**een minuut**	uhn meen-**ewt**
one hour	**een uur**	uhn ewr
half an hour	**een half uur**	een hahlf uhr
half past one	**half twee**	hahlf twee
a day	**een dag**	uhn dahgh
a week	**een week**	uhn vhayk
a month	**een maand**	uhn maant
a year	**een jaar**	uhn jaar
Monday	**maandag**	**maan**-dahgh
Tuesday	**dinsdag**	**dins**-dahgh
Wednesday	**woensdag**	**vhoons**-dahgh
Thursday	**donderdag**	**donder**-dahgh
Friday	**vrijdag**	**vraiy**-dahgh
Saturday	**zaterdag**	**zaater**-dahgh
Sunday	**zondag**	**zon**-dahgh

BELGIAN BEER AND FOOD

FISH

fish	**vis**	fiss
bass	**zeebars**	see-buhr
herring	**haring**	**haa**-ring
lobster	**kreeft**	krayft
monkfish	**lotte/zeeduivel**	lot/seafuhdul
mussel	**mossel**	**moss**-uhl
oyster	**oester**	**ouhs**-tuh
pike	**snoek**	snook
prawn	**garnaal**	gar-nall
salmon	**zalm**	sahlm
scallop	**Sint-Jacoboester/ Jacobsschelp**	**sind**-yakob-ouhs-tuh/yakob-scuhlp
sea bream	**dorade/zeebrasem**	doh-rard
skate	**rog**	rog
trout	**forel**	foh-ruhl
tuna	**tonijn**	tuhn-een

MEAT

meat	**vlees**	flayss
beef	**rundvlees**	**ruhnt**-flayss
chicken	**kip**	kip
duck	**eend**	aynt
lamb	**lamsvlees**	**lahms**-flayss
pheasant	**fazant**	**fay**-zanh
pork	**varkensvlees**	**vahr**-kuhns-flayss
veal	**kalfsvlees**	**karfs**-flayss
venison	**ree (bok)**	ray

VEGETABLES

vegetables	**groenten**	**ghroon**-tuh
asparagus	**asperges**	as-puhj
Belgian endive/ chicory	**witloof**	vit-lurf
Brussels sprouts	**spruitjes**	spruhr-tyuhs
garlic	**knoflook**	**knoff**-loak
green beans	**princesbonen**	prins-ess-buh-nun
haricot beans	**snijbonen**	snee-buh-nun
potatoes	**aardappels**	**aard**-uppuhls
spinach	**spinazie**	spin-a-jee
truffle	**truffel**	truh-fuhl

DESSERTS

fruit	**fruit/vruchten**	vroot/vrooh-tuh
pancake	**pannekoek**	**pah**-nuh-kook
waffle	**wafel**	vaff-uhl

DRINKS

beer	**bier**	beeh
coffee	**koffie**	coffee
fresh orange juice	**verse jus**	**vehr**-suh zjhew
hot chocolate	**chocola**	sho-koh-**laa**
mineral water	**mineraalwater**	meener-**aahl**-vhaater
tea	**thee**	tay
water	**water**	**vhaa**-ter
wine	**wijn**	vhaiyn

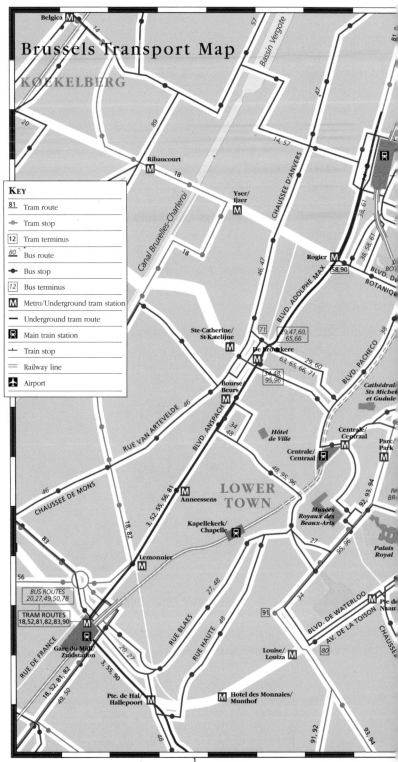

Brussels Transport Map

KOEKELBERG

LOWER TOWN

KEY

81	Tram route
●	Tram stop
12	Tram terminus
80	Bus route
●	Bus stop
12	Bus terminus
M	Metro/Underground tram station
—	Underground tram route
🚉	Main train station
—	Train stop
=	Railway line
✈	Airport

Belgica M

Ribaucourt M

Yser/Ijzer M

Rogier M

Ste-Catherine/St-Katelijne M

De Brouckère M

Bourse/Beurs M

Anneessens M

Kapellekerk/Chapelle

Lemonnier M

Centrale/Centraal

Cathédral Sts Michel et Gudule

Hôtel de Ville

Musées Royaux des Beaux-Arts

Palais Royal

Louise/Louiza M

Hotel des Monnaies/Munthof M

Pte. de Hal/Hallepoort M

Gare du Midi/Zuidstation

BUS ROUTES
20,27,49,50,78

TRAM ROUTES
18,52,81,82,83,90

Canal Bruxelles-Charleroi

CHAUSSEE D'ANVERS

BLVD. ADOLPHE MAX

BLVD. PACHECO

RUE VAN ARTEVELDE

BLVD. ANSPACH

CHAUSSEE DE MONS

RUE DE FRANCE

RUE BLAES

RUE HAUTE

BLVD. DE WATERLOO

AV. DE LA TOISON

Bassin Vergote

BOTANIQUE

Parc/Park M

 Pte de Naam

29,47,60, 65,66

63, 65, 66, 71

29, 60

34,48, 95,96

34 48

48, 95, 96

92, 93, 94

95, 96

27

91

80

20, 27

3, 55, 90

48

91, 92

93, 94

18, 52, 81, 82

49, 50

3, 52, 55, 56, 81

18, 82

46

56

83

71

57

14, 57

47

89

20

18

46, 47

38, 61

38, 58, 61

58,90

14